AF574743

THE PLUNDERED LAND

Also by Fiona Kendall

Variety of Orchids

THE PLUNDERED LAND

Fiona Kendall

HEADLINE

First published in 1989
by HEADLINE BOOK PUBLISHING PLC

British Library Cataloguing in Publication Data

Kendall, Fiona
The plundered land.
I. Title
823'.914[F]

ISBN 0-7472-0152-8

Typeset in 11/11½ pt Plantin
by Colset Private Limited, Singapore

Printed and bound in Great Britain by
Richard Clay Ltd, Bungay, Suffolk

HEADLINE BOOK PUBLISHING PLC
Headline House,
79 Great Titchfield Street
London W1P 7FN

This book is dedicated to three adventurers, my dearest uncles, who, though so far away, have been unstinting in their support and encouragement while I sought to conquer my new world. In order of seniority:

Terry Kendall, New York
Alistair Grant, Florida
Jimmy Grant, Australia

I oft have heard of Lydford law,
How in the morn they hang and draw,
And sit in judgement after.
At first I wondered at it much;
But now I find their reason such,
That it deserves no laughter.

They have a castle on a hill;
I took it for an old Windmill,
The vanes blown off by weather;
Than lie therein one night, 'tis guessed,
'Tis better to be stoned or pressed,
Or hanged, now choose you whether.

At six o'clock I came away,
And prayed for those that were to stay,
Within a place so arrant,
Wild and open to winds that roar:
By God's grace I'll come no more,
Unless by some tin warrant.

William Browne
(Seventeenth century)

PART I

Chapter One

Devon, summer 1796

'Better come, Gramps.'

The anxious young voice in Elyas Hammett's ear made him start. His mind had been far away and he hadn't seen Isaac come into the gutting shed. He stood up, at the same time flicking the scrap of bloody entrails into the bucket between his feet and dropping the pilchard into the barrel beside him.

'Did thy ma send 'ee, boy?' he asked curiously as they moved together through the crowd of chattering fishwives busy with the first of the day's catch.

Isaac shook his head. 'Nay. Ma's abed. Her's bin a-hollerin' terrible but her's stopped now babbie's come. Mrs Cherry said fetch parson an' thy gramps while babbie's still a-breathin'.'

A concerned frown knitted the shaggy brows. Mrs Cherry was the village midwife and no stranger to death-smitten infants. If she said come, then come he must – even if it did mean losing a shift at the pilchards. He stopped beside the overseer before leaving the shed.

'I best see my boy's new babbie baptised afore Almighty takes 'un,' he told the woman.

She nodded without looking up from her gutting. Dead babies were common enough, but it was proper he should see this one churched, what with the poor mite's pa out with the boats. Moreover, a baby that died before baptism joined the evil Yeth Hounds condemned to hunt for ever across Dartmoor.

'Get 'ee back soon, 'tis good fish.'

He assured her he would and went out. With Isaac trotting beside him, he set off along the quay at a brisk pace. Although it wasn't yet eight o'clock on a fine July evening, a huddle of pilchard drifters were already tied up at the wharf being unloaded. And some of the bigger boats were coming in; low in the water with a good catch, nets crammed with fish and reeked halfway up their masts.

Those silvery fish, shining like smelted tin, served as a constant reminder to Elyas that he was a tinner.

How he hated gutting! Women's work! Like sorting and dressing tin ore. He hated the slimy, wriggling bodies, the gaping mouths and accusing little black eyes. Most of all he hated the smell. Hated it as he never had the dank, dust-laden air below ground. In ten years he hadn't got used to the smell of fish. Any more than he'd got used to the fisher folk – hardy, independent breed and not unlike tinners though they were. For if fish and tin had their silvery hue in common, he'd nothing in common with these people among whom providence and pilchards had brought him. They understood only the sea. He understood only tin.

'Mrs Cherry said better hurry, Gramps.'

Elyas had unconsciously slowed his pace to take in the scene, forgetting for a moment his dismal mission. He quickened his steps again at Isaac's prompting and soon they were climbing the steep, cobbled hill which wound through the steppes of stone-built, two-storeyed cottages fronted by the sea.

The cottage which the Hammetts rented for three shillings a week was right at the top of Fish Hill. A fair distance for Elyas to walk home each day considering his chest was bad and his legs bowed from years of working cramped in the pits. He didn't mind. From the back of the cottage, on a clear day, he could see right across the mile or so of flat, stony fields to the moorland where the mine chimneys smoked among the yellow gorse and purple heather.

As soon as he entered and saw the parson's and Mrs Cherry's solemn faces he knew the news was bad. 'Be poor mite gone then?' he asked. A thin wail from the old cradle in the corner answered him. He frowned. 'Sounds healthy 'nough.'

Even as he said it, he had a morbid premonition. His pale, watery eyes went to the ceiling above which, presumably, lay his daughter-in-law, Betsy. Neither the parson nor the midwife said a word though they exchanged knowing looks. Then Mrs Cherry cleared her throat, compressed her lips and gave Isaac a pointed look Elyas couldn't miss.

'Go fetch us pail of water, boy,' he said quietly.

Isaac had gone over to the cradle and was examining his new relative with interest. ' 'Tis 'nother boy, Gramps.'

'That be right good o' the Lord. Now fetch up the water, boy.'

Isaac reluctantly left his squalling little brother and, taking up a pail, went out.

Mrs Cherry confirmed Elyas's unhappy suspicions, saying in her matter-of-fact way, 'Babbie'll live, most likely'd. Lost his ma though. Strange, cos her were proper mettlesome were Betsy.'

'We must give thanks to the Lord that in His infinite mercy He saw fit not to take both,' observed the parson and Elyas nodded solemnly.

Poor Betsy! She was a good maid. She'd looked after them well. Given her husband two . . . no, *three* . . . fine sons. Graeme, the eldest at thirteen, was 'the boy' on the same boat as his pa; Isaac was nearly eleven. There'd been some hadn't lived: four, or was it five? Elyas couldn't quite remember. Carried off by croup or some such childish ague!

'I'll tell boy,' he muttered and went out.

When Huward Hammett returned late that evening he took the news of his wife's demise in stoic fashion. 'She was a good woman,' was all he said, echoing his father's sentiment.

Graeme Hammett, ever a quiet boy, said nothing. He was ashen-faced;

but that wasn't unusual as he was always seasick when he went out with the boats, however calm the water. Huward had tried beating it out of him more than once but Elyas would always intervene, saying, 'Leave he be an' don't waste thy time! Boy's got tin in his veins, not sea!'

They christened the new baby James after his maternal grandfather, a fisherman lost at sea some ten years back, knowing that Betsy would have been pleased. Then they buried her in the little churchyard alongside her mother and a lot of other fisher folk so she'd be in good company.

With Mrs Cherry's help, Elyas found a wet-nurse for his hungry grandson. A healthy young fishwife with big breasts and abundant milk – enough for Jamie and her own big new boy. For half a crown she was pleased to come to the cottage three times a day and suckle a babe on each breast. Elyas, if he wasn't needed for the gutting and was at home, would afterwards take each baby in turn and heft them in his raw, knobbled hands, comparing their weight. The two had been born within a day or so of each other, but after two months Elyas couldn't conceal his pride because his Jamie was already a fair bit heavier than his 'tit brother'.

'That's cos I do put 'un to *left* pap . . . on account you'm payin' half crown for it,' explained the wet-nurse with simple candour. ' 'Tis fact, us left paps is terrible big wi' milk in us family.'

So impressed was he by her enthusiastic committment to his motherless grandson, he gave her Betsy's Sunday dress, chip bonnet, two aprons and a bedgown. Her old shoes he kept since there was still wear in them and they'd soon fit Isaac. The wet-nurse was overcome and, by way of showing her gratitude for such valuable gifts, kept greedy Jamie at her breast for half an hour longer than usual until his belly was round and hard and his eyelids were drooping, so exhausted was he with sucking.

The following summer there was a brief lull between the pilchards and the arrival of the summer mackerel when Elyas wasn't wanted in the gutting sheds. The fishwives were never idle. During the day they'd 'brede' new nets or 'beet' the holes in the old ones. They'd make new oilskins for their menfolk, with three coats of oil on the outer and one coat on the inner. And knit big jerseys, eight steel needles darting in their red, roughened hands. But Elyas's hands weren't nimble enough for such tasks, although he did sometimes help with the oiling in return for a new set of 'oilies' for Huward or Graeme. The rest was truly women's work and he refused to demean himself further than gutting.

Instead, he'd take Jamie, now a year old and taking a real interest in what was going on around him, across the fields at the top of the village and climb a reave of earth and stones. From there he could gaze across the wind-swept, boggy wastes towards the mist-shrouded hills and crags of Dartmoor.

'See they tors, boy?' he would mutter longingly to the solemn-faced child in his arms. 'Up the moor . . . that be where us Hammetts belong.'

Elyas was forty-two when, ten years before, he'd been driven down off the moor to the south coast for the fish. An 'old man' in the language of the tinners despite being for his age comparatively sound in lung and limb and still capable of a five-hour 'coore' at the face. But there were plenty of younger men for the contracting. And not the tin ore to be cut, so the mine captains said, that there once was. Some even went so far as to suggest that the moor was nigh worked out. Such comments filled Elyas with scorn: there'd always been tin on Dartmoor and always would be – for those who knew where to hulk.

Huward, then seventeen, had insisted on also 'going for the fish' although he was promised a new contract next setting day at the big Golden Dagger mine up along North Bovey.

'Ye'll scratch a better living from tin than fish, boy,' warned Elyas though he'd no real proof of that. Tinners and fishermen all seemed to live from hand to mouth. But Huward's mind was made up. Elyas was secretly pleased: they were the last two surviving Hammetts and it was right they should stay together.

Before setting off for the coast, Elyas had gone to the little cemetery at Cornwood at the foot of the moor. Beth, his wife, was buried there along with Huward's five baby brothers, none of whom had survived much beyond baptism.

Beth had never been strong, though she'd managed many a coore in the washing house when she was a maid, and it was there she'd first taken young Elyas's eye. But her blood had been thin; a handicap which showed itself in her unusually pale hair and dry, parchment-coloured flesh. It got thinner, it seemed, with every puny baby despite Elyas getting her a cup of warm blood to drink every time they killed a pig or sheep or even a chicken at one of the farms.

Shyly, he laid a bunch of freshly picked primroses on her grave, looking around him awkwardly though there was none to see him. 'Us'll be back a-whiles, Beth, m'dear,' he promised her conversationally, 'just as soon as they silver darlin's be harvested an' int barrels.'

But the pilchard season had been a good one. Swiftly followed that year by the summer mackerel. Then came the winter herring. So they'd stayed.

Huward took after his father: short, tough and sturdy. He soon got a berth on a fishing boat and, while at first he'd found it strangely hard, the fresh salty air seemed to suit him and soon his face lost its pit-pallor. As for Elyas, he swallowed his pride to earn five shillings a week in the gutting shed, which was better by far than idling his days with the other old men up on the moor as they waited for their ruined lungs to give a final rattle.

'Time 'ee got wed,' Elyas told Huward when he'd turned his eighteenth year, conscious of the fact that they needed a capable female to cook and knit and wash their clothes.

Huward was willing. He'd especially got an eye for the sister of one of the fishermen on his boat. She was a pretty, waif-like maiden, no more than sixteen. Her name was Rowella and she had round blue eyes which she'd lower coyly when she saw Huward on the quay. It hadn't gone unnoticed that she came to meet her brother's boat more often these days. And often with a flower in her hair.

Elyas made a point of viewing her.

'Her pretty 'nough,' he granted, 'but can her crimp a pasty?'

Huward never found out. Elyas had already picked out a likely wife for him among the maidens in the gutting shed. Betsy was a bit older than his son; unmarried on account of the fact she'd eight elder sisters, three of whom were yet to find husbands. She was the plumpest and the plainest but she'd a cheerful nature and could knit quicker and make a pasty better than any of them.

Huward was disappointed. He desperately wanted saucy Rowella but Elyas knew what was best for his son. 'Betsy be comely 'nough for 'ee, boy . . . an' won't be sparked by t'other boys when you'm out wi' boats.'

So they were wed two weeks after their first meeting. They spent just that night giggling together in the upper room of the cottage before the 'huer' on the cliffs sighted the first herring shoals and signalled the boats out. Graeme arrived, with the mackerel, eight months and three weeks later.

Now Betsy was gone, God rest her! And, apparently, so were the fish.

Day after day, the boats were coming in with the hatches still laid over the net holds.

'Fish be proper shy,' the skippers would gloomily tell those gathered anxiously on the quay to watch the fleet return.

The absence of the fish affected the entire fishing community. Word came that the Plymouth fleet weren't faring any better off Big Bury Bay Banks and they'd never been known to fail.

They said prayers on the quay. The vicar blessed the boats, the sea, the nets. Even the huer, patiently watching the sparkling water from the cliff ready to signal with his bundle of coloured rags. But the fish continued shy throughout the summer despite the fine weather and calm seas, and the oldest fisherman swore they couldn't remember a time when the sea was quite so barren.

Huward and Graeme were laid off. Elyas hadn't been to the gutting sheds for weeks. He forgot how much he hated the smell of fish as he stood for hours, Jamie in his arms, gazing silently up at the cliff top, willing the huer's rags to wave. They never did. After a month, food stores were dwindling and Elyas was having to use the little bit of money they'd managed to put by. The hard winter facing them was a daunting prospect. More and more of the younger fisherman were leaving the village to seek work in the mines and clay-pits, or to enlist in the navy – ever in need of men to protect Britain from a French invasion. When the summer mackerel didn't come, Elyas made a decision.

'Pack up,' he told Huward and his grandsons. 'We'm goin' backalong up the moor.'

They stopped at Cornwood to leave their few sticks of furniture with Hannah Rogers at the dame school until they were settled. Dame Rogers had known and liked Beth Hammett and wanted to take Jamie in for a while. Elyas refused her offer in a gruff, courteous manner, saying, 'Thankee kindly, but nay, mistress. Quicker young'n gets used t'moor better for he . . . cos ent no Hammett ever agoin' for 'un fish agin.'

Dame Rogers looked concerned. 'The mines aren't what they were. The tinning isn't good. Captains are turning away good contractors.'

'Then they be mazed!' he declared contemptuously. 'There be plenty of tin . . . copper, too . . . up'long moor. Trouble wi' they young'ns, they don't know what they be a-lookin' for, half 'em . . .'

Her concern deepened. It was clear that he'd been at the coast for so long he'd no notion of how things were with the tinning. The war with Napoleon Bonaparte had sent the price of metal soaring and the land was being plundered for ore as never before. Mines were being worked out and 'knocked' before new lodes had been channelled. The tin-bearing granite regions of the moor were a honeycomb of trial pits.

Word travelled swiftly through the community if promising mineral veins and spots of ore were found. Unemployed contractors and bal maidens would flock to the new pit, eager for work. The mine captains selected only the youngest and the fittest; and they were often expected to labour as 'tributers' for a small share of any ore extracted rather than 'contractors' guaranteed pay. Tributing was always a gamble: it took weeks for the ore to be sorted, stamped and paid for, and if the lode just petered out the tributers had lost the money they'd spent on gunpowder and candles.

'I do hear say Captain de Raddon is still taking on contractors,' Dame Rogers remembered as she saw Elyas out of her neat little stone-built cottage-cum-school to join Huward and the boys waiting for him at the gate.

He stopped dead on the doorstep and only just managed to stop himself from spitting in the nearby flowerbed at mention of the mine-owner. 'That fornicatin' limb of Satan!' he sneered. 'Why, I've forgot more 'bout tinnin' than he's ever knowed!'

She hid a smile. She, too, heartily disliked the decadent, swaggering Captain de Raddon, yet there was no denying that he'd made a fortune from his tin and copper mines, knowledgeable or not! His Wheal Blackaven on the south coast of Devon employed some 1,200 men – more than any other bal in the parish. And his Blackaven House, sitting on the cliff above a private cove, was the finest in the district.

It was as much due to this exalted position in the tinning community as it was to his friendship with the equally dissolute Prince of Wales that de Raddon had recently been appointed Lord Warden of the Stannaries on the death of his father, his predecessor. Dame Rogers was about to remark so to Elyas when another, more salient thought began to form in her mind. She sometimes called at Blackaven House at the invitation of Mrs de Raddon, a gentle, nervy creature who craved genteel conversation. Indeed, she was due a visit and was expecting the de Raddons' steward to deliver a card at any time now.

'I wonder . . . perhaps I could have a word with Mrs de Raddon about Huward and Graeme. If she could persuade her husband to give them a contract . . .'

This time Elyas forgot himself and did expectorate in the flower bed.

'Hammetts ent dyin' of the dust for that blood-sucker!' he declared. 'Nay, nor for elly like he! We'm a-going tinning on us own accounts. We'm going t'be *tributers*!'

'On your own accounts?' she queried somewhat dubiously.

Elyas's grizzled grey hair and beard, almost untrimmed, gave him a rather wild appearance, but as he stood before her, straightening his stooped shoulders beneath his frayed jersey, rheumy eyes alert, his spirit shone forth as he said: 'Hammetts will have own bal by Christmastide . . . you'm just wait an' see if'n it bain't so.'

Her faint smile appeared. 'Then I wish you well in your search for tin, Mr Hammett.'

From the gate, her eyes followed them as they set off along the main track through the village towards the moor, Elyas leading, then Huward. Both weighed down beneath picks and shovels. Graeme and Isaac were similarly laden and between them pulled Jamie in an old threshing basket set upon a sledge. Their clothes were badly in need of patching and Isaac was hobbling in his mother's old shoes, too narrow for his broad Hammett feet.

'Mr Hammett . . . wait!'

Elyas stopped and looked back at Dame Rogers. She beckoned to him and he began to retrace his steps. She darted inside and as he reached the gate reappeared with a pair of good, strong brown boots.

'I think you'll find these will fit Isaac,' she said, handing them to Elyas.

'That be right kindly of 'ee, mistress.'

'Have you money for gunpowder?'

' 'Nough . . . us'll manage.'

She took his hand and wordlessly pressed a small gunny sack of coins into his palm. His eyes narrowed as his fingers closed over it. They weren't coppers. Nor shillings. They felt like sovereigns!

She nodded, reading his thoughts. 'Twenty sovereigns, Mr Hammett.' Then, as he stuttered a protest, added: 'You may consider it a loan.'

He didn't know what to say. He half wanted to give her the money back; Beth would be furious at him for taking money off a spinster like Dame Rogers. On the other hand, gunpowder and the like were expensive and the sovereigns could mean the difference 'twixt failure and success. ' 'Twill be a whiles afore I can repay 'ee, mistress,' he warned her.

She smiled her kindly smile. 'Don't worry on that account.'

He stood there awkwardly, searching for words with which to express his gratitude but could find none sufficient. Then a notion struck him. He transferred the sack of coins to his pocket, spat on his grimy hand and wiped it on the seat of his breeches before sticking it out towards her, saying, ' 'Til I *can* repay 'ee, mistress, just 'ee consider thysel' a partner wi' a sixth share in Hammett bal.'

'Very well, Mr Hammett,' she agreed gravely, proferring her hand. She expected him to shake it, but instead he slapped her palm robustly with his own in the manner of traders and market folk concluding a deal.

She stood watching as they trudged away. She'd put the money aside to pay for her funeral. She'd always wanted a fine, polished box with brass handles and a smart hearse pulled by black horses. But she didn't regret the impulse that had made her give him the money. And if he couldn't repay her, well, the parish would just have to put her under.

The wind ruffled her silvery grey hair. She went inside, remembering that she'd soon have a class arriving to teach.

Chapter Two

They slept beneath the stars, wrapped in their oilskins against the pervading damp of the moor. Jamie hardly stirred in his threshing basket which was set upon a big flat rock and covered by an extra oilskin. During the day, he would lie gurgling happily to himself in the exceptionally warm autumn sunshine while they cut a succession of trial pits in the brown-grey granite region of the moor.

The work was hard as, with hammer and peeker, they'd hulk away sufficient of the stone to give the gunpowder a better chance to break the ground. After a week they'd found nothing. Not a likely mineral vein or the smallest trace of ore.

'Ah, well, 'twas a day lent,' Elyas would sigh at the end of every disappointing day as they watched the crimson sun slip behind the far hills. After a rest and a meal of boiled rabbit and tatties, he'd feel optimistic again. 'Mebbe try higher up tomorrow,' he'd say.

So they'd try higher up. And still find nothing but useless stuff containing not a hint of tinstone. Then October was well upon them and the days were short and the sky a dull grey. There weren't so many rabbits or pigeons for Isaac to snare for the pot so they had to buy provisions from the nearest farm, some three miles away. Or use a little of their salted meat which Jamie would spit out in disgust, yelling when Elyas forced it down him rather than see him go hungry.

Early one morning, something happened which – highly distressing though it was for Jamie at the time – changed their luck.

Isaac had been sent to buy eggs and milk for Jamie at the farm. Huward and Graeme were on the side of a hill, hulking the coarse granite to lodge the powder charge for yet another trial. Elyas sat on a rock with Jamie playing contentedly among the dry furze nearby.

Suddenly, there was a fearful flapping of wings and a great, brown sea-eagle swooped down and clutched Jamie in its talons. The child screamed in terror as the bird lifted him a foot or so but Elyas, mindful of pixies who sometimes stole winsome babes and left ill-humoured fairy children in their place, had made sure that Jamie was tethered to a bush. Grabbing a pick, Elyas charged the eagle yelling abuse. It immediately released its terrified prey and flew off.

'You'm ever come back, an' thy bald head will be smashed to un pulp!' raged Elyas, shaking his pick after the huge bird.

It glided towards a nearby hill and disappeared from view among the rocky mass crowning the top. Elyas's brain was so impeded with anger and shock at so very nearly losing his youngest grandson, that it was a few moments before the significance of the eagle and its crag dawned upon him. Of course! Eagle Tor!

Absently, he untethered the bawling Jamie and rocked him, making clicking noises with his tongue to quieten the boy. All the while he gazed towards Eagle Tor, eyes narrowed, trying to make out the eagle's nest. He was still standing there motionless, expression rapt, when Isaac returned an hour later with a canteen of milk and a crock of eggs.

Isaac poured milk into a tin mug and held it to Jamie's gaping mouth, imagining that his brother was howling because he was hungry. But Jamie pushed the mug away, spilling the milk, and continued to yell lustily.

'What be makin' babbie squall fit t'bust, Gramps?' asked Isaac. When Elyas didn't reply, he went and stood beside him, following his intent gaze to the rocks atop the hill. 'What do 'ee see, Gramps?'

'Eagle Tor,' muttered Elyas. He turned his faraway face to look at Isaac. 'Bain't bin eagle on tor for twenty years agone . . . but, by Lord Harry, there be one now!'

Isaac looked interested but faintly disbelieving. This sounded like one of his grandfather's tales! 'An eagle, Gramps?'

'Aye, boy, 'twas,' Elyas emphatically assured him, reacting to the thread of doubt in Isaac's voice. 'Near 'nough carried babbie off. Would've, too, if'n I hadn't got he snug down agin fairies.'

This was too much for Isaac: Jamie had grown into a stout little boy, too big, surely, for an eagle to lift. No, this was definitely one of his grandfather's yarns. 'Oh, Gramps!' he exclaimed in the amused, pained tone they used when they realised that Elyas was funning.

But there was no answering twinkle in the watery eyes.

'I tell 'ee, boy, I seed it happen!' insisted Elyas. He opened wide his arms. ' 'Twere sea-eagle with great wings this big!'

Isaac chewed his lip. Jamie had ceased to bawl and had begun to hiccup; his face was red and drenched with tears. Certainly something had given him a dreadful fright. Perhaps, decided Isaac, it wasn't a yarn after all. He looked towards Eagle Tor with more respect.

' 'Tis omen, I reckon,' declared Elyas with great certainty.

Isaac was about to ask what he meant when Graeme arrived at the run. 'Pa sez her be ready to hulk, if'n you'm a-comin', Gramps.'

'Go tell thy pa to save powder.' He pointed. 'That's where we'm going to hulk. 'Neath where eagle do sit. 'Tis an omen, I tell 'ee . . .!'

So that was where they hulked, in a combe beside the clear, swift-flowing, icy waters of Eagle Brook, After a week, the ground was a mass of shallow pits. They'd used almost all of their gunpowder and goosequill fuses and still found no deposits.

When Huward heard a faithful account of his baby son's narrow escape, he privately formed the opinion that his ageing father had most likely dozed off while he was babbie-watching and dreamed the whole thing – though he didn't dare suggest as much to Elyas.

Graeme had come to much the same conclusion; particularly when there was no further sighting of the eagle. Usually taciturn, even he was drawn to remark that if there *was* an eagle up yonder, it certainly wasn't troubled by pit blasting.

Another week and Huward and Graeme were for giving up and seeking work at one of the big mines along the coast. A group of itinerant tinners stopped for a while and mentioned in passing that Wheal Blackaven had opened up tunnels on the forty-fathom level and were wanting good, strong contractors. They were headed there themselves, having been tributing at another mine where their lode had petered to 'horse' ground. Huward and Graeme were keen to join up with them but Elyas forbade it.

'Ye'll not sweat blood for de Raddon save over my corpse!' he growled. 'We'm bain't giving up. That eagle 'twere an omen . . .!'

'Bad omen, most likely'd,' muttered Graeme darkly.

'Nay, boy, eagles bring good fortune,' insisted Elyas. He pointed up the combe. 'Mebbe worth a try up 'long yon creep . . .'

They were a fathom down when Elyas let out a triumphant yell.

Tin!

It was a true lode, they exultantly discovered. The granite walls of the workings were coated with gleaming, silver-black cassiterite. Elyas scrambled out of the trial pit and executed a little dance of sheer joy. His worn, dust-streaked face split in a huge grin, he snatched up Jamie and threw him high in the air half a dozen times until the child was red-faced and shrieking with laughter.

'What do we do now, Gramps?' Isaac wanted to know.

Elyas stopped his jigging and put Jamie down. '*Do*, boy? Why, us squat!'

And 'squat' they did.

Providing they built their cottage and enclosed their sett 'twixt dawn and sunset, they could claim 'squatter's rights'; the parcel of land – including the tin workings – would legally belong to them. Elyas wasted not a moment. He despatched Isaac to the farm with an urgent message asking the farmer to come at dawn to witness the commencement of building. Meanwhile he and the others began collecting the more manageable slabs of granite scattered in that region of the moor, pulling them on the sledge. But not a single foundation stone did they lay. Elyas wasn't taking any chances.

'Don't want parish fathers a-saying' as how Hammetts cheated and bain't entitled to claim us sett,' he explained when Graeme asked what harm there would be in just marking out the cottage walls with small stones in readiness.

The farmer was happy to cooperate. Having such near neighbours meant he'd be able to sell them chickens and a piglet or two to start their own smallholding, important if they were to survive in so desolate a region of the moor. He arrived astride a shaggy moor colt just as the grey dawn light began to steal over Eagle Tor. He didn't dismount. Just sat watching as the first stone was laid. Then with a satisfied nod he turned his beast towards the farm again.

The Hammetts toiled all day with hardly a break. By mid-day they'd got the walls up as far as the roof – which they could turf at a later time – and put in a fine fireplace in the biggest of the two rooms. It comprised two huge granite slabs with a conveniently-shaped stone wedge spanning near enough eight feet across the top. Graeme and Isaac would've liked to see the land boundaries extended but Elyas and Huward were careful not to be too ambitious as the day was already half done and they'd yet to build a low wall enclosing the sett.

Though it was time for mossle they didn't stop to eat. Jamie had a piece of bread and a mug of milk thrust at him while the others chewed on lumps of bread and salt brisket while they worked. Somehow they got the wall completed and managed to take in not only the mine but a good stretch of Eagle Brook which would be needed in the future to power the waterwheel which would pump out the water from the mine.

As the light began to fade, the farmer returned on his colt bearing a great stoup of strong October ale with which to celebrate the laying down of tools. And as they gratefully gulped the welcome ale in mugs clasped in hands torn and bleeding from the rough stones, he dismounted and stamped about, inspecting their efforts. He stood for a while staring into the trial pit. Then said: 'Be it good tinning you'm found?'

Elyas's jaw set and he hedged an answer to the mild question. 'That remains for us t'see. Mebbe peter out to horse.' He didn't want word spreading; didn't want to be besieged by contractors and tributers. This was a family affair and for now he was content it should stay thus.

The farmer grunted. He was a slow-witted yeoman, but not so slow as to imagine they'd go to the trouble of squatting in so desolate a valley if the trial wasn't tin-rich. Next, he went and stared into the cottage.

'Left hole for pixies to come an' go?'

Elyas gave him a withering look and pointed to an aperture no larger than his fist at the foot of the back wall. He might have been downalong coast for ten years but that didn't mean he'd forgotten what was proper upalong moor. He took a folded paper from his pocket and went and spread it out on a flat rock. It bore Dame Rogers's spidery writing. During one of his rare visits to Cornwood to spend some of her guineas on gunpowder and to have the smith sharpen their tools, he'd taken the precaution of having her draw up the document at his dictation. He gestured to them all to gather around him.

'Can 'ee read an' write, farmer?'

'Nay.'

'Make thy mark.'

Elyas offered him a lump of charcoal.

The farmer kept his thumbs firmly tucked in the armholes of his old leather jerkin. 'What do 'un say, tinner?'

Elyas couldn't read. None of them could. But he could recite the contents of the document fairly accurately from memory. He held it before his face in an impressive manner. 'This sett containing cottage, barn, pig-pen, stable, bal, blowing house . . .'

'I seed only cottage.' The farmer scratched his head beneath his wide black hat in puzzlement as he looked about him.

Elyas scowled and said curtly: 'Rest bain't bin built yet.' He continued his recitation: '. . . all buildings belong to Elyas Hammett the tinner because him and his kinfolk did build cottage and wall 'twixt sunup and sundown . . .'

'Give 'un here,' the farmer interrupted the flow. He took the paper and the charcoal and carefully drew a fat, short-legged sheep at the bottom of the page which was his mark, coming from Lamb's Down Farm.

Elyas took the document, folded it carefully and put it away in his pocket to give to the stannary steward at Plympton for entering on the Stannary Roll. He produced a crown piece and the farmer's eyes glistened. 'Now see 'ere, farmer,' he said, 'if folks ask, you'm t'say as how Hammetts squat on this sett legal belike. Say as how you'm saw first stone laid, understand?'

'I'll tell they,' the farmer said eagerly.

The coin exchanged hands.

Elyas beamed. 'Now then, what 'bout sup of yon ale?'

Tired as he was, Elyas didn't sleep much that night. He lay on the floor of his new home, staring up through the gaping roof at the dark, gathering clouds. The weather would break soon for sure. There'd be rain; mebbe a fog. And it was colder than it had been. Must get the roof turfed first thing.

Isaac, lying near him, muttered in his sleep.

Elyas felt a sudden surge of pride at all they had achieved. The cottage belonged to Elyas Hammett the tinner, pack and vardel. He chuckled at the notion. Moreover, he'd got his mine!

Dawn was approaching. As he gazed up, he saw a shadow swoop across the fading night sky towards the tower of stone above the valley. The eagle!

'There now! I knew I *seed* 'un!' he whispered contentedly, eyelids drooping. 'I knowed 'twas omen . . .'

Chapter Three

Throughout the winter they worked from first to last light of the brief days.

They finished the cottage and added another small room at the back. Built a barn and stable and, more importantly, a rectangular blowing house with a tall chimney and a big stone furnace to smelt the tin.

By the new year they were mining in earnest. Blocks of tin shone dully in the yard. It hardly mattered if they were left unattended as each one weighed 300 pounds or more and could only be carried away with great difficulty. But Elyas was leaving nothing to chance – not when they'd sweated for their metal harvest! He bought a useful lurcher dog from the farm and tied it on a long rope beside the tin.

Since Isaac spent so much time in the sweltering air of the blowing house sorting ore, he was sent out across the moor for an hour each day to clear his lungs while the lurcher hunted for its food: rabbits and hares and other small mammals fell prey to its extraordinary speed. The boy thought of the dog as his and took to calling it Wart since his hands had been covered with them until the hound licked the growths and they magically disappeared overnight.

'Call he "dog",' ordered Elyas disapprovingly. 'Give dog name and you'm git attached to he. Mebbe got to drown he one day if he sicky.'

But for once Isaac disobeyed his grandfather and continued to call the dog Wart and after a while they all did.

Early on 4 April, Elyas set off for Plympton with the tin ingots on a wagon borrowed from Lamb's Down Farm and pulled by a moor colt, rounded up and broken by Isaac who already seemed more at home upon the moor than ever he'd been by the sea.

All that week, the stannary receiver would weigh and assay the tin brought to the 'tinners' hall' where, if the quality was up to the mark, the ingots would be stamped with the Duchy coat of arms as a guarantee of purity and that the toll had been paid on them. No tin could legally be sold until it was thus assayed; yet, much to the tinners' chagrin, 'coinages' were held only twice yearly which meant tributers and the smaller bal-owners usually had to run up credit between times just to survive. Or else they'd mortgage their tin with a tin-shark for half its value. Elyas was saved from doing either, thanks to Dame Rogers's generous investment.

On his way through Cornwood, he stopped to proudly show her the tin and to have her complete the deeds of his smallholding and mine. He also insisted she draw up a proper certificate for both of them to sign, showing her to be a sixth shareholder in the project.

'It really isn't necessary, Mr Hammett. Why, I have your hand on it and that's good enough for me,' she told him.

But he was insistent. He fixed her with a direct look. 'Now then, mistress, you'm knows as well as I, tinners ne'er make old bones. You'm draw up that paper proper cos I don't want t'see you'm lose out when I'm gone.'

There was no arguing with him. Besides, she had expended her life's savings on the venture. She took up her pen. 'And what is the name of your estate, Mr Hammett?' she asked with a twinkle.

'Eaglestone.' He sucked his teeth and cleared his throat. 'I were a-wonderin' . . .'

'Yes?'

' 'Bout bal . . .' He paused.

'What about it?'

'Do ye think it be awlright if'n us call it . . . *Wheal* Eaglestone? I mean, that bain't be too falutin' for family bal, be it?'

'That will be perfectly acceptable,' she assured him.

He watched her write. Then she dipped her pen in the ink again and gave it to him to make his mark at the bottom of both documents. After a moment's hesitation, he drew an eagle with its wings outstretched.

Elyas watched as the receiver scraped off a corner of each of his six tin bars and tossed the sample across the anvil to the controller for a rapid assessment of quality.

'Best toad's-eye tin, that be,' Elyas informed him loftily.

The controller scowled, irritated at being told his business by a lowly tin-miner. 'Is this all?'

'Bal only bin a-goin' since back'long Christmas,' retorted Elyas. He pointed to the deed which he'd handed over and which now lay on the controller's desk. 'Sez so there . . . bain't you'm able t'read?'

The controller lowered at him. 'Watch thy jaw, tinner,' he warned nastily.

Elyas gave an unconcerned shrug but nevertheless fell silent: he didn't want the stannary men short-weighting him out of spite. The controller nodded to the receiver who wrote in his ledger. Elyas's tin went under hammer and punch on the anvil and was imprinted with the Duchy arms. He heaved a sigh of relief and almost cheerfully counted out his toll of four shillings a hundredweight.

The Stannary Hall was filled with traders. Tin merchants, pewterers, middle men; some local, some foreign, but mostly from London, mingled with the money men offering loans at extortionate rates of interest. Elyas stalked by them with a disdainful expression. He examined the traders' faces. Ten or so years before he'd have known them all by sight, having driven many a wagonload of tin to the coinages from the bal where he worked. But now the faces were all new. All save that of an ageing Spaniard. He went and stood before him and doffed his hat.

They settled for £3.10s a hundredweight.

The Spaniard paid in copper tokens of a high denomination. 'Bain't 'ee got proper guineas?' asked Elyas disappointedly.

The trader shrugged indifferently. The tokens were legal tender anywhere in the district. Even in London. Elyas knew that but he'd have liked to see some real gold coins for no other reason than this was the first time he'd been to a coinage with his own tin and he felt the occasion should be properly marked. He put the tokens carefully away in a gunny sack tied beneath his smock-dress, then tugged his forelock to the Spaniard and left the noisy tinners' hall.

A market and horsefair marked coinage week. The town was crammed with men and women from the surrounding farms mingling with tinners, butchers, drovers, hawkers, pedlars and tinkers of every low station. Noise resounded from every part: cries, oaths, bartering, the bleating of sheep and the bellowing of cattle. The streets were a filthy, muddy mire and the stench made Elyas's eyes water and caught at his lungs, making him cough dryly. He left his wagon hitched and went in search of an inn.

The tap-room was crowded. A plump maid brought him his food and drink: a pint of cider and some fried eggs and parsley. The pot-girl reminded him of poor, dead Betsy. She'd the same round, jolly, dimpled face and small hands and feet. A momentary sadness filled him, reminding him that once again they were without a woman to look after them at Eaglestone.

'Be you'm sparkin', maid?' he made a hopeful enquiry as to her marital prospects, but she didn't answer bee nor baw to him and just went off laughing, used to many similar, saucy questions from the customers.

The town-cryer stepped inside from the street and rang his brass bell vigorously to draw the attention of those standing at the counter and crammed along the long, wooden tables. 'Oyez!' he bellowed and, since he was employed by the town fathers, they stopped talking to listen to his announcement. 'Sale by auction of a daughter at one o'clock today in the square. Her is aged nineteen and comely wi' good hair and teeth and is of good temper. Her's had smallpox and measles and is fit in mind and body. Oyez!'

Bawdy shouts followed him out.

'Did 'un say auction of a *daughter*?' Elyas asked a man near to him, not sure if he'd heard right.

The man, clearly a townie by the cut of his short waistcoat and brown-wool frock-coat, nodded. 'Aye.' He leaned towards Elyas in a conspiratorial fashion. 'They do say as how she's a tasty piece and being sold of her own free will.'

Elyas drew a rasping breath, his eyes starting from his head at such boldness. 'By the Lord Harry!'

The townie leaned still closer to him. 'And . . .' he looked around as though he was afraid of being overheard spreading scabrous gossip. '. . . they say her reckons on ridin' to town square on horseback!'

Elyas blinked. Such goings on! 'Her must be right forthy!' he observed.

His new acquaintance shook his head. 'Nay, they say her still be undefiled!'

That made Elyas think. There they were, the Hammetts, needing a woman, and here were this maid up for sale. 'How much for a daughter, do 'ee reckon?'

The townie looked at him in surprise, saw that he was serious and gave a guffaw of laughter. 'More'n sack of thy 'tatties, farm boy,' he scoffed.

'I bain't farmer. I be mine-owner,' Elyas tetchily put him right.

The man looked him over, taking in his old calico smock-frock and leather gaiters with ill-concealed disdain. 'An' I be Napoleon Bonyparte,' he retorted with heavy sarcasm.

Elyas spat on the floor. 'Faugh! If'n you'm *were* yon Frenchie, you'm wouldn't be a-sittin' here a-suppin'. You'm be a-hangin' on Gibbet Hill!' he retorted. He took a deep draught of his cider. 'This daughter . . .'

The man gave him a lascivious wink and dug him with his elbow. 'Her be lookin' for a young buck to tap she! Not piss-proud old fumbler like thyself for a husband!'

'Her bain't for I. Her for my boy Huward on account he widdered wi' boys of his own.'

The other produced a battered silver watch and peered at it. 'Then best make haste if 'ee wants t'bid for she. 'Tis near one.' Elyas emptied his mug and stood up. 'And don't 'ee pay more'n two pound for she. Not 'less her got an inheritance coming.'

Elyas thanked him gravely for this useful piece of advice and went to join the curious, chattering crowd gathering in the square to watch the auction.

The girl arrived promptly, astride an old cob and accompanied by her father on foot. A buzz of interest percolated through the throng. She was a handsome maid. Dark haired, with intriguing, slanted, brown-black eyes and very pale skin that, unfortunately, bore the ravages of smallpox. Her coarse brown skirt was ragged and showed most of her muscular calves. Her kerseymere bodice barely hung together over her firm, ample breasts.

'Her just a *didekei* maid!' sneered a voice in the crowd.

'An' her be 'bove nineteen! Twenty-five gone, more likely'd!' enjoined another.

Disappointed by such revelations, some of the crowd lost interest and moved away as the girl's father mounted a keg in readiness to begin the auction. Gypsies often sold off their unwanted daughters; there was no mistaking his origins since his coal-black crinkled hair and swarthy skin bore witness to his Romany blood. And there was the tug. Gypsies were terrible troublesome. A lazy, thieving, pagan breed.

Elyas wasn't put off. After all, he told himself, she was only a *didekei*. Half gyppo! That was clear by her gardenia-white skin. Not that her skin was of the slightest interest to him, pitted or not. No, it was her strong legs and arms that interested him. Fine, muscular limbs that could do the work of a man in by the bal and blowing house.

He wasn't the only one with a fancy for buying her. Bidding started at five shillings and rose quickly to the two pounds that the man in the tap-room had advised Elyas to make his limit. 'Do her have an inheritance, gypsy?' he called and the crowd roared with laughter.

'Aye, her pa's thievin' ways!' came a shouted answer and the crowd gave another gleeful roar.

Despite their distrust of gypsies, the bidding climbed to three pounds. There was a shortage of marriageable females in the parish as all the newly enlisted soldiers and sailors were marrying their best shiners before they went off to fight the French. Also, this maid seemed a particularly meek sort sitting there quietly astride her nag.

'Four!'

'And five shillings, gypsy!'

'And five more!'

Some of those bidding, farmers used to cattle auctions, signalled their bid to the gypsy in their own, various, silent ways: a crooked eyebrow here, a raised finger there. The gypsy never missed a bid and soon he was calling six pounds. And there the bidding stuck.

Elyas was sorely tempted to start the bidding again at £6.5s. Yet, surveying the *didekei* he hesitated; there was something unnerving about her stillness.

'Her bain't be a dummy, be her?' he asked suddenly.

The crowd didn't scoff at him this time. They exchanged looks, surprised that this clodpated moorman had thought to ask such a question. They might well have been bidding for a mute. But her intriguing, tilted eyes swivelled to rest upon Elyas. She smiled faintly and shook her head by way of reply.

'Six pounds and five shillings from Elyas Hammett the tinner!' he bid loftily.

There was a hush. As if they were awe-struck, which is what they were. Didn't the addlepate realise *who* had made the previous bid of £6? And in such a tone as to brook no higher bids! That same voice rumbled forth again, and this time there was mistaking the menacing overtones.

'Six pounds *ten* shillings . . . from John de Raddon, Lord Warden of the Stannaries!'

Elyas blinked with the realisation of whose bid he'd topped. He searched the crowd for the mine-owner. It was over ten years since he'd last seen him: even longer since he'd slaved for de Raddon's father. So now son John, in his turn, had become the all-powerful head of the tinning community. Well, thought Elyas wryly, it was a pity Dame Rogers hadn't said. For this was boggy ground he was treading.

His eyes located de Raddon, which wasn't difficult since the Lord Warden stood almost a head above the rest of the crowd. He was a little over thirty. Wore a black frock coat, buckskin breeches and top boots. His wig, very black, was of the old style favoured by the gentry, curling over his ears and caught in a pigtail at the nape. Around his neck hung his gold chain of office. He was accompanied by his steward; a ruffianly looking fellow with wild sandy brows sprouting from his red face.

Elyas wasted not a moment in pulling off his hat in his most deferential manner. 'Good day to 'ee, zurs.'

De Raddon and his steward looked at him sourly, seeing even this small courtesy as an over-familiarity on the part of a lowly tinner who should know better than to speak before being spoken to by the Lord Warden.

De Raddon turned to the gypsy. 'Give me your hand on it, fellow. The maid's mine!'

The gypsy clearly believed that there would be no more bids. Obediently, he stuck out his palm for de Raddon to slap with his own. Elyas couldn't say afterwards what made him suddenly brush the gypsy's hand aside, saying: 'Hold thy hoss, gypsy, I ent made up my mind yet. Might want t'make 'nother bid, I might.'

A murmur ran through the crowd. They didn't know whether to pity his stupidity or admire his audacity. De Raddon roughly pushed aside those in front of him and stepped forward to loom in front of Elyas. The crowd closed in around the two of them, eager not to miss what promised to be rare entertainment. It wasn't often the Lord Warden had his nose publicly tweaked by one of his tinners. Elyas stood his ground, refusing to be brow-beaten by the other's formidable presence. 'If'n it bain't owdacious, Cap'n de Raddon, zur, might I ask after health of thy good lady wife?' he asked deferentially.

De Raddon glared. 'She's well . . . 'tho' what business that is of your's, tinner, God and the devil only know!'

Elyas hastened to explain. 'Ah now, Cap'n, I was just a-thinkin' . . . since there awlready be a Mrs Cap'n at home, I'd say you'm need 'nother bride like toad do need side-pockets.'

His words hung in the soft, spring air. De Raddon's face turned slowly puce.

A ripple went through the crowd. It was well-known throughout the parish that de Raddon's marriage hadn't stopped him from pleasuring himself with any maid that took his fancy, willing or not, so it was rumoured. He'd married sweet Emma, the daughter of another mine-owner, for her inheritance and to beget an heir. So far his wife had disappointed him on both accounts: her father was still robust and she was proving stubbornly barren.

As a young man, working as his late father's overseer, de Raddon was badly injured in a pit explosion which had claimed more than a hundred lives. The ghastly evidence of that day was a missing ear and a livid mass of scars on the left side of his face, concealed in the main by his curling wig. It was whispered that he'd left a good proportion of his manhood in the mine with his ear – sufficient to account for his lack of offspring, but not enough to interfere with his fornicating.

Elyas kept his face bland and his manner obsequious as he waited for de Raddon's response to his question. The Lord Warden's face was scarlet with anger. He'd no intention of discussing with this looby, or anyone else, his highly salacious plans for the gypsy wench. Neither was he going to be thwarted in those plans. He swung on her father. 'Six pounds ten shillings I bid. Give me your palm on it, gypsy, and I'll give you the silver.'

Elyas was sorely tempted, but decided to keep a still tongue. Weren't no sense in getting Lord Warden's monkey up, he decided, when he'd got to come to town regularly for the coinage. Yet, this time, even as the gypsy extended his hand to de Raddon, it was the girl herself who halted the sale: speaking for the first time in a voice that was oddly melodic and, like so many itinerants, without the marked accent of the West Country.

'Nay, Pa. I'm here of my own free will and I'll not be sold to Scarface.'

'You'll do as your pa sez!' snapped de Raddon.

The girl threw him a disdainful glance. Her father, not caring which of them bought her, merely shrugged. Her eyes sought Elyas. 'Is it a wife you're after, Greybeard?'

'For my son, Huward.'

'Then I'll wed your son if you'll buy me a gold ring and a new dress and swear he'll not beat me.'

'I swear.'

She slid from the cob's back. 'Slap hands wi' Pa.'

He did so.

De Raddon was almost beside himself. 'I bid six pounds ten shillings fair for you, girl, and won't be welshed 'pon!' he raged, grabbing her arm and spinning her around to face him. 'Best change your mind and come with me, if you know what's good for you!'

She was unmoved by his threat. She met his snapping eyes with a steady gaze. Her dark eyes seemed to bore right into him: into his very soul. Fear was a rare experience for him, but he felt it tug at his insides and abruptly he released her, as if her flesh seared his fingers. Aware of the curiously watching crowd, he favoured her with his most unpleasant and intimidating expression.

'I've chosen,' she said simply and turned away from him.

'God damn you to hell where you belong, you eternal bitch!' he cursed her and swung on his heel. Immediately, the crowd parted to let him and the lowering Grote through.

Elyas began to count copper tokens into the gypsy's hand. The girl stopped him when he got to £6.5s, saying, ' 'Twere Scarface bid six an' a half, Pa. Tinner bid six pounds, five shillings and that's what he'll pay.'

The gypsy didn't look pleased but he didn't argue.

'Do it include cob?' asked Elyas slyly.

By way of reply, the gypsy mounted the beast's bare back and urged it through the thinning crowd without so much as a backward glance at his daughter.

'God help yon tinner, I sez,' remarked a farmer to his companion. 'John de Raddon ent sort to be trifled wi'. And he can harbour a very long grudge.'

'And I says 'tis *didekei* will need God's help if he ever sets his eyes on her 'gin,' said the other man soberly.

Elyas bought the girl her new dress. He stood patiently sucking an old clay pipe while she sorted through a tangled pile of women's clothes on one of the pedlars' carts which lined both sides of the main street. She chose a sensible, rust-red, wool garment. She went behind the cart and reappeared a few moments later with it on. Plain though it was, it suited her glossy dark hair and pale skin admirably. Elyas nodded and paid the pedlar two shillings. At another cart he bought her a straw hat with ribbons under the chin for threepence and, since she was barefoot, an old pair of boots for sixpence. He also bought her a flannel petticoat to wear on the rare occasions they went to church since the dress clung somewhat revealingly to her muscular legs.

The promised ring cost him a shilling. It wasn't real gold but brass. She didn't seem to mind and slipped it on her hand with a smile. It was the first time he'd seen her smile. Her teeth were good: strong and white without many black bits.

Although Elyas had spent a sizeable sum buying a wife for Huward and fixing her up for him, he didn't grudge a penny; it wasn't good for a young man not to have a woman about the place, working for him. With her meekly at his heels, he set off through the mud to where he'd left the wagon, unaware that de Raddon's brooding eyes followed them from an upper, private room in the inn across the way.

'So the bitch prefers the embraces of a tinner's whelp to those of a gentleman, does she?' de Raddon fulminated.

Grote, refilling his master's tankard with ale, wasn't sure if the Lord Warden was addressing him. 'Shall I go after them, Cap'n de Raddon? Send old'n packing and bring maid back here to 'ee?' he asked.

De Raddon was tempted. His mouth curled wolfishly at the thought of teaching her a lesson, but he shook his head regretfully. He hadn't the time at present for such pursuits: he'd the coinage to attend to.

'Nay, leave 'em be, Grote. For now . . .'

Chapter Four

They were within sight of Eagle Tor, trundling along in companionable silence, when it suddenly occurred to Elyas that he didn't know his future daughter-in-law's name.

'Ruke,' she told him when he asked.

'Ruke . . .' he repeated doubtfully, scratching his head. 'Haven't 'ee 'nother handle?' She shook her head. 'Well, it be good as elly, I s'pose.' They jogged on for a while and then he pointed with his birch up the valley. 'There her be . . . Eaglestone!'

She gazed without expression at the square, stone cottage and the little group of outbuildings. The cottage chimney sent up quiet wreaths of pale peat-smoke to be scattered by the breeze. Thick black smoke belched from the tall blowing-house stack, indicating smelting was in progress. It hung over the combe like a low, dark raincloud.

Wart had begun to bark before they were even in sight. Huward, Graeme and Isaac, faces filthy and sweat-streaked, came out of the blowing house to welcome the traveller home. Day had almost gone, but even in the half-light they could make out the female figure seated next to Elyas. As the wagon got nearer they could see that she was young and comely. Isaac and Graeme giggled, nudging each other embarrassedly. They'd not had much to do with women since their mother died.

Huward hushed them by saying, 'Watch thy gobs now.'

Elyas brought the wagon to a halt outside the cottage door. 'This be Ruke,' he introduced her.

Ruke climbed agilely down with a flounce of skirts and a flash of bare, white legs which set Graeme and Isaac off nudging and giggling again. Huward scowled at them but she smiled briefly, showing her large teeth.

'Her got holes in her ears. Her be a *didekei*!' observed sharp-eyed Isaac, forgetting his shyness with this revelation.

'You'm never mind that,' said Elyas. 'Her gonna be thy new ma.'

That silenced them all. Huward stood as though dumbfounded. Graeme and Isaac exchanged amazed looks. Then they stared at their grandfather, wondering if he was funning. But there was no twinkle in his eyes. He gave his son a push. 'Where be thy manners, boy? Say thy howdedos to Ruke . . . her be thy new bride.'

'But, Pa, I d . . . don't n . . . need no bride . . .' stuttered Huward, his face growing crimson beneath its coating of grime.

Elyas's jaw set firm. ' 'Course 'ee do, boy! You'm alivin' too chaste. Ent good for ’ee . . . give ’ee gout or some such. ’Sides, boys need ma an’ washin’ house needs bal maiden!’

There was no point in arguing. His word was, as ever, final.

Huward shuffled his feet. ‘Be you’m willing?’ he asked Ruke.

Before she could answer, Elyas butted in. ‘ ’Course her’s willin’! Else her wouldn’t be here!’

‘Best I see parson tomorrow then,’ said Huward.

‘Aye, best,’ agreed Elyas. He gave a bellow of laughter and clapped his son between the shoulders. ‘Comely wench like she, you’m want to get they banns smacked off and get ’ee hitched!’

His guffawing awakened Jamie in the cottage. He started to yell with hunger. Without a word, Ruke went inside and picked him up. He forgot his empty belly in his surprise at being rocked against her soft breasts rather than a man’s hard chest. He stared interestedly at the strange face, put out a hand and explored a handful of the soft dark hair.

Elyas and Huward followed her in while the boys tended the colt.

‘Have you milk and eggs?’

Huward showed her where they stored the foodstuffs in big, earthenware stugs away from the heat of the range, then stood watching as, with Jamie balanced on her hip, she cracked an egg one-handed into a pot and poured in a measure of thick, pale yellow milk. She tossed in a piece of salt and set it on the hot iron slab to cook. Jamie kicked his feet with anticipation as she stirred his supper.

‘Best be getting back to blowing house, boy,’ Elyas told Huward, stamping out. ‘Don’t waste good furnace.’

When the fire in the granite trough had lost its heat, they trooped back to the cottage. Only to stand in a bunch just inside the door, gazing around them as if they were strangers in their own home.

Ruke hadn’t wasted a moment. The floor was swept and scrubbed and strewn with fresh rushes. She’d melted the ends of tallow and made a good-sized candle, the light of which flickered on Jamie’s sleeping face as he slept soundly on a pallet in a corner of the room near the range for warmth. She’d cut off his matted fair curls and rubbed his scalp with strong vinegar to kill the nits – ever a bane to him and inclined to make him fretful when the sun shone.

She’d scrubbed the wooden table with salt until the wood was almost white. It was set with knives and spoons, basins, tin mugs and plates. Pots boiled and bubbled on the slab.

Elyas breathed in the delicious aroma of baking and said a silent prayer of thanks for being struck with the good sense to buy her in the face of de Raddon’s wrath.

‘ ’Tis ready,’ she said and they made a rush for the wooden stools.

They ate in silence, relishing the hot beef figgen and boiled swedes mashed with dollops of lard. This was followed by a vast apple-dicky made from dried apples and currants mixed into the same unleavened pastry as the figgen and served with thick cream. The lot washed down with mugs of sugared beer.

As soon as they'd eaten, Graeme and Isaac fell upon their pallets in the larger of the two back rooms. Elyas usually slept in the front with Jamie, but they made this room over to Ruke for the time being. Elyas took his pallet into the back and Huward took himself off to the barn since it wasn't proper for him to sleep beneath the same roof as his intended.

She watched him go with her usual stolidity of expression.

Sleep didn't come quickly to Elyas. He lay coughing for a while. His lungs were troublesome of late now he was back tinning. It was the dust. He belched once or twice, tasting again the apple-dicky, and grinned in the dark at the memory of the best supper he'd eaten since before poor Betsy died. Even she, good cook though she was, couldn't make as tasty a dicky as the *didekei* maid.

He was drifting off to sleep when a sound caught his attention. It was the squeak of the front door. He rose quickly and ducked behind the curtain of joined-together flour sacks hanging between the rooms. The glow from the range lit up Jamie, still sleeping. Ruke had gone. Muttering a curse, Elyas went to the window and looked out. He fully expected to see her running away down the valley. It wouldn't be the first time a gypsy had 'sold' his daughter or his horse or his dog only to have the 'bargain' bolt home at the first opportunity.

The moon, riding a clear, star-dotted sky, shone keenly across the yard. Elyas spotted Ruke and sent her a silent apology for thinking she might be party to any such low conspiracy. She'd taken the old lantern to light her way and was hurrying towards the barn. Wart lay asleep across the entrance but as she approached he rose growling, hackles erect. Afraid he'd attack her, Elyas was about to call to the dog when Ruke gave a low, tuneful whistle. Instantly, Wart dropped submissively to his belly, his long muzzle on his front paws.

'By the Lord Harry!' breathed Elyas, impressed by what he'd just witnessed. Ruke calmly stepped over Wart and went into the barn. Elyas watched a while longer but she didn't reappear. He went back to bed chuckling. 'Her be a right cockish wench b'all accounts!'

Lying in the pitch-black, Huward heard the barn door open and shut again. A square of dull, yellow light pierced the darkness.

'Be that you'm, Isaac?'

The boy was sometimes troubled by night-hags and crept near his father for comfort. Though not as often of late, it was true, since he was going on thirteen.

'No. 'Tis Ruke.'

The square of lantern light moved towards him. He could make her out now. She was smiling, showing her white teeth. She set the lantern down carefully on a pile of peat vags and knelt beside him in the straw. He gazed at her almost sculptured face with wonder. He paid no attention to the pox marks. Or her jutting jaw. Nor did he care that she was a *didekei*. She was more handsome than he deserved.

'W . . . what do 'ee want wi' I, maid?' he asked her awkwardly.

She didn't say. For a few seconds, her strange, tilted eyes narrowed like those of a cat. Her hands slipped behind her back and she tugged at her loosened lacing. Her intention became obvious when, with a swift movement, she pulled her russet dress over her head.

'W . . . we'm ent churched,' stuttered Huward, taken aback by her boldness.

She shrugged. 'No matter. We will be.'

Her hands went behind her again, this time to undo her stays and cast them aside. Her cotton chemise had seen better days; it was mended and patched in a number of places. In a moment, it, too, was discarded. Huward gazed upon her voluptuous white body as she lay back against a straw fardel. Quicksand moved within him as she lifted her arms to unpin her hair, pushing her full breasts forth like round, ripe fruit. She shook her dark mane loose, peeping at him through it in a tantalising manner.

In the silence, Huward could almost hear his heart thudding as if he'd a drum in his chest. Yet, he made no move towards her. A frown creased his weathered brow as he sat transfixed by her pale-skinned torso. He shifted his position, first one way and then another, half-thinking that the poor light was playing tricks with his eyes. But no! They weren't birthmarks; or two identical moles; or pox-pits. Or any other such common blemishes. She *did* have four nipples! All of the same generous size and pinkish-brown colour.

'You'm got four teats,' he was drawn to remark with wonder in his voice.

Ruke grinned and nodded, running her fingers over the two extra papilla that protruded from her ribcage. They were useless as paps, merely a mistake of nature, and as the gypsies considered a woman's breasts purely functional, she didn't consider a double set important. She was, however, fully aware that the non-gypsies – the *gadje* – lusted after this particular part of the female form. 'Four are better than two, I think, husband,' she said teasingly.

He was shocked by her brazenness. And bemused by it. He felt more foolish than he had as a naïve boy of eighteen on his wedding night. He'd only ever known Betsy's plain, plump body, and then only in the dark, fumbling beneath the cotton nightgowns she always wore. Betsy had always smelled of fish from the gutting shed. Ruke smelled of herbs. An unfamiliar, musky scent which filled his nostrils and made his blood race as she suddenly moved close to him, tugging at his smock. He dragged it off. Then wriggled out of his breeches. With a stifled, hoarse cry he seized her and pressed her down into the straw beneath him. His mouth devoured hers as his big, rough hands sought the smooth orbs of her breasts. He rubbed the whole length of his sturdy body urgently against her so that she felt the tangle of coarse hair covering his torso, belly and thighs. Blushing hotly at his own frenzy, he thrust himself into her and with rampant speed assuaged his agony of longing in a surge of intense, turbulent pleasure. Almost immediately he withdrew from her with a grunt of carnal satisfaction and, rancid from his efforts, rolled on to his back.

Ruke lay quietly, muscular legs still spread, pale flesh shimmering in the dim glow thrown by the lantern.

After a while he said: 'Best 'ee go back'long cottage now.'

She rolled on her side to look at him. 'Why can't I stay? Babbie'll not stir. Besides, the old one is there if he wakes.'

'Best 'ee go,' he repeated doggedly. 'We'm not churched yet.'

She saw no point in arguing. She slipped into her clothes, took her lantern and went out without a word. Huward found his smock and pulled it on against the chilly night air. He grinned to himself in the dark: he felt new-made.

They were married within the month, and over the ensuing weeks Ruke taught Huward how to be a good lover. How to restrain his urge until she was satisfied, too, heightening the experience for himself. He forgot to be shocked by her brazenness as she showed him the things that a woman could do to excite a man other than just removing her chemise and lying on her back. Sometimes he fleetingly wondered, perhaps as she lay on top of him, or sat astride him so that he could caress her fine, firm breasts, how she came to know such things. It didn't occur to him to ask her; in the vague recesses of his mind he presumed that gypsies must in some way 'train' their young women in the craft of fornication. In which case, he told himself with deep gratification, she'd proved an apt pupil.

It wasn't long before Ruke said as they lay together in their room one night, 'I'm to have a child.'

He was pleased. It meant that she was really his now. And he felt a sense of pride that he'd so quickly fertilised this handsome, sensuous wife of his. He ran his hand tentatively over her breasts and belly: already her anatomy felt fuller and more rounded. Even her two extra nipples felt suddenly different to his probing fingers.

'When?' he asked.

She didn't answer. She was asleep.

'So 'ee still has plenty of sap in 'ee, eh, boy?' Elyas ribbed Huward when his son told him about the baby as they worked together next morning in the bal.

Elyas didn't say so, but he hadn't needed to be told his new daughter-in-law was pregnant. He'd instinctively known it even as he stood with Huward before the parson making their vows. It was all to do with the arch of the back. Elyas had seen it often enough with his own wife. And Betsy. And the moor ponies when they were in foal.

When Ruke brought their mossle bags at mid-day, Elyas gave her a playful slap on the rump. 'You'm be sure and produce a fine big boy,' he commanded her, 'wi' Isaac nigh on growed us'll be needing new apprentice in by blowing-house.'

She nodded gravely, understanding how important a son was to this family of tinners.

Elyas surreptitiously inspected Ruke as she filled mugs from a canteen of water for them to wash the dust from their throats. She was certainly burgeoning. Yet, it was, he calculated, less than two months since she'd first crept out to be with Huward in the barn. Knowing something of women's things, Elyas was now sure that she'd probably been pregnant when he bought her – which would explain her sale, and why she'd wasted no time in lying with her intended. The sly, cat-eyed creature meant to pass the child off as her new husband's.

Elyas decided it was best to say nothing; at least for the time being. Sometimes, however, Ruke caught him eyeing her growing belly speculatively. But if she sensed he'd guessed her pregnancy was more advanced than she claimed, she gave no sign of it, and, as if to prove him wrong, worked from dawn to dusk with no obvious sign of weariness.

She continued to expand throughout the summer but seemed to stop towards the end of October. Now she had to sit on a milking-stool to sort the tinstone. And Elyas noticed that when she walked, she placed the palms of her hands in the small of her back – just like his wife and Betsy always did when they were near being brought to bed.

On the last day of October, All-Hallows, Elyas's suspicions were finally confirmed. For Ruke gave birth barely seven months after she'd come to Eaglestone. And there was nothing about the long-legged baby girl with the thatch of brown-black hair to suggest she'd arrived early. Moreover, Elyas reminded himself, the Hammetts bred only boys.

The farmer's wife from Lamb's Down had reluctantly come across the moor to act as midwife. All-Hallows was a time of witches and fire and moorland spectres and not a time to be abroad. But she'd been persuaded for half a crown – providing Graeme and Isaac accompanied her to and from the farm and she was back home with all the doors bolted by nightfall.

Elyas knew that his first loyalty should be to his son, yet, as they worked together in the mine all that day, he discovered he was reluctant to tell Huward the child wasn't a real Hammett. It seemed pointless now the baby was born. Besides, if Huward divorced her they'd still have to get a woman to work for them and do a coore each day in the washing house, and good reliable workers like Ruke weren't easy to come by. So it was that Huward remained blissfully in ignorance of the fact that he'd another man's bastard fathered upon him. Moreover, he didn't seem too disappointed with his new daughter when he viewed her at crousttime.

The farmer's wife was washing her for the first time, as lore dictated, by a protective ashwood fire. Particularly important since she'd arrived on much-dreaded All-Hallows. Huward gazed at the narrow limbs, as pale as her mother's. 'Babbie got right long legs.'

'Aye, cos I'd t'pull hard on they to get she out,' explained the woman. She finished drying the yelling infant, rolled her in a clean cotton apron and gave her to Ruke to suckle.

Ruke still lay weakly on the pallet. Though she was young and strong, with wide, child-bearing hips, the birth had nevertheless proved long and difficult. Huward went and looked down into her ashen face.

'I'm sorry 'tis a worthless girl, husband,' she whispered, tears glittering in her dark-ringed eyes.

He stooped and patted her sweat-dampened head as he might pat Wart when the dog brought home a plump hare or pigeon for the pot and he was pleased with him. 'Don't 'ee fret none, wife. Maid be useful in washing house an' 'twill likely'd be boy next time, b'mercy of God!'

He left her and went back to work in the mine.

A thin mist was rising from the brook as, at dusk, Elyas and Huward made their way from the mine to the cottage along the now well-worn track. ' 'Twill be fog afore dawn,' predicted Elyas knowingly. He coughed and spat. Once he'd revelled in the soft, white moor mists which contorted every bush and rock until they loomed like giant things. These days the vapour was torture to his sodden lungs, making his chest feel tight and his breath rasp in his throat. Yet, he didn't complain. Dust and fog were, in his opinion, better by far than the stink of fish. Ruke, hearing him coughing in the night, had tried to persuade him to drink one of her vile-tasting concoctions, but he'd firmly refused, saying: 'Nay, m'dear, 'tis nawthin' save a touch of the tilly-gilly.'

Ruke was up and preparing supper when they went in. A little colour had returned to her cheeks. She'd washed her hair so that it floated about her face like a black, shining cloud. She was suckling the baby supported at her breast in a large kerchief. Jamie had been fed and was already asleep. 'Vittles is almost ready,' she told them.

They were growing accustomed to her short, clipped sentences and the way she sometimes said everything she wanted to say with little more than a gesture or a movement of her handsome head.

Elyas gave her an approving nod. 'That's the way, m'dear! Best get 'ee movin'. Ye'll heal all the quicker for it . . . like 'un cow or mare. They beasts know 'stinctively what's proper for they.'

He stripped off his smock and shook the dust from it outside the door. The others did the same.

Before she'd left, the farmer's wife had lifted the biggest of the steel cauldrons on to the slab and filled it with water carried from the brook so that Ruke wouldn't strain her healing innards and start bleeding again. They washed in order of seniority: first Elyas, then Huward, then Graeme and Isaac who had by now returned from taking the farmer's wife back to the farm.

'Her be proper frighted,' sneered Graeme. 'Her see hedgyboors back of every bush her do . . . eyes dartin' like stockin'-niddles!'

'And her wouldn't set out 'til us all had piece of bread crossed wi' salt in us pockets to save us from witches,' sniggered Isaac.

Elyas was quick to chide them. 'Don't you'm boys scoff at elly such. Best take precautions on All-Hallows . . . plenty folk have been took by they witches on moor for want of bread an' salt in they pockets.'

Isaac and Graeme exchanged looks. They'd eaten their bread and salt talismans on the way home without realising that they were truly in mortal danger.

Elyas pointed to the door, left ajar by his grandsons. 'And 'ee better close door if'n 'ee don't want some evil thing to come in and make 'un home wi' us for life.'

The very thought sent Isaac rushing to shut the door and drop the latch. 'Gramps . . . will 'ee tell us 'bout they folk as got took by witches?' he asked when he'd washed himself as best he could in the warm, muddy-coloured water in the cauldron. He loved a good yarn.

Elyas stroked his damp beard. 'Not sure as I should, boy . . . it be a right horrible tale for thy young ears. Give 'un night-widdles 'gin.'

'*Please,* Gramps,' pleaded Isaac. 'I swears I won't frighted.'

Elyas liked to tantalise. 'Mebbe I will, mebbe I won't . . . you'm just have to wait an' see, boy.'

They gathered around the table and Ruke ladled steaming soup into the basins set before them. They gulped the aromatic hot liquid and hungrily ate the meat and vegetables with their fingers, wiping hunks of bread around the basin so as not to waste a drop. She'd made a fat currant-figgen to finish supper. The baby awoke mewling so she put it back in the big kerchief she wore to suckle it as she ate.

Isaac eyed the baby. 'What's 'un new babbie called, Pa?'

His father looked surprised. He'd not given any thought to a name. After all, it wasn't as if it was a boy. He looked across at Elyas for guidance. Elyas hadn't thought of a name either. His shaggy brows knitted together and he chewed his piece of figgen meditatively. Then, after a long pause, he said to Huward: 'Best call 'un Elizabeth for thy ma . . . and thy poor, dead Betsy.'

Huward nodded. 'Aye, best.'

Ruke was cleaning the pots. She didn't stop her scouring to say simply: 'I've named the child Keziah.'

Elyas looked taken aback. Then he scowled, his annoyance manifest because she'd taken it upon herself to give the child a name without consulting him. 'Faugh!' he snorted. 'Falutin' gyppo name! You'm give 'un proper Christian handle. Elizabeth, like us sez, do 'ee hear? Show a bit of respect for thy husband's dead ma and first wife.'

Ruke didn't argue.

Two days later the Cornwood parson came rattling up the moor to Eaglestone in his ancient trap. He'd heard that he'd a new addition to his flock and came prepared for the baptism. He found Ruke busy in the cottage, alone save for Jamie clinging to her skirts and the sleeping baby in the cradle. She didn't hold much with religion, being a *didekei*, but since he was there she let the parson lift the child and hold it over a silver basin in readiness to pour holy water over the tiny, dark head.

'What is the child to be named, Mrs Hammett?'

'Keziah.' His eyebrows rose a fraction but he made no comment. After a moment, she added: 'Also Elizabeth . . . and Ruke.'

'We receive this child into Christ's flock and do sign her with the the sign of the Cross,' he intoned, his fingers touching the smooth, white brow, 'in token that ever after she shall not be afraid to confess the faith of

Christ crucified, or to fight under His heavenly guidance against the Devil and all his evil works. In the name of the Father, and of the Son, and of the Holy Ghost, I name thee Keziah, Elizabeth, Ruke . . .' He poured the holy water in a chilly gush over the sleeping infant.

Keziah Elizabeth Ruke Hammett awoke with a lusty yell which could be heard all the way down the main shaft of Wheal Eaglestone.

Chapter Five

Winter's seemingly endless dark days of icy winds and drifting snow drew to a close. It wasn't a particularly hard winter as moor winters went. Not like some Elyas could recall when the Plym, the Tavy and the Dart all had two feet of ice covering them and the wild ponies either starved or froze to death.

There'd been no visitors at Eaglestone for weeks. And most of the time they were cut off from Lamb's Down Farm by thick fogs and blizzards which made the bleak, barren waste between them too treacherous even for a seasoned moorman like Elyas to venture upon. But by March most of the snow had melted and the elms along the top of the combe were reddish-grey with blossom and alive with croaking ravens heralding an early spring.

And one clear bright morning the eagle returned to its nest high on the tor above Wheal Eaglestone.

The milder weather also brought visitors of a human kind. Dame Hannah Rogers in her jingling little trap, bearing skirts and bodices she'd stitched during the winter for five-month-old Keziah, also a cotton shirt and a good strong pair of breeches for Jamie as he'd soon be out of his frock. She went and gazed down the deep shaft of the mine but didn't venture down the swinging ladder, even when Elyas wanted her to inspect the digging at close quarters, saying: 'Best take a gunny, mistress, seeing as how you'm a-holdin' shares.'

To which, with her prim little smile, she retorted: 'I can tell quite clearly from here, Mr . . .' she paused '*Captain* Hammett, that none of you have been idle. I am most satisfied with my investment . . . most satisfied!'

Elyas turned scarlet beneath the dust caking his features. It was the first time anyone had referred to him by the courtesy title due to mine-owners and overseers. 'That be right nice of you'm to say so, mistress,' he mumbled and tugged his forelock so ferociously she half thought the grey tuft would come away in his hand.

For once, he left off working for a while though croust-time was well past, and allowed the others to do the same. They gathered in the warm front room of the cottage while Dame Rogers drank a mug of Ruke's herb tea and nursed Jamie and Keziah in turn upon her narrow lap. It was a long time since they'd heard any parish news or gossip.

The parson had died shortly after christening Keziah, she told them in a sombre tone of voice. 'Died by visitation of the Lord brought on by an ague of the spleen, I do believe.'

'Faugh!' snorted Elyas. 'Died by visitation of the Lord brought on by suppin' moonshine more likely'd!'

A new vicar had come from Exeter to minister to the parish. The Reverend Burridge Creedy. The tight-lipped way Dame Rogers pronounced his name told them that she thought little of the new minister. Each Sunday from the pulpit he professed himself concerned that his predecessor should have been so lax in collecting tithes in his waning years, which meant there were considerable arrears to collect – this Dame Rogers imparted with a pointed glance towards Elyas.

Like most moormen, Elyas considered the local parson an enemy because of his capacity to exact tithes. The tenth bar of tin, the tenth piglet, the tenth sheaf of corn or barrel of cider. The tenth sheep, if the vicar was particularly grasping. Elyas liked to tell the story of how a poor farmer had taken his tenth child, a baby girl, to the vicarage and insisted on leaving it with the parson's wife as payment in kind for his tithes. The vicar had soon returned the screaming mite, but the farmer had cancelled his debt so that was an end of it.

When Parson Creedy called at Eaglestone later that week, Elyas was less than welcoming. Creedy was a good deal younger that the last vicar. He had weasel features, shrewd little eyes and his breath smelled of ale and onions. He went straight to the pile of tin bars outside the blowing house and, while Elyas reluctantly restrained an enraged Wart, counted them.

'Twelve!' he declared, a greedy glint in his close-set eyes. 'So the tenth is mine, I think, since your tithe appears to be overdue.'

Elyas shrugged. There was no escaping payment. Besides, there were a dozen more bars in the barn, hidden there from Creedy's greedy gaze, so in truth he'd got off lightly. 'Graeme, boy, put yon bar 'pon arse of vicar's wagon for he.' He tugged his forelock to Creedy. 'I'll be a-wishin' you'm good day, Vicar, and a-gettin' back to bal. Tithes don't make theyselves!'

But Creedy wasn't leaving until he was sure he'd got his full entitlement. He looked about him at the chickens scratching in the yard. 'What number of fowl do you keep?'

Elyas shrugged. 'Count 'un for thyself, Vicar.'

So he did. 'Nine.' There was no mistaking the disappointment in his voice. Had there been a tenth he'd have had fowl for supper that night. He looked around him, sniffing the air. His eyes went towards the pig-sty.

Elyas pre-empted him. 'One sow . . . six piglets.'

Creedy had to be content with his tin.

'I shall expect to see all of you in church next Sunday now the weather is passably fine.' He climbed up behind his horse and took the reins.

'Dare say,' said Elyas noncommittally, but he knew he'd better make the effort or be in the bad books of the parish fathers.

Creedy still wasn't in any hurry to go. He sat for a moment studying Ruke as she stood barefoot in the cottage door, Keziah in her arms, Jamie peeping shyly out from behind her skirts. From where he stood watching, Elyas thought the vicar's hard little eyes lingered upon the pleasing fullness of her breasts rather longer than was seemly for a man of the cloth.

'I see your daughter-in-law is a gypsy,' Creedy remarked.

'*Didekei*,' corrected Elyas shortly.

'Ah, that would explain the whiteness of her flesh. Also the child's,' he nodded. Ruke gazed steadily back at him as he continued his leisurely examination of her as if she was a prize animal for sale in a market. 'Has she been baptised?'

Ruke nodded.

'Then she must come to church and praise the Lord.' He cracked his whip and his horse plodded forward.

They watched him set off across the moor in the direction of Lamb's Down Farm in search of more overdue tithes. As soon as he was out of sight, Elyas started to roar with laughter. They all joined in, bending double and slapping their dusty breeches with glee.

'What number of fowl do 'ee keep?' Elyas mimicked the parson and set them off again.

'Pity there be only *nine* hens, Pa,' gasped Huward, tears streaking his dirty face. 'One more and parson would have had a chicken dinner!'

Ruke had padded across to the hen-house and opened the hatch. A chicken hopped out clucking, followed by two dozen more.

'*Fifty*-nine, more likely'd!' guffawed Elyas.

Isaac opened the barn door to let out the hidden ducks and geese; the former immediately waddled off back to the brook. He went in and brought out five more piglets in sacks with their snouts tied to stop them squealing. Released back into the sty, they made a hungry rush for the sow's teats.

Elyas spat in the mud, contemptuous of the new townie vicar. 'Do 'ee reckon us would keep sow as breeds only six of a litter?'

During the first week in April, Elyas once again loaded the tin on the wagon to take to Plympton for the coinage. And since they'd chickens to spare he put some in a slatted crate to sell in the market. Graeme and Isaac were both eager to go with him to do the selling.

'I'm eldest, 'tis my place to go,' said Graeme.

But Elyas decided to take Ruke. 'Her knows somethin' 'bout sellin', bein' a gypsy an' all.' But when she insisted on taking Keziah with her he began to grumble. 'Stannary town ent no place for babbie. Best her stays.'

'She's still suckling,' pointed out Ruke determinedly.

'Faugh! Won't do she no harm t'holler for while. Good for 'un lungs. 'Sides, Isaac can always put she on cow's teat if'n we'm long a-comin'.'

'I'd rather stay.'

'I'll go, Gramps!' chorused Graeme and Isaac eagerly.

But Elyas wasn't having that. Selling chickens was woman's work. 'Ruke be a-comin' and that be that!' he told them doggedly. She opened her mouth to argue, but shut it again with a snap of her white teeth when he shot her a warning look. She'd long guessed that he knew the secret of Keziah's birth but for reasons best known to himself hadn't told her husband. It was, she decided, better not to defy him.

'I'll come.'

Plympton was a muddy, seething mass of people. Elyas set Ruke down with her chickens in a corner of the square between a mender of iron pots and an old woman selling watercress. 'Now don't 'ee waste time chittering,' he warned. 'And be sure to get least half a crown each, do 'ee hear?'

She nodded. As soon as he'd gone, she took out four of the complaining hens and held them, two in each hand, by the legs. She moved out into the square and began to shout, 'Buy my fine plump chickens!'

Elyas hitched his wagon outside the tinners' hall and beckoned to the boys grouped by the entrance to unload the tin and carry it inside for stamping. That done, he searched among the crowd of traders for the Spaniard but failed to pick him out. As he was peering uncertainly about him, a particularly flamboyant-looking trader approached him.

'I'll buy your tin.'

Elyas frowned. Slowly he looked the trader up and down, marvelling at his elaborate wig, embroidered waistcoat and lace ruffles. His face was liberally dusted with powder and he wore a diamond-shaped patch beneath his eye.

'Here, you'm bain't be a Frenchie, be you'm?' demanded Elyas suspiciously. 'I bain't sellin' no tin to Frenchies t'make slugs.'

The flamboyant one looked disdainful. 'Do I *look* like a Frenchie?'

Elyas gave a shrug. Privately he thought the trader looked like a painted Jack-a-dandy. He supposed that if the trader wasn't from Paris he must be from London. It wasn't important: both cities were as far away as the moon and the stars so far as he was concerned. He stuck out his hand. 'Slap hands and pay up, zur,' he invited and the trader obliged. There was no bargaining to be done. The stannary officials had set the price of tin at £4 a hundredweight for that coinage. Higher than it had ever been. The war with France had caused a desperate shortage and the increased price was an incentive to the tinners to double their efforts.

Elyas's eyes went wide when the trader drew him aside and produced a purse of gold sovereigns instead of the usual copper tokens. The yellow coins gleamed as they were counted into his palm and he mentally congratulated himself for agreeing to do business with this London trader with a purse full of the right-coloured stuff. Looking about him to make sure he wasn't being watched by covetous eyes, Elyas dropped the coins into his gunny sack and tied it firmly beneath his smock. He tugged his forelock to the trader, saying, 'Happy t'do business withee, zur,' and went out into the throng.

He didn't go immediately to find Ruke. It would take her a while, he decided, to sell the chickens, since the competition was so great. There seemed to be squawking hens and quacking ducks everywhere. He made his way to the nearest inn. The tap-room was predictably crowded but room was made for him at one of the long wooden tables. He emptied his first mug of cider at a single gurgling draught, then signalled to the pot-girl for another. He thought of ordering a dish of eggs and ham but decided to wait and buy two hot pasties from one of the street vendors for him and

Ruke a little later on. She needed to keep her strength up with a baby at home to feed.

'Buy some bootlaces or a tinder-box, zur, only a penny.'

Elyas scowled as an itinerant hawker pushed his wooden tray of wares in front of him. 'Take thy stuff away, tinker, I want none of it.'

The hawker persisted. 'Anything on tray a penny, zur. What 'bout a ribbon for thy shiner . . .'

Elyas roared. 'Shiner! I ent had no shiner backalong thirty years, boy! Got grandsons and a granddaughter!' But he was none the less pleased that the younger man thought him youthful enough to be interested in ribbons for a maid. He squinted at the trifles on offer. Something caught his eye. He pointed to an object suspended by a length of red ribbon from the tray. 'What be that?'

The hawker unhooked the thing: it was carved from bone in the shape of a bird. It contained dried peas and when he shook it it gave a pleasing rattle. 'For babbie,' he explained helpfully, proffering it to Elyas for a closer look.

'I didn't reckon it be for scarin' crows,' said Elyas drily. He turned it over in his hands. 'What sort of bird is what I'm asking!'

'Looks like raven.'

Elyas shook his head. 'Nawthin' like raven. More like eagle.'

The hawker smelled a sale. 'Mebbe you'm right at that, zur. Now you'm come to mention it, it *do* look like eagle.'

Elyas nodded. 'I'll give 'ee penny for it, tinker.'

'Nay . . . good rattle that. Cost 'ee threepence.'

Elyas's scowl reappeared. 'Ye said a penny for anything on tray, I 'stinctly heard 'ee.'

' 'Tweren't *on* tray,' pointed out the hawker. ' 'Twere *hangin'* from it. Threepence or I'll have un back.'

Elyas hesitated. He gave the bird another satisfying rattle. How his little Keziah would love it! But threepence! For a child's plaything! He was still considering when he suddenly noticed the hawker was supported by a roughly-hewn wooden crutch. His eyes travelled to the pinned-up empty leg of the man's breeches. 'Lost thy limb in by bal?' he asked curiously.

The hawker shook his head. 'Nay. West Indies.'

Elyas looked interested. 'And where be they then?'

The hawker didn't seem too sure. ' 'Twere fighting French and Spanish . . . backalong '73.'

'Navy, were 'ee?'

'Aye.'

Elyas felt in a pocket and produced three pennies. He dropped them on the tray. The hawker snatched them eagerly.

'Thankee, zur, may you'm have a long family.'

He hoisted his tray and moved to go.

'Hold hard, boy!' Elyas called him back. He moved along the form, making room for the tinker. 'Sit 'ee down an' I'll buy thy thirst.' The hawker licked his lips, hardly able to believe his ears. Cider was a luxury he couldn't afford. Elyas beckoned the wench. 'Give yon tinker a pint o' strong. 'Tis wisht poor thing boy like 'un should lose limb to they dratted Frenchies.'

The hawker set down his tray and lowered himself gratefully on to the form. 'God bless 'ee, zur, but I be among lucky 'uns. Died in heaps, did they . . . yeller fever. Sent to capture they sugar plantations and died horrible death. Forty thousand good fightin' men!'

Elyas shook his head in wonder at such a death toll. 'Must be terrible place, this West Indies,' he observed, interest deepening. Here was a tale which would hold them enthralled back at Eaglestone.

'Aye, terrible.' The hawker's cider arrived and he took a great gulp of it. He set the mug down. 'I'd be pleased to tell 'ee how terrible but truth is, zur, I can't stand to talk 'bout it if'n me belly's empty.' His stomach gave a confirming rumble.

Elyas signalled the wench. 'Bring us a dish each of eggs and ham, sharp now. And bread. And two more mugs of strong cider.' Ruke would have to wait awhile for her pasty. It wouldn't do her any harm. 'Now 'bout these here West Indies . . .'

'Plump young chickens half a crown!'

A woman stopped and felt the last four of Ruke's chickens with knowing hands. 'Two shillings each and I'll take the four.'

Ruke shook her head. 'You'll not find better in the market.'

It was true. The rest were sickly looking compared to these well-fed specimens. The woman, probably a cook from one of the big houses, Ruke decided, gave a brisk nod. 'Oh, very well. One pound the four.' As Ruke went to hand them over she gave them a sly shake so they began flapping and squawking. The woman recoiled, lips curling with distaste. 'Wild brutes!'

'That's because they're proper fed, mistress. Makes them right vigorous,' Ruke told her blandly. 'I'd be pleased to wring and pluck 'em for sixpence each.'

The woman didn't look pleased. She wanted the chickens but, as Ruke suspected, didn't want to be troubled by their frenzied behaviour. 'Very well, but be quick.'

Ruke pushed three of the chickens through her legs, trapping them in her skirt while she dealt with the fourth. Few could dispatch a chicken and pluck the feathers from the warm, pulsating flesh quicker than she could. In less than five minutes the job was done. The woman paid with copper tokens. Ruke tied them in a piece of rag with the rest and went and sat on her empty crate to await Elyas's return.

An hour later he still hadn't come for her. The pale sun had disappeared behind an ominous bank of black cloud and a cold, salty wind was blowing up the Yealm from the sea. She considered whether to go in search of Elyas but decided she'd better remain where she was in case they missed each other. Hunger was gnawing at her insides so she promised herself that if he hadn't returned by the time the big clock atop the Stannary Hall struck three she'd spend some of her chicken-money on a hot pasty and a mug of milk from the vendors. Meanwhile, she attended to her breasts, which, without Keziah to suckle, were uncomfortably engorged. Unconcernedly, she unlaced her bodice and pulled out her swollen breasts, gently squeezing each in turn to let her abundant milk flow forth to run in rivulets between the cobbles at her feet and mingle with the mud.

The crone selling cresses gave her no more than a bored glance, as did the pot mender. Such sights were common enough. But two pairs of eyes *were* watching her closely. So intent was she with easing her discomfort, Ruke didn't notice John de Raddon's tall, black-garbed figure, or that of his steward, as they stood among the jumble of pedlars' carts and wagons a few feet from her.

The Lord Warden had been traversing the square on his way to partake of boiled beef and carrots at the inn he patronised when, amid the milling people, he chanced to spy Ruke's familiar, statuesque figure seated upon an empty crate. The memory of the day, a year before, when she'd humiliated and frustrated him before a crowd of people was in a moment revived. An ugly emotion rose within him as he stood watching the milk gush from her big, white breasts like life-giving fountains. The carelessness of her action and the very fact that the *didekei* was letting milk enough for three children flow out upon the filthy cobbles filled him with a savage jealousy because his own wife's breasts were small and flaccid and empty. And would ever remain so, since Emma de Raddon was as barren as a desert.

He bared his teeth. The grimace puckered his scarred cheek so he looked particularly ferocious. 'Goddamn the bitch and her pup!'

'Bitch be right 'nough, Cap'n . . . if 'ee sees what I'm seeing!' sniggered Grote. Then added, in case the Lord Warden hadn't noticed: 'Her got four paps.'

De Raddon had noticed. He gazed fascinated at Ruke's remarkable torso exposed by her gaping bodice. Never before had he seen such a thing on a woman – and he'd experienced female forms of many kinds. However, he'd heard of these malformations and knew what they signified. 'Bitch? Nay, *witch*, more like, Grote. 'Tis said a witch has extra pair of teats to feed her familiars.'

Grote's eyes bulged from his head as the significance of his master's words sank in. 'God's mercy!' he breathed.

Her milk depleted, Ruke pulled her bodice together and began to relace it. Thus occupied, she didn't see de Raddon approach. His elongated shadow fell across her like a sinister harbinger of doom and she looked up startled, involuntarily clutching her bodice at the sight of his ugly, scarred face looming over her. Then she saw his gold chain of office gleaming on his solid chest and recognition dawned. The terror faded from her eyes with the realisation that he wasn't some evil manifestation but the flesh-and-blood gentleman who'd bid for her a year before. But in a moment it returned when to Grote he barked: 'Seize her!'

She moved like summer lightning but Grote managed to grab her by the hair. She screamed with pain as he dragged her back to stand before de

Raddon. Passers-by stopped to stare. The cress-seller made a half-hearted attempt to intervene, mindful that the girl's assailant was acting on the orders of his master who was clearly of the gentry and therefore entitled to do as he pleased. Perhaps the girl was a runaway servant selling stolen chickens. Even so, the old woman piped up: 'Oh leave she be, zur, her bain't doin' no harm!'

De Raddon rounded on her. 'Silence, hag! Or be counted the witch's familiar and share her fate.'

'Witch!' squawked the crone in horror and jumped up from her stool in such agitation she knocked over her basket, scattering the bunches of cress over the ground to be trampled beneath the feet of all those who were stopping to gawp. Her eldritch shriek had carried right across the square and within moments word spread that a witch had been discovered. The mob around the principals swelled.

'I'm no witch . . . I swear it!' pleaded Ruke, her eyes desperately appealing to the sea of faces. 'I'm Mrs Hammett . . . a tinner's wife. Daughter-in-law of Elyas Hammett!' She shrieked in agony as Grote gave her hair a vicious pull to halt the flow of words.

One or two of the crowd, other tinners, knew Elyas Hammett. Since they also recognised the powerful personage of the Lord Warden, they hesitated to speak up for Ruke. But one, more bold and independent than his fellows, called out to de Raddon: 'Beggin' 'ee pardon, Cap'n, Elyas Hammett wouldn't hitch his boy Huward to no witch. Reckon you'm mistook.'

De Raddon shot Ruke's champion a menacing look, his hard, grey eyes raking the man's face and fixing it in his mind for the future should their paths cross again. 'Mistaken am I?' he snarled. He moved suddenly, crossing the distance between himself and Ruke with a stride. Her fingers came up like talons and she tried to claw his face, but he struck her hands aside and ripped her gown to the waist.

A collective gasp rose from the crowd as her breasts and the extra nipples below them were revealed and a few hurriedly crossed themselves. Those at the back were pushing and jostling and craning for a glimpse of the witch-marks. Ruke tried to pull the remnants of her bodice together, covering her nudity as best she could. Tears of pain and humiliation glittered in her eyes, but as they jeered her and called her the foulest of names, her rage burst forth, eclipsing even her abject terror.

She wrenched herself from Grote's grasp, not caring that she left a lump of her hair in his fingers. He tried to catch hold of her again, but she managed to evade him and went stamping around those encircling her, gesticulating wildly and swearing her innocence in English and Romany. Some of them stepped back in alarm, treading on the feet of those behind and bumping into them. Froth appeared at the corners of her mouth and her eyes rolled like a madwoman's.

De Raddon pointed a triumphant finger at her. 'Look at her! See how she raves! Can you doubt she's possessed by evil?'

Hearing his crowing voice seemed to bring Ruke to her senses. Abruptly she stopped her ranting and stood gazing silently at him for a moment. Then deliberately, her eyes like two black chips of coal, she lifted her chin and spat full in his face.

There was an immediate hush. Automatically, de Raddon wiped the spittle from his face with his white cuff. Then, lifting his hand, he struck her brutally across the face sending her spinning into the crowd.

'Hang the witch!' someone shouted and the cry was taken up with gusto.

Suddenly it seemed as though it was the intention of all who'd recoiled from her minutes before to lay hands upon her. Like a sack of flour, she was heaved above their heads the better to be carried through the town and out to the mound known as Gibbet Hill. Her head lolled backwards, stretching her white throat; the breeze fluttered her curtain of raven hair and caught her skirts, whipping them about her waist so that her long muscular legs gleamed like white marble in the greyish light. Her lips moved incessantly, but whether she uttered curses or entreaties none could tell because her words were drowned by the cheering.

De Raddon found himself being ushered, with Grote, to the head of the unruly procession; by dint of both his exalted position in the parish and the fact that he'd found the witch he was expected to lead it. Such was his overweening self-importance, he didn't hesitate to take what he considered was his rightful place – striding forth in his long black boots with energy, the skirts of his black frock-coat swinging behind him, his steward dogging his heels.

And as the straggling line left the square and coiled through the town, more and more people left what they were doing and hurried to join in, bringing their excited noisy children and yapping dogs. For a witch-hanging was always fine sport.

Chapter Six

Elyas and the one-legged pedlar had eaten their eggs and ham and were sitting smoking a companionable clay-pipe each of three-penny shag. Their third mugs of cider sat before them. The afternoon was by now well advanced yet neither seemed in any great hurry to depart.

There seemed so much to talk about: things of which Elyas was totally ignorant but which the sharp-featured, shrewd-eyed ex-sailor knew a prodigious amount, having gleaned much during his travels both in the navy and as a pedlar. He seemed to know all about the British and French conflict and expanded upon it at great length.

Bonaparte had, a year previously, seized Malta with 30,000 picked men led by his best officers. A week later his French hordes had proceeded to Egypt and had taken Alexandria before marching on Cairo, whence, at the Battle of the Pyramids, they'd smashed the hitherto invincible warrior-race called the Mamelukes.

'*Mamelukes*!' Elyas repeated doubtfully. He gave the other a quizzical look. 'Reckon you'm talkin' up load of old ledden, boy.'

The pedlar looked pained. 'You'm ask any soldier and sailor as knows . . . he'll tell 'ee same.'

Elyas nodded. 'Go on with 'ee tale.'

Only briefly had Bonaparte been master of Egypt. Admiral Nelson had seen to that. At the head of the British fleet, he'd hotly pursued Bonaparte to Egypt and engaged the French ships in Aboukir Bay, sinking eleven and capturing six. This swiftly executed Battle of the Nile shattered Bonaparte's hopes of a French-ruled Eastern empire. Moreover, he'd found himself stranded in Egypt and, apparently, there he still languished.

'Good job, too! Keep 'un out of mischief,' chuckled Elyas, drawing contentedly on his pipe.

'He won't rot there long, matie,' declared the other with some certainty, his long face serious. 'If'n I knows ol' Bony, he'll wear a fleet together somehows and come 'cross Channel lookin' for a scrap wi' us.'

'Faugh! British will see off they stinkin' Frenchies pack an' vardel! Why, I wouldn't be 'sprised if ol' Nelson . . .'

Elyas stopped mid-sentence as an urchin rushed in cheeks glowing with excitement, clearly with some momentous item of news to impart. He stood panting between the tables, eyes flicking this way and that to see if anyone was prepared to toss him a coin in return for his information. A big farmer chucked a farthing at his bare feet, saying: 'Here, take a farden and spit it out, boy!'

'Lord Warden's found a witch an' they be hangin' she up Gibbet Hill. Her be 'un *didekei* wi' four tits an' I seed 'em,' the youngster babbled and shot out of the door in search of another paying audience.

It took a moment for the announcement to penetrate their drink-fuddled brains. Then there was a sudden emptying of mugs and a rush for the door. Elyas watched them go with disdain. 'Faugh! Ent my idea of sport t'watch some poor ol' heathen woman dancing on end of rope,' he informed his companion. But the pedlar had stuck his wooden crutch beneath his arm and was rising to follow the rest – even free cider couldn't compete with a hanging.

'See you'm again, tinner,' he said and limped out.

Elyas looked around the empty tap-room. For a moment he wondered if he might, after all, be missing something. But it was a long tramp up to Gibbet Hill and he'd seen more than one old hag hung by the neck until her eyes popped out. Anyroads, it was time he and Ruke were setting off home. She would surely have sold the chickens by now. Thinking of Ruke brought back to mind something the urchin had said about the witch: *her be a didekei* . . .

Elyas's gaunt face froze and his stomach seemed to be filled suddenly with quicksilver. No! It *couldn't* be! Ruke wasn't the only half-gypsy in the area. Why, there'd be plenty of gypsies in town for the coinage market. Cider must have gone to his brain to start him imagining such nonsense. He relaxed again.

Presently, the one-legged pedlar returned, hopeful of finding his benefactor still there and in a generous mood. ' 'Twere too many folk pushin' an' elbowin' in square . . . three, four hundred, I reckon . . . I'd have been knocked over an' tramped on most likely'd.'

'Did 'ee see 'un witch?'

'Oh aye, I seed her plain as I'm seein' 'ee.'

Elyas hesitated. 'And did 'ee see 'un witch-teats?'

The pedlar didn't answer immediately. He pointedly licked his lips. When Elyas didn't take the hint and summon the serving wench, he said: 'Aye, I seed 'em. Seed her legs an' arse an' God knows what else and all.'

Elyas found that he was sweating. 'And was her . . . an old hag?' He waited. The pedlar licked his lips again and looked around the deserted tap-room as though he hadn't heard. Elyas clutched him by the dirty rag he wore around his throat. 'Tell me! Was her young or old?' he demanded harshly as something sinister grew in his bones.

'Here, bain't no cause to take on!' the pedlar began to protest but when Elyas gave his neckerchief a sharp jerk he deemed it prudent to answer before the madman strangled him. 'Her's young . . . for a witch.' He gave a leer. 'Proper waste, ask me, hangin' maiden like she. Her ent bad save for a skin full of they drat pox-pits. Here, where ye goin', matie?'

Elyas didn't wait to tell him. He was on his feet in a moment and hurtling out of the inn as fast as his bow legs could carry him.

At the edge of town de Raddon's procession found its way impeded by the town guard and the Vicar of Plympton wearing cassock and violet stole and bearing before him a tall, silver processional cross. To the rear of the group anxiously bobbed the mayor and two local justices. Someone had slipped away and summoned help.

The baying of the mob rose to a resentful tempest at the sight of the vicar and his handful of nervous-eyed guards armed with old muskets. Gripped by unbridled barbarity, rough country faces contorted with sadistic joy, the crowd would have swept aside those blocking their path by sheer force of numbers and carried on to Gibbet Hill if de Raddon hadn't brought them to a reluctant halt with an authoritive raising of his hand.

With only feet between them, both factions faced each other. The witch-takers traded a few insults with the townsmen who made up the guard, but when they didn't rise to the bait they gave up and fell expectantly silent. Those bearing Ruke lowered her to the ground but she seemed unable to stand without support. She seemed dazed, as if in a trance, eyes staring unseeing from pits of terror in her deathly white face, not even attempting to rearrange her torn, dishevelled dress to cover the incriminating witch-marks.

Back in the town the stannary clock struck four.

De Raddon spoke: 'Step aside, Vicar, we've a witch to hang.'

The vicar didn't move. 'Best deliver her to me, Captain de Raddon, so that she may be exorcised in God's name and rid of the deceits and crafts of the Devil.'

De Raddon's mouth sneered. 'We've a rope will do it better and quicker than your Amen-bawling!'

'The law forbids witch-hanging without proper trial by the mayor and justices,' persisted the vicar.

De Raddon gave a hoarse laugh. 'Lord damn my shirt, man, I *am* the law hereabouts!'

There were a few ragged cheers at that from behind him and an impatient surging forward, as if the people felt he'd said all there was to be said. But de Raddon held them back by standing his ground, determined that the civil powers should voluntarily give way. The vicar was just as determined not to be done out of his exorcism.

'I grant that you hold sway over the tinners . . .' he started to say, but de Raddon cut across him by delivering his *coup de grâce*.

'Aye, and yon witch is a tinner's wife!'

The vicar looked startled. The woman was so obviously of gypsy origin, he'd presumed she was some teller of fortunes and seller of magical potions who'd come for market day and been taken for a witch. It hadn't occurred to him that she might be a tinner's wife. Seeing his discomfiture, the people sniggered and nudged elbows as he turned to give the mayor and the justices an eloquent look, inviting their participation. But the three shifted uncomfortably and avoided meeting his gaze directly. Even the guards had lowered their muskets and were looking almost sheepish at being there when the witch was clearly the tinners' responsibility. Only a fool would interfere with the powers of the Stannary.

As the vicar wondered what steps he should take, there was a sudden commotion among the thick mass of people. Insults were hurled at the driver of a wagon who was urging his sturdy pony through them.

'Make way, damn ye! Make way for Elyas Hammett the tinner!' he shouted, flicking his long birch in a menacing fashion over their heads. There was something about his wild-eyed, frenzied manner, inspired by his fears for Ruke, that made them give way and let him through to the front. Once there, his darting eyes took in the scene in a moment, narrowing as they settled on Ruke. Their rough handling had knocked the fight out of her and she showed no sign of recognising her father-in-law. Elyas pointed his birch at her. 'Let she be! Her bain't no witch. Her be a good wife t'my boy Huward. And her got new babbie at home a'waitin' t'be suckled.'

'Which of her four tits will she use, tinner?' jeered de Raddon and the crowd roared their approval of his witticism.

Elyas's eyes moved to de Raddon, a plea forming in his brain. But when he met the Lord Warden's steady, mocking gaze he knew he'd be wasting his breath: de Raddon hadn't forgotten he'd outbid him for Ruke and now he was enjoying wreaking his revenge on both of them at a single stroke. Instead, in a loud voice for them all to hear, Elyas said: 'Her be entitled to a fair trial by jury in tinners' court, Captain.'

The vicar supported him. ' 'Tis true what he says, Captain de Raddon. The evidence against her should be brought in a proper manner.'

De Raddon's face darkened. 'Don't tell me what's proper and what isn't, preacher!' he snarled. He pointed at Ruke. 'See? See yon witch-marks? That's your evidence!'

Elyas spat. 'Old women's widdles! Would 'ee slaughter cow for having extra pair of udders?'

'There's your jury, Hammett!' de Raddon swept his arm in a wide arc indicating the crowd. He called to them in ringing tones: 'How say you? Is she guilty or not guilty?'

'*Guilty*!'

They answered with one leather-throated roar. De Raddon swung on his heel and strode forward, unceremoniously pushing the vicar aside. A man caught hold of Ruke and tossed her over his shoulder like a rag-doll. For one, hopeful moment, Elyas thought perhaps the man was going to carry her off and save her, but he charged after the Lord Warden with the rest. They swarmed by Elyas's wagon, rocking it on its axles, and on through the scattered ranks of the town guard. One guard was foolhardy enough to fire his carbine over their heads and promptly had it seized and smashed to pieces. His comrades put up a show of resistance for appearance's sake but were brushed aside like hovering gnats.

'In the name of God, have mercy upon our sister!' the vicar tried desperately to appeal to them, but they were drunk with malice and his cry went unheeded.

There was nothing Elyas could do but to follow his daughter-in-law's dangling raven head to Gibbet Hill.

There was already an old gallows on the mound. Just a wooden crossbar on two weathered posts. Someone found a rope, made a noose and threw it over. Ruke was thrust forward and the rope dropped around her neck. She hardly seemed conscious of their actions.

Elyas's face was waxen and streaked with sweat. 'Dear God in heaven . . .!' he muttered disbelievingly as he clambered down from his wagon and pushed his way to the front. It was too late to help her.

Suddenly, as if she'd come to her senses and realised her end was nigh, Ruke gave a thin wail which seemed to rouse the crowd to a frenzy. Women rushed forward and shook their fists in her face. The vicar pushed through them and extended his cross so that it was just a few inches from Ruke's lips.

'Kiss the cross and let the Lord be with thee and thy spirit!' he urged. 'Save thy soul . . . in God's name, repent!'

The crowd was strangely mute. A few spots of rain fell and there was a roll of thunder in the distance. Ruke's slanting eyes were fixed to the silver cross as though she was mesmerised by it. A shadow flitted across her wan features, leaving them contorted and ugly so that Elyas no longer recognised her as the handsome young woman he'd bought for his son to wed. Chill fingers gripped him.

'Ruke . . . kiss the cross!' he called to her, suddenly in fear for her soul. But she didn't look in his direction or give any sign that she had heard.

Her eyes moved from the cross to rake the sea of faces. 'God's apes!' she hissed at them, her teeth drawn back so that her gums showed a vivid red against her white teeth. Then, throwing back her head, she spat full at the cross.

They howled their fury. Elyas knew now that there was no saving her. 'Sorceress!' shrieked a woman and threw a handful of stones at her. Others began to do the same and for a moment Elyas thought they intended to stone her to death. But a dozen pair of hands were hauling on the rope and Ruke was jerked upwards, arms and legs threshing. Her eyes bulged from their sockets and her tongue protruded. A few feeble kicks and it was over. Urine and slimy wet faeces began to drip from the body. The vicar made the sign of the cross and began to intone the litany.

They would have torn Ruke's body to pieces but de Raddon stopped this final act of barbarism, saying, 'Let the tinner take his witch back up the moor. We don't want her evil carcass in Plympton bone-yard!'

So they took her down, squabbling for possession of the rope which was thought to have magical properties, and tossed her on to Elyas's wagon for him to cover with the flour sacks used to cover the tin bars. People jostled around him, howling insults and expectorating at his feet and on the wheels of his wagon. He said nothing. His throat felt as if it was closed up. Besides, there was nothing to say. Despite the presence of witch-marks, he couldn't believe Ruke was a witch. Granted, she was a little 'fey' – just like all gypsies were with their charms and cure-alls. Yet he'd swear she was no sorceress, no maker of evil spells! But what was the good in telling them, when, with her last defiant, pagan act, she'd damned herself absolutely? Grim-faced, he climbed up and took the reins amid loud jeering. His departure was followed by a hail of stones and dung. And de Raddon's crowing voice: 'You would do well to drown the witch's pup, Hammett! Like mother like child!'

Elyas reined in for a moment and swivelled in his seat to look back at them. He found his voice.

'By the liver of Christ, I hope you'm right, John de Raddon! Then when her growed, her can put curse on lot of 'ee for what 'ee did to her ma this day!' he raged and shook his fist at them.

But they weren't listening. The rain had begun in earnest and they were scattering down the hill for home.

Chapter Seven

'Why doesn't Jamie have to go to school, Gramps?'

It was a question that Kezzy often asked. Usually on Monday, Wednesday or Friday mornings – being the days when she must set off down the moor for Cornwood to attend the dame school.

Elyas's reply was similarly routine and very much to the point. ' 'Cause un be more use in by stamps.'

' 'Cause I'm a boy an' you'm just a maid,' Jamie would taunt her, sticking out his chest. 'So off withee an' hang 'round dame's skirts.'

Whereupon Kezzy would stick her tongue out at him and try her best to land him a hard kick beneath the table as they ate their morning oatmeal. Fiercely, she'd retaliate, saying: 'I'm as good as elly little ol' boy . . . I can pull bigger cart of ore than you!'

It was true. Kezzy was tall for her age and her bony childish frame and long arms and legs were surprisingly strong. Her mother had been a strong young woman, though sturdier built. Elyas saw much of poor, dead Ruke in his granddaughter's dark, tilted eyes and unruly mass of raven hair. There was, of course, no Hammett in her – which was hardly surprisingly considering the circumstances – but only Elyas seemed aware of that. Jamie, on the other hand, was all Hammett: short and stocky with mousey, fair hair. No, he wasn't yet as strong as Kezzy, and it wasn't strictly true that he was a better worker than his sister. Elyas knew, though he wouldn't say so, that the *didikei*'s daughter was brighter than all of them put together. So when Dame Hannah Rogers had offered a year before to take Kezzy as a pupil without payment, Elyas had jumped at the chance of having his granddaughter educated.

Kezzy didn't mind going. Not really. In fact, once she got there she was a model scholar and thoroughly enjoyed scratching words on a slate and learning to read from the dame's books of verse. And she very much liked her prim, grey-haired schoolteacher who, despite her gaunt features and beady eyes and sharp manner of speech, was a kindly, good-humoured soul. Also, the example of feminine gentility which the dame injected into Kezzy's otherwise male-dominated life on Dartmoor ensured that she grew up less of a tomboy than she might have.

But sometimes Kezzy would dawdle on her way down from Eaglestone to the village and sit on a stone, dreaming and gazing up at the high tors sticking out of the ragged brown mantle of furze covering the downs. Then she'd be late and would be told off by the dame and kept in after school to make up. And once, just once, she didn't turn up for lessons at all.

It was a Monday morning in October, shortly before her eighth birthday. Kezzy set off as usual for school with Jamie for company for part of the way as he was to go to Lamb's Down Farm to buy bread and oatmeal. But when they reached the ford on the Erme where they were to go their separate ways, she was loathe to part from Jamie.

'Go on withee, or ye'll be late and make un teacher mazed so her takes dab at 'ee with un birch,' he warned Kezzy of the fate that awaited her if she didn't hurry along.

'Her don't use birch. Her reckons it ent right to birch boys and maids.'

'Then her be soft,' sneered Jamie. 'Won't learn if 'ee ent birched.'

But still she tagged along behind him. The morning, though crisp, was bright, with scarcely a haze glittering above the groups of rocks on the high land above them and school lessons couldn't compete with the spirit of adventure which suddenly gripped Kezzy. She stopped.

'Let's climb Eagle Tor, Jamie!'

He stopped, too, looking back at her with concern on his fresh young face. 'I've got to go to farm, Pa says.'

She tossed her dark head. 'Then do what Pa says. I'm going to climb up and look at the eagle's nest.' She set off determinedly up the moor with a flounce of her shabby brown-wool skirt.

'Kezzy!' he called anxiously after her but she didn't stop.

'You're scared, Jamie Hammett!' she shouted over her shoulder. 'Scared the eagle will carry you off like when you were a babbie!'

'I bain't scared!' he bellowed angrily. But he was. The incident with the great sea-eagle was only distantly remembered in his subconscious, but Elyas often repeated the story of how the eagle had lifted little Jamie in its talons – higher off the ground with every telling – which was sufficient to make Jamie very wary of the eagle, indeed. Not that it had been seen that year: in fact, it hadn't been back to its nest since that time years back when the Hammetts came looking for tin and found it beneath Eagle Tor. Yet, the thought of climbing up to its nest terrified the boy. Perhaps the eagle would choose that very time to come back.

He watched his sister's receding figure, her old shawl flying behind her for all the world like the wings of an eagle, as she cantered on her long, colt-like legs over the bracken and the scattered rocks towards the base of the southernmost mass where the nest was.

'I bain't scared!' he muttered uneasily. Then, after a moment more, he began running after her. 'Kezzy! Wait for me!'

It took them the best part of the morning to reach their goal, what with stopping to pick and eat some small, hard blackberries and then to lay on their stomachs, silent and quite still, for an hour or longer watching a mountain fox scrabbling at a rabbit hole. Jamie would have been content to lie there for another hour, until the fox had clawed out its lunch, but Kezzy grew restless, and in truth felt sorry for the rabbit, so she gave a ringing 'view halloo' and sent the fox scurrying.

'Now you'm frighted un and I wanted to see un eat yon jackrabbit,' grumbled Jamie and gave Kezzy a push so that she rolled back a way down the slope.

She was up in a moment and took a retaliatory kick at his rump as she shot by him and continued on up the moor, defiantly singing a verse she'd learned at school: 'The fox went out one winter's night, and prayed to the moon to give him light, for he'd many a mile to go that night, before he reached his den, O! . . . his den, O! . . . his den, O . . .!'

Her well-aimed kick brought forth an indignant roar from Jamie. He jumped up and ran after her as fast as he could, intent on pulling her long, raven braids. But she was already far ahead, agilely clambering up the jagged rocks to the collection of sticks and twigs at the very top of the tor. For a moment, she balanced precariously on a high, jutting slab of grey granite, surveying the moorland far and wide below, giving Jamie a chance to catch up with her. Then she was off again, singing loudly. 'For he'd many a mile to go that night, before he reached his den, O! . . . his den, O! . . . his den, O!'

The nest, which neither had seen close to before, was something of a disappointment when, panting, their hands and knees skinned by their efforts, they reached it.

'It's nobbut a few ol' sticks and dried leaves,' said Kezzy peering disappointedly into the hollow of the crumbling structure.

Even so, Jamie nervously scanned the skies, half-expecting the eagle to descend at any moment with flapping wings. And when Kezzy gave the nest a prod, he let out an apprehensive squawk which ensured she repeated the action. 'Don't Kezzy!' he begged.

'You're frighted, Jamie Hammett! I'm going to tell Graeme and Isaac . . . Jamie's frighted of an ol' eagle! Jamie's still a babbie!' She suddenly left off taunting him and stared. Her prodding had dislodged, through a hole in the nest, a shower of pebbles. The clinking they made as they bounced down the stones made Jamie jump. He backed away. 'C'mon, us best be getting back'long home . . .'

'They're only stones you great lubbut!' Kezzy picked one up and tossed it at him, but not spitefully, not so as it might hurt him. He caught it and chucked it back at her, making her squeal. For the next few minutes the pebbles from the nest hurtled between them as, shrieking, they dodged back and forth among the tumbled rocks, until Kezzy had one pebble left. She hefted it in her little hand as Jamie popped cheekily up from behind a rock and quickly ducked down again, drawing her aim. She looked at the stone: it was different from the other pebbles, being oval in shape and quite smooth and of a delicate shade of grey. She dropped it in the pocket of her fustian apron. 'C'mon, Jamie, we best be going,' she called and began the long climb down.

It was late in the afternoon by the time they reached Lamb's Down Farm. The farmer's wife eyed Kezzy as the little girl stood waiting for Jamie to hand over the coppers he had knotted for safety in the tail of his shirt. 'What 'ee a-doin' here, child? Why bain't 'ee at school? 'Tis Monday, bain't it?' she questioned Kezzy.

Kezzy shrugged. 'I didn't go to school today, missus.'

'Oh, and why be that, my dear?' persisted the woman as she counted the coppers on her kitchen table before dropping them into a tin on the dresser.

Jamie fidgeted uncomfortably; as the older of the two he felt guilty for not insisting his sister had gone to school. Except that no one save his Gramps could order Kezzy to do anything she didn't want to do. 'Gramps said it 'twas awlright for Kezzy t'come with I today,' he lied.

Kezzy's elfin face set. 'Jamie Hammett, that's a lie! Gramps said no such thing! I didn't go to school off my own hook!'

His face turned red because he'd been shown up for a liar. He picked up the sack of oatmeal and slung it across his back. 'Take up they loaves and come 'long withee,' he muttered.

'If'n 'ee bain't at school 'ee should be working in by bal and not playing games,' scolded the woman as she saw them out of the door.

Kezzy gave her an unconcerned smile and rolled her slanting dark eyes up at the red-ringed sky. 'Ah, well now, missus, 'twas a day lent,' she said, sounding so much like her grandfather that the farmer's wife blinked in astonishment. 'Ay, best make most of fine weather while 'tis upon us. Good day, to 'ee missus . . . remember me to thy good husband.'

Speechless, the woman watched the two children set off across the moor following the narrow track which, after eight years, now ran like a pale seam across the moor between mine and farm. Later, when the farmer came home at dusk, she said: 'Kezziah Hammett were here. Right forthy maiden, her be.'

Her husband nodded and gave a chuckle. 'Her would be . . . Elyas Hammett's gran'child.'

The woman pushed a bowl of stew at him, saying darkly, 'Don't 'ee laugh, husband. Her have old head on young shoulders. I reckon her be a *pixie* child!'

He looked up from his stew in alarm. Certainly the Hammett maid looked like a pixie with her pointed face, neat little ears and upturned nose. And pixies could be mischievous creatures, tormenting the hens so they stopped laying and turning the milk sour. 'You'm tell un tinner to send only they boys in future . . . yon Hammett maid ent welcome here 'gin,' he growled.

She didn't look pleased. 'I can't tell he that. Have 'ee no better sense? Might offend he . . . and his coppers come handy.'

But the farmer was resolute. He was having no pixie things on his farm. 'You tell he, wife,' he said.

The light had all but faded by the time Jamie and Kezzy reached Eaglestone. Wart barked a welcome as they entered the yard with the sacks on their backs. Graeme came out of the blowing shed, followed by Isaac, their faces streaked with grime.

'Where've 'ee been all day?' demanded Graeme scowling. There'd been no bread for their croust and they'd had to make do with boiled turnips and a lump of the dried pork they were storing for winter.

'Gramps is proper mazed with 'ee. Reckon you'm forrit,' declared Isaac with a certain amount of relish. The younger ones always seemed to be sliding out of work, what with school-learning and trips to the farm and the like, while he and Graeme worked the mine day in and day out with their pa and grandpa until they were dropping with tiredness.

In the dim light, Jamie's face was concerned by the news that their grandfather was mad at them. Kezzy looked unconcerned. She could, she knew, twist the old man around her clever fingers. At that moment, two flickering lights appeared one after the other at the gaping entrance to the mine. With a whoop, Kezzy dropped her sack of bread and bounded across the yard to greet her father and grandfather. The burning tallow candles stuck in clay atop their dented tin hats illuminated their dust-covered faces as they stared down at her sternly. Quickly, she seized Elyas's hard, knobbled hand, tilting her face anxiously to return his gaze. 'Isaac says you're proper mazed with Jamie and me, but you aren't, are you, Gramps?' she asked him winningly and his weary face creased in a smile.

He never could resist this prettily spoken maid. It warmed his heart to see her there when he emerged from the choking damp below ground and he forgot in an instant how angry he'd been when she didn't come home at four o'clock or soon after to help wash and sort the day's harvest of tin ore for smelting. However, her father's displeasure didn't evaporate quite so readily; he scowled at her, then across at Jamie.

'Come here, boy,' Huward commanded. Reluctantly, his son set down the sack of oatmeal and went and stood beside Kezzy in front of the two senior Hammetts. 'Where's pair o' 'ee bin?'

Jamie shuffled his feet and stared at the ground. 'Us got lost, Pa. Reckon us were led right dance 'cross moor by they piskies.'

Huward started. 'Piskie-led!' he gasped and Graeme and Isaac, still standing watching, exchanged glances, suddenly interested.

Jamie nodded vigorously. 'Ay, Pa. Us couldn't find way home no matter how hard us tried. Us walked round and round in circles.'

Elyas cocked an eye at Kezzy. 'Be this true, Kezzy?'

She shook her head. 'Nay, Gramps. We climbed up to look at the eagle's nest.'

Jamie shot Kezzy a reproachful look and would have darted away only Huward grabbed him and shook him hard, saying in a voice thick with fury, 'I'll give 'ee piskie-led!'

Kezzy's voice rang out as she leapt to Jamie's defence. 'Please, Pa, leave him be! 'Twere my idea to climb Eagle Tor!'

Huward gave Jamie a final shake, clouted his head so he yelped loudly and released him. 'Get 'ee inside, pair of 'ee and start un supper before I take switch to 'ee.'

They snatched up their sacks and ran. Later, after they'd all eaten and Huward and Elyas were in a better frame of mind, Elyas drew Kezzy to him, stroking her glossy, dark head affectionately. 'What made 'ee want to shirk school and go climbing Eagle Tor, child?' he asked her. 'Ent nawthin' up there save that old nest.'

'It had stones in it, Gramps.' She took the smooth, grey stone from her apron pocket and showed it to him.

His shaggy grey brows rose. He took the stone and rolled it in his palm. 'Ye took un from nest?' She nodded. 'Why, this be an eaglestone, child. Mustn't take un or eagle won't come back 'gin.'

' 'Twere lots more, Gramps, but her throwed they at me,' piped up Jamie. He hadn't forgiven Kezzy for not supporting his story about them being pixie-led and sought now to get his own back for the painful clout she'd earned him.

Elyas frowned. 'Did 'ee do what 'ee brother says, Kezzy?'

She nodded again. 'Ay, Gramps.'

'Her left they stones scattered all over, Gramps,' crowed Jamie.

'Just 'ee pipe down, boy!' Elyas told him sharply. He turned his attention to Kezzy again. 'Did 'ee pick up they eaglestones and put they back in nest?'

'Nay, Gramps,' she admitted and tears filled her eyes when she saw his disappointment.

Huward peered at the stone, unimpressed. He rose and went to lie on his pallet. 'Don't know what all fuss be 'bout. They just stones,' he yawned.

Elyas shook his head sadly. 'Not *just* stones, Huward boy. *Eaglestones.* Eagle won't lay her eggs wi'out they. Like as not her won't come back ever 'gin.'

Kezzy felt icy fingers steal over her. Her lower lip trembled. 'Oh, Gramps!' she exclaimed, mortified by what she'd done when the eagle had been good to the Hammetts, showing them where to hulk for tin so that now they were mine-owners and not scratching a living as tut-workers for a greedy captain. 'Oh, poor eagle,' she whispered and her tears began to fall.

Elyas patted her cheek. 'You'm weren't to know, child.' He handed her back the eaglestone. 'Here, 'ee may as well keep un. Eaglestone be proper fey. Right magical. Cure all manner of ills and keep 'ee from harm if'n 'ee got un.'

Kezzy brushed a hand over her eyes and stared in wonder at the stone. Being told that it was magic made her wish more than ever that she'd taken perhaps just this one, pretty grey eaglestone and left all the others where they were in the nest. Dragging her feet miserably, she went and lay on her pallet in the back room with her face to the wall. When Jamie and Isaac came through a little later and lay on their pallets whispering together she kept quite still, pretending to be asleep. She couldn't make out what they were saying but was sure they were talking about the eagle and blaming her for driving it away for ever. After a while, the boys fell silent and all she could hear was the sound of their soft, even breathing. Kezzy waited until she was sure they were sound asleep, then she rose and crept over to the curtain covering the door between the two rooms; peeping round it, she saw that her grandfather was still sitting beside the dying fire deep in thought. And, as young as she was, she could tell by the hunching of his shoulders that his thoughts were gloomy. She longed to run to him and comfort him: to tell him that the eagle would come back one day. But her father and Graeme lay sleeping and she dared not disturb them.

With a last, wistful look towards the mournful figure of the old man, Kezzy went back to her pallet. After what seemed like hours, she heard him get up from the wooden settle and shuffle across to his pallet; he groaned as he knelt to murmur his nightly prayers, then again as he stretched out. Within minutes he fell into a fitful sleep, his snores carrying through the curtain to his granddaughter's ears.

The Hammetts woke with the crowing of their old cockerel. The morning was grey and leaden, with a chill current of air creeping into the cottage to tell them that the 'St Luke's' fine October spell had gone.

And with it, apparently, had gone half a loaf of bread and Kezzy!

'Where would her have gone skulking off to afore dawn?' Huward asked, annoyed and puzzled, when Isaac had been sent to search the outhouses to make sure she wasn't hiding somewhere to tease them. It was particularly irksome that she wasn't there to make their oatmeal porridge; she was already a dab hand at it and the boys made it too lumpy.

Elyas gave a chuckle. 'Reckon I knows where her gone.'

'Where?' they demanded with one voice.

'Up Eagle Tor, most likely'd . . . to find they eaglestones and put they back in nest!'

They didn't expect to see Kezzy before mossle. Even when she wasn't back by mid-afternoon they weren't unduly concerned. She was only a child and her legs would soon grow tired climbing all the way up the tor.

'Likely'd her stopped to rest and eat her croust,' said Elyas with a bluff certainty when they stopped themselves for a bite at croust-time. He was growing a shade uneasy but didn't want to show it.

There was still no sign of Kezzy as evening drew near and a thick fog had descended, swathing the hills and the moorland in its grey folds. For once, Elyas and Huward left off working what promised to be a useful lode, judging by the abundance of quartz traversing the granite face, and hauled themselves back up to the surface by the pulley. They walked a hundred yards or so up the valley, treading carefully since they couldn't see more than a yard in front, and shouting for Kezzy as loudly as their dust-tormented lungs allowed so that if she was nearby, and lost, she'd be guided home. Every so often they stopped and listened, but there was no plaintive, answering call and after a while they went back to work.

'Her be awlright, Pa,' insisted Huward with more confidence than he truly felt. 'Her have a right good brain-box on her . . . for a maid. Her knows to sit tight where her be 'til mist lifts.'

Elyas nodded. It was true: he had warned all his grandchildren to beware wandering around if a moor mist suddenly descended. With that comforting thought, he swung on to the pulley and let his son lower him into the gloom.

The fog hadn't lifted by evening; if anything it was thicker. And much colder. And Kezzy had only her scrap of a shawl for warmth. Her family ceased now to hide their fears for her from each other.

'Put bridle on Rats, Jamie boy,' instructed Elyas as he and Huward and the two older boys dressed in jerseys and oilskins in readiness to go and search for her. The moorland pony wouldn't be troubled by the dark or the fog, and would lead them safely over the treacherous ground which lay between the head of the creep and the foot of Eagle Tor. Elyas got out some new tallow candles and fitted them in the lanterns; they wouldn't be much use in the fog but there was just a chance that Kezzy might glimpse a light through the eddying white curtain.

'Best take ol' Wart with us, Gramps,' said Graeme putting on a stout pair of shoes. 'Mebbe pick up Kezzy's scent.'

Elyas nodded grimly. Anything was worth trying.

Jamie came rushing back inside having tethered Rats in the yard. Feverishly he began dragging on a thick jersey.

'You'm stayin' here, boy,' said Elyas.

Jamie's face crumpled. 'Please let me come, Gramps!' he begged.

'Nay, boy, bad 'nough losin' one young un. Besides, what if her were to find her own way back and there be nobody home? Fine thing, *that* would be . . .'

'But I know what way us took up tor yesterday, Gramps,' Jamie interrupted him, desperate to be allowed to go with the search party.

'Don't 'ee argue with 'ee grandpa, boy!' said Huward gruffly. 'You'm stayin' and that's that! And mind 'ee keep fire mended . . .'

'Hist!'

Elyas's sharp ears had heard something. He pushed open the door and peered out into the swirling mass of white, listening.

'What do 'ee hear, Gramps? Be it Kezzy?' asked Jamie eagerly.

'Hist!' muttered Elyas again and they fell silent as he strained his ears: Surely they weren't playing him tricks! No, there it was again: the chink of metal horseshoes against stone. And coming up the valley. 'By Lord Harry, we'm got visitors!' he announced, his wrinkled face incredulous.

They could all hear the sound of approaching hoofbeats now, but muffled by the fog. Who would be out on the moor on such a night? They stared, trying to penetrate the grey wall, but it was more than a minute before the shapes of a score or more horses loomed out of the mist. Half a dozen of the animals had riders, the rest were being led in a string. And astride the leading pack animal was perched Kezzy!

Her family's relief was palpable as she slid down from her mount with an excited little cry and ran across to them. It was her grandfather around whom she threw her arms, gazing up into his relieved face, her dark eyes aglow.

'I put the eaglestones back, Gramps! As many as I could find. Only then . . .' She bit her lip, her enthusiasm fading as she prepared to admit the next part of her escapade. 'Only . . . I got lost. I walked and walked . . . then these gentl'men found me and took me up. I know you said stay put if mist come down, but I was sure I knew the way!'

He nodded. It was a misjudgement easily made by a seasoned moor-man let alone a slip of a maid. His eyes moved to the band of men who had brought her home. They hadn't dismounted but sat with their horses reined, and though Elyas couldn't see them clearly he sensed that they were watching the Hammetts closely. He took a step towards them, lifting his lantern the better to see them.

'Thankee, friends, for brunging home my granddaughter. Her pa, here and me be right 'bliged.'

They were, Elyas saw with a slight feeling of concern, rough, hard-featured and mainly ill-clad. Two carried muskets slung across their backs; the other four had silver-hafted pistols in their belts. Their leader wore an old stocking cap, the end wound around his lower face, masking it. His eyes were unfriendly in the flickering light. Not the eyes of a man who would care what happened to a small girl lost on the moor. Anyroads, mused Elyas, not sufficiently to travel out of his road to carry her safe home without good reason. And he had a fair suspicion what that reason was.

They were at home on the moor, that was obvious. Even in the fog. Probably free-traders who made the journey regularly. Elyas eyed the special trappings on the pack animals. *Flaskers!* The men were 'flaskers', specialising in smuggled cognac. Although there wasn't a single brandy keg to be seen, the steel and leather supports worn by the sturdy beasts bore witness to the transportation of barrels. They had probably run a cargo the previous night and taken it up the moor under cover of the fog to hide it far from the keen eyes of the Revenue. Perhaps at some farm where they'd bribed or, more likely, bullied the farmer into being their custodian. Perhaps their contraband was hidden in some isolated mine . . .

'What's thy name, tinner?'

It was the leader of the band, his harsh voice muffled by his woollen mask, who interrupted Elyas's train of thought. At least, Elyas presumed the man was the leader since he was mounted on a handsome chestnut and wore a good cloth coat with a shoulder-cape and silver buttons.

'Elyas Hammett,' he answered after the slightest pause. He kept both his face and his tone bland. 'And who might us Hammetts be beholden to, friend?'

But the flasker ignored the question, instead asking, 'Do ye own yon mine, Hammett?'

'Ay.'

The flasker twisted in his saddle, eyes probing the shifting fog to make out the dark shapes of the stack and the whim at the bal entrance. 'How deep is main shaft?'

'Deep 'nough,' replied Elyas non-committally. Even in the poor light he didn't miss the veiled glance which passed between the leader of the band and the man mounted nearest to him.

'It be ever so deep, zur! More'n five fathoms!' Jamie was quick to boast.

Elyas put a warning hand on the boy's shoulder. The flasker's next question put him thoroughly on his guard.

'How many tunnels has thy mine, tinner?'

He knew exactly how many, long and short, broad and narrow, but he pretended to give the matter some consideration, removing his oilskin sou'wester and scratching his head. 'Now, let's see . . . I s'pose you'm talking 'bout *dry* tunnels, friend?'

'Ay, dry or middling dry.'

'Thought you'm be,' chuckled Elyas and gave the man a sly wink. 'Dare say you'm a-looking to store drop o' Frenchie moonshine where Preventy men can't trip over it?' The flasker's eyes were like flints above his muffler and Elyas knew his suspicions were correct. He kept his tone amiable but allowed a note of regret to creep in. 'Well, now, friend, we'm would *like* to help 'ee. 'Specially after you'm brung home young Kezzy none the worse. But 'tis only right to tell 'ee, they tunnels is terrible for flooding on account they be close to leat. Proper irksome it be. One minute we'm working dry as bone, next we'm flooded nigh to head of' shaft.'

It wasn't true. Although some of the tunnels were damp, especially those beneath Eagle Brook, they collected just a few inches of sodden muck on the floor. Elyas had long since installed a waterwheel to work a pump so there wouldn't be any serious flooding.

Fully aware of this, Jamie's mouth had dropped open in amazement. Why would his grandfather be telling the gentlemen different? He found his voice. 'But, Gramps, they tunnels ent never fl . . . Ouch!'

It was quick-witted Kezzy who stopped him giving the game away by delivering a hard kick to his bony ankle, making him gasp with pain and bringing tears to his eyes.

The flaskers exchanged looks. A mine which was apt to flood badly was no good to them as a hiding place for contraband. A surfeit of water could seep into cognac and ruin it. A moment later, without another word said, they were riding away through the fog, back down the valley. Elyas raised a hand, ensuring none of his family unthinkingly made an unwise comment which might bring the smugglers back to examine the mine for themselves. When he could pick out the hoofbeats no more, he dropped his hand and let out a loud, relieved breath. 'They've gone,' he said.

Graeme and Isaac grinned at each other then looked towards Elyas with respect manifest on their faces. Huward clapped his father on the shoulder. ' 'Twere well done, Pa. You'm saw they smugglers off Eaglestone pack and vardel!'

'Smugglers!' exclaimed Jamie in astonishment.

Kezzy gave him a push. 'And you nearly give it away, you silly boy! Gramps don't want smugglers hiding their moonshine in by bal, do you, Gramps?' She looked up at his expectantly but he gave her no answering nod and his face remained as hard as moorland granite.

'Hold thy tongue, Keziah,' he told her and she winced at the sharpness of his tone and the uncommon use of her full name. 'Isaac, take bridle off Rats. Inside with the rest of 'ee.'

He was angry with Kezzy for all the trouble and worry she'd caused, they could tell. It wasn't often that Elyas was angry with any of his family, and never without good reason, and never for long. But this time not even his favourite grandchild's appealing little face could disperse his ill-humour. Once inside the cottage, he sat down on the settle with the lantern nearby, then pointed to the rush-covered floor in front of him, silently indicating to Kezzy that that was where she was to stand while he admonished her.

Slowly she obeyed. But the bolt of wrath didn't immediately fall.

Presently, however, in a voice that was almost gentle, Elyas asked her, 'Now, Keziah, what have 'ee to say for thyself?'

She stood plucking at a fold in her apron. 'I'm sorry,' she muttered.

'Ye fright us half to death, and all 'ee can say is you'm sorry?'

'I wasn't in any danger, Gramps,' she told him with a certainty that made him blink.

'But 'ee were lost on moor, child! Mebbe have got stagged in mire if'n they rogues hadn't taken 'ee up with they!'

'But you said I wouldn't come to any harm as long as I'd got my magic stone, Gramps,' reminded Kezzy. She slipped her hand in her pocket and brought it out to show him. Seeing his frown deepen, she hastily added, 'I put back all the rest, 'pon my honour! I didn't think the eagle would miss just this one.'

Still the old, hard face didn't soften. Abruptly he said: 'Do 'ee know what might have happened if'n they rogues hid un moonshine in by bal and Preventy men found un?' Kezzy shook her head. 'Then I'll tell 'ee. We'd have been took before tinners' court and found guilty. Then me an' thy pa an' thy brothers would've been sent on convict boat to Australia for seven year or more.'

Kezzy's dark eyes flew across the room to where they sat around the table watching and listening. Her lips trembled. 'Even Jamie?' she asked doubtfully.

'Ay, even young Jamie,' Elyas soberly confirmed.

There was a long silence then while Kezzy digested her grandfather's terrible revelations and theories. She was trembling now and her strange, narrow eyes swam with tears at the thought of what might have befallen them all through her thoughtlessness. Then she rallied, swallowed her tears. Her head came up.

'How was I to know they were moonshiners?'

Elyas eyed her at length. Seeing, as he always did when she turned stubborn, an almost overwhelming likeness to Ruke in her vivid and changing features. *Ruke's stubbornness had been the death of her! If only she'd kissed the cross . . .* He shook the painful memory from his thoughts.

'Do 'ee knows what I'd do to 'ee if'n 'ee was a boy?'

'Ay, you'd take birch to my bare arse, Gramps,' she answered him carelessly.

'Hammetts don't birch un maidens, thy knows, Kezzy.'

'Ay, Gramps. Ent right.'

Elyas looked across at Jamie. 'Fetch birch, boy.'

They all looked startled. The pink in Kezzy's cheeks was wiped out as something cold and terrible gripped her heart. Surely he wasn't going to mete out a boy's punishment to her! Hesitantly, Jamie rose from his stool and fetched the birch from its hook behind the door. He gave Kezzy a sympathetic look as he handed it to Elyas, having tasted its stinging swish more than once. As he moved to return to his seat, Elyas stopped him.

'Stay here, boy.'

Jamie stood obediently, staring at Elyas wide-eyed, curious as to what he wanted with him. He wasn't kept in suspense for very long.

'Now then, Jamie, seeing as how I can't birch maiden, you'm must take thy sister's punishment,' Elyas told him gravely.

Jamie's face turned as pale as Kezzy's. 'B . . . but G . . . Gramps . . .!' he began to plead against the unfairness of it but his father's brusque voice silenced him.

'Don't argue with thy grandfather, boy!'

Kezzy stared horrified at the hazel switch in Elyas's hand. She lifted her eyes pleadingly to his face. 'Nay, Gramps . . .' came her broken whisper. 'Jamie had nothing to do with it. He only climbed Eagle Tor with me 'cause I played bully with him.'

Elyas was in no mood for clemency. What she'd done was both foolish and dangerous and he believed that being made to watch as her brother was thrashed in her place would teach her a lesson she wouldn't forget. He rose and pointed with the birch to Jamie's stool.

'Bring thy stool an' drop thy britches, boy . . .'

Chapter Eight

Cornwood was a small world of its own. Marooned as it was in a wooded hamlet through which the Yealm cascaded after quitting the moors, the village was independent of outside help save when a physician or tooth-puller was summoned from Plympton.

There were just a few greystone cottages straggling along the single main track, yet, besides the church, vicarage and Dame Rogers's school, there was a smithy, carpenter's shop, bakehouse, chandler's and draper's, and a good inn. There was even a kiddleywink which the locals called the 'Brandy Keg' though they had never known it sell anything but the roughest ale and cider – or swore they hadn't.

Since actual residents were few, the village relied to a great extent upon the bounty of the gentry. For it was they who owned the surrounding tenant farms, the Wheals employing hundreds of tinners, and, of course, the stately homesteads which employed armies of liveried servants, grooms, maids and skivvies.

It was to one of these fine houses, Fardle Hall, the seat of the Raleighs, though not the birthplace of Sir Walter, that Elyas went one morning, a brilliant, clear, fresh April morning in 1805 when Graeme was twenty-two and Isaac almost twenty years of age. For he had been led to understand by Dame Hannah Rogers – who always seemed to know such things – that there were two young sisters, Morgenna and Bethinda, who were desirous of marrying two local brothers so that they wouldn't be separated, on account of the fact that they were exceptionally close to each other. Moreover, their mistress was prepared to release them on the understanding that they continued to work from home as her seamstresses since they were particularly clever with their needles.

'And will her ladyship pay they sisters a shillin' or two for they stitchin', do 'ee know, mistress?' Elyas had enquired of Dame Rogers with a crafty glint in his sharp, pale eyes.

'Oh, surely! Lady Raleigh is most generous to her servants.'

'Then I best be a-callin' at Fardle an' paying my respects to they there sisters.'

The notion that, as well as keeping house and working their coore as bal maidens, Morgenna and Bethinda would bring in a bit of silver for doing, after all, what came naturally to women in the evenings, made them all the more acceptable to Elyas as wives for his grandsons. That was why the very next morning after his conversation with the dame, without a word to his family until he'd viewed the sisters, he set off for Fardle wearing his

Sunday clothes of cotton shirt, corduroy trousers and long fustian waistcoat.

Lady Raleigh's steward received him at the kitchen door, listened to what he'd to say and then sent for the two sisters so he could decide if they were suitable.

They stood giggling, peeping shyly at Elyas from beneath springy, kipper-coloured hair. They were clearly twins. And were just seventeen, according to the steward. Any question Elyas put directly to the sisters was met with yet more giggles. Still, he told himself, they had plenty of 'beam and bust' and looked as if they'd plenty of work in them.

'Well, now, are you'm maidens willing to marry my Graeme and my Isaac?' he asked them and had to wait a full minute for the giggles and the nudging to subside before one of them, Morgenna, recognisable from her twin only because she'd a mole on her jaw, replied: 'Thankee, mister, for askin', but me and Bethinda can't say bee nor baw to it afore us have met thy boys.'

Elyas looked taken aback. 'Bain't no call to meet un first! Give me thy answer an' we'll slap hands on it. Ye won't find more rampant pair of boys in whole of Devon, I promise 'ee that!' he boasted and started them off giggling again, this time until their ruddy faces were a dark red and tears were squeezing from between their brown lashes.

But for all their mirth and coyness, they knew what they wanted and refused to agree to the marriage without a prior meeting with Graeme and Isaac. The steward announced that he was in agreement with them. ' 'Tis only right,' he muttered to Elyas. 'Ye wouldn't buy stallion without straddling he first, would 'ee?'

So it was agreed that the sisters would attend church the following Sunday and Elyas would bring his grandsons. Then, if all parties were in agreement, the vicar would be asked to call banns there and then.

Graeme and Isaac were apprehensive when, at supper that evening, Elyas informed them of the arrangements he'd made for them.

'Bain't be squint-eyed, be they?' asked Graeme suspiciously.

'Or toothless?' put in Isaac with an ill-concealed shudder, since this was something he found particularly abhorrent. The farmer's wife at Lamb's Down had scarce a stump in her head when she laughed, and so repulsive did Isaac find the sight of her gnashing grey gums he would have been content with even a squint-eyed wife rather than a toothless one.

But Elyas put their doubts to rest, saying, 'Nay, nay, they be right buxom, nut-brown pair of wenches. An' good tempered, or I'm no fit judge . . . even if they do giggle fit to strip feathers off hoody-crow.'

On Sunday, Graeme and Isaac stripped off their working clothes and waded into the brook to wash themselves before putting on their Sunday shirts. Neither had much facial growth, but they trimmed each other's unruly locks and cleaned their fingernails.

Kezzy wandered down to the brook and viewed them. 'My, oh my! Look at pair of you! Shining like shitten barn door to go sparkin'!' she taunted, and Isaac, turning scarlet, grabbed her and would have ducked her in the brook if Graeme hadn't intervened.

'Leave she be, brother. Her's got good frock on. Gramp'll skin 'ee if'n her gets wetted afore church. Mebbe stop us a-goin'.'

Now they'd had a chance to consider, they weren't against meeting the sisters. Reluctantly, Isaac released Kezzy and she darted away back to the cottage, shouting irritatingly over her shoulder, 'Sparkin'! Sparkin'! Graeme and Isaac are going sparkin'!'

Morgenna and Bethinda were as good as their word. Wearing identical blue-cotton dresses and white aprons and chip-straws tied under their chins, they were seated in a pew at the back of the church among other members of the Raleigh household when the Hammetts arrived. Elyas directed his family into a pew just across the centre aisle so his grandsons and the sisters could form a nodding acquaintance before the service commenced.

For the next few minutes, the congregation were continually rising and sitting with much tugging of hair by the men as the local gentry arrived to take their family pews at the front of the church. Lady Raleigh was among the first; followed by Mr and Mrs John Dudley Pode and the four Misses Dudley Podes from Slade Hall up by Piall Brook. The Hawns and the Dendles, farmers and mine-owners, came in together since the two families were always marrying each other. Old Lord Blachford arrived leaning heavily on the arm of his steward.

By now, Graeme and Isaac were thoroughly taken with the kipper-haired maidens across the aisle. Since they looked as alike as two peas, for the sake of convenience Graeme whispered to Isaac that he would take the one sitting nearest to them, which was Morgenna. Using dumb signs, they let the sisters know this and they, in turn, indicated with much rolling of eyes behind their prayer books that they were 'willing'. Noting this, and receiving a discreet nod from the Raleigh steward who had the sisters in his charge, Elyas beckoned over the hovering curate to whisper his request for the banns to be read after the service.

Mrs Creedy, the minister's wife, came in, rustling slightly in stiff grey calico, her straw bonnet trimmed with a black ribbon. She took her place at the organ and began to play a gentle hymn, her black shoes pumping the pedals in a businesslike fashion as her neat, pale hands worked the keys and stops. She was just beginning her second hymn, 'Ye Servants of the Lord Each in His Office Wait', which let the Reverend Burridge Creedy know in the vestry that the pews were now full, when the church doors opened to admit two more worshippers.

Elyas turned and craned his neck to see who had the audacity to arrive so noisily after Mrs Creedy had begun her hymn playing. Kezzy, seated between her father and grandfather, felt Elyas tense and the hands holding her grandmother's old prayer-book gripped it so tightly it seemed as if the sharp knucklebones were in danger of piercing the skin.

The rest of the congregation had also recognised the Lord Warden, John de Raddon and his wife, Mrs Emma de Raddon, and were hastily rising to show their respect, with much tugging of forelocks from the men and boys. Elyas, however, remained firmly seated. As de Raddon passed him by, their eyes met for a moment. Kezzy looked curiously from face to face, trying to make out what was meant by this silent, cold-eyed exchange and her grandfather's daring display of disrespect towards a high official of the Stannary.

Then de Raddon was gone, marching on down the centre aisle with his black coat-tails swinging and the light from the altar candles catching his gold chain of office. His wife followed him meekly, eyes lowered, delicate features and flaxen hair almost hidden by her lace-trimmed lavender velvet bonnet. Her high-waisted gown was of the latest fashion, lavender silk with a fine, Brussels lace overskirt, and she wore milk-white pearls around her neck and wrists. Even her prayer-book was of softest white kid with tooled gold letters on it. The Lord Warden, Kezzy concluded, was terrible rich: probably the richest man in Devon.

Lord Blachford, seeing them approaching, rose as quickly as his bent form permitted and moved along his prestigious front pew to make room for the de Raddons. Spotting them out of the corner of her eye as they settled themselves on the wooden form, Mrs Creedy swiftly changed key and began to play 'Hail to the Lord Who Comes' so as to let the vicar know that he'd an unexpected, illustrious addition to his flock.

The de Raddons generally worshipped at Plympton St Mary but occasionally they came to Cornwood church or one of the other small parish churches to see and be seen by the tinners who made up a large part of the congregations. No one quite knew why the Lord Warden behoved himself to come; some thought it was because he wanted to see which tinners were God-fearing and which weren't so he'd know whose contract and whose not to renew the next 'setting day'. But others thought he came because he liked the vicars to see how he was more respected and feared than them. While those who knew his libidinous ways swore that he came to see the maidens, noting which were the prettiest so he'd know where to dally when next he was in the neighbourhood.

'If'n 'ee have a fair-faced wife or daughter, keep they from Lord Warden's sight,' was an oft-whispered warning whenever tinners' families congregated.

Remembering it now, Isaac scowled at the back of de Raddon's coarse, black bag-wig. He nudged Graeme. 'Do 'ee reckon Lord Warden will cast his eye on us sweethearts?' he whispered anxiously.

Graham shook his head. He wasn't so headlight for love of his ruddy-cheeked intended that he imagined she, or her twin, would appeal to de Raddon. He didn't, however, say as much. Kezzy, on the other hand, seated behind her brothers, her ears pricked to hear their confidences, leaned forward and dug Isaac between the blades.

'Don't worry, Isaac,' she whispered saucily, 'Lord Warden has got any number of cart-horses in his stables already.'

Isaac turned crimson and would have turned round to remonstrate with his young sister, but Elyas shushed them because at that moment the Reverend Burridge Creedy was making his solemn entrance.

The service was gone through and the hymns sung. Then the minister climbed into the pulpit with his sheaf of papers to deliver his sermon, taking for his text Job 1:7 'And the Lord said unto Satan, Whence comest thou? Then Satan answered the Lord, and said, From going to and fro in the earth, and from walking up and down in it.'

Seeing de Raddon's scarred, satanic face glowering up at him from the front pew, Burridge Creedy couldn't help but feel his text was rather apt. If ever there was a devil come among them to walk and plunder the earth, it was the Lord Warden of the Stannaries.

For fifty minutes the minister preached, warning them of the wrath of God, of dire and dreadful punishments should they sin; that irreligion was insanity. The congregation grew restless and the younger members began to whisper and giggle, bored by thunderbolts and fiery, everlasting torment. Even Mrs Creedy stifled a yawn and began to turn the pages of her hymn book, hopeful that her husband would take the hint. But their waning interest only made him raise his voice and continue for another twenty minutes. When at last he did finish, with a ringing, 'The blessing of God Almighty, the Father, the Son and the Holy Ghost, be amongst thee and remain with thee always . . .' Elyas woke up in time to say 'Amen'.

Outside the church, the Raleigh steward permitted Graeme and Isaac to walk with Morgenna and Bethinda as far as the wagon which had brought the lower orders from Fardle to morning service. Kezzy and Jamie tried to slip away after the enamoured four but Huward stopped them, the memory of his own brief, tantalising courtship of their dead mother, Betsy, nibbling at his memory.

'Leave thy brothers alone, pair of 'ee! They bain't want 'ee stringin' along while they be sparkin' they shiners,' he told them sternly.

Kezzy pouted and tossed her dark head but she soon forgot her pique when Elyas and Huward began discussing the wedding plans with the steward.

'Next month will be convenient for her ladyship to release they maids,' said the steward.

Elyas shook his head. 'Not next month, 'tis May . . . marry in May repent for ay,' he quoted. 'And Lent will soon be 'pon us . . . marry in Lent, live to repent! Since banns is read, best they be hitched in a two-week.'

So it was agreed.

Kezzy was unusually quiet as they clopped back up the moor behind Rats. She didn't even bother to jump down and grab up an armful of daffodils and catkins from the wayside. Presently she said in an enquiring tone of voice, 'Gramps . . .?'

'Spit un out, Kezzy! What's botherin' 'ee?' He could usually tell when her busy brain was taken up with some fanciful notion which she'd eventually voice by way of a question.

'When I'm growed, will you go up to one of the big houses to get a husband for me?'

Elyas nudged Huward sitting grinning beside him on the box. Gravely he said, 'Well, ay, Kezzy. If them boys don't come up moor in they droves to sue for thy hand . . . which I think them will, mind.'

'It's just . . .' she hesitated.

'Ay, chield?'

'If you *do* go looking for a husband for me, can he not be a servant?'

Elyas choked. He coughed raspingly to clear the phlegm that had gathered in his throat. 'Not a servant?' he gasped, bemused.

'I don't want to marry a servant, Gramps,' said Kezzy solemnly.

The others began to titter but Elyas quietened them with a, 'Hist, let Kezzy have her say. Now then, m'dear, who 'zackly *do* 'ee want to marry when time comes?'

'I want to marry someone . . .' she paused, remembering Mrs de Raddon's lavender-silk gown and her pearls and the fine coach which had been waiting for her and her husband outside the door. 'I want to marry someone rich like Captain de Raddon.'

Elyas half turned. Two bright spots of red coloured his cheeks, a rare thing for him. All the humour had left him and there was an icy edge to his voice. 'If 'tis Lord Warden 'ee has a-hankerin' to wed 'ee may as well bequeath thyself to the Devil, body and soul an' save thyself trouble!'

With that, he cracked his whip over Rats's startled head and lapsed into a moody silence which lasted all the way home.

But by then Kezzy had forgotten all about lavender-silk dresses and pearl necklaces. And the Lord Warden.

With the double wedding so close, Elyas allowed Graeme and Isaac to miss their forenoon coore and spend the time building on two more small rooms at the back of the cottage in readiness for their brides. On the days she didn't attend school, Kezzy was sent out with Jamie and the wagon to collect suitable stones, taking with them a lump each of cold figgy pudding in a mossle bag and a canteen of water – a task they didn't mind at all since running free on the moor in the crisp, spring air was infinitely preferable to being cooped up in the washing-house sorting ore. They always made sure, however, that they'd a good load of stones to take home at croust-time, and of the right size and shape, so that their days out wouldn't be curtailed.

By the following Sunday, Graeme and Isaac had got the walls up and the stones packed with mud-and-straw 'cob' to keep out the draughts. A morning spent thatching the roof and they'd be done. Since there was time enough before their wedding day on the following Saturday, Elyas let them go to church to meet their sweethearts and take a stroll afterwards to talk about whatever it was that sweethearts talked about.

Kezzy was to go with them to church, since Dame Rogers would always remark upon her absence when next the schoolmistress saw Elyas or Huward in the village. 'But you'm to come straight back 'long home after service,' Elyas warned her. 'Ye can ride part of way with they folk from Lamb's Down.'

He wasn't going himself that Sunday. Neither was Huward. And they were keeping Jamie with them to collect barn eggs and clean out the pig-sty.

'I'd as lief work a coore than sit through that poxy God-botherer's sermon,' growled Elyas to his son as they watched the wagon trundle off down the valley.

'I'd as lief work *fifty* coores,' said Huward from the heart.

After church, the Hammett boys and their sweethearts were quick to disappear. Kezzy stayed for a while to chat to Willy and Jane Beckwitt, the smithy's children who also went to the dame school. She forgot all about asking for a ride partway up the moor on the Lamb's Down wagon and it had gone by the time she'd parted from her schoolfriends. She didn't care. It was a fine spring day and she knew where she might find some garlic mustard to take home and crush into the figgens.

The spot she had in mind was Fernfires Wood. It took her a good hour to get there since she stopped at Wisdome Mill to say 'Good morning' to the miller and his wife and to eat a thick slice of soft white bread covered in yellow butter. It was the finest bread Kezzy had ever tasted and she said so which greatly pleased Mrs Wisdome who pressed another slice upon the visitor.

'When I'm growed I shall have white bread every day,' declared Kezzy graciously accepting the proffered delicacy.

Mr Wisdome laughed heartily at that. 'Then 'ee must marry a miller, my dear.'

Kezzy chewed reflectively. Then she said: 'But not only millers eat white bread.'

' 'Tis true. Gentl'men wouldn't eat no other.'

'Then with respect to your good self, Mr Wisdome, I think I shall marry a gentl'men.'

The couple gaped as she politely thanked them for their 'hospitality to a wayfarer' and set off up the track towards the wood. They went to the door and watched her receding back view.

'That Kezzy Hammett be a right queer maiden,' commented the miller.

His wife looked knowing. 'Ent s'prising, Mr Wisdome, when her sprouted from witch's guts . . . and on All-Hallows, mark 'ee.'

Wisdome grunted. He only half-believed the idle talk of the village, which was, he wisely thought, half due to a deep-rooted distrust of gypsies with their secret language and magic charms and potions. Down the years, the facts of what happened the day Ruke Hammett was hanged for a witch at Plympton had become cloudy with repetition. True, many Cornwood folk had been there for the coinage and had been among the throng on Gibbet Hill, but each told a different, highly coloured version that reached the miller's ears as women's gossip. He'd heard it said that Ruke's dark mane had turned into a mass of slithering black snakes when the vicar held his cross before her face. Another 'witness' claimed that, as Ruke kicked her last, three witches on broomsticks had obscured the sun so a terrible darkness fell. All nonsense, of course, Wisdome told himself. Still . . .

'Ay, her be a queer un,' he repeated.

'End like her ma, if'n 'ee asks me,' said Mrs Wisdome darkly. 'Ill weeds grow for cutting.'

Blissfully unaware of her mysterious and gruesome heritage – for who was going to speak of it to her and risk her evil eye? – Kezzy skipped on her way and presently disappeared into a thicket of sapling which skirted the outer edge of Fernfire Wood.

Once through the thicket, she came to the broad green ride which led through the trees to Broadall Lake where it joined the Yealm. It was a particularly pretty spot in the spring as the banks were bright with primroses and yellow-green bedstraw and, Kezzy hoped, white garlic mustard flowers. She hadn't walked far when she began to notice hoof marks and wheel ruts in the green path where the turf was softest: a horse and cart had passed that way not long since. A few minutes later she arrived at the lake and, as she half-expected, saw the Eaglestone wagon and Rats contentedly cropping the grass. Of her brothers and their sweethearts, there was no sign. There was, however, plenty of garlic mustard. She was collecting a bunch when she heard a giggle from somewhere quite close by. Peering through a gap in a hawthorn bush she could make out Graeme's prone figure. He murmured something and again came the girlish giggle. A malignant impishness seized Kezzy. The sound of her movements drowned by the rippling water, she began edging closer to the unsuspecting lovers, intent on playing a trick on them by jumping out with a wild shriek from behind the trunk of a nearby tree. But, once she was in position, her eager interest was caught by the activity in the long grass and she forgot her purpose as she craned her neck to watch.

Morgenna had discarded her chip-straw and was stretched on her back with Graeme beside her. Her skirts were twisted up around her hips and with a sense of shock Kezzy realised that it wasn't just her hat that her future sister-in-law had discarded. She'd also removed her drawers. Her plump belly and sturdy thighs were strangely white in contrast to her ruddy face and arms, and were covered by a luxuriant tangle of springy red-brown hair which glinted in the dappled light. As Graeme shifted his position, Kezzy saw that his shirt and the flaps of his breeches were agape, revealing his pale, freckled chest and gold-tufted belly. He was clearly all of a-tremble and was fumbling with the strings of Morgenna's bodice. When at last he managed to loosen them so her immense, soft white breasts came tumbling out, Kezzy had to clap a hand over her mouth to stop herself from giggling out loud. How funny, she thought, the lovers looked, lying there with their clothes abroad! Moreover, they were gazing at each other in such a mutually foolish manner Kezzy was reminded of a pair of cows gazing upon their new-born calves.

But what happened next drove the impudent grin from her face, making her almost ashamed to look. Yet, look she did, so curious was she to observe a boy and maid doing what the wild ponies and the farm animals did as a matter of course. Elyas even had Kezzy and Jamie drive their house-cow, Pansy, over to Lamb's Down every ten months or so to be put to William the bull, thereby ensuring a good supply of milk – the resulting calf being the farmer's payment for William's services.

It seemed as though Morgenna was quite used to the sport whereas

Graeme seemed uncertain of what was expected of him. She wrapped her brown arms and her white legs around him and began to heave up and down beneath him so that their naked bellies smacked together, all the while moaning and groaning as if she was complaining. Just like Pansy when William mounted her, it occurred to Kezzy. Impelled by instinct, Graeme began to kiss her noisily and his body plunged to and fro.

'Oh!' he cried, so abruptly that Kezzy started, although there was no likelihood of him seeing her as he lay atop Morgenna. 'Oh . . . oh! What's happening?' he panted.

Morgenna's big rough hands travelled swiftly down his back and clutched at his heaving backside. 'That's it, m'dear!'

Graeme gave one final, tremendous lunge, a shuddering yell and collapsed on her breast. Morgenna wriggled a moment or two longer, shifting his weight up and down, then she gave a final wailing groan and was still.

Kezzy crept away and made her way back along the ride. 'Same as cows and colts,' she muttered to herself a trifle disappointedly, 'only quicker and they don't kiss one 'nother.'

She had almost reached the thicket when she saw a flash of blue among the saplings and heard Isaac's cheerful laugh. Ducking off the path, she crouched down behind a holly bush until her brother and Bethinda had passed by. Peeping between the green prickles, Kezzy saw that their faces were flushed and their eyes strangely bright. Isaac had his arm around Bethinda's waist. A shrewd guess told Kezzy what they, too, had been up to in the dim recesses of the wood. Their quietly spoken, amorous words confirmed it.

'Us'll be wed come Sat'day next,' said Isaac squeezing Bethinda more tightly around the waist.

'Will 'ee be such a rude fellow then, Isaac?' she simpered from beneath her flat straw hat.

'Ay, 'tis husband's right to be as rude as he wants.'

'Be that so? Well, now, us'll have to see 'bout that, won't we?' she whinnied and, giving him a hard push that nearly sent him flying backwards into the holly bush where his sister was hiding, Bethinda picked up her blue skirts and, with her muscular white calves flashing, ran away, laughing.

Isaac recovered himself and gave chase. As soon as they'd disappeared around a shoulder in the ride, Kezzy darted from her hiding place and hurried through the thicket to rejoin the track which led to Eaglestone.

It was a good half hour later when the Eaglestone wagon caught up with her. Isaac had the reins and Graeme was sprawled on the backboard staring dreamily up at the floating white clouds. The length of time suggested that they had made a detour to set the sisters down at Fardle.

'Ye were s'posed to go straight back'long home after church,' Isaac told Kezzy as she scrambled up beside him on the box. 'Gramps will be proper mazed.'

'No, he won't,' retorted Kezzy airily. 'I went to pick some garlic for the figgens. See?' She thrust the slightly wilting bunch of stems and buds towards him. Clutched in her hand, it was already giving off a musky odour.

' 'Tis lucky for 'ee,' grumbled Isaac. He clicked at Rats and the colt went on at a brisk walk.

They travelled without speaking for a while, the silence only broken by Kezzy softly singing a hymn. 'O day of rest and gladness, O day of joy and light, O balm of care and sadness, Most beautiful most bright . . .' Every so often she'd glance sideways at Isaac but he was hunched over the reins with a faraway look in his eyes. Once or twice Graeme yawned behind her but she didn't turn around. She broke off pieces of garlic mustard and crushed them between her fingers to make the smell stronger before flicking them over her shoulder at her eldest brother.

Presently, irritated by the strongly scented volley, he said: 'Will 'ee stop that, Kezzy, afore I dab 'ee one?'

'Don't you like the smell of garlic, Graeme?' she asked him innocently.

'Nay . . . save in figgens.'

'Fancy.' She said it in the same disbelieving way that Dame Rogers did.

Graeme frowned. 'What do 'ee mean . . . *fancy*?' he mimicked.

'I thought you must like it very much . . . Morgenna, too, since all forenoon you were lying next to a big patch of . . .'

Kezzy didn't finish what she was saying. Graeme reached above him and hauled her down off the box on to the backboard, scattering her garlic mustard and making her squeal. 'What do 'ee know 'bout me and Morgenna?' he demanded furiously, guilt stamped all over his face.

Isaac gasped. 'By Jesu! I *told* you I thought I saw someone dive 'mong bushes!'

'Let me go or I'll tell Gramps,' threatened Kezzy, struggling beneath Graeme's weight as he pinned her down.

'Were 'ee peepin' on she and me?' he demanded, face crimson. 'Ye were, weren't 'ee?' He shook her hard.

But Kezzy clamped tight her lips and refused to answer and after a while he let her up. She stuck her tongue out at Graeme and began collecting her garlic plants while he sat with his chin on his knees scowling at her. They were almost home and could hear old, near-blind Wart barking a welcome when he roused himself to say: 'Swear 'ee'll say n'owt to Gramps or Pa, or I'll cut thy arse wi' birch . . . maid or nay! May I be everlastingly goshwoggled if'n I don't, Miss Keziah Hammett!'

Her dark eyes narrowed like a cat's and flew to his face. She was about to deliver some impudent, challenging retort inviting him to risk their grandfather's wrath by doing so, when the stern set of his features and the glint in his eye made her bite her tongue. *How like Elyas he was!* It was as if he was no longer a callow boy but a man. And a very angry man at that.

As the wagon rolled to a halt in the yard, Graeme gripped her arm hard. 'Do 'ee swear?' he persisted.

Kezzy nodded.

Graeme still wasn't satisfied. 'Say it . . . swear on thy ma's soul!'

'I swear on my mother's soul I'll say nothin' 'bout . . . anything,' she acceded meekly.

'Well, just 'ee remember 'ee sweared . . . or thy ma'll be sent out of Heaven down to Hell,' said Isaac darkly as he climbed down.

Kezzy shivered. The sun had gone behind a bank of grey cloud and a breeze had got up. From the distant hills came the echo of thunder.

Chapter Nine

Unlike the other children who attended the village school, Kezzy wasn't in the least in awe of Dame Hannah Rogers. She did, however, greatly admire the schoolmistress and on her way to and from Cornwood practised speaking out loud in the same, clear, slightly clipped, accentless manner as the dame.

Dame Rogers was a 'foreigner', having been born in London rather than the West Country. She seldom spoke about her past, other than once to mention, when asked by the forthright Kezzy, that, no, she'd no brothers or sisters, alas, or, indeed, any living relative. She'd looked quite sad-eyed when she'd said it, so after school that day Kezzy picked her a big bunch of primroses and took them back to the school.

For some strange reason which Kezzy couldn't fathom, her modest floral offering made her teacher sadder than ever: her eyes became quite swimmy and she had to dab at them with a linen square. But she took Kezzy into her neat little parlour and let her help put the flowers in a china bowl. After which, she'd given Kezzy some sweet, cinnamon biscuits and a mug of milk and told her a secret.

Oh, and how Kezzy loved secrets!

It seemed that Mr and Mrs Rogers had died within a week of each other from a fever despite the attendance of numerous doctors and the hourly administration of Godfrey's Cordial which used only the purest laudanum and grain spirit. This medical attention was expensive which meant that fourteen-year-old Hannah was left destitute. An elderly aunt took her in as a companion but she died two years later from a similar complaint after similarly costly treatments, which meant that Hannah was once again left destitute. But her aunt's chaplain had taken pity on her and found her a place with the Devonshire de Raddons as governess to their daughter, Georgina, sister of the present Captain John de Raddon, Lord of Blackaven. Sadly, her charge had died of smallpox aged fifteen despite the devoted nursing of her young governess. But old Captain Cosmo de Raddon had been grateful to her; he was, she told Kezzy, remembering, as just and benevolent as his son was corrupt and cruel. It was he who had suggested that she open a dame school in the village and had given her the money to buy a suitable cottage plus books and writing materials.

It wasn't long before she had a sweetheart. Captain Francis Morgan . . .

Kezzy hadn't understood quite everything which was being confided to her since Dame Rogers's murmuring voice was at times almost indistinct – as if she was speaking to herself and not to Kezzy at all. Furthermore, the biscuits were delicious and took her mind off much of what was being said, until the dame mentioned her sweetheart. Then Kezzy pricked up her ears: she found it hard to imagine the grey-haired, bird-like dame with a sweetheart and doing with him the things that sweethearts did, like Graeme and Morgenna. Especially since they were near-gentry, being a schoolma'am and a captain.

'Where was he captain of? Which bal?' asked Kezzy interestedly.

The woman gave a little laugh. 'He was an army captain.'

Kezzy looked disappointed. 'Oh, he wasn't a proper captain then?' She found a last crumb and transferred it to her mouth. 'Why didn't you marry him if he was willing and you were, too?'

For a moment she thought Dame Rogers hadn't heard. She was sitting quite still, her neat head cocked as though she was listening to something far away. But after a pause she said in an oddly toneless voice: 'He went to fight the Yankees in '76 and never came back.'

Her sad words hung in the air. She seemed to stoop and grow older before Kezzy's eyes. 'How . . . old was he?' asked Kezzy hesitantly in a low voice.

'Twenty-two.'

'The same age as our Graeme.'

'Yes.' After another pause, Dame Rogers seemed to pull herself together. She blinked rapidly behind her pince-nez and straightened her narrow back. In an almost matter-of-fact voice she said: 'It's all so long ago it's hardly worth the thinking of, but I'd be obliged if you'd treat everything I've told you as our secret. Will you do that?'

Proud to have been confided in, Kezzy said: 'I'll say naught.'

'Thank you, Keziah . . . and thank you for the primroses.'

Kezzy shrugged, embarrassed. 'There's millions of them up'long moor if you know where to pick.'

Dame Rogers never mentioned her young army captain again. And Kezzy kept the secret; it must have been truly dreadful, she thought, to love somebody only to have them go away to war and not come back.

That melancholy thought was still nagging at the back of her mind the following Friday, the eve of the double wedding, when through the window of the dame school she spied a solidly built man wearing the glazed top-hat of the bosun and dangling a rattan from a leather thong looped around his wrist. He was tramping briskly through the village at the head of half a dozen brutal-looking sailors. The foremost pair also carried rattans and all of them had manacles clinking from their broad leather belts. Kezzy's eyes widened with alarm: though they were close to the sea, sailors were a rare sight in the village. There were far more lively places than Cornwood's Kiddleywink for their entertainment in Plymouth's back alleys.

Dame Rogers was reading aloud from the Book of Common Prayer but Kezzy didn't hesitate to interrupt her. 'Please, mistress . . .'tis the press!'

The needle-sharp eyes went straight to the window. In the silence they could hear the thud of the gang's feet. She nodded quickly and the children made a rush for the door. They all had male relatives of an age and physique that would make them liable to be taken unless they were warned and given the chance to hide.

'Where are you going, Keziah?'

The dame's clipped voice stopped Kezzy as she was about to bolt out of the door with the rest.

'Please, mistress, my brothers are in the village . . . they came to buy new shirts to get wed in tomorrow.'

'Return to your stool, Keziah.'

'But, mistress . . .'

'Do as I say, Keziah. Your brothers are tinners and are therefore exempt from the army and the navy.' She watched as Kezzy reluctantly resumed her seat, her face still mirroring her concern.

The dame picked up her prayer book and began to read again in a steady voice. But all the time she was listening, for the sound of the church bell which would warn the young men in and around the village that a press-gang was in the vicinity. For the children knew exactly what to do; while some of them ran to the inn and the kiddleywink tucked away behind the smithy to warn those who might be there – men in their cups being easy targets for the press to round up – other children ran to the church to see that the bells were rung.

Dame Rogers paused in her reading as a bell began to toll mournfully. 'There!' she exclaimed with satisfaction. She read on for a while but, glancing over her book, she could see that Kezzy wasn't listening. 'Now I want you to read the next verse, Keziah.'

Kezzy dragged her eyes away from the view beyond the window with difficulty and lowered them to the pages of the book lying open in front of her. Haltingly, she began to read. It was of course true what Dame Rogers had said: because they were tinners and therefore deemed to be already in the King's service, her brothers weren't liable for enlistment unless they wished it and volunteered. And even then they had to ask permission of the Lord Warden. Yet, the very appearance of the press made everyone anxious, and Kezzy, with two strong young brothers, was no exception.

It was a good while, or seemed like it, before they heard the heavy tramping of feet as the press returned the way they'd come, heading back towards Plymouth. Only now the thud of feet was louder and accompanied by the sinister cries and wailing of women. Clearly the press had netted some victims despite the children's quick actions.

Kezzy rushed to the window. The dame hurried to join her.

'God bless the poor souls!' she murmured as the press and their eight or nine ill-assorted, manacled captives drew level with the window.

For the space of seconds the woman and the child stood so still each could hear the pounding of her own heart, hardly able to believe what they were seeing. Two of the pressed men were a head shorter than the rest, broad-shouldered and fair-faced. Both had bloodied faces and seemed dazed, dragging their feet. Surely it couldn't be . . .! A tremor ran through

Kezzy and she gave a shriek. Her feet flew, carrying her to the door and out after her brothers almost before the dame had registered the fact that it was, indeed, them.

'Stop! Stop! You can't press them, they're tinners!' Kezzy shouted throwing herself at the bosun with such force his top-hat rolled off into the mud. He thrust her aside angrily.

'Off withee, child!' he growled.

She ran to Graeme and Isaac. Close to, she could see that blood was seeping from a deep cut above Graeme's left eye and one of Isaac's eyes was shut and already turning blue. They'd obviously put up a fight for their liberty. 'Tell them you're tinners!' she sobbed, clinging to Graeme.

But he could only shake his head and mumble something she couldn't make out as though his wits had gone.

One of the sailors gave her a push to move her out of the way, but she lashed out at him with her old boots, catching him straight between the legs so that he sank to the ground moaning, whereupon another sailor and two of the pressed men tripped over him and landed in a tangle of bodies and manacles.

'You can't take 'em! You can't! They're tinners and the King will send his soldiers after you with guns!' Kezzy shouted.

'Stow yon maid's luff!' snarled the bosun and another of the sailors raised his rattan as if to strike her. But Kezzy was too quick for him and butted him hard in the stomach, doubling him up, gasping.

'Ye steal our boys an' beat our children!' screamed one of the women whose husband had been taken. Emboldened by Kezzy's furious attacks on the press-gang, she jumped on the nearest sailor's back and brought him down with a blood-chilling yell that froze the rest of them where they stood, adding to the mêlée.

During the commotion, Isaac, less dazed than Graeme, seized his chance and ran stumbling towards the open door of the school. The dame saw his bid for sanctuary and, in a trice, was across the room to drag him in and slam the door. He almost got there. The bosun spotted his fleeing figure and lunged after him, catching him on the doorstep even as the dame had her hands upon him and setting about him with his rattan.

'Don't!' shrieked the dame as the polished length of wood delivered a rain of blows to Isaac's defenceless head and body, splattering her starched white pinafore with crimson spots. 'I tell you he and his brother are tinners and not to be taken. Twenty-five guineas each! That's what it will cost your master!'

But her threat was to no avail. The bosun dragged Isaac, in a daze of pain, to his feet and hustled him back to join the rest, saying, 'Taste o' the cat will cure this fellow's turn o' speed!'

The sailors had restored order with much flaying of rattans and shouting of vulgar oaths. Kezzy had taken a sharp crack to the jaw, but she hardly noticed the pain as she joined the men's wives, children, sisters, mothers or sweethearts as they ran alongside the enforced gang of marchers, weeping and begging for their release. Two of the women clutched babies to their breasts, another carried a frightened, screaming toddler; one old, bent and wizened mother couldn't keep up and collapsed weeping by the wayside for her lost son and only means of support.

Kezzy's long legs meant she could keep up long after the rest had fallen behind the gang as they were prodded into a sharp pace down the road to Plymouth. Graeme seemed to recover his senses and turned his bruised and battered face towards Kezzy loping beside him. His eyes focused on her tear-streaked face and recognition dawned. 'Go home, Kezzy! Go home!' he shouted. 'Tell Gramps! He'll know what to do!'

She knew she must do as he said if she was to help her brothers. There was nothing a child could do, even if she managed to keep up all the way to the port. She slowed, then stopped, and watched them go through eyes near-blinded by scalding tears. She was trembling from head to foot and every breath hurt, but she turned and began running back to Cornwood as fast as she could.

Dame Rogers had removed her bloodstained pinafore and put on her good black-velvet bonnet. Two of the bigger village boys had brought her fat pony from the paddock at the back of the cottage and hitched it to her trap. She was just climbing up when Kezzy came panting up.

'Come, child, look sharp and climb up.'

Thankfully, Kezzy did so. Only to be seized by panic when they set off at a trot down through the village instead of up the track and across the moor to Eaglestone. 'We're going the wrong way! I must get home and tell Gramps what's happened!'

'There's no time for that,' said the dame, tight-lipped, her face grave. 'It may be they plan to sail with the tide.'

She urged the pony into a canter.

Kezzy had to hang on to keep from being thrown about as the old trap swayed alarmingly at the unaccustomed speed. What could an elderly schoolmarm and a child do? she pondered anxiously. Certainly not stop one of the King's ships sailing! She wished her grandfather was there: like Graeme said, he'd know what must be done and would do it.

But Dame Rogers knew where the Hammett boys' only chance lay. Nothing would be gained by going to Plymouth: no ship's master would bother with an old woman and a weeping little girl. So when she came to a fork just outside of Cornwood, she turned off the Plymouth road along a less-used track which would eventually take them to the wild, sea-lashed coast south-east of Plymouth. It was a fair distance to travel, though mostly downhill. Once or twice they stopped to rest the sturdy, willing pony and to water it at a stone trough by the way. Then they were off again at a smart pace.

It was well after two o'clock when they reached the coast. The Sound stretched grey-green in the thin sunshine. Unerringly, Dame Rogers turned them along a narrow track along the cliffs. Clearly she'd come this way many times before.

'Are we nearly at Plymouth, Mistress?' asked Kezzy.

'We're not going to Plymouth. We're going to Blackaven.'

Kezzy felt a stab of hope. Of course! The Lord Warden! How clever of the dame to think of him! Then doubt began to nibble at her insides again: would he be at home at such an hour? And if he was, would he deign to see them? She hadn't long to wait before her silent questions were answered. With a final burst of speed, the sweating, wheezing pony swept them through the iron gates and up to the great, brass-studded oak doors of Blackaven House.

The dame handed the reins to Kezzy with a sharp, 'Wait here.'

Agilely, she swung down and hastened up the stone steps. Even before she could lift the big, brass knocker, the door swung open. A liveried footman listened stony-faced to what she had to say, then stepped back to let her enter. She turned and motioned to Kezzy to join her and a few minutes later they were shown into a small, dark chamber off the main hall with its handsome staircases.

'Is the Lord Warden at home?' ventured Kezzy when the footman had departed.

'I know not. But Mrs de Raddon is in . . . and it is she whom I asked to see.'

Mrs de Raddon came hurrying to see them less than a minute later, her black-taffeta afternoon gown rustling, pale-blue, wax-doll eyes wide with concern.

'Mistress Rogers!'

The dame wasted no time with the usual niceties. 'Please forgive this intrusion, Mrs de Raddon, but it is most vital that I see the Lord Warden immediately.' she said in a rush.

'My husband is partaking of nuncheon, Mistress Rogers.'

The delicate-looking young woman quailed visibly at the notion of interrupting her husband while he was nunching but the dame wasn't to be put off. 'I *beg* of you, madam,' she pleaded desperately. 'This child's brothers are tinners and have been pressed against their will, not an hour past.'

The doll-like eyes flickered across to Kezzy standing tense and silent, a plea in her almond eyes. The girl's tear-stained elfin face and the blue swelling on her jaw moved Mrs de Raddon as no words could have done. Immediately her taut expression softened to one of sympathy. 'Wait,' she said and swept out.

The dame paced agitatedly. 'I feel so *culprit*!' she exclaimed. 'If only I'd let you go with the rest to warn them!'

Kezzy shook her head, not wanting the woman to blame herself. 'I wasn't zackly sure where Graeme and Isaac were!' she admitted. 'Mebbe at inn. Mebbe kiddleywink. Gramps give 'em half-crown for themselves to buy ale on account they're getting wed tomorrow . . .' She stopped and bit her lip, reminded suddenly of Morgenna and Bethinda. How frightened they would be for their future husbands if they knew what had happened.

They both started as the door swung open. Mrs de Raddon rustled in. 'Come,' she said.

Chapter Ten

There were wonderfully carved double doors leading from the galleried hall to the dining room. The room itself was spacious and a good deal brighter than the rest of the house as candles were lit in four great silver-branched candlesticks along the centre of the polished wood table.

It was the array of food on the table which first caught Kezzy's attention as she shyly entered with Dame Rogers. Never had the child seen so much food outside Plympton market. It momentarily made her forget even her brothers' plight. There was a huge ham, glowing pink in the candlelight; a cold roast chicken – plumper than any the Hammetts had scratching in the yard; cold pheasant; a massive, golden-crusted pie and a succulent lump of hot roasted beef glistening with fat. Plus any number of other dishes which she couldn't name since she'd never met their like before. And all of it set out on big silver platters, the type of which she'd imagined that only the King would use in his fine palace in London.

So this was a nuncheon, she repeated the new word to herself.

A manservant, elderly and somewhat furtive-eyed, and a young woman, wearing a maid's black alpaca dress and starched white apron but with a sullen rather indolent manner, were waiting upon the only diner. The Lord Warden was seated at the head of the table, two foxhounds sleeping on the floor beside him. He wore a plum-coloured coat, the small cuffs faced in black velvet, and a green-and-white striped waistcoat with hair-buttons. He'd removed his cravat and wig, both of which lay on the table near him.

It was the first time that Kezzy had seen him thus: without the black, curled wig which hid his thin lank hair and most of his cheeks. She stared, edging still closer to Dame Rogers's sheltering skirts though she was more fascinated than fearful of the mass of red, ridged scars disfiguring the left side of his face and the pulpy flesh where the ear had been torn off.

He hardly glanced at them when they came in, continuing to chew on a piece of chicken breast as Dame Rogers explained in brisk, courteous tones their reason for being there.

'Since they are hard-working tinners, Captain de Raddon, I felt sure you would most urgently intervene with the ship's master and have the Hammett brothers restored to their family,' she concluded.

De Raddon dropped the chicken carcass on the floor and watched for a moment as the hounds tore at it. Then he said: 'His Majesty has decreed that tinners can enlist if they are of a mind to fight the French.'

Dame Rogers couldn't help sounding impatient. 'But they were *pressed*, Captain de Raddon . . .'

'So you said, mistress,' he interrupted brusquely, 'but since neither you nor I were there when the event occurred, it must be presumed that these two boys were suddenly seized by a patriotic fancy and volunteered. *That's* what the master will say, you may be sure.'

Dame Rogers blinked at him from behind her pince-nez, hope fading with his lack of interest in the brothers' predicament. If he would just try and get them released. 'Captain de Raddon . . .' she paused, took a steadying breath. 'Many years ago, when you were a youngster, you said that I might come to you if ever I needed help.'

He scowled and wouldn't look at her as she stood there, erect, hands folded calmly before her, the child peering from behind her skirts. 'I don't rightly recall the occasion, mistress,' he bridled but his shifting eyes revealed that he remembered perfectly well.

It was on the day his sister died. None could have tried harder to save the dying girl than her young governess. And it was because Hannah Rogers, with total disregard for her own health, had isolated herself and her charge in an empty cottage on the estate that the dread disease hadn't spread throughout the de Raddon household. John had been a surly youth, yet even he had shown some semblance of gratitude for her selflessness, informing Hannah that he would be glad to be of service to her should she ever require his help in the future. He'd said it with an air of youthful extravagance as he'd mourned his adored little sister, but Hannah hadn't forgotten during the thirty years which had passed since then. It had never entered her head to approach him purely on her own account; and she hated doing so now, particularly as she was having to plead for his help. But she'd no choice: she felt responsible for what had happened to the Hammett boys.

De Raddon wouldn't meet her pleading eyes. 'If I did say such a thing once, well then, it was a foolish youth talking. You were paid for what you did for the de Raddons, mistress. And given a good living by grace of my father,' he reminded her.

Her heart sank. She'd played her final card and failed to move him. Surprise tempered her deep disappointment; it wasn't like the Lord Warden to let the navy undermine his authority by taking his tinners without first asking his permission – whether they'd volunteered or not. Despite his age-old, half-forgotten feud with Elyas, the dame would have sworn de Raddon would have demanded the Hammett boys' immediate release. She couldn't understand his strange detachment under the circumstances.

She stood silently, watching as he pulled apart a cold pheasant and fed it to his dogs. Every now and then, she noticed, he looked briefly at Kezzy. She gazed steadfastly back at him, her quaint, slanting dark eyes as candid as his own and burning with a silent entreaty that he help her beloved brothers.

'How old is yon child?' asked de Raddon abruptly.

Kezzy didn't wait for the dame to answer but spoke up for herself. 'I'm nearly nine, Cap'n . . . and my name is Keziah Elizabeth Ruke Hammett.'

'Is it your older brothers who have been pressed?'

She nodded. His voice was harsh and his eyes unfriendly, yet Kezzy had lost her awe of him. She came out from behind the dame's skirts and went and stood near to him, almost at his elbow. One of the dogs growled at her impudence, but he quieted it with a sharp word. 'We can't work bal without 'em, Cap'n. Only leaves Pa and Gramps and Jamie and me . . . and Gramps is old and has lung-rot. And I'm more use than Jamie on account he's runt o' litter.'

Then a strange thing happened. De Raddon briefly grinned at the little girl's vivid descriptions of her kinfolk. Dame Rogers held her breath. Could it be that Kezzy might succeed where she'd failed? It was impossible to know what was going on in de Raddon's mind as he eyed this miniature version of Ruke. Something the dame didn't see any sign of in his face, however, was remorse for the death of the child's mother. The dame had hardly been able to believe it when Elyas had told her that it was the Lord Warden who'd instigated the witch-taking. Yet Elyas wasn't the sort of man to lie about such a terrible thing.

De Raddon left off feeding his dogs and ran a hand over his damaged cheek and jaw. 'Do I frighten you, child?' he asked noticing her interest in his scars.

Kezzy shook her head. 'I seed worse face on tinker in Plympton. Some naughty boys set fire to pook he were a-sleepin' in . . . near burnt off his face. And *both* his ears!'

Again the rare, tight grin showed itself for an instant. He picked up a silver comfit dish and held it towards Kezzy. It contained small rectangles of marchpane made from pounded almonds and pistachios, sugar and flour. She gazed longingly at the pretty sweetmeats but didn't take one, putting her hands firmly behind her back.

'Come . . . taste some of these sweetstuffs,' he invited gruffly.

She shook her head stubbornly.

'Don't you like marchpane?'

'I don't rightly know, Cap'n, not having tried it.'

'Then try it, child.'

She stared at the marchpane, struggling against temptation. Then her bright gaze shifted to his face. 'Will you help my brothers, Cap'n?'

His voice was impatient. 'King George has need of them to fight the Frenchies.'

'Then if you won't help them, I'll not eat your sweetstuff.'

He scowled. 'Lord damn my shirt! You're as pig-headed as your grandfather!' He turned the bowl over, emptying the sweetmeats on the floor so that the dogs went diving for them.

Kezzy's face was as dark with anger as his own. 'When I'm growed, I shall have white bread every day and eat as many sweetmeats as I want! *Better* than those! Those are just fit for dogs to eat . . .!'

'Kezzy!' The dame's voice sharply reprimanded her but the pointed chin came up and she stared down her little nose at the ugly big man who wouldn't help her brothers.

'Grote!' shouted de Raddon.

The dame imagined that they were about to be shown unceremoniously out. 'I'm sorry, Captain de Raddon . . . the child is distraught at losing her brothers . . .'

Her voice faded as a door behind him opened and his steward came in. 'Ay, Cap'n?'

'Bring me paper, pen and ink. Then saddle a horse. You're to ride to Plymouth. Find out which ship has pressed the Hammetts and hand a letter to her master demanding their immediate release.'

'Ay, Cap'n.'

'Oh, *thank* you, Captain de Raddon!' exclaimed Dame Rogers, her relief manifest in the two spots of red which appeared on her sallow cheeks. She looked at Kezzy, her snapping sharp eyes telling the child to show proper appreciation to the Lord Warden. Kezzy was staring hard at Grote, her high, white brow creased with thoughtful interest.

The Lord Warden waved a hand, dismissing the need for thanks. 'Good day to you, Mistress Rogers.'

She bobbed him a curtsey. 'Good day, Captain de Raddon . . . and thank you again. Now we must just pray that they haven't sailed with the tide. Come along, Kezzy . . .'

Kezzy bent her knees quickly to de Raddon but her eyes were still fixed curiously upon Grote who gave her a black look, uncomfortable beneath her frank gaze. 'You will ride *dreckly* to Plymouth, won't you, sir?'

Grote glanced sideways at his master. Then nodded. Kezzy had to be satisfied with that. She turned and skipped out of the room behind Dame Rogers and the big double doors were shut behind them by a liveried footman. She didn't speak until they'd left Blackaven House behind and were almost at the fork in the road where they were to turn off back up the steep road to Cornwood.

'Could we stop here a while, Mistress?'

'Stop? But why?'

Dame Rogers looked and sounded surprised. They'd a good way to go and it was nearly all up hill. Moreover, Elyas and Huward were yet to be informed of what had befallen Graeme and Isaac.

'Please . . .'

She reined in the pony to a walk. 'What's the matter, Kezzy?'

Kezzy pointed to a copse not far from the fork in the road. 'Can we sit for a while among the trees?'

Now Dame Rogers understood: Kezzy wanted them to lie in wait to see if Grote *did* leave for Plymouth immediately. 'I'm sure Captain de Raddon won't allow his steward to waste a moment . . .' she began to say reassuringly.

'Please can we?' persisted Kezzy, her face serious.

They'd reached the fork and Dame Rogers was turning the pony for home. Surely, she thought, Captain de Raddon would be as good as his word? Why, the man Grote might pass them at any moment heading for Plymouth. Still, what was a few minutes if the sight of him galloping by brought some measure of solace to the worried little girl?

'Very well. But just a few minutes, mind, if we're to be at Eaglestone before dark.'

The few minutes spread to half an hour.

'He didn't mean it!' said Kezzy angrily, swallowing tears of disappointment. 'He lied! He only pretended Grote would go to Plymouth.'

'Perhaps some urgent matter arose to delay Grote,' ventured the dame optimistically but something told her, just as it did Kezzy, that de Raddon had played them false.

They waited a little longer, the last shreds of hope fading as the westering spring sun lost its warmth and started to disappear behind pale scudding clouds. Dame Rogers took up the reins with a heavy heart. Had de Raddon purposefully lied to them? she wondered. Would he deliberately raise their hopes just to dash them? Alas, yes. As a boy he'd been as spiteful as his sister was gentle. And from what poor Emma de Raddon had confided to her, he'd become a very cruel man.

'He lied and I hate him!' declared Kezzy in a trembling voice as they set off for home. 'One day I shall kill him! That pig Grote, too! And watch the crows pick their eyes out!'

'Hush, Kezzy. You mustn't say such wicked things. God will hear and punish you,' warned the dame, dismayed by the ferocity of her small companion's outburst.

'They're the wicked ones! They're the ones God should punish! And by Lord Harry, if He doesn't then I will when I'm growed! I'll be death o' that pair o' rogues, I swear it on my mother's soul!'

'Hush, Kezzy!' said the dame again, her tone sharper. This was near to blasphemy.

Kezzy began to sob compulsively. Weariness, fear for her brothers, her disappointment at the Lord Warden's treachery, all these things combined to rouse in her a feverish sense of emotion bordering on hysteria. And there was something else: something strange which she couldn't begin to understand but which, instinctively, she was loath to speak of to the dame before she'd a chance to tell her grandfather, for it concerned the Lord Warden's steward.

The moment that Grote had entered the room, Kezzy had thought there was something familiar about him. She'd seen his hard eyes and shaggy sandy brows before. They were all that were visible of him on the previous occasion they had met as then he'd covered most of his face with the tail of his stocking-cap.

It came as something of a shock to Kezzy to know that the Lord Warden's man was the leader of a band of flaskers.

Grote had brought Captain de Raddon the writing materials and then gone to the stables to order a horse to be saddled. De Raddon had interrupted his nuncheon to write a strong letter of complaint to the unknown ship's captain, pointing out that stannary law was not to be flouted, and threatening to inform the King if the pressed tinners weren't immediately returned to work. He signed it with a flourish and pressed his big seal of office into the hot wax.

When Grote returned for the letter, de Raddon was sitting staring at it deep in thought. He didn't look up at his steward or make a move to hand the letter to him.

'Horse be saddled, Cap'n.'

De Raddon grunted. Eventually, frowning thoughtfully, he asked Grote, 'How many of a family are the Hammetts, do you know?'

Grote conjured the image of them all standing outside the cottage that foggy night. 'The old man, his son . . . two more what's pressed . . . then just a boy and yon maid as was here.'

De Raddon nodded. That's what Kezzy had said. An avaricious glint came into his eye. Without his two strong grandsons, Hammett would be struggling to work his mine. And Eaglestone was tin-rich. Good lodes of toad-eye were wasted on the Hammetts' pathetic little work force. Far better in the hands of a big mine operator like de Raddon.

The Lord Warden picked up the letter and tore it in half. 'Unsaddle your horse, Grote. I reckon a taste of the sea will do the Hammett boys a power of good,' he chuckled nastily.

When Kezzy and Dame Rogers reached Cornwood they found Elyas, Huward and Jamie were eagerly awaiting them at the school. Their worried and unhappy faces revealed that they already knew about Graeme and Isaac and it transpired that one of the farm boys from Lamb's Down had been in the village and just escaped the press himself by diving into a cart of manure. He'd returned to the farm by way of Eaglestone and told the Hammetts what had befallen their kin. Also that he'd seen Kezzy Hammett and Dame Rogers set off in the dame's trap at a fast lick.

On seeing her grandfather, Kezzy jumped down and ran to him. 'I tried to stop the press taking 'em, Gramps! And got dab on the jaw for it. See?' She pushed out her jaw for him to see the blue and red proof that she had done all she could.

Elyas touched the dark, glossy head gently with his bony hand, too choked for the moment to speak. It seemed as if he'd aged ten years since morning. His rheumy eyes went to the dame.

'I'm sorry, Mr Hammett, I did what I thought best by going to Captain de Raddon,' she said, her pinched face grave.

Elyas seemed to tense at the mention of the Lord Warden, and the faint light of hope in his eyes died instantly.

'Them can't be took . . . them be tinners,' said Huward in an anguished voice.

'The King has decreed that tinners might . . . volunteer,' explained Dame Rogers and Elyas spat on the ground, for once not caring about his manners in front of her.

'Cap'n de Raddon said he'd help 'em but he didn't, Gramps,' Kezzy told him, her eyes welling with tears of frustration at the memory of how the Lord Warden had so callously tricked them.

Elyas handed the dame down from the trap. In her clipped way she told them what had occurred at Blackaven House. 'I was so *sure* he would get your sons released, Mr Hammett,' she ended by saying, shaking her head with disbelief at his out and out duplicity.

Elyas spat again. 'Don't 'ee blame thyself, mistress. De Raddon wouldn't help Hammetts if'n he could hang 'em!'

'He offered me sweetstuffs but I didn't eat elly,' said Kezzy proudly and with a sidelong look at Jamie to see if he was suitably impressed by such heroic abstinence.

Jamie's face filled with disbelief. 'You'm a liar,' he hissed. 'Cap'n de Raddon wouldn't waste sweetstuffs on maiden.'

Kezzy's eyes flashed. She forgot Graeme and Isaac as she squabbled with her remaining brother. 'I'm not a liar. I *never* tell lies! When I wouldn't eat his sweetstuffs he fed 'em to his dogs. You ask Dame Rogers.'

But Dame Rogers had walked away a few yards with Elyas and Huward, and the three were deep in serious conversation.

'What's to be done, Pa?' The children heard their father ask their grandfather wretchedly. But for once the old man was bereft of ideas.

'Don't know as there be aught we can do, boy. I'll go to Plymouth at first light, tho' I reckons them be gone b'now. Ye best get over to Fardle first thing and tell they sisters there bain't no weddin'.'

Elyas set off in the wagon before dawn, taking with him a well-filled mossle bag and a canteen of water since he didn't know how long he might be gone. He also took what money they had, £30, in case the opportunity arose to purchase his grandsons' release from the Royal Navy.

It took the best part of the morning to reach Plymouth as he saw no point in tiring Rats unnecessarily, and in his innermost heart he felt sure that Graeme's and Isaac's ship would have sailed with the tide the previous evening. Elyas's years on the coast with the fish had taught him something about the navy: a newly pressed crew wouldn't be kept long in port for fear they'd jump overboard or, worse, bribe their way out of their chains and mutiny.

The port was a noisy, violent place. A licentious, ruffianly element ruled supreme among the backstreet dives and kiddleywinks, avoiding, by methods best known to themselves, the law in the weakling shape of the city guard. Moreover, these ruffians managed to avoid the press themselves although it was rumoured they knew the names of all those most recently press-ganged and the ships upon which they were to serve. They knew every bosun on every ship, so said the fisherfolk, and if it was possible to buy a man out of the navy, they knew how to go about it.

Hence it was towards the sea of chimneys that Elyas went, rather than the dock. His wagon barely managed to pass through the narrower streets and from his elevated position on the box he could see into the bedrooms of the two-storey houses through the leaded windows so that the doxies therein came running to look out and call enticingly after him. Mostly they were young, some little more than children. He didn't stop until he was almost at the end of one dingy street which was particularly well served by swinging inn-signs. A buxom figure leaning out above a sign which aptly proclaimed 'The Sailor's Dream' caught Elyas's eye. He reined in.

‘Good day to ’ee, master, won’t ’ee come inside and refresh thyself?’ she asked simperingly.

Elyas didn’t answer. He sat with his shoulders hunched beneath his best shirt and fustian waistcoat, considering her powdered and painted face. She was older than the others; and there was a knowing glint in her needle-sharp eyes.

‘Ent refreshin’ I’m a-needin’, mistress,’ he told her shortly.

She smiled at being called ‘mistress’. ‘Well, master, what is it you’m a-needin’?’ she enquired with a great fluttering of soot-blackened eyelashes.

‘I’m a-needin’ information.’

The rouged smile faded immediately and she began to back away from the window, wrapping her brightly patterned Chinese robe more tightly about her ample form. ‘I don’t know any information,’ she muttered and reached for the window to shut it.

‘Not even for a half crown?’ Elyas had the coin ready; he opened his palm and showed it to her. The sight of it stayed her hand.

‘What do ’ee want by ways of information?’ she asked warily.

‘I wants to know where to find they as knows ’bout pressed men and how to buy they out of navy.’

She considered, eyeing the half crown. Those who lived and worked and had business in that part of the port all knew where to find the band of men who passed for authority thereabouts, so what did it matter if she told this stranger? Clearly, he wasn’t a Preventy man but had lost kin to the press. She stretched out her hand.

‘Half crown first,’ she demanded.

He hesitated. She was quite likely to snatch the coin and slam shut the window. ‘You’m tell I information first.’

‘Ye can trust me,’ she riposted.

He spat. ‘Mebbe so.’

‘You’m wants Harbour Lane . . . the mermaiden. Ask for Muffler. Failin’ he . . . Fat John,’ she grudgingly directed.

She leaned out until her outstretched hand was just inches from him. He gave her the half crown and she grinned hugely as she quickly transferred the coin among the folds of her bosom, darting a look up and down the street. It was, Elyas guessed, the easiest money she’d made in a long time. Sailors preferred younger, tenderer flesh.

‘Which way to Harbour Lane?’

She pointed down the street, making an arc with her fingers to indicate he should turn right. He clicked to Rats and moved off again. It took him only a few minutes to reach Harbour Lane but none of the signs displayed had anything to do with ‘The Mermaiden’ and he began to think that the doxie had stung him after all. He spotted a couple of merchant seamen, recognisable as much by their rolling gait as their high boots, caps and jerseys, and called out to them.

‘Do you’m boys know un Mermaiden?’

The tipsy pair collapsed with mirth.

'Ay, matie,' spluttered one, 'knows her like we knows our old mothers!'

Elyas tried again. 'Be un Mermaiden un tavern? Don't 'zackly see a proper sign for un.'

One of the seaman wiped his streaming eyes on his sleeve and attempted to answer the question. 'Nay, matie, ain't no grog house. Her be a proper mermaid.' He pointed across the street. 'See yon door? If'n ye knocks an' asks for Muffler he'll take penny of ye an' show ye mermaid, right 'nough.'

Sniggering and elbowing each other, they left Elyas and began wending their way unsteadily up the street. They began to sing raucously.

Elyas got down and secured Rats to a post. Approaching the door to which he'd been directed he saw it had a wooden sign nailed to it. Most of the paint had been worn away by the salty elements but he could make out the shape of a mermaid with long flowing hair and naked breasts. There was a line of writing beneath the crudely done painting. He gazed uncomprehendingly at the words, and as he did so, he saw a shadowy figure peering out from the small dim window beside the door. He rapped with his knuckles. Footsteps came clumping to the other side of the door. It swung open on rusting, creaking hinges and a rancid stench came wafting out.

'Yus?'

'Mr Muffler?'

'No, I ain't.'

He had to be Fat John. His massive body filled the doorway and his great, round stomach protruded over the stone step. Atop his huge head he wore a brown horse-hair wig. He was dressed in a voluminous flannelette shirt which would have made a balloon sail and gargantuan breeches and stockings which would as easily have encased a pair of tree trunks as his bulbous legs.

'Be you Mr Fat John then, zur?'

'Who's arskin'?'

'Elyas Hammett, Cap'n of Wheal Eaglestone up'long Dartmoor.'

Fat John looked him up and down with a contemptuous sneer. 'What do you want, tinner?'

'I was 'drecked here to see Mr Muffler or Mr Fat John.'

'Who sent 'ee?'

'A lady back'long street . . .'

Fat John wobbled as he laughed heartily. 'If you saw a lady in this quarter you're seein' things, tinner. Where's your twopence?'

'What for?'

Fat John jerked a broad thumb over his shoulder. 'To see the mermaiden.'

'That ent why I'm here. 'Sides, it be a penny to see she. Sailor told me,' said Elyas curtly.

There was a movement in the shadows behind Fat John. A man as tall, bony and fiddle-faced as Fat John was rotund, loomed behind the fat man. Muffler, presumed Elyas.

'What do you want?' growled the tall individual.

'My two grandsons were pressed yesterday over Cornwood. I'm looking to find out ship they be on . . . mebbe buy they back. Graeme and Isaac Hammett be their names. They be tinners and 'zemp from navy.'

Muffler shrugged. 'Ain't no men 'zemp what with ol' Bony planning to cross Channel and invade us.'

Elyas stared. 'Are you'm saying they Frenchies is a-comin' over here interferin'?'

Muffler nodded. 'Unless our Nel can sink 'em in Channel before they can land! Needs every man Jack he can get, do Lord Horatio! 'Specially now those poxy Spanish jacks have run up their colours on side o' Frenchies. Press from one ship o' the line or 'nother have been out huntin' afore most every tide this past two-month, far 'way up as Widecombe, they do say.'

'On account they 'long coast as fit for it have been pressed already,' put in Fat John. 'They've even been takin' merchant Jacks out the kiddley-winks . . . and they be 'zemp like tinners.'

'Ay, they masters don't seem to care if'n it do cost 'em fine for taking men they aughtn't,' confirmed Muffler. He considered for a moment. 'If'n your boys were took yesterday they'll have sailed by now, methinks.'

It was no more than Elyas had expected. Yet, to have it confirmed by one as undoubtedly in the know as Muffler made his insides lurch sickeningly. He was silent for a while, steadying himself. Then he said: 'Can 'ee find out name o' ship my boys be on?' That would be better than nothing.

Muffler's eyes narrowed. 'Cost you.'

'How much?'

Experience told Muffler what to ask. 'Five guineas.'

Elyas snorted. 'Giddaway! I could go down'long docks an' find out from Admiralty men for free.'

Muffler sneered over Fat John's massive shoulder. 'They wouldn't tell you at docks. Like as not they'd swear blind they ain't got your boys.'

'Well, I've only got a guinea. Ent that 'nough?' lied Elyas.

'Show us.'

'Ent got it on me,' he lied again, wary of being robbed.

Muffler stroked his long, sparcely bristled jaw. 'Graeme and Isaac Hammett pressed at Cornwood yesterday, you say?'

'Aye. Took eight or nine boys they did, drat they lily livers!'

'Be here at six o'clock with the guinea and I'll have news of 'em.'

Muffler and Fat John retreated inside and shut the door.

Aware of them watching him from the grimy window, Elyas went and unhitched Rats and climbed up on the wagon. He continued on down Harbour Lane and came out at the sea-front. For once it was almost devoid of loungers and gossiping fishwives. Even the bumboat women's small boats were tied up and deserted. The stout-bellied little shops and taverns fronting the quay were gloomily empty of customers. The few men Elyas did see were either old men or swaggering naval officers. The young men had gone: to sea or to ground.

The row of market carts along the harbour wall were busier. The market women bawling their wares in coarse, carrying voices to attract the milling wives.

'Crabs! Alive O . . .!'

'Winkles penny a bag!'

The heaps of shining, silver fish reminded Elyas of the years he'd spent in the gutting shed and he shuddered at the memory of the bloody guts and the smell. But he bought a penn'orth of winkles and took his time choosing a pin from those stuck in an old cushion which unbeknown to him bore the embroidered legend: SIN NO MORE. He went back to the quay. The tide was in, lapping against the stone wall. It was about two o'clock, he thought, judging by the light. The sun had gone and a misty rain was blowing in from the sea. Elyas didn't care; it helped clear his lungs after the dust of the mine. He went and found a coil of rope right by the quay-edge where he could sit and eat his winkles, accompanied by a lump of bread from his mossle bag and a draught from his canteen.

There were a few merchant ships bobbing in the harbour. They looked deserted. Two privateers were anchored out in the Sound and every so often a sturdy, ruddy-faced bumboat woman would row to and fro from the shore, ferrying provisions and seamen in her barge. Once, tying up close to Elyas, she cackled: 'You'm don't want to squat there too long, matie. Press will have 'ee, grey hair or nay.'

Elyas looked alarmed for a moment, then he realised that she was only joking. No ship's master would waste a berth on an old man like him. Mournfully, he told her how his grandsons had been pressed on the day before they were to be wed.

'Tch! That's a terrible thing,' sympathised the bumboat woman. She sat down beside Elyas and brought out a clay pipe, then some navy plug which she shared with him. He told her about the 'mermaiden' and her two ruffianly keepers, Muffler and Fat John. She knew them well. 'If'n anybody can winkle name of thy grandsons' ship, 'tis Muffler,' she told him reassuringly.

They sat smoking in companionable silence for a while. Then Elyas asked her curiously: 'Have 'ee seen yon mermaiden?'

Her big bosom heaved as she chuckled. 'O ay, matie. We'm all seen Muffler's mermaid.'

'And is her like mermaiden painted on Muffler's door?'

She chuckled again. 'Well, now, mister, I ent a-goin' to do Muffler out o' penny. You'm pay up an' see for thyself.'

'But is her a *real* mermaiden?'

But the bumboat woman refused to say. And a little later three seamen came with slatted crates of squawking fowls and wanted rowing out to the Sound. Elyas was sorry to see her go: he still had almost two hours to pass until he could return to Harbour Lane. Leaving Rats to rest with his nosebag on after the long journey down from the moor, he took a turn about the port. A group of young naval officers about the same age as Graeme and Isaac emerged laughing from one of the taverns. He wondered if pressed men ever laughed like that.

Chapter Eleven

Muffler's door opened as soon as Elyas knocked.

Once again the rancid air wafted out so that he caught his breath chokingly. The stench was reminiscent of the gutting shed, but stronger. Fat John squeezed aside so he could pass.

'Muffler says you're to go up.'

The interior was lit by a couple of tallow-dips flickering in old clay bottles. Elyas found himself in the lower room. It was almost bare; just a few squares of old matting and a trestle table bearing a canvas-draped object about the size of a five-year-old child. Fat John pointed to a narrow flight of steep stone steps in the corner.

'Up there.'

He made no attempt to follow Elyas as he began to climb – which was as just as well, for he'd have most certainly got wedged as tight as a bung in a barrel.

The upper room was better furnished, with a table, two chairs and a pallet in the corner. Muffler sat at the table, a stoup of ale and a pewter mug before him. A wooden trencher bore the remains of his dinner: the empty claws and shell and yellow guts of a big crab. A lantern hung from a nail in the overhead beam, casting an eerie glow that turned his bony face parchment coloured and shadowed his eye sockets so that Elyas started when he saw him, so like a skull did he look.

'Good evening to 'ee, Mr Muffler.'

Muffler wasn't one to waste time on such civilities.

'Have you got the guinea?'

'Ay.' Elyas sat down opposite him uninvited. He made no move to produce his gunny sack. 'What news of my boys?'

Unlike the doxie who'd directed him to Harbour Lane, Muffler wasn't going to disclose any information until he'd been paid. He kept his bloodless lips tightly shut, his skeletal hand outstretched across the table towards Elyas. Reluctantly, Elyas plunged a hand beneath his shirt and brought out the little sack. It clinked as he untied the drawstrings. Muffler's eyes glittered greedily.

'Thought you'd only got a guinea,' he sneered and before Elyas could stop him, he reached across and snatched the gunny sack. He shook out its contents eagerly. A guinea and four farthings! His face fell; he was sure Elyas had been holding out on him and had more guineas in his sack than he said. He pocketed all the coins. 'Hardly worth the effort,' he complained. 'Still, I'm a man of my word . . .'

He hadn't found out a great deal: there wasn't a great deal to find out. Graeme and Isaac, along with the other Cornwood pressed men, had sailed aboard the *Royal Sovereign* on the tide the night before. None knew save her ship's officers where they were headed, but Muffler had found a doxy who'd spent time with a talkative midshipman from the *Royal Sovereign*. He'd bragged that they were off to join the great Lord Nelson himself who, aboard the *Victory*, was commanding the fleets which were blockading the French harbours.

The stoup of ale had loosened Muffler's tongue. 'I knows a flasker who reckons ol' Bony has got 100,000 soldiers quartered at Boo-loin just waitin' to come at us 'cross the water.'

Elyas was hardly listening, he was wondering what fate might now befall Graeme and Isaac if they were pitched into battle against the French. But now he pricked up his ears. 'Giddaway!' he exclaimed scornfully. 'How's ol' Bony to get army like that 'cross Channel when our Nel's keeping un at home?'

Muffler didn't know. His flasker friend wasn't as well informed as that.

Elyas got to his feet. 'Better be true, cully . . .'bout my boys being aboard *Royal Sovereign*. I got ten more at home like they and they'll come after thy blood if'n you'm talkin' up load of ol' ledden.'

Muffler sneered at the threat. 'If you've got ten more you won't mind King George havin' couple, Two less to feed.'

Elyas didn't like being bested. He scowled ferociously and stamped down the narrow stairs. Fat John was sitting on the floor with his back to the wall since no chair or stool would have taken his weight. Elyas's eyes went to the canvas bundle on the table.

'Be that un mermaiden?'

'Yus,' said Fat John.

'Can I see un?'

'Got a penny?'

Elyas jerked a thumb up the stairs. 'I give it to he.'

Muffler was standing at the top listening. 'Show him,' he said to Fat John.

The big man took his time getting to his feet. He ambled across to the table and flipped back the cover. Elyas picked up one of the dips and held it aloft so he could get a better look at the wonder which was revealed. After taking a good, long look, he said: 'That be a seal, I reckons. Wi' un whiskers shaved.'

He reached out a hand to remove the long, silvery horse-hair wig which was sitting rather crookedly on the thing's head but Fat John dropped the canvas back into place before he'd a chance.

'Go to boogery!' he said rudely.

Elyas turned to go but found Muffler blocking the doorway, face sly. 'Let's just see if tinner has any more guineas on him.'

Elyas shrugged and lifted his arms so he could be searched. 'You'm took every farthing. See for thyself, cully,' he invited.

It took only a moment to confirm that he'd nothing more of value on him. Muffler even made him remove his shoes and shake them before allowing him to leave. They watched him from the doorway as he unhitched Rats and took off the old flour sack used as a nosebag. He tossed it on the back of the wagon, climbed up and flicked his whip over the colt's head.

As soon as they were out of the town and along a quiet wooded track, Elyas reined in and reached for the nosebag. Delving in among the oats, his fingers found the small wrapped bundle of coins he'd hidden right at the foot for safety. It gave him some measure of satisfaction to have outwitted Muffler. He unhitched Rats and tethered him on a longish rope in a grassy glade. Then, rolled in his oilskin against the dew, he settled himself on a soft, mossy bank to sleep.

Sleep was a while coming. The sky had cleared and through the budding branches he could glimpse the stars and the shining crescent moon. He wondered if Graeme and Isaac could see the moon. Or if they were down in the dark, cold bilge of the *Royal Sovereign*, sleeping the sleep of the exhausted after their first twenty-four hours in the service of the King.

'Black hell and worse to His Majesty!' Elyas ranted aloud as he lay there in the bright moonlight of a March night. His outburst disturbed a corncrake resting in the branches above him; it fluttered peevishly and set up a rasping cry. After a while it settled again, leaving only a sense of dread and desolation.

Wart didn't bark his usual welcome when the wagon trundled into the yard just after noon the next day. The lurcher just lay in his usual place across the barn door and didn't even prick his ears when Elyas whistled to him. He could have been dead, save that his deep ribbed chest rose and fell.

Kezzy was the first to appear. She'd been watching for Elyas from the washing house as she sorted ore. Huward and Jamie heard his piercing whistle above the roar of the furnace in the smelting house and came running, their faces blackened by cinders and glistening with sweat. The disappointment was plain on their faces when they saw that Graeme and Isaac weren't with Elyas.

'Did you find 'em, Gramps? Are they coming home?' clamoured Kezzy. Her eyes were red-rimmed from crying.

'Mebbe, m'dear, mebbe,' was all he could say. Weariness was etched in the deep lines of his face. He got down stiffly and looked across at Wart. 'What ails hound?'

'Hasn't eaten since yest'day mornin'. Pinin' for they boys,' said Huward heavily. His own face was tired beneath the layer of grime: his eyes red-veined from lack of sleep.

'Best put he down,' said Elyas.

'Aw no, Gramps!' Kezzy and Jamie entreated in unison and Kezzy ran across to put her arms around the near-blind, broken-hearted old dog that had been such a faithful friend to all of them.

' 'Tis best for he,' said Elyas, depressed himself at the prospect.

'But what if Graeme and Isaac come back and we've put Wart down?' asked Jamie desperately.

'Poor brute'll starve heself long afore they come back 'gin. They be sailin' t'war on the *Royal Sovereign*,' Elyas said disconsolately.

Kezzy left Wart and went to Elyas, her face lifted seriously to his. 'They *will* come home again . . . after they've been to war . . . won't they, Gramps?'

'The Lord will decide, Kezzy, m'dear,' replied Elyas.

He took her hand and together they led the remnants of the Hammett family into the cottage.

That evening, when Kezzy and Jamie had fallen into a restless sleep on the pallets, Elyas and Huward sat talking in low voices by the dying fire. They had important things to discuss. Foremost, the mine.

'How we'm going to manage wi'out un boys?' said Huward, shaking his head worriedly.

'Jamie'll have to start workin' in by bal wi' us. He be nigh on ten year old.'

Huward nodded. 'Ay, 'twere time he worked a man's coore,' he hastened to agree but he knew it wasn't what his father wanted.

Elyas had always said he wouldn't use children below ground, unlike the other mine-owners who'd no such conscience about employing boys and girls, some as young as six or seven, to work the airtraps and to pull heavy corves of stuff along the tunnels by a 'dog belt' worn around the child's body.

Huward bent forward and poked the fire. It flared briefly.

'If Kezzy were to stop the school her could work three more coore a week in by washin' house,' suggested Huward.

'Nay, boy!' Elyas's voice was suddenly harsh. 'Kezzy is to be learned proper, whatever happens.'

'Mebbe us could look to tributers,' was Huward's next suggestion.

'I'll not share Eaglestone wi' strangers, boy!'

'Tut-workers then . . . We'm could take on mebbe six strong boys.'

Elyas snorted contemptuously. 'And where 'bouts do we'm find un? If'n they ent workin' in by big Wheals, they been took by press.'

They lapsed into silence, each pondering the calamitous position they were in without Graeme's and Isaac's brawn. After a while, in a voice much less sharp, Elyas said: 'Us'll get by 'til they boys come home 'gin, don't 'ee fret.'

'If the Lord sends they home,' muttered Huward.

Elyas pretended not to hear him. The absence of his grandsons was burden enough to bear, without the terrible thought that they might never return. He changed the subject, saying: 'What 'bout Wart?'

'I tried he with rabbit . . . fresh killed, but he wouldn't take un.'

'Best put he down though 'tis a wisht poor thing.'

Huward's face was expressionless. He moved to rise. 'Best do it now. I'll drop he in river wi' brick lashed to he.'

Elyas stopped him. 'Nay, boy. I'll slice un throat quick.'

They sat a while longer. Presently, Elyas stood up, went and got his sharp knife and went out without a word. Huward heard him whistling for Wart. He was back inside ten minutes. The knife in his hand was clean and wet from being washed in the brook.

' 'Twere good ol' dog that,' he said as he made for his pallet.

'Ay, 'twere,' agreed Huward yawning. 'Mebbe get 'nother from farm tomorrow. Must have dog t'guard tin when we'm in by bal.'

Elyas grunted. He wished his grandsons were as easily replaced as Wart. He was just dozing off when he remembered that this would have been their wedding night. Something within him stirred. Vividly he pictured his own wife's pale, shy face when he'd brought her as a bride to his father's shack across the moor on the banks of the Bovey Tracey, where, for three generations, Hammetts had washed ore from the river. His hard old face softened as he was reminded of those other, sweet, distant days. And nights. And as he savoured the memories, his thoughts turned to Morgenna and Bethinda.

'Be 'ee 'sleep, boy?' he asked in a low voice.

'Nay, Pa.' As exhausted as he was, Huward was finding sleep elusive. Every time he shut his eyes he saw a warship slewing through a great swelling sea, her towering expanse of canvas tinted pink from the sky. And somewhere on her decks amid the scurrying figures of the hands, were Graeme and Isaac . . .

'Did 'ee go to Fardle like I said?'

'Ay. Took on terrible did they sisters. Weepin' and sobbin' and tuggin' they hair.'

'Roarin' cow do soon forget calf.' It was a pity though, mused Elyas, they could have done with the two strong young women at Eaglestone. Especially now. An idea occurred. 'Mebbe ye could marry one of they sisters thyself, boy. And have other sleep in wi' Kezzy if'n they don't want separating.' His answer was a rumbling snore. 'Mebbe not,' Elyas changed his mind. 'Young maidens like they would sap thy strength an' that be needed in by bal.'

Elyas closed his eyes and in a short while his snores and grunts were mingling with those of Huward. He didn't sleep for long. Less than an hour. He was awakened by Kezzy plucking at his beard and whispering to him to wake up.

'Worramarra?' he mumbled.

'Gramps, I want to tell you something. Something 'portant.' She pulled his beard again.

'Tomorrow, m'dear.' He turned his face to the wall, shifting his beard out of the way of her tormenting fingers.

She shook him determinedly and leaned over to peer into his face. Her curtain of black hair tickled his nose and brought him back to full consciousness. He sat up, squinting in the dark to make her out.

'What is it, Kezzy? Night-hags botherin' 'ee, child?'

'No, Gramps . . . I want to tell you something. A secret.'

He rolled off his pallet and went to the fireplace. He found a candle but the fire was quite dead by now so he had to fumble a while longer to find flint, iron and tinderbox.

'Now then, what be this secret?' he whispered when he'd got the candle lit and he could see her troubled little face.

She went and sat very close to him on the settle. 'It's about the Lord Warden's man.'

'His steward?'

'Yes.'

Elyas frowned. 'By name of Grote? That he?'

'Yes.'

'What about he?'

'He's the cap'n of the smugglers, Gramps. The ones as brought me home cos they was looking for somewhere to hide their moonshine.'

Elyas's face showed no surprise at this revelation. 'How can 'ee know, Kezzy, when he had face covered?' he asked her in a level voice.

'I knowed 'twere him the minute I saw him at Blackaven House. He's got funny sprouting brows . . . and a funny way of looking at me. 'Tis same man, Gramps!' In her eagerness to convince him, she forgot to whisper.

'Hush, child, ye'll wake thy pa.'

She cast a look at Huward's sleeping form. 'Aren't we going to tell him?' she asked, sounding surprised.

Elyas put a hand on her shoulder. It was few moments before he spoke again. 'Kezzy, m'dear, I don't 'spect 'ee to understand 'bout Grote an' the flaskers an' such, on account you'm but a maid as yet.' He hesitated, choosing his words as she stared at him with wide eyes. 'What I'm trying to tell 'ee, is that sometimes we'm must close our eyes to certain things . . .'

'But I *did* see Grote . . . and he *is* the cap'n of the flaskers,' she said quickly, interrupting.

'O ay, m'dear. He's that right 'nough.'

She registered utter amazement. 'You already *knew*, Gramps!'

He squeezed her thin shoulder slightly. 'Ah, m'dear. I recognised Grote instant he brung 'ee home that night. But I said naught . . . not even to thy pa. Like I said, sometimes best to pretend us don't elly know nothing. Especially if'n it concerns gentry.'

'Grote isn't gentry.'

'Mebbe not, but there won't be much he gets up to that de Raddon ain't back of.'

Kezzy's eyes were bright. 'Do you think Cap'n de Raddon is a smuggler, too, Gramps?' she breathed.

'Mebbe he is, mebbe he ain't. Mebbe *he* turns blind eye to his steward's doings if'n it do mean he has a choice keg or two in his cellar.'

Kezzy sat silent, resentful that the mighty Lord Warden of the Stannaries should be embroiled in such nefarious goings on. He was supposed to uphold the law thereabouts, not break it. If a lowly tinner was caught with contraband he was taken across the moor and locked up in Lydford Castle for years and years with only bread and water given to him.

Or he might be put on a boat and sent far across the sea. She couldn't decide which was worse: the prison at Lydford, probably, since she'd heard there were big black rats in there that nibbled the prisoners' toes while they slept. She couldn't help a shudder at the thought and Elyas, feeling the tremor run through her small, cotton-clad frame, presumed she was chilled.

'Go to thy bed afore 'ee gets a chin-cough,' he said, gruffly solicitous. Sometimes he forgot that she was just a small girl so little fuss did she make about the hardships of her life high up on the windswept moor with no mother to care for her. She was just going when he thought of something else.

'Does Grote know 'ee spotted his phiz?'

She looked quite indignant. 'I never let on. Not even to Mistress Rogers. She'd have said I were half rocked!'

He nodded approvingly, marvelling at her maturity. She was a shrewd one. Most children would have kicked up a to-do and pointed fingers and blabbed to all who'd listen. 'You'm did right, Kezzy. Best it be our secret. Understand?'

She nodded, though she didn't understand. But if her grandfather said it must be their secret, then wild dogs wouldn't drag it from her.

Elyas waited until she disappeared round the curtain before he snuffed the candle. He grinned wryly to himself in the dark as he found his pallet and lowered himself stiffly on to it. Clearly, the child had been shocked to discover that a personage of such high rank as the Lord Warden kept company with gentlemen of the night. Despite his low spirits and his deep concern as to how they were to manage, he actually chuckled as another thought came to him: what would Kezzy have to say if she knew that just about every mine-owner, land-owner, farmer and priest in the West Country cleared the dust from his gullet with moonshine? Wouldn't be the first time he'd parted with a few coppers himself for an illicit tot of brandy down at the Cornwood kiddleywink while his wife, Beth, was taking a dish of tea with her friend Dame Rogers.

Elyas's soft chuckling ceased suddenly and he caught his breath painfully. Thinking of the Brandy Keg brought to mind an image of Graeme and Isaac as he'd last seen them, young faces flushing with pleasure as he handed them each a half crown for their pocket along with the money to buy their new shirts and two pairs of brass earrings for their brides as a symbol of their new marital status.

He'd guessed that his grandsons would spend the best part of the day supping in secret round the back of the smithy but he hadn't told them nay since it was their wedding eve. Now he bitterly regretted that grandfatherly display of generosity. For if they'd not dallied in the village they'd not have been pressed.

Damn the press! Elyas cursed the faceless sailors. Probably pressed men themselves, since they were usually the most zealous when it came to depriving other men of their freedom, he mused with a rising sense of anger which pushed sleep further away still. And damn John de Raddon!

For that double-dealing limb o' Satan could have got those boys released if he'd been of a mind to. Something Kezzy said flew to mind: 'Cap'n de Raddon said he'd help 'em but he didn't . . .'

So why hadn't he?

Out of cussedness because they were Elyas the tinner's kin. That, apparently, was the answer to the question. Yet, Elyas thought it not quite credible. Did their feud over the *didekei* still rankle so deeply with de Raddon that he'd allow the navy to prick his self-importance if that meant getting a leg up on the Hammetts?

Nay, there was more to it than that, Elyas was totally convinced. He experienced a small surge of dread, like a tiny, icy dart which momentarily pierced his heart. De Raddon could be a determined and savage foe, as he had proved at poor Ruke's expense.

'He's got some game afoot, drat his dirty soul!' muttered Elyas.

He rolled over on his side, coughing. After a while he fell asleep.

Chapter Twelve

It was April and the quarterly coinage in Plympton and Elyas was taking their blocks of tin for assaying.

It was a bleak, damp Monday and he bore with him a deep feeling of depression. This would be their last good tin harvest without Graeme's and Isaac's young brawn helping to work the lode. There would be no more fistfuls of copper tokens from the merchants for him to turn into gold coins and hide in a hewn-out stone in the pig-sty. They would be lucky to make a few pennies, an old man, a middle-aged man, and two children, if they worked all God's hours digging and sorting and washing and smelting. There was just one small consolation: what they did harvest was theirs and not to be shared with greedy tributers or lazy tut-workers.

The sweetly toned tenor bell of Plympton St Mary was welcoming the tinners to the coinage as Rats wearily hauled his weighty burden through the river of mud towards the Stannary town. Elyas reined in for a few moments as he always did whenever he passed Gibbet Hill. Needles of rain battered his wizened face as he gazed up at the wooden gallows; the old, rotting gallows upon which Ruke had been hung had been taken by the townspeople virtually splinter by splinter to be worn as protection against witches' spells. The city fathers had erected a solid new one; from which now hung a body in a metal cage. A highwayman or cattle thief. It was difficult to know what the felon might have looked like in life as the crows had been well and truly occupied with his face and the naked, putrid flesh showing through his prison rags.

At least by taking Ruke home up the moor and burying her in a secret grave in the lee of Eagle Tor, he'd saved Kezzy's mother from the ignominy of their scavenging beaks. Sad-eyed, Elyas raised his whip in brief, silent salute before he moved on. It was a gesture uninspired by any emotion other than pity for all those unfortunate men and women who'd come to such an immoral and degrading end there.

The rain grew heavier as Elyas trundled down through Bottle Hill Mine and passed Loughtor Mill into the outskirts of Plympton. The rain fairly danced on the cobbles in Market Square and the mud along the main street reached almost as far as Rats's knees which slowed progress to a crawl. Despite the weather, there were plenty of people milling about the market stalls and cattle pens and Tinners' Hall was packed tight. But somehow Elyas found a place to tether Rats and counted his ingots of tin as they were unloaded and carried inside by the soaking youths whose job it was.

Elyas was by now an old hand at the formalities and even managed to catch the eye of a controller who knew the excellent quality of his tin. This meant he was brought to the top of a long line of tinners, many of whom had been standing for an hour or more. In no time he was back outside with his tokens stowed safely next to his skin. He set off through the mire in search of refreshment, unaware that his progress was being carefully followed by Grote stationed at an upper window of the Fighting Cocks inn.

'Here he comes now, Cap'n.'

Grote spoke over his shoulder without taking his eyes from the stooping, bow-legged figure wading purposefully through the mud below him.

There was a good deal of rustling from behind the drawn hangings of the big bed which dominated the low-ceilinged room. John de Raddon's voice was muffled as he said: 'Bring him to me.'

Grote went out.

Once he'd gone, de Raddon wasted little time. He pushed the naked wench from him impatiently and swung his legs out of the bed, at the same time dragging open the drapes. Giggling, she tried to detain him by catching hold of his shirt but he was in no mood for frolics and lashed out at her. She yelped as the back of his hand caught her cheek. He snatched up her russet dress from where she'd dropped it on the floor and threw it at her.

'Get out.'

Sulkily, she got out of bed and dropped the dress, her only garment, over her head.

'Shall I come back later, Cap'n?'

He didn't answer, didn't give her another look as he pulled on his own clothes. She looked disappointed. The money she was given by the owner of the inn was in proportion to the amount of time she'd spent with a customer in an upstairs room. Captain de Raddon was a good customer, he usually kept a wench for an hour or more. She'd been there less than half an hour so would get just a few coppers rather than a shilling or two. Dimpled, walnut-skinned face still sullen, she threw more logs on the fire in the wide stone fireplace, straightened the bed and went out.

De Raddon set his wig upon his thinning locks, poured himself a glass of claret and carried it across to the window. He could see Grote talking to Elyas Hammett in the street below.

Elyas's thoughts were on a dish of salt herrings and plenty of thickly buttered bread so he visibly started when he found his way blocked by Grote's thick body. His face darkened with annoyance when he recognised de Raddon's man. Recovering himself, he hooked his thumbs in the arms of his waistcoat and leisurely looked Grote up and down.

'Well, now. Master Grote, if'n 'ee stops there, ye'll likely'd be took for strayin' porker an' rounded up,' observed Elyas.

Grote's face hardened at the tinner's deliberate insolence and he clenched his big fists longingly. But his orders were to fetch Hammett in, not to beat him to bloody pulp. 'Cap'n says yer t'come,' he growled.

Elyas's eyebrows rose. 'Oh ay? And where be his lordship?'

Grote tilted his head towards the Fighting Cocks. 'Inside.'

Elyas's eyes travelled as though drawn to the overhanging upper storey of the inn. His eyesight wasn't too good so he sensed rather than saw the Lord Warden's shadowy bulk behind the leaded panes of one of the windows.

'What do 'ee want?' he demanded, making no move to follow Grote who'd begun walking towards the open door.

Grote stopped and looked back, scowling. 'Ye'll find out soon 'nough. Best come, Cap'n don't like t'be kept waitin'.'

Elyas was sorely tempted to continue on his way to the tavern of his own choice but decided it wouldn't be prudent to antagonise the Lord Warden more than he'd already done. Besides, he was curious to know what de Raddon wanted with him. A spark of hope kindled in Elyas: perhaps there was some news of Graeme and Isaac. He spat in the mud, shrugged his shoulders nonchalantly, and squelched after Grote.

Moments later, cap in hand, he was pushed into the Lord Warden's presence. Grote withdrew and shut the door. De Raddon was still standing at the window, his back to the room. It was a while before he deigned to turn and face the visitor he'd summoned, during which time Elyas stood twisting his cap and viewing his surroundings with interest. It was the first time he'd been in a private room at a posting inn.

Though not particularly large, the room would have swallowed Eaglestone with room to spare. The cedar wall-panelling and the two Jacobean chairs needed a rub with beeswax, and the Turkey carpet, like the red silk-brocade bed hangings, had been attacked by moths in places. But none of this detracted from the room's sumptuousness in Elyas's naïvely uncritical eyes. Never had he seen such a bed. He wondered how many of a family it was meant to take.

There was a marble washstand and a side table covered in the whitest of linen clothes and bearing the remains of a pigeon-pie, a round of cold beef and some kidneys. Elyas felt hungry. He wished de Raddon would have his say so that he could go and buy his herrings. He considered speaking first, though it was never the done thing to do so with the gentry. As a rule, he wasn't much concerned with such conventions. Wasn't he a better tinner any day than Captain de Raddon? And wasn't he also a mine-owner, though admittedly on a much smaller scale? However, these fine surroundings had a humbling effect on Elyas so it was as much as he could do to give a small, rasping cough.

Even that didn't have any immediate effect upon the man at the window. But eventually he did turn and, stony faced, surveyed Elyas from beneath his heavy black brows.

'Good day, Cap'n,' Elyas risked saying.

De Raddon grunted. He went to the side table and poured himself another glass of claret, then sat in one of the dark oak chairs. 'Help yourself to what's there, Hammett,' he said abruptly and in a tone of voice which was verging on the amiable. 'And take yon chair.'

Elyas's jaw dropped. For a long moment he stood rooted with surprise.

He eyed de Raddon suspiciously but could read nothing in his florid voice to explain what might have brought about this unexpected show of generosity. Perhaps he was regretting not helping Graeme and Isaac and was looking to make amends.

'Thankee, zur, I'll take a drop o' that there brandy,' said Elyas when he'd found his voice and his legs were prepared to carry him across to the glass decanter. He ignored the glasses, afraid of their fragility in his clumsy hands, and splashed a good three inches of brandy into a pewter tankard. He cut himself a large wedge of pigeon-pie and carried it, and his brandy, over to the chair on the opposite side of the fireplace to de Raddon. Elyas's sunken eyes were still rather wary as he raised his tankard. 'Thy health and that o' yourn,' he said in as cordial manner as he could muster.

De Raddon nodded but he didn't drink with him.

He said, 'You can't be making much progress in by mine, Hammett.'

It was true. They hadn't shifted above four or five sacks of ore-bearing stuff a day since they'd lost Graeme and Isaac. But Elyas was too proud to admit it. 'Us bain't doin' too badly, 'sidering. Reckon us have opened up 'nother twenty-three or -four yards this past two-week.'

De Raddon didn't believe it. The ground was hard up there at Eagle Tor. 'They do say you're troubled by watering.'

If it wasn't that his mouth was full of pigeon-pie, Elyas would have denied this with some exasperation; Wheal Eaglestone had always been a middling dry mine considering her position. But as he chewed he suddenly remembered the flaskers. And Grote. He guessed the source of de Raddon's inaccurate information. Swallowing, he said in a voice laden with regret, 'Ay, Cap'n, 'tis terrible for floodin' like 'ee say.'

De Raddon wasn't taken in. He'd been near enough to the Hammett mine to see the waterwheel and pumps that kept the seepage at bay. He'd laughed scornfully when Grote, who knew more about flasking than mining, repeated what Elyas had said about the mine being wet; he guessed, correctly, that the wily little tinner didn't want his tunnels used as a cache by flaskers.

There was silence while Elyas finished his pie and sucked the crumbs from his fingers. Then, abruptly, de Raddon came to the point. 'Look here, Hammett, you'll not be able to work Eaglestone without tut-men. And they'll want paying. So I'm offering to take the mine over. You'll be kept on as overseer, mind, and receive a share of the profits. Your son will be put in charge of the blowing house and he can have his boy with him . . . So, what do you say?'

For a long while Elyas didn't say anything; his tongue was trapped to the roof of his mouth. So this was de Raddon's reason for letting the navy keep Graeme and Isaac. Deviously, he'd imagined that without their muscle Elyas would be so hard put to keep his mine working he'd be easy meat to be picked off. He frowned, and de Raddon, anticipating what was to come, said briskly: 'The war with France has increased the demand for tin. His Majesty has sent word that I must do everything in my power to ensure every mine maintains a high production. I fear that Eaglestone's production will drop drastically.'

'Then 'ee shouldn't have let my boys be stolen by the navy to suit thy own greedy game,' snapped Elyas rashly, not caring if de Raddon took offence.

De Raddon's eyes narrowed dangerously; the tinner was shrewder than he'd credited him. 'You crossed me once before, Hammett, to your great cost. Or have you forgotten the woman, Ruke?'

Elyas rose, his tankard gripped forgotten in his hand. Deliberately he spat in the grate. 'I bain't forgot un *didekei* . . . and I'll not forget my grandsons, blast thy lily liver!' He spat again.

De Raddon's disfigured face contorted with rage so he resembled some crumbling, grotesque gargoyle. Yet, he somehow restrained himself from shouting for Grote to come and seize the insolent dog and whip him through the town. He also rose, and stood towering over Elyas.

Savagely, he said: 'By Jesu, man! I could seize your mine in the King's name to make sure 'tis properly worked. And if you dared to set your face agin me, I could have you and your son boated with the convicts for treason. Ay, and set the boy and his sister to work so deep below grass they'd forget what clean air was. What then of the Hammetts, hey? What then?'

Elyas was gripped by a sickening dread at the very thought of Jamie and Kezzy being condemned to this living hell; starved, beaten by a cruel overman, dragging corves of stuff until they dropped from weariness. 'Goddamn you to black hell and worse . . .!' he began to curse, then stopped himself, fighting grimly to hang on to a semblance of control. This was boggy ground he was treading. He must step warily for all their sakes.

There was silence. Broken only by the beating of rain on the windows and the crackling of the logs in the grate. The two of them stood facing each other, their stance hostile. One the brutal bear, the other the watchful weasel.

De Raddon was bluffing but he had the satisfaction of seeing the angry defiance fade from Elyas's face and be replaced by uncertainty. True, the Stannary was empowered by ancient Royal charter to seize at whim any piece of land, be it arable, wood, farm, field or common, in the unremitting search for tin. Towards that end, they could even alter the course of the streams so that vast areas, once lush and green, became barren wastes seamed by parched beds. But to seize Wheal Eaglestone wasn't as callously simple as de Raddon would have Elyas believe. After all, it was a working pit properly registered in the owner's name and entered on the Stannary Rolls. The only legitimate means by which the Lord Warden could seize it in the name of the Crown would be if Elyas seriously transgressed tinners' law so that his property was forfeit. This usually meant that he himself would be either transported for life or hung. Even so, he would have to be charged in the proper manner and brought before the Stannary Court at the next Lydford sessions to be tried by a jury of tinners.

De Raddon had no intention, however, of seizing Hammett's pit for the Crown. He wanted it for himself. Over the years he'd taken a surreptitious interest in Eaglestone's production figures; the amount paid in coinage and the quality of the tin being produced. And it rankled with him that this grey, wizened, dust-ruined moorman had not only spawned a strong son to follow him (when the Blackaven nursery remained disappointingly empty) but could also produce better tin with his ramshackle pulleys and pumps than any dug from the Blackaven wheals with their horse-gins and steam-winches.

De Raddon grew suddenly impatient. He wanted Eaglestone and he would have it! 'Well?' his harsh voice broke the silence. 'Do I take the mine for the Crown? Or will you make her over to me and receive a fair share of the profits? Which is it to be, Hammett?'

Elyas surveyed him with deep hatred. He was still ashen-faced and wheezing slightly, but his immediate panic had subsided, enabling him to apply a modicum of logic to the situation. Powerful the Lord Warden might be, but he couldn't just help himself to another man's mine because he'd got green in his eyes. Not even in the King's name. As for his threats – Elyas's lip curled with disdain. He wasn't so simple that he didn't know that all convicts were being pressed into the King's service, so there were no convict ships. Even the old tinners were being taken on again if there was a coore in them.

Elyas straightened his shoulders and lifted his chin, the old, defiant glint returning to his pale, watery eyes. His voice was hoarse from the fit of coughing as he said: 'Well, now, Cap'n de Raddon. I've this to say to 'ee so mark un well. If'n ye ever sets one foot on Hammett land I'll take 'ee by yon fine gold chain 'ee wears an' hang 'ee from nearest tree for the stinkin' thief you'm be!'

The colour drained from de Raddon's face. 'I'll have you horse-whipped!' He raised his voice. 'Grote!'

When the steward didn't instantly appear, Elyas said knowingly, 'Mebbe un be out ridin' wi' they flaskers you'm got in thy pay, Cap'n.'

De Raddon's face froze and his fingers tightened on the claret glass he was holding so that it seemed in danger of being crushed. For once he was rendered speechless.

Elyas chuckled, but without humour. 'Oh ay, I knows all 'bout Master Grote an' his smugglin' friends. Reckon Preventy men might find cellars at Blackaven mighty interestin'. Now there would be a thing! Gentl'man like thyself, Lord Warden an' all, taken in charge for freetradin' wi' they Frenchies . . . an' they lookin' to invade us! King would have plenty to say 'bout that, I reckons.'

There was no mistaking the implication.

'A pox on your tongue, you dog!' snarled de Raddon, his florid face turning dark red with frustrated fury. He wasn't sure how much the tinner knew about his illicit activities, but a wrong word in the right ear could prove embarrassing – and very expensive, if he'd to buy a zealous Preventative or two.

Elyas read his thoughts. 'I'll not blab if'n 'ee stays 'way from me an' mine.'

'Get out!'

Elyas stepped across to the fireplace and threw the untouched contents of his tankard on the fire, sending blue flames leaping and crackling up the chimney. 'I'll not drink withee, de Raddon,' he said sourly. He set down the tankard, went out and slammed the door.

De Raddon glared at the closed door. Elyas's parting gesture suddenly reminded him of an elfin-faced little girl. What was her name? Keziah? She'd refused his sweetstuffs even though she'd probably never tasted anything so delicious in her young life. And when he'd fed them to his dogs in front of her, she'd lifted her jaw at him in exactly the same wayward, rebellious way as her grandfather!

'Goddamn and take you, Emma, and your cursed, barren body!' he muttered and with all his might smashed the claret glass into the fireplace so it disintegrated into thousands of tiny, glittering shards.

At the foot of the stairs, Elyas met Grote coming out of the tap-room wiping his mouth on his sleeve. They looked fiercely at each other.

'Thy master's whistling for 'ee, cur,' sneered Elyas. 'Likely'd wants they fancy boots o' his licked.'

He didn't wait for Grote's irate response but swung out into the street chuckling gleefully to himself. Nevertheless, this latest clash with Captain de Raddon had somewhat unnerved him, although he wouldn't have admitted it, even to himself. He went straight to one of the less salubrious taverns and downed a pint of strong cider, followed straightaway by another. He wasn't hungry, having eaten a big piece of pigeon-pie. But he ate a dish of herrings anyway. To take away the taste of de Raddon vittles.

Shrovetide, Lent and Easter went by at Eaglestone mostly unmarked save for a visit to church. Without Graeme and Isaac getting up to their usual seasonal capers it wasn't the same. Though Kezzy did make egg pancakes on the hot iron which Elyas swore were the best he'd ever tasted. That pleased her greatly, but she knew in her little heart that they were doughy and black at the edges and nothing like as good as the farmer's wife made – something which aggravating Jamie took great delight in telling her.

On Lent-crocking day which was always a Tuesday, she slipped out of the cottage just before bed-time, went to the barn and dressed in Elyas's old smock and her father's hat trimmed with straw and twigs. She blackened her face with mud save for two circles around her eyes, and went and rapped loudly on the cottage door. Jamie came to open it and was so taken aback by the sight of this apparition, that he gave a startled yelp and stumbled backwards. Elyas and Huward roared with amusement. For they'd immediately recognised the pair of sparkling eyes beneath the brim.

With her thumbs tucked in the smocking, Kezzy launched into the Lent-crocking song, broadening her accent and turning up the corner of her mouth like the cheeky farmboys who usually went knocking for a pancake.

> I be come a-shrovin'
> Vor a li'l pan-cake
> A bit o' bread o' yourn bakin',

Or a li'l truckle cheese
O' yourn own makin'.
If you'll gi' me a li'l, I'll ask 'ee no more,
If you'm don't gi' me nawthin' . . . I'll rattle thy door!

Elyas and Huward laughed and stamped, even Jamie joining in grudgingly.

'Well now, reckon we'm et all they fine pancakes, young fella,' said Elyas seriously, stroking his chin and entering into the spirit of it. 'Mebbe find 'ee crust un hens have turned they beaks up at . . .'

Kezzy brought her hand from behind her back and showed them the chipped cloam pot she was hiding. To let a Lent-crocker go unrewarded was asking for a cannonade of old crocks against the door.

Elyas pretended alarm. 'Quick, Huward, boy! Give un a penny!'

Kezzy whipped off her hat. 'It's me, Gramps!' she shrieked.

So Kezzy got a penny. And then nothing would do but Jamie must go out to the barn and dress up in the smock and the hat and come knocking and threatening a cloam attack so he, too, would get a penny from Elyas for desisting.

Towards the end of May rumours reached Devon, later to be confirmed, that the French Admiral Villeneuve had managed to slip through Nelson's blockade at Toulon. Thence he'd sailed to Cadiz where he'd routed the British ships blockading the Spanish fleet. It was Bonaparte's plan that all the smaller fleets should sail for and unite in the West Indies, there to take on food and water before returning to give him his longed-for supremacy in the Channel. But only part of his plan was maturing since Admiral Cornwallis was still managing to hold the major part of the French fleet at Brest.

News of the war was slow reaching the west. Shorthanded as they were at Eaglestone, Elyas had taken to going up the moor now and then to visit a cousin of his who was a cowman at Cherry Brook Farm near Princetown. French prisoners of war came daily to the farm from the nearby prison camp to help till the fields as the farmboys had either volunteered or been pressed. Elyas viewed these truculent 'furriners' with a certain amount of enmity. Nevertheless, he forced himself to disregard his personal feelings to go into the fields when they stopped for mossle since they were a good source of information.

Most of them spoke a ragged form of English, having been captive for more than five years. They had been farmboys in their own country until impressed aboard a raiding party of four ships under American command. They'd landed on the north coast of Devon near Ilfracombe, burnt the first farmhouse they'd come to and then had either surrendered to the furious pitchfork-armed locals or were chased back to their ships.

Rumour soon swept the country that the west was in enemy hands. There was a rush on the banks by those who felt their gold was safer from the invaders hidden beneath their own stone flags than in a bank vault; long lines of anxious customers stretched from the bank doors. More rumours reached their ears. The country was virtually bankrupt. The Bank of England added to the panic by suspending all repayments. Elyas had been with the fish then; his small savings were well hidden among the straw in his pallet as he'd never trusted banks anyway. As for the invasion. Well, be they Frenchies or Yankees they'd still want fish, he'd told his family unconcernedly.

Now the remnants of that 'invasion' boasted to any who passed the time of day with them in the fields while they ate their mid-day figgens that it was only a matter of weeks before the great Bonaparte, now Emperor Napoleon, launched his mighty army across the Channel in a flotilla of 2000 flat-bottomed small boats to do the thing properly. Then it would be the men of Devon who'd find themselves interned in a camps like the one at Princetown and be forced to slave in fields which once had been their own.

On his return from his visit, Elyas had imparted this chilling piece of gossip to Huward. His son pondered over it for a good hour while they got ready the goose-quill fuses and powder charge needed to hulk the tunnel another few feet. Then he spat and said: 'Seems as they Frenchies knows more'n ol' Bony do, Pa.'

Elyas tapped his nose. 'They've way of findin' out what's what, do they furriners,' he said knowingly. He looked over his shoulder as though he might be overheard although they were alone, Jamie being in the washing-house and Kezzy at school. 'Them got *spies* everywhere!' he hissed.

Huward was singularly unimpressed. He lapsed into thought again. He'd never been as sharp-witted as his father, or even his sons and daughter, yet what he'd next to say on the subject made Elyas pause to think.

'Couldn't float all they row-boats in less'n six tides or more. An' first out would soon be spotted by one o' our Nel's men-o'-war. Be picked off one after t'other like squattin' ducks, they Frenchies.'

Cussedly, Elyas would have liked to argue with this fine piece of logic but was silenced for once. His years with the fish, waiting for Huward's and Graeme's boat to come in with the tide, had taught him enough about the sea to recognise that there was truth in what his son said. And, though disappointed that he couldn't disagree, he was secretly relieved that the invasion wasn't as easy or as imminent as all that. As he set light to the fuse and retired with Huward to safety, he said carelessly: 'Never did believe word o' furriners. Our Nel be fitty for they, boy!'

During the following month, however, Elyas never could resist regaling all those he met with this disquieting piece of gossip. And always without Huward's comforting conclusion. Consequently, the moor folk, various itinerate tinners, tinkers and gypsies, even the Reverend Creedy after he'd come looking for his overdue tithe, carried this new 'invasion' rumour far and wide through Devon and Cornwall. Unbeknown to Elyas, the situation became quite serious when people began withdrawing their savings from the local banks. One or two of the smaller ones closed their doors but there was no such rush on Clotworthy's bank in Plympton since it was generally known that it was shored up by the vast fortune and industrial might of the de Raddon family.

Even so, Thomas Clotworthy, who was John de Raddon's father-in-law, was a troubled man when he called upon his daughter and her husband at Blackaven at the beginning of June, summoned by the Lord Warden to confirm that he truly had nothing to fear financially. Clotworthy hastened to do this, not being so much concerned for himself or his bank, but for the economic state of the country in general.

' 'Tis the fault of these cursed wars. I blame those damned war-mongering ministers!' Clotworthy grouched as he and de Raddon paid a post-dinner visit to the stables to view a new hunter de Raddon had recently acquired. 'The French! The Yankees! The French again! Now the Spanish! What's the matter with His Majesty?'

He stopped in dismay, casting an embarrassed, sidelong look at his son-in-law who was, he'd just remembered, close to the King and the Prince of Wales both by dint of both friendship and office. But de Raddon waved a concurring hand.

'His Majesty, alas, is as witless as a Jack Hare!' he declared disparagingly. 'If only people had clamoured for Prinny to keep the Regency as loudly as they did for Pitt to be returned to office it would be a different story.'

'Pitt is a consummate master of economics,' said Clotworthy wryly.

They had entered the stable yard. De Raddon stopped and looked down at the slight, pale, freckled man at his side. 'Pitt has been walking a financial cliff-edge for years because of these damn wars. If we've got a gold crisis on our hands it's thanks to him.'

Clotworthy shook his head. 'No, de Raddon. 'Tis thanks to his war-mongering ministers . . . and the tittle-tattlers who make up all this non-sense about invasion.'

At that moment a groom came out of the stables leading a fine big grey by the bridle. De Raddon immediately forgot all else.

'Now, Clotworthy, tell me honestly, have you ever seen a finer animal? Worth every penny of the sixty guineas I paid for him, wouldn't you say?'

It was also at the beginning of June when two unexpected visitors came up the moor to Eaglestone – Morgenna and Bethinda. They walked up from Fardle early one evening and, as they entered the valley, the new dog, also called Wart but part foxhound, barked to let the Hammetts know strangers were approaching.

Jamie was out with the wagon cutting peat, so it was Kezzy who came shyly from the washing-house to welcome them. She ran to the mine entrance and tugged on the rope hanging in the shaft, rattling the cowbells tied on the end as a signal to her father and grandfather below. A couple of minutes later, Huward emerged blinking in the late sunshine. He saw the sisters standing there in their identical blue dresses, shawls around their shoulders against the moor breezes. He still couldn't tell which was which.

'Us ent heard n'owt o' they boys,' he told them regretfully, presuming that was why they'd come.

They looked at one another. One said: ' 'Tis old man us want to see.'

Kezzy, standing quietly by, knew that this was Morgenna who'd spoken: she was the one with the tiny brown mole on her jaw.

Huward shrugged and began to lead them towards the cottage. 'Shake bells for thy Gramps, Kezzy.'

She did so and waited at the mine entrance until Elyas climbed the last of the stepped, leaning ladders and emerged. 'They two sisters from Fardle want to see you, Gramps,' she told him eagerly.

He squeezed shut his eyes for a few seconds against the bright light, coughing in the fresh air. 'Did thy pa not tell they maidens un boys bain't home yet, an' no sayin' when them shall be?' He sounded peeved at being called from work on account of social visitors.

'Yes, Gramps, but 'tis you they've come to see.'

If Elyas had an inkling that there was a special reason for the sisters' visit, he didn't let on. He dropped his tin hat and stamped off towards the cottage, Kezzy trotting at his heels.

On entering, he greeted them cordially enough but didn't waste any time. 'What ho, you'm maidens! What have brung 'ee?' He sat himself down at the table opposite them and waited.

Again they exchanged veiled glances.

Kezzy curled herself in a corner behind the vags of turf used to fuel the range. She sensed that something interesting was about to be forthcoming and didn't want to be shooed out. With luck they'd forget she was there.

'Come' long . . . us have work t'do,' groused Elyas.

At that point they burst simultaneously into tears. Elyas and Huward looked at each other, at a loss as how to cope with this unexpected turn of events.

'No need t'take on,' said Huward in a kindly tone. He patted the shoulder of the sister nearest him. 'If'n they boys don't come back . . . God help 'em! . . . why, ye'll soon find 'nother pair o' boys. Handsome pair o' maids like you'm be . . .'

But this made them weep all the more.

'Best gi' un drop of shrub,' suggested Elyas generously.

Huward went and got the stoppered cloam jug and four mugs down from the shelf and set them on the table. Elyas poured liberally pushed two of the mugs across to the sisters. The room was filled with a pungent aroma. The shrub was strong, since it was good rum that had only been a little tainted by seawater during a run. The landlord of the kiddleywink added sugar and herbs and spices to make it more palatable and sold it cheaply at twopence a flask. A long draught seemed to steady Morgenna and Bethinda so they stopped their sobbing and sat smacking their lips.

'Now then,' Elyas tried again.

They both began at once. 'Us came . . . us *had* to come . . .'

Elyas held up a hand. 'One of 'ee at a time!'

' 'Tis I as had to come most urgent like, zur.'

Elyas frowned. 'Which be you'm? Damned if'n I knows 'ee 'part.'

'Morgenna, zur.'

'Urgent, 'ee says?'

' 'Tis a terrible thing, zur . . .'

'Spit un out, maid!'

Her face seemed to crumple. 'I be wi' child. By you'm boy Graeme.'

Elyas and Huward sat stunned. It was a while before either of them could speak. Then it was Elyas who said disbelievingly: 'Aw no, m'dear! More'n likely'd fart doubled up, that's all.'

' 'Tis true! All these weeks I've spent an hour mornin' an' night-time on my knees a-prayin' it bain't so. Oh, the shame of it!' She threw her apron over her head and began to weep in earnest.

Impatiently, Elyas turned to her sister for sense. 'Has her missed havin' rags on this month?'

'Ay, an' last month.'

Dumbfounded, Elyas and Huward exchanged astonished looks. Could it be so? They made mental calculations, Elyas arriving at the answer well ahead of Huward. It was now seven weeks since the boys had last seen their intendeds, so, yes, it was possible. 'But you'm was only sparkin'!' exclaimed Elyas perplexedly, forgetting that the boys had spent most of their last Sunday with the sisters. Time and enough to do more than hand-holding.

Huward was staring at Morgenna with something akin to wonder. *She was carrying his grandchild. Elyas's great-grandchild!* He felt a surge of something which he didn't immediately recognise as pride. 'What's to be done, Pa?' he asked awkwardly.

Elyas didn't answer. He was watching Morgenna as she sniffled into the corner of her shawl. She avoided meeting his eyes. Doubt nibbled at him. They had only her word for it. And her sister's, which amounted to the same thing. If Graeme had enjoyed her favours then likely'd other boys had, too. He sneaked a look at his son: saw the gleam of interest in Huward's eyes as he gazed at the young woman who claimed to carry Graeme's child in her womb. And suddenly a memory of other days stirred within Elyas, when Ruke had given birth to Kezzy, and only she and Elyas had known that Huward wasn't the father. Huward had been quite content with the bright-eyed *didekei* child, often gazing into the cradle with much the same look on him as now. As Kezzy grew, the fact that she didn't resemble the Hammetts in the least became even more obvious. She took after her ma, which wasn't unusual with a girl, so Huward never did suspect. And over the years, Elyas had almost forgotten that his beloved granddaughter wasn't his own flesh and blood. It hadn't mattered then, so what did it matter now whether Morgenna's child was or wasn't a Hammett? mused Elyas. Providing it was a boy, of course. One girl in a generation was enough! You fed them, clothed them, taught them how to wash and sort the ore, and then they were off and getting wed and using their nimble fingers to help fill their husband's pockets before you'd had any benefit from them. Yes, one girl was quite sufficient.

'Do 'ee come from a family o' boys or maids?' Elyas asked Morgenna cagily before coming to any decision.

She looked surprised. 'Us be the only maidens . . . fourteen brothers we'm got. All livin' . . . an' three pair o' twinnies.'

Elyas's face lit up. Now there would be something! *Twin* boys! Double the hands to help Kezzy and Jamie in by the bal when the time came. He poured them all another tot of shrub, then lifted his mug high in the air. 'Morgenna, m'dear! Us hopes 'ee do live to a fair age and rear a long family!' he said and downed the shrub.

Her tears dried instantly. 'Do 'ee intend helpin' I then, Mr Hammett, zur?' she asked hopefully.

He wiped his mouth on the back of his hand. 'O ay,' he confirmed and didn't miss the triumphant look she shot her sister. He got down to business. 'Now then. Have 'ee spoke of this to elly o' they over to Fardle?'

'We'm not said word to anyone save thyselves,' Morgenna assured him.

'Good. Best 'ee comes to Eaglestone soon as thy mistress lets 'ee. Else they Fardle folk'll be chitterin' like a tree vull o' sparrows soon as thy gut starts to sprout.'

'But us don't want to be sep'rated,' the sisters chorused in dismay.

'Then best 'ee both come. Soon as they boys come back 'long home 'ee can be wed as intended.'

They looked relieved.

It suited Elyas to have them both there when they were so short handed. Morgenna could keep house and Bethinda could help Kezzy in the washing-house. Which meant that Jamie could work his coore in the mine.

There was just one other thing worrying the sisters. It was Bethinda who managed to voice it, her nut-brown face solemn. 'Fardle steward do say likely'd they boys will be shot or drownded.'

Elyas's jaw tightened. Huward glared at Bethinda. Curled up in her corner, Kezzy bit her lip. She and Jamie and her father all knew that to suggest such a terrible thing sent the old man wild with anger. But instead of roaring like he usually did, he said in an almost kindly way, 'Don't you'm be worrin' 'bout they, m'dears. Them'll be back one o' these days . . . just like eagle to un tor!'

When Jamie returned with the wagon and the peat was unloaded and stacked in the barn, Elyas put the sisters on the backboard to take them back to Fardle. He wanted to see the steward there and arrange for them to move to Eaglestone as soon as their mistress allowed it.

Kezzy crept from her hiding place.

'Can I go with you, Gramps?'

He shook his head. 'Be plenty o' daylight left for working.' But her tilting dark eyes entreated and he never could resist her. 'Mebbe blow o' air in thy lungs won't do 'ee elly harm,' he relented and she scrambled eagerly up on the box beside him before he could change his mind.

Kezzy waited with the wagon outside the servants' and tradesmen's entrance while Elyas went inside with the sisters. She couldn't see much of the house but sufficient to tell that, although very fine, it wasn't as grand as Blackaven. After a while, Elyas reappeared looking satisfied. The sisters were to move to Eaglestone at the end of June. He climbed up, took the reins and clicked to Rats.

They travelled in silence for about a mile. Every so often, Elyas would give Kezzy a sidelong look. That there was plenty going on in her dark head, he'd no doubt. After a while, he said: 'Well, now, m'dear, now we'm by ourselves, what's all this 'bout, eh?'

She turned her head to gaze candidly at him. Not in the least surprised he'd guessed she'd wanted to come so that she could talk to him privately about something that was troubling her.

'Gramps . . .' she hesitated, uncertain how to begin. 'Gramps, if you swear on your mother's soul not to tell something, you mustn't ever, must you?'

Elyas glanced down at her; there was something amiss, he could tell. 'Who made 'ee swear on thy poor dead mother's soul, Kezzy?' he asked gently.

She pursed her lips, considering for a moment. Graeme had made her swear not to tell anyone what she'd seen him and Morgenna do that Sunday down by the river where the garlic grew. But surely if she answered her grandfather she wouldn't be breaking her word.

'Graeme made me swear not to tell something . . . before he was pressed.'

Elyas grunted. He'd guessed that her mysteriousness had something to do with her brothers and the two Fardle maids. Clearly she desperately wanted to tell him her secret, but he'd always taught her that if she gave her word she must keep it. He glanced at her again: her little face appealed to him to find a solution. It was probably nothing: some childishness. Yet . . . she was a wise little mortal, was Kezzy, and not given to childishness as a rule.

They were descending Houndle Hill. Below stretched fields and small copses. On one side of the road was a gateway to Lord Blachford's estate. On the other, was the old Moor Cross. Elyas reined in and got down, leaving Rats to graze by the wayside. Kezzy did the same, following him over to the simple, grey-stone Latin cross.

No one really knew why the cross stood there; the elements had taken their toll and the ancient inscription was too faint to make out. Some said it was merely to mark the track across the moor; others of a more futile imagination said it was to protect the moorfolk from witches and hedgyboors and other fearful entities.

Elyas lowered himself stiffly to the grass at the foot of the cross and brought from a pocket an old pipe. Kezzy knelt beside him, watching as he found a plug of tobacco and pushed it into the clay bowl, once powdery white but now grimy and chipped with use.

'I be going to tell 'ee something now, Kezzy, on account you'm growed enough to be told. 'Tis about thy ma,' he told her gravely when the pipe was drawing to his satisfaction. She was gazing at him intently. 'Some wrong-minded folk reckoned that thy ma was witch.'

He had always known that one day he would have to tell her the truth, but had put off the moment for as long as possible, believing it was too great a burden for very young shoulders. Now, however, she was a few months off nine so he felt she was entitled to know. He'd always wondered what her reaction would be, imagining that she – so God-fearing – would be shocked by his revelation, so he was utterly taken aback by her lack of surprise.

The glossy, dark head bobbed. 'Yes, I know. They hanged her for it over Plympton and she spat on sacred cross.'

Elyas blinked. 'How do 'ee knowed, child?'

'Willy and Jane told me. They have cousins live over Plympton who reckon they were at the witch-hanging.'

Elyas looked annoyed. 'They Beckwitts should mind they own interference,' he growled, promising himself that next time he went to have his peekers sharpened by the smithy he'd have a few strong words with Jim Beckwitt. 'If'n 'ee knew 'bout thy ma, why didn't 'ee say summat, Kezzy?' he asked, scratching his head perplexedly.

'I thought mebbe 'twere secret because mama spat at cross,' she explained. Her eyes searched his face. ' 'Tis true, isn't it, Gramps! Willy says you were there and tried to save mama's life.'

'Ay, 'tis true. But I did more un tried to save her life. I tried to save her soul. Begged her, I did, to kiss cross and repent.' He drew his granddaughter closer to him, his old face softened by his deep and abiding love for her. 'Now I reckon this . . . swearin' on thy ma's soul don't hold on account her were *didekei*. Her were pagan, may Lord grant her peace!'

Kezzy took her time to digest this, her eyes dark, sad, troubled. A few silky tendrils of raven hair had been loosened by the wind from their braid and she brushed them impatiently back from her face. She supposed that if her grandfather said her oath didn't count then it must be so. Her sense of relief at being able to unburden herself made her gabble. 'Gramps . . . I seed Graeme and Morgenna being rude by Broadall Lake only Graeme made me swear not to say and now it ent Morgenna who has been got with child but Bethinda.'

Elyas looked bemused. He led her through the verbal maze again more slowly. 'Ye saw Graeme and Morgenna sparkin', ye say? Kissin' and cuddlin' and such?'

She gave him a withering glance. 'More than *that*, Gramps. Graeme did to Morgenna what William does to Pansy when we take her over to Lamb's Down to put calf in her. Only he lay on her, his face to hers.'

There was no mistake, thought Elyas half amused, she'd seen them all right! 'Graeme catched 'ee out peepin' and pryin', did he?'

Kezzy nodded. 'Made me swear on mama's soul not to tell.'

'And what be all this 'bout it being Bethinda and not Morgenna who's bin got?' he asked tapping out his pipe and putting it away.

She hesitated, lowering her eyes. There was nothing for it, she'd have to own up! 'I was behind vags listening to what sisters had to say.'

'Proper Miss Long Lugs, bain't 'ee?' he chided her and she had the good grace to turn pink.

'Those sisters have swapped their names. 'Tis *Bethinda* who says she's been got by Graeme, not Morgenna. Morgenna is the one with mole on her face, Gramps.'

'By the Lord Harry, you'm right, Kezzy!' he exclaimed, slapping his leg. He'd got his own doubts as to the father of the child but hadn't spotted that the sisters had actually switched places. He sat considering for a while, brow creased with the effort of concentration. It was plain what they were up to. Bethinda had been made pregnant by a boy other than Isaac but didn't dare claim the baby was Isaac's on account he hadn't lain with her. He'd be proper mazed to get home and find she'd foisted some by-blow on the Hammetts. Graeme, on the other hand, had lain with his Morgenna though she hadn't been got with child through it. So she switched names with pregnant Bethinda and they had set off for Eaglestone looking for a roof over their crafty heads. Chances were Graeme and Isaac wouldn't recall which twin was which when they got back, mused Elyas wryly. Nor were they likely to care providing each had a woman to warm his bed.

He got stiffly to his feet.

'Are you going to tell Morgenna and Bethinda you know, Gramps?'

'Nay. Least, not yet awhile. Do 'ee recall me sayin' as how 'twere sometimes best not to see a thing?'

'Yes. Like Grote being leader of flaskers.'

'Well, this be one of they sometimes. So not a word to thy pa or Jamie or un dame while us plays along wi' they pair o' slyboots. Now, we'm better get a-goin'. I smell mist a-comin' in quick from sea.'

She didn't follow him to the wagon. 'Gramps . . .?'

'Ay, Kezzy?' He turned back, shaggy brows raised questioningly.

'You are sure my oath don't count because mama was *didekei*?'

'Ye were right to tell me what 'ee did, Kezzy.'

Even now she wasn't totally convinced. 'Graeme said if I *did* tell then mama would be sent from heaven into hell.'

'He shouldn't have said such a thing,' sighed Elyas. He had an idea. He went back to where she still stood before the cross. 'Why don't we'm kneel down and tell God 'bout thy ma? Ask He to keep she safe in His hands?'

Kezzy's face shone. 'Oh, yes, Gramps! Let's pray for mama!'

And so, with the mist wafting about them, they knelt together and prayed for Ruke Hammett.

Chapter Thirteen

'Jim Beckwitt's shifted un anvil, Mr Hammett, zur.'

This observation was accompanied by a conspiratorial wink.

Elyas's informant was Old Jacob, a farmboy from Lamb's Down whose real purpose for being at Eaglestone was to carry a message from the farmer warning the Hammetts that Parson Creedy was out and about on the moor counting pigs, lambs and anything else that caught his eye. Another month or so and tithes would again be due.

Jacob was invited into the cottage and given a quart of cider and a slab of currant figgen for his trouble. The shrub reminded him of the kiddleywink – and Jim's anvil. When the smithy had an especially fine drop of moonshine going cheap in the Brandy Keg he shifted the position of his anvil to let his best customers know.

'Ent got money for moonshine,' was Elyas's grumbling response to Jacob's well-meaning intelligence. 'We'm scratchin' t'keep food in us bellies wi' Graeme and Isaac pressed.'

Old Jacob nodded sympathetically. ' 'Tis wisht poor them were took, zur. 'Tis terrible hard times we'm livin'. Anyroads, like I says, Jim Beckwitt's anvil be as squint as Lob's eyes if'n 'ee do fancy drop o' what un gentles be suppin' in by they big houses.'

He finished his cider and set off again on his errand of mercy. He'd another two small mines and half a dozen smallholdings to call upon. All those he warned would in turn send out a farmboy to their own neighbours so that word would quickly spread throughout the parish, thereby ensuring Parson Creedy's barn wasn't as full as he might have hoped come tithe collection.

June was set fair. Even the moor breezes were still which meant they weren't troubled with the sudden mists that sometimes swept in from the sea even in summer. It was exceptionally warm, which also meant that the blowing-house with its great peat-fuelled stone furnace was stifling. None the less, after Elyas and Huward had worked their long coore in the mine, they worked until dark smelting the ore with Kezzy and Jamie taking turns to work the bellows.

It was dusk on Friday, two days after Old Jacob had called at Eaglestone, when Elyas loaded the wagon with as many blunted tools as he could find with the intention of taking them to the smithy for sharpening. This was generally Jamie's chore, and although he pleaded to be allowed to go with his grandfather, Elyas was immoveable, saying firmly, 'Time 'ee were abed. I'll brook no sleepy-heads come sun-up.'

So he went alone. Because he had business to attend to which was more important than blunt peekers.

It was a bright, clear, starry night and Elyas wasn't by any means the only one abroad. They were coming from all around; farmhands to sharpen their scythes against the coming hay harvest; and itinerate tributers who'd not waste daylight doing what could be done at night when the price of tin was rising because of the war. The sound of metal set against the massive grindstone in the smithy's yard reached Elyas's ears some distance from Cornwood.

There were a handful of men in the yard waiting their turn at the grindstone. Jim Beckwitt was busy at his forge and anvil, shoeing a horse.

'Good evenin' Jim Beckwitt,' said Elyas dourly as he approached.

Jim looked up briefly to see who it was. 'How are 'ee then, Elyas Hammett?'

'Proper. Thyself?'

'Ay, proper.' Jim plunged the red-hot shoe sizzling into the trough of cold water. Through the pall of steam he saw that Elyas carried a sack out of which poked boyer drills and peekers. 'Thy boy Jamie could've brung they for grindin' first light when grinder bain't so busy,' he observed.

'Ay, could've,' responded Elyas non-committally.

Jim lifted the horse's hoof, bringing it through his legs, and fitted the shoe. He knocked in the nails with skilful strokes and dropped the hammer. 'Thirsty work. Makes 'ee as dry as tinning.'

'Ay. See anvil's squint.'

'Ay. 'Tis that.'

'You'm treatin'?' enquired Elyas.

Jim looked surprised at being asked such a thing when everyone knew that he never spared a drop of even his cheapest brew. 'Why should I be treatin', Elyas Hammett?'

'Reckon you'm owes me noggin' of you'm best cool, Jim Beckwitt. On account ye opened thy gob too wide 'bout un *didekei* gettin' hung for a witch. 'Twere for Hammetts to tell Keziah, not Beckwitts.'

Jim untethered the horse and gave it a smart slap on the rump to shift it and make way for another. 'Her would have heard soon 'nough, if not from I, then somebody else as saw her ma strunged up,' he said carelessly.

'Nevertheless,' protested Elyas shaking his head in a disapproving manner.

As they were talking, a steady stream of farmboys and tinners ambled through the yard, heading for the Brandy Keg. Jim would give each a sharp look in the bright light from the forge, checking that he knew them. It wouldn't be the first time Preventatives disguised as farmboys attempted to worm their way into a kiddleywink, though they were brave men who tried it since they risked being caught and handed over to flaskers who would certainly cruelly beat them. Then, depending on the ferocity of the gang, they might be bound and gagged and left suspended in a disused mine-shaft. Or dressed in a sailor's suit and dumped in

France on the next run to meet a bloody, gruesome fate at the hands of the French peasantry.

Elyas licked his lips. 'Still reckon 'ee owes me noggin.'

Jim Beckwitt said nothing until he'd finished his shoeing.

'If'n I give 'ee sup o' brandy will 'ee pay for 'nother sup?' he asked Elyas grudgingly.

Elyas frowned. 'Not sups, noggins.'

A sup would barely wet his throat. A noggin was at least a quarter of a pint if one of Jim's daughters was pouring.

Jim nodded. 'Fair 'nough. But ye bain't t'say . . . I've got bellies t'keep an' can't put food in they if'n I'm givin' away good brandy for nought.' He turned and stamped off. 'C'mon then if'n you'm a-comin'.'

Elyas dropped his sack of tools and followed Jim out of the yard and through the orchard at the back to where a cheerful buzz of voices came from a rough wooden shack. Jim rapped on the door. A tiny shutter covering a hole no bigger than a bung slid back and an eye was applied. On seeing it was the landlord, the owner of the eye was quick to drop the latch and swing open the door.

The inside was lit by three lanterns hanging from the rafters. Blue-grey smoke from more than two dozen clay-pipes hung in the air like a moor fog, making Elyas's eyes stream and starting him coughing until his lungs grew accustomed to it. A cock-fight was in progress with much squawking and flapping of feathers. Willie Beckwitt was taking bets, dropping the coins into his leather apron. He wasn't as old as Jamie, yet in seconds he could calculate the odds in his head. Hence the reason his father was prepared to pay Dame Rogers a weekly shilling to teach him. Willie's sister Jane, also an able pupil, took the money behind the counter in the kiddleywink while her mother and elder sisters served. Jim whispered to his wife, nodded to Elyas and went straight out again. Shortly, Mrs Beckwitt slid a tankard to Elyas across the rough-hewn plank supported on barrels.

'You'm to pay this time. Next be free,' she muttered in case he'd the audacity to drink his free one and slip away without keeping his part of the bargain.

He counted out the money and stood sipping his drink at the counter. Over the rim, he carefully scrutinised the faces of the other men. He knew most of them quite well, the rest, like the young grooms and gardeners and under footmen from the big houses, by sight. There was a small group of young men and boys from Fardle standing together watching the cock-fight. They cheered as the victorious bird, torn and bloodied from the loser's wicked spurs, was held aloft. Willie paid the winners, his small hands diving in and out of his apron pocket, a rapt expression on his face as he did his mental reckoning. Elyas was pleased to see that the Fardle boys received a handful of coins which they immediately passed across the counter to Jane in exchange for strong ale. Elyas sipped his noggin of brandy; content to wait until the last two cocks had met in bloody, crowning combat and the floor had been swilled of the slippery, crimson mess and sawdust strewn. By now the Fardle bunch were well in their cups and gathered around one of the wooden tables on stools and forms. Elyas requested his free noggin and carried it with him when he went to join them.

'Be yon seat took by elly chance, young zurs?' asked Elyas, pointing to an empty stool.

They made great play of looking under the stool and the table, even lifting the lids of their tankards to peer in exaggeratedly.

One of them, a cocky, good-looking young rascal – probably an under valet, Elyas thought, since he wore a plum-silk waistcoat which had presumably once belonged to his master – said slyly: 'Nay, old man, don't *look* like yon stool's been took. Unless 'tis by the pixies so we can't see them sittin' on it.'

They sniggered as Elyas carefully set his tankard down upon the table and lowered himself towards the stool. As he guessed would happen, one of the youths kicked the stool from beneath him. Protected by his thick corduroy breeches and long fustian waistcoat, he threw himself backwards in mock-surprise, feet in the air. How they laughed at the slow-witted yokel rolling about in the sawdust.

He took his time getting up and sitting on the stool. 'Reckon pixies done whip un from under I,' he said wide-eyed, and they hooted with mirth. When he picked up his tankard it was, as he suspected it would be, quite empty by now. 'Why, they pixies have supped my noggin!' he exclaimed in a voice filled with wonder and set them off again laughing and slapping their legs with delight at his foolishness.

But they weren't bad boys at heart and quickly refilled his tankard from their stoup of ale. In no time he was the best of friends with them and enjoying their confidences about the various voluptuous maidens employed at Fardle. The under valet, whose name was Horace Drigg, adopted a somewhat blasé expression as he boasted that he'd indulged in carnal rompings with all those fair enough to warrant his attentions.

'Giddaway!' Elyas sounded and looked incredulous.

Horace shot him an annoyed look. ' 'Tis true I tell you!'

Elyas still looked sceptical. 'What 'bout they nut-brown sisters? They twins . . . Morgenna and Bethinda?'

Horace couldn't resist this opportunity to brag about his prowess. He lounged with his back to the wall and set his tricorne – another trophy discarded by Lord Raleigh – at a rakish angle. He feigned a bored yawn behind his cuff. 'Oh ay, I've been very rude with them two. As luck had it, both at the same time.'

The circle of faces were filled with astonished envy. It was well known that the sisters were keen to be wed and to that end were freeish with their favours to likely swain. But both at same time! This was a quite shocking revelation.

Nothing now would do save Horace must describe every detail of his scandalous adventure. At first he pretended to be reticent, whetting their appetites with sly winks and leers. Then he leaned forward in a conspiratorial manner, beckoning them to do the same.

' 'Twere beginnin' of April. Them was walkin' in the garden and by chance so was I. Suddenly one of 'em starts crying, "Oh! Oh! 'Tis cramps in my legs!" Well, t'other sister didn't seemed to know what to do. So I helps the one what's hurtin' cross to summer-house and sits her down. "Best chafe thy legs," says I. "Ay, Horace, best 'ee does," says her . . . dunno which one her was to this day . . . alike as two peas in pod they are . . .' He winked. 'Dressed or stripped!'

'What happened next?' prompted one of the boys eagerly.

'I pulls up her skirts and chafes her legs.'

'Were her legs bare?'

' 'Course . . . what d'you think? Skivvies wear silk stockin's?' retorted Horace sarcastically. 'Anyroads, I rubs her legs all the ways to the tops. Then suddenly her sister starts cryin', "Oh! Oh! Oh! My legs!" So she sits and I chafe her legs same way. Then first sister says all sly like, "Why, Horace, you're better than a doctor, how can we ever repay you?" '

At this, the boys grinned lasciviously and elbowed each other.

'I'll wager 'ee soon found 'way, eh, Horace?' Elyas chuckled.

Horace took a long draught of ale and wiped his lips. 'I did an' all! Though mebbe I shouldn't speak open 'bout them on account they were of the virgin type at the time.'

This brought forth a collective gasp and a chorus of 'Tell us, do, Horace!' But he became reticent again – until they'd passed around his hat for ale money and refilled the stoups.

'Well now,' he said and they leaned forward again attentively. 'There I was, sitting 'twixt pair of them, an arm 'round each, and them giggling and blushing. Anyroads, one thing leads to 'nother and before I knows it we're as nekkid as Adam an' Eve!' This produced more gasps. Horace took another long draught and wiped his lips, relishing his bawdy tale. 'Soon as they saw my affair they were fighting and squabbling to be first. So I spins coin and one of 'em shouts "Heads", and down it come King George, so 'twere her. "Oh! Oh! Oh!," her started to cry when I got busy on her maidenhead . . .'

'Had her got un cramps 'gin?' asked one of the younger boys innocently and couldn't understand why they shouted with laughter.

Horace waited until they'd quietened down again before continuing. 'Ay, boys, I soon made women of them two maids. Near killed them with delight! Groaning and trembling like aspen leaves, them was. After, when I'd been rude wi' both, one of them says, "Horace, you're a real Adonis!" That's what she said . . .'

'You'm sure 'twere same sisters . . . that Morgenna and Bethinda?' interrupted Elyas doubtfully.

Horace's lip curled scornfully. 'Buck up thy brains, old man!' he said rudely. 'There's only *one* set twins up 'long Fardle, ain't there, boys?'

They nodded vigorously.

Elyas scratched his head. 'I don't understand it,' he muttered.

Horace winked at his friends: here was perhaps another chance of a bit of fun at the clodpate's expense. 'What's too much for thy dim wits, old man?' he asked sneeringly. 'Have you forgot what 'tis like to have stiff affair?'

'I be just remembering . . . they sisters called banns back'long April,' said Elyas thoughtfully. 'So what would they be a-wantin' wi' you'm stiff affair when them had boys of they own?'

'Oh ay!' exclaimed one of the others. ' 'Tis true what old un says! Them *were* 'spectin' to wed Hammett boys back'long spring.'

Horace scowled, annoyed at having his story questioned. And by some fool who dug in the earth like a mole to earn his bread! 'Shall I tell you why they preferred me to have their maidenheads? 'Cause they wanted to try a right randy fellow instead of they daft Hammett boys. They hadn't nouse t'keep out of way of press even though they're 'zemp.' he sneered. 'Good riddance to 'em, I say!'

Elyas's hand tightened on the handle of his tankard and it was all he could do to restrain himself from throwing the contents in Horace's arrogant young face. He set down his brimming tankard and rose, saying sourly: 'I'll bid 'ee good-night.'

'Finish thy ale, old man,' urged Horace, sorry to see this excellent butt of his jokes depart.

'I'll not drink any more of thy poison, Horace Drigg,' said Elyas curtly. 'Just be thankful I bain't called 'ee out round back o' shed an' muddied that fancy wesskit of yourn.'

Without another word, he stamped out.

Horace looked bemused. A silence had befallen the group; they were looking decidedly discomfitted. The mention of the Hammett brothers alerted their ale-sotted brains to something which hitherto had escaped them. *Their drinking companion was Elyas Hammett the tinner!* One of them sought to enlighten Horace, who'd the decency to look somewhat dismayed.

'Should've said who he were, come drinking our ale,' he groused. 'Anyroad, why should I recognise likes of *him*? I work for gentry . . . not diggin' in ground like a bleddy dawg!'

Recovering his bravado, he picked up Elyas's tankard and drained it. But as he did so, for all his show of bravado, he silently warned himself to stay out of Elyas Hammett's way if ever he happened across him in Cornwood. The old man might not be so peaceable when he'd had time to brood.

Elyas didn't brood on the parentage of 'Morgenna's' child. Having made a point of finding out that the sisters had a reputation among the boys at Fardle, he promptly put it to the back of his mind.

He sent Jamie in the wagon to fetch them and their few belongings on the last day of June as arranged. It wasn't a day too early if they were to be saved the gossips' barbs: the pregnant sister was beginning to swell beneath her apron.

Darkness was falling when they arrived at Eaglestone. Kezzy was in the kitchen preparing supper. Elyas and Huward came in from the blowing-house, hot, weary and dirty, to welcome the new arrivals. Elyas led them into one of the little bare back rooms.

' 'Tis clean straw in thy pallets,' he told them setting their basket down. He pointed. 'Bucket for slops.'

They looked around them in a disgruntled fashion. Even the kitchen skivvies lived like queens at Fardle compared to this.

'Us 'spected to be more comfortable,' complained 'Morgenna'.

'Us needs stool and chest each. And candlestick,' put in 'Bethinda' discontentedly.

Elyas was tired and his chest ached. He'd been digging and smelting since dawn with barely a break for mossle and croust. He wasn't interested in their grievances; especially since one of them was fallen, pregnant and penniless. Bluntly, he said: 'Count thyselves lucky you'm roof under un circumstances. Lady Raleigh would send 'ee to Workhouse, pack and vardle, an' no arguin'.'

' 'Tis fault of Graeme Hammett I'm under un circumstances,' she was quick to remind him with a peevish toss of her brown hair.

He sighed inwardly. Already he was beginning to regret their presence. How he disliked crabby females. He frowned at her. 'Which maid be you'm, did 'ee say?'

She began to answer without thinking. 'Beth . . .' Her sister stopped her with a fulminating look which didn't escape Elyas. 'I mean Morgenna,' she blustered turning red.

The real Morgenna attempted to cover the slip by saying, with a giggle, 'Us be so 'like, us gets properly mixed up ourselves sometimes. 'Tis on account folk keep callin' us by each other's names.'

Elyas grunted. 'Best call 'ee *both* Morgenna then,' he declared. He stamped out saying over his shoulder. 'Supper be on table. Make haste.'

Kezzy had been listening in the next room as she stirred the soup. When they were all seated and she was ladling the steaming vegetables and pieces of fat pork from the crock into their bowls, she said shyly to the sisters: 'There be a good stool and a chest and a proper oil-lamp in me and Jamie's room. They were Grandma Hammett's. You can take them in with you if you like. Me and Jamie don't mind, do we Jamie?'

Jamie didn't answer. He was more interested in sucking up the delicious, scalding liquid in his bowl than in fancy furnishings.

The sisters looked interested. 'Be there anything else us can have?' asked the real Morgenna.

Kezzy thought. 'There's a wood box with a pretty comb and a brass ring in it. And two big red shawls to cover the pallets.'

'Jamie's ma knitted they. Right fine they be,' remarked Huward.

Morgenna nodded. 'Bring all they things in to us after supper, girl. And anything more 'ee has in there would do us.'

'Her will not!' They all looked up at the sound of Elyas's harsh voice. Loweringly, he looked from one to other of the sisters. 'Ye can make do with what's there . . . or bring in own stuff. We'm givin' 'ee roof an' food in return for thy labour an' nawthin' else.'

Resentful and sullen, they began noisily to slurp their soup, eyes on the crock for second helpings.

Kezzy forgot her own soup as her dark eyes sought her grandfather's questioningly. She was puzzled as to why he wouldn't allow the sisters to have the things. They were, after all, grown-up women and she was just a maid. Surely that meant that they were more important than she was in the household?

Elyas's worn face softened as he smiled at Kezzy. 'Ye did right thing to offer, m'dear,' he assured her. 'But they things be yourn an' Jamie's,' he darted a warning look at the sisters from beneath his straggling grey brows, 'an' if elly should take un . . . well, that be stealin' to my way of thinkin'. We'm don't have much save cottage an' bal, but by the Lord Harry, we'm keepin' what we do have!'

It wasn't long before Elyas found out that the sisters were as lazy as they were greedy. They were always last up in the mornings and needed no end of tellings to stir themselves. Kezzy always had the range lighted and the oats on to boil by the time they came through yawning. They were slovenly about the home, never bothering to sweep the floors or carry out the ashes unless Elyas barked at them. He began to understand why Lady Raleigh had been so willing for them to leave her service.

But even Elyas had no true idea of just how idle they were. When he was in the mine, it was constantly, 'Kezzy, do this, Kezzy, fetch us that,' and, good-natured child that she was, she would trot off to do their bidding without a word of complaint. One day Graeme and Isaac would come back from the war and marry them so they became proper Hammetts, but until then, she felt duty-bound to make them as welcome as she could in her brothers' absence – even if in her heart she didn't much care for them. She'd always secretly longed for female company at Eaglestone but as such they were a wretched disappointment, the way they huddled and whispered together and left her out of their secrets.

Morgenna and Bethinda liked Kezzy less than she liked them. Partly it was because, mottled and ruddy-faced themselves, they were jealous of her clear, pale skin – as soft and fine as that of a gentlewoman. But then Kezzy always heeded Dame Rogers's advice and, young as she was, never went out in the sun without her old shady straw tied beneath her pointed chin. However, the sisters' dislike of the child went far deeper than mere jealousy; sometimes they caught her watching them and would find themselves involuntarily shrinking from her strange, slanting gaze.

'What her always starin' at?' the real Bethinda whispered to her sister as they lay awake one night on their pallets a week after they'd come to Eaglestone. 'Fair gives I creeps. Mebbe her pixie child wi' second sight.'

'Hush, in case pixies hear 'ee and swap thy own babbie for one of they fairy children. Them can do it! Even afore babbie be born!'

Morgenna's grim warning made Bethinda tremble in the dark. She pulled her cotton bedgown protectively between her thighs. As the baby had been made by way of this entrance she imagined that any exchange by the pixies would be achieved by the same route while she slept. She wished they were back in the big house, for all they had to share a room no bigger than the one they were in with a dozen other skivvies. She didn't like this lonely cottage and the barren moorland with its mischiefs; pixies and witches and hedgyboor monsters lurking behind every shrub to jump out at the unwary.

'I wish us hadn't come here,' she sighed unhappily.

Morgenna rose on one elbow and glared across at her sister's form, just discernible in the sullen light of the waning moon shining through the tiny, uncurtained window. 'Us would have been thrown out on parish if'n us hadn't been took in by Hammetts,' she pointed out in a low, sharp voice. 'So be mighty thankful!'

'Mebbe we'm better off in Workhouse,' whispered Bethinda bitterly. 'We'm no more'n unpaid skivvies here.'

Morgenna lay down again and pulled the coarse blanket up to her chin. There was little point in bickering with her sister. It was true that old man Hammett was always nagging them to work harder or complaining that they were greedy for having second helpings before the children had eaten first. But it was better by far than being sent as paupers to the Workhouse where life was truly harsh and food meagre and Bethinda's baby would be lucky to survive above three-month. Morgenna shuddered with dread at the thought of it. No, they'd much to be thankful for. Besides, if Bethinda hadn't been got with child by one of the Fardle boys they wouldn't be in this position. Morgenna rose on her elbow again.

'Be you'm 'wake, Bethie?'

'Mmmm . . .'

'Th'art *sure* babbie bain't Isaac's?'

She waited but Bethinda didn't reply. Then her sister's even breathing reached her ears. No matter: she'd already asked her sister the same question more than once and been told that if definitely couldn't be. That Isaac had proved himself a daft boy without the least idea of fun with maids. Oh, they'd played games of slapping and romping in the woods that last Sunday, Bethinda had admitted, and he'd become quite alloverish with excitement, chasing her and lifting her skirts to cut at her arse with a hazel switch. But no more than that, for he'd said it was wrong until they were properly churched and she hadn't liked to seem too yielding in case he thought her wanton.

Morgenna lay down again and closed her eyes. Kezzy's face with its solemn dark eyes and high white brow appeared behind her lids. Whether or not she was a pixie child, Morgenna sensed that Kezzy knew their secret. Her fingers went to her sun-coarsened jaw, seeking the tiny, brown protruberance. It was hardly noticeable among the freckles, but Kezzy's sharp eyes could well have spotted that she could thus be told apart from her twin.

Bethinda moved restlessly and muttered in her sleep.

Morgenna's brain, always more active than that of her slower-witted sister's, refused to let her drop off. It had been her idea that they trade places so as to pass off Bethinda's by-blow as Graeme's – since neither cared which brother they wed. It had all seemed so simple when they'd planned it at Fardle, stealing away into the grounds so they wouldn't be overheard. And, sure enough, Elyas Hammett had been easily taken in. *But would Graeme be so easily duped?* Morgenna began to feel less confident. Her fingers went again to the treacherous mole on her jaw. Supposing he returned and recognised her, Morgenna, as the twin who had introduced him to the joys of the flesh? He'd know Bethinda's by-blow wasn't his.

Their trickery would be exposed. They would be driven from *Eaglestone!*

Morgenna's heart began to hammer in her ribs as the threat of the dread Workhouse loomed large. A succession of terrible images presented themselves to her. Pauper women and children. Some so thin their bones seemed in danger of piercing their flesh, some whose tissue of rags hardly covered their nakedness, some in stained and torn finery of silk velvet. Women carrying sickly babies. Pregnant. Deformed. Blind. Consumptive women. Women with running sores. Pox-ridden. Lice-ridden. All cramped together, screeching and wailing and praying for more than a pail to piss in and a morsel of stale black bread.

'Please, God, no!'

Morgenna's anguished cry woke Bethinda. 'What? What?' she sat bolt up peering about her nervously in the gloom.

Morgenna had wakened herself. She was bathed in sweat, yet she shivered as if she'd a fever. ' 'Twere n . . . night-hags,' she said, teeth chattering.

'Shurrup thy chitterin'!' Elyas's muffled sleepy voice reached them.

Bethinda lay down and promptly fell asleep again but the memory of her nightmare was too vivid to allow Morgenna to do the same. Although she wasn't pregnant, it didn't enter her head to think only of herself. She could have stayed at Fardle until Graeme came home to marry her. Indeed, found herself another boy if he didn't survive the fighting. But nothing would have made her desert her twin in Bethinda's hour of need; bond like their's, born in their mother's womb, could never break. Morgenna was even prepared to go with her sister into the Workhouse – if God willed it and she could think of no certain way to avoid it.

The next day was Wednesday. As soon as Kezzy had eaten her hot oatmeal with buttermilk and honey, she put bread and butter and cheese in a mossle bag and set off down the moor to the village.

'What do her want with schoolin'?' sneered Bethinda. 'Givin' she fancy airs an' her nowt burra tinner's chield.'

Elyas looked up from his bowl to give her a cold look. ' 'Cause I say her's to be learned. An' I'll thankee to watch thy own interference while 'ee be under my roof,' he growled.

Bethinda looked sullen but didn't dare answer him back as she'd have liked to have done. It would be different when the boys came back and wed them so they were proper Hammetts, she told herself. Then they'd be four . . . five, counting the baby. Her hand went to her belly, smoothing the coarse stuff of her towzer possessively over her growing bulge. And any God's number of babies to come. Ay, then there would be changes at Eaglestone, and old man Hammett would have to learn to keep a civil tongue.

Elyas, Huward and Jamie didn't linger a moment after they'd finished their oatmeal, but pulled on their boots and set off for the mine. Elyas turned at the door.

'Get un pots scrubbed an' bread baked. Then get 'ee to washin' house and do what Kezzy showed 'ee. I'll have no lazy lollops sittin' 'bout when there be work t' be done.'

He stamped out after the others and shut the door with a bang behind him.

Bethinda pulled a face after him. 'Mean ol' goat! He'd skin turd for hide an' tallow!'

Morgenna went and fetched the oatmeal pot and they finished what was left, using their fingers to push the sticky, congealing mess greedily into their mouths. When they'd even scraped up with their nails the layer stuck to the bottom, Bethinda took the pot and the crocks to the brook and cleaned them. She remembered to fill the pot with water to be heated on the side of the slab throughout the day ready for the men to wash in at night, but slopped a great deal of it carrying it back so that it was barely two-thirds full. She also managed to drop and chip one of the bowls.

'What do I care?' she sniffed as she went in. 'They only got us here for pair o' lubbuts to do the rough work!' She saw that Morgenna had hold of the length of iron used to poke the fire and had it stuck in among the hot ashes. 'What 'ee 'bout, sister?'

Morgenna viewed the end of the poker, decided it wasn't quite red enough for her purpose and pushed it back in for a while longer. She straightened up and looked at Bethinda.

'I reckon that Kezzy has guessed us have swapped 'cause of babbie.'

'Didn't I reckon her were pixie chield wi' second sight?' exclaimed Bethinda worriedly. 'What'll us do? Tell Parson?'

Morgenna looked horrified. 'Nay, nay! If'n us says one word 'gin she, old man Hammett'll get proper mazed and send us to Workhouse. 'Sides, bain't be pixie sight . . . chield must have spotted mole as makes I Morgenna.'

Bethinda's eyes went to the tiny brown speck on her sister's jawline. For once her dull brain seemed to manage to follow Morgenna's way of thinking. 'S'pose Graeme has seed it? He'll know I bain't right one!'

Morgenna pulled the red-hot poker from the fire. 'Then better I don't have mole . . . better we'm two burn marks in same place.'

Bethinda's mouth dropped open. She looked doubtful. Then fearful. 'Won't it hurt terrible?'

Morgenna shook her head. 'Only need quick dab.' She suddenly lunged at Bethinda with her free hand, catching her by the hair, she jerked her head backwards. She touched the end of the poker to the skin in the approximate position of her mole. Bethinda gave a yell as a tiny wisp of smoke rose from the blistered flesh. Morgenna released her.

'There . . .'tweren't much for fussin' 'bout.'

Bethinda ran and splashed water from the pot on her face. 'God preserve us, that do smart!' she gasped.

'Now do it to I,' commanded Morgenna.

Bethinda took the poker gingerly. 'I don't like to . . .'

'Do it!'

When Kezzy got home from school she went straight to the wash-house. Morgenna and Bethinda were giggling together as they rather half-heartedly worked the timber block between them, packing the ore in the keeve ready to be skimmed. They started guiltily when Kezzy appeared. Morgenna was the first to recover herself.

'Well, if it bain't little Miss Scollard!' she sneered and dropped Kezzy a deep, mocking curtsy.

Kezzy said nothing. She tipped out a sack of stuff and began picking out bits of granite and stone, her small fingers flying industriously. The sisters put their heads together and began their silly giggling again.

Later, when the sky had darkened with the fall of evening, Kezzy crept out to sit with her grandfather on the low stone wall circling the Hammetts' sett. He usually sat there on a fine evening, quietly smoking his pipe and staring down the valley with unseeing eyes. For a while she sat silently, loath to interrupt his deep thoughts. There was something in the hunch of his shoulders and the dark, etched furrows of his face that told her he was thinking about Graeme and Isaac. She occupied herself with trying to capture one of the fluttering clothes-moths drawn by the pungent scent of smouldering tobacco. When she and Jamie were much younger, they called the moths 'piskies' because they came flickering like strange, darting shadows on the outside of the windows drawn by the light. She caught one and held it in her two hands, peeping in at it through a tiny gap between her thumbs. The big brown wings flailed helplessly. She opened her hands and let it go.

'Gramps . . .' She touched his arm. 'Morgenna and Bethinda have burned their faces so Morgenna hasn't got a mole any more. Now we don't know which of them is which.'

He looked up at the sky. It was darkening, the bright crescent moon and the stars had all but disappeared. 'Do look like rain,' he remarked and tapped out his pipe. A few drops fell, he rose and took her hand, leading her inside. 'Come 'long, chield, day has pissed on her heels.'

Kezzy didn't mention the marks on the sisters' faces again: obviously this was yet another of those occasions when it was best not to see something however plain it was.

Elyas had spotted the sisters' fresh burns at supper although he'd made no comment. The following morning, as he and Huward were shovelling stuff in the mine, he mentioned the twin marks to his son.

Huward stopped for a moment, resting on his shovel as he thought. He hadn't noticed anything different himself about the two women.

He shrugged and got on with his work again. 'Likely'd them'll say cinders from range did burn they.'

'In *zackly* same place?' snorted Elyas. 'Mighty convenient, that be, I'm a-thinkin'.'

'Well, them do be twins, Pa.'

Elyas spat. 'Them do be now.'

Chapter Fourteen

So it was Lammas – 1 August. The season of fairs and first fruits.

Elyas allowed Kezzy and Jamie to go with Farmer Lamb's Down to the Michaelmas Goose Fair at Tavistock to help sell his geese. They got back late in the evening, dirty and exhausted but thrilled to have been given a shilling each for their trouble. After a mouthful of food they fell on to their pallets and immediately fell asleep. However, they were up at cockcrow the next morning and set off before breakfast to pick 'hurts'. They knew just where to find the biggest, juiciest wortleberries and were back in little over an hour with their baskets full.

At Lamb's Down, the wife baked two dozen loaves from the first of the wheat. Some of them had currants and peel, sugar and spices in them, and she sent Old Jacob across to Eaglestone with two of these special loaves, with a shoulder of mutton and a crock of new butter. She'd also entrusted to Old Jacob a stained, fishy-smelling, torn copy of the *Western Daily Mercury* which had been used to wrap mussels with the instructions that he was to have Kezzy read it out whereupon he was to remember as much as he could.

' 'Specially 'bout they Frenchies,' said Old Jacob. 'Missus do want to know if war soon be done an' farmboys comin' back'long home.'

Elyas called Kezzy in from the washing-house. The sisters came, too, curious to know what was afoot, and since a newspaper was a rarity, Elyas didn't drive them back to work but sent for Huward and Jamie to come and join them so that they could listen to 'the reading' as well. 'But just you'm all t'keep thy gob-boxes shut,' he warned them.

Kneeling on a stool, Kezzy smoothed out the newspaper on the table, wrinkling her pointed little nose at the fishy smell. She began to read, haltingly at first, shy because she'd to demonstrate her ability to such a large audience, but with growing confidence when she found that she could make out very well the lines of black-printed words.

' "Landslip at Sidmouth . . ." ' she read.

Elyas grunted knowingly. 'Coast always be slippy 'twixt Exmouth an' Lyme. Elly they Dorset folk hurted?'

Kezzy read on. ' "The landslip began in the night of July the twenty-seventh and next day slight movements of the undercliff were noticed by a shepherd. A few fissures appeared in the fields above . . ." '

'What be they fishhoors when they be home?' enquired Huward interestedly.

'Them be cracks,' said Elyas. He tapped the newspaper. 'They noospapery folk don't write like 'tis proper spoke.'

Kezzy continued. ' "The face of the new cliff is most interesting as the tumbled fragments of varying sizes give the appearance of fairy castles and towers. It is likely that the upward movement was sim . . . sim . . ." ' Kezzy paused, took a deep breath and tried again. ' "Sim . . . ul . . . taneous with the downward shift of the land." '

This was beyond even Elyas. 'Read us somethin' else, chield.'

' "Smugglers sighted at Wembury . . ." ' This interested them. ' "On Sunday night last a small vessel was observed nearly on shore not far from Blackaven Cove . . ." ' Kezzy paused as the realisation of what she'd just read registered. '*Blackaven Cove . . .*' she breathed, looking up at her grandfather to see what effect this was having upon him. Knowing Steward Grote's involvement with smugglers, her shrewd little brain leeched on to this mention of a smugglers' vessel near Captain de Raddon's private cove.

Elyas shot her a warning look: the little they knew of Grote's nefarious doings was to remain their secret. 'Read on, m'dear,' he urged.

' "The lugger . . . the *Three Brothers of Plymouth* . . . was observed to drop twenty half-anchors weighted with stones over the ship's bulwarks when a revenue cutter approached. The *Three Brothers* was pursued round land to Gurnard's Head where the smugglers managed to escape the revenue aided by a lucky slant of wind. The contraband cognac was recovered." '

Elyas gave a rasping chuckle. 'There'll be a dry throat or two up'long Blackaven.'

'Listen to this,' said Kezzy excitedly. ' "His Majesty, in order to discover and bring to justice those concerned in this felony, promises his most gracious pardon to any one or more of the smugglers who shall supply the names of their accomplices so that they might be apprehended and convicted." '

Elyas gave a contemptuous snort. 'Pardon they, ay, then press they in navy most likely'd!'

'Be there elly writin's 'bout Frenchies?' asked Old Jacob.

Kezzy ran her eye over the rest of the page.

'Events at sea. The British and French war.'

'What do un say?'

' "A fleet was gathered under the command of Admiral Calder who on July the twenty-second fought an in . . . de . . . cis . . . ive action against the French Admiral Vill . . . Villen . . ." ' Kezzy shook her head, flummoxed by Villeneuve's foreign name.

'Never 'ee mind if'n 'ee can't make un out. What it do mean, is all they Frenchies be villains. But us knows that already,' said Elyas.

Kezzy read on ' "After the action, the French fleet ran for Corunna where they remain as at time of reporting . . ." '

'Where be Corunna?' piped up Jamie.

Their faces turned expectantly towards Elyas.

'Never you'm mind,' he said.

Kezzy was spelling out the next paragraph to herself. She drew their attention with a sudden squeal. 'Listen to this bit . . . "Admiral Lord Nelson first sailed for Cadiz with his squadron but, on finding the French were not in the south, sailed north to join Admiral Collingwood aboard the *Royal Sovereign*." '

The Hammetts looked at one another excitedly. The *Royal Sovereign*! Graeme's and Isaac's ship!

'Do it say 'owt else 'bout our boys' ship?' Elyas's voice was strangely gruff.

Kezzy's dark head bent over the newspaper again, her finger moving along the line as she read the words. ' "As soon as Emperor Napoleon received news of the French rout he recognised that the invasion of Britain had collapsed. It must however be remembered by our readers that Bonaparte still has an army large enough to overrun Europe." '

They looked at each other again, this time perplexedly. *What did it all mean? Was the war over*?

'Be that all it says 'bout Frenchies?' Old Jacob wanted to know.

Kezzy nodded.

There was a silence, eventually broken by Morgenna. 'Be they boys a-comin' home then, Mr Hammett?' she ventured to ask, her fingers going involuntarily to the small pink scar on her jaw.

'That remains to be seen,' was all Elyas was prepared to say on the subject.

Old Jacob went and got his crook in readiness to set off back across the moor. 'That remains t' be seen,' he repeated, memorising the phrase so he could repeat it to the missus by way of an answer as to whether the pressed men would soon be back at work in the fields. He pointed at the newspaper. 'Reckon maid can keep un . . . bain't no use t' Lamb's Down save for wrappin' fish.'

Kezzy had folded the newspaper ready to hand to him. It hadn't entered her mind that she might be allowed to keep such a wonderful thing. Apart from a bible which had belonged to Grandma Hammett and a prayer-book which had been Betsy Hammett's, she hadn't any reading matter and the newspaper was filled with all sorts of interesting things.

'Please, can I, Gramps?' she asked him, her dark eyes pleading to be allowed to accept the gift.

He nodded without hesitation. 'Ay, best 'ee do keep it . . . seein' as how you'm can read it,' he told her and he couldn't keep the pride out of his voice.

Kezzy's eyes glowed with pleasure and she hurried off to put the precious newspaper under her pallet to read later.

Old Jacob bid them farewell and went on his way, muttering to himself. 'That remains t' be seen . . . that remains t' be seen . . .'

Huward and Jamie had already returned to the mine. Elyas wouldn't be long in following them. He scowled at the sisters as they fiddled with this and that in the cottage rather than return to the toil of the blowing-house with Kezzy.

'Mebbe Lammas but bain't no tinners' holiday,' Elyas remarked coldly.

Morgenna pointed at her sister's swollen belly. Sullenly, she said: 'Can't 'ee see her bain't fitty for heavy work?'

Elyas scowled at her for daring to cross words with him. 'No call for 'ee to dawdle. You'm ent been got. Anyroads, which be you'm?'

'Bethinda,' said Morgenna after only the slightest pause.

'Humph! Ain't so easy to tell 'ee 'part now'days,' said Elyas dourly. His eyes moved to the real Bethinda and she flushed guiltily as he ran a speculative eye over her spreading girth. 'Ent twins,' he said disappointedly. 'When will 'ee pup?'

'October . . . 'bout middle d'pendin' on moon's change,' she mumbled.

'An' 'ee reckons 'tis boy chield?'

Morgenna answered for her sister. 'Can't *swear* it 'til un born, but us hung mutton bone 'bove door an' Ol' Jacob were first under it so 'tis most likely'd boy chield.'

'Best be,' said Elyas darkly. 'Hammetts only breed boys.'

Before she could stop herself, Morgenna snapped: 'Then what 'bout Kezzy? Or be they stories 'bout her bein' witch's by-blow true?'

Bethinda gasped audibly at her sister's reckless impertinence. She went and stood close to her sister as Elyas's face lost the little colour it had and his eyes kindled dangerously. The instant she said it, Morgenna regretted it: before now she'd got his monkey up for saying less and found herself with an extra coore to work at the tin.

Yet, the expected storm wasn't forthcoming. Elyas's voice was harsh but controlled as he said: 'Just you'm pray 'tis boy chield. I'll not feed elly more female mouths, hear?'

He went out and banged the door.

Bethinda clutched Morgenna in alarm. 'What if 'tis girl?'

Morgenna's face was white. Bluntly, she said: 'Then 'tis my guess he'll pack us off to Workhouse.'

Bethinda began to cry. 'I'll not go to that terrible place. I'll go in river first an' take babbie with I!'

The baby was a girl. Born on 21 October 1805, just ten days before Kezzy's ninth birthday on All-Hallows. It was, anyway, a day far more memorable for the death of the great Admiral Lord Horatio Nelson than for the birth of the puny, ill-tempered, red-haired child Bethinda produced with little difficulty early in the morning. The day would ever after be known as Trafalgar Day, although those who lived on the moor hadn't yet heard of the momentous sea-battle off Cape Trafalgar.

Later in the day it was Dame Rogers, having heard of the British victory from her friend Mrs de Raddon, who came hurrying up the moor track as fast as her pony could pull her to share her exciting news with the Hammetts.

She could hear the baby's piercing yell, drowning even Wart's barking, as she approached Eaglestone. 'Oh dear,' she said to herself, feeling a surge of sympathy for the unfortunate mother and child. Kezzy had whispered to her after school that Elyas was greatly disappointed it wasn't a boy to take Graeme's place and was refusing to even acknowledge his new 'grandchild'. 'That's because it isn't really Graeme's . . .' Kezzy had begun to say but bit her lip at the look of astonishment on the schoolmistress's face, remembering that her grandfather wanted it kept secret even from the dame.

Kezzy wasn't at school that day. She and Morgenna came from the washing-house, wiping their hands on their towzers, to greet the dame. They saw immediately that the woman's eyes were unusually bright; also that her usually immaculate grey hair was wispy beneath her straw bonnet – the strings of which were tied any old how.

'Fetch your grandfather and father, Kezzy . . . I have important news! It most certainly concerns your brothers,' she quavered.

Kezzy ran to pull on the bells hanging in the mouth of the mine.

They were busy below, so Elyas sent Jamie up to see what the signal was for. He began climbing up the slanting ladders. Kezzy spotted the halo of light which was the candle set in clay atop his hat and shouted down to him: 'The dame's here. Tell Gramps, quick! 'Tis 'bout Graeme and Isaac!'

So quickly did he descend the ladders again, that Jamie got splinters in his hands, but he didn't care, and in a few moments the three of them emerged blinking in the bright autumn sunlight. Elyas went straight across to the dame without removing his hat and snuffing the candle. She saw that his eyes were ablaze with hope and immediately regretted making so much of the scant news she'd heard, thrilling though it was.

'I can't tell you exactly about your boys,' she had to admit and some of the hope faded in their faces. Hastily, she went on: 'But what I *can* tell you is this . . . the war with France is over! All pressed men are to be discharged to return to their homes if they so wish. Lord Nelson, God rest him, has won the day for us!'

'*God rest him*, did 'ee say, mistress?' asked Elyas, shocked.

She coloured. To speak of the hero's death in such a cheerful manner was unbecoming to her. She schooled her face to a suitable sadness. 'Alas, yes. His Lordship perished . . . killed by a slug fired from the rigging of a French ship. Fortunately, he lingered long enough to hear of the victory.'

So astonished were they all, no one thought to invite the dame inside the cottage in the proper manner but kept her standing in the yard holding the bridle of her own colt. They stood silently. Then suddenly Elyas let out a loud whoop and sent his hat flying in the air, candle and all. Grabbing the startled dame about the waist he twirled her, skirts flying, in a wild, exultant jig.

'The boys be a-comin' home! The boys be a-comin' home!' he sang.

The others were quick to join in, clapping and shouting and stamping their feet with joy because Graeme and Isaac would soon be home. Wart barked furiously, diving to and fro among the whirling bodies. It was as if months of worry and sorrow had given way to a mad outburst of ebullience. None danced more high-spiritedly than Kezzy. She leapt and bounced and hopped through the mud, not giving a care for her boots or the hem of her skirt, her face aglow and her eyes sparkling, rejoicing because their prayers had been answered and her beloved brothers were coming home.

The furore brought Bethinda to the cottage door, her baby in her arms wrapped in an old shawl. The child was still giving forth a loud, thin wail. Frightened by the commotion, her cries increased to ear-jarring shrieks.

It was the dame, breast heaving, bonnet swinging from its ribbons, who brought them to order, 'Cease, Mr Hammett!' she begged, pulling away from him. 'I'm quite giddy and out of breath!'

He released her, out of breath and wheezing himself. 'Ay, fair takes it out of un, good step-dance,' he chuckled. His jovial air evaporated and his brows knitted over his beaky nose in a scowl when he spotted the child. 'Why she always roarin' like hedgyboor?'

Dame Rogers experienced a similar surge of pity to the one she'd felt on arrival. She knew – because Beth Hammett had told her once – that so far as Elyas was concerned baby girls roared like monsters, whereupon boy babies 'aired their lungs just like they aught'.

'The mite is your grandchild, Mr Hammett,' she reminded him quietly, with just a hint of censure in her voice.

He swivelled his pale lachrymose eyes and stared hard at her for a moment, as if weighing whether she was probing because she suspected all was not as it seemed between the Hammetts and the sisters.

Dame Rogers was suspicious: Kezzy's slip had seen to that. Also, she'd heard rumours about the sisters since they'd left Fardle. The news that one of them had given birth to a daughter, allegedly Graeme Hammett's, had soon percolated through the village. It was whispered by those who claimed to know what went on at Lord Raleigh's seat that both sisters had been exceedingly free and easy-going with the menservants. Some even went so far as to suggest that if the baby was a Hammett it would be the first miracle seen on the moor.

The dame's prim features told Elyas nothing about what was going on in her head. He gave the howling child another scowl. 'Take un in, will 'ee?' he ordered Bethinda and she immediately disappeared inside and shut the door. He turned again to Dame Rogers. 'Babbie be proper sickly . . . probably won't last.'

'Then all the more reason to have her christened this Sunday. Would you like me to have a word with Parson Creedy?'

He looked her straight in the eyes. 'There'll be no baptisin' 'til Graeme comes home to see to un, mistress,' he said, and there was a note in his voice warning her not to interfere with Hammett family matters.

She bowed her head briefly in acceptance of that. Then she gave a faint smile. 'I brought some things for the child . . . cottons and such. Necessities, you understand? Perhaps I could . . .' She glanced towards the cottage.

He took the hint. 'Oh ay, mistress. Take they inside an' thankee kindly. Tell she t'make 'ee mug o' cream tea 'stead o' sittin' 'bout playin' nanny games wi' babbie.' He clapped his hands smartly together. 'Rest o' 'ee back t'work! Plenty time for jawin' when we'm bone-weary.'

They obeyed immediately and went off grinning hugely. Nothing, not even hard work, could dull their sense of happiness. They still couldn't get over it. Pressed men to be released . . . Graeme and Isaac home, God be praised!

'You'll be a married woman soon,' remarked Kezzy to Morgenna as they worked the wooden block, toasing the tin for the furnace.

Morgenna stopped to wipe the sweat from her eyes with a strong, brown forearm. She didn't miss the flickering glance Kezzy gave the scar on her jaw where once she'd had a mole and her fingers went to it, touching it almost lovingly.

'Ay,' she said smugly, 'that us will . . . then there'll be some changes for better 'round Eaglestone.'

Kezzy looked uncertain. 'What sort of changes?'

'That's for I to know and you'm to guess!' she said mysteriously. Then she smiled across the keeve at the child.

It was the sort of smile Kezzy didn't particularly like so she didn't smile back at her.

There was still no sign of the boys a week later.

The Hammetts spent the time they weren't working gazing down the valley, fully expecting that any day they would see two figures making their weary way home. Then a dense fog closed in blocking out the landscape. It remained for three days and three nights, and throughout that time the usually economical Elyas kept a big candle burning in the window to guide the boys home should they come.

'Well now, 'tis while since them were up'long moor . . . mebbe got they foolselves piskie-led,' he rationalised this waste of good tallow, for waste it turned out to be since Graeme and Isaac remained disappointingly absent.

When the fog lifted, Elyas hitched the colt to the wagon and set off down the moor for Plymouth to learn what he could of the *Royal Sovereign* and her crew.

It was late in the day by the time he'd found cheap stabling at the top of Anchor Street. There were many more people on the streets than there had been on his last expedition to the town and he thought it prudent to pay a couple of shillings to ensure no one made off with his pony and backboard.

His footsteps took him straight to the harbour. Even though it was almost dark and the market stalls at the entrance had been packed up for the night, there was a busy toing and froing of people. Fisherman, sailors, officers, youngsters staring out to sea in wonder at the many big ships anchored in the Sound, their yards hung a-cockbill as a mark of respect for a dead hero. One or two had lamps burning along the quarter-deck, dipping and blinking with the swell. The people on the quays were also in mourning for Lord Nelson; they spoke in muted tones, even the usually raucous crowd of bumboat women who were kept busy with so many ships in the bay. Elyas searched their weathered faces for the friendly woman with whom he'd struck up an acquaintance previously, but they all looked the same in their old oilies and men's shapeless woollen hats.

Spotting his interest in the women, one of the parading dockyards trulls sauntered up to Elyas.

'I got whiter meat on me than those ol' bloaters, darlin',' she informed him in an inviting tone and with a swish of her cheap, blue velveteen dress.

He paused to squint at her in the half-light, not sure what she'd said since she wasn't from those parts. Not even from Cornwall. 'Where 'ee from, mistress?' he asked curiously.

She was tickled at being addressed as 'mistress' and struck what she thought was a haughty pose, one hand to the yellow ringlets at the nape of her neck, the other catching up her skirt to show a grubby ankle in an old, buttoned shoe. 'La, sir, I'm from the court of King George hisself!' she tittered.

Elyas still didn't catch what she'd said. 'S'pose you'm here for the fish,' he said, unable to think what a 'foreign' female would want to come to Plymouth for.

She gave a shriek of laughter, revealing black teeth and a yellow-coated tongue. 'Lord luv us! Do I *look* like a bleedin' fishwife, darlin'?'

He had a closer look. Her neck and the ample bosom rising from her low bodice weren't overly clean. And she had one or two running pustules which suggested she carried what was called the 'French Pox', a painful disease for those men who were unfortunate to catch a dose. But she smelled sweet – like musk roses – so she was certainly no fishwife. He was about to apologise for his mistake, blaming the poor light, when a group of sailors lurched up to them. Elyas caught a strong whiff of rum as he was rudely elbowed aside.

'Who be you'm a-shovin', boys?' he asked testily.

'Move over, grey-beard,' said one, 'let dog see rabbit!'

'Ay,' agreed another, 'we want more'n pass time o' day wi' yon doxie. We've been at sea more'n six months fightin' for King and country.'

'We got salt needs blowin', matie' added a third coarsely.

'Which ship 'ee from, boys?' asked Elyas eagerly.

'*Revenge*.'

'Were ye wi' our Nel, God rest him?'

The question seemed to sober them.

'That we were. And never was there such a battle as Trafalgar!' said the first sailor proudly.

'An' where be this Trafalgy then?' asked Elyas interestedly.

The sailor's brows shot up. 'Haven't you heard all 'bout it?'

Elyas shook his head.

They stared at him in astonishment, hardly able to believe that there could be anyone in Plymouth who hadn't heard all about the great British victory outside of Cadiz, off Cape Trafalgar. Returning sailors were packing the taverns, happy to recount their experiences to anyone prepared to buy them a noggin to wash the battle smoke from their throats. Suddenly the yellow-haired trull was forgotten as they swarmed around the moorman, all talking ten to the dozen in their eagerness to relive their various moments of glory for ears as yet unenlightened. From *Revenge* they might be, but they all seemed to have a brother, cousin or uncle aboard Lord Nelson's flagship, *Victory*. All of which kin were actually present when the great man fell. He didn't say so, but it occurred to Elyas that it was a miracle a slug had found his lordship considering the number of bodies around him.

The French and Spanish ships numbered thirty-three against Nelson, who could muster twenty-seven. He'd shown his brilliant seamanship when, instead of breaking the enemy line at one point, he attacked it at two – with *Victory* leading one squadron and Admiral Collingwood in the *Royal Sovereign* leading the other.

Elyas grew excited on hearing this. 'That be my grandsons' ship, that be! *Royal Sovereign*!' he declared, bursting with pride.

That silenced them for a moment. They hadn't realised he'd kin at Trafalgar, and aboard Collingwood's ship. One of them asked: 'Volunteers or pressed, cully?'

'Pressed.'

The sailor curled his lip slightly as he straightened his back and stuck out his chest. 'Volunteers, us. Wanted t'do our duty,' he declared loftily.

Elyas didn't waste time taking issue with him over this inference that pressed men were inferior to volunteers. He was too impatient to hear about the *Royal Sovereign*.

'What happened next?' he prompted and started them off again vying to tell him.

'We attacked under full sail. First time ever . . .'

'Crashed clean through their huddle and peloton, the Frenchie swabs!'

This unusual tactical move ordered by Nelson had apparently left isolated the van of Villeneuve's fleet of five ships, stopping them from so much as striking a blow while the centre and rear were being raked and sunk by British gunfire. The *Victory* ran aboard *Redoubtable* stoving her lower ports but, as the British boarders drew cutlasses and ran up the rigging, they were felled by riflemen in *Redoubtable*'s mizen.

'Tyrolese, my brother reckons. Dead-eye shots every one of 'em, drat their livers!' said one of the sailors half-admiringly.

It was one of these sharpshooters who had picked out Lord Nelson in full uniform on the quarter-deck and had lodged a bullet in his spine. The battle was far from over, however. Despite the surprise opening manoeuvre on the part of the British, the French guns battered them remorselessly. The decks ran with blood and the dead were pitched unceremoniously overboard. By three o'clock in the afternoon it was all over bar the mopping up. Nineteen enemy ships had been captured, the rest sunk or disabled. Not a mast was left in the French or Spanish flagships. Lord Nelson had lived just long enough to hear of the victory.

One of the sailors pulled up a striped trouser leg to show Elyas a flesh wound on his calf. 'Took a caulk, I did. Lucky not to have lost whole bloomin' leg!'

Some of the others had similar small trophies and the trull, joined by two or three others, gathered around for the free show, gasping and

'Oooohing' and 'Ahhhing' at the gore while flirting with their eyes and running determined fingers along the Jack Tars' sinewy limbs with an eye to business. Night had fallen. The sailors and their trulls began to drift away, laughing raucously, arms linked.

Elyas called after them. 'What 'bout *Royal Sovereign*? Where be her docked then, boys?'

One of the sailors turned, remembering the old man had kin at Trafalgar. 'She's at Chatham, cully,' he called. He was dragged away by a giggling whore old enough to be his mother.

'Chatham,' repeated Elyas to himself. That was probably the reason why the boys hadn't managed to get home yet. Got to wait until the navy released them.

The sailor disentangled himself from the purposeful clutches of the trull and walked back to Elyas. His expression was self-conscious. He wasn't above Isaac's age.

'Are your grandsons not home then, mister?'

'Nay.'

'Should be.' He chewed his lower lip, as if he was trying to choose the right words to express what was in his mind. 'You see . . . tars is all on shore-leave . . . or been sent home proper if they was pressed. I just thought . . . well, there were lot of men wounded an' killed on *Royal Sovereign* . . .'

His voice faded awkwardly. Not a muscle moved in Elyas's face.

'How do I find out?'

'They . . . post list of dead an' wounded outside each naval base.'

Elyas nodded. He moved to go, then, as an afterthought, took out a crown piece and flipped it to the delighted sailor, saying, 'Here, boy, you'm blow thy salt on Elyas the tinner. You'm done thy duty by us all.'

'God bless you and yourn, tinner!' He touched the brim of his hat to Elyas. He stood gazing after the stooped, bow-legged figure. 'Hope you find your boys, mister!' he called.

Elyas didn't turn round.

That night Elyas spent the night in the same copse outside Plymouth as before. He lay on the mossy bank, gazing up through the branches just as he had then. Only then the branches had been budding with the promise of spring, and a bright moon and stars had shimmered through the trees. Now the branches were stark and bare, like long, skeletal fingers against a sullen grey November sky.

Dead men's fingers! thought Elyas. *Reaching and clawing their way up to Heaven from a watery grave!* And he wept. Sobbing as he hadn't done since he'd laid his darling Beth in the cold, dark, lonely earth.

Kezzy should have gone to school that day but she'd persuaded her father to let her stay at home so she'd be there when Elyas got back, hopefully with good news of the boys. She spent the forenoon cleaning ore alone in the washing-house – the sisters having taken the chance offered by Elyas's absence to stay by the fire drinking hot cream tea.

Kezzy didn't care that they were shirking their coore. She much preferred her own company. She didn't, however, mind the baby. She quite liked her. And the baby liked Kezzy. The moment she leaned over the old threshing basket in which the mite lay – Elyas having refused to allow the sisters to bring the Hammett cradle from the barn where it was stored – the mewling stopped as if by magic. Convenient though this was when a little peace and quiet was required, Bethinda would have preferred Kezzy to keep away from her baby.

'Her puts evil-eye on she, I reckon,' she grumbled to Morgenna, but for once Morgenna refused to support her sister's fanciful notion. Evil-eye or nay, anything was better than the constant crying.

The open front of the three-walled shelter faced down the valley so Kezzy worked standing in such a position that she could watch for the wagon. It was drizzling. And a chill wind blew in the rain soaking her thick jersey, an old one of Isaac's. She began to shiver and her hands were so numb she could hardly pick out the 'deads' from the heap of stuff in front of her. A rumble of thunder came from the direction of Eagle Tor, followed by a flash of orange light and a louder roll of thunder. Even Wart took himself off to the barn, his tail between his legs. But Kezzy remained at her post, watching and waiting.

The storm quickly passed and around mid-day the rain stopped. Far below, Kezzy spotted a tiny, moving speck. She raced to the cottage and stuck her head in.

'Boil up some stew for mossle! Gramps is coming!' she said excitedly. She withdrew and dashed to tug on the bells hanging in the mine. 'Gramps is coming!' she shouted down into the deep, dank hole and her voice echoed against the walls.

They gathered in the yard, standing in a silent group as Elyas reined in, bringing the wagon to a squeaking halt. He remained sitting on the box, his shoulders drooping, his sopping grey beard on his chest, as if he was too weary to get down.

It was impatient Bethinda who broke the silence: 'Well, when they comin' home then?'

Elyas didn't move. And at that moment, with the same cold dread gripping their hearts, they knew that Graeme and Isaac weren't coming home. Not ever.

The Fardle steward reluctantly took Elyas to the little room adjoining the pantry that he used for study, prayer and private meetings such as this. Elyas came straight to the point. Since his grandsons were listed as dead, the sisters were surplus to requirements. Particularly as one had an illegitimate daughter – not fathered by either of the Hammett brothers – and they were little more than useless about the cottage and in the washing-house. In short, he wanted rid of them.

'They ain't coming back here!' said the steward in alarm. 'Her Ladyship won't have it!'

Elyas professed himself not to be in the least bit surprised at that. 'I bain't never known lazier pair o' lollops! An' eat!' He paused, frowning, as another grievance began to form. 'An' what 'bout this stitchin' trade them was s'posed to do for Her Ladyship? Don't see elly o' that bringin' in shillin's as were promised.'

'Her Ladyship is newly returned from London with any number of new gowns so don't require their needles at present.'

Elyas snorted. 'An' likely'd her never shall, cully!'

The steward looked annoyed. 'Are you suggesting . . .?'

'I'm suggesting, Master Steward,' interrupted Elyas, stabbing the table with a grimy finger, 'that this 'ere stitchin' trade 'twere yarn to get they pair o' wantons settled wi' my boys.'

The steward looked shocked. 'God Almighty, Her Ladyship wouldn't stoop to such a connivance!' was his fervent assurance.

'Never you'm mind Almighty, her be a woman, bain't her?'

Elyas sat with his elbows on the table while the steward spluttered forth about his 'wretched and contemptible insolence' among other scathing condemnations. When he paused to draw breath, Elyas said: 'Lookee here, friend. Mebbe there be a bit o' the right coloured stuff in it for 'ee if'n 'ee helps I out on this occasion.'

The steward had his mouth open to continue his castigation but shut it with a snap. His eyes glinted. 'What have you in mind?'

Elyas told him.

Horace Drigg, the under valet, was sent for. He wasn't wearing his fancy waistcoat and jaunty tricorne, but his sombre Raleigh livery. Neither did he swagger. His young face was anxious at being summoned urgently before the steward, and seeing Elyas Hammett he visibly quailed.

The steward surveyed him severely. 'Now Drigg, Mr Hammett says as how you've been bragging in Brandy Keg as how you pleasured yourself with Morgenna and Bethinda while they were employed here.'

Horace swallowed hard. He was no longer the cocksure braggart and he was sweating with nerves. 'I didn't mean no harm. 'Twere the ale talkin' . . .' he began to whine.

Elyas wasn't having that. He leaned forward, a look of contempt on his face. 'By the Lord Harry, be you'm a-sayin' all un talk 'bout legs an' zummer houses were load of ol' ledden, boy?'

'Ay . . . no . . . leastways . . .' Horace stopped and bit his lip.

'Speak out, boy, let's have truth now!' commanded the steward.

Horace swallowed hard. His reputation as a rakehell was at stake. To deny the sisters would bring into question all his other tales of procuring and dispensing pleasure with which he kept the other male servants entertained at night around the kitchen hearth. The steward never deigned to join them, but he would ensure Horace Drigg's admission was well published. And that, thought Horace with a sinking feeling, would make him a laughing stock! No, he'd gone too far to turn back. Besides, the Hammett boys were lost at sea and no danger to him. And as for Elyas Hammett . . . well, if the oaf was looking to restore the sisters' reputation, he'd not help him at the cost of his own.

He straightened his shoulders, adopted a defiant attitude. 'I had no complaints from twinnies 'bout my stiff affair!' he bragged.

Elyas and the steward exchanged a triumphant look.

Horace fell silent. He'd steeled himself to be challenged; to be called an out and out liar. Yet, here was Elyas Hammett actually grinning at him in full approval!

'How old are you, Drigg?' the steward asked.

Horace blinked, surprised by the question. 'Seventeen . . . eighteen come January.'

'Old 'nough,' said the steward, and Elyas nodded.

Horace looked uncertainly from one to the other. 'For what?'

'Why, to be wed to mother of your child, boy,' the steward told him sternly.

Those servants working in the kitchens could hear the angry voices behind the closed door of the steward's room, mainly that of Horace Drigg who, in a high-pitched, querulous voice, was seemingly refusing to comply with whatever it was being demanded of him. Far from wise since the steward was a martinet with the power to dismiss any servant without reference to master or mistress. The altercation grew very loud indeed and those listening stopped what they were doing to strain their ears in an effort to discover what it was about.

'You'll do as you're told, Drigg, or be dismissed without a character!' the steward was heard to threaten and that seemed to bring the under valet to his senses as his voice became an almost imperceptible mumble.

In the room, he was close to tears at the thought of an enforced marriage to Bethinda and what his father would have to say about it. He was the youngest son of a good family, Dorset horse-breeders, and might have expected to marry at least a farmer's daughter. To declare his intention to marry a skivvy . . . Horace trembled at the thought. He would be forbidden the family home. Cut off without even a youngest son's expectations.

'No good 'ee blubberin',' growled Elyas. 'Should've thought o' consequences when 'ee started playing' wi' un legs. Now, I'm not a hard man, even tho' them sisters tried t'pull fast un an' pass thy by-blow off as our Graeme's. So I'll tell 'ee what I'll do. If'n ye stand up like man an' admit babbie be yourn, I'll make 'ee weddin' present of . . .' He hesitated. He'd come with the intention of offering twenty-five pounds, but that was before he'd discovered how cooperative the steward was prepared to be in return for a guinea or two. '. . . of ten pounds.'

Horace sniffed and dashed his hands across his eyes. He forgot the steward was there and flew into a resentful rage. ' 'Tis a damned insult! I earns that in a year, ay, an' more!'

'You'll not be earning it for much longer if'n you don't watch your tongue, Horace Drigg,' warned the steward. He stroked his jaw. 'Ten pounds . . . hmmmmm . . . Of course there's her sister to consider. They won't be parted, those two.'

'True 'nough,' agreed Elyas. He'd no wish for the spinster sister to remain at Eaglestone after her sister had married.

Horace gasped. 'I won't, Goddamn you! I'll kill myself!'

Elyas chuckled. 'Nay, nay, no need for that talk. Strappin' boy like thyself . . .' He gave a knowing wink. 'From what ye had to say down'long Brandy Keg, you'm already had carnals wi' *both* un merry-legs down'long zummer house.'

They settled for twenty-five pounds.

Bethinda made no objection to the marriage. Nor did Morgenna, since she was provided for in the arrangement. Moreover, it meant that they no longer need fear the Workhouse. When they'd time to mull it over, they agreed that things had turned out quite for the best as they were a deal better off with an under valet than a lowly tinner.

All being well, as Horace's dependants they would live in a cottage on the estate. Or, if none were vacant, they could rent one near the village. Either way, they could take in sewing to supplement his wages so they would live fairly comfortably, all things considered. Far better than at desolate Eaglestone, high up on the windy moor.

So Bethinda and Horace were married in the little chapel at Fardle. Horace, ashen-faced and utterly miserable, looked absurdly young beside his hefty, kipper-haired bride. Morgenna was in attendance upon her sister, and a friend of Horace's, a young footman, stood up for him as groomsman. Of the Hammetts, only Kezzy was there, and then only because she was needed to keep the baby quiet during the service. Afterwards, the wedding party gathered around the font and the newlywed's daughter, now legitimate, was christened Victory Morbeth Drigg.

Outside, in the hoary November air, while the wedding party bethought themselves of their manners and thanked Parson Creedy for coming from the village to officiate, Kezzy cuddled Victory for the last time. It was she who'd suggested the name, in honour of the late admiral who Dame Rogers called 'our saviour on earth', and that morning, she had begged a shilling from her grandfather that she might press it in the little hand for luck.

Although still pale and delicate-looking, the baby had gained considerably in size and weight during the month since her birth, and as the little body had grown, so had Kezzy's affection for her. The girl had even gone so far as to suggest to her grandfather that they might keep the baby and let the sisters go, seeing that neither mother or aunt seemed to care much for her. But Elyas was adamant.

'Best her keeps by-blow,' was all he said and that was that.

In Kezzy's arms, the baby gurgled happily and waved tiny fists, one of which firmly gripped the silver coin. Kezzy stroked the fine red-gold tuft of hair on Victory's crown. The bright hair was clearly a legacy from her mother yet, try as she may, Kezzy's sharp eyes could detect no likeness whatsoever to Horace Drigg. If anyone, Victory resembled Isaac. She'd precisely the same nose and heavy-lidded eyes, and even her little mouth was like his. Suddenly, Kezzy ached to keep the baby, so much did she remind her of her dead brother. A childish notion of running away with

Victory flitted through her brain, but she knew that it wasn't right. It would be stealing. God would punish her.

'I'll take babbie now, girl.'

Kezzy started guiltily at Bethinda's sharp voice. So intent was she on gazing into the contented, cherubic face, that she hadn't heard Victory's mother approach. It was time for her to relinquish her charge. Involuntarily, she clutched Victory tightly to her and Bethinda had almost to drag the child from her arms.

'Give un here!' snapped Bethinda impatiently. 'Bain't a raggy-doll for 'ee t'play with!'

Tears stung Kezzy's eyes as she reluctantly let go of Victory. Bethinda hefted her baby carelessly in her arms so that the little fair head wobbled as if only skin anchored it to her little shoulders. Victory dropped her shilling and Bethinda quickly bent and scooped it up and dropped it in her pocket. The sudden movement frightened the baby. Kezzy's last sight of her was over Bethinda's shoulder, red face screwed up, mouth wide open and screaming in terror, as she was carried off towards the servant's quarters where a quantity of bride ale and a big pigeon-pie were waiting to be consumed.

Kezzy wasn't invited. Neither did the sisters bother to say good-bye to her. She stood watching until they'd disappeared around the corner of the house and Victory's frantic howls had receded in the distance. Then, dejectedly, she turned and started back up the moor.

Chapter Fifteen

Kezzy didn't go straight home from Fardle. She stayed on the narrow goat track which skirted the Eaglestone valley and eventually dwindled to nothing among the granite-strewn turf below the southernmost hump of Eagle Tor. There was a nip in the air which promised frost to come. But the light was good with an eye or two of blue in the clouds. Kezzy had brought with her a mossle bag of bread, butter and cheese, and a skin of water, since she'd guessed she wouldn't be included in any of the marriage celebrations. She'd a ravenous appetite from being out in the air but she didn't stop to eat. Above her beckoned the great jagged mass of rock atop the hill.

The ground grew slippery with a slight frost as Kezzy ascended into the colder, thinner air. She took her time, placing her stout shoes carefully, enjoying the climb, enjoying the freedom. Her grandfather had told her to come directly home and would be angry with her for disobeying him, especially now that they were so hard put to keep the bal working. It was almost more than they could manage. She felt a surge of guilt because she wasn't hard at work in the washing-house. But she didn't think of stopping, or of going home. Up and up she went. Panting a little now, and red-cheeked from the biting wind.

At last she was there. Cautiously she peered into the eagle's nest wedged between the two rocks. The stones were just as she'd replaced them over a year before. Kezzy took from her pocket the eaglestone that she'd kept. It lay, smooth and grey in her palm. Perhaps if she put it back with the rest the eagle would return and bring another good omen to the Hammetts. It occurred to her that if only Graeme and Isaac had each carried a magic eaglestone they would be alive now. For hadn't her stone saved her the time she'd got lost in the fog by bringing the flaskers to save her? She hadn't admitted it to her family, but she was near frozen to death and very scared when they came across her, having almost blundered into a mire. With a shudder, Kezzy remembered the awful squelching underfoot and how she'd only just managed to scramble back on to firm ground before she was sucked under the mud. The terrifying memory of it decided her and she dropped the eaglestone back in her pocket. Better to keep it in case any such danger befell her again.

Kezzy found a place to sit, tucked down in a hollow in one of the rocks where she was out of the wind. She opened her mossle bag and ate a slice of bread and butter with some cheese. Then she took a draught of the icy water in the skin. From where she sat she could make out the distant bulk of Heddon Down, way beyond Cornwood, and even the loom of Crownhill

Down in the Plympton St Mary parish. Closer than that, however, she could clearly see all of Eaglestone valley with the cottage and mine buildings huddled on the banks of the brook, lonely in their isolation. Wispy grey smoke rose from the tall stack of the blowing-house. The furnace had been started ready for the evening coore at the smelting. By Jamie, probably, mused Kezzy with a twinge of conscience. Her father and grandfather would still be deep below grass, cutting the ore. Kezzy experienced a greater twinge of conscience. With the sisters gone, there was now only her to lower their mossle bags and canteens to them at noon. And if she didn't begin her descent quite soon she wouldn't be home in time for croust either. Yet she made no move to leave her craggy hideaway: she was out of the wind and snug in her woollen dress and old jersey. Besides, her legs ached from the long walk to and from Fardle, followed by the steep, slippery climb up the tor.

Kezzy crouched still lower. She thought about baby Victory and wondered if the poor mite was missing her badly. Tears pricked her eyes. How she wished her grandfather had let her keep the baby. Bethinda wouldn't look after her – not properly. Oh, she'd feed her and change her if she messed herself, but she wouldn't sing to Victory or rock her on her knee or amuse her with the rattle that was carved out of bone in the shape of an eagle. The rattle had been hers when she was a baby: she'd wanted to give it to Victory but Gramps wouldn't let her.

'Those two will only sell un for a few coppers . . . babbie'll get no joy from un, mark my words,' he'd said. ' 'Sides, one day when you'm growed ye'll have own babbie an' be wantin' good rattle.'

He was most likely right: he usually was. But as she had only just turned nine last All-Hallows it was too far in the distance for Kezzy to contemplate. Right now she wanted Victory to love and to hold. Just thinking of it made her suddenly burst into tears, a loud, desperate sobbing which tore at her throat. A passionate revolt against the injustice of it all. First she'd lost her brothers, now Victory. How lonely she was! She sobbed harder, wallowing in her misery until her eyes were swollen and she was too exhausted to cry any more.

'I'm *not* going home. I shall stay here for ever!' she muttered petulantly to herself. 'I *hate* Eaglestone!'

Below her, Wheal Eaglestone was belching out a thicker, blacker pall of smoke for the wind to disperse through the valley like thin, grey fog. But Kezzy wasn't aware of it.

She didn't hate Eaglestone. She loved the homely cottage and the mine as passionately as Elyas. He'd fostered in his little granddaughter, more than in any of his family, an innate sense of pride in this modest heritage which the Hammetts had hulked for themselves from the naked desolation of the land. *This was theirs!* And if anybody tried to tear it from their torn, blistered hands, they'd have to reckon with Elyas the tinner and his grandchild Kezzy.

Yet, since he'd returned from Plymouth with the heartbreaking news that Graeme and Isaac were listed among the dead at Trafalgar, the whole of Eaglestone had seemed to change. Or so it seemed to Kezzy who was particularly sensitive to such things. The place seemed to be brooding with shadows of sorrow, as if the grey granite from which it was built shared their bitter grief.

Sometimes in the night, as she lay half asleep, she thought she could hear her brothers calling her out in the yard in soft, moaning voices. *'Kezzzzyyy!'* But it was only the wind in the thatch of the barn.

Once, early one morning as she collected eggs in the barn, she could have sworn she heard Isaac's teasing chuckle and felt a ghostly hand tweak her long, dark braid just as he often did to torment her. She'd screamed and dropped her basket, breaking four big brown eggs. Eyes starting from her head, she'd rushed out and back to the cottage to fling herself into the safety of her grandfather's arms, knocking aside his bowl of oatmeal and spilling it over the table as she did so.

As a rule Elyas would have been annoyed at seeing good food spilled. God knew, it was hard enough earned. But he saw immediately that Kezzy had had a bad fright. So instead of scolding her, he calmed her with soft clicking noises and gentle pats on the head, as though she was a nervous moor colt he was trying to put a bridle on.

'What frighted 'ee, chield?' Elyas asked the little girl when she'd stopped trembling and the colour had started to come back into her cheeks.

She told him, falteringly.

Jamie sniggered. Elyas shot him a dark look.

'Just you'm watch thyself, boy,' he warned 'or eagle will swoop an' carry 'ee off to un nest.'

The unlikely threat made Jamie turn red and he lowered his eyes to his bowl. His narrow escape as an infant was for ever imprinted in his mind so that he recoiled in terror if so much as a black grouse rose flapping from the furze in his path.

' 'Twere Isaac, Gramps,' insisted Kezzy. 'I heard his laugh . . . like this.' She gave a fair imitation of her brother, not unlike a broody hen.

Elyas's worn face was serious. 'Mebbe 'twere he. Or mebbe you'm were a-missin' they boys so hard ye sort of imagined Isaac up in thy mind. Could that be it, do 'ee reckon? Were 'ee missin' they somethin' terrible?'

Of course she missed them, more than any words could describe. And thought about them all the time. Yes, Gramps was probably right, she must have imagined the whole thing, concluded Kezzy relieved, and the tension left her face. 'I was bending 'neath colt's tackle,' she said thoughtfully. 'Mebbe I snaggled my hair . . .'

Elyas instantly turned her around so he could examine her braid.

'Why lookee here! 'Tis proper mussed 'bout! Ay, chield, you'm snaggled un on tackle right 'nough!' he proclaimed, winking over the top of her head at Huward and Jamie. The braid was as smooth and tidy as it was when she'd plaited it first thing but he made a to-do about tucking in imaginary wisps and swung her round to face him again. 'There now. No harm done. But I'll tell 'ee this, Kezzy. They dear boys wouldn't have hurt hair on' thy head when them was 'live, an' nawthin' will have changed now them dead.'

His sage words went some way to curing her qualms. However, it was a while before she'd venture alone in the barn again.

'I bain't 'fraid to go in barn,' Jamie hadn't been able to resist boasting.

'Glad to hear 'ee say that, boy,' Elyas said swiftly, ' 'Cause 'ee can go an' c'lect rest o' they eggs dreckly you'm et thy vittles.'

Jamie looked alarmed: he hadn't expected to have actually to prove his courage. Kezzy took pity on him and so they both went, staying very close to one another as they investigated the straw beneath the complaining hens.

'By the Lord Harry, her be like her ma!' exclaimed Elyas when he and Huward were alone in the cottage. There was concern in his voice.

Huward nodded soberly. 'Ay, Ruke were terrible wi' second sight. Proper fey, her were.'

He was packing peat vags beneath the slab so the cauldron of water would heat ready for them after work. He stood quite still, clasping a forgotten slab of turf, a faraway look in his eyes as he vividly pictured his full-bodied, sensual *didekei* wife. How lustrously her black, slanting eyes had sparkled in the candleglow as she'd unlaced her bodice for him to fondle her big, white breasts. He could almost feel her soft, warm flesh against his palms . . .

'Wake up, boy! We'm work t'do!'

Elyas's rasping voice brought him back to the present.

That was more than a week before Kezzy climbed Eagle Tor.

Her eyelids began to droop as her exertions and the fresh air brought sleep. But not for long. She awoke with a start, vaguely conscious that something had disturbed her. She lay for a few moments of semi-wakefulness, unsure where she was, then her eyes focused on the valley below and the smoking chimney. The wind had sharpened and the light was beginning to fade. It was getting late. In alarm, she scrambled to her feet. She'd have to run down the hill as fast as she could if she was to reach home before dark. Then again came the sound that had roused her and she stopped to listen. Curlews, perhaps. She strained her ears. No! Not curlews. Human voices!

Boys' voices. Two of them. Coming closer. They were ascending the northern hump of the hill to reach the crag, laughing and shouting encouragement to each other now their goal was in sight. Kezzy stood trembling for a moment in the grip of poignant recollection.

Graeme and Isaac!

They'd come looking for her! Who else could it be? Eyes fever-bright, her mouth forming a shout of welcome, she began quickly to edge around the rocky shoulder. Abruptly, like a blow, the truth came to her. *It couldn't possibly be them*! She sank down, feeling weak as her excitement suddenly ebbed to be replaced by an overwhelming and renewed sense of loss.

'I can see a big nest, Peter! Eagle's . . . or buzzard's!'

The eager voice was so clear, the boy couldn't have been more than a few feet from Kezzy now, around the jutting rock. Evidently his friend, Peter, hadn't managed to keep up since his response came from further away.

'Wait for me, Jordan!'

Kezzy could hear him panting and scrabbling for a foothold. He dislodged a shower of small stones.

Jordan spoke again: 'Give me your hand.'

Further gasps and scraping noises told Kezzy that Peter was being hauled the rest of the way up. That achieved, there followed a few moments of silence while the boys caught their breath. The she heard Peter say: 'Let's see if there's anything in the nest . . . look's a right old'n to me . . .'

Anger surged within Kezzy, sweeping away all other emotions. *How dare these strangers intrude upon Eagle Tor!* As agilely as a monkey, she swung around the rock, landing, as luck would have it, right in front of them with a clatter of her sturdy old boots and a flapping of her woollen skirt and her bleached-cotton towzer. Her sudden appearance, as if by some form of magic, startled the boys so much they yelped in fear and clutched one another, their eyes wide and staring.

'If you touch so much as a stick of that nest I'll . . . I'll . . .' Kezzy began to threaten in the fiercest tone she could summon, then she hesitated, searching frantically for a truly horrible fate with which to cow the interlopers. She had a flash of inspiration. 'I'll burn you on the brawn with a red-hot iron!'

She recalled hearing her grandfather telling her father that a tinners' court had condemned four thieving tut-workers to just such a punishment. She wasn't absolutely certain what it entailed – or even where the brawn was located, but it certainly had the desired effect. The two boys stood gaping nonplussed at Kezzy while she glared ferociously back at them, standing between them and the nest. She was a good bit taller than one of them, but a whole head shorter that the other. It was the taller boy who broke the silence with a hoot of relieved laughter.

'Why, you're just a little girl!' he exclaimed and Kezzy knew from his voice that he was the one called Jordan.

Stung by his observation, her chin came up and her long eyes narrowed. 'I am not little. I am nine years old.'

'Well, I'm ten,' returned Peter triumphantly. He jerked his mousy, tangled head at Jordan. 'Jordan is *eleven* . . . goin' on *twelve*!'

Kezzy's scowl deepened. 'That may be,' she said petulantly, 'but I go to school.'

Peter gave a snort of disbelief. 'Where do 'ee go t'school?'

'Down 'long Cornwood . . . Dame Rogers's school.'

'Don't believe you. Why, you'm just raggedy-arse med'n!'

Kezzy's eyes flickered and a faint flush rose in her pale cheeks. This was open warfare. But Jordan, standing silently by listening to their hostile exchange, plucked admonishingly at his friend's frayed and torn sleeve.

'Mebbe she does go to school, Peter,' he said quietly. 'She doesn't talk like bal maidens. She talks more like gentry, come to think of it.'

Kezzy turned her gaze upon the taller boy. At least he recognised her superiority. She began to smile, then checked herself, remembering the reason for this confrontation. She scowled instead. 'What are you doing climbing tor, anyroads?'

'What's it to 'ee?' retorted Peter.

Kezzy pointed down to the valley. 'That's Eaglestone mine.'

They turned and stared at the cluster of buildings and the smoking stack.

'What of it?' asked Jordan with a shrug.

'Elyas Hammett owns yon mine.'

The boys exchanged uncomprehending looks. The name meant nothing to them.

'So who's he zackly when he's at home?' enquired Peter.

'My grandpa,' declared Kezzy proudly. '*Everybody* knows Elyas Hammett.'

'We don't,' said Peter candidly.

'Well, you must be right pair of oafs. He prack'ly *owns* this tor . . . least, he says who can and who can't climb it,' Kezzy told them with a toss of her head.

Peter jerked a contemptuous thumb towards the valley. 'Huh! Yon workin's ent much bigger'n trial-pit,' he sneered, making Kezzy's eyes flash with indignation. 'Wheel Emma . . . now her's *proper* mine . . . ouch!'

He gave a yelp as Jordan kicked his bony ankle to silence him. It was too late: Kezzy had heard. Her eyes narrowed shrewdly as she looked them up and down. Their thin bodies and their rags told of their wretched poverty; their calloused hands of their cruel labours.

'You're run'ways from Lord Warden's Wheal Emma!' she blurted.

The boys exchanged anxious looks. They were, indeed, runaway apprentices from the big de Raddon-owned mine near Plympton. Two days before, early in the morning, they'd crept out of the big barn-like building where the youngsters slept in rows on pallets, and slipped away in the darkness before dawn. They had made their plans carefully, whispering together as they toiled in the mine, struggling on all fours, harnessed to the corves of stuff they pulled along the narrow seams. The bigger boys, thirteen- and fourteen-year-olds, took it in turns to sleep across the dormitory entrance to discourage runaways – on pain of earning a beating for themselves if any of the apprentices did manage to abscond. One of these young 'overseers' was particularly vicious to his younger companions, some of them boys and girls of only six and seven, kicking and punching them for the fun of it. Jordan and Peter agreed a thrashing would serve him right and purposefully picked a night when he was the guard, wriggling out through a hole in the rotting wood and stealing away like shadows. It had been their intention to run away to sea but neither had been quite certain in which direction the sea lay. So they'd just kept walking across the seemingly never-ending humped and crouching hills. They hadn't known the name of the tor when they decided to climb it to get their bearings, or that it belonged to a man called Elyas Hammett. It was the highest, and they'd hoped to see the sea from its crown of rocks.

'You are runaways, aren't you?' persisted Kezzy when they didn't immediately answer.

'What of it?' muttered Peter surlily.

'Cap'n de Raddon will have his monkey up, right 'nough, when he catches pair of you,' Kezzy said warningly.

'He won't catch us,' said Jordan determinedly.

'We're going to sea,' announced Peter.

'My brothers were pressed,' said Kezzy sadly. 'Now they're dead. Killed by the poxy French, drat their murderin' lily-livers!'

The boys stared, fascinated by this fair-faced, tilt-eyed little girl who'd all the aplomb of the gentry yet who was capable of cursing in the same tongue as the bal maidens. Peter's eye fell on her mossle bag and canteen of water and he felt a pang of hunger. They'd long eaten the hunks of bread they'd managed to save to carry as rations. Apart from a few old windfalls they'd found lying on the ground in a farm orchard, they'd not eaten that day. They hadn't dared to knock at the farmhouse to beg for food in case the farmer turned them in.

Peter jerked his chin at the mossle bag. 'Have 'ee any bread?' he asked hopefully.

Kezzy saw the hunger in his eyes. Without a word she reached down and picked up the bag. Opening it, she took out the remainder of the bread and cheese and shared it equally between them. She watched pityingly as they ate ravenously, wishing that she'd more to give them. They drained the canteen, wiping their mouths on their torn cuffs.

'God bless you, little girl,' said Jordan gratefully.

She didn't mind him calling her a little girl: after all, he was almost twelve and therefore nearly grown. 'My name is Keziah,' she said shyly. 'Gramps calls me Kezzy, though . . . so I s'pose you can too, if you want.' Speaking of her grandfather reminded her that it was growing dark and he would be getting worried if she wasn't back soon. 'I must go now,' she said, slipping the empty mossle bag and canteen on her back. She looked from one to the other, concern in her face. 'Will you promise not to touch the eagle's nest after I've gone. If you take the eagle's stones it won't ever come back.'

They promised fervently. It was the least they could do when she'd been kind enough to put some food in their bellies.

She pointed. 'Coast's that way. Goodbye!' She was off, slipping and sliding down the slope.

'Good-bye, Kezzy,' they shouted, disappointment manifest in their voices because they were so quickly losing their interesting new friend. They stood watching her receding back view.

She was a good way down the hill when she suddenly stopped and turned to look back up at them. They stood silhouetted against the darkening sky. She found she was shivering although she'd a thick jersey on. How cold they must be in their thin rags, poor boys!

It was strange, how she'd thought they were Graeme and Isaac: they were nothing like her brothers. Save they were young and strong enough to work men's coore in by bal. Her heart beat faster as a fascinating notion occurred to her: perhaps some magical force had drawn these boys to Eagle Tor as a replacement for Graeme and Isaac.

On an impulse, she called out to them: 'You can come with me if you want.'

The boys looked at each other, sorely tempted but uncertain. Since her grandfather owned a mine, he might well be in cahoots with Captain de Raddon. Big or small, the mine-owners all seemed to be cheek by jowl what with their stannaries and their coinages.

'Won't your grandpa turn us in then?' shouted Jordan.

'He'll not do that,' floated back Kezzy's unhesitating reply. She hadn't forgotten how he'd taken in Morgenna and Bethinda in their time of need. 'He'll give you roof and food and work . . . if you're willing to bestir yourselves.'

Yet still they hesitated, hopping from one foot to the other to keep warm in the icy wind.

'C'mon!' shouted Kezzy encouragingly. 'I promise he won't turn you in. 'Sides, he hates Cap'n de Raddon worse'n geese hate fox on account he didn't save our boys from press like he aught've.'

That settled it. By tacit agreement the boys took off down the tor after her.

By the time the three of them had reached Eaglestone, Kezzy's confidence in her grandfather's benevolence towards runaway apprentices was on the wane. It would be best, she told them, if they hid out in the barn until she'd had a chance to break the news to him, also her father and brother. They would be warm among the hay and she would smuggle what food she could to them.

Wart came snuffling and growling at the boys' heels as they slipped into the barn, suspicious of the two strangers even though they were in Hammett company. He flopped across the entrance to the barn, head on his front paws, eyes watchful as Kezzy hastened across the yard and disappeared into the cottage.

When she went in, Elyas, Huward and Jamie were already seated at the table tucking into an enormous salt-pork figgen and a giant mound of mashed tatties dripping with yellow butter.

Kezzy fetched her bowl and sat down.

Elyas looked up from his supper. 'Where 'ee been all day, Kezzy?' he asked her by way of greeting.

It didn't occur to her to lie; to pretend that she'd been kept late by the sisters to help with the baby. 'I climbed Eagle Tor.'

Elyas nodded. He'd guessed as much. He didn't scold her for missing the afternoon coore in by the stamps, understanding her desire to seek peace and solace upon the grey summit away from the mournful atmosphere shrouding Eaglestone.

'Eat thy supper, chield.'

Huward wasn't as tolerant, growling: 'You'm no right to be shirkin' thy coore, Kezzy. Ent fair on rest o' us.'

'I had t'make figgen,' grumbled Jamie.

Kezzy helped herself to a good-sized piece and eyed it speculatively. 'Huh! Best sole our boots with it,' she told him cuttingly.

'Well, figgen-trade be maid's work, anyroads,' he justified his somewhat doughy effort.

'Well, I do boy's work in by stamps, don't I?' Kezzy shot back, silencing him with her quick wit and tongue.

Nevertheless, not a crumb remained of the figgen, or the pile of buttered bread which was meant for the morning as well as supper. And it seemed to be Kezzy's hand that reached out again and again for what was on the table, which greatly surprised Elyas, although he made no comment, since usually she wasn't a big eater, and it was unlikely her excursion up the hillside had suddenly given her a man-sized appetite. He watched her surreptitiously from beneath his shaggy brows and just caught a quick movement as she transferred a piece of figgen from her plate into her apron. Still he said nothing, sitting after supper as he usually did on the settle by the fire, apparently dozing by the fire while Kezzy washed the pots and Huward and Jamie prepared a brace of goose-quill fuses ready for hulking a new run the next day. Elyas had located some promising mineral veins and spots of ore, but the ground was hard just there and would need a good charge of powder to start the work.

Presently, with a wary eye on her grandfather, Kezzy slid quietly out of the door. In her apron she clutched some good-sized pieces of figgen, still warm, and almost a whole loaf of buttered bread.

Out in the yard, she collected a bucket and filled it at the brook so Jordan and Peter would have water to drink. Wart rose as she approached the barn door, letting her by him somewhat unwillingly, aware that strangers were in the barn. He gave a sharp bark, as if to warn her, and would have followed her in but she made him stay outside, firmly pulling to the door behind her.

' 'Tis me . . . Kezzy!' she called softly into the pitch blackness. 'I've brought you some food.'

She heard a rustling above her head and some of the roosters began to cluck, complaining at the intrusion. Then came Jordan's answering whisper.

'Up here.'

Kezzy peered in the direction of his voice. Her eyes were growing used to the dark and she could make out dimly the grey patch of his face. He was kneeling at the top of the wooden ladder slanted against the hay-loft. Peter was a shadowy figure at his shoulder. She handed them up the bucket, then the food, upon which they fell hungrily.

'I mustn't stop . . . Gramps might wake and wonder where I am,' said Kezzy agitatedly.

Jordan quickly swallowed a mouthful of figgen. 'When will you tell your grandpa 'bout us?'

'When he's lit his second pipe o' baccy.'

It was clear from her tone that she didn't relish the task.

However, it had to be done, so better to get it over sooner rather than later. Elyas didn't trust strangers. 'Furriners' he called them even if they just came from the other side of the moor. Kezzy hadn't forgotten how angry he'd been with her for bringing the flaskers to Eaglestone, though they'd rescued her in the fog. But she was sure that once he was over his initial surprise, he'd see that she'd acted for the best by bringing the boys back with her. True, they were as thin as a cat's elbows, but they'd soon fill out and be a good, strong pair of workers to take her brothers' place in by the bal.

'Mebbe best if'n you wait awhile afore telling him,' suggested Jordan worriedly, sensing her trepidation.

Ever cautious, he was beginning to think that it might not be a bad idea if they stayed just the one night, creeping away before dawn so that Elyas Hammett need never know he'd harboured runaway apprentices in his barn. He and Peter had been discussing this while they were waiting for Kezzy to return. Peter was all for staying and throwing themselves upon the tinner's mercy; he was nowhere near as robust as Jordan and was already weary of tramping the bleak wastes on an empty belly. Moreover, from the stories told by the returning Wheal Emma tut-workers who had volunteered to fight the French, thinking to escape the living hell of the mines, life in the services was just as harsh, whether on land or sea. On the other hand, Jordan was of the opinion that anything was better than tinning, and that no ship's master could possible be as flinthearted as 'Cruel Caplan', the overseer at Wheal Emma.

'Jordan don't want us to stay, Kezzy,' revealed Peter between mouthfuls. 'But I reckon we'm better here than a-goin' t'sea. Us bain't never been on briny afore.'

'Mebbe 'tis best we go . . .' Jordan began to say apologetically.

Kezzy spoke quickly. 'Please don't go. We need help in bal . . .' She stopped, ears pricked as Wart whined softly outside the door. A murmuring voice hushed him. A second later, the barn door creaked slowly open and the interior was lit by the sullen orange glow of a lantern. There was no mistaking the bent and bowed shadowy figure holding the light.

'Gramps! I was just . . . just . . .' she faltered, her face flushed and guilty.

Wart had followed Elyas in. Now he began to growl and bark, making little runs at the foot of the ladder. Without a word, Elyas lifted the lantern to shoulder-height so he could see the strangers in the hay-loft, blinking stupidly in the light.

'Two of 'ee, eh?' he growled. 'Well, you'm best come down here and no tricks or 'twill be worse for 'ee, cullies.'

He called Wart to heel while they climbed down to stand quaking before him. By the tone of his voice they could tell he'd no intention of treating them leniently, regardless of what his little granddaughter might say. Elyas held the lantern close to their faces. What he saw surprised him.

'By the Lord Harry! You'm just pair o' shrimps!' he burst out. 'An' I was a-thinkin' young Kezzy must've took pity on convict who'd skiddaddled from Princeton.' He shouted over his shoulder. 'In 'ee come an' have a geek at what us have here, boys!'

Huward and Jamie appeared armed with peekers. Elyas had left nothing to chance: if there had been an escaped convict hiding in the barn, he'd not have easily escaped the Hammetts' clutches.

There was, Kezzy saw with relief, a gleam of amusement lurking in her grandfather's eyes. She wasted not a second in playing on his present good humour. Going to him, she hung on his hand, turning her face up to him with her most appealing expression. 'Oh, Gramps, they're two poor boys who've run away from Wheal Emma 'cos the captain beat them terribly. They can stay here and work in by bal, can't they?'

His eyebrows met in a bristling frown. 'Wheal Emma, 'ee say?' He gazed hard at the boys as they stood in deepest penitence before him. 'When did you'm boys skiddaddle then?'

Jordan told him. Also about climbing Eagle Tor and meeting Kezzy.

'Yon med'n promised 'ee wouldn't turn us back in, Cap'n Hammett,' Peter chimed in with an accusing look towards their 'saviour'.

'Did her now?' said Elyas gruffly. But his eyes twinkled with gratification because the boy had addressed him so respectfully.

'They *can* stay, can't they, Gramps?' Kezzy asked coaxingly.

Elyas muttered something unintelligible.

Kezzy looked uncomfortable. She'd given her word in a folly of bravado that the boys would be well received at Eaglestone. 'Gramps . . .' she began to implore, eyes moistening.

Some slight involuntary hardening of his face told her that her pleas wouldn't on this occasion be sufficient to move him if he was dead set against them staying. He turned on his heel and stamped out in an irascible fashion, saying, 'Best us go in and talk 'about this.'

In the cottage, Elyas sat the boys down opposite him at the table and motioned to Huward to join them. Huward's usually placid face was troubled. He knew as well as his father the consequences if they were caught harbouring runaway apprentices. Jamie tried to slide quietly on to a stool, a keen eye cocked on the boys – one of whom was much his own age, he guessed – but Elyas pointed to the dividing curtain.

'Bed for 'ee, m'boy,' he said curtly.

Jamie scowled but didn't dare argue. He was reluctant to leave these two interlopers so cosily ensconced in the bosom of his family. As he went, he scooped up a little carved frigate – his heart's treasure – which Graeme had made for him when he was younger in case either of these shifty-eyed boys took a fancy to it.

To Kezzy, Elyas said brusquely: 'Make us some tay an' put in a spoonful or two of honey an' plenty of cream.'

'Yes, Gramps.' She hastened to do as she was bid, glad that she hadn't been packed off to bed like a runny-nosed child in front of Jordan and Peter.

Elyas looked across at Jordan. 'How old are ye, boy?'

'Nigh twelve, Cap'n,' he answered, looking back at the old man with steady, grey-green eyes.

Elyas looked at the younger boy.

'Ten, Cap'n,' muttered Peter without prompting.

Elyas nodded. 'Then you'm old 'nough to knowed runnin' 'way from bal is a terrible crime gin tinners' law.' It was more of a statement than it was a question but the boys nodded sullenly. 'Why, 'prentices have been strung up for it. Certain t'earn ye a floggin' you'm not forgit if'n they catches 'ee . . . which them likely'd shall.'

'Ay, an' same goes for us Hammetts if'n we'm caught givin' 'ee roof an' vittles,' adjoined Huward dourly.

'Worse'n that, most likely'd,' said Elyas grimly. 'Keepin' 'nother cap'n's 'prentices be stealin' 'cording to tinners' law. An' what withee bein' Lord Warden's boys . . . well, most likely'd tinners' court will boat us to Botany. Jamie an' Kezzy 'long wi' us . . .'

Kezzy was setting steaming mugs of tea before each of them. Her grandfather's ominous words startled her and she split some of the hot, milky liquid on the table. She knew she'd acted impetuously by bringing the boys to Eaglestone but it hadn't occurred to her that she was putting her family in danger.

Jordan and Peter exchanged an unhappy glance. With so much at stake, the old man would be a fool to let them stay. He must, surely, turn them in.

'Oh, Gramps, I promised you wouldn't send them back,' whispered Kezzy, mortified. Her face was ashen and she fought the tears swimming in her dark eyes.

'Ay, I knowed that, m'dear,' said Elyas, nodding his grey head. 'An' I'll stand by thy promise since a Hammett's word bain't t'be broke . . .'

'But, Pa . . .' Huward started to protest, his face aghast.

Elyas lifted his hand, silencing his son. 'Rest o' us Hammetts must 'bide by Kezzy's word whatever the consequences.'

Jordan and Peter exchanged another look, hardly able to believe what they were hearing: *the old man wasn't going to turn them in.*

'You'm bain't sayin' them can *stay*?' gasped Huward, eyes staring.

'Ay . . . if'n them choose to.'

Kezzy gave a little shriek of delighted relief and threw herself at her grandfather to hug him, jarring the table and spilling more tea. 'Thank you, Gramps! Cap'n de Raddon will never find out, I'm sure of it! And I know they'll work ever so hard and not be elly trouble and not eat too much . . .'

Elyas put her from him, gently but firmly, his expression grave. 'I said them could stay . . . if'n them *choose* to, Kezzy.' He looked across at the boys; they were looking thoroughly bemused. 'I'll not turn 'ee in, boys. But I'm askin' 'ee to think 'pon what it do mean to Hammetts if'n ye choose to stay. You'm would be puttin' us in terrible danger.'

There was a silence for a moment or two. Then Jordan said: 'Best we go back, Peter.'

'Nay!' Peter half rose, fear gripping him, swamping his natural reticence. 'I'll not go back t'be hung or whupped like a cur!'

'Sit down, boy!' ordered Elyas. His voice was sharp but his face had softened. 'You'm bain't goin' out on moor t'night. Most likely'd walk into swamp an' be lost.'

'I don't care!' There was a break in Peter's voice and his lower lip trembled. ' 'Twould be quicker'n hangin' or floggin'.'

Elyas shook his head. ' 'Tis clear 'ee bain't seen a man stagged in mire. He do sink terrible slow . . . shoutin' an' screamin' for help afore mud sucks he under.'

Peter sat down. He gave Kezzy a venomous look and began to berate her. 'Us should've known better'n trust word of med'n . . .'

She hung her head, face colouring with shame. Seeing her discomfiture, Jordan cut across his friend, saying, 'Hush, Peter, Kezzy meant t'help us. She wasn't to know about tinners' law. 'Sides, Cap'n Hammett says we can stay if we choose . . . so what she said was true. Only 'tis best we leave and not bring grief to these good folk when we've eaten their vittles and rested 'neath their roof.'

Kezzy looked up at him shyly, grateful for his understanding words.

Elyas brought his watchful gaze to bear upon Jordan's serious young face, impressed by the boy's maturity. 'Thankee, boy, for thy consideration,' he said quietly.

'Best un sleep in barn t'night,' said Huward, ever cautious. 'If'n de Raddon's men come a-lookin' for un boys us can swear we didn't knowed un were there.'

' 'Tis cold in barn an' we've got two good pallets going beggin',' ventured Kezzy as she sipped her tea.

Her father scowled at her for interfering in men's talk, but Elyas unexpectedly nodded his agreement.

'Ay, m'dear. One night won't hurt.'

He preferred them to sleep in the cottage so that they couldn't slip away in the dark without him knowing. The moor was too dangerous for them to go blundering about upon. Privately, he thought it a near miracle they'd survived as long as they had since they couldn't possibly know how to recognise the various fens and bogs and quaker swamps. But that wasn't his only reason for letting them stay in the cottage – for Wart would have made sure they stayed put in the barn. It was good to have them there, so greatly did they remind him of Graeme and Isaac when they were about the same age. That was soon after he and Huward had left the fish and brought them, with little Jamie, backalong up the moor to hulk for tin. Gazing at the boys as they drank their tea, Elyas found himself wishing with all his heart that he dared to let them remain at Eaglestone. God knew, they could do with their strong, young muscles. But more than that, the harder Elyas looked at Jordan, the more like Graeme the boy seemed to become. He'd the same shock of tousled, sandy-coloured hair growing over his brow through which, like Graeme, he'd run his outspread fingers whenever he was troubled or perplexed about something. And Peter, mousey-headed and sturdy with pale, wary, questioning eyes, bore more than a passing resemblance to Isaac. *Damn the Stannary! And damn de Raddon!* Elyas silently cursed, but not for a moment did he weaken. Word travelled swiftly: *if Eaglestone was suddenly to boast two apprentices and Wheal Emma was missing two . . .*

Huward broke into his reverie by yawning hugely. 'I'm for bed,' he announced and without more ado rose and went and threw himself on his pallet in the corner. Although they'd rooms to spare at the back of the cottage now, he and Elyas still preferred to sleep near the fire; their bones craved the warmth in winter and a freezing room always set Elyas off coughing for an hour.

Seconds later, Huward began to snore.

Kezzy collected the mugs and rinsed them in the water bucket ready for morning. The boys remained seated at the table, still and silent, waiting to be told what to do – conditioned by years of Cruel Caplan's discipline. Elyas rose and went and tapped out his clay in the fire. He banked the fire with vags so it would smoulder throughout the night and boil the water for the morning gruel, aware that Jordan and Peter were watching these small domestic actions with a certain wistfulness. Clearly, they'd never known what it was to be part of a family. He felt his resolution ebbing away. Perhaps he could shave their heads. Pretend they were two convict boys newly released from Princeton camp. But he couldn't keep their heads shaved for ever and if the flaskers ever came again with the Lord Warden's man Grote at their head there was a chance they'd be recognised as Wheal Emma runaways. Alas, 'twas too dangerous to keep them when they were bonded to de Raddon. All this went quickly through Elyas's mind as tired as he was. He frowned as some new notion began to form. Perhaps he could take the boys to Blackaven House and ask de Raddon to release them from his bondage. Buy them! He'd got a cache of gold coins hidden beneath the mud in the pig pen.

His initial enthusiasm for that plan quickly subsided. Most likely the Lord Warden would trick him out of his savings and somehow wangle it to keep the boys. Maybe even accuse Elyas of enticing them. Nay, decided Elyas regretfully, best get rid of the poor young wretches as quick as he could and forget about them.

He was standing gazing at the glowing embers deep in thought. He stirred himself, aware that Kezzy had spoken. 'What did 'ee say, chield?'

'Shall I show them where they're to sleep?'

He nodded, turned to poke at the fire so he'd not have to see their woebegone faces. 'Ay. Goodnight and God bless to all o' 'ee.'

'Good night, Gramps,' murmured Kezzy in response.

The boys followed her dispiritedly. For a few moments, Elyas could hear them whispering; Peter's voice despairing; Kezzy's dejected and remorseful; Jordan's urgent. He heard the words 'sea' and 'Plymouth' mentioned and guessed their intention was to seek berths as 'boys' on a merchantman. Elyas was stirred by a distant memory of when he was a boy bonded along with his three brothers at White Works near Fox Tor Mire. They, too, had dreamed of running away to sea. They used to say to one another 'If ever I escape from this dark, dusty world, I'll never, never go in by bal 'gin.' At night he'd dream they had run away; he and his brothers would be running and running through a moor mist. Running so fast and so hard that it seemed as if they'd wings on their heels. Ahead of them shone the sea, but it never got any nearer. And they never did run away for real. One of his brothers had died of lung-rot when he was only fifteen. The other was killed in a pit blast.

Elyas the tinner went to bed.

Elyas half expected the boys to try and sneak out past him during the night and he slept with one ear cocked just in case. But they were so exhausted, they'd fallen asleep almost as soon as they'd lain down and didn't stir until cock crow. After breakfast, eaten in a silent circle around the table in the light from the range because Elyas wouldn't burn tallow unnecessarily, Kezzy was sent to fetch Rats and the wagon round into the yard.

Jordan's and Peter's gloom deepened noticeably at the sound of the creaking wheels outside the cottage door.

'Best this way,' muttered Huward as he and Jamie rose to go to work. They were good, strong boys to be sure, but not worth swinging for. But he was moved by their plight. He'd a bundle of Graeme's and Isaac's clothes ready to give them. Jerseys and breeches.

Gratefully, they went and swapped their rags for them.

With Jordan seated beside him and Peter sitting on the flatboard with his legs dangling, Elyas set off down the moor. Kezzy came and stood at the break in the wall surrounding Eaglestone with Wart beside her, watching them go. Jordan twisted around and saw her standing there, a small, dejected figure. He waved and she waved back. Then the grey morning light closed in around her and he couldn't see her any more.

At the foot of the valley, Elyas turned Rats along a narrow goat track which would lead them eventually to Cadover Bridge over the Plym. For what seemed a long time they plodded along in silence. Then Jordan asked in a faintly anxious tone of voice: 'Where are you takin' us, Cap'n Hammett?'

'Ye'll see soon enough,' said Elyas gruffly. He gave the boy a sideways look. 'Reckon I'll not keep my word and hand 'ee over to Wheal Emma overseer? Be that what's a-botherin' 'ee, boy?'

'No, zur,' returned Jordan swiftly, though it had crossed his mind.

Nothing more was said. Presently, Elyas looked up at the thick, dark clouds racing across the sky. They foretold heavy rain: perhaps snow. And a long, strong blow at sea.

'If'n wind afore rain, hoist thy topsails agin.'

'Cap'n?' queried Jordan uncomprehendingly.

Elyas hadn't realised he'd spoken aloud. ' 'Tis sailor's warnin',' he explained. 'But . . . if'n rain afore wind, ye topsail halyards 'ee must mind.' Jordan was still looking mystified. Elyas chuckled humourlessly. 'Ye'll learn, boy. Have to, if'n 'tis life at sea 'ee craves.' He felt Jordan tense. 'You'm boys are reckonin' on runnin' 'way t'sea, bain't 'ee?'

Slowly, Jordan nodded.

'Thought as much. Well, ye can tekkit from me what's bided wi' un fisherfolk . . . the sea be as cruel a master as the land. Either of 'ee ever been t'sea?'

'Nay, zur.'

'Thought not. Then there be the sharks.'

There was a pause. Then came Peter's voice from behind them.

'What be sharks?'

'Devils in fish skin,' said Elyas darkly. 'Swallow pair of 'ee whole an' not knowed they'd vittles in they guts!'

'They m . . . must b . . . be t . . . terrible b . . . big fish,' stuttered Peter in alarm. He hadn't known about sharks when he'd agreed to run away to sea with Jordan.

'What odds . . . be et by shark or be hung by Cruel Caplan?' said Jordan miserably.

'Well, now, boy,' said Elyas. 'if'n 'ee turn *thyselves* in an' be proper penitent 'bout it, I reckons 'ee'll get no more un a good whuppin'.'

At that moment, Rats reached a high ridge. Below them ran the swift-flowing dark waters of the Plym spanned by Cadover Bridge. Beyond, the scene was desolate: humped boulders and withered trees. And the smoke-belching chimneys of de Raddon-owned mines. Among them Wheal Emma. Elyas flicked Rats with his switch and the colt took the descent at a gallop. He reined in at the little clapper bridge.

'This be as far as I'm a-takin' 'ee, boys.'

They got down. Elyas leaned down and produced a mossle bag from beneath the box seat. He tossed it to Jordan, shrugging aside their mumbled thanks and forelock tugging. He pointed with his birch across the bridge towards the track on the other side. 'See where un do fork?' They nodded. 'Take that fork for Wheal Emma . . . an' that one for Plymouth. 'Tis thy choice . . . an' God go withee whichever 'ee do choose.'

Elyas turned Rats and set off the way'd they'd come, leaving the boys standing there indecisively. It began to snow. He didn't look back.

It snowed heavily for the rest of the week. Pelting barbs of frosty white which blew into great drifts and blocked the moor tracks and waterways. The Hammetts were prepared to be snowed in. There was plenty of vags of peat in the barn; hay for the animals; a whole pig salted and hung to smoke in the big chimney in the cottage and a whole big pit of vegetables dug in behind the barn. Work had to cease. The buildings were piled high all around with frozen snow. It was as much as they could do to keep open a narrow alley between cottage and barn by dint of taking turns with the shovel throughout day and night. It was Kezzy's job to watch the fire as melted snow trickled down the chimney threatening to put it out. If that happened the range would quickly become too chill to light again, and there was a real danger they would all freeze to death.

On Saturday, it stopped snowing and the sun came out. But there was no warmth in the thin, pale shafts. If anything, it seemed colder. That evening, came a frost the like of which even Elyas couldn't remember. Huward took over the tending of the fire for Kezzy was in danger of falling asleep so diligent had she been, merely dozing for a few minutes now and again between using the bellows and swabbing the dripping water. Every iron pot was kept filled with snow and set to heat on the range, the hot water being used to keep open the path now the ground was too hard for a shovel.

Stones were placed beneath the vags to be carried red-hot across to the barn and there doused with cold water so that the hot steam saved the sheltering livestock and fowls from freezing to death.

Late that night a big fall of snow came down the chimney and smothered the fire with a triumphant hiss. Huward's loud cursing brought the others scrambling from their pallets but there was nothing any of them could do. They did try: swabbing out the wet with whatever they could lay their hands upon and immediately getting to work with dry wood and tinder-box. But even as the sticks kindled, another fall of slush quenched the feeble flames. They lit a candle, just the one; not daring to light more when they didn't know how long the frost might last. Above the candle they rigged up a small pot of water to make a hot drink. Elyas put a small stone in it to heat for the children's feet. They put on whatever clothing they could find, layer upon layer, and huddled together around the candle.

'Will it start to thaw tomorrow, Gramps?' asked Jamie.

'Mebbe.'

And then they heard a terrible sound: a strange snapping and crackling, but muffled – as though from a distance, yet carrying to their ears through the silent white world outside.

'What's that, Gramps?' asked Kezzy in alarm, clutching his arm.

'Don't you'm be fright, chield . . .' he started to soothe her.

Huward had half-risen. 'Do sound like gunfire!'

'Nay, nay, boy. Sit 'ee down,' Elyas bade him. ' 'Tis only trees top o'creep splittin' wi' un frost.'

Huward sat down again. 'Mebbe us should try an' kindle fire gin,' he suggested, desperate to do something other than sitting shivering and waiting for the thaw. But even as he said it, he knew it would be a waste of time. The fireplace and range were flooded, the iron slab wet and glistening in the candlelight.

They sat there for what seemed like hours. Until the candle began to gutter. It was impossible to say whether it was getting light outside because the windows were blocked by frozen drifts like dense white curtains. Elyas rose stiffly and went to the door but found he couldn't open it. The frost had buckled the timber, jamming the door. Huward went and helped him, pulling and pushing until it gave way and swung open. Light flooded the cottage. It was morning. Well after cock-crow by the look of it – only the cock hadn't heralded the dawn in his usual manner. When they went into the barn, they discovered why. The old rooster sat frozen rigid on his high perch in the roof. Half a dozen or so hens had suffered the same fate. Elyas bade Kezzy collect the dead fowls in a sack and take them back to the cottage for plucking ready for the pot. They'd save on the salt pork and make a change from their monotonous winter diet. A check of the livestock showed that, though lethargic, they'd weathered the terrible frost fairly well, being sheltered from the worst of it. It crossed Elyas's mind that Lamb's Down would have suffered badly, being higher up the moor and mightily exposed.

'Most likely'd lost terrible lot o' ewes,' Elyas remarked to Huward with a regretful shake of his head. If they were nearer they might have been able to give the farmer a hand to dig out his buried flock before the frost, but only madmen would have attempted to cross the moor when it was blanketed in snow. More dangerous even than fog.

Huward made no response; he was leaning over the side of the makeshift pig-pen vigorously rubbing the porker's bristly skin to get the blood flowing in its veins. Jamie was doing the same for their cow Pansy. Rats was a hardy moor colt and needed no such attention and Wart had had the sense to lay where he best benefited from the pony's warm, steamy breath.

Kezzy went out with her sack of chickens. A moment later, she could be heard frantically calling them from the yard.

'Gramps! Pa! Jamie! Come quick!'

Her sense of urgency galvanised them and they hurried out, slipping and sliding on the snow-packed ground, to see what was agitating her. Kezzy had dropped her sack and was staring towards the purple-grey heavens. She pointed.

'Look! The eagle!'

They followed her hand, squinting against the dazzling light reflected by the snowy mantle. Against the sky soared wide, brown wings. Elyas shaded his eyes the better to see.

'By Jesu! 'Tis eagle, right 'nough!' he crowed delightedly.

It was, he saw, a female. A good third bigger than a male eagle, as was to be expected in birds of prey. For a while she wheeled and soared and plunged high above her interested audience, then suddenly she dropped on the air current and slanted towards them, circling the yard as if she was as curious about them as they were about her. As her broad shadow slid over them, Jamie turned and hurtled sliding and slipping back into the barn in terror.

Wart ran barking and jumping across the yard after the feathered intruder only to go sprawling. When the eagle suddenly turned and swooped low over his head, the hound was seized by a belated prudence and disappeared cringing, tail between his legs, into the barn after Jamie. Elyas couldn't help chuckling. Of course, this couldn't be the same eagle that had tried to carry off Jamie years before. But it was a sea-eagle, and of similarly impressive proportions.

The eagle circled over the yard again, this time so low they could see her black, hooded eyes and vicious-looking talons. She uttered a plaintive 'Kee-iah! Kee-iah!'

'Her be hungry,' said Elyas.

'Shall we pitch her one of the dead hens, Gramps?' Kezzy asked him eagerly, reaching for the neck of her sack. But Huward snatched the sack from her.

'Ye'll not waste good food on birds,' he said sharply.

'Her deserves better un scrawny hen, boy,' murmured Elyas as he gazed in wonder at the eagle, never having seen one this close in flight before, marvelling at the adroit way in which she floated upon the icy currents of air.

'Kee-iah! Kee-iah!' she cried again, and to Kezzy's ears it sounded as if she was calling her name in a piteous fashion. The little girl slipped her hand beneath her jersey, feeling for the eaglestone she carried always in her pocket.

'We *must* feed her, Gramps!' Kezzy cast desperate eyes towards the sack her father was possessively gripping. The eagle might well deserve better than frozen hen, but it would be better than starvation for there was nothing to be found across the vast white wastes of the moor.

Elyas was already picking his way carefully over the ice to the barn. 'You'm wait there . . . I'll bring un eagle proper dinner,' he chuckled.

In the barn, he went and viewed the rabbits Jamie kept in a run along the back wall. The boy came and stood with him.

'Has eagle gone, Gramps?'

'Nay, boy. Not wi'out un dinner.'

Leisurely, Elyas selected a good plump specimen from among the jackrabbits, ignoring the nursing does and the young ones, and lifted it out kicking by the ears.

'What do 'ee want wi' buck, Gramps?' There was a faint note of reproach in the boy's voice which Elyas didn't miss. Jamie was aware that he was allowed to keep the rabbits for fattening on some of the scraps and vegetable peelings meant for the pig because they made a tasty stew sometimes. But it was always left to him to choose which of his stock would go in the pot. The big buck Elyas was holding was a prize specimen, something which had saved it from the dinner table in the past.

Elyas held the kicking creature aloft and chuckled. 'This'n bunny should gi' eagle fine bit o' sport as well as fillin' her vittlin' office.'

'But, Gramps . . .' Jamie started to protest then bit his tongue as Elyas began to frown.

'Now, lookee here, Jamie boy. If'n us don't feed eagle . . . why, us can't 'spect no more good omens.'

Jamie couldn't argue with that piece of logic. But he remained where he was, safe from flapping wings and wicked claws, peering out warily after Elyas as he carried off the rabbit, calling 'Hoke! Hoke! Hoke!' to attract the eagle's attention as he might cattle.

The eagle quickly spotted the wriggling creature and began to cry out in a frenzy of anticipation. 'Keeee-iahhh! Keeeee-iahhhh! Keeeeee!' Recklessly, she circled ever closer. So that they could hear the swish of the air through her feathers.

'Lerrit go, Pa, or her will snatch un . . . ay, an' thy arm wi' un, most likely'd,' Huward warned, cautiously eyeing the wheeling bird. Hunger had clearly subordinated her natural fear and distrust of man.

But Elyas paid no heed, he took his time, carrying the struggling rabbit clear of the buildings before releasing it. For a moment it sat frozen. Then, scut bobbing, set off in giant bounds for the nearest cover, a snow-laden bush some yards away. The eagle rolled over, backing her wings as she plunged after her leaping prey. Sensing danger, the rabbit began jumping evasively from side to side, but the eagle stretched wide her massive wings and dived upon the buck clasping its hindquarters with her needle-sharp talons. She gave a scream of triumph and flapped her wings in an attempt to carry it off. It struggled frantically and she dropped it. Caught it again, only to drop it again. Blood poured from the buck's torn hindquarters but still it managed a great, twenty-foot leap, almost reaching cover. Hunger had weakened the eagle. For a while it seemed that Elyas had overestimated her strength and the big buck might prove too much for her. But she rallied and with another scream, this time of rage, she dropped on her prey again and managed to grip it securely with both her curved feet. Slowly and clumsily, with much beating of wings, she rose. Then her wings took hold on the current and, with her tail fanned to help buoy her, she soared high above the valley and the moorfolk who'd fed her, away towards her eyrie on Eagle Tor.

Silently, they stood watching until she was a distant speck.

With an impulsive rush of feeling, Kezzy skidded across to her grandfather and threw her arms around him so exuberantly he nearly lost his balance. Joyously, she cried: 'Oh, Gramps, isn't *wonderful* the eagle has come back?'

He hugged her to him. 'Ay, 'tis wonderful, indeed, m'dear. 'Tis right good omen for Hammetts.'

'Will us have good luck now, Gramps?' asked Jamie, agog. Now the eagle had gone, he and a chastened-looking Wart had emerged from the barn.

'Ay, boy, ye may be sure of it,' replied Elyas with solemn confidence.

Kezzy gazed up into his face. 'Will the eagle stay, Gramps?'

Huward spat. ' 'Twill, if'n us keep feedin' un fat jackrabbits what's reared for our own bellies.'

Kezzy took no notice of her father's dour response but kept her bright, dark eyes fixed questioningly upon her grandfather's face. He didn't answer. He was far away. High above the valley upon the frosted, tumbled mass of rock where the sea-eagle was hungrily devouring her gift. Ay, she'd be grateful to the Hammetts and work her magic, Elyas told himself. It was a comforting thought. Some of the pain, the deep, ever-present longing for his gentle Beth, for his fine, young grandsons, even the sadness which a fleeting memory of Ruke could send stealing over him, subsided and he felt strangely comforted. His old, misted eyes shone as brightly as Kezzy's, his stooped shoulders straightened and his grey, bristly chin jutted with all the old spirit and determination of the Hammetts. Suddenly, he began sniffing the air. His hooked nose twitching this way and that like a hound after the scent.

'By the Lord Harry!' he exclaimed. He sniffed again, to make sure he'd correctly located the direction of the milder, westerly breeze. 'Yon eagle has brought us a good snow-eatin' wind!'

The thaw had begun.

Chapter Sixteen

The eagle did stay. And the following spring she brought a fine young mate to Eagle Tor where together they rebuilt the old nest, interlacing new twigs with the old and padding it with dried furze and soft green moss. They added to it every succeeding season until the nest was almost three feet round and nigh on as high: a warm secure place to lay eggs and hatch eaglets.

Elyas strictly forbade Kezzy and Jamie to go near the eyrie, warning them that the eagles would most likely attack them if they felt their eggs or young were threatened. Jamie didn't need telling: the very thought of their loathsome hooked beaks and claws made him quake. But to begin with, Kezzy longed to climb up and look in the nest: especially when, from the open-fronted stamps where she worked, she could see the female wheeling and plunging over the moor, busily catching small rodents to feed her hungry brood.

After a year or two, the Hammetts became used to the eagles being there. The amusing antics of each season's young birds as they took shakily to the air, flapping and wobbling and tumbling among the heather as they learned to hunt for themselves, became a familiar sight. Kezzy, as she grew, no longer felt the urge to view the nest at close quarters. Even Jamie forgot his fear of the eagles, and old Wart ceased to cower and whine if he spotted flat, brown wings gliding above the yard. The old birds grew accustomed to the industrious humans in the valley and in bad weather would swoop fearlessly to pick up whatever meaty offering Elyas was only too pleased to sacrifice.

For just as he'd predicted, the eagles brought them good fortune.

It seemed that in whichever direction they hulked, they exposed dark glinting veins of cassiterite. When so many other mines were going 'horse', Eaglestone consistently produced a good harvest of the best quality tinstone, something which didn't escape the Lord Warden's notice at the quarterly coinages. At least twice a year he sent Grote up the moor offering to buy Eaglestone outright or, at the very least, offer a handsome shareholding in the Hammett mine. Each time de Raddon's price increased; each time Grote's visit was in vain and he'd be contemptuously sent packing. Once, Captain de Raddon actually came himself but couldn't make himself heard above Wart's furious barking. Elyas's manner was deferential enough, the way he stood, cap in hand, a hand cupped to his ear in an effort to make out what de Raddon was saying. In the end, thoroughly exasperated, de Raddon remounted his horse and galloped off down the valley. As soon as he was out of earshot, Elyas quietened Wart with a simple, muttered, ' 'Nough, Wart.'

When Kezzy was ten, Huward married again.

Jeanne Hammett was the widow of Elyas's cousin who'd been cowman at Cherry Brook Farm near Princetown until the previous winter when he'd succumbed to pneumonia. The farmer had given Jeanne until Candlemas day, less than two weeks, to vacate the cottage her husband rented from him, saying it was needed for his new stockman. With the Workhouse looming, Jeanne had sent word to Elyas. He didn't hesitate, immediately set off up the moor to fetch her back with him – on the condition that her three sons, Jake, Cleve and Ebert, respectively twenty-eight, twenty-two and seventeen years old, left the farm and came with her to live and work at Eaglestone. They were perfectly willing; being simple-minded boys they didn't much care where they laboured or at what. They had a sixteen-year-old sister, Young Jeanne, who was in Elyas's opinion, a sight too forthy. He wasn't in the least disappointed when she insisted on remaining at the farm to marry her sweetheart, one of the stockboys.

With eight of them now at Eaglestone Cottage, the two extra tiny bedrooms built by Graeme and Isaac came in useful. 'Cousin Jeanne' was given a choice: she could share the third, slightly larger room with Kezzy and Jamie, or marry Huward and share one of the smaller rooms with him. She chose the latter, happy at her age to find a man willing to marry her. In truth, Huward wasn't all that taken with the idea: she was exceedingly fat and had straggly, grey hairs on her chin. As usual, Elyas prevailed upon his son, pointing out that it was strictly a marriage of convenience, without the necessity of marital duties of a carnal nature – in part due to their advanced ages.

Once married, however, the new Mrs Huward Hammett had other ideas. The first night, Huward tucked himself well down beneath their shared cover, his back sternly towards her, pretending to be asleep.

She gave him a determined dig in the back. 'You'm s'posed to oblige I, husband.' When he only grunted, she slid her big, rough hand beneath the cover and touched his buttocks through his cotton shirt. Quicksilver quivered in his entrails. Not for ten years, not since Ruke, had a woman touched his body: suddenly, he was rediscovering sensations he'd all but forgotten. The blood began to beat in his veins and he began to breathe hoarsely as, persuasively, her hand travelled over his hip. She was wheezing slightly, and her hand was hot and moist. Purposefully, she pulled up his shirt, moving her palm over his protruding navel and down over the wiry pelt covering his belly and groin, boldly seeking to arouse his ardour.

'That's the way, my lover!' she panted gleefully when her administrations proved successful and he was mounted on her big, flaccid body, thrusting between her massive thighs as best he was able.

Afterwards, she went straight to sleep. Exhausted as he was by his exertions, Huward lay for a long time listening to her snoring and grunting beside him. He was bemused. He found her revolting, yet not even with comely, sensuous Ruke had he experienced such an intensity of pleasure.

It became a regular nightly occurrence. Jeanne would demand. Huward would demur. She'd coax him, her pleasure-giving hands slipping stealthily beneath his long shirt. After a while, he'd haul himself atop her and bury himself to the utmost among the loose, sweaty folds of flesh. The moment he'd satisfied his compulsory lust and flooded her vitals, she'd push him off her, roll on her side and almost immediately begin snoring.

Huward was no longer a young man; moreover, he'd been celibate for the past ten years. So it didn't take many nights with the robust Jeanne to find his strength began to ebb away. Sometimes Elyas, whose sharp ears told him what went on between the newly-wed pair once the candle had been snuffed, caught him yawning as they worked in by the bal and his son seemed to be growing all the more lethargic. When he saw that Huward was taking twice as long as he once did to haul a corve of stuff back along the tunnel, he decided it was time to speak out.

'What's matter withee, Huward, boy?' he grumbled. 'Her bain't proper bride. Her be here on 'count o' they boys an' 'cause we'm needin' woman t'look after us. You'm daft t'waste thy sap grindin' ol' nanny goat when there be tin t'be dug, boy.'

After that, Huward did try and impose certain restraints upon the voluptuous Jeanne, even telling her that his father disapproved of their too-frequent couplings. But she was used to a wife's physical entitlements and refused to be deprived of them on Elyas's say so. Consequently, she continued to arouse and provoke Huward whenever the mood was upon her at night – which was most nights.

During the day, she went quietly and diligently about her chores and never revealed by so much as a coy glance what passed between her and Huward during the dark hours when they were crushed together on their narrow, adjoining pallets.

Kezzy and Jamie grew very attached to her. Unlike the crabby, bullying Morgenna and Bethinda, big Jeanne was always smiling. She wasn't very bright and had to be shown over and over again which were the 'deads' to be picked from the spalled tinstone in the stamps. But it didn't matter: she saw to it that her three dim-witted boys worked their coore and she could crimp a fine, tasty pasty for mossle.

They were all saddened when, like her previous husband, she fell victim to pneumonia and died the following winter, the weather being exceptionally cold and foggy. Elyas also suffered the symptoms of lung-inflammation and coughed a lot as he sat snug by the fire rolled in a sheep's skin, drinking hot brandy and honey.

' 'Tis nawthin' burra touch o' tilly-gilly,' he'd gasp, but even Kezzy knew that his agonising cough was the same as that which had carried off poor Jeanne. She'd shed tears for her kindly stepmother. But she trembled with fear for her beloved grandfather.

'Gramps won't die like Jeanne, will he, Pa?' she whispered anxiously as they all sat around the table after supper, silently staring at the frail old man dozing by the fire.

'Death do come to us all, chield,' murmured her father mournfully.

At that, Elyas stirred, opened an eye, and croaked: 'Nay, nay. Death do come to young men . . . old men *go* to death. An' I bain't ready t'go yet.'

That night his fever reached its peak and by noon the following day he was enquiring of his relieved and delighted granddaughter if there was any stew for mossle.

It was a while before Elyas was strong enough to work a coore again. In truth, he never did fully recover his previous, wiry strength. But that no longer mattered, not now that Jake, Cleve and Ebert had worked their apprenticeship and were putting their muscular young backs into their work.

Like their dead mother, they were jolly souls. Always happy to be teased by young Jamie and laughing loudly when they found that he had popped a fat toad in each of their mossle bags. Ebert was a simpleton: he continually wore a silly grin and didn't talk much, save to Kezzy. She never quite understood what he was saying as he would put his hand in front of his mouth and giggle like a pixie, at the same time hopping clumsily from foot to foot.

'Yon Ebert bain't got all his'n apples on tree,' observed Elyas more than once. Nevertheless, he'd no complaints about the boy's work and soon discovered that Ebert was twice as strong as his elder, bigger-built brothers.

Kezzy was always especially kind to Ebert since he was weak-witted. Like his mother used to do, she always made sure he got his fair share of whatever was on the table. And she wouldn't let naughty Jake and Cleve bedevil him with stinging-nettles and hazel switches until he cried like a small child. And sometimes, in the summer evenings when there was yet light enough for such things, she read the Bible aloud to him. He would sit on the front step, totally enthralled, not perhaps understanding the scriptures but enjoying her sweet, lilting voice. Presently, one by one, Jake, Cleve and Jamie would sidle out and find somewhere to perch so that they, too, could listen to the wonderful stories which she somehow managed to make so much more interesting than the Reverend Creedy, whose long sermons were mostly about unholy fires and scorched souls.

So it was against this background that the Hammetts' lot continued to improve.

Wheal Eaglestone extended to a great depth, too deep for the stuff to be brought up by manpower and windlass. Elyas bought a whipsederry with a good, strong pulley wheel in Plympton and paid five guineas to a young man called Richard Trevithick to come to Eaglestone and fix it in the shaft. Trevithick was the maker of a steam engine which was being tried out on winding work at Captain de Raddon's Wheal Emma. Since he hadn't yet received any money for his wonderful contraption he was glad to take what work was offered.

When the whipsederry was in place, a pair of sturdy moor colts were hitched to it and Jamie and Kezzy took it in turns to drive the animals and hoist the kibbles of stuff to the surface.

Come the next coinage day, Elyas needed two colts to pull the glittering blocks of tin to Plympton for weighing and stamping. And as his beasts plodded down the main street of the stannary town, straining in their harnesses beneath the weight, he was aware of the envious looks he was receiving, for his was a tin harvest worthy of one of the bigger wheals. Some of the men, tinners from around Cornwood, recognised him and ran along behind him, shouting out to him jeeringly.

'What ho, Cap'n Hammett! 'Tis rich ye is, by looks o' it!'

'Remember un paupers an' they dry throats, good Cap'n, zur . . .!'

He ignored their sarcasm, sitting atop his wagon in a dignified manner as befitted the owner of a tin-rich mine like Eaglestone. But as he passed the Fighting Cocks inn, he couldn't resist a quick, triumphant look up at the windows, certain that Captain de Raddon was standing there in the shadows, drawn from his libidinous pleasures to look out when he heard voices in the street shouting the familiar name. Grote, too, most likely. And Elyas's swift look from beneath his grey, old-badger brows spoke more clearly than words.

So ye thought sendin' Hammett boys to they deaths would crush Elyas the tinner, did 'ee, Cap'n John de Raddon? Bring un ol' clodpate to heel, once an' for all? Well now, cullie, just you'm take a geek at what this'n ol' clodpate has on arse o' wagon. Have ye ever seen tin as silver-bright and pure? Nay! An' ye bain't likely'd to, not if'n ye plundered the land from now 'til ye last death rattle! B'cause this be Hammett tin. Eaglestone tin!

Then, his eyes as hard and grey as moorland granite, Elyas tugged his forelock exaggeratedly and trundled on.

Thereafter, every coinage saw Elyas in Plympton with a good tin harvest and after a while those who shouted after him, calling him 'Cap'n Hammett' in a derisory fashion, ceased to do so and began using that title in the proper, respectful manner.

Chapter Seventeen

It was one of those shining golden November days, just after Kezzy's thirteenth birthday on All-Hallows, when the sheltered elms at the top of the valley still had dry red leaves clinging to them and the moorland was covered in stubbly, russet furze.

Kezzy was the first to spot the eagles restlessly gliding and dipping above Eaglestone – male, female, and that season's two young eagles, their white natal down all but gone. Kezzy went out of the washing-house into the yard the better to view them, curious as to why all four should be there. Save in the winter, they seldom saw any save the female, and then only as she swept up the valley towards the eyrie.

After a moment, Kezzy called across to Jamie who was driving the colts round and round as they worked the horse whim. He turned and she pointed wordlessly up at their feathered visitors. He peered, shading his eyes from the bright, autumn sun. So? Eagles. He no longer feared them, but that didn't mean he was interested in them. He shrugged carelessly and gave his attention to the colts again, reining them in as the full kibble reached the surface.

The female eagle suddenly dropped right down and perched on the low stone wall surrounding the Hammetts' sett.

Kezzy hurried across to the blowing-house where Elyas and Ebert were busy smelting. She stuck in her head and a wave of hot, dry air hit her in the face and made her catch her breath. Ebert's silly grin widened at the sight of her looking in; he was standing patiently by the bellows waiting for Elyas to order him to start pumping them again. Elyas was carefully pouring a trickle of silvery tin into a mouldstone with hands so steady they'd be the envy of any younger man. Kezzy restrained herself until he'd finished the delicate task.

'Gramps, the eagles have come . . . all of them.'

His bushy brows shot up in surprise. He dropped the smelter in the water trough with a hiss and a cloud of steam and hastened to stand with her in the yard. The old female eagle was still sitting hunched on the wall, her brittle, thinning feathers slack, black button eyes alert. As Elyas and Kezzy took a few steps nearer to her, she rose abruptly and went to join her mate circling in the clear, chill air overhead. The two young birds – a male and a female – were preoccupied making short, rather graceless flights between the rocks and burrows on the banks of the brook.

'Are they hungry, Gramps?' Kezzy asked him, bewildered. There was still plenty of small prey on the moor because of the fair weather.

Elyas stood for a moment gazing into her pale, oval-shaped face with its high forehead and slanting dark eyes, almost on a level with his now she'd grown so tall. It was a tender face: so guileless. Slowly and sadly, he said: 'Nay, chield. Them ent hungry. Most likely'd come to say good-bye.'

'Oh no, Gramps . . .!' she quavered, face crumpling.

But she'd known, just as he did, that one day the eagles would grow restless, lured, perhaps, by a fresh, salty breeze from the sea, to seek less harsh climes than high up on the desolate, wind-swept moor.

The old female gave a sudden scream. '*Keee-iahhh!*'

Immediately the young birds left their watery playground and swooped to answer her summons. Abruptly breaking her circle, she led them down the valley all the while climbing strongly on an updraft. The old male soared away to the west for two hundred yards or so, then swung and flew after them.

'Goodbye, eagles,' called Kezzy. 'Dear friends.'

Elyas said nothing. He was silently praying that they hadn't taken the Hammetts' luck with them on the winter flight.

Many of the villagers swore they'd heard the explosion and felt the earth tremors in Cornwood, though it was unlikely.

It was three months to the day after the eagles had left. Kezzy was in the village that afternoon. Later, when she allowed herself to go back over the terrible events, she couldn't recall whether or not she had heard anything. She did recall that it was late on Friday and she was at the dame school. In truth, she was, at thirteen, too old to attend as a pupil, but since she so hated the thought of not going, when every well-thumbed school book was as much an old friend as Dame Hannah Rogers herself, Elyas permitted her to spend one afternoon there a week helping to teach the smaller ones their letters – which was a great help to the dame whose sight, sadly, was beginning to fail.

And she remembered the smoke. A great, black pall which rose above Eagle Tor and gathered above the moor like the darkness of a winter's night. Never, never would Kezzy forget that.

One of the children spotted it first from his place – Kezzy's old seat – by the little leaded window. Excitedly, he pointed, exclaiming, 'Lookee, mistress! 'Tis terrible smeech up'long moor!'

They went out on to the doorstep for a better view.

'Reckon 'tis barn afire,' piped one of the boys.

'Bain't no flames, clot'ead!' snorted another.

Doors began opening and the miners who were home because they worked night coore began spilling out, ropes and shovels and lanterns on their backs. None spoke. Tired faces grim, they set off at a smart pace up the village street towards the moor.

Towards Eaglestone.

'Oh, mercy!' gasped Dame Rogers.

Comprehension crossed Kezzy's face, swiftly changing to horror.

She began to run after the miners, her long legs speeding over the uneven ground, her long, dark hair flowing behind her. Unhampered by tools, she quickly overtook the rescuers. They recognised her as she sped blindly by, saw her white, stricken face and despairing eyes. But none called her name or uttered any word of encouragement. The tinners were no strangers to disaster; their lives were fraught with danger, every coore spent below ground among the flying dust and the splinters of stone and the fire-damp. Fire-damp! Satan's breath! That was what tinners called the seeping, suffocating, unwholesome vapour which could suddenly erupt with the noise of ten cannons and claim God knew how many victims.

The breath was torn from Kezzy's lungs as on and on she went, up over the wasteland towards the towering crags. Once she stumbled ankle-deep into a mire which she escaped by throwing herself among a tussock of rushes and getting a good foothold. In a trice, she dragged herself up from the sodden ground and was off running again. Her body ached and she had an agonising pain in her side, but she didn't stop. Not until she heard the sound of hooves behind her and, turning, saw that Dame Rogers was fast approaching in her horse and trap. Gratefully, with no word passing between them, Kezzy scrambled up beside the solemn-faced schoolmistress and let herself be carried the rest of the way up the moor.

Kezzy's worst fears were realised as soon as they came within sight of Eaglestone. Puffs of smoke still wafted from the main shaft of the mine, feeble witness to the terrible holocaust below ground. The cluster of buildings stood deserted; like grey granite ghosts glimpsed through the fine, choking dust which hung in the air.

Kezzy leapt recklessly from the still-moving trap as they galloped into the yard. She called frantically: 'Gramps! Pa! Jamie . . . where are you, Jamie?'

For a moment she stood looking desperately about her, taking in the scene of desolation. The two ponies used to work the horse whim had wrenched themselves free in their panic and bolted. One lone hen scratched in the yard. The cottage door swung, creaking slightly on its rusty hinges, as though somebody had just gone out for a few moments and hadn't bothered to shut it properly behind them. To take the miners' croust to them, perhaps. *Oh, no!* Horror gripped Kezzy anew with the sudden realisation that even Jamie must have been caught in the blast.

Coughing and spluttering as the dust bit into her lungs, eyes streaming as it raked her eyeballs, she tore across to the gaping entrance to the mine and pulled violently on the bell rope. Far below in the choking blackness she heard the cowbells jangling. No pinprick of light appeared, growing bigger until it was discernible as a candle atop a hat worn by one of her family as he climbed the slanting ladders. No voice called up to her in response to the merry, echoing peal, asking what she wanted.

'Hollooo, Eaglestone!' she shouted with all the force her tortured lungs would allow.

But Wheal Eaglestone was silent. As silent as a tomb.

PART II

Chapter Eighteen

1813

'Horses, Gramps.'

When Elyas gave no sign that he'd heard, Kezzy leaned across to where he sat hunched on the settle by the fire and touched his arm so that he looked up into her face. 'Horses, Gramps,' she repeated louder, mouthing the words so he could make out what she was telling him.

'Ay, I hear they,' he muttered.

She knew it wasn't so. The explosion in the mine over two years before had all but ruined his hearing, just as the falling rubble had all but wrecked his body. Concernedly, she watched as he picked up one of his crutches and used it to steady himself as he hauled his frail, twisted frame off the seat. She longed to go and help him, but he grew angry if ever she did, insisting that he could manage quite well given time and didn't need 'babbyin' '.

The horses came into the yard and stopped.

Kezzy looked out of the window. It was night, but the moon was a silvery eye in the dark sky revealing the outlines of two score riders and their heavily laden pack-horses. She spoke over her shoulder forgetting he wouldn't hear. ' 'Tis the flaskers, Gramps. With a fair-sized cargo, by the looks of it.'

The flaskers were expected. Exactly which night they would appear, Elyas and Kezzy hadn't known. But with a good moon and fair weather for February, they were bound to run a cargo of cognac, of that the Hammetts were sure. Therefore they'd sat up for the past three nights, dozing by the fire and waiting for them.

Captain de Raddon's steward, Grote, led the band of flaskers. Now that the Hammetts were involved, he didn't bother to hide his face from them. Nor did he hide the fact that he and the other men – drawn from among the ostlers and grooms and gardeners at Blackaven – were free-trading with the full knowledge of their lord and master.

Grote dismounted from his big chestnut. 'What ho, tinner!' he growled in greeting to Elyas. He ignored Kezzy.

Elyas scowled at him from beneath his overhanging brows. He hadn't heard, and couldn't lip-read in the poor light, but he always set his face harshly at Grote since he hated him almost as fervently as he did Captain de Raddon. Had he heard, he would have felt a deep resentment at being referred to as 'tinner' instead of as 'Cap'n'. Although Wheal Eaglestone was 'knocked', he still expected this mark of respect. Indeed, there were few in the tinning community who didn't continue the courtesy and speak of him with awe for surviving the pit blast which had shifted hundreds of tons of rubble, crushing his son, grandson and Jake, Cleve and Ebert.

Elyas jerked his head towards the mine. The cage above the disused horse whim rattled slightly in the sharp night breeze coming up the valley. 'Best get un cargo stowed 'neath grass . . .'twill soon be dawn.'

Kezzy took over. First she made sure that Grote's big chestnut was securely roped to the whipsederry so the pulley moved the kibbles freely up and down their shaft. Then, carrying a lantern, she led the way down the first sloping ladder inside the main shaft. Grote followed. Then a dozen of his men. The rest remained at the surface to unload the draught-animals and work the horse whim. Elyas stood propped on his crutches carefully counting the half-ankers of cognac being loaded into the kibbles as they were paid half a crown for each tub hidden in the mine.

Kezzy agilely descended another ladder, pausing at the foot with her lantern held aloft to light the way for the lumpish smugglers in their clumsy sea-boots. As soon as they had attained her level, she was off down the next ladder, then the next. Down and down, she went, until she reached fifty fathoms deep, which was the full depth of the shaft though they didn't know it. There they waited until the first full kibble descended. The half-ankers were still roped together in pairs as they'd been taken from the horses so they could be strung across the chest and shoulders of the burly tub-carriers. Even Grote carried his two, weighing over fifty pounds each, so that the job would be done as quickly as possible.

With Kezzy at their head, her lantern lighting the way, the laden column trudged along the winding, low-roofed tunnels to the small chamber where they stacked their tubs, the lower ones standing on rocks so that the filthy water, impregnated with an acrid, earthy smell, wouldn't seep in and spoil the fine brandy rendering it fit only to have herbs added to turn it into cheap, kiddleywink shrub. There was water everywhere. Or so it seemed to Grote. He'd not forgotten that Elyas had once dissuaded him from using Eaglestone to hide contraband, saying that it was likely to flood.

'You'm sure mine won't flood?' he'd ask Kezzy doubtfully each time he came, either to cache a run or pick up tubs previously left for delivery to the gentry.

' 'Tis dryer'n most upalong moor,' she'd tell him curtly.

With that Grote, and his master, had to be content. One thing was certain: no safer place existed in which to hide their valuable cargos. If the Preventatives did come demanding to search Eaglestone they'd not find their way through the veritable warren of tunnels to the secret chamber. Kezzy would see to that. Even the flaskers weren't absolutely certain of the way to and from the foot of the shaft as all the passages looked similar in the pale lantern glow. Grote, quite correctly, suspected that their innocent-looking young guide sometimes led them in circles to confuse them. Once, he attempted to surreptitiously mark the way with a piece of chalk but shrewd Kezzy was alert to such tricks and added a few chalk-marks of her own, utterly confounding him.

This cargo was unusually large and took almost two hours to unload and stash. During that time, Kezzy had a chance to examine the tub-carriers, a rough-looking bunch in dark-dyed jerseys and crinkled sea-boots. She knew most of the flaskers by now: Grote generally used the same men, drawn from the Blackaven household. Yet on this occasion he'd seemingly brought with him a stranger who greatly stirred her curiosity. He stood head and shoulders above his companions and wore Grote's old red stocking hat with the long tail wound around his face in the manner of a man with tooth-rot. And Kezzy couldn't help noticing that he showed a great deal of interest in his surroundings: twisting his head this way and that, peering and sometimes probing the walls with an enquiring finger while he waited his turn to pick up his two kegs. Something which he did with ease, hoisting them across his broad torso as though they were half the weight.

The tubs were all secreted away at last and the underground party could wearily ascend the seemingly never-ending ladders into the fresh air again. The horses were taken to the brook to be watered and the men threw themselves down along the bank to smoke a pipe of plug and rest for a while before setting off back down the moor to the coast.

Kezzy noticed that the big stranger didn't go with the rest of the men but remained silently standing in the yard with Grote while the steward grudgingly counted out the half crowns into Elyas's work-scarred hand. Grote disliked having to pay the Hammetts for hiding contraband when fear of a vicious beating or seeing their home in flames was usually sufficient to force tinners or yeomen into helping free-traders. It was Kezzy who, three years previously when she'd her seriously injured grandfather to nurse and no income, had sought out Grote and offered to be the flaskers' custodian in return for payment. He'd laughed in her face and had called her a foolish maid for imagining she might profit in such a way but he'd thought it prudent to tell Captain de Raddon of her offer. The Lord Warden hadn't laughed. His ugly, scarred face had twisted in a thoughtful frown at mention of her name.

'Keziah Hammett, you say?' he'd mused, picturing the small girl glaring defiantly at him as he fed sweetstuffs to his dogs after she'd refused to take them from him unless he helped to save her brothers from the press. It was then that de Raddon had envied Elyas Hammett his *didekei* granddaughter, more than he'd ever envied the old man his sturdy son and grandsons. De Raddon himself had witch-hunted Ruke Hammett; branded her dark-haired, dark-eyed baby a witch's pup and best drowned. Yet, had his own pale-haired, nervous, barren wife given him just such a daughter he'd have been well satisfied.

'Is Eaglestone dry enough for our needs?' he'd asked Grote.

'Ay, Cap'n. Dryish . . . so Hammett maid says.'

'How much storage is she asking?'

Grote's lip had curled scornfully at her very impudence. 'Half crown a tub. For what should be free if'n her knows what's healthy for she.'

'She's got her grandfather to keep back and belly,' de Raddon had observed, but without any note of compassion in his voice.

They were in the library at Blackaven House. Grote restrained himself from spitting in the fireplace at the mention of his old antagonist. 'Faugh! That crippled no good limb of Satan . . .!'

'Take the next run to Eaglestone and pay Keziah Hammett her storage . . . I want no spoilt barrels, mark me. Tell her that: or she'll be held liable and made to pay for them.'

His steward had looked dumbfounded. He found his voice and spluttered. 'Did 'ee say *pay* her, Cap'n? Why, I could take whip to the forthy baggage and . . .'

'Don't argue with me, Grote!' snapped de Raddon. 'Or 'twill be your hide tastes the lash.'

Grote had departed without another word. It crossed his mind that his master was turning soft-headed in his middle years. But it didn't enter his head to disobey: just in case Captain de Raddon's unexpected indulgence was directed solely at maidens and not crafty stewards with thin purses.

De Raddon had sat for some time after Grote had gone, conjuring other images. In particular, one of Elyas Hammett as he was pulled from the rubble, torn and bleeding and barely alive. As Lord Warden of the Stannaries, de Raddon had been notified immediately of the pit blast. When he'd arrived at Eaglestone, the rescuers were on the verge of giving up, certain that none of the Hammetts could have survived the massive roof-fall. The new run where they would have been working, pointed out by Kezzy, was solidly blocked by tons of granite. But Kezzy had pleaded with them to keep digging, tearing desperately at the debris with bare, bloodied hands, driven by some strange, deep-rooted instinct which guided her to where he lay.

'I know Gramps is alive! I know he is!' she kept saying when they gently pointed out the impossibility of his survival.

So they kept digging. And she'd been proved miraculously right. One of the solid wooden stiddles had wedged itself across Elyas, saving his upper body and head from being crushed.

Afterwards, people round about whispered of magic and spells and other dark mysteries whenever the name Keziah Hammett was mentioned. For wasn't her ma a witch born and bred and hanged for it? And they became wary of catching her sharp, black, undaunted gaze on the rare occasions she left her crippled grandfather and came down off the desolate moor to the village.

It wasn't fear of sorcery that made de Raddon agree to Kezzy's terms for storing contraband. In truth, he didn't believe she had witch-like tendencies or was in any way demonic. She was fey, undoubtedly, and had an almost uncanny extra sense as she'd proved, but that was hardly surprising with gypsy blood in her veins. Neither had de Raddon's decision anything to do with pity: though he guessed that, like other families who'd lost the breadwinner, the two remaining Hammetts lived from hand to mouth. No, his enmity towards the arrogant, defiant old tinner who lay broken and gasping for life was as strong as ever. Yet, for the first time in his life, he, Captain John de Raddon, Lord of Blackaven, Lord Warden of the Stannaries, friend of Royalty and the largest mine-owner in Devon, had something in common with Elyas the tinner. For they both knew what it was like to be caught in a skin-searing blast of fire-damp. To hear the terrible roar of splitting pit-props and falling rubble. Then to lie in agony listening to the thundering silence closing in about them like the soft, dark brown earth they plundered.

So Kezzy had got her half a crown a tub 'storage'.

Elyas, once he'd recovered sufficiently to know what was going on in by his beloved bal, didn't share her enthusiasm for de Raddon silver. But his utter inability to work meant he'd no choice but to accept the position or see them both lousterers on the parish – which would be an even bigger blow to his pride.

Even though Elyas carefully counted the coins as Grote reluctantly dropped them into his hand, he always made him stand waiting while he counted them again, now and then biting on one of the clinking pieces if it didn't shine as brightly as the rest. It was a ritual that never failed to make Grote furious, which was partly why Elyas did it.

Always Grote would round scornfully on the crippled old tinner. 'Ye grizzlin' ol' labbut! Ye should be tied t'bulls arse an' shit t'death!' he'd roar, or something equally as insulting which Elyas didn't hear, or pretended not to.

Yet, on this occasion Grote said nothing, contenting himself with a scowl while Elyas tallied his fistful of silver with the number of marks, one for each tub, he'd made on his crutch with a lump of chalk. Kezzy, standing watching the scene, didn't miss the quick, sidelong look Grote gave the tall stranger, as though to judge his reaction to her grandfather's obvious distrust. With a start Kezzy realised that the stranger, far from being interested in Grote, was gazing intently at her. For a brief moment their eyes met. Her own, bright with curiosity. His, speculative. So that for some strange reason she found herself flushing. Then, abruptly, he moved into the shadows, away from the flickering orange circles thrown by the lanterns.

'Ay, do tote proper,' acceded Elyas grudgingly. He dropped the silver in the gunny sack fastened to his belt. 'Now, off withee, boys. Afore some meddlin' tinker gets geek at 'ee an' goes squealin' like hog t'un Preventy men for reward.'

Grote and his companion moved to go.

Kezzy's voice rang out. 'A moment, Captain de Raddon. Won't you step inside an' take a swallow of tay afore you start back to Blackaven?'

The two men stopped dead.

Elyas's damaged ears had picked up his granddaughter's high, melodic tones – just as she meant him to. He'd started to swing away towards the cottage but he, too, stopped dead, his hands gripping the struts of his crutches until the knuckles looked in danger of bursting through his papery grey skin. His hawk-eyes pierced the gloom, raking the tall figure in the long leather boots and jerkin.

Slowly, the stranger unwound the stocking-hat that concealed all but his stony eyes.

Elyas stared. Then began to curse.

' 'Tis 'ee, John de Raddon, blast thy liver! Sneakin' round my land like cunnin' fox!' Turning to Kezzy, he blazed: 'Tay? Tay? Fetch un evil an' cloppy-legged or nay I'll run he off like some thievin' tinker . . .!'

Quickly, Kezzy laid a pacificatory hand on her grandfather's arm as de Raddon stiffened in anger and Grote took a menacing step forward. She said reproachfully, 'Gramps, we must show gratitude for Cap'n de Raddon's patronage. Least we can do is offer him some tay . . .'

It was as if her soft, reasoning words acted as a trigger to the bitter resentment gnawing deep within him.

'Patronage!' Elyas raged. He swayed dangerously as he put his weight on one crutch and lifted an arm towards the mine in a sweeping gesture. 'Yon dark hole is bal, ent some illigant lady's parlour room. Nay, an' us ent fancy ladies' maids. We'm in pay o' moonshiners . . . an' that could put bless'd rope round our necks if'n we'm caught. So don't 'ee talk up weak 'bout bein' grateful to his'n high an' mighty Lord Wardenship!'

'Please, Gramps . . .' Kezzy attempted to stem the tirade as de Raddon's scarred face turned as hard as moorland granite.

But Elyas wouldn't be silenced.

'I'll show 'ee what I think of de Raddon *patronage*!' he snarled. And before Kezzy could stop him, he twitched the gunny sack from his belt and upended it, sending a silver stream of coins scattering in the mud. Then, for good measure, he spat on them. Turning clumsily on his crutches, he started off towards the cottage, saying, 'C'mon 'long inside with 'ee, chield. Hammetts filled they bellies afore wi'out de Raddon silver an' shall do 'gin.'

He went in.

'I'm sorry, Cap'n de Raddon. Gramps is a proper mazegerry these days. Ever since the pit blast.'

Her tone was curt, as though by apologising for him she felt she was being disloyal. All the while her eyes, so dark and sorrowful, appealed to him: God knew how much they needed his patronage. She was all too aware that they were fortunate to receive storage when so many others were made to assist the free-traders for no payment.

De Raddon's cold look of anger remained but he nodded briefly.

To Grote he said: 'Send the men on their way. Then wait for me along the valley.'

Wordlessly, Grote strode away to do as he was bid. Shortly, the column of flaskers and pack horses streamed by at the gallop down the valley. De Raddon remained, standing silently, watching Kezzy as without a thought for her clothes she knelt in the mud and began to hunt for the scattered coins. Because skirts were too hampering during her forays in by the mine, she wore an old pair of corduroy breeches and an old jersey, both of which had belonged to her brother Isaac. Since he'd been narrow-shanked, her long, slim legs were tightly encased and the jersey emphasised the contours of her fine young breasts. Her abundance of glossy hair was drawn back from her pointed, elfin face and captured at the neck with a scrap of ribbon.

De Raddon's stony eyes roamed over her appreciatively. He was forty-six and had grown somewhat jaded with the ways of the flesh, yet something about Kezzy stirred his interest. There was a vibrant sensuality about her which was lacking in the tavern wenches and maid servants with whom he usually pleasured himself. With some surprise, he suddenly realised that Keziah Hammett was no longer the tinner's little girl whom he'd coveted all these barren years, but a tantalising young woman.

'How old are you, girl?'

He spoke abruptly, the sound of his harsh voice startling in the quiet of the yard. Kezzy looked up sharply and saw his expression. It was one she often saw on the faces of the men in the village as she passed them by. She avoided his eyes, busying herself with finding the last of the coins and dropping them in her pocket as she told him, 'Fifteen last All-Hallows, Cap'n.'

He gave his brief nod again.

Kezzy straightened up. She'd found all the coins but still she kept her head lowered, her eyes on the muddy ground, sensing his eyes boring into her. Presently, he said: 'Are you not curious as to why I should come clandestinely to Eaglestone?'

Kezzy could guess why he'd come. Undoubtedly, it was to do with his avaricious determination to wrest the mine from her grandfather. However, she looked straight at him and nodded, prepared to hear him out.

'There's talk that Eaglestone is too dangerous to be worked now. 'Tis likely there would be more explosions.' He was watching her face, judging her reaction. 'My man Grote knows stewarding and flasking but he doesn't know mining, so I came to look for myself.'

'Well, Cap'n de Raddon, now you have seen it,' Kezzy heard herself saying grimly, in an almost perfect imitation of Dame Hannah Rogers. There was also a cool note of dismissal underlying her words which he attuned to but chose to ignore.

'Yes, and I'm prepared to venture an increased offer.'

'Venture?' she repeated, frowning.

'Risk,' he simplified.

'I do know what venture means, Cap'n,' Kezzy told him crisply. 'I've had an education.'

He blinked. Momentarily taken aback because she'd the temerity to talk back to him. No wench had ever dared to do so before. Scowling, he snapped: 'Then I would hope you've more sense than your addle-brained grandfather. You said it yourself, pit-blast has left him mazed. Now you're full-grown, or near enough, best take the reins yourself and sell Eaglestone to me.'

There was a long pause, during which he watched her closely, awaiting her reaction. She'd taken the initiative and allowed the flaskers to use the mine as a cache, but that had been out of necessity to buy food when the old man lay for weeks half-senseless and hovering 'twixt life and death.

Clearly, it hadn't occurred to her to seize control of Eaglestone while Elyas Hammett had a rational thought in his head.

When the import of what de Raddon was suggesting registered, Kezzy stood gazing at his unpleasant countenance in astonishment. He was her grandfather's sworn enemy. Did he really believe that she would connive with him against her beloved Gramps? Her fine-moulded lips thinned with disgust as she struggled against giving vent to her sense of outrage, her pocketful of coins serving as a reminder that to antagonise de Raddon was to risk poverty and starvation.

'I regret that you have wasted your time coming her, Cap'n de Raddon,' she said with as much civility as she could muster. 'Eaglestone is not for sale and never will be.'

His own tone became urgent and persuasive.

'Lookee here, girl, sell to me and you and your grandfather can leave this godforsaken place. Live in comfort in the village . . .'

As she doggedly shook her head, he was again reminded of her as a small, obstinate girl standing before him at Blackaven House pleading for her brothers' freedom. 'You could buy all manner of sweetstuffs . . . eat white bread every day . . . wear a fine silk gown . . .'

That had been her dream. Then. But now her head continued to move stubbornly from side to side. De Raddon grew impatient with her.

'Come, name your price for the mine, Keziah!'

She stopped shaking her head and stood quite still, frowning slightly, surprised by his unexpected use of her name. That he'd even remember it: to one so exalted in the parish she expected to be no more than just another nameless bal maiden. She found even this small familiarity disturbing, almost as disturbing as his levelled, piercing gaze.

'Cap'n de Raddon . . .' she hesitated, not quite sure what she was going to say. She'd spoken only to break the unnerving silence. 'Cap'n de Raddon, Gramps and me . . . we can't sell Eaglestone. Not to you or anyone. Not now. Pa and my brother Jamie and my cousins are buried in Middle Alley behind Bess and Graeme. 'Tis their grave.'

He made a gesture. 'Bones!' he snapped and saw her flinch at his callousness.

'Nevertheless, Parson Creedy did say words over them just as if they were buried down'long church.'

So that was that. The ground was sacred to the two remaining Hammetts. De Raddon knew that however much he offered for Eaglestone, they wouldn't sell what amounted to the family grave. 'You'd do well not to thwart me!' he snapped in frustration and felt a certain satisfaction at the anxious look which flitted across her face. He seized upon his advantage. 'It may well be that after this run has been dispersed I must look for another hiding place. One that doesn't cost half a crown a tub.'

The implied threat wasn't lost on Kezzy. He stood between them and the degradation of poverty. 'You'll not find a safer place for your tubs, Cap'n,' she said quickly. 'We'll not squeal to Preventy men if they come sniffin' round, I swear it.'

He knew it was true. 'Just see you don't' he said curtly.

He turned and walked away. In a moment the dark had swallowed him. Presently, Kezzy heard his and Grote's horses cantering down the valley. She stood listening until the sound of hooves receded. Then went in and closed the door behind her.

Chapter Nineteen

Elyas was sitting propped on the settle staring moodily into the dying embers of the fire. As Kezzy came in, his scowl deepened but he didn't look up or enquire as to what had kept her talking with de Raddon for so long out in the cold night air.

She was used to his truculence and compassionately put it down to frustration at his uselessness, and the fact that he silently suffered terrible bone-aches from his poorly knitted limb as well as the trying chin-cough. She poked the fire into life and put on two vags from those piled by the fireplace; a small chore, but one that he couldn't do save with great difficulty.

'They vags bain't dry 'nough,' he began to grumble. 'Won't blaze nor burn proper. Jist give out smeech an' smoke.'

'Nevertheless, 'tis better than freezing bones, Gramps.'

He grunted at that. It was because his bone-aches had worsened of late and he needed a constantly burning fire, that they'd used up all the vags she'd cut and stored in the barn the previous autumn to see them through until spring. In desperation, she'd taken the wagon up to the turf ties and cut a load of damp peat vags, setting them to dry around the fireplace.

There was silence for a while. Then Elyas's curiosity got the better of him. 'What did un skulkin' fox de Raddon want, as if'n I don't know?' he asked bitterly.

'He wanted to buy Eaglestone.'

'Eh, what you'm a-sayin'?' He peered into her face.

Wearily, she raised her voice and repeated herself.

Elyas coughed and spat in the fire. 'Thought as much. An' ye told he t'be gone pack an' vardel!'

'I told him we wouldn't sell.'

'Eh? Speak up . . . I can't abide un talkin' up weak!'

'I told him we'd never sell . . .'tis Pa's and the boys' grave.'

He nodded. Sat wheezing to himself for a while, watching from beneath his eagle-brows as she took the coins from her pocket and scraped the mud from them before hiding them behind a loose stone in the wall.

'*Patronage*!' he sneered. She pretended not to hear, not wanting to enter into further altercation regarding what was after all their only means of income at present. Instead, she said: 'Cap'n de Raddon reckons that even if he did buy Eaglestone he'd have trouble finding men to work it because of the fire-damp.'

'Fough! Don't stop he wantin' t'buy un,' retorted Elyas. 'Yon mine bain't be any more noxious than his own Wheal Emma.'

Kezzy replaced the stone. 'He said I . . . we could name our own price.'

Elyas wasn't so addled that he missed her swift change to the plural. His eyes flickered shrewdly. 'Tried t'get round 'ee then, did un? What did un slimy toad say? I be proper mazed an' bain't fitty to own good tinnin' works? Eh? Eh?'

He began to gasp and choke, a sure sign he was growing agitated. Kezzy went to him. 'Come, Gramps, lay down a while and rest,' she said soothingly, taking his arm.

He let her help him up and across to his pallet in the corner.

'Mustn't sleep too long, Kezzy chield,' he wheezed. 'I be first coore to bal.'

'Yes, Gramps, I know . . .' she said, humouring him. She helped him lie down and propped him up on another rolled-up pallet so he wouldn't suffocate on the blood-tinged emission from his dust ruined lungs.

'Can't leave hulkin' o' Middle Alley to un boys . . .'

'No, no, of course not, Gramps.'

She went and fetched from the wooden shelf the precious bottle of laudanum that Dame Rogers had given her. She held it to Elyas's lips and carefully tipped a few drops down his throat. Then sat with him, waiting for it to work its small, calming miracle.

Eyes wild, he suddenly jerked himself bolt upright and began shouting orders. 'Fetch us fuses an' look sharp, Jamie boy! Huward! Huward! Come here, son! Look! Look!' He stabbed the air with a hand that was hooked and yellow and fleshless like the claw of an old hen. There was a look of exaltation on his face. 'See there! 'Tis copper, boy! *Copper*!'

Gently, Kezzy pressed him down to rest against the rolled pallet and pulled the blanket up to his chin. For a while longer he ranted, then his eyelids began to droop.

'Are ye there, Kezzy chield?' he murmured drowsily.

'I'm here, Gramps.'

She touched the worn old face and he smiled contentedly. A moment later he fell into a restless sleep. Bone-weary, Kezzy went into her little back room and threw herself on her pallet fully clothed save for her muddy boots.

Distantly, an owl screeched in the coppicewood at the top of the valley, complaining at the encroaching dawn. Kezzy didn't hear. She, too, was asleep.

The morning was well advanced when she woke. Elyas's pallet was empty. His delirium had passed as he slept, as it always did. Kezzy knew where to look for him. As soon as she'd changed into her grey woollen skirt and bodice and set a pot of oats to boil, she went out into the yard and across to where he sat on the low wall, the same wall he'd built around Eaglestone sixteen years before. He was sitting with a faraway look in his eyes and she could tell by the way his grey head was cocked, as though listening, that he was remembering what Eaglestone was like when the great smelting furnace was roaring, sending black smoke belching from the tall chimney. And the waterwheel and whim were going at full tilt. And the eagles soared high over the valley . . .

He didn't hear her approach or realise she was there until she touched his shoulder. He looked up into her smiling face and his own face puckered like that of an impish child.

'Oats is boiling, Gramps.'

'I'll be 'long in a minute, chield.'

He continued to sit clasping one of his crutches in front of him to support his crippled frame. Kezzy perched on the wall beside him and for a while they sat, the old man and his granddaughter, in companionable silence, each lost in their own thoughts. There was something about which she'd wanted for some time to talk to him: something concerning the mine. Now seemed a good time. So presently, not wanting to disturb the tranquillity of the crisp, bright morning, she touched his shoulder again, causing him to turn and look at her questioningly.

'Gramps, the mine . . .' she mouthed tentatively. Then paused, uncertain whether she should give credence to his hag-ridden rantings.

'What 'bout un, chield?' he prompted, seeing her hesitancy. He was familiar with every twist and turn of the girl's mind and knew instinctively if there was something troubling her.

' 'Tis something you said when they brought you out after the blast.'

He shook his head wryly. 'Can't say as how I remember too much 'bout that day . . . thank the good Lord!'

'An' sometimes even now, at nights, when you're . . . restless . . . you keep talking about . . . copper.'

He just sat staring at her, face expressionless. For a moment she thought he hadn't understood what she'd said. Then he nodded. 'Terrible wi' rantin' an' ravin', am I, chield?' he said ruefully. 'Ay, well, 'tis lung fever shiftin' up'long my brain-box. 'Twere same wi' my Pa an' his brothers t'wards end. Why, I do recall . . .'

He stopped to wipe his eyes on the rag he always carried for that purpose, and to draw a rasping breath. He began to cough.

Kezzy had heard time and again about her Great Gramps and all the other Hammetts who'd died of the dust before their fortieth birthdays. Her own pa, Huward, had begun to show signs of advanced lung disease when he'd been killed in the explosion, yet he, and Elyas, were the fortunate ones to have survived the miners' scourge for so long.

When Elyas's fit of coughing showed no immediate sign of subsiding, Kezzy rose, saying: 'I'll fetch the stuff for your chin-cough, Gramps.' But he pulled her back down beside him, keeping her there with his hard, veined hand gripping her wrist as he fought to control his choking. At last he managed to hawk, dislodging the foaming, yellow, blood-speckled mucus obstructing his airway and his breathing became calmer.

'What zackly did I say about this copper when they pulled I out o' mine?' he wanted to know. Since the blast had part stunned him, he remembered little of events and what followed afterwards.

'You kept shouting "Copper! Copper! We'm rich . . . rich!" It was as if the terrible pain didn't matter . . . only copper.'

He chuckled wryly. 'An' I 'spose folks tapped they forreds an' whispered that poor ol' Elyas be half rocked?'

She said nothing. For that was exactly how it had been. In fact, some folk had actually sniggered as the old tinner continued his ranting about his copper strike, even as they carried his battered and broken body to the cottage. Others, with cruel thoughtlessness, had whispered within her hearing that it would have been better if he'd perished with the rest of their kin. She was so young. It was a terrible thing for her to be burdened with a crippled old half-wit.

Yet, if there *had* been copper in Eaglestone . . . It didn't bear thinking of. Such wealth! So near yet so far. For there was no coinage to be paid on copper: and little labour involved in the dressing of the ore. Unlike tin.

'An' de Raddon, were he here a-gloatin' an' a-listenin' an' a-tappin' his big ugly head?' Elyas demanded bitterly, breaking into Kezzy's thoughts.

' 'Twere right and proper Cap'n de Raddon should come, Gramps . . . him being Lord Warden,' she was quick to point out, knowing how agitated it made him even to think of de Raddon setting foot upon his beloved Eaglestone.

He grunted. 'Anyroads, do 'splain why that skunk do crave un bal so bad. He do know Elyas Hammett bain't ravin' lun'tic what do 'magine copper lode where bain't un . . .'

It took a few seconds for what he was saying to sink in. Then Kezzy's eyes widened.

'Gramps! Are you saying that there *is* copper in by bal?'

He turned and studied her seriously for a moment. Suddenly his eyes twinkled and he grinned, showing a row of chipped, yellowed teeth. 'That be *zackly* what I'm a-sayin', chield. 'Twere just 'bout last thing I did seed afore fire-damp done bring roof in.'

Kezzy's mouth opened but no sound came out. She could only stare at him speechlessly. He gave a watery chuckle, enjoying her incredulity.

'Ay, 'twere beaut'ful'st sight I ever did seed that ol' malachitee! Sparklin' like wall of emeralds . . . an' as bright green Cap'n John de Raddon's greedy eyes!'

Grote returned to Eaglestone a little over a week after he'd been there with his master and the flaskers as it was common practice for him to oversee the delivery of some of the tubs to eager customers.

As usual, he brought a covered wain pulled by two sturdy nags. The flasker driving the horses and his comrade on the box wore farmers' smocks to hide flint-lock pistols tucked in their belts just in case anyone might be inquisitive enough to examine the sacks of swedes, potatoes and cabbages among which the tubs were hidden for transportation. As the wain bore the Blackaven insignia and it was well known that the Lord Warden, with unusual generosity, always sent his surplus vegetables to be distributed among the poorest tinners in the parish, his men fully expected to move freely and unmolested.

Consequently, it came as something of a surprise to Grote and his waggoners when, on this occasion, they were followed some distance up the moor by a patrolling riding officer who'd chanced upon them just outside of Cornwood. Grote recognised him as coming from over Salcombe way. As a free-trader, he made it his business to know by sight the six riding officers operating inland along the south coast of Devon. In the main, they were a fairly ancient bunch of individuals, renowned for their inefficiency and therefore quite easy to outwit. Moreover, their supervisor was in de Raddon's pay. However, this particular riding officer who, Grote recalled, went by the name of Dorrity, had only recently been appointed by the Customs Commissioners on the sudden demise of his elderly predecessor. He had a brown, square-chinned face and pale, questioning eyes, and couldn't have been more than twenty. And not only was he considerably younger than his comrades, he was also a great deal more zealous.

As Grote astride his big cob and the Blackaven wain passed Dorrity by on the moor tract, he slowed his own horse and gave each of the men a hard, searching look. The two on the wain avoided his eyes, but Grote stared arrogantly back. Since they'd nothing but vegetables in the wain he felt no cause of concern: the riding officer should search them if he was of a mind to.

'What do 'ee reckon Master Nosey be up'long moor for, Mister Grote?' asked the driver of the wain a shade anxiously as soon as they were out of earshot.

Grote gave a nonchalant shrug. 'Mebbe takin' gunny at Cornwood kiddleywink.'

They plodded on. Every so often, Grote glanced back the way they'd come. And there behind them, about a hundred yards back, was always the riding officer.

'What's he takin' rare interest in us for?' Grote, worried and perplexed, wondered aloud. 'Can't dratted fool see wain belongs to Lord Warden?'

One of his companions fingered the pistol beneath his smoke. He looked about him, scanning the deserted wasteland. 'Bain't none t'see if'n I plug he, Mister Grote,' he offered.

Grote considered, sorely tempted. They could bury the nosey young cub up on the moor and none need ever know. His superiors would think he'd been taken by a bog. Like all smugglers, Grote hated Preventatives and would have relished the death of this one, but he was more in fear of his master than he was of any lawman. And Captain de Raddon was insistent that they were never to attack, only to defend themselves if needs be – such was his 'agreement' with those in authority who turned a blind eye to his 'venturing'. There was hardly a Devon flasker whose runs weren't financed by him for a great lump of the profit.

'Best leave him be,' decided Grote regretfully. 'If'n we take yon Princeton fork mebbe he'll reckon we're delivering fodder up'long prison for them French and Yankee curs. Throw him off our scent . . .'

So at the next fork they turned off along the narrow, rutted track which would eventually lead to the great, desolate grey-stone prison which housed some 9000 French and a few hundred American prisoners of war, crammed into every cell on lice-ridden pallets and hammocks strung three deep.

Grote's ruse apparently worked: when next he looked behind them there was no sign of the riding officer. They plodded on for a short distance, constantly checking their rear, until they were satisfied he'd given up his pursuit of them. Then they swung around and returned to the main track to continue their journey to Eaglestone.

Grote was triumphant. 'Preventy man should be in diapers 'stead o' riding officer's togs!' he scoffed.

They were within sight of the cluster of granite buildings in the valley when Grote chanced to look up at the brow of the hill to his left. Fleetingly, he saw the outline of a mounted figure silhouetted against the dark gathering clouds.

'Preventy man is still on our heels, blast his lily liver!' growled Grote, furious at being taken in by so simple a ploy as doubling-back.

Alerted by his rasping curse, the two on the wain followed his gaze. The hill was deserted. They exchanged a disbelieving look.

'Where? Don't see un. You'm got piskie sight,' scoffed one.

'I tell you, I saw him,' insisted Grote, annoyed that they should think he was imagining things.

'Should've let I plug he back'long track.'

'Do we pass Eaglestone by up creep and wait 'til Master Nosey has gone?' asked the other.

Again Grote considered carefully as they moved slowly on, closer to the cottage and mine. His wits weren't quick, but he soon came to the conclusion that Preventative Dorrity must by now have a fair idea where they were heading. There was no other habitation save Eaglestone in that remote region of Dartmoor.

'Bain't no point hidin' from him now. Reckon he's got us dead to rights. We'll rest horses 'while, but best we leave tubs o' Cousin Jack be. Gentry shall have t'go thirsty this'n month.'

Wart, the old foxhound, gave a sharp bark as soon as he caught the flaskers' scent on the chill breeze blowing up the valley. Kezzy heard and came out of the cottage to wait for them in the yard. As soon as she could make out their faces, she could see that Grote's expression was even more dour than usual.

'We got problems,' he declared ill-humouredly by way of greeting.

Kezzy frowned, anxious. 'What?'

'Preventy man sniffin' our heels. Thought we'd given him the slip down'long Cornwood way 'til he showed himself just now 'top barrow.'

'You shouldn't have led him here,' was Kezzy's immediate reaction.

'He'd know where we were headin' this'n far up.'

She stared beyond him, eyes scanning the forbidding landscape. Nothing. Not even a bird soared. She wondered if they'd all seen him, or just Grote. It was easy to mistake the long, dark shadows streaking the moor for mysterious figures. Men and horses and tall, raggedy witches. Even to her eyes, it sometimes seemed as if the moor teemed with life-like forms. Was Grote the sort for such fancies, though?

'Well, there's no sign of him now,' she observed.

'He's out there somewheres . . . a-spyin' on us, you can be sure o' that,' grumbled Grote.

He seemed uncertain just what to do.

Kezzy said: 'Best unload some of the vegetables and carry them into the barn . . . as if that's the reason you've come.'

Grote saw the logic in that and they went off to do as she suggested. Kezzy stole a fleeting look in the direction of the hills but wasn't rewarded with a glimpse of the riding officer. She went back into the cottage. Elyas was sitting hunched and wheezing in his usual place by the fire.

'Be it that dog, Grote, for un load o' tubs?'

'Yes.'

She didn't tell him about the Preventative man in case it agitated him. And there was always the chance that Grote was mistaken.

'How many tubs be he movin'?'

'I don't know.'

He reached for his crutches. 'Best I go an' count un . . . make sure the thievin' dog don't finger tun for hisself an' swear we'm nabbed un.'

' 'Tis cold out, Gramps,' she told him quickly. 'Start you coughing terrible, 'twill. I'll go.'

She didn't wait for him to argue but threw her shawl around her shoulders and went out to find the flaskers.

They'd unloaded a sack of potatoes and one of swedes into the barn and taken the horses down to the brook to water and rest them before starting back to Blackaven. Kezzy drew Grote a little aside from the other two.

'How many barrels were you supposed to shift?'

He frowned. 'What's it to you, med'n?'

Kezzy ignored his brusqueness. 'How many?' she persisted.

'Dozen.'

She did a quick mental calculation. As each half anker of brandy weighed about fifty pounds that meant a load equivalent to three hefty men. Yes! Rats could do it!

'Where were you to take the barrels?'

Grote's frown deepened to a scowl. 'Bain't none of yourn business, med'n . . .'

She cut swiftly across him. 'I might be able to deliver the barrels for you . . . right under the Preventy man's nose.'

Grote stared. Then his lip curled. 'You?'

'Yes. For an extra half crown a tub.'

'Now lookee here . . .!' he began to splutter but Kezzy forestalled his protest.

'I'm sure you'll find that Captain de Raddon will be happy to pay . . . rather than disappoint Sir Ryden Bliss and Mayor Gill and of course Mr Land at the New London . . .'

Grote's jaw went slack.

'You *were* intending taking the tubs over to Exeter, were you not, Master Grote?'

'How the Devil . . .?'

He stopped, a wary look twisting his florid features. Better not invoke the Devil, he thought. Not when the maid had shown she had a power. For how, save by sorcery, could she possibly have known who the brandy was meant for? She was the daughter of her witch-mother for sure! He dropped his eyes from her bright slanting gaze and shuffled his feet, humbled and discomfitted by this apparent proof of her dark gifts. Reluctantly, he said: 'Ay, Mistress Keziah, 'tis to Exeter we're s'posed to go.'

Kezzy hid her satisfaction. There was nothing magic about her knowledge of the flaskers' Exeter patrons. But if believing otherwise cowed de Raddon's bullying head steward why, it occurred to her, reveal the truth? That once, long ago, when they'd come to collect tubs, she overheard him telling the waggoner that Captain de Raddon insisted that the first load should always go to the three at Exeter since they never quibbled about the quality or the price, and paid on delivery.

Kezzy stood quietly considering for a while. Grote found the silence unnerving. 'What's to be done then, Mistress Keziah?' he asked submissively.

She told him.

It was necessary to wait until nightfall before the first part of Kezzy's plan could be put into action. Meanwhile, at her instigation, the three flaskers made a great show of taking a wheel off their wain and pretending to mend it for the benefit of the watching Preventative. If they'd sat around idly waiting for dark he might have guessed what they were up to.

'Yon med'n be proper shrewd,' observed the driver of the wain to Grote at one point during the afternoon. He was lying on his back beneath the wain, striking the iron axle at random as though trying to straighten a buckle in it.

Grote scowled, not liking the note of admiration in the man's voice. But he had to admit it was so; Keziah Hammett had an old head on her young shoulders.

Kezzy was satisfied that the Preventative *was* hidden near by. Every so often, she would call Wart to heel and take a turn around Eaglestone's perimeters. Sure enough, the old foxhound would sniff the air and give a low warning growl, his hackles rising. Once or twice he stood with his paws splayed, head straining and barking frantically towards a small copse of dwarf oaks growing among the scattered rocks on the nearest hillside.

'Hush, Wart! 'Tis only a rabbit or weasel!' she'd loudly reproach him, then move casually on her way as if taking the air, never for a moment allowing her eyes to rest upon the hill.

Wart's behaviour confirmed what her strange sixth-sense told her: *Eaglestone was being watched.*

She wondered what it was about Grote and the others that had aroused the riding officer's suspicions when he saw them on the moor. The Lord Warden's coiled snake insignia carved on the tailboard of the wain should've been enough to ensure impartiality. Yet, he'd purposefully followed them to lie in wait, watching to see what they were up to. Well, she'd make sure his efforts proved fruitless. And that he'd be loath ever to spend another cold, supperless night out on the moor.

The moon was kind to them, conveniently staying behind the leaden clouds. Kezzy was careful to cover the cottage windows with touzers so that no pool of candlelight lightened the pitch black of the yard. Then, under cover of the inky darkness, their faces and hands smeared with soot so they wouldn't show as white patches moving to and fro, the three men brought up the dozen barrels and loaded them on the Hammetts' wagon. That done, they settled themselves in the barn to wait for first light.

Kezzy boiled some of their vegetables for their supper, adding a lump of fat pork, garlic, leeks and salt, and carried the pot out to them with some bread as Elyas refused to have them at his table.

'Barn's best place for they . . . wi' rest o' un rats!' he said. crustily. 'Why them still here? Should've been gone pack an' vardel by now.'

'I told you, Gramps. They buckled a wheel coming here.'

'Faugh! Wouldn't have took three Hammetts best part o' day to mend un.'

'Well, it's mended now and they'll be on their way at cock crow.'

'An' not moment too soon for I,' groused Elyas.

The morning was still very cold but a much brighter day than the one before. As Kezzy fed the chickens, Grote and his companions hitched the horses to the wain and set off with loud farewells. At the foot of the valley, they whipped up the horses and set off across the heath at a cracking pace. Watching from the opening in the hay loft, Kezzy spotted the uniformed rider emerge from the copse and canter after them.

Quickly, she returned to the cottage. She'd prepared everything in advance so there would be no delay. A big pot of hot stew on the slab for her grandfather to eat during that day and the next; plenty of vags piled so he could reach them without too much difficulty. A mossle bag of bread and cheese and a canteen for herself. And, to avoid being molested travelling alone, she'd put on her old breeches and jersey and tucked her long hair under an old woollen hat.

'Gramps, I must go to Exeter,' she told him simply.

He stared. Uncertain whether he'd heard right.

'I'll explain when I come back . . .' she was making for the door.

'Ye'll 'splain now or 'ee bain't a-goin'!' he declared.

She hesitated. Any moment the Preventative might appear. Having stopped and searched the wain – good chase though Grote swore they'd give him – and found nothing, he might be sharp enough to guess their intention.

' 'Tis de Raddon business, Gramps. You'll be all right for a couple of days . . .'

Instinctively he knew what it was she was planning to do. His eyes narrowed to slits in their deep sockets. 'If you'm deliverin' tubs for that varmit . . .'

' 'Tis worth the doing for six crowns, Gramps.'

He spat. 'Will it be worth un boat t'Botany if'n you'm caught?'

Kezzy had tried not to think of the consequences should she be found in possession of the smuggled cognac. But his words made her heart suddenly start thudding in her chest. What she was doing *was* highly dangerous. If caught, she could expect no mercy because she was a female with an old and dependent relative. They might even hang her for helping the free-traders. Her eye fell on the small phial of laudanum which she'd put close at hand should he be seized by a bad coughing fit when she was absent. Laudanum was expensive, as were lung syrups. Rich men's medicines. She still owed Dame Rogers for the last two bottles. That decided her. She was out of the door and running.

'Good-bye, Gramps. I'll be as quick as I can!'

By the time he'd struggled on to his crutches and made it to the door, she was aboard the wagon waiting ready behind the barn with Rats between the shafts.

'Ye bain't t'go, Keziah. Do 'ee hear? I forbid it!' shouted Elyas after her receding back view.

She turned and waved.

Chapter Twenty

When she left Eaglestone, Kezzy purposefully swung nor'westerly along a little-known sheep track rather than taking the obvious route which would lead her eventually to Exeter. It was a more circuitous track but, she thought, a sensible precaution in case the Preventative guessed that the hard-driven wain was merely a diversion to lead him away from the valley while she set off with the barrels. Had he that much wit, he would also guess that the cognac was intended for Exeter gentry.

Her chosen route took her across trickling streams and through shadowy gullies tucked between the hills topped by great scarps of rock. By mid-morning she was within sight of Sheepstor. She ignored the tiny village below it and kept on the sheep track as it looped due north, running for a mile or so parallel with the main Plymouth to Princeton road.

She intended to stop at Crazywell Pool and roughly knew its location. It was a while since she'd been near the vast, water-filled hole. Not since she was a child roving the moor with her brothers. They'd come to see if the pool really was haunted, as was claimed, by the old tinners who'd dug the 'bottomless" pit and magically kept it filled.

Graeme had bravely plunged in and emerged to announce that the pool was no more than fifteen feet deep and filled by an underwater spring. Little Kezzy had been disappointed at the time. Now, it came as almost something of a surprise to top a spur and discover the blue-grey rippling expanse immediately below her.

The sure-footed Rats plunged down the slope to the water's edge and Kezzy left him to slake his thirst while she got on with the chore in hand. Taking a sharp reap hook in one hand, and wearing a leather 'cuff' to protect the other, she began to cut tasks of dried bracken and gorse to cover the barrels which, at present, were covered only by old flour sacks.

Furze was sparse so early in the year. And others had had the same notion as she – that there would be tussocks still to be cut where in summer the water-fed land was particularly green and lush. It took her a good hour to fill the wagon. But fill it she did, packing the prickly tasks tightly around the tubs so that none but the most determined searcher would discover what lay concealed there.

That done, she led Rats back up the slope to the ridge. She was about to climb up on the wagon when the colt sniffed the air and gently whinnied. Her eyes swept the boggy terrain but saw nothing. A copse of wind-battered trees clung to the flank of a hill near to her left. Among the gaunt trunks and branches Kezzy glimpsed the gleam of bridles and silver buttons and pistols in holsters. The riding officer must have trailed her. Fear gripped her. But it was futile to try and escape. Poor Rats would have been no match for a Preventative's fast horse. With a fast-beating heart, she prepared to try and bluff her way out of danger. Schooling her expression to one of, she hoped, boyish interest, she sat quietly atop her wagon watching as the uniformed figure emerged from the trees and walked his horse along the track towards her.

It took Kezzy a moment to realise that the rider wasn't a riding officer but a dragoon officer. So then she hadn't been followed. Relief flooded her. There was a good chance he'd come to Crazywell Pool merely to water his horse. Seeing other shadowy figures among the trees, and hearing the tramp of feet, she realised he wasn't alone.

They emerged from the copse behind him. A slow-moving column of some 300 tired, dusty, foot-sore prisoners-of-war escorted by the rest of the troop of dragoons armed with carbines. A few of the prisoners wore French sailors' uniform but mostly they were Yankee sailors captured in the Channel. Officers and men linked together by heavy steel chains without consideration for rank or origin. Their once spruce uniforms were grimy and ripped and, in many cases, bloodied.

The young dragoon officer gave Kezzy no more than a cursory glance in passing. Peasant boys collecting fuel were a common enough sight. Careful to play her part, she lifted her hand to her forehead and made a respectful tugging gesture. Calmly, she sat with Rats reined in, watching interestedly as the long column of men wound past her along the sheep track above the pool. She saw that some of them tried to break ranks, pulling on their chains like dogs straining on the leash towards the cold, clear inviting water below.

'Water, for mercy's sake!' croaked one and some of the others took up the cry, pleading that they'd not had water since setting off from Plymouth many hours before.

'No stopping! You'll get water at Princeton!' barked the dragoon officer and the stumbling, thirsty prisoners were roughly prodded along with the dragoons' carbines between their shoulderblades. Those who were slow to respond and dragged their feet, like those who dared to utter a word of dissent, were clubbed viciously about the head. Stunned, they had to be dragged and half-carried along by those to whom they were chained before and behind.

The officer, with something of a languid air, tossed his canteen to a trooper. 'Refill that,' he commanded. Then urged his horse down the slope to the water so that it might drink.

An almost overwhelming anger rose within Kezzy as she witnessed the officer's inhumanity. Why, the prisoners were treated worse than animals! Granted, they were the enemy. But most of them were just boys. And such a thoroughly dejected and bedraggled bunch of winnards she'd never seen before! Probably pressed – like the Hammett brothers – into fighting in a war not of their making or choosing. Indeed, probably even beyond their simple-minded comprehension.

The sudden, heart-wrenching memory of Isaac and Graeme being dragged in manacles through Cornwood made her totally forget her own rather precarious position as guardian of twelve illicit tubs of cognac. Her voice rang out, plaintive and pleading but with a strong note of censure as she addressed herself to the officer.

'Oh please, Cap'n, zur, for love of God let they poor souls drink!'

The prisoners slowed to a shuffle, heads turning in amazement at this unexpected intervention on their behalf.

The dragoon captain, like all mounted cavalry officers, had the art of sitting his fine, lean grey as if nothing save the way ahead and his horse's twitching ears were of importance. Yet, even he twisted in his saddle to glare loftily at the youngster. He saw dark flashing eyes gazing at him accusingly from a pale, pointed, beardless face. Some gypsy's by-blow, by the look of him, it fleetingly crossed his mind as he observed the boy's almost ethereal paleness.

'On your way, boy, or I'll beat you soundly for your interference,' he threatened. 'Then hand you over to the magistrate to be hanged. 'Tis treason to help the enemy, don't you know that?'

Kezzy didn't move. Careful to maintain her piping boyish tone and broad accent, she determinedly tried again: ' 'Tis fair distance up'long Princeton Prison, zur. Best let un prisoners drink to yon pool. Make they step out all more lively.'

A dragoon sergeant urged his horse forward so he drew level with the captain. Kezzy's sharp ears picked up his murmured words.

'Beggin' ye pardon, Cap'n, mebbe boy be right. If'n they curs start laggin' for want o' mouthful o' water, mebbe us won't get they to prison afore dark. Ent safe t'be out on moor in dark wi' parcel o' Yankees, Cap'n. French, mebbe. But they Yankee boys is proper troublesome. I know. I 'scorted they afore. Slit thy throat wi' blade o' grass.'

The young captain was silent for a moment. There was sense in what the sergeant, an older, more experienced man, had to say. The American prisoners were certainly a dangerous bunch, not resigned to the humiliation of defeat and incarceration like the French prisoners mostly were. No, the Yankees were a hard-faced, eagle-eyed lot of men, ever alert for the chance to escape. And not caring if dragoon blood was spilled in the process. This was, the officer conceded, no time for misplace pride.

'Water the prisoners, sergeant. Five minutes,' he barked and wheeled his horse, making for a suitable vantage point from where he could keep a far-reaching eye on proceedings.

The prisoners had trudged on, but now they were brought back and herded down the slope to kneel along the water's edge. Aware that it was the youngster on the wagon who'd brought about this welcome respite, the eyes they turned to her were filled with gratitude.

One of the Americans, to the rear of the column, held back, tugging on the chains that linked him to his two, protesting companions. As the wagon passed within a few inches of him, he called out, 'God bless you, boy!'

Kezzy was vaguely aware of a tall, loosely built young man, fair-haired, firm-jawed with streaks of blood on his bronzed face.

An irate dragoon was already bearing down on him. One of the others spotted the danger and growled a warning.

'Enemy bearing port quarter, Matt!'

But the young man stood staring up at Kezzy as though transfixed, until the dragoon's swinging carbine landed with a paralysing thwack against his upper arm. Kezzy flinched, sensing his pain. But he clenched his teeth and uttered not a sound.

'Get down to that water, you Yankee scum!' snarled the dragoon and swung his carbine again as the vivid blue eyes shot him a look of defiant loathing.

The young man's companions bundled him with them down the slope after the rest before all three sustained a concussing blow. He knelt reluctantly in line but his thirst was forgotten. His fair head swivelled as he watched the departing, narrow-backed figure.

Feeling his eyes boring into her, willing her to turn, she did so. Their eyes locked. And in that brief moment he knew! Knew for sure that his suspicions were correct. The smooth chin which had tilted so aggressively at the dragoon officer, the soft red mouth, the rounded pliant frame . . . these belonged to no youth but a girl! A slender, nubile girl who was undoubtedly wise to dress as a boy so as to avoid the unpleasant attentions of lewd rogues while roaming the moor in search of fuel for her parents' fire. A girl who had been touched by their plight, who had risked a severe beating to beg water for the vanquished foe.

And Lieutenant Matthew Youngmay of the United States Navy raised a hand and saluted her.

Kezzy dipped her head in acknowledgement, then she flicked the reins and the wagon jogged on across the moor.

It took Kezzy rather longer than she anticipated to reach Exeter. In truth, on suggesting to Grote that she deliver the barrels, she hadn't an idea as to the real distance between Eaglestone and that big city, having never before been further than the stannary town of Plympton.

The going was particularly slow because, not wanting to wind the valiant Rats, she stopped often to let him rest and crop the scrubby grass along the way. But she didn't regret taking such a roundabout route; nor did she forget the reason for it. Not until, she was well on her way did she stop looking nervously over her shoulder.

By dusk, she'd gained the ancient Dartmeet crossroads where she could fork nor'easterly along a wider, well-rutted track towards Exeter. The night was bitterly cold but she was too tired to care. She unhitched Rats in a wooded valley where the East and West Dart met and, wrapped in a thick woollen shawl and an oilskin, lay beneath the wagon to sleep. She thought of her grandfather, wondering how he was faring without her. Quite well, probably. He was as tough and enduring as the tumbled rocks along the Dartmeet riverbed.

But it wasn't Elyas's worn, weathered, canny old face which floated behind her closed lids as she lay waiting for sleep. It was a young man's face. Strong and intelligent with brilliant, deep-set blue eyes and a straight, broad nose. A young man whose curling hair was so fair it had glinted like gold in the dull morning light.

What was it his friend had called him . . . Matt?

Matthew . . .

Kezzy whispered the name to herself in the dark and a swift, warm current ran through her veins. Her meeting with the tall, bronzed foreigner with the bold, fascinating eyes had stirred within her desires which, hitherto, had remained dormant. Never in her sixteen years had a boy troubled her young heart. Yet, as brief as was her encounter with the American, she found herself possessed by the fire of some strange emotion which was at the same time both disturbing and pleasurable.

Matthew!

This time she called his name loudly and joyously so that the night-breezes might carry her voice to him across the moors to the bleak, forbidding grey prison where he was held captive.

Enemy! reminded a small, insidious voice.

Kezzy quickly stifled it. Had not that one, lingering, ardent glance exchanged by Crazywell Pool not inexorably linked their two minds and two hearts across the graves of feud? Once their countries had been allies, and surely would be again. One day. And one day she and Matthew would meet again. Of that, she was in no doubt. Her strange second-sight told her it was so.

Matthew . . .

She sighed his name and presently the weary purple eyelids dropped and the strained lines relaxed and she fell into a deep, motionless sleep.

Not so far away across the moor, at Princeton, in a cramped, granite-walled cell was the fair-haired object of Kezzy's first maidenly adoration. And as Matthew lay in the chill dark on a thin, hard, verminous pallet, breathing the fetid air and listening to the groans and snores of three dozen other captives, he saw again a pair of solemn dark eyes in an elfin face on a shapely, lissom body garbed in boy's clothes. The memory of the girl's compassion cheered him in his state of unutterable weariness and despondency and after a while a restless sleep stole over him. He dreamed terribly that night, just as he had done every night since his capture three days previously. He dreamed he was back aboard the United States Navy brig *Maryland*. He dreamed he saw the lift and recoil of her guns and heard their infernal thunder. He dreamed he smelled the smoke, heard the screams of the dying, saw the decks running red with their blood. Until, in a sudden access of horror he woke with an anguished cry to find his shoulder being shaken by the *Maryland*'s purser, John Dagge.

It was dawn.

Chapter Twenty-One

Kezzy's first impression was that Exeter wasn't so very different from Plympton. Just bigger. And noisier. And a great deal smellier.

As soon as she descended into the valley and passed through the old Water Gate, a terrible stench assailed her nostrils. It grew still stronger as she trundled slowly along the one great unflagged street thronged with carts and wagons and coaches making her feel quite nauseous. It emanated, she shudderingly deduced, from the putrid filth and rotting garbage strewn along the walkways. Didn't city women clean their doors like country women? wondered Kezzy, wide-eyed with astonishment. Apparently not. Well, the parish fathers would have something to say to them if they lived in a stannary town!

As she travelled deeper into the town she soon forgot the vile atmosphere with the strangeness and excitement of it all. Everywhere there were people: haggling in the market for meat and fish and fowls; strolling along the pillared walks; coming and going from the shops and inns and noble public buildings. And so many different people. From blind beggar to baker's boy to high-born lady. So enraptured was Kezzy with gazing at the fine ladies entering or alighting from their ornate coaches, fine silk and muslin peeping from beneath fur-trimmed cloaks, that she didn't pay attention to where she was going and crashed wheels with a big coal cart.

'Watch out, boy! Ye'll have us locked!' the coalman shouted a good-natured reproach.

'Sorry, sir,' Kezzy was quick to pipe. Then, just he was whipping up his team of big horses again, she shouted, 'Please, sir, can you direct me to the New London Inn?'

He pointed down the street with his whip. 'Can't miss un . . . biggest there is, boy.' He spotted the load of furze and his black-ingrained face split in a grin. 'Take more'n few twigs to heat New Inn . . . best take un kindlin' home to thy ma, boy.'

He cracked his whip and pulled away.

Rats was unaccustomed to so much noise and traffic and was swerving and skittering and tossing his head. Afraid that he might rear up and overturn the wagon, smashing the hidden tubs, she got down and took his bridle to lead him the rest of the way. 'Easy, Rats, easy . . .' she kept saying soothingly and her familiar voice and touch seemed to calm the agitated colt.

Thankfully, just as the coalman had said, the New London Inn wasn't far, its many-latticed windows aglow with candlelight in the dusky, late afternoon light. Kezzy led Rats through a handsome stone arch into a big stone-flagged courtyard extravagantly lit by a myriad of hanging lanterns. A post-chaise was filling with passengers in readiness to depart. Another was disgorging weary, crumpled travellers to be led by liveried lackeys into the inn to refresh themselves. The ostlers were busy hitching and unhitching teams of six horses, while stable boys scurried and hither with buckets of water and bales of hay. No one paid any attention to Kezzy. And in her breeches and jersey and woollen hat, she looked just like one of the stable boys. She found somewhere to tether Rats and fetched him a bucket of water and some hay.

A mail-coach arrived and she stood watching as four passengers alighted. Then, slightly nervous because she'd never before been in an inn, not even the Cornwood kiddleywink, she attached herself to the group of passengers as they were shown inside. She got as far as the warm, welcoming lobby with its roaring log fire. Then her ear was seized and painfully twisted. She yelped.

'Here, what's your game, boy?' demanded an angry voice. 'Get back out t'stables an' mind your place. Comin' in here wi' your mud an' horse muck . . .'

Kezzy gave another yelp as her ear was twisted again.

'I'm not one of the stable boys. I've come to see Mister Land. I've a . . . message for him from Cap'n de Raddon.'

Her ear was released. She glared at the man who'd assaulted it. He was clearly of some importance since he wore a watch-chain across his grey waistcoat and a look of condescension on his long, pallid face.

'This way,' he commanded. Abruptly he turned and strode off.

After a second's hesitation, Kezzy followed him.

He took her into a small, low-ceilinged chamber containing a desk covered with ledgers. There was a chair behind the desk and another, a straight-backed one, nearby. He didn't sit down or invite Kezzy to do so. Curtly, he said: 'What is the message?'

'Are you Mr Land?'

He hesitated, tempted to say he was and be done with it. 'No. But you can give me the message and I'll make sure he gets it. I'm his clerk.'

Kezzy considered. She wondered if Mr Land's clerk was party to the knowledge that the fine cognac he served to his patrons was the best moonshine. She decided that it was better to be discreet.

'I'm sorry, the message is for Mr Land's ears only.'

'He's a very busy man . . .' the clerk started to say. He could see that the youth wasn't to be persuaded. 'Wait here.'

He returned in a few minutes accompanied by the proprietor of the inn, John Land, an exceedingly ancient, stooped man wearing a handsome diamond pin in his cravat. He came straight to the point.

'A message from Captain de Raddon, you say?'

Kezzy flicked an uncertain look towards the clerk. Land saw it and gave a quavering guffaw.

'Don't you worry about Mr Digby, here.' He winked a red-veined eye.

'There's not much Mr Digby don't know about my business. So speak out frank, boy.'

'I've got six tubs of cognac for you on my wagon outside.'

That took Land and his clerk aback. They exchanged a surprised look. Some of Land's joviality evaporated. Frowning, he asked Kezzy, 'Who brought you here, boy? The man Grote? Where is he?'

'I came alone.'

He looked her up and down, his frown deepening. 'What folly is this? Has de Raddon taken leave of his senses, sending an apprentice to deliver the necessary? And with no batman for protection! Dear heart alive! We could all be discovered!'

Kezzy couldn't help a slightly tart note creeping into her voice, shades of Dame Rogers, as she said. 'Fret not, Mr Land, believe me when I say that I am perfectly able for the task. 'Tis by far the safest way. Mr Grote was followed by a Preventative and dare not risk another delivery . . . which is why I shall be delivering the . . . er . . . necessary in future.'

There was a pause while the two men gazed in some surprise at their fresh-faced caller, taken aback by the boy's totally unexpected articulateness. Clearly, this was no ordinary apprentice. Perhaps John de Raddon wasn't so foolish after all. Land suddenly gave another of his loud guffaws.

'Well said, boy!' he exclaimed. To Digby he said, 'Go with him. See the tubs are unloaded away from prying eyes.'

'I'm to collect payment for them,' reminded Kezzy.

Land nodded briefly. He turned to go. 'Mr Digby will give you a banker's note for your master.'

'And I must ask you for a further half a crown for each tub for delivery. In coinage,' Kezzy said.

Digby began to protest about the extra charge but the ancient proprietor flapped a hand at him dismissively. 'Pay up, Digby! Pay up! And be glad our cellars boast the finest those damnable Frenchies can offer!' He departed chuckling.

Digby went with Kezzy out into the courtyard where he snapped his fingers at the head ostler, a burly individual who was clearly in Mr Land's confidence. The ostler led Rats into one of the huge stables, each of which could house a hundred horses. At the end of the stable was a door and beyond it a flight of stone steps which led, Kezzy presumed correctly, down into the cellars. She and the clerk stood watching as the furze was lifted and six of the tubs, two at a time, were lifted out across the ostler's massive shoulders and carried out of sight below. Then she was taken back into the clerk's chamber where she was given a banker's note made out to de Raddon and three crowns, grudgingly produced with much jangling of keys from a locked money chest.

'I'll see you in a two-week . . . if the weather permits a run,' said Kezzy as she took her leave. At the door she paused, a thought occurring. 'Perhaps you'd ask Mr Land if there is anything else he requires. Cigars . . . or tea, perhaps. Please let me know next time and I'll make the necessary arrangements. Good-day to you, Mr Digby.'

He went to his window overlooking the courtyard and watched her lead Rats at a plodding walk out beneath the arch. What an extraordinary boy he was! thought Digby, a nonplussed expression on his colourless face. Quite, quite extraordinary!

Kezzy next made her way to the address Grote had given her for the Mayor of Exeter, Mr Humphrey Gill, owner of Exeter's largest serge-making business. He lived in a handsome three-storied house in James Street right next door to the new Presbyterian Meeting House which he'd donated to the city – for which philanthropic deed he was awarded the much-coveted mayorship.

He was also a hard-headed businessman and refused point blank to pay the extra half a crown a tub delivery charge on his three tubs, shrewdly guessing that the money was for the delivery boy's own pocket and hadn't been authorised by Captain de Raddon. Kezzy stood her ground patiently while he huffed and puffed, calling her 'a crafty young whippersnapper' and accusing her of stealing from her master.

'I shall inform Captain de Raddon that an extra fee has been forthcoming for delivery . . . and will be in future,' declared Kezzy in a calm, firm voice.

Mayor Gill positively squawked with anger. 'I won't pay it! I won't!'

'Then I'll bid you good-day, sir,' said Kezzy turning to leave the room into which he'd taken her to settle the account. 'I shan't, of course, be coming again . . .'

'Wait!'

She waited. She could read what was passing through his mind. If he wanted the finest cognac he'd no choice but to do business with de Raddon. And in his position, he had to be careful; better the devil he knew than some blackmailing scoundrel he didn't.

He paid her.

It was quite dark by the time Kezzy arrived at the tradesman's gate set in the high, creeper-covered walls of Sir Ryden Bliss's town house. She tugged the bell-chain and sent a jangling peal through the cold night air. Through the iron bars of the gate, she could make out dimly the rambling, gabled building. No light burned in any of the rear windows. She was about to pull the bell again when she saw a glimmer of light as a door opened. A dark shape emerged and moved towards her across the small courtyard carrying a lantern. As he came up to the gate, she saw that he was a manservant wearing a striped black and grey waistcoat and a huge green touzer tied about his waist. He held the lantern aloft and peerd at her.

'What do 'ee want, boy?'

'I have business with Sir Ryden Bliss.'

'Who sent 'ee?'

'Cap'n de Raddon.'

The lantern shifted while the man took a closer look at Kezzy up and down. He seemed satisfied. He produced a bunch of jingling keys and unlocked the gate to admit her. He eyed Rats and the wagon with ill-concealed distaste, 'Best put thy nag in orchard . . . away from Mrs Hibbit's kitchen garden . . .'

He showed Kezzy the way, waited while she unhitched the weary Rats and let him loose among the stumpy, naked trees, then led the way across to the house and in through the kitchen door. A log fire blazed in the huge chimney place throwing dancing lights on the brass pots hung on hooks on the chimney breast. The huge scrubbed wooden table held various dishes and jugs. A skivvy of about twelve years old, with a simple, pock-marked face, was on her knees scrubbing congealed fat off the stone tiles with a coarse, wooden-backed scrubbing brush. When she glanced up at Kezzy, a big woman in a stiff white apron standing mixing something in a bowl at the table gave her a kick, saying, 'Get on withee work, Annie. Bain't aught t'do withee.'

The man said: 'This'n boy has come t'see the master, Mrs Hibbit.'

She looked Kezzy up and down, much as the man had done at the gate. 'How old are you'm boy?' she asked.

'Sixteen . . . near enough.' Kezzy answered politely although she failed to see why her age should be of account. 'May I see Sir Ryden Bliss now, please?'

'All in good time.' The man looked across at the woman and gave a scornful laugh. 'In proper hurry, bain't he, Mrs Hibbit?'

'That he is, Mr Hibbit . . . more fool he,' she responded.

Kezzy felt a twinge of unease. Why were they weighing her up in such a scornful manner? And why was the skivvy giving her strange, pitying sideways looks? It was all most odd. It had been in her mind to ask Sir Ryden Bliss if she could sleep the night under her wagon in his orchard, but now she just wanted to deliver her barrels and be on her way.

'Hold out your hands,' ordered Mrs Hibbit. 'Master can't abide grubby hands.'

After a moment's hesitation, Kezzy stuck out her hands for inspection. Her hands were as grimy as any boy's would be. Mrs Hibbit seized one of her wrists, the better to examine the proffered hand. She peered at it closely, almost suspiciously.

'Soft as maiden's,' she remarked sourly.

Kezzy said nothing. Dame Rogers had shown her how to use a piece of pumice on her work-scars. One day, the dame had assured her, she would be glad that she hadn't rough hands like the bal maidens.

'Wash in yon pail boy,' directed the woman returning to her mixing bowl.

Kezzy did as she was told. And brushed down her dusty breeches and jersey as well, since Sir Ryden Bliss was apparantly so particular about such things. She tucked a few wisps of hair beneath her woollen hat and presented herself to the Hibbits.

The woman nodded. She poured whatever it was she was mixing into a big pewter mug, added to it a small ladle of hot water from a kettle suspended in the chimney, then, taking out a red-hot fire iron, plunged it into the brew. The steam which rose smelled of brandy and herbs. Placing the mug on a salver, she handed it to her husband. He had removed his apron and donned a black serge coat trimmed with grey.

'Come, boy. This way.'

The interior of the house was well lit by scores of candles set in sconces on the wall. Sir Ryden Bliss was extravagant in his use of tallow; the thought heartened Kezzy as she followed Hibbit up an ornately carved staircase since it meant that the man she'd come to see would be unlikely to quibble over a few shillings extra for his brandy.

Hibbit led her along a gallery and gently tapped at the very last door. A man's voice responded curtly from within.

'Come.'

Hibbit entered, Kezzy close behind him. A few steps into the room, she stopped dead in consternation on seeing a big four-poster bed, the hangings agape to reveal the long handle of a copper warming-pan protruding from the bedding. She hadn't expected to be received in the gentleman's bed-chamber. She felt herself flushing and came close to running from the room. But the sight of the elderly figure seated by the fire reading a large bible was very disarming so she stayed where she was, waiting to be received.

'Your night cordial, sir,' announced Hibbit.

His master didn't look up from his bible. 'Yes, yes, set it down.' He was prepared for bed and wore a blue velvet robe over his nightshirt and a knitted woollen bed-cap. His bare feet were pushed into velvet slippers trimmed, like his robe, with red-squirrel fur.

Hibbit placed the steaming tankard on a table at Sir Ryden Bliss's elbow and stepped back. He stood waiting to attract his master's attention and, when it wasn't forthcoming, gave a polite cough.

'Yes, yes, you can go, Hibbit.'

'There's a young person to see you, sir. A boy . . .'

When his face lifted from the bible, Kezzy saw that he was much younger that she'd first assumed; thirty or just above, rather than nearly seventy. It was his brows and whiskers, light brown but heavily streaked with grey, which aged him prematurely. It had once been a handsome face. Now it was ravaged by dissipation. The jowls were loose and the once fresh complexion was blotched and purple-veined. The purple veins reminded Kezzy of old Lord Blachford's countenance. Once, after church, she'd heard Dame Rogers discussing Cornwood's most illustrious citizen with Mrs Wisdome, the miller's wife. The latter had referred to Blachford an 'evil old debauch'. Later, Kezzy had looked up the meaning of word 'debauch' and had been quite shocked. Now, she had the unpleasant feeling that, despite his bible reading, Sir Ryden Bliss was also a 'debauch', and she silently blessed her boy's clothes and the protection they offered her.

None the less, he was eyeing her in a very strange, speculative fashion. For a moment Kezzy thought he must have seen through her impersonation. But he made no comment; just continued to gaze at her, his eyes travelling up and down, admiring the litheness of her adolescent body.

Then closing his bible with a snap and setting it aside, he rose and crossed the room to where she stood stiff and silent.

'What is your name, boy?'

She answered without thinking: 'Kezzy.'

He burst out laughing. 'What a funny name. Kezzy . . . Kezzy . . .'

'Sir . . . I come from . . . from Captain de Raddon . . .'

Kezzy tried to explain her purpose for being there but her voice faltered nervously. He clearly wasn't listening. He began to walk around her, viewing her as if she was a prize exhibit in a meat market.

'Go,' he said sharply to Hibbit.

Hibbit bowed and left, closing the door quietly behind him.

'Sir . . . I was sent by Captain de Raddon to deliver brandy . . . three tubs,' said Kezzy, edging away from him.

He gave a shrill laugh. 'How very convivial of him! I'll say this for the Lord Warden, he has an eye for a pretty youth . . .' He put out a hand and stroked Kezzy's cheek. She recoiled from his touch and his eyes turned dark with sudden anger.

'I . . . if you would pay for the brandy I'll see the tubs are put in your cellar, sir,' Kezzy stammered, edging towards the door.

The anger cleared from his face. 'Brandy!' he exclaimed. 'Do you like brandy?' He lurched towards her and grabbed her by the wrist, dragging her with him across the room to a side table upon which were fine crystal decanters and glasses.

Thoroughly alarmed now, Kezzy struggled to free herself, but he was unusually strong and easily held her pinioned by the wrist with one hand while he poured amber liquid into a glass, half filling it. He picked up the glass and thrust it towards his captive.

'Drink it, boy!'

The strongest drink Kezzy had ever had was a drop of her grandfather's kiddleywink shrub, well-watered. She shrank away from the proferred glass and the strong aroma.

'Thank you, no . . . I don't take brandy . . .'

He thrust it against her lips, spilling some on her chin in the process. 'Drink!'

Kezzy clenched her lips, shaking her head. In a second, he had released her wrist and transferred his hand to the nape of her neck. Wrenching her head back, he forced the rim of the glass between her lips and upended it. Most of it streamed over her chin, but as she gasped for breath some of the fiery liquid poured down her throat making her splutter and choke.

'There! Isn't that fine brandy? I get it from my friend . . . my very good friend who sends me pretty youths!'

His eldritch cackle rang out and he gripped Kezzy tighter by the back of the neck, at the same time flinging the fine cut glass away from him so that it smashed against the wall. He pushed his face to within inches of hers, eyes staring wildly.

'Shhhh! I must not speak of my good friend to anyone. Hear me? *Not to anyone* . . . or we shall all be hanged. Hanged by the neck until our eyes pop out! Yes, even you, my pretty youth. Only then you wouldn't be so pretty . . . dancing on the end of a rope!'

He was mad! Quite insane!

The realisation came to Kezzy in a flash of sickening dread as she was reminded of the Mad Woman of Plympton, a tinner's wife who'd taken a peeker to her husband and five children as they slept. Kezzy had been eleven at the time. She'd been in the stannary town with her grandfather on the day of the hanging and watched as the cart carrying the crazed creature passed by on the way to Gibbet Hill. Just like Sir Ryden Bliss, the mad woman had slavered and rolled her eyes until all the white was visible.

She must escape from this madman!

Kezzy tried to wrench herself free of the fingers digging cruelly in the flesh beneath her ears but her threshing made him grip her all the tighter. The pressure of his fingers seemed to numb her shoulders and arms, as if her upper body was paralysed.

His maniacal laughter rang out again. 'You shan't escape me, boy! You're my prisoner!'

Kezzy wasn't prepared for what happened next. Before she could summon her strength to resist, she was propelled across the room to the four-poster and thrown across it face down. With one swift, practised movement, her attacker dragged down her breeches laying bare her round, white buttocks. Kezzy tried to scream but he was pressing her face into the featherbed so that she could hardly breathe, let alone cry out.

'Ahhh . . .' he groaned as he abandoned himself to his erotic frenzy, stroking and kneading and biting the soft flesh of her loins and thighs.

Through the mists of terror, Kezzy became aware that he had cast aside his velvet robe and was rending his flannel nightshirt from neck to hem with one hand, a hand to which madness gave a titan's strength. She felt his naked, clammy flesh against her buttocks, pushing and thrusting. *Merciful God, he was trying to mount her like a beast in a field!*

Terror, rage and disgust gripped Kezzy, giving her the strength to fight him. And she fought him any way she could: violently twisting her body, bucking and arching and kicking. Yet her struggles only seemed to delight him, and he laughed interminably in his gloating, imbecilic way. But after a while, as the battle raged and he received a hard kick from one of Kezzy's flailing boots, he grew angry at being thwarted.

'Do not resist me, boy!' he hissed. 'Or I shall have you chained like a cur! And then I shall beat you like a cur!'

His high-pitched voice faltered. With a sudden exclamation he released Kezzy. Her hat had fallen off and an abundance of raven hair cascaded around her shoulders.

'By Jesu! It's a woman!' he squeaked in horror, backing away from her as though she was the Devil incarnate.

Free of him, Kezzy rolled quickly across the bed and scrambled to her feet, hauling up her breeches. Her eye fell upon the handle of the warming-pan and she seized it, dragging it from the bed to use as a weapon if necessary, not trusting the madman's sudden aboutface. She flipped off the lid with a clatter and, holding the heavy pan with both hands, extended it towards him so he could see the smouldering coals.

'Come near me again and I'll throw these hot coals in your face,' she threatened him.

He stepped back convulsively, clutching the remnants of his torn night-shirt about his plump pink body. 'I . . . I thought you were a boy. De Raddon sometimes sends me boys . . . apprentices from his mines . . . if they are pretty fellows and he thinks they might amuse me,' he said sulkily.

Kezzy stared at him aghast. She'd never heard of such goings on! Free-trading was one thing – how else would gentlemen come by their liquor and cigars? – but this unscrupulous use of boy apprentices was . . . well, *evil*! There was no other word to describe it.

The warming-pan was growing heavy. She gave Sir Ryden Bliss a scornful look and pushed it back among the bedclothes, satisfied that by dint of her sex he was no threat to her. He was standing, plucking bemusedly at his torn nightshirt. She went and picked up his robe and held it out to him.

'Put this on,' she ordered.

Meekly, he obeyed.

'Where do you keep your money?'

He thought. Then looked crafty. 'Hidden,' he whispered dramatically. His eyes darted towards the closed door. 'Hidden from *them*. They would steal it . . . all of it . . .'

'*Where* have you hidden it?' Kezzy interrupted him.

He eyed her suspiciously. 'If I tell you then you will steal it,' he said plaintively.

'No, I won't. I only want paying for three tubs . . . and half a crown each for delivering them.'

There was something reassuring about her masterful manner and the direct way she looked at him. He nodded, took the robe and put it on and then tiptoed across to the door. He put a finger to his lips and beckoned.

They crept stealthily along the gallery and down the staircase. He paused in the hall, his head cocked, listening. Then pulled Kezzy quickly with him behind a pillar until a liveried footman went by, for all the world as though he were an intruder in his own house, it occurred to her. Catching sight of his rapt expression, she realised that he was enjoying himself. It was a game.

'Come,' he hissed and, grabbing her wrist, hurried her across the hall and into a small dark chamber.

He lit a candle and Kezzy looked about her in the flickering light. It was an anteroom, furnished with a carved oak side table upon which visitors might leave their hats, and four uncomfortable-looking oak chairs. Sir Ryden Bliss went to the fireplace and, giggling quietly in his imbecilic way, touched a hidden spring so that part of the fireplace creaked open to reveal a tiny secret room behind the chimney. Taking the candle, he went in and beckoned Kezzy to follow.

She hesitated. Was it safe to enter the secret chamber with this madman? The secret door was constructed of bricks set in a wooden frame and was so thick no one would hear her if she shouted for help.

He saw her hesitation. 'You're afraid of me,' he taunted.

Her chin came up. 'No, I'm not.'

She followed him in and he shut the door behind them.

Evidently there was a concealed ventilation duct as the air was quite fresh and the candle guttered slightly. The room was bare save for a large wooden chest. Setting the candle down on the floor, Sir Ryden Bliss lifted the lid with an eerie creak and dropped it back on its brass hinges.

A gasp escaped Kezzy's lips.

The chest was filled almost to the top with gold and silver coins, glinting in the sullen orange glow of the candle. Sir Ryden Bliss got down on his knees beside the chest and began to trickle the coins through his fingers, crooning softly to himself. Presently, he remembered Kezzy's presence. He looked up at her, grinning inanely. Then grabbed a fistful of coins and proferred them to her, saying, 'Here, for the brandy.'

The gold he was offering her would have paid for ten tubs. Without hesitation, Kezzy shook her head. 'Twenty-five shillings a tub, and seven shillings and six pence for delivery,' she told him, and refused to take a penny more, unable to bring herself to take advantage of a man who, through no fault of his own, was a proper mazegerry. If it wasn't for the fact that he used apprentices in such a shocking fashion, she would have been inclined to feel pity for him despite his vast wealth and fine big house.

He appeared to have forgotten her again. He remained crouching beside his money-chest, gazing at the glinting coins as though mesmerised by his riches.

'I must go now,' Kezzy announced loudly, breaking into his abstraction.

He looked up at her with his petulant frown. Then, as though recognizing her, his florid face cleared and he nodded. He closed the lid of the chest and straightened up. Picking up the candle, he worked the hidden spring and the secret door swung open with a faint creak.

He led her through the house and into the kitchen. There was no sign of the woman, but Hibbit was polishing silver cutlery at the table. From beneath the table, where she slept on a pallet, protruded the skivvy's dirty bare feet. She peeped out at the sound of footsteps and her mouth gaped like Hibbit's upon seeing the master there in his nightclothes. Rarely did he venture into the kitchen or into those parts of the house where the servants lived and worked. But what was even *more* surprising, he was accompanied by the boy who was not only in good health, but also in good spirits. Usually, the unfortunate boys taken to the upper regions of the house reappeared bruised and shaken and often weeping, to immediately be whisked away somewhere by Hibbit. Some of the other servants, those who knew of their employer's desire for young boys, whispered among themselves behind Hibbit's back, saying that the head steward took the boys into the woods and strangled them and buried them so that they couldn't prove an embarrassment to Sir Ryden Bliss. In truth, Hibbit took the boys to the Half Moon Inn where Grote put up for the night before his return journey to Blackaven, whence he'd take them back with him and return them to the mines, threatening that if they spoke of what had occurred in Exeter to anyone they would be taken back there on another visit.

Hibbit and the skivvy gaped still more when Kezzy, very much in command of the situation, said curtly, 'I have three tubs for the cellar. Who will shift them?'

Hibbit darted a look at Sir Ryden Bliss's enigmatic face. After a second's hesitation, he kicked the skivvy beneath the table. 'Go and rouse pair o' boys, quick,' he ordered sharply. She slithered out, scrambled to her feet and raced away. She returned in less than a minute with two brawny, yawning, grumbling manservants with their shirts hanging outside their breeches. They stopped grumbling and became instantly alert on seeing that it wasn't merely the head steward who demanded their presence at such a late hour, but the master himself.

Kezzy led them out to where the wagon stood outside the orchard gates. Sir Ryden Bliss followed, not caring that his velvet slippers were being stained by the damp grass or that the fur on the bottom of his robe was dragging in the mud. He stood silently, candle guttering in the faint breeze, while the kegs were unloaded and carried away to his cellar beneath Hibbit's eagle eye. When that was done he dismissed Hibbit with a jerk of his head, but he made no move to return yet to the house himself. He remained standing there as Kezzy went and slipped the bridle on Rats, led the colt from the orchard and adroitly hitched him to the wagon.

She climbed up, ready to depart.

'Will you come again?'

The suddenness of his question took her aback. She gazed down at him, surprised, also, by the clear note of appeal in his voice. In the dim light, his flabby face was taut and strained.

He took a deep, audible breath.

'Please . . . Kezzy . . .'

'Very well,' she said solemnly and his child-like smile split his face, 'but only if you swear that no more boys will be brought here to be so . . . so wickedly preyed upon.'

His smile instantly faded to be replaced by a petulant scowl. 'No! I'll swear no such thing!' he declared querulously.

'Then I'll not come again.' She lifted the reins purposefully.

'Wait!'

She waited. After a long pause, she asked: 'Well . . . will you swear?'

Again the petulant scowl. 'Why should I? Such trade is common enough among gentlemen . . . and not just boy-trade, girl-trade, too.'

Kezzy was half afraid of that: if de Raddon supplied young boys to this deviant then it was highly likely that he also supplied girl apprentices to other perverts in his illustrious circle of friends and acquaintances, along with his smuggled cognac. She *must*, she told herself worriedly, discuss the matter with Dame Rogers as soon as possible – she would be bound to know what action might be taken to halt the filthy trade. Kezzy set great store by the elderly schoolmistress's good sense. Once upon a time, it was to her grandfather she'd have gone with her terrible account. Sadly, there was little point in doing so now. He would only rant and rage and bitterly curse de Raddon, dredging from the past every grievance, real or imagined – not least being his, Elyas's, insistence that the mine-owner was directly responsible for the death of Kezzy's mother in that he'd led the witch-hunt against her by way of revenge for her spurning him. Kezzy didn't know for certain if his version of that terrible day was accurate; what she did know, was that old sores still festered between Elyas Hammet and John de Raddon.

'Very well. I swear,' he cunningly agreed without any intention of keeping his word.

Kezzy had been deep in thought. Sir Ryden Bliss's sudden capitulation brought her back to reality with a start. 'Then I shall continue to bring you brandy,' she declared graciously. 'Do you require any tea next trip?'

'Tea . . .?' he faltered.

'Or tobacco?'

He was gazing at her in stupefaction.

'Snuff, perhaps?'

'Brandy.'

'Yes, I'll bring brandy . . . three tubs as usual,' she reassured him. 'But is there anything else that you require? Gin or rum . . . fine lace for your cuffs, perhaps . . .'

He brightened. 'Yes, snuff.'

'How much?'

'A pound tin.' Frowning, he considered. 'French pomade . . . the finest . . .'

'Of course.'

'. . . and six dozen silk handkerchiefs.'

'I'll see what can be done.'

'Oh, and a Leghorn hat.'

'If I can.'

'*Please* . . .' he begged. 'Such a hat is *most* important! They're quite the thing, you know. Prinny says that only the French know how to make the damned things properly.'

'I'll see what can be done,' she repeated, eagerly committing his handsome order to memory. She slapped the reins and Rats moved forward at a slow walk. Sir Ryden Bliss walked beside the wagon as far as the rear gate where he pulled on the bell-pull to summon Hibbit with the keys to let her out.

'When will you come again?' he asked her, again with the note of appeal in his voice, loath to part from his new friend.

'When I have the goods.'

'Will that be soon?'

'Yes. Soon,' she said optimistically.

Chapter Twenty-Two

After Grote and the Blackaven wain left Eaglestone, the wagoner, following Kezzy's instructions, kept the team moving as briskly as the rutted track allowed.

Every so often, Grote would slow his mount and drop back a ways to scan the wild terrain behind them, each time fully expecting to catch a glimpse of the riding officer on their heels. The Hammett maid had been so sure that Dorrity would take the bait and give chase to them, but of the Preventative, there was not a sign.

Approaching Dendles Wood, with still no Dorrity behind them, Grote gave the order for the hard-driven team to walk.

'Reckon Master Nosey got tired wid a-peepin' an' a-pryin' an' took hisself off for some shuteye,' opined the wagoner jeeringly as he reined in his sweating horses.

Grote wasn't convinced. The previous day he had imagined they'd shaken Dorrity off their backs and had been very much mistaken. He reminded his companions of the fact, adding darkly, 'I'll wager he's somewheres 'bout, drat 'im! If Hammett maid do say he'll follow . . . he'll follow! Got the power, her has.'

'You'm a-sayin' her's got second sight, Mister Grote?' asked the wagoner's batman in astonishment.

Grote nodded. 'When roof come in up'long Eaglestone, her looked straight through hundred ton o'stuff an' saw where her grandpa were trapped.'

'Geddeway!'

' 'Tis true, I tell ye,' said Grote annoyed. He suddenly recalled how she'd be able to pluck from the air the names of those for whom the cognac was meant. He shivered involuntarily. 'Best tread wary 'bout she, I say. Got *didekei* in she. *Cohani* like her ma.'

'Bain't frighted of yon med'n, are ye, Mister Grote?' asked the batman slyly and Grote flushed. 'Just 'cause her looks *didekei* wid they black eyes an' hair, don't make she *cohani*.'

The wagoner had been quietly listening to their exchange as the team plodded along. With a look of rapt concentration he was searching the recesses of his brain for a titillating piece of gossip he'd once heard in the stamps at Wheal Emma.

'Mister Grote bain't talkin' up load o' old plod,' he joined in eagerly. 'I heared yon med'n were just a babbie at tit when her ma were hung for a witch at Plympton.'

'Geddeway!' exclaimed the man beside him disbelievingly. He caught sight of Grote's face in the grey early morning light. The head steward's usually stern face was troubled. Nay, he'd go so far as to say fearful. 'Bain't so, is it, Mister Grote? Hammett woman weren't hung for a witch were her?' he asked incredulously.

Grote said nothing.

The wagoner recalled something else. '*And* I done heared that the master was there when they strung she up!' he announced with relish. 'Bin feudin' wi' Hammetts ever since . . .'

'Ye hears too much. More'n good for ye,' Grote interrupted him, a warning note in his voice. 'Master don't want no loose jaws workin' for him, so just you button it. Or he'll button it for ye an' 'twouldn't be first time.'

The two on the wain swapped nervous glances. They knew what was behind Grote's veiled threat. Only recently one of the flaskers, ostensibly employed at Blackaven as a groom, had been overheard by Grote boasting of his night-time pursuits to a pretty serving maid. It was no coincidence, the rest of them were convinced, that the very next day the talkative fool was snatched by the press in Plymouth while on some trivial errand for Captain de Raddon. Generally, if any of de Raddon's servants or tut-workers were taken by the press, a word from him secured their immediate release. But not this time. The luckless groom had remained impressed. Probably never to be seen again. It was a sobering thought; one that silenced the two flaskers.

Entering Dendles Wood just above Cornwood and with still no sign of Dorrity, Grote began to worry. Maybe they'd underestimated the Preventative! Maybe he'd guessed what they were about and had waited instead for the Eaglestone wagon with its load of tubs. If that was the case, there was nothing he could do now – save hope and pray the Hammett maid kept her mouth buttoned. Mostly, Grote didn't trust females with their gossiping tongues. And they'd likely'd squeal like hogs to Preventatives if it was a case of saving their own skins. Yet, something told him that Keziah Hammett was different from most other females. She'd a head on her shoulders. If that damned interfering, long-nosed Dorrity had nabbed her with the tubs, she'd not squeal. Grote felt certain of that.

So deep in thought was he as they plodded around a bend in the track through the trees, that Grote didn't immediately notice the mounted figure blocking their path. The wagoner was the first to spot Dorrity; his muttered volley of oaths was drowned by a ringing shout.

'In the King's name, I command you to halt!'

Taken by surprise, Grote uttered an exclamation and pulled so sharply on the reins, his horse swerved and kicked. Peering ahead, he could see that the riding officer had a pair of pistols levelled at them. The wagoner, seeing the weapons, swiftly obeyed the command and brought the wain to a rolling halt a few feet from Dorrity. Grote calmed his mount, then walked the horse forward to stand docilely beside the wain. Close to, he saw that Preventative Dorrity was every bit as young as the rumours concerning him maintained he was: probably no more than twenty years of age. He was clean-shaven, with keen, pale eyes and a shock of mousey hair which curled on to his forehead from beneath his cap.

When the Preventative stops you, do not look guilty.

Remembering Kezzy's warning, Grote hastily collected his scattered wits and addressed him in a voice which was both surprised and impatient. 'By Jesu, friend, I took ye for a robber! What do ye want with us?'

Dorrity gestured with one of his pistols towards the wain. 'What are ye carrying?'

'Vegetables.'

'Whither are ye taking these *vegetables*?'

The faintly sarcastic manner in which he emphasised the word 'vegetables' was lost on the flaskers. Grote scratched his jaw, giving every impression that he was carefully considering his reply. *Delay him*, Kezzy had said, *for as long as possible. Give me a chance to get well on my way.* 'Well now, friend, if 'tis names of the poor tinners as are to receive Lord Warden's bounty, I can't help ye on 'count I don't know 'em . . . just where they bide . . .'

Dorrity glared at him, annoyed by his familiar manner. 'Ye must call me "sir",' he informed them stiffly.

They didn't speak. They didn't stir.

'These vegetables . . . a gift to the poor from the Lord Warden, you say?' Dorrity returned to the business at hand.

Grote pointed to the insignia on the side of the wain. 'There's his emblem. Right generous hearted is the Cap'n.'

Dorrity's gaze followed the pointing finger to the carved snake of Blackaven. *So the wain belonged to Captain de Raddon!* He felt a stirring of excitement. He'd heard it said that there weren't many free-traders in Devon who hadn't de Raddon's backing. He viewed Grote and the two, burly, swarthy-faced men on the wain with new eyes. Especially Grote. His icy gaze swept Grote from head to toecap.

'What's thy name, fellow?' he asked abstractedly.

'Septimus Grote.'

Dorrity nodded. As if he already knew the answer. 'What is your employment?'

'Head Steward at Blackaven House.'

Again the thoughtful dipping of the head, as if he knew that also. After a while, he seemed to shake himself. Abruptly, eyes narrowed, he asked: 'Are ye sure 'tis *just* vegetables ye carry? Sure ye didn't take on load of moonshine while ye were up'long that old mine?'

Grote shook his head vigorously. 'Nay, nay, friend . . . I mean, sir! 'Tis just vegetables . . . see for thyself.'

'I fully intend to!' He gestured with the pistols. 'Unload the wain.'

They took their time in doing so. When at last all the sacks were unloaded and standing along the side of the track, Dorrity stuck one of his pistols in the belt beneath his cloak and drew his sword. This he plunged into each sack in turn. He looked quite crestfallen when no obstruction met its sharp point.

Resheathing his sword, he said: 'Pull up your smocks.'

They hesitated. The wagoner's batman looked anxious.

'Lookee here, friend . . . sir . . . we'm ent armed . . .' Grote started to say.

Dorrity's pistol moved. 'Lift 'em!' he snarled.

Reluctantly, they obeyed. An unpleasant smile twisted the Preventative man's face when the aspied the flintlock stuck in the batman's belt.

'Tis for shootin' rabbits,' lied its owner, refusing to meet the Preventative man's eyes.

An unpleasant, disbelieving smile twisted Dorrity's boyish features. 'Remove it carefully and drop it.'

The man did so.

'Now get down, both of you, and go and stand over there.' Dorrity indicated a spot a good twenty yards away where they couldn't easily jump him. He jerked his head at Grote. 'You, dismount and stand with them.'

When they were at a safe distance from him, he swung up inside the wain's canvas to investigate the interior for secret compartments. For a good few minutes he methodically tapped the wooden sides and the floor, having learned during his period of training that smugglers often used quite elaborate hides and could conceal a fair quantity of tea or snuff or tobacco in the smallest of holes. Having found no kegs hidden among the vegetable sacks, Dorrity was sure he'd find another sort of contraband tucked away somewhere.

He found no such secret places. Disappointed, he climbed down and stood for a while lowering at his smirking audience. He was convinced that they were free-traders, had thought so the instant he had chanced upon them while he was patrolling out on the moor the previous day. No farmers' boys wore long, crinkly sea-boots such as they had on. Suspicions aroused, he'd followed them, guessing when they had suddenly forked towards the Plymouth-Princeton road that they were aware of his presence and were trying to shake him off. Doubling back, he'd concealed himself in a creep and, sure enough, back they'd come a short while later.

He had lain hidden in a copse above the mine for hour upon hour. Watching. Waiting. Sure they were there to fetch kegs from their hide. Once or twice he'd thought himself discovered when the dog had caught his scent and begun to whine and bark. Luckily, the dim-witted maid with the animal hadn't the sense to know what the hound was trying to tell her: that there was a stranger in the vicinity. The night had been bitterly cold and the damp had soon crept through his cloak and tunic. Moreover, he'd just had the remainder of his patrol rations of hard biscuit to keep hunger at bay. But he'd remained steadfastly at his post, not daring to close his eyes for a moment in case they slipped by him in the dark.

'If'n ye've done with us, we'll be on our way, sir. Else there'll be folk without food in their bellies this night,' said Grote, not liking the long silence.

Dorrity had no further reason to keep them there. He was about to let them go when a sudden thought occurred to him. 'What was wrong with the wheel?' he asked sharply.

They exchanged slanted looks. Here was proof, indeed, that he had kept constant vigil. Grote answered, a little hesitantly.

'Hit a rock . . . broke two spokes and bent axle.'

Dorrity walked around the wain. There were no new spokes in the wheels. Grote was lying.

'You can go.'

He stood watching until they were out of sight among the trees.

Dorrity muttered an oath. Yes, they were free-traders. He'd stake a year's pay on it. His eyes darkened to slate. *Captain John de Raddon's moonshiners!* And they'd outwitted him. This time.

He turned and gazed absently along the track, back up towards the moor. Presently, he untethered his horse, mounted and set off at a gallop.

Captain de Raddon was in his study, the oak room, long and narrow and cheerless, writing at his big leather-topped desk when Grote came knocking at the door to report to him.

De Raddon's black brows knitted in a frown when he saw his head steward, knowing that Grote couldn't possibly have made the round trip to Eaglestone, then to Exeter and then back to Blackaven House in the time he'd been absent.

'What went wrong?' he immediately demanded.

Grote launched into his account.

'Dorrity, you say his name is?' de Raddon interrupted Grote to query, his scarred face darkening at mention of the Preventative.

'Ay, Cap'n, from over to Salcombe. Nobbut a young hobbledehoy, by looks of him, but proper cunning for all that.'

De Raddon nodded. 'I heard the Commissioners had appointed some zealous young buck to replace Old Squinty Dawlish.'

'He's that awlright, Cap'n,' growled Grote with feeling.

'Go on,' de Raddon ordered tersely.

Grote did so, his voice occasionally faltering when he met his master's cold gaze. He concluded by reluctantly admitting that he'd handed over six crowns to Keziah Hammett by way of payment for delivery.

There followed a long pause.

Presently, in a low, dangerous voice, de Raddon said: 'Are you saying, man, that the Hammett chit has taken twelve tubs to Exeter *alone*? In a wagon fit only for kindling and pulled by a half-ton of bones done up in horsehair? *And* you handed over six crowns by way of reward for this . . . this *harebrained escapade?*' His voice rose to an enraged bellow.

Grote swallowed hard. 'Ay, Cap'n,' The reply seemed safer than silence.

'It didn't enter your numb skull just to leave tubs be?'

'No, Cap'n.'

'Then you're a fool, Grote. A damned fool! Better a few empty cellars upalong Exeter than risk having the Revenue down on us.' He rose and stamped across to stand staring out of the window at the waves crashing against the rocks far below in Blackaven Cove. 'Goddamit, Grote! I thought you could be trusted!'

Grote could see by the set of his shoulders that one of his boiling rages was not far away. He sought to avert it, saying reassuringly, 'I'll warrant young Mistress Hammett will come to no harm, Cap'n. Her's proper plucked, I'll say that for she. I'll wager they tubs o' Cousin Jack is awlready wid they meant t'have 'em.'

'I hope you're right, Grote,' said de Raddon grimly without turning round, '*for all our blessed sakes*!'

Chapter Twenty-Three

It was in June 1812 that the United States of America, rebelling at last against the English blockade which was so effectively stopping Yankee skippers trading with starving, desperate-to-trade Napoleonic Europe, had declared war on Great Britain.

Matthew Youngmay, then aged twenty-two and an ordinary seaman in the Revenue Cutter Service, was among the first to volunteer for naval warfare. He was accepted for a commission, trained, and the following January sailed as First Lieutenant aboard the United States Navy brig *Maryland* for the line-of-battle in the English Channel.

He looked older than his years, which was hardly surprising since he had already endured over eight years of the privations and hardships that accompanied a life before the mast. When he was thirteen, he had run away from home to join the Revenue Cutter Service as a 'hurricane jumper' – rather than risk rejection by the masters of the harbour training ships.

As well as being lackey to the captain and officers in those early days, he'd been drummer-boy, 'powder monkey', cartridge carrier, and had lost count of the stormy nights he'd spent aloft as lookout, tied to the crow's-nest so that the plunging motion of the ship wouldn't send him plummeting into the boiling foam.

On more than a dozen occasions he'd received a sound thrashing, usually from a midshipman little older than himself and usually for no good reason that he could fathom. He accepted this casual brutality with hardly a flinch or a moan, just as he accepted the long hours and the drudgery as being all part of naval discipline.

The alternative, had he remained at home in east Pennsylvania, to his mind, would have been a lot worse. A living death. Hour upon hour, day upon day of back-breaking, mind-numbing labour deep down in the hot, suffocating blackness of a coal mine.

No blue sky above him. No scolding sea birds swooping above the spread of taut, white sails. No stinging gusts of wind to weather his boyish skin. And, more terrible than anything else he could imagine, no mighty, surging, white-capped ocean to lift his spirits and stir his blood.

Once, when he was a very small boy, he'd told his father he wanted to be a sailor. Youngmay Senior had cuffed his ears, though not unkindly, saying: 'What romantic notions you got in your head, boy. You'll be a collier like me an' your brothers an' be glad of it.'

His father's fatalism only served to intensify Matthew's rebellious spirit though never again did he speak to his father of his yearning for the sea. As young as he was, however, he inwardly vowed that somehow, someday he would escape from the sunless pits of the coal fields and make a better life for himself in the bright, clean air.

Before Matthew could achieve his ambition, he experienced the horrors of the mines. When he was only eight years old, he was employed at the same pit as his pa to move the cut coal from the face to the shaft, pulling corves weighing a good half ton or more. By the time he was a strapping twelve-year-old, he was hewing coal alongside his father and elder brothers, contorted and cramped in the narrow tunnels, stripped naked against the intense heat, knee-deep in the filthy morass of black dust and seeping water.

At close hand he saw what breathing that dust did to a man over the years. He saw two uncles die; physical wrecks at thirty-six and forty years of age, from the miners' scourge called 'Black Spit', terrible, black-and-blood streaked mucus choking their lungs. Already Matthew's father, at thirty-three, was showing signs of the disease in his wheezing breath and the increasingly frequent, blinding headaches. Once the 'Black Spit' took hold of a man his fate was written. Sure enough, in no time at all, Alice Youngmay was a widow.

Her sister had married a sailor, Uncle Mort, a big, jolly man who felt sorry for poor, young, fatherless Matthew and brought him strange objects back from his voyages – fancy gourds and seashells; and once a shrivelled head, every line and wrinkle horrifyingly preserved. But best of all, his nephew-by-marriage loved to hear the amazing stories he had to tell of his travels. And there was nothing Uncle Mort liked better than an audience. Long after Mrs Youngmay and her eldest boys had gone to sleep in their wooden shack, one of many clustered near the coal field, Uncle Mort and Matthew would sit outside by a log fire.

'Now then, young Matt, did I ever tell you 'bout the time a mermaiden saved the lives of every one of us aboard the *Elzevir*?'

He would always begin by asking some such tantalising question, whereupon the tousled fair head would be shaken and the boy's grey-green eyes would gleam with anticipation.

'We were in a raging sea and headin' for the rocks . . .'

Launching into one of his fantastic yarns, Mort had no concept of the effect he was having on his impressionable young relative. Not that Matthew believed utterly his far-fetched stories; rather he was exalted with the visions they conjured of valiant ships sailing upon surging, white-capped seas. And, as he listened enraptured, he could almost smell the keen salt wind and feel the cold spray cleaning the coal dust from his blackened pores.

'*Are* there such things as mermaidens?' Matthew had ventured to ask his mother one morning as she stirred the breakfast corn in a cauldron over the fire.

'Don't you set store by Uncle Mort's braggings,' she'd replied dismissively. Then, as if reading his mind, she gave the boy a sharp look. 'You'll not make a living at sea . . . not like you will down the mines . . . and the work's as hard. You ask Uncle Mort. And they whip the skin off you for slightest thing . . .'

He hadn't heeded her warning. One morning she found her youngest son had run away. She guessed to sea, but wasn't particularly concerned. She'd miss the small amount of money he'd earned working down the mines, of course. But she had two more strapping sons digging coal – and earning men's wages, such as the pittance was. Besides, young Matthew's departure meant there was one less belly for the filling.

The *Maryland* was his first experience of service aboard a first-rate ship of war, having previously only ever served aboard the old sailing ships used by the Revenue Cutter Service to enforce maritime law in home waters. Like the rest of her officers and crew, he was looking forward to 'blooding Mad King George's swabs'.

Matthew's first taste of real sea warfare was short-lived.

Almost as soon as the *Maryland* had reached the dark, choppy waters of the Channel, her lookouts spotted the small upper sails of a British man-of-war some miles astern of them. The roll to quarters had sounded and they had sprung excitedly to their posts, clearing the decks for action. Their preparations, it had turned out, were somewhat premature. It was almost three hours before they got a clear view of the enemy ship bearing down on them with her Union Jacks and ensigns streaming from her tops and mizzen rigging. Through his eyeglass, Matthew had made out the name of the side of the mighty hulk – *HMS Pelican*. In his heart he, like the rest of *Maryland*'s crew, had known they were hopelessly out-classed.

The *Pelican* attacked under full sail.

The *Maryland* returned her fire but without inflicting any real damage on the colossal ship sailing nearer and nearer to them. Then a thunderous crash of splintering timber and falling spars over their heads told them the *Pelican* had their range. They lost a midshipman and the quartermaster, crushed beneath a falling mast. Minutes later, their commander fell, mortally wounded by a slug fired from the *Pelican*'s mizzen shrouds. In precisely twenty minutes the brief but ferocious engagement was over with a final, resounding crash which stove in the *Maryland's* lower ports. She foundered before her small boats could be launched and Matthew was among the survivors plucked from the sea.

Twenty minutes.

Matthew could hardly believe that that was all the time it had taken for Mad King George's swabs to rout them. The thought rankled. Twenty minutes, which at the time seemed to pass in a moment, yet seemed like an eternity when Matthew's restless brain recalled every second with agonising clarity during the long nights in the remote, grey-walled prison to which providence had condemned him.

He continued to have nightmares, reliving over and over the action which had deprived him of his liberty, as if he was a spectre at the bloody scene of destruction aboard the *Maryland*. Sometimes, as he saw Commander Allen fall, clutching his bloodstained chest, he would hear his own urgent voice shouting above the battle noise: *'Surgeon! Surgeon! For the love of God!'*

He would be roused by the grousing of those around him, in the main also survivors from *Maryland*, and know he'd cried out again.

'Stash it, matey!'

'Stow his luff for pity's sake, somebody!'

But in the morning none uttered a word of reproach. For they, too – hardened war veterans that they were – felt the loss of their commander and harboured a deep and abiding hatred for the anonymous sharpshooter whose slug had downed him.

Commander Allen's body was eventually washed ashore at Falmouth and buried there. None of his crew was allowed to attend. Indeed, the first the *Maryland* survivors heard of his funeral was through one of the prison guards who was slightly more talkative the the rest. However, the magnanimous parish fathers, as a mark of respect towards one who had until recently been an ally, erected and inscribed a tombstone proclaiming: *Here sleeps a brave son of his country.*

Matthew's nature was too rational for him to wallow in anger and grief for very long; neither would he allow himself to become embittered by adversity. So, after a while, the night-hags came less often and in due course quit tormenting him altogether. In retrospect, he began to realise that it was something that so many of the *Maryland*'s crew had survived. And if he did ever find himself feeling depressed, well then, he had an antidote for it. He would quickly conjure up a face: a young, creamy-skinned face, only briefly seen by the pool on his way 'up the moor', yet a face in which he soon discovered he could lose himself during that morbid, half-dreaming time before dawn. A face which was a strange mixture of stubbornness, vulnerability and solemn-eyed watchfulness. And after a while Matthew grew to love the face.

The day after Kezzy returned from Exeter, she prepared to set off again, this time for Blackaven House, to pay Captain de Raddon a visit.

'Off 'ee go gin, gall'vantin'! Leavin' me t'manage best ways I can,' grumbled Elyas when she appeared early that Thursday morning wearing her red woollen Sunday dress.

'You'll be all right, Gramps,' Kezzy told him firmly. 'And 'tis important I see Cap'n de Raddon . . .'

Even as she uttered the name, she regretted it: it would have been better not to have told him where she was going and whom she was to see. She sighed inwardly as Elyas began to rant.

'Ye'll not go near the scurvy varmint! I forbid 'ee, Keziah Hammett! Do 'ee hear?'

He was seized by a violent fit of coughing. Kezzy ran for his lung-syrup. Once he was breathing easier, she continued to get herself ready, putting on her Sunday shawl and bonnet and putting bread and cheese in a mossle bag. He watched her swift, determined movements with eyes filled with reproach.

'Never did I think day'd come when ye'd defy me, chield,' he said shaking his head like a mournful, grey old badger.

' 'Tis business . . . important business I have with Cap'n de Raddon.'

He was sitting in his usual place by the fire. He spat on the smouldering vags. 'Business! Faugh! Only business Hammetts should have with that limb o' Satan is *killin'* business. By the Lord Harry, 'tis wisht poor thing I didn't take peeker to he when I were fitty in the legs!'

'Well, I'm very glad you didn't, Gramps,' Kezzy told him with a faint smile. 'He's not worth hanging for.'

'Then why ye a-rushin' round deliverin' his'n bleddy moonshine for he? Eh? Tell me that? Be *that* worth hangin' for then?'

'He pays me to deliver it . . . at least he will. That's what I want to see him about. Among other things . . .'

'What other things?' demanded Elyas suspiciously.

Kezzy pretended not to hear.

'What other things?' he asked again, louder. 'Eh? Speak up!'

'I'll tell you all about it when I get back, Gramps,' she told him soothingly. She checked he had a stoup of water near at hand and another of cider, and that the big pot of stew on the slab wouldn't catch and spoil. Finally, she made sure he had his lung-syrup and the laudanum bottle close by. 'You will be all right, won't you, Gramps?' she asked him a little anxiously. While she'd been away in Exeter, the time had hung heavily on him, she knew.

'Why should 'ee care 'bout me?' he griped.

She put out a hand and touched one of his. It felt cold. 'Well, I *do* care,' she said. She went and fetched the blanket from her pallet and put it around his shoulders.

'I don't need babbyin'! Be off withee if'n you'm a-goin'.'

'I'll be as quick as I can.'

'Oh, don't 'ee hurry on account o' me,' said Elyas sarcastically. 'Mebbe Cap'n de Raddon will invite 'ee to sit at his'n table.'

Kezzy picked up her mossle bag. 'You know I wouldn't accept even if he did . . . which, thank God, is hardly likely.'

He knew what she was saying. She was prepared to do business with de Raddon if needs must but she'd not forgotten that he had led the witch-hunt again her mother. Nay, she'd not sit and sup with the black-hearted devil.

'Don't 'ee be too sure he won't ask. That de Raddon . . .' Elyas spat in the fire again. 'Got an eye for young maidens, he has, drat the dirty, seducin' dog! You'm just watch thyself, Kezzy. You'm growed. You'm bain't a chield now'days . . .' He paused as an idea occurred. 'Mebbe best if'n 'ee weared boy's togs . . .'

Kezzy had already thought of that. And decided against doing so. It was *because* she was no longer a child that she wasn't keen to appear at Blackaven wearing breeches. To reveal the shape of her limbs in such a way would be thought quite shocking. Besides, de Raddon was all too well aware that she wasn't a boy. If he entertained any ideas about seducing her, breeches might well serve to give him the wrong impression by suggesting she was a forthy piece.

'I'll be all right, Gramps,' she said in a ringing, confident voice as much to reassure herself as her grandfather.

He waved to her with a gesture of dismissal. She went out.

The day was fair, calm and quiet with just a small amount of mist in the distance blotting out the furthest line of hills. Rats set off at his lumbering trot. Kezzy sang to herself in time with the creaking of the wheels.

Whose ragg'd togs be this you wear?
'Tis mine, said the sailor,
But I could dress fine as any squire
If you'll pay the tailor . . .

The little ditty made her think of one ragged sailor in particular. Matthew. Something told her that the wasn't a pressed man but proud of being a volunteer. A trained man whose years before the mast had left an unmistakable stamp on him from the set of his fair head upon his muscular shoulders to the way he moved, with a brisk rhythm to his step.

O Sailor, O Sailor, what can you know,
Of the sorrow and pain I undergo?
Come, lay thy head 'pon my breast,
Hear how my beating heart takes no rest . . .

Kezzy stopped at Cornwood. The plight of de Raddon's boy apprentices was playing on her mind. Perhaps the dame could think of some way of putting a stop to their shameful torment.

Hannah Rogers's pupils hadn't arrived yet, so she took Kezzy through into her tiny sitting room and brought her a cup of milk and some small sweet biscuits, exactly as if she was still a small child. Only now her movements were tentative because of her poor sight. Yet, physically, the years had been kind to her, and to Kezzy's eyes she looked much as she always had: neat and slender in an ankle-length skirt of grey alpaca. Her starched white blouse fastened high at the throat with an over-crowded line of mother-of-pearl buttons. Her hair was perhaps greyer, but still pulled back in its immaculate bun from a long, thin, pale face criss-crossed with fine lines.

'And how is Captain Hammett?' asked the dame when they were seated opposite each other at her highly polished mahogany table. She always paid him the courtesy of calling him 'captain' even though his Wheal Eaglestone was 'knocked'.

'He's as well as can be expected,' answered Kezzy politely. She took a biscuit and nibbled it. After a while, she said hesitantly, 'He gets so angry . . .'

'Yes, my dear, I expect he does. But he's not angry with you. He's angry at himself. For being so helpless. For a man like Elyas Hammett to be crippled . . . well, I dare say he's asked the Lord more than once why He didn't take him and be done with it.'

This was true. For a while after the explosion, when Elyas had realised that he'd never walk again unaided, he would indeed rage at God – almost to sacrilege – waving his fist at the ceiling as he lay on his pallet and shouting that 'Even Satan don't give as much trouble to them as belong to him'. Eventually he'd resigned himself to the crutches made for him by the Cornwood carpenter and had ceased to vilify the Almighty. Instead, he would take out his frustration upon Kezzy, grousing at her over the slightest thing as he would never have done once upon a time.

'I know . . . I try not to mind . . .' she said with a sad little smile. She finished her milk. 'I must go . . .'

Yet, she made no move to rise.

Dame Rogers felt sure that there was something else Kezzy wished to say but was having trouble putting into words. She searched her mind. 'Do you have enough . . . laudanum?'

Kezzy was miles away. She looked up with a start. 'Oh, yes! at least . . .' she took out her purse and counted out the money she owed the dame for the last bottle. Then added to the pile of coins enough for another bottle and also one of lung-syrup, saying, 'If you would be so obliging. I'm sure I wouldn't know where to go to purchase such medicines.'

The dame put out a tentative hand and touched the coins, grey brows raised in surprise. 'But where . . .?'

She just stopped herself asking outright how Kezzy had come by such a sum (and with plenty more in her purse by the sound of it), which would have been the very height of impertinence.

Kezzy thought quickly. She didn't want to confide in her friend. Not this time. She suspected that the dame had guessed the Hammetts were hiding contraband for the flaskers to eke out their living but was loath to tell the schoolmistress that, all being well and de Raddon willing, in the future she would also be delivering their moonshine. She made herself lie.

'I . . . sold some eggs. And half a dozen hens.'

The questioning brows remained raised. 'Yes, of course . . .'

They both knew that such paltry sales wouldn't have raised anything like the amount on the table between them.

'I must go,' said Kezzy again. This time she rose, pulling her shawl around her. Still she lingered, clearly troubled.

Dame Rogers racked her brains. *If not medicine, what then?*

Kezzy's careful attire – worthy of Sunday – hadn't escaped her notice. 'Have you . . . far to travel?' she ventured. 'Perhaps some biscuits and apples for the journey?'

'Thank you, no, Mistress Rogers. I have a mossle bag.'

Kezzy couldn't help a wry little smile as she fleetingly wondered what Dame Rogers's reaction would be if she suddenly informed her that she was calling upon Captain de Raddon with a business proposal. She would undoubtedly be shocked. And would call her overly forthy. She might even insist on accompanying her as chaperone, God forbid!

Kezzy's expression changed to one of deep concentration as she pondered the best way of telling the dame about the terrible events of Sir Ryden Bliss's house but without revealing that she was a participant – albeit a frightened and unwilling one.

'May I ask you something, Mistress Rogers?'

The dame had also risen. Encouragingly, she said: 'Of course . . . please speak quite frankly, child.'

'Do you . . . I mean, *have* you ever heard before of . . . well, gentlemen who prefer . . . in a certain way . . . boys? Youths . . . in preference to maidens . . .?' her voice trailed. She found herself blushing furiously. How absurd the question sounded!

The dame's face was quite impassive. She didn't appear in the slightest bit embarrassed or put out by the candour of the question. 'You mean, I think,' she said quietly, '*sodomites*.'

Kezzy chewed her lip. *Was* that what she meant?

Dame Rogers sensed her uncertainty. She clasped her hands before her as she did when she was addressing a class and proceeded to quote by heart from the relevant chapter in Genesis.

'And they called unto Lot . . . where are the men which came to thee this night? Bring them out, that we may know them . . .'

Kezzy slowly nodded. 'Yes, sodomites,' she said musingly.

Dame Rogers waited but Kezzy continued to ponder in silence. So eventually she asked, promptingly, 'And what would you know, child, of such . . . such *wickedness?*'

It came out in a rush. 'Captain de Raddon sends boy apprentices to Sir Ryden Bliss to use in such a way. So that Sir Ryden Bliss will speak well of him to the Prince of Wales.'

There was silence. The dame thought it over.

'How can you know this, Keziah?'

Even if she could bring herself to lie again to her friend, Kezzy doubted the dame would believe her if she claimed to have heard it from some itinerant tinners or bal maidens. Dame Hannah had a way of getting at the truth. 'I'd rather not say . . . but please believe when I say that I do know that it is so. 'T'isn't a load of ol' plod I heared . . . heard . . . from bal maidens over at Wheal Emma.'

Despite the seriousness of the matter, the ghost of a smile played about the dame's prim, colourless lips. Despite all her efforts over the years, both as a schoolmistress and as a friend who tried her hardest to set a good example, she knew that Kezzy would always remain at heart as wild and untamed as the moors which were her home. She was suddenly grave. In a rare gesture she reached out and felt for Kezzy's hand, taking it in both of hers. She spoke slowly, carefully choosing her words.

'Keziah . . . Kezzy, my dear. There are some things, horrible shocking, vile things which revolt and sicken us but about which we can do nothing. This terrible proclivity of Sir Ryden Bliss's is, alas, not unusual among those of his class.' She felt Kezzy tense. A note of bitterness entered her voice. 'Yes, child, I know all about it. Do you imagine that I haven't racked my brains for some way of putting a stop to this perverted trade? And it isn't just boys who are defiled by these monsters, but girls, too. Some of them no more than five or six years old. The poor mites are sold to . . . to certain houses in London. Houses of ill-repute. Some of them are taken across to France and sold to houses there . . .'

The dame stopped as her emotions threatened to overwhelm her.

'But surely something can be done to help them?' said Kezzy, aghast at what she was hearing.

The dame released her hand and made an impatient gesture.

'Who would listen to an old village schoolmistress? And if I could get someone of influence to listen . . . what could they do? The common laws of England are twisted against women and children. And I dare say they always will be.'

Captain de Raddon wasn't at home when Kezzy arrived at Blackaven House. Mrs de Raddon was at home but had given orders that she wasn't to be disturbed, the footman who had answered the door told Kezzy with ill-concealed disdain as he looked her up and down.

'My business is with Captain de Raddon,' she told him icily. 'So I shall wait.'

Grudgingly, he showed her into a small, dark, fireless anteroom and left her. An hour passed. Then another, the hands of the big long-case clock in the corner creeping with agonising slowness. Bored, Kezzy went and looked out of the small casement window. She could see trees. And a hedge. That was all.

The clock was striking four when she heard de Raddon return. The house, hitherto almost as silent as a tomb, was suddenly astir with hurrying servants, barking dogs, slamming doors and, above all this noisy activity, the Lord Warden's booming voice issuing a volley of commands, mostly to Grote.

Kezzy opened the anteroom door a few inches so she could peep out into the hall. She saw the footman who'd let her in bow as de Raddon strode by, but couldn't quite make out what the footman said to his master in his low, obsequious voice. There was, however, no mistaking de Raddon's loud, scornful reply.

'Some scrounging tinner's widow, I suppose. Tell her to apply at tinners' hall over at Plympton like the rest of them. Or take herself to the Workhouse.'

So saying, he stamped into the oak room with his dogs at his heels and the footman closed the big doors behind him. Once again, peace reigned. Grote ambled off about his duties, as did the other manservants. The footman who'd admitted Kezzy approached the anteroom, scowling at seeing her peering out.

'You'm heard Lord Warden, girl! So off with 'ee!'

'You didn't tell him my name,' complained Kezzy, annoyed. She had made a point of giving her name to the footman on arrival, sure that de Raddon would agree to see her.

'What difference would that make?' sneered the footman. He took hold of her arm and began propelling her through the hall to the rear of the house, intending to throw her out.

'Take your hands off me!' she spat.

Wrenching herself free, Kezzy made a dash for the doors through which de Raddon had disappeared. Taken aback, it was a moment before the footman could collect his wits and lunge after her.

'Come 'ere, ye bitch!'

She was too quick for him. In a trice, she'd the door open and was inside, slamming it in his furious face.

De Raddon was standing by the fireplace about to light a pipe with a burning tallow dip. He paused, glowering across to see who'd entered in such a cavalier fashion. His eyebrows shot up beneath his black horse-hair wig at the sight of Kezzy standing there pink-cheeked and straightening her bonnet.

'Good-day, Cap'n de Raddon,' she said courteously. 'I have come . . .'

She was interrupted as the door behind her was hauled open and the footman, red-faced and mortified, plunged in after her. He grabbed her, struggling, by the arm and stuttered his apology to de Raddon, fearful for his job.

'B . . . beggin' thy pardon, sir . . . her just run p . . . past m . . . me!'

'Let her be,' said de Raddon sourly, and the footman reluctantly released Kezzy. 'Leave us.'

The astonished footman bowed out, giving Kezzy a poisonous glance as he did so for outwitting him, whereupon she responded with a triumphant grin.

De Raddon took his time lighting his pipe. All the while he kept his eyes on Kezzy, roaming speculatively over her in a most disconcerting way. She had grown into a tall, slender young woman, very tall, yet very graceful, with narrow wrists and ankles and a fine pair of shoulders beneath her woollen dress. And her bosom, he decided with quickening interest, was most womanly. Not voluptuous, not yet, but nicely upthrusting.

Kezzy stiffened with embarrassment, hating this blatant appraisal of her body. She was fully aware of what was going on behind his hard, heavy-lidded eyes and found herself wishing that she had, after all, confided in Dame Rogers and brought her along as a chaperone. Mentally, she pulled herself together, reminding herself why she was there. She needed, desperately *needed*, to earn money. A lot of money. If her grandfather was to have the costly medicines for his lung-rot purchased from a proper doctor, rather than some weak cure-all made from herbs and sold by the gypsies. And then there was the price of corn! Three guineas a bushel now because of the war, if it could be found for sale. Mr Wisdome the miller at Cornwood always had wheat and corn for those that had the right stuff to buy it. Gruel and white bread was virtually all Elyas could manage to keep down nowadays. That and a little stewed beef or chicken.

She forced herself to meet his gaze calmly, without revealing anything of her deep-seated loathing for him, or the revulsion she couldn't help but feel whenever she caught a glimpse of the torn, twisted flesh he tried to hide beneath his wig.

Eventually, he seemed to get his pipe going to his satisfaction. Exhaling a cloud of blue smoke, he addressed her in a voice laced with disdain. 'Well? Why have you come? What, pray, can be so important that it can't await Grote's next visit up the moor?'

Kezzy had had plenty of time in which to rehearse what she wanted to say to him. She took a deep breath and began. His face revealed nothing, but he listened attentively, puffing at his churchwarden, until she had said her piece and had counted out the money that she'd collected in Exeter on his behalf into his big hand.

'So you see, Cap'n de Raddon . . . I can do it,' she concluded. She fully expected him to sneer at her, to pour scorn on the very idea of her acting as tub-carrier to his band of flaskers. She'd even prepared various arguments. But, unexpectedly, he needed no persuasion.

'Yes. 'Tis a sound idea. Preventatives won't concern themselves with a boy driving a furze wagon.' He paused, considering gravely. 'Of course, your wagon will need strengthening . . .'

Kezzy had already thought of that. 'Yes . . . with iron struts. But underneath, and covered with thin planks so they can't be seen. Can it be done here by your smithy?'

He nodded.

'And the wheels . . . they'll need steel rims. But scratched and rusted-looking.'

'You'll need a good, strong horse.'

She'd thought of that, too. 'A big farm horse would be best. With its coat roughened so it looks old and broken down.'

'I'll have Grote buy it at the horse-fair and bring it to Eaglestone.'

They were silent for a while. Somewhat thoughtfully, de Raddon knocked out his pipe and placed it on the marble chimney piece. He went and poured himself a large measure of cognac and sipped it. He didn't offer Kezzy any refreshment although there was a decanter of port and another of madeira wine on the side table, Perhaps, thought Kezzy, he was remembering how he'd once offered her sweetstuffs and had been rebuffed.

'Is there anything else?' he asked.

'The names of those who are to receive the tubs.'

'Grote will tell you when he brings the cargo. We write nothing down.'

She nodded, seeing the sense in that. 'There is just one other thing, Cap'n de Raddon.' He waited. 'I don't want to be paid in money for storing and delivering tubs.'

Again his black brows shot up. 'If you don't want money, how do you want paying?' he asked bemusedly.

'In tea . . .'

'In tea?'

'. . . and snuff and tobacco . . .'

'Tobacco?'

'Yes. Also some French pomade, six dozen silk handkerchiefs and a Leghorn hat.' He was gazing at her in utter bewilderment. 'On second thoughts, will you get me a *dozen* Leghorns, please, Cap'n? They're quite the thing, you know.'

'So I believe . . . among the foppish,' he said disdainfully.

'And Prinny says that only the French can make the demned things properly.'

'So those nonsensical hats enjoy Royal approval, do they?'

'Yes, indeed. All your gentlemen patrons will want one of my Leghorns!' She paused, chewing her lower lip while she pondered. 'Might I ask . . . how many gentlemen *do* you . . . er . . . supply, Cap'n de Raddon?'

He stared at her for a long time with narrowed eyes. As the silence drew out, she began to wonder if he was going to reply. Then, abruptly, he said: 'The cargo you hide at Eaglestone is but a small part of what I bring in. Most weeks I land over 2000 gallons of cognac.'

Kezzy blinked. So *many* patrons!

'In that case, perhaps we should say *two* dozen Leghorns, Cap'n de Raddon . . . Just to begin with . . .'

His great bellow of laughter carried through the heavy oaken doors into the hall. Mrs de Raddon heard it as she descended into the hall from her apartments where she'd spent most of the day abed. Her fragile face lit up – it was such a long time since she'd heard him laugh like that. It boded well. He might even be agreeable to her at dinner . . .

Chapter Twenty-Four

Matthew soon discovered that Dartmoor Prison was not unlike an island, with barren wasteland instead of sea all around, marooning them from even the cluster of little stone and slate houses at nearby Princeton – mostly the dwellings of the prison guards.

There was virtually no contact between the majority of the prisoners-of-war and the world beyond the high grey prison walls. A few, a lucky few – always Frenchmen never Americans whose word as gentlemen wasn't to be trusted – were allowed out in parties of three or four to work on the local farms. They had to swear an oath before the prison captain, these young Frenchmen, solemnly and ceremoniously with their hand upon the tricolour. Prison Captain Gilpin well knew what a crucial thing it was for them to swear this oath – any oath. Such fervent patriots – savage in battle, gullible and superstitious in thought – would sooner perish than break their word so honourably given. Moreover, these Frenchmen were mostly farmboys and since one farm, French or English, was much alike, and since farmers' daughters on both sides of the Channel were equally as saucy-eyed and rosy-cheeked, they seldom thought of escape.

Those prisoners who could write were permitted to send occasional letters, with Captain Gilpin's permission. Their letters had to be tendered to him unsealed for approval. Composing a letter that was in any way acceptable to Gilpin wasn't easy, and somewhat risky. The smallest criticism or hint of a complaint about the hellish conditions was construed as mutinous, earning the author at best a visit to the triangles, or, worse, a visit to the makeshift yardarm. Some prisoners morbidly believed that it was better to be hanged quickly than flogged slowly by the bosun's mates – one a burly right-hander, the other an even burlier left-hander, and both as big a pair of sadists as ever swung a cat-o'-nine.

Consequently, few letters got written. And there was some doubt whether those that did get written were ever sent. Notwithstanding, towards the end of his first month of incarceration, Matthew put in a formal request for permission to write a letter, and early one morning, a week hence, was marched before Prison Captain Gilpin in his quarters at the top of the central block from where he could look down upon the main prison yard: a stark, well-tramped grey square. He was standing at the window watching a group of prisoners exercising beneath the watchful eyes of armed guards when the master-at-arms brought Matthew in.

'Prisoner . . . atten . . . shun! Prisoner . . . salute! Off cap!' roared the master-at-arms. 'Prisoner Youngmay requests permission to write a letter, sir!'

Gilpin left the window and went and seated himself behind his big polished teak desk. He sat back, sternly viewing the prisoner as if estimating him. Youngmay was, he knew, just twenty-three. He saw a tall, fair-haired man, well-set up about the shoulders and with piercing blue eyes. He spoke brusquely:

'To whom would this letter be directed?'

Matthew stood absolutely straight, his broad-arrowed cap correctly beneath his arm as if it was his officer's cocked hat.

'To the Admiralty in Whitehall, London, sir.'

Gilpin's small, cold, hard eyes positively bulged.

Behind Matthew, on sentry before the door, the master-at arms shifted his weight creakingly and harrumphed his disbelief and disapproval of this display of unsurpassed impertinence. He looked across at Gilpin and braced himself for the storm, fully expecting to be ordered to remove the prisoner and see he was flogged or thrown into solitary.

The expected storm never came.

Gilpin's face was in dark contrast to his white neckband but his voice, though icy, was controlled. 'What would this letter say?'

'I wish to inform the Admiralty that conditions within this prison are in direct contravention of the Articles of War pertaining to the treatment of prisoners. In particular, the overcrowding and the meagre rations, sir.'

There was a long pause. Then Gilpin said tersely: 'You are presumptuous, Prisoner Youngmay. I will not tolerate such presumption. I'll have your blessed guts for it!'

Matthew continued to stare straight at him. In the same, clipped, correct tone of voice, he said: 'Sir, the Articles state that all officers are to be addressed by rank and name.'

Another, longer pause, during which the master-at-arms creaked and coughed some more and the prisoner and Prison Captain continued to stare frigidly as each other across the desk. From experience, Gilpin had already sized up the American – patriotic, courageous; clearly an enemy of the prison authorities and not one to do his loathing stoically. The other prisoners would instinctively respect him and that made him dangerous. A natural leader who was likely to start a mutiny, given the chance. Gilpin intended making sure he wasn't given that chance. Yes, there had been others like Youngmay – a few, who had soon been controlled and taught to obey. Such was Gilpin's hatred of Britain's enemies, he actually looked forward to breaking, both mentally and physically, this fine young specimen standing before him. His dispassionate tone, however, revealed nothing of what was going through his mind.

'What date were you brought here?' He already knew. He had before him on the desk a list of those prisoners brought up from Plymouth during the previous month.

'Twenty-third of February, sir.'

'A month ago,' observed Gilpin musingly.

'Three weeks and four days, sir.'

Sarcasm entered Gilpin's voice. 'It seems that you have lost no time in becoming the mouthpiece of the resentful scum it is my misfortune to control . . . *Prisoner* Youngmay.'

Matthew's mouth tightened but he made no response. He thought it wise not to antagonise Gilpin while there was still a chance permission for the letter might be granted, though he had to fight the temptation to point out that it was because he was a 'short' prisoner that he was so outraged by the conditions in which they were expected to live. The 'long' prisoners had, to some extent, become inured to the cramming in like hens for market, the sickening stench, the spartan food full of worms and weevils.

Other officers, Matthew knew, having been told by a Yankee midshipman who'd been a prisoner almost from the start of war, had in the past petitioned Gilpin for better conditions – to no avail. The middy was called Jim Doherty, known as 'Knuckles' because he'd 'put up his dukes' to a guard and got a month in the dumb-box for it. Knuckles was twelve and had been pressed from his father's farm in New England. Yet there was nothing boyish about his hollowed eyes and gaunt face.

It was then that Matthew, looking about him at all the haggard, dispirited faces of the long prisoners, determined to approach Gilpin for permission to write his letter, while he still could. Before the soul-destroying degradation took its toll on him, as it had on them, becoming a solid wall over which they no longer had the will to look, let alone to climb.

He was aware of Gilpin's cold eyes watching him closely, trying to force him to lower his gaze as all the prisoners were brutally trained to do. He refused to be intimidated, and held Gilpin's gaze without blinking while schooling his face to utter blandness.

From outside, far below in the prison yard, came the muffled shouts of the guards ordering the exercise party back into their cells.

Gilpin spoke abruptly. 'Permission refused. Remove the prisoner.'

Matthew hadn't expected that Gilpin would deny his request out of hand. The Articles were quite clear on that point: prisoners-of-war were entitled to petition a higher authority than the prison captain if they considered they had a valid complaint.

'Prisoner . . . atten . . . shun!' barked the master-at-arms.

Matthew ignored him. 'Sir . . . the gruel ran out this morning before all the prisoners were fed . . .' he told Gilpin sharply, fighting the urge to lean over and haul the complacent, corpulent prison captain across his desk by the throat and shake some humanity into him.

'Come on, you!' snarled the master-at-arms, enraged at the prisoner's disobedience. He stepped forward and would have struck Matthew with his cudgel but Gilpin motioned for him to return to his place in front of the door.

Gilpin glared at Matthew. He'd purposefully refrained from ordering an increase in rations to accommodate the last influx of prisoners, instructing those who worked in the cookhouse to stretch existing rations still further. Though Gilpin entered the oats and vegetables thus saved in the stores ledger as having been distributed, they found their way to a local farmer as horse feed and pig swill and at a mutually satisfactory price.

'Can I be held responsible,' he demanded coldly, 'for the greed of those at the head of the line?'

'Sir . . .' Matthew forced a note of appeal, trying another tack, 'I'm sure that it isn't an easy task . . . the administration of nearly 10,000 prisoners . . .'

'Indeed, 'tis not!' barked Gilpin, not interested in honeyed phrases. 'Particularly when a vainglorious young hot-head stokes the filthy scum just to prove he's plucked!'

Matthew's face drained of colour as he finally lost the battle with his simmering temper. 'I insist . . . *demand* that you adhere to the Articles of War or answer for it!'

The master-at-arms stepped forward unbidden with his cudgel menacingly raised. 'Watch thy gob-box when 'ee speaks to the Cap'n!' he growled but once again Gilpin waved him aside, his eyes locked, full of contempt, to Matthew's defiant blue ones.

'*Insist? Demand?*' he sneered. 'And who, pray, will I *answer to*? Not to you, *Prisoner* Youngmay! No, not to you. Take him away, Mr Brett! And see he gets a month in solitary for his presumption.'

Matthew was taken to the tiny subterranean cell the prisoners called the 'dumb-box' because the walls were so thick that no sound could permeate in or out. The guards fastened leg-irons and manacles on him and left him with barely enough bread and water for a week.

For the first few hours solitary meant little more to him than dark and silence and a certain dismount of discomfort from the irons. He had no way of knowing the time, only when it was night because then it grew exceedingly cold. He couldn't tell where the icy, fetid draughts came from: he guessed a grating, but since he was chained to the wall he was unable to investigate. By stretching out his legs he could just touch the opposite wall – something he did often to keep his powerful leg muscles from wasting.

He was careful to eke out his bread and water, uncertain if he would be given more, though it was hard to see how a man could possibly survive on such a meagre diet. Perhaps, it occurred to him, that was the idea. Perhaps he was meant to starve to death – forgotten by all save Gilpin. But just when he was down to his last morsel of bread and sip of water, the heavy steel door suddenly swung open with a faint clang that sounded like thunder to Matthew's ears. Involuntarily, he squeezed shut his eyes as lantern light – as strong as the sun after a week of pitch black – flooded the cell. He heard a clatter as a steel plate and a pail of water were pushed in. No one spoke to him.

'How . . . long have I been here?' he asked.

No one answered him. The light receded and the door clanged shut again. This ritual was to be repeated twice more before he was released. Meanwhile, when he did manage to sleep he was plagued by all his old nightmares – crying out in anguish and pain but with none to hear. During his waking hours he concentrated his thoughts on his beloved 'face'. *Where was she now? What was she doing? What colour was her hair beneath her stocking-hat? What was her name? Where did she live?*

These few simple, unanswered questions and fleeting recollections of a tender, elfin face, saved Matthew from becoming totally disoriented. These, and his plans for escape . . .

> 'O Sailor, O Sailor, what can you know,
> Of the sorrow and pain I undergo?
> Come, lay thy head 'pon my breast,
> Hear how my beating heart takes no rest . . .'

The ragged boy atop his furze wagon pulled by an old cob with drooping head, became a familiar sight. And if the song he sung in a high, sweet lilting voice was a strange one for a boy, none thought to remark upon it. For it seemed the boy was half-witted. To begin with, he didn't like to be looked at and would drop his chin and hide his face whenever he passed anyone on the moorland tracks. No one knew precisely where he came from, and no one much cared; there were plenty of boys apprenticed to farmers on Dartmoor.

It was well into March and spring was promising to come early. Smokey-red blossoms were covering the nakedness of the elms above the creep and on the slopes above Eaglestone, and the heathlands were already patched with heather and liverworts and clumps of greenish-grey lichen. But Kezzy had little time to enjoy the changing scenery: the flaskers were keeping her well occupied. For, after some consideration, Captain de Raddon had decided that Eaglestone should become their sole hide, believing his cognac safer beneath Kezzy's bold eyes than forced upon farmers and tinners who'd squeal like hogs at the very sight of a Preventative.

So never a week went by without at least one nocturnal visit – and usually two or three – from Grote and his men leading their strings of heavily laden pack-horses. And with the half-ankers of cognac would come Kezzy's payment – packets of tea and snuff, silk handkerchiefs and sweet-smelling pomades. And Leghorn hats by the score, until it seemed that every gentleman in Devon sported one. And always Grote had a name to whisper in Kezzy's ear along with details: to wit, how many tubs and to where they were to be delivered. And as the tubs had to be brought up in the kibbles from their secret chamber, there seemed always to be two or more hefty carriers about the place. Then there was her grandfather to look after, and their smallholding; since he could do little other than feed the hens. All this activity made Elyas fractious, particularly since the sight of Grote brought it home to him just who was back of it all, so he would bitterly harangue Kezzy.

'You'm a traitor to thy name, chield,' he'd rage, 'doin' business wi' he as hung thy ma an' sent thy two brothers to they deaths!'

It was always the same. And he would not be reasoned with. But when the coughing was upon him, he was glad of the soothing lung-syrups and, if the fever took his brain, the laudanum which de Raddon money bought. Though sometimes, if he was in a particularly vexatious mood, he would spit his medicine out, saying, 'I'd lief take poison than elly of thy quack stuffs bought wi' Devil's gold!'

Yet he had periods of complete lucidity, when he would say to Kezzy, 'Get that jug o' shrub down, will ye, chield?' And he would sit in his chimney corner, mug in hand, with the fire – which he demanded was kept burning day and night – lighting his worn features, telling Kezzy stories of long ago. Of his father, who'd been a tut-worker for old Captain de Raddon, the present Lord Warden's father, a good and kindly master. And of his Grandfather Hammett, who'd been one of the 'old men' working the streams for tin in the old days. And he would tell Kezzy how he'd left the moors when his beloved Beth had died and, with Kezzy's pa Huward, had gone for the fish, only to return after ten years, drawn by this windswept, desolate land and the tin that was in their blood. And Kezzy, as weary as she usually was, would listen, thrilled, an expression of fierce joy lighting her face, while within her surged pride and admiration, and a deep, abiding love for this old man who had seen and suffered so much.

'One day, chield,' Elyas would tell her, bright vistas dancing before his faraway gaze, 'a fine boy will come thy way. An' then ye'll slave no more for that devil de Raddon! Because this boy will take good care o' 'ee, ay, an' the sons ye'll give un. An' he'll knowed, this boy, how to work yon bal an' bring out un copper. An' then ye'll be rich. An' wear fine silk and live in a big house . . . bigger an' better un Blackaven!'

'But, Gramps,' she would ask him teasingly, 'how shall I know this boy when he comes my way? Just so I snare right one?'

'Ye'll know him, chield! I promise 'ee that . . . ye'll know him,' Elyas would assure her, chuckling delightedly.

Easter approached. And the Reverend Creedy put in a surprise early morning appearance at Eaglestone – ostensibly to ensure that the Hammetts would be attending church on Palm Sunday, but in truth to count their stock before they'd a chance to hide pigs or hens out of the way of his avaricious gaze. However, he quickly discovered that Keziah Hammett was every bit as cunning and troublesome as her grandfather.

'Fine sucklings ye have this year, Miss Keziah,' he observed, peering in the sty and mentally counting them.

'Pretty fair,' she agreed curtly.

'Eleven, I make it . . . this time.'

'Yes. A right good sow this time, for sure,' Kezzy told him nonchalantly, leaning over the gate to scratch the mottled-pink bristly back.

'Then the tenth is due to me for tithing. Perhaps ye'll bring it down to Cornwood and put it in my yard.'

Kezzy shook her head. 'Not me, Parson Creedy.'

He frowned. ' 'Tis due me.'

'Yes. But I'm not your servant. So I won't bring it.'

His frown deepened. 'This is most, er, unusual . . .'

Kezzy shrugged. 'I've enough to do looking after Gramps and this place to go deliverin' pigs to parsons.'

'I tell ye, 'tis mine by right of tithing.'

'Then take it yourself . . . I shan't stop you.'

He looked the piglets over and picked out the plumpest. 'I'll take that one. Have ye a sack?'

'Yes.' She made no move to fetch one from the barn.

Creedy threw a leg over the gate and climbed in. The sow stopped her snuffling about in the filth and stood watching him suspiciously as he moved towards the piglet of his choice. But the moment he grabbed the little back legs and swung the piglet in the air it began squealing in terror, setting all the rest off squealing as well. The next thing, Creedy was prostrate in the mud with the snorting, furious sow treading on him.

'Help! Help!'

The parson's squawks reached even Elyas's dulled ears and he came hurrying out of the cottage as fast as he could on his crutches to see what the commotion was all about. He arrived just in time to watch Kezzy open the sty gate, drive back the sow and haul the parson unceremoniously up and out.

'Oh dear, Parson, you seem to have some bad rents in your good black suit!' exclaimed Kezzy concernedly as she attempted to brush some of the mud from his clothes.

'Should take care wi' mother pigs, Parson,' chuckled Elyas. 'Now, what *I* should do, if'n I were 'ee, is distract sow wi' un rag waggled afore her face . . . red un be best . . . an' *then* grab thy piggy.' He held out the tattered red kerchief he always wore. 'Take un' an' have 'nother go, if'n ye likes,' he invited generously.

'Do ye imagine I've taken leave of my wits?' demanded Creedy indignantly. From his pocket, he produced an immaculate white silk handkerchief (which Kezzy instantly recognised as being one of the half dozen she'd sold him the previous week while delivering his monthly brandy) and proceeded to wipe the mud from his eye-glasses. He set them back on his long, thin nose and pointed at the sty. 'Yon sow, why, she could have trampled life out of me!'

'Ay, that her could,' nodded Elyas sagely. 'So best leave her little uns 'lone, I reckons. Good day to 'ee.'

He swung off inside whistling to himself.

'I *am* sorry . . . about the rips,' said Kezzy with as straight a face as she could manage. 'I do hope Mrs Creedy is handy with a needle.'

'Bah!' was Creedy's response. He gave the sow a last, venomous look and turned away. 'Now. How do 'ee intend payin' thy tithe . . . if not with piggy?'

Kezzy looked surprised. 'But, Parson, there's none to pay. I made you a fair offer of that piglet and you didn't take the offer. By my reckoning, that quits us.'

Creedy scowled. She was sharp. These vulgar tinners often were. 'I'll see ye come Sunday, then,' he said peevishly, limping slightly from his tumble as he went across to his trap.

Kezzy said nothing. Perhaps he would see her; perhaps not. It all depended on the flaskers.

In the event, Kezzy *did* attend church on Palm Sunday, and insisted that Elyas went with her dressed in his Sunday trousers and a clean shirt. It was as well, she decided, if folk saw them there: she didn't want any well-meaning busybodies calling upon them uninvited because they'd not be seen over Easter and perhaps coming face to face with the flaskers. So she'd hitched Rats to the wagon – the big cob being kept well hidden in a secret glade a short distance from Eaglestone – and helped Elyas on to a pallet laid on the buckboard. All the way down the moor he loudly protested that it was nothing but torture expecting him to sit on a wooden pew listening to that 'Amen bawler' for an hour or more.

'You can sit on my shawl, Gramps,' Kezzy told him mollifyingly but that didn't stop him grumbling. He even tried a coughing fit but quick as a wink she produced his lung-syrup and fed him a spoonful.

'Please, Gramps. 'Tis for the best,' she appealed to him. 'We don't want any well-meaning busybodies calling on us unexpectedly because we haven't been seen over Easter and maybe walking into the flaskers.'

He saw the sense in that although he wouldn't admit it out of sheer cussedness. 'Arsk me,' he muttered scornfully, 'you'm right daft for showin' thyself at all t'they busybodies in village. 'Spose one o' they spots ye an' furze boy as one an' same? Eh? What then?'

But they both knew it was extremely unlikely. Of late, Kezzy had taken to wearing her luxuriant dark hair loose about her face instead of pulled back into a child's braid down her back; moreover, partly at the dame's instigation, she'd begun to wear stays so that her outline took on a more mature and womanly shape. Both these changes in her appearance were in direct contrast to the image she presented while masquerading as a boy, when she wore a head-hugging woollen hat, and dirtied her face and hands and bare calves as her skin was unusually soft and fair. Also, she'd begun to bind her burgeoning breasts beneath the ragged ploughboy's smock she wore in place of the old jersey now the fine weather had come. She was quite safe: there were neither eyes nor wits in Cornwood or thereabouts sharp enough to discover her secret.

So Easter arrived, with silky greyish-yellow willow buds for Palm Sunday, and spicy crossed buns on Good Friday and roast spring hare on Easter Day itself (though Kezzy never could understand why hares, which were said to cause melancholy, should be eaten to celebrate such a happy day). And the Reverend Burridge Creedy's sermon was every bit as long as Elyas dreaded it would be, As its basis, Creedy took St Matthew 27.1: '*And when they had bound Him, they led Him away, and delivered Him to Pontius Pilate the governor. Then Judas who had betrayed Him, when he saw that He was condemned, repented himself, and brought again the thirty pieces of silver . . . saying, I have sinned, in that I have betrayed innocent blood . . .'*

'Youngmay, you say?' said Captain Gilpin musingly.

'Ay, Cap'n, zur. Ever since he come out o' dumb-box he bin a-whisperin' an' a-plottin' in corners wi' they other Yankee boys from his'n ship.'

Gilpin's informant was Shem Frost, an old convict gaoled for eight years for sheep-stealing and one of the few to be sent 'up the moor' rather than to Botany Bay aboard the convict hulks.

Despite Shem's certainty that it was Matthew Youngmay who was behind whatever mischief the American prisoners were planning, Gilpin's small, prominent eyes were deeply suspicious as they surveyed the ragged individual standing on the other side of his desk. It was the way Shem's eyes kept darting slyly towards the hollowed-out elephant's foot in which he stored his tobacco – the usual reward for information received – that made Gilpin wonder if, perhaps, Shem's addiction to Navy Plug might not have coloured his imagination.

'But you don't know exactly what they're planning?'

'Not zackly, Cap'n, zur . . . bit 'tis just matter o' time.' Shem tapped his nose. 'I'll sniff un out . . . like bleddy dawg!'

A shadow of repugnance crossed Gilpin's features. He thought the analogy a fair one, save he deemed Shem even lower than a dog; firstly because he was a convict, secondly because he was a Judas. However, he needed the likes of Shem to tell him about any furtive goings-on among the captives.

He flipped open the elephant's foot and tossed a plug of tobacco across the desk to Shem. 'Get along now. And keep after Youngmay . . . find out what he's planning . . . *if* he is.'

Shem snatched his reward and it vanished among his rags. ' 'Tis he at back o' they, I tell 'ee, Cap'n, zur. You'm count on Shem Frost t'sniff un out . . .'

'Get out!'

Shem got out.

He returned regularly once a week but seldom had anything fresh to report in return for the scant pipe of baccy which Gilpin allowed him just to keep him alert. 'That Lootenant Youngmay, he be the big fish now'days,' he'd tell Gilpin with a certain relish, knowing that the very mention of the American's name was enough to send the prison captain's colour soaring. 'Ay, they all look up to he, right 'nough! If'n 'tweren't *blasphemious* belike, I'd say them do seed he as some sort o' second messi-ahry. If'n 'ee follow my meanin', Cap'n zur . . .'

Shem knew how to stoke Gilpin's hatred. But on that occasion he pushed his luck a mite too far. Gilpin slammed shut the lid of his tobacco jar this time without extracting the craved plug.

'Get out! Get out and don't show yourself to me 'til you've something well founded.'

Shem got out. His longing for tobacco made him even more vigilant than before. His eyes were everywhere, So much so, some of the prisoners – both French and American – began to wonder just why it was that whenever they met in quiet groups, half-witted Shem Frost could be counted upon to come lumbering up to sit near them, mouth abroad, eyes staring, fingers moving beneath his verminous rags in a steady scrat-scratch movement. If they spoke to him, all he said was, 'Elly baccy, boys? Elly baccy?' And if they'd a twist – smuggled in by the French who worked on the farms – they would take pity on the poor old simpleton and share it with him.

Yet, despite all his efforts, which included virtually dogging Matthew's every move, Shem Frost discovered nothing worth so much as a grain of Gilpin's excellent navy plug.

'The more of us there are scattered across the moor, the harder it'll be to round us all up,' Matthew told his fellow conspirators as they plotted in whispers at night. 'Some of us will surely make it to the coast. Then aboard a privateer heading for Spain and work your passage home from Cadiz aboard a Yankee trader.'

He made it sound so simple. And to a man they were with him.

Of course, if they were caught they would be flogged. Probably to the death – depending upon the number of lashes and the fitness of the man. And after just a few weeks cramped in these diseased conditions, breathing fetid air and existing on rations which were purposefully meagre to damp down their aggression, no man could be deemed fit. But wasn't it worth the risk? They could hardly contain their impatience.

'And just exactly how are you going to get three dozen men out of this bilgy pest-hole, Lieutenant?'

The man who asked the question uppermost in all their minds was Moab Austin, one of the *Maryland*'s bosun's mates. He was older than the rest of them, so small he was almost dwarf-like, with long, muscular arms and thick bow-legs. He had spent a lifetime aboard merchantmen, but patriotic zeal – fueled by a flagon of Blue Pig whiskey – had sent him lurching after the drum.

'Aye, how *are* you going to do it, sir?' young Knuckles echoed Moab eagerly.

There was a long pause. Then, slowly, as if he was ashamed at not trusting them implicitly, Matthew said: 'I want you each to take an oath . . . that you won't divulge our plans . . . or talk carelessly that you might be overheard . . .'

'None of us will blab, sir,' growled John Dagge, the *Maryland*'s purser.

'Lieutenant's right,' said Moab, 'best we all swear with our hands on our hearts.'

'But we won't know in the dark who has and who ain't got their hands on their hearts,' pointed out Knuckles.

Another voice spoke up – that of Lordy Sleeve, a copper-skinned mountain of a man, half Mohawk Indian. '*I'll* know and if there's any who don't swear proper . . .' He cracked his knuckles ominously in the dark.

Lordy had the reputation of being able to kill a man with his bare hands inside a few seconds. None of them had actually witnessed this phenomenon. Not yet. But since he was part-savage none of them doubted his extraordinary powers – not least being his ability to see in the pitchest black.

So they swore a whispered oath. And spontaneously elected Matthew their leader, and Moab, Dagge, Lordy and, since Matthew asked for him, Knuckles, the Special Escape Committee.

That done, Matthew revealed his plan.

It was quite simple. They would tunnel their way out. During the three months he'd been imprisoned, and particularly during his month of solitary, Matthew's heredity had risen within him as it had never done before. Moreover, his experience as a young collier meant that he could speak with some authority regarding shafts and tunnels and removing rubble with hand-winches. They listened attentively, fired with enthusiasm for the project, straining their ears not to miss a word.

'I'm for it,' said Moab positively when Matthew's voice died away, and a chorus of supportive whispers echoed his sentiment.

'Aye, and if I'm caught,' said Lordy, 'well, you can send a lock of my hair to my poor ol' ma and tell her I died brave!'

Which made them all chuckle since Lordy was completely bald.

Matthew brought them to order with a quick 'Shhh!' in case they brought a suspicious guard to investigate what it was they found so amusing amid such squalor. It wouldn't be the first time all those in a cell had been split up because they were suspected of plotting at night.

'We'll need tools,' said Knuckles.

But Matthew had already thought of that. He waited until Brett, the master-at-arms, was making his morning inspection, and then kicked over a slop pail, soaking the officer's highly polished, buckled shoes. Matthew was suitably apologetic, swearing that it was an accident, but this venial sin earned him a place on the next stone-breaking party taken out on the moor. Whereupon, on the first day, he managed to purloin a pick and drop it down the back of his shirt, strapping it around his waist with a length of rag to smuggle it back to the cell, and the following day obtained a shovel the same way. Work on the tunnel, beneath a slab in the corner of the cell, began. When the pick blunted and the shovel bent, Matthew committed some other transgression which took him out stone-breaking so he could swap the tools for good ones. Once, however, he overstepped the mark by tripping up a guard and received five lashes instead, and on yet another occasion got himself chained to the wall in the dumb-hole for a week for offering dumb insolence to 'Old Blessed Guts' as the prisoners referred to Captain Gilpin. Such spectacular heroics increased Matthews prestige among his companions and there was no shortage of volunteers to do the actual digging.

At first they tried working as quietly as they could with look-outs posted at the bars to warn of approaching guards. That meant progress was slow. So Matthew traded his leather shoes with a French *matelot* for a squeeze-box to drown the noise. Night after night Moab would play and they would sing until their voices grew hoarse. And each morning the stone flag would be fitted over the entrance to the shaft and covered by a pallet, and the fruits of the nightly labours – earth and small pieces of rock – were smuggled out and surreptiously scattered upon the moor by those on stone-breaking duty. And as the tunnel grew, so did their hope of freedom.

For a year they toiled thus, unaware that Shem Frost had at last discovered their secret and was making regular reports on their progress to the prison captain.

'Let them burrow like the worms they are,' was Gilpin's sneering reaction when he first learned of the tunnel. 'Keep 'em out of other mischief. When they've dug a fair distance . . . then I'll take 'em. And then I'll have their blessed guts for it!'

Chapter Twenty-Five

Once, as Kezzy crossed the Plymouth-Princeton road on her way to deliver tubs to a member of the Yelverton gentry, she passed near to a stone-breaking gang. Her ragged sailor was among the fifty or so men engaged in hard labour along the side of the road but she didn't know it, and, although some of the prisoners stared with casual interest at the 'boy' with his furze-load – glad for any change in the tedium of their stark surroundings – Matthew did not. He was too busy scattering the contents of the 'rubble-bags' hidden about his person to waste time looking about him for other than alert-eyed guards who might spot the small stream of earth and stones which accompanied his every swing with the pick.

For sure, Kezzy's sympathetic gaze swept the line of ragged, sweating men swinging their picks against the scattered rocks, or shovelling the resulting small lumps of granite into heaps, but she didn't distinguish one man from another and purposefully kept her distance. The guards accompanying the stone-breakers suffered excruciating boredom and tales were told of how they sought to relieve it at the expense of any unwary passer-by. Only the week before, an apprentice from Cherrywood Farm had his load of hay set alight by a guard while another took his attention with some small sleight of hand. The boy had jumped down in panic when the flames suddenly shot around him and could only stand helplessly watching while the wagon was turned to ashes. The colt pulling it reared up with its tail afire, broke fee and bolted amid the guards' hooting laughter. The unfortunate apprentice had a five-mile walk back to the farm, received a terrible beating for his carelessness and was given to the next press-gang that came that way.

Sailors were still needed to protect home waters. The war with America wasn't going as well as the Admiralty had complacently expected it would. While the British Navy boasted bigger ships and more of them, the American men-of-wars carried a far superior array of armaments. British ships were being sunk or seized all too regularly, although the British newspapers harked mostly upon the sinking of the US brigs *Maryland* and *Chesapeake* in twenty minutes and fifteen minutes respectively. However, the United State's invasion of Canada was being so stoutly resisted by the colonists it was already being hailed a failure in despatches home.

News of the various campaigns, successful or doom-laden, took weeks to reach the moor folk – if it ever did. And so for them life went on much as it always had, with only the heathlands changing with the seasons from purple to gold to dun. And if Kezzy didn't think so often of her golden-haired, blue-eyed sailor, it was because the passing months misted the memory of their one brief meeting by Crazywell Pool.

Also, as the months passed, she ceased to worry about Preventative Dorrity, or to fear another clandestine visit from him, although Grote always posted men at either end of the valley and atop the hills whenever the flaskers came with a run of contraband. Kezzy almost ceased to bother scanning the hills at other times for the glint of bridle or buttons; or to walk in the soft evening air with old Wart, his nose twitching for a stranger's scent.

It was after one of her trips across the moor to Yelverton, to deliver tubs to Squire Tomlin and Parson Membury, that something occurred which made quite sure she was never so complacent again.

She had tethered the cob in his secret glade and walked the half mile to the head of the creep. There, alone, 'twixt the setting sun and approaching dusk, her strange sixth sense told her that all was not as it should be. She stared down into the valley, but it stood deserted. Where was Wart? Why hadn't he caught her scent and barked a welcome? She listened, but heard nothing save the restless 'caw-caw' of the rooks in the battered elms clustered on the slope below Eagle Tor. Yes! The rooks! They should have been settling to sleep on their smudgy blobs of nests high in the branches. What could be disturbing them? Like a wraith, she entered the trees, treading carefully so that no snapped twig should give her presence away. Almost immediately, she caught the warm, faintly acrid smell of horses. She moved deeper into the copse, eyes alert to penetrate the shadows ahead. She heard rustling and a bridle chink near by to her right and began to edge in that direction. She could hear the animals blowing now. Moments later, peering through some low, prickly branches, she could make out saddle horses tethered in the shelter of the trees. They weren't flaskers' mounts, to be sure. The saddles and harness were uniform and highly polished. She spotted a pair of gleaming black boots among the hooves and fetlocks and carefully shifted her position so she could see to whom they belonged. Her heart gave a lurch at the sight of fringed epaulettes and a beaver hat trimmed with a red cock-hackle. *A dragoon!* Just the one; left to watch the horses. Kezzy slipped away. She stood for a moment at the edge of the copse, forcing herself to consider calmly the significance of the troop of horses. Their riders were, she was quite sure, lying in wait around Eaglestone – in the barn, and the old blowing-house and such places – ready to ambush the flaskers.

Kezzy was gripped with a sudden poignant fear: *what of her grandfather?* She fought the desperate urge to tear down the creep to the cottage to see if he was unhurt, knowing that he wouldn't take quietly to these unwelcome visitors, even if they were dragoons led, a shrewd guess told her, by Preventative Dorrity. It wouldn't help her or her grandfather if she were simply to barge into Dorrity's trap without the least idea how to extricate herself.

Her thoughts whirled. Dorrity had picked the wrong night, thank the Lord! The flaskers had been there two nights before and, according to

Grote, probably wouldn't return for a few days – maybe longer, depending upon their mistress the sea. There had been some gusting winds along the coast warning of imminent March gales too violent for the free-traders' small luggers to make the crossing to France and back.

It was quite dark now and Kezzy saw a candle had been lit in the cottage so the little front window glowed dimly. It had long been a habit of the Hammetts to pull the thick curtain made out of an old bleached flour bag so as to shun tinkers or gypsies or, indeed, Preventatives, who might otherwise be drawn to their isolated dwelling. The light was, Kezzy felt sure, a sign from Elyas letting her know that all was not well. Her thoughts whirled. Well, she couldn't remain where she was! Swiftly, she pulled up her smock and unbound her breasts, then took off her breeches and, rolling them up, tucked them out of sight in a hollowed tree trunk. Her hat joined them and she shook free her long raven hair, running her fingers through it to untidy it. Pulling up a few tufts of furze, she scattered the stalks in her hair and added a few twigs as if she had been lying on the ground.

She set off down into the valley.

As she entered the yard, Kezzy could feel the watching eyes. She kept her face impassive, her eyes almost dreamy as she softly sang to herself:

Oh Sailor, O Sailor, what can you know
Of the sorrow and pain I undergo . . .?

As Kezzy swung open the door, Elyas rasped out a warning: 'Run, chield!'

She couldn't have done so if she'd wanted to as she was immediately grabbed by the arm and hauled stumbling inside. Straightening up, she found herself staring down the muzzle of a pistol held by a riding officer. An exceptionally young riding officer, she fleetingly noticed with some surprise. Her gaze moved quickly around the room. Elyas was sitting in his chimney corner, apparently unharmed, though in a towering rage. As a precaution, the riding officer had taken his crutches from him and stood them out of his reach. Also, he'd tethered a doleful-eyed Wart to a table leg and bound his muzzle with a rag to keep him from barking.

'*How dare you*!' Kezzy rounded furiously on the riding officer, dark eyes flashing. 'What gives you the right to push into folks' home?'

She made as if to go to her grandfather but stopped as the pistol was waved at her in a menacing manner.

'Don't move!' snapped the Preventative. With his eyes still on Kezzy, he moved to the door which was still standing open. He gave a low whistle, immediately answered by another which came, so far as Kezzy could judge, from the vicinity of the pig-sty. He closed the door and stood looking Kezzy up and down, his pale eyes resting a shade too long, perhaps, on her shapely legs, bare from the knee below the thin smock.

Elyas didn't like this candid assessment of his granddaughter's slim figure. 'You'm lay so much as finger on she, an' I'll break thy neck, cully!' he croaked.

Preventative Dorrity flushed. 'I wasn't . . . I meant t'say, I meant no disrespect . . .' he stuttered, embarrassed by his own wayward emotions. There was something strange about the girl: something about her high cheekbones and slanting dark eyes and the way her brows soared like wings. Something which nagged at the back of his mind, refusing to come to the fore.

Kezzy was staring back at him just as intently, her memory similarly jogged by some half-forgotten recollection. He was older, of course. And taller. But from beneath his shako his mousey hair still flopped low over his brow, shadowing his pale, questioning eyes. She took a deep breath and spoke his name. 'Peter . . .?'

He looked startled, hearing his name on her lips. Then, slowly, he lowered the gun he was pointing at her breast.

He began looking about him, as if he was seeing the inside of the cottage for the first time. His eyes rested on Elyas and he frowned, trying to recall the old, crippled figure.

' 'Tis you, Peter!' exclaimed Kezzy, hardly able to believe it.

His eyes locked with hers. 'Keziah Hammett!' he blurted, the years falling away. 'By Jesu! 'Tis little Kezzy from upalong Eagle Tor!'

Elyas's old ears just managed to catch this familiar usage of Kezzy's name. He scowled at the sight of them standing there, smiling awkwardly at each other. 'What's this, chield? Do 'ee *know* un?' he asked Kezzy gruffly, unable to conceal his displeasure.

She raised her voice so he could hear. ' 'Tis Peter, Gramps. The apprentice from Wheal Emma . . .'

Elyas shook his head uncomprehendingly.

'Don't you remember, Gramps?' Kezzy tried gain. 'I hid him and his friend in the barn one night . . . years ago . . . when they ran away from bal.'

'Isaac?' asked Elyas, hopefully. 'Be it Isaac come back?'

'No, Gramps,' Kezzy told him gently, 'Not Isaac. 'Tis Peter.'

Then suddenly the mist lifted from his befuddled brain. ' 'Tis one o' they hobbledehoys as runned 'way from de Raddon bal. Do *look* like Isaac. What were name o' t'other boy?'

'Jordan,' said Kezzy, remembering.

'Now, *he* looked just like Graeme,' recalled Elyas a faraway look in his pale, watery eyes.

'I'd forgotten . . .' muttered Peter, his astonished gaze shifting towards the door, as if he could see through it into the yard around which were grouped the barn and thc mine buildings and the tall, smoke-blackened stack. 'How could I have forgotten?'

' 'Twas dark that night, when you were here,' Kezzy reminded him.

He nodded. Moreover, he was but a boy then, and all these old tin-mines scattered across the moor were, like the tinners' grey-stone cottages, like so many peas in a pod. Ay, like the old tinners themselves.

Kezzy was watching him closely. 'Why have you come?'

Elyas read her lips. 'I'll tell 'ee why un's here!' he burst out before Peter could answer. 'Got some daft widdle in un brain tells he we'm helpin' free-traders. Hidin' they moonshine for they in by bal!' He leaned forward and spat slantingly into the fire to show his contempt of such a thing.

Kezzy feigned surprise, gaze flicking from one of them to the other. 'Oh but surely you're mistaken, Gramps,' she chided him, praying that he would remain in control of his wits and not blurt out anything which might endanger them.

Luckily, nature was being generous and allowing Elyas a period of complete lucidity. 'Arsk he!' he growled, glaring over at Peter.

'Is that why you've come, Peter?' Kezzy asked him.

Suddenly all the good-humour had left his young face, all the pleasure at seeing her again. Once again he was the cold eyed, determined riding officer there on Customs Service business. Curtly, he nodded in answer to her anxious question.

'Faugh!' declared Elyas scornfully. 'An' to think I let 'ee go, boy! Jordan, an' all. 'Stead o' givin' both 'ee over to Emma overseer to have skin stripped from thy arses! Fed 'ee and give 'ee roof that night, did Hammetts, when us could've been boated for helpin' run'ways. An' now 'ee shows thy gratitude by a-comin' back in un man's togs wi' dragoons to plague us . . .'

He lapsed into a fit of violent coughing. Kezzy started to move towards the shelf where his lung-syrup stood; her eye went to the gun in Peter's hand, hanging limply by his side, but he made no move to stop her. He stood silently watching while she fetched the medicine and carefully gave the old man a measured dose.

' 'Tis my sworn duty to seek out the free-traders and those that help them and to bring them to justice,' Peter announced pompously, but also a shade defensively.

Shielded from his view by Kezzy; Elyas looked up into her face and winked slyly. She smiled back at him and gave his hand an encouraging squeeze. Turning to Peter, she said simply: 'Gramps has lung-rot.'

Peter nodded briefly. Few tinners escaped the dust, few lived as long as Elyas Hammett. He frowned suddenly. 'There was another man . . . and a boy . . .' he recalled.

'Yes. Pa . . . and my brother, Jamie.'

A triumphant glint entered the pale eyes. As though he'd caught her out. 'Where are they?' he demanded to know.

She paused. It always hurt, even now, to think of them.

Peter's eyes narrowed at her hesitation. 'With the free-traders? Is that it?' he quizzed her determinedly.

She looked him straight in the eyes. 'No. They're dead,' she told him levelly and had the satisfaction of seeing his colour heighten with embarrassment.

'I . . . didn't know . . .' he muttered, unable to meet her eyes.

'In pit explosion. Backalong three . . . four years now. My three cousins from Cherrywood, too, God rest them. Gramps . . . he was crippled.'

Elyas had lapsed into a reverie. Peter looked across at the hunched, wheezing figure in the corner. Kezzy couldn't guess exactly what was passing through his mind but his face, though stern and grave, mirrored his inner compassion as he stood biting his lip, seemingly at a loss what to do.

Ever since he'd followed Grote and the wain to Eaglestone, Peter Dorrity had been totally convinced that the old mine was a free-traders' hide. However, he'd had trouble convincing the area collector and the assistant collector of revenues, or, indeed, his fellow riding officers, that Captain de Raddon's head steward, Grote, perhaps even the Lord Warden himself, was involved in free-trading. The very idea was pooh-poohed by all he approached and he was refused permission to keep watch on Grote's coming and goings. Instead, Peter had found himself kept busy over at Salcombe, as far along the coast from Blackaven House as the riding officers' jurisdiction allowed.

That was until the collector received a letter from His Majesty's Commissioners of Customs in Whitehall, London, in effect, demanding to know why so little revenue had been paid and so little contraband had been seized in the area which he administered in comparison to the other ridings. Fearful for his comfortable sinecure, the collector had hurriedly summoned his newest and most zealous young riding officer and given him his orders.

'You are to uncover a good-sized cache of contraband, Mr Dorrity,' the collector told him, standing there, swag-bellied and red-faced, in his office in the Customs House at Plymouth. 'A *really* good-sized cache, mind! Not just a few kegs hidden in some old parson's vestry! And I want to see some arrests. Round up some of these rogues . . . and their accomplices. I'm relying on you, Mr Dorrity.'

'Do I have a free hand, sir?'

The collector had considered for a moment. The threat of Whitehall loomed largely; he had to be *seen* to be doing something about the amount of free-trading that was going on seemingly beneath his nose. Of course, he could always tip the wink in a certain direction when next he called at Blackaven House to have his palm greased.

'Yes, you've a free hand, Mr Dorrity.'

'Then I'll need a troop of dragoons, sir.'

He had expected to find a nest of desperate felons in league with smugglers high up here on the moor, but had found just a crippled old man and a girl. Moreover, they had once extended the hand of friendship to him. Yet, watching them, Kezzy saw that his face took on again that set look. He wasn't altogether satisfied that they were as innocent as they made out.

Abruptly, he asked Kezzy: 'Do you deny that a man called Grote came here with two other men driving a wain?'

'Grote . . .?' she murmured, frowning in concentration. 'I don't recall . . .'

'From Blackaven House.'

Her face cleared. She was a supreme actress. 'Ah, I *do* recall! Why, it must be more'n twelve-month past. They came with some vegetables . . . and stopped a while to mend a wheel . . .'

Elyas stirred himself and joined in again, saying sourly: ' 'Tis wisht poor thing t'have t'fill our bellies wi' de Raddon charity.'

Peter wasn't listening. He was eyeing the shelf upon which sat Elyas's medicine bottles. An impressive array. And most incongruous in a poor tinner's cottage. Particularly the silver-topped vial of laudanum which wouldn't have disgraced a lady's toilet table in one of the big houses. Obviously, they weren't as poor as they made out.

Kezzy followed his gaze, cursing herself for her stupidity in leaving the expensive syrups and potions and medicines on display. 'Dame Rogers . . . the village schoolmistress . . . has been most generous,' she murmured.

Peter's eyes were moving around the cottage. They alighted on a loaf of fine white bread, some slices temptingly cut and thickly spread with creamy, yellow butter. Also on the table stood a stoup of cider and – luxury of luxuries! – a small wooden box of China tea.

'And can this generous friend of yours, this charity school dame, can she afford gifts also of white bread and tea?' demanded Peter coldly, angry with himself for momentarily forgetting his duty and feeling sorry for them.

Kezzy's chin came up at the sarcasm in his voice. 'No,' she said constrainedly. 'I have . . . another friend who gives me such things to make out life here a little more comfortable.'

'And who is this . . . other friend?'

She paused, then gave him a defiant look, and said: 'A *gentleman* friend. Whose name is no concern of yours.'

Peter stared at her. 'I . . . don't believe you.'

Kezzy shrugged.

He turned to Elyas. 'Is this true?' he snarled, for some unknown reason not wanting it to be so.

Behind his back, Kezzy nodded at her grandfather. Her reputation mattered not a fig if it meant saving their skins.

'Her don't lie,' said Elyas with a suitable note of regret in his wavering voice. He stabbed a finger at her. 'Look at un maiden, boy! Clothes all abroad an' straws in her hair! Ay, her's been nannyin' wi' some gentleman, awlright . . . drat she for her shamelessness!'

Peter seemed to freeze at his words. His mouth thinned and an ugly gleam lit his eyes. 'And what did this generous gentleman give you in return for your favours?' he asked Kezzy nastily.

There was a long pause. Then, slowly, with a great show of reluctance, Kezzy took her purse from the pocket of her smock. She shook it so that the contents – some of which was payment due to de Raddon for tubs she'd delivered – chinked.

'Do you wish to count it, Peter?' Kezzy asked him, holding it out to him.

He shook his head, eyes full of reproach because the fine, courageous, God-fearing little girl who had befriended him among the rocks at the top of Eagle Tor had come to this. Selling her favours to some fumbling old squire, or, perhaps, the arrogant son of one of the mine-owners – for a loaf of white bread and a fancy, silver-topped bottle.

Kezzy flinched, reading the disgust in his face. How ready he was to believe the worst of her. Her chin came up and a militant light flared in her dark eyes. Well, then, let him believe what he liked, the snobby-nosed skiddamalank! she told herself angrily.

With every passing moment, a paralysing coldness was spreading between the two of them, like an icy fog which blotted out the sweet memories of childhood. They stood glaring at each other, like two enemies instead of two friends of old.

With a sudden fierceness, Elyas said: 'Go! Leave us in peace!'

Without another word, Peter swung on his heel and went out.

Kezzy fetched Elyas's crutches and released Wart, keeping her hand on the furious hound so that it wouldn't bound out after Peter and attack him or one of the dragoons. There was nothing to be gained in asking for trouble. They stood in the cottage door, the dim glow of the candle within illuminating the yard just enough for them to make out the armed dragoons as they materialised, stretching and yawning, from their various hiding places. Peter spoke quietly to the dragoon officer. They saluted each other, and the officer set off up the creep with his men. A few minutes later they rode by Eaglestone down the valley.

Only Peter remained.

He seemed, thought Kezzy, almost reluctant to leave. Ignoring the two of them watching from the door, he stood gazing about him, at the mine-buildings, and at the old barn where she'd hidden the two boys from her grandfather, and smuggled food out to them.

'Why don't 'ee quit his'n nosin' an' go?' muttered Elyas.

'Be patient, Gramps,' Kezzy whispered, forgetting that he wouldn't hear, 'best he goes away satisfied he was mistaken.'

Peter wandered across to the mine and stood for a while just staring up at the whim-cage, creaking slightly in the stiff night breeze. Kezzy felt no more than a twinge of concern at his apparent deep absorption with the tackle. As a precaution, she always made sure the ropes were grimed and all metal parts 'aged' with scrapings of rust from an old pail she kept for the purpose. Her handiwork would pass a much closer examination than he was giving it – and in a better light. Still, she would be glad when he *did* go . . .

Peter put out a hand and touched the whipsederry tentatively. Then, almost in surprise, gazed at his fingers. He rubbed his thumb over his fingertips. *Grease*! The hoisting tackle had recently been greased. He turned and barked a command across the yard:

'Fetch a lantern! I wish to search the mine!'

Kezzy grinned in the dark. He could search all night long if he liked: He wouldn't find so much as a keg of four-penny shrub in by Eaglestone.

Kezzy lowered the lantern on its chain down the main shaft to the first sollar, then skimmed agilely down the ladder after it. She stood watching as Peter made his own, rather more cautious descent, feeling for each rung in turn and testing it beneath his weight before continuing. Once beside her, he took a quick look about him, decided that the smugglers were unlikely to cache their kegs in quite such an accessible part of the mine, and commanded: 'Deeper.'

Kezzy shrugged unconcernedly and lowered the lantern again.

Once down on the next wooden shelf, Peter paused to consider. Would they take the time and trouble to carry the kegs lower than this? He stared at the white patch which was Kezzy's face but it showed no positive expression.

'I can help you, Kezzy, if only you'll let me.'

Her eyebrows rose. She stood quite still, gazing at him, her hair loose about her shoulders. He expected to see veiled interest in her eyes – certainly curiosity, perhaps even gratitude. But scornful amusement . . .!

There was a long moment of silence.

'Aren't you going to ask how I might be of help to you?' asked Peter tartly.

'Very well. *How* can you help me?' she humoured him.

'I can put in a good word for you and your grandfather . . . with the authorities . . . if you show me where the contraband is hidden.'

Her gaze was unwavering.

'I could give evidence for you. Tell the magistrate that you were bullied into helping the smugglers. That you led me to their hide and . . .'

'Peter,' she interrupted him wearily, 'there is no hide here.'

His jaw set stubbornly. 'The whim an' tackle are newly greased.'

'Gramps insists 'pon it. Stops rust. 'Tis his dream that we might open bal again.' After a moment she said: 'Peter . . .'

'Yes.'

' 'Tis so silly . . . this. You'll find nothing here.'

'Which isn't to say it isn't here!'

She grew angry suddenly. 'What can I say that will convince you? Make you go away and leave us alone? You're like old Wart . . . when he catches a rat in the barn. He'll shake it and shake it 'til you'd think his silly head'll fall off. Even when the rat's dead, he'll just go on and on shaking it! Go away, Peter! Leave us be!'

For a long moment they stood staring belligerently at each other.

When next he spoke, Peter's voice was less harsh, with almost a note of appeal in it. 'Please, Kezzy . . . try and understand. 'Tis my sworn duty. It matters not who the felons are . . . or who their accomplices are. I'm solemnly sworn to track them down in the King's name and bring them to justice.'

She gave a rueful smile. 'Then I reckon you're the only riding officer in parish who *does* set store by sworn oath.' Again the laugh, but scornful this time. 'Peter the Preventative!'

He scowled. He was used to respect from the maidens he met in the execution of his duty. And sometimes more than that. Quite often, some sly-eyed girl invited him into the barn to 'see the varmint'.

Sometimes he went; mostly not. None of them were anything like Keziah Hammett. There was about her an air of delicacy and sensitivity which these other maids lacked. He was aware of her standing close to him on the small, jutting shelf. There was a tantalising, musky smell about her – as if she'd bathed her body in sweet rosemary.

'There isn't any gentlemen who buys ye pretty things in return for your favours, is there?' he heard himself asking her, not wanting it to be so, and at the same time resenting the fact that he would never be able to afford such extravagances on his riding officer's annual pay of £35. ' 'Tis all bought with money got from the flaskers, isn't it?' he persisted when she didn't answer immediately.

She sighed loudly. 'I've said all I'm going to say, Peter. Now, is it above grass you want to go? Or down? Or along Run Isaac?' She pointed to the tunnel entrance on the left. 'Or Run Graeme?' She pointed right. 'Which is it to be?

He took the lantern, the candle within guttering in the reeky, vaporous air, and moved it so that its circle of orange light picked out the low, narrow entrances to the runs. He chose Graeme, handing Kezzy the lantern.

'You lead.'

He found nothing remotely suspicious in Graeme or Isaac. Or in the runs on the next level: namely Betsy, Ruke and Hannah. And Run Kezzy he discounted because its mouth was hardly big enough to take a tub, let alone a tub-carrier. However, had Peter investigated further, he would have found the opening most deceptive. With a bit of a squeeze it took a full-grown man and led into a quite roomy tunnel leading to a dryish cavern which was filled floor to roof with barrels and chests, The latter containing Kezzy's payment in kind of tea and pomades and silk handkerchiefs. The Leghorn hats were hung in nets from the roof to keep them dry.

They descended the last ladder to the floor of the mine.

Stepping off the last rung, Kezzy immediately sank up to her knees in reddish-brown mud beneath her short smock.

Peter let out a stifled curse as the feculent mess squelched over the cuffs of his boots and soaked his breeches. The air was so foul this deep below ground, that their lungs rebelled and they were forced to breathe shallowly, speaking in gasps. Even the candle was guttering and threatening to extinguish itself. Sweat ran in rivulets down their faces. Peter's tunic was soaked and his cravat hung around his neck like a limp white rag. Kezzy's hair hung down her back like a sleek, wet curtain. Her smock clung to her damply so that the roundness of her breasts and buttocks could be seen. She's somehow tucked up the smock to keep it from the mud and in so doing was revealing an immodest amount of her white, curving thighs. Peter fought to avert his gaze, but, as he followed Kezzy along the tunnel of his choice, his eyes returned again and again to the tantalizing sight.

They were in Eagle Alley which drove west under Eagle Tor.

This was cruel, hostile ground. The scarred walls bore bitter witness to just how hard the stockwork had been, as did the number of slits hacked out along the way in which the miners could take shelter during gunpowder blasting. And as the lode had been a drift-lode, it was apt to meander, much of it sloping upwards. Peter began to think it went on for ever into the dark.

Presently, he reluctantly called a halt. 'I must rest . . . for a minute,' he gasped sinking down upon a shattered pile of broken granite, earth and stones.

Kezzy smiled.

He scowled at her, hating to be beaten. When he'd caught his breath, he looked about him, sure that they were looping back on themselves. 'Where are we? This isn't still Eagle, is it?'

'No. Middle Alley. Eagle crosses it.'

Peter grunted. He kicked a stone.

'Don't!'

The sharpness of her tone startled him. He looked at her. Her face was like carved stone. Her eyes shot venom at him. He looked around him again with new eyes.

'Is this . . .?' He paused.

'Yes.'

Their grave! Her father. Brother. Cousins. He took off his cap. A simple gesture of respect.

Kezzy retrieved the lump of stone he'd dislodged with his foot and replaced it lovingly on the heap from whence it had come. 'It was a miracle Gramps lived,' she told Peter in a hollow voice. 'They say the blast must have blown him back along the tunnel away from worst of it.' She pointed to a solid wall of rubble, clammy with moisture. 'Thousands of tons of stuff blocked the rest of the run. We filled nigh on fifty kibbles looking for Gramps. They near gave him up . . . said he couldn't still be alive. But I knew he was . . . I *knew*, Peter! Just as if I heard him calling for me . . .'

She stopped, looked at him almost embarrassedly, remembering suddenly that he was the enemy – that he'd come to Eaglestone in search of contraband and to arrest those who were hiding it for the flaskers; not caring whether they were hung or boated or left to rot in some filthy prison for it. What mattered one old tinner and his daughter when he'd his sworn duty to perform? Tears welled.

'Goddamn you, Peter Dorrity!'

'Kezzy!'

He shouted after her. But her long legs were already carrying her away from him back up the tunnel. The speed at which she was moving caused a guttering draught which blew out the lantern, plunging them into total darkness. Not the darkness of night above grass – for even the blackest night shows a glimmer of grey – but a pitch dark so dense it was as if a black velvet cloak had been thrown over Peter's head. He moved to follow Kezzy but in just those few seconds he's lost his sense of direction and bumped into the wall. He stretched out his arms, feeling his way.

'Kezzy!' he shouted again, this time in alarm, but she didn't answer. 'Light the lamp, Kezzy! *Please*, Kezzy . . .!'

The total darkness made no difference to Kezzy, so well did she know the twisting, turning labyrinth of passages. Somewhere behind her, she could hear Peter frantically calling her. She didn't stop, kept on going until she reached the foot of the main shaft. She stood there for a while, straining her ears to hear if he was approaching. Silence. He must have blundered left instead of right halfway along Middle Alley: that would have set him off back on himself along Leat Side Alley which ran parallel. Well, let him go blundering about, chuckled Kezzy. If nothing else, it should put him off venturing in by the mine again.

After a while, hearing a rather desperate and long-drawn, 'Kezzzy . . .!' from quite close at hand, followed by an anguished, and receding, 'For pity's sake . . .!' she did, indeed, take pity upon him. Taking tinder and flint from her pocket, she relit the lantern and went in search of him.

Peter was, though he wouldn't have owned it, filled with unutterable relief when he saw the cheerful yellow glow of lantern-light approaching along the tunnel and heard Kezzy singing a cheerful little song.

She stopped singing suddenly, as if surprised by the sight of Peter. 'Dear heart alive!' she exclaimed, 'I'd quite forgotten you were still down here!'

'I doubt that!' retorted Peter through gritted teeth.

She stifled a giggle. 'What happened to your uniform?'

He was covered in mud. Even his face was daubed with it. Kezzy was suddenly reminded of Parson Creedy when he tried to help himself to a piglet.

'I slipped,' said Peter stiffly.

'Tsh! You should've waited 'til I came with the lantern. I only went to get a tinder-box to relight the candle.'

'I thought . . .' He stopped.

'You thought I'd left you to rot down here, didn't you?'

He nodded dumbly.

'Well, and might you deserve it! Coming to bully innocent, God-fearing folk!' she told him severely.

Peter, intensely mortified and furious at himself for putting himself in such danger, said nothing. His eyes, however, spoke of his relief that she had not left him entombed alive. It would have been quite simple for her to pull up the ladder. Such dreadful acts were far from uncommon among the ruffians it was his lot to track down.

'Come along,' said Kezzy, starting back along the tunnel. 'And we'll see if we can't scrape some of the smeech off your fancy togs. Unless . . .' she stopped and turned to face him. 'Unless you'd rather continue your search?'

He'd the good grace to turn pink beneath the caked mud. 'Nay, I'll not trouble you further,' he muttered.

'I should think not!'

Her cutting rejoinder precipitated a sullen: 'For now . . .' from Peter.

They were almost at the top of the shaft and could feel the fresh night air in their faces and could make out a circle of stars above them, when Kezzy suddenly recalled something she'd meant to ask Peter.

'Did Jordan join the Preventatives, too?'

'Nay. He stayed with the tin. Head tut-worker for de Raddon.'

'So you *did* go back to Wheal Emma?'

'Ay. We went back.'

She couldn't see his face but something in his voice – a lamentative note, no, more than that, something akin to self-reproach – told her that her questioning had unlocked doors he preferred to remain closed. Behind those doors must lie so many painful memories, thought Kezzy with a rush of sympathy. Yes! It was for the best that he kept them – the misery and the torment – locked away and buried. No man could go forward weighed down by such a burden.

They stepped out into the yard. After the dark below ground it seemed almost light, although blue-grey clouds were banking above the distant hills and a faint rumble of thunder warned of a storm.

Kezzy wasn't prepared for what occurred next.

Peter gave a sob. A strange, strangled cry and, without warning, twin tears rolled down his face. He brushed them quickly away with his cuff. He was no longer the arrogant young riding officer on the trail of desperate rogues, but a sad-eyed, bewildered, hurt, angry boy. Kezzy said no word. She put out her hand to him. He took it and held it tightly. Without passion.

'I know,' whispered Kezzy. 'Poor Peter . . .'

Only she – who could guess what terrible and depraved evils he had suffered as one of de Raddon's apprentices – could understand. She could feel a pulse racing in the fingers gripping hers. There was another, much louder, roll of thunder and a few raindrops, carried on the wind, spattered their cheeks so that there was no telling which droplets were rain and which were tears.

'Kezzy . . .' Peter gripped her hand tighter. 'Kezzy . . . I'm going to kill that evil bastard de Raddon. And his man Grote. Not yet . . . when I'm ready . . . then I'll kill them . . .'

A vivid flash of blue and orange lightning zigzagged over Eagle Tor, seeming almost to dance off the jagged rocks. The air seemed to be filled with an ominous roaring which grew and grew and then exploded in a thunderous crash which made the earth tremble.

It began to rain heavily.

Chapter Twenty-Six

'Who is the Judas? Just tell me that.' Matthew entreated the master-at-arms.

Brett said not a word. He stood watching as one of his guards prised up the stone flag – so well-fitting it looked just like any other – which hid the shaft in the corner of the cell. It was no coincidence, Matthew felt sure, which brought Brett to that particular cell for a surprise, early morning inspection and guided him straight to that particular flag. Matthew had been asleep on the pallet covering it and had been swiftly rousted and the pallet stripped away. And it was certainly no coincidence that one of the guards had about his person a crowbar with which to prise up the heavy flagstone. For a while it defied all his efforts (it usually took Lordy's massive strength to lift it). Another guard came to his assistance and together they managed to get sufficient leverage upon the bar to lift the slab and send it crashing back.

The shaft yawned black and deep.

Matthew exchanged a worried glance with Moab as they stood grouped among the thirty or more occupants of the cell.

'Ah,' grunted Brett smugly.

He stooped and grabbed a fistful of the straw sticking out from a split pallet, lighted it, and tossed it into the shaft. He peered after it, judging the depth, surveying the small, dark mouth of the tunnel some ten feet down.

Matthew stepped forward. 'Permission requested to see the Captain, sir.'

Brett's grin wasn't pleasant. 'Oh, you'll see 'im, right 'nough, lug. I can promise you that.'

Gilpin sat iron-faced behind his desk as Lieutenant Matthew Youngmay, quietly and with great dignity despite his ragged garb, claimed full responsibility for the tunnel.

With heavy sarcasm, Gilpin said: 'An amazing feat, Prisoner Youngmay, to dig single-handed a ten-feet-deep shaft and a fifty-yard tunnel!'

'Nevertheless, sir, I and I alone am responsible,' Matthew insisted in a taut voice.

'Do you think I'm a half-wit?' snarled Gilpin, striking the desk with his fist. 'Every man in that cell – and probably many more besides – had a hand in this diabolical conspiracy!'

'No, sir. There was no conspiracy. I acted totally alone.'

'Do not lie to me, Youngmay! Or I'll have your blessed guts!' He paused, tight-lipped, considering. From the very outset, some fifteen months ago, the American had been a poisonous thorn within him. He'd made life as difficult as possible for his custodians, and had encouraged the other prisoners – who looked upon him as some sort of hero – to do the same, stealing rations and tools and even prison uniforms to be cut up into bags for the removal of the rubble from the tunnel. Oh, yes, it hadn't taken old Shem too long to learn just how they managed that! And then, out on moor, with the stone-breakers – falling over and pretending to have a fit while one of the others swapped a blunted pick for a honed one. Well, here was his chance to be rid of that damned thorn once and for all. What did it mattered who or how many helped Youngmay? He was the ringleader. Let him shoulder the blame since he was so damned eager to do so.

Even as Gilpin came to this decision, there came a smart rapping at the door. Brett scowled, put out that anyone would have the audacity to come knocking when he'd a prisoner on captain's orders.

Gilpin nodded curtly to him. 'Very well, Mr Brett.'

Brett opened the door a few inches and glared at the sergeant-at-arms who stood there. They spoke in low voices for a moment.

'Yes, yes, Mr Brett? What is it?' demanded Gilpin impatiently.

'The prisoners, sir . . .' Brett couldn't conceal his astonishment. 'Youngmay's cellmates. To a man they've owned up to helpin' dig tunnel. They're askin' to be allowed to stand 'longside Youngmay . . .'

Matthew looked anxious. Because the tunnel had been his idea he'd wanted to save them from being flogged. 'Sir . . .' he began to voice an urgent appeal on their behalf.

'Silence! Prisoner will speak only if spoken to!' barked Brett, giving Youngmay a sharp dig in the kidney with his rattan.

Gilpin had opened his snuff-box. He took a leisurely pinch, sniffed, waited a second, then sneezed violently into a large silk handkerchief. Only then did he say in strangely mild voice: 'Very well, Mr Brett. Batches of ten.'

He dealt swiftly with the culprits. Each man was to receive forty lashes with the cat. Except for Youngmay. Gilpin dealt with him separately and with great relish.

'Prisoner Youngmay, since by your own admission you are the instigator of this heinous conspiracy, it is my intention to see you are punished with severity. One hundred lashes!'

Even Brett was visibly startled. Forty lashes was grievous enough; one hundred was as good as a death sentence, only not as mercifully quick as hanging.

Matthew hid his emotions behind a blank façade as he heard the barbaric sentence pronounced. He wasn't prepared to give the prison captain the satisfaction of knowing that his stomach churned with the dreadful realisation that he was as good as dead. He'd long had Gilpin's measure. Disgruntled at being sent up the moor as captain of a prison rather then to war as master of a frigate, he used the suffering of others as a salve for his frustrations. He positively wallowed in brutality.

* * *

On the appointed day, on Gilpin's orders, every American and a further 350 French prisoners were herded into the main prison yard to witness the punishment.

They stood silently in tight ranks, every so often glancing up at the window where Gilpin stood watching from his quarters. Even from that distance, they could tell by the hunch of his shoulders and the angry, jutting position of his head that he was in a black and sadistic mood. And that spelt potential danger for every one of them. One untoward gesture or careless word of sympathy towards Youngmay and his followers could prove sufficient to merit a flogging at the triangles along with them.

One by one, those to be punished were led out and spancelled to the triangle erected in the centre of the stone-flagged yard. Their shirts were stripped from their backs and the bosun's mates wielded their cats, turn about. The soft spring air echoed with their agonised cries and pleas for mercy. The ground around their feet ran crimson as the knotted, leather throngs relentlessly scourged their naked flesh.

Matthew was kept to last.

It was past noon before he was brought out between two guards and paraded before the crowd in the yard. A restlessness ran through the watching prisoners; they shuffled their feet and threw compassionate looks towards the tall, blond American. The previous floggings, the dragging away of bloodied, half-conscious men, these were merely preliminaries to this, the major event of the day.

'Have you anything to say before punishment commences?' the master-at-arms asked Matthew in a sharp, formal manner.

Those watching expected Youngmay to say something in a final attempt to avert what could only be called judicial murder. He held himself proudly, his blue eyes lifting briefly to rest upon the motionless figure at the window. Yet, surprisingly, there was no animoisity in his glance. Matthew considered it the solemn duty of every prisoner-of-war to try to escape in order to be able to fight another day; alas, he'd failed to do so and must therefore face the consequences, however harsh they might be.

'That,' he'd told the disconsolate Moab, Dagge, Lordy and Knuckles – his Special Committee – quite cheerfully as they all awaited the dawning of punishment day, 'was war!'

Matthew lowered his eyes from Gilpin and turned towards the master-at-arms, bringing himself to attention.

'I have nothing to say, except . . . God bless America!'

He defiant cry brought grins to the faces of the watching prisoners. Brett stared, incredulous. Gilpin, hearing Matthew's ringing cry, began turn to a dark angry puce. He nodded curtly to Brett, ordering punishment to commence.

Matthew was immediately seized and dragged across to the triangles. His wrists were spancelled to the top and his ragged clothes were stripped from him.

His fair hair shone brightly in the April sunlight. Freed from its officer's ribbon, it fell in waves to his collarbone and, save for his impressively muscled physique, would have given him a rather feminine appearance.

The bosun's mates stepped forward and unfurled their cats. They both stood for a moment as though measuring the distance between themselves and Matthew's naked, sinewy back. They raised their cats.

'God help him!' muttered one of the watching prisoners, and those who heard him nodded, tight-lipped, in agreement of this sentiment.

During the long months of captivity, a strong sense of trust and comradeship had developed between the American prisoners, transcending the usual barriers of rank: many of the men – both young middies and hardened veterans hero-worshipped Matthew to such a degree that any number would have gladly taken his place on the triangles.

'Commence punishment!' barked Brett.

Matthew's body tensed. He heard the sound of the flail flying through the air, felt himself lifted and swung between the steel struts with the force of the blow. Yet, for a moment he felt nothing. *Then* he began to feel pain, a terrible burning like the branding of a red-hot iron as the skin was scourged from his back.

'One!' rang out Brett's voice. 'Two! Three!'

Long, welling welts criss-crossed Matthew's back. After the first dozen lashes, blood oozed steadily from the lacerations down over his buttocks and thighs to mingle on the ground with that of his fellow conspirators. Yet, unlike them, his lips remained clamped shut over his clenched teeth.

'*Fifteen*!'

'Cry out, damn your eyes!' Gilpin mouthed to himself vindictively. He wanted no martyr for them to lionise after Youngmay was dead and buried out on the windswept moor in the shadow of the prison walls. For he would die: Gilpin was convinced of that. No man weakened as the prisoners were by such privation could survive a hundred lashes, not even if he'd the courage of ten lions and God to help him!

'*Twenty*!'

Matthew had by now entered into an existence of rabid, brain-numbing pain. He no longer heard the number of lashes being called. All he knew was that the torture went on and on. His lips were now bared over his teeth and his fists were balled so tightly that his nails tore into his palms. Still he uttered no sound other than the gasping of air into his lungs.

'Cry out!' Gilpin willed him resentfully, noticing that even the guards were standing absorbed, mouths agape, their expressions showing that they were mightily impressed by this show of stoic endurance at the triangles.

'*Forty*!'

This was the number of lashes received by all those punished that morning before Matthew. But unlike them, his ordeal didn't cease. No welcoming bucket of cold water sluiced the blood from his torn flesh. No guard came to take him down and carry him away to lie on his belly in a cool, granite-walled cell.

Fifty-one! Fifty-two!'

The knotted tails kept falling, wielded turn about by the bosun's mates who were sweating now and breathing heavily from their exertions. Those watching had ceased to wince as every lacerating blow found its mark, turning the flesh and muscle to pulp.

Eighty!'

Matthew's body gave a tremendous jerk and he sagged so that his weight was supported by the steel manacle fixed to the top of the three struts. His head lolled, his jaw went slack.

'He's finished!' a voice whispered, hoarse with emotion. The ranks of prisoners darted looks up towards Gilpin's window, their eyes filled with resentment and loathing. Brett marched across to Matthew and wrenched back his head by the hair so he could look into his face and judge his condition. There was no point in flogging a dead man. The eyes beneath the pale brows were shut, the aquiline features were ashen. Brett was about to announce that he was dead when he saw a slight movement of the eyeballs behind the lids. He put his ear to the slack, waxen lips and heard a faint sigh. He wasn't dead. Not yet, though more punishment would doubtless finish him. Brett turned and looked up at Gilpin for guidance, something almost akin to a plea for mercy in his questioning expression. Eighty blows he'd taken; he'd not be the same ever again. He'd not cause them any more trouble.

This silent communication didn't pass unnoticed by the front ranks of prisoners. They held their breath. Would Gilpin show Matthew mercy? Would he let Matthew live?

Gilpin was feeling far from lenient. He hadn't forgotten that it was only due to Shem Frost that he hadn't lost a whole host of prisoners through that accursed tunnel. Matthew Youngmay's cunning would have lost him, Gilpin, his position. Better prison captain than the disgrace of being dismissed the service through incompetence. If Youngmay was allowed to live, it was quite possible that he'd start stirring them up again – even if he was a mere shadow of the young man he'd been. And next time, knowing that there was a Judas among them, they'd be doubly careful. No! decided Gilpin. He met Brett's gaze straight on, raised his hand and pointed at Matthew.

'It's cold-blooded murder!' shouted a voice from the prisoners' ranks, daring to voice the general opinion. Instantly, two guards fell upon him, rattans lifting and falling until he dropped to his knees. He was hauled away to await Gilpin's adjudication at a future time.

'Continue punishment!' barked Brett.

'*One hundred*!' Brett swung on his heel, stood to attention and saluted the prison captain. 'Sentence carried out, Sir!'

Gilpin returned the salute, eyes fixed to the shredded figure suspended from the triangles below him. The clawed hands and blood-streaked limbs no longer twitched spasmodically. He must be dead! Gilpin's gaze shifted to rake the sea of sullen, upturned faces. He experienced a surge of satisfaction. What if they did dub the American a martyr and a hero for dying without as much as a whimper? What good was a dead hero to them? He'd lead no more escapes.

Brett had approached Matthew and was listening to his heart as formality demanded, prior to declaring that life was extinct. To his amazement he detected a heartbeat, and a fairly strong, steady one at that.

'Prisoner is still alive. Take him down,' he ordered.

Gilpin started as a ragged cheer echoed through the yard almost immediately dying away as the guards moved forward towards the prisoners with their carbines menacingly raised.

In total silence, Matthew was taken down. His lips moved. All those in the yard strained their ears to hear what it was he was trying to say. Gilpin was too far away, but somehow he knew.

'*God bless America!*'

It was little more than a sigh, but they heard him and in a single leather-throated voice his fellow countrymen took up the cry, so that the prison rang with their patriotism.

'*God bless America!*'

In a moment, the guards were among them, viciously laying about them with the butts of their carbines. A few of the prisoners went down under the volley of blows with blood streaming from their heads. Even as they lay in the red mire, they kept shouting: 'God bless America and death to the British!'

The French who until now had stood dazedly watching the scene, edging away in a milling crowd to avoid the swinging carbines, were suddenly fired with a similar patriotism.

'*Vive la France*!' yelled a gaunt-eyed Frenchmen and this cry, too, was taken up with gusto.

A Frenchman lobbed a stone. Then another. A guard spotted the culprit and made a dive for him but he ducked the hail of blows raining down upon him and for good measure butted the guard in the stomach so that he collapsed groaning among the stamping feet of the prisoners who were being ineffectually pushed and prodded backwards by the handful of guards who were having trouble keeping their balance on the slippery, blood-stoned flags. In the mêlée, the triangles were toppled and sent crashing. Brett began frantically blowing his whistle to summon more guards to assist quell what was quickly turning into a riot.

Gilpin stood as though rooted; only his thick neck quivered in anger as he gazed in utter disbelief at the scene. The terrible floggings they'd witnessed that day should have been enough to cow the bravest among them. Yet, such was Youngmay's influence, they were to a man, American and French alike, obviously prepared to risk similar, agonising retribution simply to demonstrate their support.

Gilpin felt a chill sense of foreboding as he glimpsed the silvery head and pallid face through a gap in the wall of prisoners who were defying the guards' cudgels to form a protective circle around Matthew's prone figure to keep him from being trampled upon. Something told Gilpin that the American would survive to cause him a great deal more trouble yet. Damn him! he should've given him the maximum four hundred lashes! Or, better still, hanged him when he'd the chance, even if it was a quick and painless death and better than he thought Matthew deserved.

Gilpin jumped, startled as a stone struck his window. It chipped the glass and sent a myriad of small silvery cracks running across like a cobweb. He stared. This was too much.

'I'll have your blessed guts!' he snarled aloud, eyes darting here and there trying to pick out the culprit. But it could have been any one of the six hundred men bunched in the yard refusing to obey the guards who were trying to force them back to their cells and with a savage ferocity were voicing their hatred of their British captors. Brett emerged from the throng, eyes turned despairingly aloft towards Gilpin for guidance; he'd lost an epaulette and there was an unsavoury splodge of something which looked suspiciously like saliva adhering to his cravat. Gilpin caught his eye and made a signal, as if reaching for a holstered pistol.

Brett understood immediately. He ordered the nearest guards into a ragged, defensive line. 'Fire warning volley!' he commanded.

The clatter of carbines brought the riot to an immediate end, but just for good measure Brett ordered another volley fired over their heads.

'I'll have their blessed guts!' muttered Gilpin vindictively.

In the event, the entire prison was put on bread and water for a month. Gilpin would have preferred to have flogged the six hundred or so rioters in batches of ten, but such an extreme measures would have to be entered on the punishment roll and then sent to his masters in Whitehall for ratificaton. He didn't want to risk a visit from anyone at the Admiralty, asking questions and, perhaps, checking stores.

'You tell 'em, Mr Brett, that they can count themselves lucky. But any more trouble an' I'll have their blessed guts! You tell 'em that!'

By that spring of 1814, the tenacious British commander Sir Arthur Wellesley had cleared the French from northern Spain and was on French soil, occupying Bordeaux. The southern front had crumpled. Thus heartened, the Czar of Russia and the Allied armies of Prussia and Austria pushed into France in the east. Brilliant though Napoleon's strategies were in the face of this combined European onslaught, they couldn't save him. France turned against their Emperor. Paris surrendered. And on 3 April Napoleon deemed it prudent to abdicate and retire to the island of Elba. The long, bloody war with France was over. All French prisoners were released, though many chose to stay and marry their sweethearts rather than return to their homeland. By June, Princeton Prison housed only Americans, despite the fact that, with the end of war in Europe, the reasons for the British-American struggled ended, too. Britain no longer needed her naval blockades: American skippers could once again put into the French ports. But, until the diplomatic wranglings of peace at the Congress of Vienna were concluded to the satisfaction of the powers, the American prisoners remained captive.

Dame Hannah Rogers came personally to Eaglestone to tell the Hammetts the exciting news of Napoleon's abdication. Tom Beckwitt, the smithy's eldest son, brought her up the moor from the village in her little trap since her poor eyesight meant she could no longer take the reins herself. Kezzy was feeding the chickens in the yard when Wart gave a bark. Looking down the valley she half expected to see Grote. Or perhaps Peter Dorrity, who'd taken to paying occasional, surprise calls at Eaglestone whenever his duties took him up the moor. Kezzy didn't dare to discourage him in case she roused his suspicions again, though it meant that she and the flaskers had to be extra careful. But it was neither Grote nor Peter. Seeing the dame's neat figure on the box beside Tom, Kezzy ran to the cottage and shouted to Elyas.

' 'Tis Dame Rogers coming, Gramps!'

He was lying on his pallet although it was almost mid-morning. Having suffered one of his brain-fevers in the night, he was still sleepy from the effects of laudanum. However, on hearing that the dame was coming, he immediately sat up yawning and reached for his crutches. Such a rare visit could only mean that she had important tidings to impart.

Elyas and Kezzy stood in the yard to greet her. At close quarters they could see that her usually pale face was pink with excitement and her grey hair was escaping from the confines of her straw bonnet. She was waving a newspaper. 'War's over, praise be to God!' she cried before Tom had even reined in.

There was a long silence while it sank into them and Tom helped Dame Rogers down. It was Tom who broke the silence, saying pettishly, 'I wanted to go for a soljur an' kill they Frenchies, but Pa said I mustn't on account he do need I to help wi' shoein'. Now I'll *never* get to kill they Frenchie dogs!'

'And a good thing, too,' said Kezzy sharply. 'There's been enough killing.'

Tom's young face showed surprise. 'But they be our swornest an' bitterest foes, Keziah,' he told her earnestly, quoting his father near enough.

'Not any more, Tom,' said the dame happily. 'And soon, our boys will all be coming home . . .' She stopped short, covered with confusion, suddenly conscious of what she was saying.

Not Graeme and Isaac Hammett. They wouldn't be coming home. Not ever. Elyas's worn features twisted as if he was in pain. He closed his eyes to keep back the burning tears.

'I'm so sorry,' whispered the dame, mortified. Her eyes went to Kezzy's sad face. 'I . . . was so excited, what with the news about Bonaparte abdicating . . . I . . . well, my tongue just ran on wheels . . .'

'Don't fret yourself, Mistress Rogers,' Kezzy told her, forcing a smile. 'Indeed, 'tis wondrous news! And we're mighty grateful to you for taking trouble to bring it. Aren't we, Gramps?'

He opened his eyes, brushed his hand over them. Swallowing hard, he said: 'Ay, we'm glad to see thee, Mistress Rogers. We'm always that. An' thee, young Tom Beckwitt . . . even if'n thy Pa do water un beer in kiddleywink.'

They all laughed at that, Tom a trifle uncertainly, and the painful moment was passed.

They went into the cottage. Kezzy made tea and cut up a fresh-baked lardy cake to pass around. Once they were all seated at the table, Kezzy spread out the *Western Daily Mercury* brought by the dame.

'I know *very* little of what it says,' said Dame Rogers regretfully, 'as I can't read such small print these days. I had to rely on little Carrie Cooper to read it to me and, poor dear, she really isn't the best of readers.'

Kezzy stroked the newspaper as though it was some wondrous treasure, which, indeed, to her it was. It was all there. The cessation of hostilities. Napoleon's exile to Elba. How they had created Sir Arthur Wellesley, the victorious commander of the British forces, Duke of Wellington and British ambassador in Paris. And, nearer to home, how eager for repatriation were the American prisoners still incarcerated at Princeton.

'Never mind 'bout they Yankees,' said Elyas dismissively when Kezzy read out that item. He was clear-minded and awake now; revelling in the French defeat. 'Read us gin 'bout how we'm whupped ol' Boney.'

Kezzy didn't hear. She was sitting with a faraway expression, remembering . . . An irregular line of men in chains kneeling by the water's edge at Crazywell Pool. Among them, an American with hair the colour of wheat and eyes as vivid as the sea on a clear summer's day. *Matthew! Soon he would be free. Soon he would leave these shores for his homeland, never to know that she loved him*!

'Might I have 'nother slice o' lardy, Keziah?' asked Tom.

Kezzy nodded abstractedly, still half lost in her dreams.

He helped himself to a large piece. ' 'Tis best I ever did taste. Do fair stick to thy guts, it do.'

'Say belly, Tom, not guts,' corrected Dame Rogers primly.

Kezzy wasn't interested in Tom's innards. Or the empty mug which her grandfather was pushing beneath her nose to be refilled with tea. Her eye had been caught by a piece in the newspaper which had nothing to do with Napoleon or Wellington or a handsome young American prisoner . . .

'God in heaven!' she gasped, horror-struck.

Dame Rogers stopped with her mug halfway to her lips and turned her short-sighted gaze towards Kezzy. Tom stopped chewing and looked across the table questioningly, curious as to what Kezzy could have read which had sent her all of a dither. Elyas hadn't caught his granddaughter's exclamation, but seeing her abject astonishment he was prompted to ask: 'What is it, chield? What do 'ee see in yon noospapery?'

Kezzy looked at them with wide, shocked eyes. ' 'Tis Mrs de Raddon . . . she's dead!'

'Dead!' squeaked the dame. 'She can't be! I was only with her a week ago!'

'Don't take week to go to thy Maker if'n thy time has come,' said Elyas. 'Well, 'tis wisht poor thing, an' her wi' no children to follow she, but I'm a-thinkin' her's well at peace an' out o' that devil de Raddon's reach!'

'Poor Emma always was delicate, God rest her soul,' sighed Dame Rogers.

' 'Twas an accident.'

Tom had resumed chewing but stopped again. His mother would box his ears hard if he didn't memorise every word that was said so he could repeat them to her when he got home.

'An *accident*?' The dame looked shocked. 'What sort of accident?'

'She fell . . .'

'Fell? Where?'

'Over the cliffs at Blackaven Cove.'

They sat digesting that in silence for a while. The dame kept shaking her head, as if she couldn't take it in. Tom finished his cake and eyed the last slice. 'If'n slice is to be wasted I'll eat un,' he offered. When no one said anything, he shrugged and helped himself.

Presently, Elyas, in his forthright way, put into words the terrible notion which was already going through Kezzy's and the dame's thoughts. 'I'll wager he shoved she.'

This time it was Dame Rogers who gasped while Tom almost choked on a crumb.

Kezzy looked quickly up from the newspaper. 'I don't think we should say such things, Gramps. 'Tisn't right to make wild guesses.'

Elyas gave a wheezing snort. ' 'Tisn't right to shove thy wife off cliff top on account her got empty womb.'

Dame Rogers spilt her tea. 'Oh, Cap'n Hammett . . .!' she, too, began to protest.

Kezzy shot Tom a look to see if he was taking all this in. Tom's mother would publish it all around the village in no time. 'Tom,' she said, 'won't you please go and look at Rats? I do believe he's shedding shoe.'

Tom couldn't hide his disappointment at being sent out just as the conversation was becoming interesting. His mother would also be disappointed, but he could hardly refuse Kezzy when he'd eaten her cake and supped her tea. Reluctantly, licking sugary crumbs from his fingers, he ambled out.

'Gramps . . .' Kezzy started to scold Elyas as soon as the door shut on Tom, but he interrupted her before she'd the chance.

'Now, now, Kezzy chield, I knowed what 'ee a-goin' to say. An' I don't care scrap if'n Ma Beckwitt *do* wag her blessed tongue for all o'parish to hear! I knowed de Raddon well 'nough to swear he wouldn't stop at murder if'n it suited he . . .'

'Captain Hammett! That's a most terrible and unfounded slander!'

'. . . an' you'm knowed it, too, Hannah Rogers! So don't ye be a-sayin' elly different!'

'Captain Hammett, I must protest . . .!'

'Shame o' it is,' continued Elyas, 'murderin' skunk won't be given neck-party he deserves. 'Twill all be covered up like dog's dirt, mark me.'

He was probably right, the dame thought, but wouldn't have dreamt of saying so out of misplaced loyalty to Captain de Raddon. He was, after all, the brother of the sweet, dead little girl to whom she had once been governess. She rose. 'It is time I was on my way home. I have a class at one o'clock.'

Kezzy folded the newspaper reluctantly. 'I'll fetch Tom.' She moved towards the door.

'You may keep the newspaper, Keziah.'

Kezzy turned and gave her a warm, grateful smile. 'Thank you.'

She would read it and re-read it over and over. Everything that was in it. Not just about the war and poor, tragic Emma de Raddon but even the smallest item and all the advertisments for saddles and animal fodder and for the Clotworthy Bank at Plympton, Mr Thomas Clotworth being poor tragic Emma's father. All of this provided Kezzy with a fascinating glimpse of the world beyond her wild moorland – albeit the somewhat narrow world of the *Western Daily Mercury*.

Tom was tidying Rats's hooves when she went around the back of the barn to where the colt was let loose in a pen.

'Don't seem to be no loose shoe, Keziah.'

'I must have been mistaken.'

'Anyroads, I done trim un coffins for he.'

'Thank you.'

'Best be thinkin' o' gettin' new Rats.'

'He'll do.'

'Gettin' on.'

'He doesn't have much to do these days.'

She patted Rats's nose and he blew affectionately at her. He was the fifth moorland colt – all called Rats – that they'd had at Eaglestone. And her favourite. Bought for five pounds from gypsies who'd rounded up some of the shaggy wild 'gossies' to sell at the October horse-fair. Graeme and Isaac had each caught and broken the first two Rats . . .

'Tom Beckwitt!'

Her reverie had been abruptly and rudely interrupted by Tom. He'd seized her around the waist and was pulling her close to him. Before she could struggle free, he'd planted a kiss full on her mouth. Having done so, he released her, red in the face but triumphant.

'There now,' he said, pleased with himself, 'I reckon that makes us promised.'

Kezzy didn't know whether to be angry or amused. She started to laugh, then stopped, not wanting to hurt the foolish boy's feelings. 'It makes us no such thing,' she said firmly.

'But I'm terrible headlight for love of ye, Keziah,' he told her plaintively. 'I do want to take 'ee for I's wife.'

He tried to catch her in his arms again but she ducked away from him. 'No, Tom!'

'Please, Keziah,' he begged, lumbering after her as she danced further out of his reach. 'Pa says 'tis time I were wed an' brought in a good wife to help Ma. 'Course, they said I weren't to get hitched to 'ee on 'count o' you'm un witch.'

Kezzy stopped fighting him and stared into his flushed, eager face. 'Your ma and pa said *that*?'

'Ma says you'm got the power. Piskie sight. An' witch-spells belike.

Mebbe you'm put spell on I awlready,' he said worriedly, 'way I do feel 'bout 'ee. I do love 'ee fitty to burst I's britches.'

He made a lunge for her and pulled her close to him again as if to prove the fact. Since she twisted her head away he buried his face in her neck, slobbering over the soft, white skin and groaning loudly such was his need of her. He reeked unpleasantly of boiled onions and garlic and stale tobacco.

'Even if'n you'm *is* witch like thy ma, God rest she, I'll marry ye, Keziah. Straight'way. An' not care if'n it do mean everlastin' hell-fire like ma say,' he boldly declared.

Anger surged within her: so *that* was what they were saying about her in the village. She was a witch like Ruke Hammett.

'Your ma's tongue need's shortening, Tom Beckwitt.'

Their scuffles and her sharp, raised voice agitated Rats and he danced sideways, tugging at his tethering rope and softly whinnying.

Tom wouldn't release Kezzy and although she was taller than he was, he was too strong for her to push away. She was aware of his hard, bony body pressed against hers. He managed to slip a hand between them to grip one of her breasts and she gave him a hard kick on the shin. Still he held on to her.

'I love 'ee, Keziah.' He tried to kiss her mouth again.

'No, Tom!' Frantically, she jerked her head from side to side. 'I'm promised to another!'

He released her instantly, face scarlet and crumbling with remorse and disappointment. 'Who you'm promised to?' he demanded jealously.

'Matthew. His name is Matthew.'

He frowned, trying to recall if he knew this rival and if so, what Matthew would have to say about him trying to spark Kezzy. 'Be it Matthew Skinner? As got cloppy leg?'

'No.'

'Matthew Butler from over to Land's Down then?'

Kezzy shook her head. 'He's not from round here. He's from far away.'

'Ah,' observed Tom, understanding, 'from over to *Plympton*, thy means.'

She didn't pursue the subject. 'Best be gettin' in. Mistress Rogers won't be kept.'

He looked suddenly guilty. 'You'm not to say 'owt.'

She frowned at him. 'Very well,' she agreed 'providing you never behave like that again.'

He shook his head. 'I'll not. But 'tis terrible pity for 'ee. I'd have made 'ee good husband. Worked for 'ee. An' given 'ee plenty o' chillun to fill thy belly. Not like yon Mrs Cap'n de Raddon as got she murdered on count her be barren.'

Kezzy tutted. 'You're not to repeat such things, Tom.'

He shrugged. ' 'Tis most likely'd true.'

Chapter Twenty-Seven

Shem Frost, unwittingly, proved something of an inspiration to Matthew when he eventually recovered from the flogging and his back had healed, thanks to frequent administrations of some stinging, evil-smelling decoctation brewed by Lordy. For Matthew adopted a similar slouching gain and addlebrained manner to that of the old convict. Only his Special Committee knew it wasn't genuine. All the other prisoners and the guards were fooled into believing that Matthew was a broken man, incapable of planning another escape.

To begin with, Matthew's performance fascinated the guards, and Prison Captain Gilpin in particular. He would watch from his window as Matthew shuffled around the exercise yard, eyes downcast, arms hanging limply at his sides.

'Funny how a floggin' can break a man,' Gilpin remarked once to master-at-arms Brett. 'Now, solitary . . . that didn't touch Youngmay. Come out pert as a pearmonger, blast him! But hundred strokes . . .' he smiled unpleasantly, '*that* brought him into line.'

'Aye, Cap'n,' agreed Brett without quite the same enthusiasm, 'an' left him as mad as a May loon.'

After a while, Gilpin lost interest in Matthew and the guards grew so used to his shambling figure they forgot that he'd ever been anything other than a witless, cowering human wreck. And that suited Matthew perfectly. For, far from witless, his brain was never idle, it was ever searching for a new method of escape.

But on 14 December 1814, before he could formulate anything worthwhile to put to his loyal Special Escape Committee, the war between Britain and America officially ended. Captain Gilpin had all American prisoners assembled in the main yard and made the brief announcement in dour tones which were quickly drowned by a rousing, relieved cheer. That night, Matthew and Knuckles had braved the bitter cold and scaled the icy roof of their block to run up a United States flag. Seeing it fluttering defiantly in the morning, Gilpin had been so incensed he'd placed all Americans on half rations for a week. None had minded. It was worth it. Particularly as the flag remained there for the entire week because the blizzard had worsened suddenly and none of the guards was prepared to risk life and limb to remove the offending article.

'We'll be out of here quicker'n Hell can scorch a feather!' Moab kept saying.

He spoke too soon. January came – mercifully nowhere near as bad as the previous year with its great snow storm – then February, and still they languished, half-starved and growing increasingly desperate for freedom. Matthew and his Special Committee composed a round-robin which every American in the prison signed, asking why they hadn't yet been released, weeks after the British-American war had ended and months after the last French prisoner had left; also, the petition requested better conditions in the meantime. Since Matthew was still maintaining his useful veneer of insanity, the rest of the Special Committee drew straws to see who would present the petition to Old Blessed Guts.

John Dagge drew the short straw.

Gilpin had barely glanced through the round-robin.

'It's nothing to do with me if the Admiralty has stopped sending funds to buy rations. If you've any complaints, write to London,' he told Dagge peevishly, forgetting the Lieutenant Youngmay had received a month in the dumb-box for once requesting permission to do just that.

So they wrote to the Admiralty. No reply was forthcoming. Had Gilpin even sent the letter? they asked themselves. March came, and with it high winds. They could sniff salt in the air and it made the blood in their veins pound with the longing to feel a deck beneath their feet.

Night after night, Matthew lay awake, agonising over the problem of how they were to be delivered from their harrowing plight before they died of starvation. Then one morning, as the prison bell clanged six bells to rouse them, the solution came to him. *Why not seize the prison and release themselves?*

For the rest of that day, Matthew mulled over the idea, sitting in a corner of the prison yard gnawing half-wittedly on a stone. It was a ploy he sometimes used when he wanted peace and quiet to think, having discovered that the guards – apart from a few amused grins and initially a sneering remark or two – left him alone. Exercise parties came and went and still he sat there chewing his lump of rock, blue eyes vacant. It also gave him a chance to observe the other prisoners. Ever since the tunnel had been discovered, Matthew had remained convinced that they had a traitor in their midst. A French prisoner, perhaps, now gone, of course; possibly even a fellow American, though he shuddered at the thought. But more likely one of the handful of old convicts who would have been sent to the penal colonies if it wasn't for the fact that all ships and crews were needed to fight the French. And of the old convicts, it was Shem Frost who niggled at Matthew's suspicions the most, despite the fact that the old sheep-stealer gave every impression of being half-witted. But then so did Matthew himself. So perhaps they were both faking.

Yes, Shem should certainly be watched.

It wasn't until late in the day that Matthew had an opportunity to put his idea to Moab, Dagge and Lordy (Knuckles having earned himself a week in solitary for stealing rations). They had gone to the prison church, St Michael and All Angels, to work on the furnishings for an hour or two before the light went. The French prisoners had built the church but hadn't quite finished the interior before being released. Gilpin had given the Americans, and John Dagge in particular, permission to form a working party to complete the work, little knowing that Dagge's representation was Matthew's idea and that the working party would always include him to sweep up after the wood-workers.

The church made the perfect place for the Special Committee to hold their low-voiced meetings. As soon as they were ensconced and going about their various tasks, Matthew informed them of his proposal that they should seize the prison.

They stopped what they were doing and stared at him in amazement.

Dagge was the first to speak: 'That's mutiny you're talking, Matt.'

'I prefer to call it justifiable insurgence.'

'Call it what you will, matey, Old Blessed Guts will call it mutiny pure an' sweet!' declared Moab.

Mutiny, they were all fully aware, was deemed a crime far more serious than mere escape. And the punishment fitted the crime: death at the end of a rope for those leading the conspiracy, flogging for the rest, and with such savagery, the treatment meted out to Matthew would pale by comparison.

Lordy was rubbing gum resin vigorously into an oaken pew. He stopped, straightening his massive back, and looked across at Matthew, his big, flat, brown face shining with eagerness. 'I'm with you, Lieutenant. You kin count on Lordy Sleeve. I'd face Hell an' all its demons to get outa this stinkin' place.'

'Oh aye,' Moab was quick to agree, 'I ain't turnin' goosey. Don't think that. *Somethin's* gotta be done and mighty soon. My belly's stuck to my backbone.'

Matthew looked across at Dagge. 'What about you, John? Are you with us?'

'You don't have to ask, Matt.'

Matthew nodded. He thought for a moment, leaning on his broom. Even in repose, his air of authority belied his ragged appearance. He began to elaborate on the plans he'd formed during the day.

'We'll need some sort of weapon. Musket or, better still, a pistol as its easier to hide.'

'Do we spread the word 'mong the other prisoners?' asked Dagge.

Matthew hesitated, remembering how they had been betrayed over the tunnel. If Gilpin got so much as a hint of what was in store he'd send for reinforcements. Then it would be nigh on impossible to seize the prison. Yet, they needed to enlist support.

'Yes,' he said slowly, 'test them out. But keep a weather eye on Shem Frost.'

'Old Shem ain't got all his oars in the water,' snorted Moab stepping back and viewing the genteel piece of carving he was engaged upon.

'I'm not so sure,' Matthew told him seriously.

'Reckon he's blabbing to Gilpin?'

'Let's say that I'd like to know how the old hayseed keeps that pipe of his filled.'

Moab chuckled. 'Smoke any damned thing, would Shem. Even his own dung, I reckon.'

'Since when has dung smelled like Navy Plug?'

They were quiet for a while. They, and many more besides them, had worked long and hard on the shaft and tunnel until it had been discovered. They all bore the scars of brutal punishment on their backs. Now their fury was scorching.

'Plague take the snitchin' cur!' spat Moab. 'I'd like to rip out his infernal tongue and feed it to the rats!'

Lordy cracked his huge brown knuckles. 'Just say the word, Lieutenant, and I'll snap his neck quicker'n heart-beat.'

'There's to be no murder!' said Matthew sharply. His vivid eyes raked each of them in turn, silencing the ripple of muttered objections. 'It'll go better for all of us if we do this without shedding blood. We'll seize the arms chests and . . .'

Matthew stopped dead as Lordy held up a warning hand. The Indian in him had given him exceptionally keen senses so that he had detected the faintest rustling from outside the porch chamber. Soundlessly, he slipped away among the shadows only to reappear a few moments later.

'Shem,' he said. He aped the convict. 'Elly baccy, boys? Elly baccy?'

'Could he have heard?' asked Matthew concernedly.

Lordy shook his bald head with certainty. 'He couldn't have got close enough without my hearin' him.'

The vast majority of the prisoners approached by Youngmay and his confederates were ripe for mutiny and pledged their support with enthusiastic willingness. Here and there a man refused, fearful of the terrible price to be paid if the prison officers managed to restore the situation and halt the mass escape. Why risk their lives unnecessarily when they would be sent home anyway before long? argued these non-participants.

'Sent home in an eternity box most like! Dead from rat-fever or starvation!' Moab would scoff by way of knocking such arguments to the ground.

But even these few, wary individuals wished the committee well and swore to do nothing which might endanger the success of the 'justifiable insurgence'.

Word of the mutiny spread quickly through the prison. Too quickly, thought Matthew in agonised frustration. He'd hoped to keep it a guarded secret among those he could trust for a few days, until he'd schooled his immediate band of supporters in the vital parts they were to play. But everywhere, in the cells at night, in the yards during exercise, he heard the eager whispering.

'We're going to seize the prison! Are you with us, matey?'

'Aye, matey, I'm with you!'

If Gilpin *did* still have a spy in their midst, he must surely be aware now that a conspiracy was afoot. That worrying thought brought home to Matthew the need for swift action. There was not a moment to lose now he'd sufficient supporters to carry out his plan.

* * *

'*Mutiny!*' The very word sent a tremor through Gilpin's portly body. 'Are you sure?'

Shem Frost's grizzled head wagged up and down.

'Sure an' I'm sure, Cap'n, zur.'

Gilpin was astonished that a state of mutiny could not only exist, but could gather full support right under the noses of the guards. He surveyed the scrawny individual standing on the other side of his desk through narrowed, suspicious eyes. It occurred to him that it was the contents of his tobacco jar which had fostered this tale of an imminent rebellion. A rebellion, moreover, planned by Matthew Youngmay.

'None of the guards have reported anything amiss.'

Mention of the guards produced a contemptuous snort from Shem. 'Daft as carrots half-scraped, they be.' He tapped his nose with a filthy forefinger. 'Didn't find tunnel, them didn't. Took ol' Shem to sniff un out.'

Grudgingly, Gilpin had to admit that his informant had been proved right before. Yet, still he had reservations: mainly because Frost was so insistent that Youngmay – half-crazed, shuffling, broken-spirited Youngmay – was behind the conspiracy to take over the prison. Goddamit, it just could not be, Gilpin told himself.

True, Youngmay had survived a hundred lashes against all odds. But afterwards he had developed a raging fever and had lain mostly unconscious on his pallet for days hovering 'twixt life and death. When eventually he'd managed to drag himself to his feet, the guards reported that he was a broken man, both in mind and body. Such had been Gilpin's near-obsessional mistrust of Matthew, that he had ordered the prisoner brought before him so he could view him personally. Gilpin knew from experience that a severe flogging took its toll but even he had been startled by the marked change in Matthew. He'd become a pathetic, squinting parody of the golden young god who'd promised his fellow inmates freedom. And when Gilpin questioned him closely, demanding to know if he'd learned his lesson, he'd muttered a docile, 'Yes, sir. Thank you', as he stood there with his eyes downcast.

Gilpin had been satisfied; the other prisoners had been shown beyond any shadow of a doubt what became of even the strongest and bravest who dared to try and escape.

Now Gilpin was anxiously asking himself if Youngmay had been shamming. The slow, monosyllabic speech. The slack mouth. The cowering mien. Could these all have been a brilliant piece of fakery?

'Be that all, Cap'n, zur?'

'Yes, yes, you can go,' Gilpin dismissed his informer in a preoccupied manner.

Shem didn't move. For a while he stood there silently, twisting his dirty hat in filthy, calloused hands. Presently, he ventured a gentle hawking to attract attention.

Gilpin looked up, seemed surprised to still see him there.

'Well, what is it?'

'Beggin' they pardon, Cap'n, zur . . .'

His voice trailed and he stared pointedly at the elephant's foot. Gilpin took the hint and flipped open the silver lid. He inserted a thumb and forefinger. Shem's eyes glistened with anticipation as a good-sized plug was produced and pushed across the desk towards him. Swiftly, he scooped up the offering and dropped it in the gunny sack he used as a tobacco pouch.

'Thank 'ee, Cap'n, zur, thank 'ee,' he muttered, tugging his forelock and edging towards the door.

'If this should turn out to be some trick to get a twist of baccy, Frost . . .' He didn't complete the threat; there was no need to.

'I bain't talkin' up load of ol' plod, Cap'n, zur,' Shem said, looking quite pained. He paused, halfway out of the door and looked back at Gilpin. 'Beggin' thy pardon, Cap'n, zur . . .'

'Well? What now?'

'Terrible thicky fog a-closin' in.'

Gilpin glared at him. He was fully aware that a wispy white vapour was creeping across the moor and would soon reach the prison walls. But with a possible mutiny on his hands he'd neither the time nor inclination to discuss the worsening visibility with this traitorous bumpkin. 'Get out!' he snapped.

Shem edged through the door, then stuck his head back in. 'I was just athinkin', Cap'n zur . . . s'pose that Youngmay has got they other Yankees proper fired up and fitty to cut thy throats any time now? If'n I was 'ee, I'd send messenger to Plymouth for they dragoons. While they can still get here . . .'

The grizzled head was withdrawn and the door shut.

The first part of Matthew's plan went smoothly.

During the afternoon exercise period, a handful of prisoners led by Knuckles – now released from solitary and eager to join the conspiracy – began pelting the guards with stones. In the ensuing mêlée, Matthew collided with one of the guards and with a deftness which would have shamed a magician, appropriated a loaded pistol. Immediately, he passed it on to Moab who in turn passed it to Dagge, and so on around the shuffling circle of men until it found its way among the remnants of Gilpin's lunch which a trustee happened to be carrying across the yard at that moment, having only moments before cleared the dishes from the prison captain's table.

The disturbance had been quelled and the prisoners herded back to their cells before the guard noticed his loss. The cells and the prisoners were thoroughly searched. Every pallet was ripped open; every nook and cranny probed and probed again. But the pistol had apparently vanished into thin air.

Brett had no alternative but to report the loss of the pistol to the prison captain.

'*Lost*, Mr Brett?' Gilpin's voice was dangerous, his heavy features twisting with rage.

Brett gulped. 'Aye, sir, from his belt. I do now believe that the affray was a diversion . . .'

'Any fool would guess that, Mr Brett!' snarled Gilpin. 'And has this pistol been recovered?'

'No, sir. But we're still searching . . .'

Gilpin made a deprecatory gesture. 'Was it loaded?'

'Yes, sir.'

'God Almighty!'

Gilpin crashed his fist on the desk.

'I'm confident that we'll find the missing pistol, sir.'

'I wish I was, Mr Brett!' retorted Gilpin bitterly.

He rose and went to the window. Was this then the start of it? Shem Frost's mutiny and bloody massacre? Of one thing, Gilpin felt sure: Matthew Youngmay knew exactly where the pistol was though he would never reveal it, not if he was flogged to the death. The mist was thickening – perfect conditions for an uprising since before long the guards wouldn't be able to differentiate 'twixt friend and foe. Gilpin came to a decision.

'Send a messenger with all haste to the Plymouth garrison, Mr Brett.'

'Dragoons, sir!'

There was a definite note of dismay in Brett's voice. For the navy to request army reinforcements was tantamount to admitting they couldn't handle a handful of defenceless, half-starved Yankees. They'd be the laughing stock of every mess.

'Yes, Mr Brett. Dragoons. And I want a full complement of guards. They must be extra vigilant.'

'Aye, aye, sir.' Brett saluted and made for the door.

'And Mr Brett . . .'

He paused and turned. 'Sir?'

'At the first suggestion of trouble the guards are to open fire. Is that clear?'

Brett's face registered his concern. 'Surely, sir, drawn cudgels would be sufficient. The prisoners only have one pistol. And one slug.'

'In the right hands, Mr Brett, that's all they'd need.'

Chapter Twenty-Eight

Old Wart gave a single sharp, warning bark.

Kezzy set aside the basket of woollen vamps she was mending and rose to blow out the candle. Elyas watched her movements from his corner, his elbows on his knees, both hands clasping a mug of hot, sugared tea.

'What do 'ee hear, chield?'

'Horses.'

His brows went up in surprise. Clammy wisps of fog crept in beneath the door despite the sand-filled stocking 'snake' put there to keep it out. Who would be foolhardy enough to venture out on the moor when a terrible black mist was sweeping in from the distant sea to mantle the dykes and bogs?

'Mebbe flaskers wi' run,' suggested Elyas watching her intent face as she listened.

Kezzy shook her head. The horses were moving too freely to be led draught-animals. And the flaskers always muffled the trappings. They were so close now she could hear the clink of steel: stirrup-irons and bits. And probably swords and carbines.

'Preventy men, I reckon,' she said grimly.

Elyas hawked in the fire. 'Damn they to black hell and worse!'

'They've stopped. Beyond wall.'

She strained her ears. The horses – and there did seem to be an exceptionally large troop of them – had come to a halt a short distance from Eaglestone. Their stamping hooves and the muffled shouts of the riders indicated that they were in a quandary as to which direction they should take. Just there, outside the yard, the track became a mass of ruts and hoofprints leading in all directions.

'Perhaps they'll pass us by,' mouthed Kezzy.

'If'n they don't sniff smeech from chimbley.'

They sat waiting to see if they would be left in peace or not. Not that either of them was overly concerned. It wouldn't be the first time of late they had received a random visit from Preventatives demanding to search for contraband. Smuggling, as the Hammetts were all too well aware, was getting out of hand and the collector was growing quite desperate to uncover a worthwhile cache to satisfy his London masters.

Elyas and Kezzy always cooperated with them; willingly she'd lead the Preventatives into the mine, then round and round in circles just as she had Peter Dorritty, until they were wet and filthy and heartily wishing that they hadn't troubled the Hammetts. Occasionally, Peter himself was the riding officer leading the dragoons. He would keep his manner purposefully brusque, as if he wasn't already acquainted with them. His search would be cursory and, as soon as he could, he'd lead the dragoons away to tear apart some unfortunate farmer's barns and ricks further up the moor. But once the big cob Kezzy used to pull the wagon-loads of brandy was tethered in the yard because she hadn't had time to return it to its secret glade. Although Peter had walked around the sweating horse, and had examined its teeth and hooves, he made no comment.

Nevertheless, Kezzy had felt some sort of explanation was called for.

' 'Tis from Cherry Brook Farm,' she'd quickly lied. 'We have cousins there. One of them rode down to visit us.'

If Peter was curious as to the whereabouts of this 'cousin' he hadn't shown it. He had merely grunted, apparently with little interest. Yet, for a few moments he had engaged Kezzy's eyes, staring deeply into them, as if trying to tell her something, before turning abruptly away to remount and ride away with his dragoons strung out behind him.

After that, Kezzy was always careful only to bring the cob into the yard to be hitched or unhitched when the flaskers had watchers posted on the hills to warn of any approaching danger.

Old Wart began to bark madly out in the yard.

'Here they come,' said Kezzy.

The horses entered the yard and came to a muffled stop right outside the cottage door. A voice rang out.

'Open up in the King's name!'

Elyas frowned. 'What un say?' he asked Kezzy, hearing the loud command but unable to make out the words.

Kezzy told him.

There was no point in ignoring the command. Kezzy took a dip and relighted the lantern. Elyas rose stiffly, taking his time, balancing himself on his crutches. He jerked his head towards the long-handled pitchfork behind the door. 'You'm take un evil an' don't be 'fraid to use un if'n they don't show 'ee proper respect.'

Kezzy took no notice. It annoyed her just as much as it did her grandfather when the Preventatives leered at her, but threatening them with an evil wouldn't stop libidinous thoughts passing through their minds.

Those outside were growing impatient. The door was hammered with the stock of a gun and the voice grew more threatening.

'Open up, or I'll burn down your hovel about your blasted ears, do you hear?'

'Awlright! Awlright!' groused Elyas as Kezzy ran to lift the latch. 'War's over. So 'ee can quit bangin' fit to frighten French.'

The door swung open and they stepped out, Kezzy holding the lantern aloft, to see who it was who had risked the treacherous weather.

Visibility was all but gone. Dimly through the shifting vapour, like grim spectres, loomed a troop of some fifty or more dragoons. Kezzy and Elyas eyed them concernedly: usually a troop consisted of no more that twenty. Something serious must be afoot. And there was no riding officer with them. They were led by a dragoon captain swathed in a multi-caped grey cloak, astride a big, lean grey; a ghostly-looking, slightly fearsome figure in the swirling fog.

He addressed Elyas: 'Are you Elyas Hammett?'

Elyas cupped an ear. 'Eh?'

The captain raised his voice. 'Elyas Hammett?'

'Who be a-lookin' for he?'

'Answer civil, tinner!'

'Ay, I'm Hammett. *Cap'n* Hammett, to 'ee, cully. An' this be my gran'daughty Miss Keziah Hammett. Her be used to gentles touchin' they forrids to she.'

Kezzy couldn't make out the captain's face but sensed he was sneering. He was young: his voice told her that – a pompous, snobby-nosed fellow who wouldn't waste pretty speeches on bal maidens.

Behind him, a ripple of amusement ran through the double rank of troopers because their officer had been so audaciously given a lesson in manners by the old tinner. They fully expected him to retaliate in some way, yet he let the gibe pass. He drew himself up in the saddle and in a clipped, urgent tone announced: 'Elyas Hammett, by the authority vested in me by His Majesty King George, you are hereby sworn as guide to the Eleventh Dragoons. God Save The King!'

Kezzy's dark eyes lightened with alarm as the captain swivelled in the saddle and barked out an order for a spare mount to be brought forward. *Surely they weren't expecting her grandfather to ride with them?*

It took Elyas just a moment longer to arrive at the same conclusion. He gave a hoarse laugh and grinned up at the captain showing his snaggly yellow teeth. 'An' did 'is Majesty not mention as how I be crippled an' can't sit no hoss, cully?'

'If necessary I'll tie you on, Hammett!' snapped the officer as a trooper led forward a big chestnut.

Elyas's laughter turned to a choking cough and Kezzy made to run inside to fetch his medicine but he stopped her, clutching her arm to keep her there. 'Begob, Kezzy chield!' he gasped. 'What do un say to that? I bin pressed for a soldjur an' me turned seventy!'

'He can't go! It would kill him!' said Kezzy aghast.

'Now, now, I bain't a-goin' nowheres wi' they fancy coats,' he said, patting her hand reassuringly. He began to cough again but wouldn't let her fetch his medicine, determined to remain alert until the dragoons had gone. He peered up at the officer from beneath his straggling brows. 'So 'ee be lost, cully? he chuckled. 'Shouldn't have left Plymouth road, I reckon. Where ye headin' over to?'

'Princeton.'

'Oh ay.'

'They say you know Dartmoor better than any man.'

'Folks will say anything but their prayers,' snorted Kezzy.

'An' who might "they" be?' asked Elyas curiously.

'Smithy downalong Cornwood.'

'Jim Beckwitt do have mouth like barn door!' declared Elyas scornfully. He frowned, gave a wheezing chuckle. 'Hear un, Kezzy? *Cornwood*! Reckon they been piskie-led in fog.'

A note of anxiety crept into the captain's voice. 'It is true, isn't it? You do know the moors better than any man?'

'Ay, 'tis true,' admitted Elyas proudly.

'Then 'tis your duty, fellow, to guide us to Princeton Prison with all haste. The prisoners are planning mutiny and we're needed.'

As his words registered, Kezzy felt a little shiver of dread. *Matthew*!

'But the war's long over. They should be free men!' she heard herself exclaiming.

The captain ignored her. He was impatient to be gone. 'Help the old man mount,' he commanded the trooper holding the spare horse, a fine chestnut. 'Tie him on.'

'Sir,' Kezzy appealed to the captain, 'my grandfather has lung-rot . . .' As if to confirm it, Elyas was seized by a spasm of coughing as the fog attacked his chest. 'Hark! he should be in by the fire, not out here at all!'

'He'll be well paid for his trouble, girl.'

Elyas stopped coughing immediately. He shook the trooper's hand off his arm, cocked an eye at the captain. 'How much?'

The officer hesitated; he'd hadn't any idea as to a guide's pay, never previously having needed to employ one. At that moment the fog seemed to close in still tighter around them, emphasising his dire need of Hammett's services. 'A shilling,' he hazarded.

Elyas gave a disparaging snort and began to cough again. They got more for storing a single tub of cognac for the flaskers.

'*I'll* take you,' said Kezzy abruptly.

'You?' The captain sounded scornful.

'For a guinea.'

'A guinea!'

'In advance.'

'Out of the question!' He turned to the trooper. 'Get the old man mounted, I said.'

The trooper moved to seize hold of Elyas again but Kezzy put herself between him and her grandfather. 'Wait! I know the moor as well as he does. Besides, he'll perish long before you reach the prison.'

Even as she spoke, Elyas was wracked by another coughing fit, more savage than before. He doubled up, mouth foaming with blood-flecked spittle. Kezzy darted a warning look at the trooper, set down the lantern and dived back inside the cottage to reappear with a flask of lung physic. She held it to Elyas's lips and he took a good swallow.

Watching them, the captain was forced to accept that what she said was true: the old man wasn't in any fit state to guide them. Yet, he hesitated to take the girl instead. He eyed her shapely, slender body in its coarse woollen kirtle. The hands which held the flask to the old man's lips were, though work-roughened, as graceful and well-formed as those of the fragile, silken creatures in his mother's drawing room.

'But you're a female!' he blurted anxiously and a ripple of amusement ran through the ranks at this patently obvious observation.

Kezzy nodded. 'So I am, Captain. But I can sit a horse as well, maybe even better than any of those sniggering jiggins you've got with you.'

'Very well. Consider yourself sworn,' he said brusquely. 'Now mount up and look sharp.'

Kezzy held out her hand. 'A guinea, if you please.'

Another ripple ran through the troop. It was more than any of them earned in a two-week. The captain moved aside his cloak and let his hand rest on the silver stock of the pistol he wore. There was no mistaking the implied threat.

'A shilling, I said. And that's what you'll be given,' he snapped. 'I *could* order you to guide us across the moor *without* payment.'

'So you could. But the piskies wouldn't like it.'

'Piskies!' he sneered.

'They're my friends,' Kezzy told him solemnly. 'If you *were* to make me lead you with pistol to my back . . . why, those piskies would be terrible angry! Likely'd lead you into boggy mire so none of you was ever seen again.'

He knew what she was saying; every so often someone did disappear into a mire. Reluctantly, his hand left his pistol and produced his purse. He shook out a guinea and dropped it into her palm.

Kezzy gave it to Elyas. 'Keep it safe now, Gramps,' she bade him, 'and I'll be back by and by.'

'I wish ye wouldn't go wi' un, chield,' he told her worriedly, ' 'tis over dangerous for a maid.'

'I'll be all right. Don't worry.' She pressed his hand reassuringly, then picked up the lantern and held it up so she could see the horse she was supposed to ride. The chestnut was exceedingly handsome but wouldn't be as much use as their own colt who wasn't affected by the fog and could pick his way instinctively over the rough ground. She told the captain so, slightly regretful because she wouldn't be riding his fine animal.

'As you please, girl! But for God's sake, make haste!' came the terse response. 'Even now we may be too late . . .'

When the trusties brought the prisoners' supper of gruel – all that they could expect now that the Admiralty had stopped providing a ration allowance – they were accompanied by twice as many guards as usual and with carbines cocked and at the ready. Matthew exchanged veiled looks with the four members of his Special Committee: Gilpin must know something was afoot and was taking certain precautions.

Shem Frost was one of the trusties. He took his time moving along the line of men crowded against the thick steel bars, holding out their tin bowls for a scant ladle of the thin, grey mess. He scanned their faces: they were unusually quiet, he thought. Too quiet. None of their usual baaing and bleating for a larger helping.

'Wait thy turn, Injun,' he growled as Lordy's long arm reached over the backs of those in the front line to hold his bowl almost beneath Shem's bony nose. He slopped a dollop of gruel in Lordy's bowl; less than all the others got.

'That ain't fair shares!' protested Lordy.

Shem sneered at the big man. 'Serves ye right for pushin'.'

He found himself opposite Matthew. He eyed the tall, stooping, fair-haired figure, trying to see behind the bovine expression.

'Don't know as there be elly loblolly left for 'ee, Mister Snobby Looutenant!' he taunted.

'Give him his share, blast you, Shem Frost!' growled Moab. 'Poor bastard ain't got all his oars in the water. Any fool can see that!'

Shem's grin was sly. 'Be that so, now?'

Matthew's face didn't alter: he stood stock-still, his bowl held out through the bars. Shem dipped the ladle in his pail and held it over Matthew's bowl. But just as he was about to tip the contents into the bowl, he seemed to fumble with the long handle of the ladle so that the gruel would miss the bowl and fall on the floor. Instinctively, Matthew quickly shifted his bowl so that it neatly caught the pulpy stream.

Damn! Matthew inwardly cursed himself for falling into Shem's little trap.

Shem's leathery face split in a triumphant, toothless grin. 'Well now, Mister Lootenent, seems you'm terrible quick wi' un mits . . . for un addlepate,' he crowed.

Matthew kept his head: he remained utterly implacable, met Shem's watchful gaze vacantly then turned and slouched off to a corner to eat his gruel. Shem gave him a final, jubilant grin and moved to the next cell, satisfied that at last, for just a moment, he had penetrated Matthew's veneer of insanity. Moreover, he'd be willing to wager his most prized possession – his old clay pipe – that Youngmay was behind the planned mutiny. And, if he wasn't very much mistaken, Shem told himself more with interest than concern as he eyed the lines of taut faces, the uprising wouldn't be long in coming.

Matthew and those around him remained tight-lipped until the gruel-pails were empty and the trusties had left the cell block. Even then, they noticed that a guard remained standing just inside the door with his loaded carbine held at the ready. Gilpin was taking no chances.

They spoke in whispers.

Worriedly, Knuckles said, 'Shem's guessed, Lieutenant. Guessed you're shammin'.'

Matthew pulled a rueful face. 'I should have let the filthy stuff fall on the floor. Captivity is dulling my wits.'

Moab shrugged. 'Ain't worth the frettin', Matt. 'Tis surprisin' you got 'way with it for so long!'

It was true. But Matthew still couldn't help feeling angry with himself; his carelessness could have put their plans in jeopardy. Appetite gone, he handed his bowl to the grateful Lordy, saying: 'Here, you eat it. It would stick in my craw.'

Dagge placed a judicious hand briefly on Matthew's shoulder. 'It's going well for us, Matt. Won't be long now,' he breathed.

Matthew nodded. After a while he looked about him. The presence of extra guards was disquieting. How much did Gilpin know? How much had Shem managed to find out and tell him? Goddamn the Judas to hell! Maybe Gilpin had had the sense to send for military reinforcements before the fog got too thick for them to find their way across the moor. Yes, it was just as well that – as Dagge had said – it wouldn't be long. He scanned the faces of the other prisoners as they sat waiting for the signal which would tell them that he and his Special Committee had taken the prison. Here and there he spotted an anxious face or nervous, darting eyes, but the great majority were dark-eyed and calm, anticipation of what was soon to come quenching all other emotion.

The main double doors crashed open to admit half a dozen trusties carrying pails of water. They were followed by two armed guards.

Matthew tensed. The second part of his plan was about to be performed.

Once again, the prisoners surged up to the bars. This time to receive their ration of water: a couple of brackish mouthfuls each from a communal tin mug passed among them. It was the first water they had been given that day and was barely sufficient to moisten their parched mouths.

The trusty dispensing water to Matthew and his cellmates was a committed insurgent and the same man who had cleverly smuggled the stolen pistol from the yard hidden in the pail containing Captain Gilpin's gnawed chicken bones. Now, twisting his body to mask his pail from the guard standing near by, he quickly dipped in a hand and brought out the pistol wrapped in oilcloth. It took no more than a second for him to thrust the dripping parcel through the bars and for Matthew to snatch it and to conceal it among his rags as the jostling bodies closed in about him, hiding him from the view of the guards.

The trusty moved on down the line.

Matthew experienced a surge of exhilaration. The second part of his plan had been successfully completed. Now all that remained was the last desperate, dangerous deed – the actual taking of the prison.

As soon as the trusties and their guards had left the block, leaving just the one guard on sentry duty, the prisoners made a show of settling down on their pallets to sleep.

Matthew quietly unwrapped the flintlock pistol and examined it in the dim light from the single lantern which hung on a nail by the front door. The trusty had wrapped the weapon well, sealing the edges of the oilcloth with melted tallow so that no moisture had seeped in to ruin the powder in the pan. Though Matthew was determined not to fire the pistol, it was none the less comforting to know that he could do so if forced by some unforeseen emergency.

He looked across at Moab, meeting the other man's expectant gaze. He nodded. That was Moab's cue.

Moab opened wide his mouth and let out a blood-chilling wail. Prepared though the other prisoners were, they froze at the suddenness of the terrible cry. The guard, leaning boredly on his carbine, was startled out of his reverie. He grabbed his carbine in both hands, swinging the muzzle in an arc to cover all of the cells.

'What's t . . . to do down there?' he demanded, stuttering in his anxiety.

Moab emitted another agonised cry.

'He's sick, turnkey!' shouted a voice.

'Aye, looks as if poor bastard's done for!' added another.

The guard, still with his carbine at the ready, took a few wary steps along the passage so he could view the sick man who was rolling on the floor clutching his stomach.

'Rat fever!' he announced authoritively. 'Dab he one to stow his luff for he.'

Moab wailed louder and increased his convulsions.

'That ain't rat fever. No sir!' said Dagge emphatically.

Curiosity got the better of the guard. He swung his carbine on his shoulder and came right up to the bars, peering in at Moab's writhing form. 'What's up wi' he, then?' he demanded.

The prisoners had put on a show of grumbling, as though annoyed at being disturbed, Now they fell silent, waiting for Dagge to deliver his all-important line. Dagge took his time, pausing for effect.

'Looks to me . . . as if he's got the Deuce in him,' he declared dramatically.

The prisoners gasped on cue.

The guard, a deeply superstitious Devon man, almost dropped his carbine as he recoiled visibly and fumbled to cross himself. 'Best I fetch priest dreckly,' he said, edging away.

Dagge stopped him going, saying sharply: 'Too late for priests. Lordy, here, is an injun mystic . . . he knows what to do.'

Lordy stepped forward and began to pass his big brown hands over Moab's jerking form, at the same time uttering an eerie chant. After a few moments, Moab gave one huge, spasmodic twist and lay absolutely still, eyes tight shut, holding his breath.

'Is he dead?' asked the guard.

No one answered. They stood in hushed groups, willing him to take the bait. Moab was turning scarlet with the effort of holding his breath. The guard seemed uncertain what to do. He gestured with his carbine. 'Back 'gin wall an' look sharp.'

They obeyed. All except Matthew who remained crouching dazedly in his corner. The guard ignored him, more concerned with Moab than some harmless half-wit. He reached for the keys hanging from his wide leather belt. 'Reckon I better take look at un . . .'

Watching them warily, he placed his carbine in the crook of his arm and unlocked the cell. He stepped inside and advanced cautiously towards Moab's prone figure. He peered into the strained, scarlet face. 'Well, cheeks look proper ruddy! He don't *look* dead . . .' He stopped dead as a cold steel muzzle was pressed beneath his jaw.

'Keep it buttoned, turnkey, and maybe . . . *just maybe* . . . you won't look dead either,' Matthew murmured in his ear.

Kezzy rode a little ahead of the dragoon captain. Mostly she let Rats pick his own footing, guiding him only when they came to a crossing of the track, or slowing him so the column could keep up if the track wound perilously down a stony gully, difficult to traverse in the fog save for the moorland-bred. Few words passed between guide and officer. Once, when they paused at a brook to rest the horses for a while, his anxiety rose to the fore and he stood looking desperately about him, trying to penetrate the dense, white curtain.

'Are you sure we're right for Princeton?' he asked, voice concerned. 'This track doesn't look like Plymouth road.'

'That's because it isn't the Plymouth road,' Kezzy told him quietly. 'We're crossing the moor direct.'

He grunted. Then said: 'Are you sure we aren't lost?'

'Quite sure.'

He had no choice but to trust her.

Dawn brought a soft wind from the south-west to clear away the fog and to speed progress. They skirted the mires below Fox Tor and then breasted the hump to the ancient stone Nun's Cross where the captain called a halt. Below them, in a shallow valley not far off, lay the circular site of the prison with its high surrounding wall. The captain took out his eyeglass and trained it on the bleak grey buildings. Kezzy's sharp eyes watched his face, noting the tightening of his cheek muscles and the hardening of his mouth.

He uttered a sharp expletive, not caring that she was there to hear. 'They've taken the prison, the Yankee scurfs! They're flying the American flag! We're too late!'

Wild hope leapt to life within Kezzy.

'Does that mean they've escaped?' she asked eagerly.

Without lowering his glass, he said scornfully: 'Think you they'd linger longer than it took to open gate? They'll be scattered all ways across Dartmoor by now and take the very devil to round up.'

Matthew was free! Kezzy's heart seemed to sing it.

The captain swept the prison with his glass for a few moments longer but was too far away to make out much more than the grey walls and that cursed Yankee flag. He snapped shut his glass angrily and stowed it away. 'You can go,' he dismissed Kezzy curtly. He lifted a gauntleted hand, commanding the column to follow him, and set off down the slope at a gallop.

Kezzy watched them go, tempted to follow and discover for herself what had occurred during the night, but the thought of her grandfather and the long ride home stopped her.

And then, of course, there was Matthew.

Her eyes shone with the pleasure she felt because he was free. He was free. Her strange power told her that. She sensed him somewhere out on the fern and heather-covered moor, gazing upon the wild peaks upon which the blue sky rested, and she filled her lungs with the same crisp morning air as he was breathing and felt close to him. *Soon, very soon, those same strange powers told her, they would be together . . .*

Chapter Twenty-Nine

On the way home, Kezzy stopped to rest for a while at Crazywell Pool. She loosed Rats so he could wade knee-deep and drink the cold, clear water. She drank some herself and then spread her oilskin on the chill, damp ground and sat with her back against a rock. There was no real warmth as yet in the spring sunshine but it reflected prettily on the water turning the wind-churned ripples to gold and silver.

Rats left the pool, glistening droplets falling from his shaggy coat, and ambled over to a patch of green to graze. Kezzy was aware of a gnawing hunger in her own belly and wished she'd thought to take a mossle bag. The dragoons had rations with them and had eaten on the move. She had been given a strip of tough dried beef and a hard biscuit and had had trouble getting them down. A dragoon's life was terribly hard, no doubt about that. As hard as a sailor's? She sat and pondered upon that for a while. Dragoons were on land so could therefore seek occasional comforts when not on duty but a sailor was away at sea, often for two or three years at a time, with no comforts save his hammock and a daily ration of grog. No, a sailor's life was much, much harder than a dragoon's, she decided. Yet, however hard it was, Matthew and his shipmates would have preferred it to being prisoners-of-war. She could only guess at the terrible conditions they must have endured – fever, scurvy, starvation, floggings – and which had led to rebellion.

Kezzy was half dozing. Suddenly she was awake, listening intently, uncertain what had roused her to consciousness. She looked towards Rats. The colt had stopped grazing and was standing with his ears twitching, as though he too sensed something or somebody close by.

Probably just a toad or a grass snake among the rushes, Kezzy told herself, eyeing the spiky tussocks of bur-reed and pond-sedge. Then she heard it again. A groan. Faint but unmistakable. Rats heard it at the same time and whinnied gently, pawing the ground to tell her. Warily, Kezzy got up and approached the water's edge, eyes probing the rushes. A glint of gold caught her eye. She parted a tangled mass of reeds to see what it was and, startled, found herself gazing down at the figure of a man. Save that he had groaned, she would have been sure that he was dead, so drained of blood was his face. He wore ragged prison garb, streaked with blood, and the lower half of his ashen face was covered with fine, blond bristles. But it was his hair – bright golden among the dark green reeds – that caught and held her attention. Heart thudding, she knelt down beside the unconscious man.

Matthew.

Kezzy mouthed his name, or thought she did. His eyelids flickered and his eyes opened. Vivid blue, just as she'd remembered in a thousand dreams. Tentatively, she put out a hand and touched his cheek as if to convince herself that he was, indeed, real and not just another half-waking dawn image. Matthew gazed up at her dazedly, without recognition. But that was hardly surprising since on the occasion of their first meeting she had been wearing breeches and a woollen hat to hide her hair. Now she wore an old dimity gown and her hair fell in a silken stream to her shoulders. Yet, as she ran her fingers gently over the stubbly growth on his face, he smiled and tried to say something. The smile quickly faded and his whole body tensed as if he was suddenly wracked with pain, a shadow passed over his features and beads of perspiration appeared on his brow. His eyes closed and he seemed to slip into oblivion once again.

Blood was seeping through his shirt in a dark, spreading patch over the right side and blood trickled down his arm and through his fingers. Carefully, Kezzy pushed his shirt aside to examine the wound. A slug had entered the fleshy part of his shoulder and was, by the look of it, still embedded in his shoulder between breast and collarbone. She had nothing, no knife or other instrument, with which to dig it out while he was mercifully unconscious. All she could do was to wad her apron and tie it tightly over the wound to stem the flow of blood until, somehow, she got him back to Eaglestone.

She fetched Rats.

'Kneel, Rats! Kneel! Kneel!'

It took the colt a few moments to get the idea. Then, amenably, he went down on his front knees so that his solid, round belly touched the ground. Kezzy got hold of Matthew beneath the armpits and pulled him out of the reeds. She was surprised how light he was; then ceased to be so when her hands felt his ribs protruding through his skin. Half hauling, half carrying Matthew, she managed to get him astride Rats and over the colt's shaggy mane. She brought his arms around Rats's neck and secured his wrists with her kerchief to keep him from falling off.

Kezzy was well used to walking and her long legs easily kept up with Rats's brisk, ungainly pace. Every so often she would stop to look at Matthew's wound. It had stopped bleeding, which was something, but the blood had dried so that the wadded apron was stuck to his shoulder and breast. She didn't touch it for fear of starting the bleeding again. He was still unconscious. Sweat ran down his face and soaked his shirt. He was already in the grip of fever. She knew they must keep moving if his life was to be saved.

Kezzy followed the same little-known goat track she'd used the night before to lead the dragoons across the moor. It twisted and turned in the general direction of Eaglestone, skirting the stark, smoke-belching chimneys of Captain de Raddon's Wheal Fortune and Wheal George and dipping down to the head of Fory Brook nestling in a small lush, wooded valley. Rats strained towards the babbling waters so she released his bridle that he could lower his head to drink. She didn't dare relieve him of his insentient burden in case she couldn't get Matthew back up upon the animal's back again. But she untied Matthew's hands and soaked her kerchief to swab his pale, sweating face.

As she was doing so, Kezzy heard musket fire. A short volley. She strained her ears, heard another volley. Dragoons! It had to be, probably searching for escaped prisoners and, by the sound of it, with some success, God save the poor souls. She tugged Rats's head up and set off again through the copse, alert for danger. Near the end of the trees, Rats's ears twitched. Kezzy stopped, looking about her and listening. She could hear the clatter of hoofbeats and, peering ahead, saw six dragoons approaching the wood across the heathland. Two of them had a brace of rabbits apiece tied to their pommels. She thought they were from the troop she'd led up the moor but couldn't be sure. Obviously, they intended to build a wood fire and cook themselves a meal.

There was no time to escape. The dragoons would be upon them within minutes. Kezzy didn't hesitate. Quickly, she led Rats behind a stunted, curling oak set amid a patch of brambles and looped the reins loosely over a low branch. It wasn't good cover but the best the small copse could offer.

'Shhhh!' she hissed commandingly in Rats's ear, at the same time squeezing his muzzle gently shut in the hope that he would understand and not give himself away by whinnying. Then, snatching up a few sticks as she went, she ran to the edge of the trees and emerged to confront the dragoons. They were about fifty yards away and were clearly startled by her sudden appearance, pulling on the reins, so that their horses reared and skittered, and automatically reaching for the carbines strung across their backs. Kezzy stopped dead, eyes wide, feigning similar surprise on seeing them there. Then it registered with them that this wasn't one of the American escapees but a peasant girl and a comely one at that.

'Here's sport, boys! Better'n huntin' Jack Rabbit!' exclaimed one, kicking his heels into his horse's flanks so it surged towards her.

She saw the gleam in his eye, heard the note of menace in the laughter of his comrades as they moved to circle her like hounds surrounding a cornered deer. Her eyes darted this way and that as she backed away from the instigator, a big, ruddy-faced corporal. At all costs she must lead them away from the thicket and Matthew. The corporal leaned in the saddle and made a lunge for her, grasping her by the shoulder with fingers that dug painfully into her flesh so that she gasped and the colour drained from her face.

'What ho, bal med'n! Remember us then do 'ee?' asked the corporal leering down at her. His bulging eyes were red-rimmed and his cheeks above his gingery beard were a net of tiny red and blue veins. ' 'Cause us remember 'ee, right 'nough . . . on count ye has proper pair o' tits on 'ee!'

Pain turned to anger and Kezzy's clawed hand flew at his face, raking the skin so that red, welling grooves opened the flesh of one florid cheek. This time it was he who winced and gasped with pain. His clasping fingers opened involuntarily and, seizing her chance, Kezzy was off and running, ducking between the horses and heading for a substantial covert of prickly yellow gorse something like a hundred yards away. If she could reach the gorse bushes and disappear in among the narrow channels between them she would stand a chance of escaping her tormentors since their horses couldn't follow without being torn to shreds and she could easily outrun the men on foot, hampered as they were by riding boots and heavy uniforms.

Her attempt to escape proved in vain. Another of them wheeled his mount and charged after her, leaning from the saddle to scoop her up with an arm around her waist.

'Come 'ere, ye young limb!' he laughed. 'An' show us un tits!'

Frenziedly, she fought him, kicking and twisting and clawing at him with her nails, all the while hissing and spitting vile curses at him, learnt, much to Elyas's disapproval, from a band of itinerate bal maidens who'd once stopped a while at Eagle Brook – curses the like of which the dragoons hadn't heard even from the painted lips of the sailors' doxies down in Plymouth. So taken aback was the trooper who held her, he was momentarily rendered immobile so that her nails found another mark, much to the raucous delight of the remaining and so far unscarred four troopers, and she raked his cheek from eye to jaw.

'Why ye . . .!' he grunted as the stinging pain registered.

'A med'n wi' spirit is worth the takin', I reckon!' declared another, edging his horse alongside her so he could reach over and grab the shoulder of her dress. Deliberately, he wrenched the faded, oft-washed cotton so that, with a soft crack of breaking stitches, it tore to the waist, baring one of her full, round, copper-tipped breasts.

The dragoons crowed lewdly.

Kezzy redoubled her efforts to free herself from the encircling arm of the man who held her off the ground, clasped uncomfortably to his thick body. He had managed to pinion her wrists with his free hand, but when he was unwise enough to try and kiss her, she sank her teeth in his lower lip so that blood spurted down his tunic. At the same time one of her flailing shoes dug his horse, startling it so that it reared, tossing them both on the ground. The dragoon fell with a thud which temporarily winded him. Kezzy, however, was physically lighter and landed in the cushioning heather without hurting herself. Instantly, she was up and running. By chance, the dragoon's skittering horse had carried her nearer to the gorse-thicket so she'd less than a hundred yards to cover. And cover them she did, leaping and bounding over the ground as sure-footedly as a moorland colt. The unseated dragoon clambered to his feet and remounted to join the rest as they streamed in pursuit of her, gleefully holloing at the tops of their voices like huntsmen after the kill. And, as cunningly as any fox, instead of taking the most direct route to her covert so that they would easily ride her down, Kezzy dodged first this way and then that, diving between jagged boulders which they were forced to ride around.

Lungs bursting, blood pounding in her ears, she reached cover just yards ahead of them and, heedless of the prickles tearing her skin and ripping the rest of her tattered dress from her torso, she threw herself into the nearest, narrowest gorse-channel and forced her way deep into the covert where they couldn't reach her. She collapsed, panting and gasping to her knees. She paused only for a moment to catch her breath, then began to crawl deeper in among the bushes so that they would lose track of her completely.

Presently, she heard one of the dragoons trying to force his way in among the gorse after her. She rolled herself into a ball and held her breath. She heard him cursing as the brush caught at his uniform and after a while he gave up rather than condemn himself to hours picking thorns out of the serge.

The corporal's voice rang out, deploying his men.

'You an' you . . . t'other side. You an' you, take the flanks. I'll soon flush young longlegs out o' her burrow!'

Kezzy heard the four gallop off to take up their positions. She strained her ears, wondering what the corporal intended. She could make out the creak of leather as he dismounted and the chink of his pistol or sword as he approached the edge of the thicket.

He called out to her: 'Do 'ee hear me, med'n?'

She didn't answer.

'Best for ye if'n ye comes out o'there. We'm only wantin' t'jaw 'while withee while we'm restin horses,' he told her persuasively. 'Mebbe even find ye a silver sixpence to buy pretty ribbons wi'. Eh? So what do ye say to that then, eh?'

Kezzy kept absolutely still and breathed shallowly, terrified that he might locate her hiding place and plunge in after her and drag her out. Lust, she knew, did strange and terrible things to men, particularly, so she'd heard said, to dragoons. Indeed, two maids from Raleigh had been found once hung upsidedown on the north fence, speared by their petticoats and draws, whereupon they'd claimed that dragoons had been responsible for their predicament. On the way to Princeton, Kezzy had sensed through the shifting fog the troopers' hot eyes fixed to her back. Purposefully, she'd ridden well ahead of them and hadn't turned around so as to avoid their lascivious grins. Had it not been for the captain, who was more interested in reaching the prison before the uprising, she wouldn't have trusted them, any more than she trusted them now, or believed the corporal when he said that they only meant to while away the time 'jawing' with her.

A trooper had remained with the corporal. Now she heard his slightly anxious voice ask: 'What are ye intendin', corp?'

The corporal didn't answer other than to give a low, unpleasant chuckle. Then her stomach gave a sickening lurch as new sounds reached her ears: the clink of flint and tinder followed by the crackle of flaming furze.

The corporal called to her again.

'Come on out o' there, girl, or I'll burn ye out!'

Evidently, the trooper with him wasn't quite so cold-blooded, or, perhaps, so determined to satisfy his lust, for he said: 'Her's but a med'n, corp . . . mebbe us should leave she be . . .'

'Did her scratch *thy* face, boy?' demanded the corporal surlily.

'Nay, corp.'

'Then keep it buttoned, boy. Her don't claw Corporal Adams wi'out payin' for it.' He gave a sneering chuckle. 'An' since her give un guinea to her grandpappy for safe keepin', her'll just have to pay in kind, won't her?'

The flaming furze torch went sailing through the air to land a few feet inside the thicket. He'd aimed it at roughly the place where he'd last seen Kezzy but as she'd crawled a few yards since then it fell well clear of her. The gorse was green so it didn't immediately catch alight as the corporal intended. He scrubbed up more tussocks of old, dried furze, lit them, and tossed them into the thicket in roughly the same direction to help the fire get going.

A flock of stonechats rose flapping.

'What if fire do spread, corp?' asked the trooper worriedly.

' 'T'wont. Too green. But good smeech an' smoke'll flush she out.'

Near them, a rabbit shot from the gorse, scut bobbing, also smoked out. The corporal pointed at it delightedly. 'See . . . all we has to do is wait for young longlegs to show.'

The smoke reached Kezzy, stinging her eyes and making her choke. She tried to escape it by crawling yet deeper into the thicket but came up against a tangled wall of prickles. She turned down another gorse-tunnel.

'I can hear summat, corp!' shouted one of the flankers hearing rustling. But it turned out to be another rabbit, bobbing out to disappear among the heather.

The smoke was biting into Kezzy's lungs now and she couldn't keep from coughing.

'Harken to she coughin'! Over there . . .!' yelled the other flanker triumphantly, pointing with his carbine.

'Her's movin' 'cross to ye, boys! Keep thy eyes skinned!' ordered the corporal of the two watching the far side of the thicket. He called out to Kezzy again, taunting her. 'Give up, girl. You'm as good as on thy back wi' they long legs o' yourn spread for us.'

For good measure, he sent another half dozen or so burning tussocks sailing into the thicket although a fair few bushes were now smouldering. The thicket trapped the smoke so that just a few pale-grey spirals escaped to be scattered by the breeze.

There was nowhere Kezzy could crawl to escape the suffocating smoke. Heaving for breath, she fell prostrate on her face in the soft, moist earth. Oblivion wasn't far away. As she collapsed prone a sharp pain bit into her hip and percolated her dulling consciousness. She knew instantly what had caused the bruising pain. Rolling on to her side she groped blindly in her pocket for the hard, smooth, slightly oval-shaped Eaglestone she always carried. As her fingers closed around it, an image of her grandfather flashed before her raw eyes. She heard his voice, an echo of long ago when he'd instructed her and Jamie, when they were very young, what to do if fire broke out in the mine. Instinctively, she followed his instructions. *Cover thy head wi' summat . . . skirt or shirt. Crawl on thy belly like un snake. Keep thy snout right to the ground . . . not so much smoke there . . .*

The dragoons' voices gave her a good idea of where they were. Her skirt over her head to protect her, she began to slither in a westerly direction where the smoke seemed thickest and they'd least expect her to break cover. The gorse-channel began to narrow and she prayed desperately that it wouldn't go 'horse' on her so she'd have to turn back and try another direction. The prickles tore at her already lacerated skin and all but ripped her head-covering to shreds but she continued to worm her way between the bushes until, abruptly, there was no more gorse.

Luckily, the dragoon didn't see Kezzy's head suddenly appear. She stole a look at him and ducked out of sight again. He didn't see her until she suddenly rose and stumbled out into the open. His jaw dropped and he could only sit blinking at her as though transfixed, giving her precious seconds in which to recover herself sufficiently to bound away across the moor – this time heading for a crumbling mine chimney. There would be a disused shaft there; and a labyrinth of tunnels in which she would be at home in the pitch-black and they would be at a disadvantage.

By the time the dragoon collected his wits and shouted to alert the others, Kezzy was a good distance away, leaping the stones scattered among the heather like a startled deer.

'There her goes. Don't let she gerraway!' shouted the corporal, furious at her outwitting him.

But the lumps of granite hidden in the furze were a serious hazard: they didn't dare risk their horses falling and maybe breaking a leg so they had to pick their way carefully over the ground. Luckily, that enabled Kezzy to put an even greater distance herself and her pursuers.

'We'll have she yet, boys!' sang out the corporal determinedly. 'I tell 'ee, her'll be proper bandy time I done with she!'

Kezzy didn't dare look over her shoulder to see what was happening. She could tell from the clipping hooves that they had reached clearer ground and were beginning to gain on her. Her heart was thumping like a stamp-engine and her lungs felt as though they would burst at any moment, yet from somewhere she found a hidden reserve of energy and surged forward towards the cluster of ruined mine buildings and the mossy burrows of dumped rubble among which she could hide if the shaft was sealed.

So intent was Kezzy on reaching the sanctuary of the old mine it was a few seconds before her bemuddled brain told her that the thundering hooves were no longer pursuing her. She could still make out the shouts of the men though strangely muffled now, as if she was outstripping them. Safety was tantalisingly close but she stopped dead with the sudden realisation that the distant commotion she was hearing wasn't born of revelry. The shouts she could hear were those of terror-stricken men, intermingled with the frenzied whinnying of fear-maddened horses.

Kezzy spun around.

God in Heaven!

Oblivious of her near-naked torso, she began running back to where the six horses and their riders were floundering in a great expanse of mire.

The horses were sinking fast, rolling their eyes and emitting pitiful screams as they struggled frantically to free themselves without success. Of their six riders, four, including the corporal, had the sense to remain mounted, which meant that although the poor brutes sank faster beneath the weight, the dragoons at least gained precious moments during which they could seek some means of escape. Two, however, had dismounted in panic as soon as the solid ground had gone, thinking that they could wade to safety, only to sink instantly up to their waists. They were threshing about in a futile manner shouting for help in high, fear-filled voices.

Nearing them, Kezzy's ears were filled with noise. The struggle of doomed men and horses was terrible in its desperate intensity. There was nothing she could do to help the two: even as she approached, the heaviest of them went under, to be followed quickly by the other man who emitted one last, blood-chilling roar before his mouth filled with mud and he was drawn beneath the surface. One of the riderless horses had gone; the head of the second one, eyes baleful, protruded above the tremulous green mire. Then it, too, was gone. One by one the remaining four horses slipped under, dragging with them their petrified riders so that the mud began to seep over their high boots and stain their doeskin breeches.

'Help, for the love of God!' bellowed the corporal, his eyes wild.

Recollection was born of grim need and once again Elyas's sage words came to Kezzy, telling her what was to be done if they stood a chance of being saved. It was agony to run and shout at the same time but somehow she managed to call to them.

'Stand on the saddles. Throw off anything heavy.'

They rallied to her commanding voice, clambered to their feet and unbuckled their cross-belts and swords, tossing them and their plumed helmets aside. Reaching the mire, Kezzy saw that a good twenty yards separated her from them.

'Save us, missy, save us!' pleaded one of the dragoons plaintively. He was no more than eighteen or nineteen. His face was ashen and beaded with sweat and he was trembling violently, as though he'd a fever.

Kezzy's eyes were scanning the few clumps of rushes which dotted the surface of the mire, searching for a route by which she might reach them. She took a chance and leapt to the nearest clump, prepared to leap back again if it proved too tremulous to take her weight. It held. She measured the distance to the next foothold, coiling herself ready to spring. Four more such leaps took her to within a few feet of them. Tantalisingly close yet still too far away to grab the hands they were desperately stretching towards her.

'Throw me your belts,' she shouted, brain racing.

They did so. She seized the portly corporal's, which was some inches longer than those belonging to the thinner men.

'You must lay prone on the mud . . . flat as you can,' she called. 'Hurry, or you'll be stagged too deep to free yourselves.'

Even using their poor submerged beasts for leverage and leaving their boots stuck in the mud, the dragoons found it virtually impossible to lift themselves clear and lay prone as she suggested. One just gave up trying to save himself; soon the mud was up to his shoulders and creeping steadily towards his chin. There was a strange, almost faraway look in his eyes as he waited for the mire to take him.

'The long sleep is a-comin', boys,' he said dreamily, 'the long, bless'd sleep . . .' Softly, he began to pray.

'Then sleep, damn you! I ain't done yet!' snapped the corporal. With a massive effort he managed to lever himself above the mud so that momentarily he appeared to hang in the air before pitching forward across the mire on his face. With his weight evenly distributed, he hardly dented the surface.

'Now work your way towards me,' shouted Kezzy,' like rowing a boat.'

Heartened by her proximity and the corporal's achievement, the two troopers made one last tremendous effort to lift themselves clear of the mire as he had done. One succeeded. One, the younger dragoon who earlier had pleaded with Kezzy to save them, was stuck fast. He began to weep. The soft praying of the fourth dragoon suddenly ceased as he disappeared below the mud with a soft, sucking sound.

The corporal wasn't making much headway paddling towards Kezzy. The remaining trooper, slighter bodied, managed to get within a belt-length of her; she threw the end of the corporal's belt towards him, keeping hold of the buckle with one hand and gripping the rushes with the other to steady herself. Fumbling, he managed to get a grip on it. Slowly, pulling with all her might, Kezzy began to inch him towards her. But, alas, his legs were beginning to sink, dragging him down; he kicked and threshed with all his failing strength but it was hopeless. The belt slipped from his clawing fingers. The last sight Kezzy had of him was his stricken face and staring eyes vanishing beneath the mud.

Only the corporal was left. Although he was the heaviest of the six, his superior strength gave him the advantage. Somehow, whenever the matted surface began to give way under his prone body, he managed to find it in him to almost lift himself clear and belly flop to another, more stable position.

He stretched out an imploring hand towards Kezzy.

'Throw me yon belt, missy . . . gimme chance . . . I didn't mean ye no harm, honest. I were just funnin' . . .!'

The surging strife which had linked her with those who so recently had been her tormentors had temporarily driven all memory of their cruel pursuit of her from Kezzy's brain; even the corporal was no more to her than a hapless man stagged in the mire and doomed to die unless by some miracle she managed to pull him free.

The belt went flying through the air. Her aim was good: it landed within reach of his flexing fingers. And so the battle for his life began in earnest, the grim silence broken only by their gasping and panting as he fought to keep himself from sinking and she hauled on the belt until her torn dress was soaked with sweat from her exertions. Both her hands were bleeding; one cut by the metal buckle, the other by the sharp, spiky rushes as she strove to drag him towards her. Inch by inch, they made a little headway, but her strength was failing and she was having difficulty hanging on to both rushes and belt. And all the while, the corporal was slipping deeper and deeper into the mire. His fingers grew slippery with sweat and slush and he lost his grip on the belt and could not reach it again, however hard he tried.

'Try . . . try!' Kezzy urged him frantically, knowing in her heart that it was hopeless. The battle was lost.

'Good-bye, missy . . . good-bye and God bless ye for tryin'. 'Tis better un we deserved.'

Once again, leaning over the mire at a precarious angle, she threw the belt to him. 'Try, for God's sake, try and reach it!'

He tried, even managed to touch it with his fingertips, but couldn't get a grip on it. Even had he been able to do so, they both knew that it was impossible for her to pull him free now that only his head and one shoulder and arm showed above the surface.

'Mebbe 'tis God's will, missy,' he told Kezzy mournfully. 'Punishment for houndin' ye like we did. Most likely'd sendin' us all to burn in Hell for our sins.'

Tears caught in Kezzy's throat. Surely God would be merciful?

'I forgive you . . . absolutely,' she said in an agonised voice.

'God bless ye for that, missy. Tell 'em that I died brave. Tell 'em . . .'

He began to choke as the mud filled his mouth and nose so she couldn't make out his final few words. Then the ooze closed over his head so that only his one, clawing hand remained sticking out. Then it, too, sank soundlessly from view.

Kezzy stood as if paralysed. Hardly able to believe that the mossy green expanse before her had swallowed six men and their horses virtually without trace. Even their swords and helmets and tunics had vanished. Only a few disturbed surface patches and four belts remained to show that they had ever existed. Kezzy shivered as though a cold wind had caught her. She shook herself. She must go. To Matthew, pray God he was still alive! She bounded from tussock to tussock back across the swamp. Paused for a few seconds at the edge of the mire to mutter a quick prayer for the souls of the lost.

'Almighty God, grant them forgiveness and everlasting life, Amen.'

Matthew was as she'd left him, and mercifully the bleeding appeared to have stopped. She unrolled her oilskin and put it on over her torn dress. Then, taking Rats's bridle, she set off for home.

Chapter Thirty

When Kezzy arrived home with Matthew, it was with a sense of relief that she discovered Elyas hadn't, in her absence, had to resort to the laudanum bottle. Consequently, he was in one of his more lucid frames of mind and able to assist her to remove the slug from the wounded man.

'Best he has proper doctor,' says Elyas doubtfully, peering beneath the bloodied apron at Matthew's shattered shoulder.

'By the time I fetched a doctor it would be too late.'

Elyas lifted one of Matthew's eyelids with his thumb and viewed the eye beneath it. 'Ay, bain't much life left in he. Best get move on . . . if'n he has any chance at all.'

Neither of them had ever removed a slug before.

'Saw my pa take ball out o' huntin' dawg once,' said Elyas. 'Can't be much different. We'll need cauldron, hot water an' rags an' thy strongest lye soap to wash wound. An' a knife.'

Kezzy hurried to collect the necessary items. Elyas took the knife and pushed it into the fire where the peat glowed reddest. Meanwhile, Kezzy soaked Matthew's shirt with warm water to loosen the dried blood so she could strip it off him. She winced when she saw the criss-cross of scars on his back.

Elyas eyed them with distaste. 'Been flogged. For tryin' to 'scape most likely'd. Don't hold wi' floggin' . . . men nor beasts.'

'He must have been near enough torn to the bone,' said Kezzy angrily. 'How could they be so inhuman? Treating helpless, starving men like that?'

Without his shirt, Matthew's ribs could easily be counted.

' 'Twere lucky for he you'm come 'long afore soljurs. If'n they'd catched he this'n time, they'd have flogged he then hung he, most likely'd.'

Kezzy shivered. How close the dragoons had come to recapturing him! And to ravishing her! Her concern for Matthew had pushed the ghastly memory of all that had occurred at Crazywell Pool to the back of her mind. Now, with a rush, she heard again the terrified screams of men and horses, saw them floundering in the mud, wild-eyed with the knowledge that they were doomed to drown in the shifting, brown ooze. She began to shake. So much so, that her hands could hardly ladle hot water from the cauldron into a bowl. Elyas saw. He peered into her face, saw that it had blanched and was shiny with sweat.

'What ails ye, chield?' he asked her, concerned. 'Not sicky 'cause o' yon slug-hole?'

She shook her head. Her voice shook. 'I'm . . . all right . . .'

He grunted disbelievingly. Something had occurred to bring about this belated attack of the cold sweats. 'Were ye there when yon Yankee boy were shot?' he probed.

'No. I told you . . . I found him in the rushes by Crazywell.'

He grunted again. She'd spoken sharply. Unusual for her.

And immediately she was contrite: 'I'm sorry, Gramps . . . I . . .' She paused.

'Spit it out, chield,' he invited.

Suddenly, she put down the bowl, splashing water on the hot slab so that it sizzled, and ran to where Elyas sat in his chimney corner. She dropped to her knees, her head buried in his long woollen jersey, and began to sob, quivering from head to foot. He said nothing, just stroked the glossy raven head, waiting for the storm of tears to abate. He hadn't long to wait. After a few moments, she looked up at him through her tears.

'They went in the swamp, Gramps. It was . . . *horrible*,' she gulped.

'They?'

'Dragoons. Six of them . . .'

Matthew let out a gentle moan. Kezzy promptly forgot her own distress and, rising quickly, went to him. Kneeling down beside his still figure, she whispered his name. 'Matthew.'

But there was no movement in the eyes behind the closed lids.

Looking up, Kezzy saw Elyas was watching her, an unspoken question in his pale, watery eyes. There was nothing she could do for Matthew until the knife was red-hot, so she took a stool across to Elyas and sat at his knees, her hands clasped comfortingly in his as she told him all that had happened. How she had first met the young American by Crazywell Pool and heard him referred to as Matt – which surely meant his proper name was Matthew? How she had found him, all this time later, hidden in the rushes by the same pool, and led the dragoons away from him, to their deaths, as it transpired, in a 'Dartmoor Stable' – so-called because many a pony had found such a resting place.

'I tried to save them, Gramps. I did every thing you said . . .'

He shook his head gravely. ' 'Twere will o' God, chield. No better'n they deserved.'

'That's what the corporal said, near enough, before . . . before . . .' her voice caught.

He continued to stroke her head, saying soothingly, 'Don't 'ee fret, m'dear. 'Twere they fault, an' they knowed it. Damned fools!' He was silent for a moment. It was so unlike her, he mused, to take risks: she was too aware of her position as bread-earner. His eyes went to Matthew as, slowly, he said: 'What I don't understand . . . is why ye did what ye did. For boy who be little more'n stranger.'

Colour mounted in Kezzy's cheeks.

'He wasn't a stranger. Leastways, it didn't seem as though he was. You see, after that first time . . . at Crazywell . . . he was so often in my thoughts, I . . . Oh Gramp, I do so love him!'

Elyas gave a wheezing chuckle and pinched her flushed cheek.

'Sort o' crept up on 'ee unawares, this love business, eh? Well, didn't I always say as how ye'd know right boy for 'ee when he happened 'long?'

Kezzy turned her head and gazed at the pale, still figure on the pallet before the fire. 'Do you think he's the right boy, Gramps?' she breathed, hardly able to believe the feeling of joy she felt just having Matthew beneath the same roof. 'Do you, Gramps? Do you?'

He patted her shoulder. 'Only time can say, chield. Now . . . I reckons that knife be ready . . .'

For the next three days and nights, Kezzy sat with Matthew in the fireglow as his fever raged. And during that time, a gale swooped and roared across Dartmoor, shrieking in the thatch and hammering at the windows and doors and shaking all of Eaglestone to dizziness.

The tempest was, however, a blessing since, along with accompanying torrential rain, it forced the riding officers and militia to temporarily abandon their search for the escaped prisoners. And that meant that the Hammetts could safely nurse Matthew in the cottage rather than hide him in a cold, damp tunnel in the mine.

She occasionally dozed in a chair for a short while, but only when she was too exhausted to keep her eyes open. And now and then she'd let Elyas watch over the unconscious man while she prepared food or another poultice of stewed groundsel and marshmallow leaves to apply to the solid, purpled flesh around the wound.

Elyas had dug a musket-ball from Matthew's shoulder with the white-hot knife-blade, and in doing so, discovered that the ball had entered through the back of the shoulder.

'Hard to b'lieve it, chield,' he'd said, shocked by his discovery, 'but yon Yankee were shot in back.'

'How *could* they, Gramps?' Her voice was bitter. 'The war's over.'

But Elyas could only shake his head as he gazed at the musket-ball rolling in his calloused palm, as appalled as Kezzy that any man could shoot in the back, in the name of duty, another who was unarmed. 'If'n Yankee do live, I'll give un this ball . . . do have his'n name on it for sure.'

As she sat watching over Matthew, Kezzy prayed fervently he would live to claim it.

He would often moan but without ever wakening or moving. With Elyas's help, Kezzy eased off the rest of his rags and bathed him with warm soapy water. Only then was the true extent of his bruises and lacerations and scars revealed and it was as much as she could do to keep from weeping, knowing that he must have suffered almost beyond belief.

'Ay, 'tis a wisht poor thing, treatin' he like that,' declared Elyas, seeing how affected she was. 'But worse to shoot he in back, an' he entitled to be free man. Now *that*, to *my* way o' thinkin' be little short o' 'tempted murder. An' if'n prison cap'n did give order to fire . . . well, then he should be strung up for it!'

On the fourth day the storm began to abate. Grote rode up the moor to

Eaglestone. Kezzy was careful not to let him in the cottage, instead she walked over to the brook with him and stood talking there while he watered his horse.

'Best ye don't deliver any tubs for a few days,' Grote had come to tell her. 'Moors is runnin' 'live wi' dragoons lookin' for 'scaped Yankees.'

'Oh.' She longed to pump him, to discover what he knew of the break-out, but didn't care for fear of appearing too interested. Grote wasn't as slow-witted, Kezzy had discovered, as the impression he gave.

'Ay,' he went on in his dour fashion, 'there was trouble upalong Princeton four, five days back. Nine Yankees killed, fifty or more wounded. 'Bout hundred 'scaped. Bain't seen any Yankees, have 'ee?'

'No.'

He looked across to Eaglestone, surveying the barn and blowing-house. 'Have ye searched out-houses 'case Yankee snuck in?'

'There's nobody hiding here, Master Grote. Wart wouldn't have it.'

He grunted disappointedly. 'Prison authorities be offerin' reward for recaptured Yankees. Five pounds a head . . . fifty pounds for the ring-leader.' He reached inside his leather jerkin and produced a crumpled advertisment torn from the *Western Daily Mercury*. 'Ye can read, can't 'ee?'

She took it from him and looked at it.

He watched her face with a slight sense of grievance because this slip of a maid could read the printed words and he couldn't. 'It do say there's a reward, don't it?' he asked gruffly. 'Cap'n did say so.'

Kezzy was silent. She had tensed but Grote didn't notice. Nor did he see that her eyes, lowered over the torn piece of newspaper, were gazing in wonder at what they saw there.

ESCAPED PRISONERS

Whereas it has been humbly presented to the King, on the 16th Day of April instant, a Mutiny occurred at Princeton Prison whereupon 93 American Prisoners-of-War did successfully make good their escape.

His Majesty, for the better apprehending and bringing to Justice the Prisoners concerned in the said Mutiny, is hereby pleased to promise his most gracious Pardon to any Persons succouring any of the Fugitives, and to pay a reward of FIVE POUNDS for each Prisoner recaptured and returned to the Prison Authorities.

As a further encouragement, His Majesty does hereby promise a reward of FIFTY POUNDS to any Person or Persons who apprehend and return to the Prison Authorities the leader of the Mutineers, one MATTHEW GEORGE RUDOLPH YOUNGMAY, Lieutenant, United States Navy. The Fugitive is aged twenty-five, Fair of Skin and Hair. Eyes particularly blue. Above six feet in height. He speaks the American accent strongly but not so markedly that it affects his intelligibility to an English ear. Any Person or Persons to be discovered succouring the said Matthew Youngmay will be deemed to have committed treason and upon conviction will be hanged and their Property forfeited to the Crown.

God Save The King

Distractedly, Kezzy handed the advertisement back to Grote.

'It do say 'bout reward, don't it?' he persisted.

'Yes.'

'Five pounds for each swab, and fifty pounds for the cove back o' the mutiny. That's right, ent it?'

'Yes.'

Smugly, he folded the piece of newspaper and stowed it back in his jerkin. 'Fifty pounds' he said musingly, a look of greed in his eyes. He turned and surveyed the cluster of buildings again. 'You'm sure ent no prisoners tucked away? In by mine, mebbe?'

'See for yourself,' invited Kezzy briefly.

But Grote didn't fancy that. He didn't like the long climb down the dark shaft, or crawling along the damp, pitch-black tunnels with just a lantern to show the way. It wasn't so bad if he'd a couple of his men with him, but he wasn't keen to stumble around down there with just this half-gypsy, half-witch for company.

He shook his head. 'If'n ye be sure, then I'll take thy word on it, missy,' he said with something nearing respect. He mounted his horse. 'Best I do take cob with me, Cap'n says. In case soljurs do find he hidden an' guess what's afoot. Likely'd tear Eaglestone apart lookin' for moonshine.'

'Yes,' said Kezzy, relieved. She'd been worrying about that. 'He's tethered in the glade.'

'We'll bring no more kegs . . . not 'til it be safe 'gin.'

She nodded, secretly glad that she had no deliveries to make. It meant she would have time to properly nurse Matthew back to health.

'Where's the moonshine to be hidden meanwhile?' she asked, casually, more from curiosity than anything.

He viewed her from his lofty seat in the saddle through narrowed eyes. He never quite trusted her: for no other reason than she was a female and he wasn't used to dealing with females. Cagily, he said, 'Down'long coast. Too close to home for comfort, Cap'n de Raddon do reckon, but needs must.'

She watched him ride off up the valley. '*Down'long coast . . . too close to home for comfort . . .* ' he'd said. That probably meant in one of the disused de Raddon mines. There were a couple that had been knocked on the coast near to Blackaven House, their old stacks sticking almost straight out of the cliffs among those still being worked.

Kezzy didn't go straight back to the cottage. She busied herself carrying pails of fresh water from the brook to fill the pig's trough. In case Grote stopped again, having remembered something he was meant to tell her. She didn't want him pushing into the cottage to find her and seeing Matthew, not now that she knew the steward had a hankering to claim the fifty pounds on the young American's head. That Matthew was the 'leader of the mutineers' mentioned in the advertisement, she was absolutely certain.

Lieutenant Matthew Youngmay!

Kezzy repeated his rank and name silently to herself, her heart suddenly very full.

Let him live, dear God! Let him live . . .!

Old Wart, laying in his favourite sheltered, sunny spot before the barn door, gave a bark to let Kezzy know that Grote was returning. He didn't stop, but continued on down the valley leading the cob with just a nod in Kezzy's direction.

Kezzy stood in the yard a few moments longer, considering. With the moors swarming with dragoons and a price on the prisoners' heads, she would have to try and move Matthew in by the mine and hide him. It shouldn't be too difficult providing she could get him into the kibble, for then Rats could work the whim and lower him down the shaft. If only he would regain consciousness!

Kezzy turned to go back in. As she did so, she glimpsed a fleeting movement out of the corner of her eye. She stood rooted, narrowing her eyes as she scanned the scudding clouds. Nothing. She must have imagined it. Her heart-beat had quickened; it slowed again to a steady thud-thud. She moved to go. *There!* A dark shape soaring across the top of Eagle Tor! She stared hard, scared to blink in case she missed it. *Please don't let it be a buzzard,* she prayed inwardly. Tears squeezed from the corners of her squinting eyes. Her patience was rewarded. Soaring on a gust of the strong northerly wind, the great white-tailed sea-eagle swooped down across the cloud-darkened valley as if to view the girl.

'Halloooo, Eagle!'

Kezzy sang out, happily, waving to the eagle as if to an old friend. It was an immense female: the largest she'd ever seen. Yet, it was a young bird; hatched no more than four or five seasons past, she hadn't entirely lost her youthful grey plumage, nor had her head completely turned from dark brown to brown and yellow-white. She circled at a wary distance from the waving figure. Then suddenly dropped low over Eaglestone uttering a chattering call as if to answer Kezzy.

'Kee-kee. Kee-kee. Kee-kee.'

The shadow of her immense wings passed over the yard, sending Wart into a frenzy of yapping. The eagle didn't seem unduly disturbed by this four-legged antagonist. Again she circled the yard, viewing the old fox-hound as it stared white-eyed back at her. Then, catching an up-draught, she soared higher and was away up the valley towards Eagle Tor with one final cackling call.

'Kee-iahhhhhh!'

Kezzy ran to the cottage. She bounded in with an exultant cry of 'Gramps! The eagle! It's back!'

Elyas was squatting on a stool beside Matthew, holding a mug of water to the young man's lips. Over the rim of the mug, a pair of rather bewildered blue eyes stared at Kezzy who, finding herself so surveyed, stopped dead in the doorway.

'So eagle's back, eh?' chuckled Elyas. 'Seems her's brought this'n Yankee boy back'long with she. Back from the dead.'

They didn't dare keep Matthew in the cottage, especially after Grote's warning that soldiers were searching the moors again now the worst of the storm had passed. Kezzy explained this to Matthew with infinite patience. He seemed dazed, unable to take in that he had been seriously wounded but was recovering with people who meant him no harm. His eyes watched the Hammetts warily, as though he would get up and run away from them if only he had the strength to do so.

As it would be chilly in the mine, Kezzy found him a pair of her father's breeches, one of his shirts and a jersey. But when she tried to help him dress, his pale face went pink and he clutched the blanket about him, gasping the first words she'd heard him speak.

'I can . . . dress . . . myself.'

So she went out, leaving Elyas to watch over Matthew from his corner in case he was in truth too weak to manage alone. But when she returned, Matthew was dressed and had tied back his long fair hair with a scrap of cotton torn from the foot of the shirt. He was seated on a stool and removing the bristles from his chin as best he could with Elyas's sharpest knife.

'Mighty present'ble, ain't he, chield?' remarked Elyas with a wink when he saw Kezzy's astonishment at this change in her patient. 'Why, you'm might almost think he'd come a-sparkin'.'

His teasing brought a flush to Kezzy's cheeks. 'Pshaw, Gramps!' she admonished him. She went to Matthew. 'You must come with me, Matthew. Into the mine. It's too dangerous here.'

He stopped scraping his chin and gazed at her, frowning. Slowly, he raised a hand towards her cheek but seemed to stop himself from actually touching her. Kezzy struggled to read what lay behind his apprehension, why he didn't seem to comprehend that they were trying to help him. It was quite simple; too often he had reached out for images of her pointed, elfin face and bright, tilting eyes only for her to dissolve into nothingness. He daren't now believe she was real.

'Go with her, boy. 'Tis best for us all,' said Elyas firmly.

The blue eyes flicked across to the old man. Then, as if obeying a senior officer, he rose, swaying slightly, arms straight at his sides. 'Aye, aye, sir,' he said.

He stumbled once or twice as they crossed the yard and Kezzy would have taken his arm to help him, but he drew away from her, preferring to manage alone.

She had everything ready at the head of the mine shaft. Rats was harnessed to the whim and a kibble swung in the cage ready to lower Matthew below ground. Gently, Kezzy explained what everything was for. The doubt in Matthew's eyes seemed to clear and he nodded. Without argument, but still refusing to let her help him, he swung a long leg over the edge of the kibble and climbed in. Unsteadily, he lowered himself to his haunches. Kezzy clicked to Rats and the colt lumbered forward. The whipsederry creaked into action and the kibble slowly descended to the first level which was as far down as Kezzy felt it necessary to take Matthew.

She climbed down the ladder and joined him on the wooden platform, only this time she made no attempt to help him as, somewhat shakily, he climbed out of the kibble. He leaned against the wall of the shaft, looking about him in the dim light which entered from above in a strangely anxious and bewildered way.

'We're in by Wheal Eaglestone,' Kezzy told him gently.

He seemed almost to flinch at the sound of her voice.

She lighted a lamp. 'There's a narrow tunnel. Just big enough to wriggle through. The entrance is easily hidden by a few rocks but it leads into a good, dry chamber. You'll be safe there.'

'Thank you.' He said it in a dull, polite voice. He was, however, watching her intently.

'This way.'

Meekly, he followed her. She took him almost to the end of the slightly uphill tunnel. Then stopped. All the way along, as in the other tunnels, lay fallen lumps of rock and stones and earth from the old workings. Now, Kezzy stooped and quickly rolled away two biggish pieces of granite to reveal a low, narrow entrance at the foot of the wall. In the past, she'd led Peter Dorrity, and, on more than once occasion, searching dragoons, along the tunnel without them having the least notion that a secret chamber ran off it. There were many such small 'secret' tunnels and chambers in the bal; hulked over the years by the Hammetts in their search for tin lodes.

Matthew was standing staring uncertainly at the hole.

'It's quite easy,' Kezzy told him coaxingly. She dropped to her knees. 'I'll go first.'

Holding the lantern carefully in front of her, she crawled into the tunnel. It was only a few feet long and a few moments later she was standing in the small chamber she'd prepared for Matthew. She heard a faint scuffling but it was a full minute before his fair head appeared. His face was wracked with pain and she suddenly realised that it must have been agony for him to worm his way through the narrow gap with his injured shoulder. Yet, he uttered no word of complaint, just stood looking about him with the same anxious expression.

She held the lantern aloft so that he could take in his surroundings. The chamber measured roughly ten feet square. She had brought down a pallet, freshly filled with clean straw, and covered by a big woollen blanket. She had also placed a pail of clean water to hand and a mossle bag of bread and butter and cheese.

'It's a good way from the brook and quite dry,' she told him reassuringly.

'Yes. Thank you,' he responded in his dispassionate way.

There was another lantern there, in readiness. Kezzy lit it. Took her own and moved towards the hole in the foot of the wall. 'I'll roll the stones back . . . just in case any dragoons insist on searching the mine. Don't worry, they wouldn't ever find you . . . and the walls are solid granite so they won't hear you . . .'

Kezzy stopped, frowning. Matthew's features had distorted with anguish. Abruptly, he lurched away from her and dropped upon the pallet, crouching there with his head in his hands as once he had done when locked for a long, solitary month in the pitch-black of the dumb-box at Princeton Prison. He began to shake uncontrollably as the terrible memory of it flooded him until he could no longer tell reality from nightmare.

Kezzy stood gazing at him, at a loss to know what to do or say that might pierce the veil of horror enclosing Matthew as absolutely as had high grey prison walls. She went to him, knelt on the pallet beside him. Tentatively, she put out a hand and touched the side of his face. He shivered, kept his face buried in his hands.

'Look at me, Matthew.'

His violent trembling lessened at the sound of her soft voice; he'd forgotten that a voice could be gentle and sweet and filled with . . . yes, love. He lowered his hands and looked at her. This face before him, this beloved face, had given him hope when there had been none – helped him keep his courage, his sanity, his self-respect. Now, by some miracle, the face was before him – soft-skinned, framed by an abundance of gleaming raven hair – exactly as he'd always pictured her without her boy's woollen hat.

'Are you real?' he whispered.

She nodded. 'Oh yes.'

Suddenly his arms went around her, holding her so tightly they hurt. The movement was so quick and reckless she wouldn't have had time to escape him even had she wanted to. He buried his face in her soft herb-scented hair and she felt the tension drain out of him. Slowly, hesitantly, then with a sudden surge of passion, her arms went around him, holding him almost as tightly as he held her. He buried his face in her soft hair, groaning with joy because the mists of shock had lifted from his brain and he knew for certain that she was no dream.

They remained liked that, wrapped in each other's arms, shy, ecstatic, loving, for a long time. Their passion for each other reached far beyond the mere needs of carnal pleasure.

'I must go,' Kezzy whispered presently.

His answer was to hold her still tighter.

'I must.'

'Stay . . . please.' There was a note of terror in his voice.

She drew a little away from him so she could look into his face. She saw mirrored in his blue eyes fear at the thought of losing her again, having just found her. She said: 'I'll be back by and by.'

He didn't release her. 'Swear it.'

'I swear.'

Reluctantly, he let her go. She pushed him gently back against the pillow. 'Rest a while, Matthew.'

He frowned. 'You know my name.'

'I've always known it. I heard one of the other prisoners call you Matt.'

He nodded, sank back and closed his eyes. He was still weak. Just moving from the cottage to the mine had wearied him. Kezzy got to her feet with a faint rustle and immediately his eyes flicked open.

'I won't be long,' she told him. His eyes followed her as she picked up her lamp and went across to the hole in the wall. She dropped to her knees in readiness to crawl back through the short tunnel into the main alley.

'Wait . . .!'

She paused, looking back. He'd risen on his good elbow. 'I must go, Matthew.'

His voice was plaintive. 'But I don't know your name.'

'Keziah.'

'Keziah,' he repeated softly.

'Kezzy.'

He smiled then and it was as if the sun had come out in that cramped, dark chamber.

Kezzy. Kezzy. Keziah.

He repeated it to himself over and over, long after she had gone. His face – his beloved face – at last had a name.

Chapter Thirty-One

Dragoons came twice to Eaglestone, that week. With hardly a word, certainly without asking permission, they searched the cottage and the outhouses, then ordered Kezzy to take them down into the mine. There was no doubt who they were looking for but they found nothing. Kezzy had long burned Matthew's prison rags and his bloodied bandages. And she always made sure that the rocks guarding the entrance to his chamber were wedged securely in place and the scuff marks on the dusty floor dispersed with her apron.

On Thursday evening a family of tributers crossing Dartmoor to seek work at Mary Tavy asked the Hammetts' permission to camp for the night beside Eagle Brook. Elyas wasn't happy that they should do so, muttering to Kezzy that it wasn't wise at such a time, what with an escaped prisoner hiding in by the bal.

'Tributers is as tricky as tinkers,' he muttered. 'Sniff out lay o' the land like bluddy sniffin' dawg.'

But Kezzy overruled her grandfather for once and gave the tinners her permission to stay, knowing that she would undoubtedly hear some interesting gossip from them. They numbered six men, two women and half a dozen children – one a baby. They were thin and ragged and, presently, Kezzy took them a big iron pot of steaming vegetables with a big piece of fat pork in it. And she spared them some milk and a few chunks of bread for the children.

'God bless you, mistress,' the elder of the two women thanked her gratefully. She probably wasn't more than thirty but her face was wrinkled and sunburned like an old woman's and she'd lost most of her teeth so that her jaw was sunken. The family name was Dinion and they had been tributing over near Bovey Tracey until the lode had gone horse on them. Ma Dinion, as her family all seemed to call her, and her daughter, Rose, who sat suckling her baby on a stone by the brook, were only too pleased to chat with Kezzy. And they had gleaned a great deal of news and gossip during their recent travels.

Corn was in short supply again. And the price per quarter had more than quadrupled since the war. But Kezzy already knew that; luckily, she earned enough from her smuggling activities to pay the miller's prices. Ma Dinion said that a crowd of tinners and bal maidens, more than two hundred, had stormed a mill at Ashburton and shared out the grain – sacks of it – that they had found hoarded there, paying the miller the old price per quarter. But it wasn't, said Ma Dinion, anything like the riots back in the 1790s when ten thousand miners had marched on Camborne Village where some twenty millers had their mills and seized every grain there was.

'Proper battle 'twere,' declared Ma Dinion, who'd been there along with her husband and eldest son, both of whom were taking their ease by the water's edge, along with her younger son and Rose's husband, all having filled their bellies with Kezzy's good hot food.

Kezzy knew all about the Camborne riots: those tinners who'd been there never tired of reminiscing about their great corn victory. None the less, she gave every impression of listening attentively to Ma Dinion's colourful version of events.

The shortage of corn was a terrible thing. Vegetables and bread were the miners' staple foods. Mr Wisdome, the Cornwood miller, insisted that he'd no flour hidden away (though he could always find some for Kezzy when she showed him a gold coin). The previous year's harvest had certainly been poor and many farm workers had been thrown out to go on the parish. The war had also brought about a slump in the demand for tin and bands of tinners wandered the countryside, like the Dinions, in search of work and food. Some, the lucky ones, found work in the quarries, potteries or down by the coast with the fish. Others found work in the copper mines; not the underground work they were used to, but on the surface, in the blowing and washing houses, sorting and grading the ore. Like gutting fish, it was women's work and they hated it. However, it meant they could buy food for their families, so they swallowed their pride as Elyas Hammett had once done almost thirty years before when he went for the fish.

Ma Dinion came to the end of her lengthy tale, concluding: 'And if'n they don't gi' us cheap bread, we'm ready to take on they snobby-nosed millers 'gin! And I'll tell 'ee whose likely'd come off worst!'

Kezzy saw her chance to change the subject. 'I heard there's been a mutiny upalong Princeton Prison.'

Ma Dinion seized upon this new topic with enthusiasm.

'We was stopped five times in as many days by dragoons searchin' for Yankees,' she told Kezzy. She jerked a thumb towards the four recumbent forms beside the brook. 'Made yon boys speak out in turn in case they was really Yankees pretendin' else.'

'Searched wagon an' all,' put in Rose. She hefted her baby on to her shoulder and pushed her plump pink breast back inside her cotton blouse. '*First* time we was stopped was over to Haytor . . . so that do show how far they soljurs be a-searchin'.'

'Do you know if they have recaptured any of the prisoners?' Kezzy asked.

The two women shook their heads. They hadn't heard.

'Them's offerin' reward for elly Yankees catched, mind,' said Ma Dinion. She chuckled. 'May as well save theyselves trouble. Bain't none as I knowed would give over elly prisoner to Preventy men. Not even for handful o' tin!'

It occurred to Kezzy that there was a great deal of truth in what Ma Dinion said and that it was highly likely other moorfolk were hiding Americans despite the severe penalties for doing so. Those whose few pleasures in life included a drop of moonshine and a plug of baccy deemed Preventatives their natural enemies along with tithe-demanding parsons. She made up her mind to ride over to Lamb's Down the first chance she got. Perhaps the farmer and his wife would whisper the truth to her if that was indeed the case.

Ma Dinion was eyeing Kezzy with interest as the girl sat perched on a boulder near to the old rocking chair in which she, herself, sat; it travelled atop the wagon and was always put in last so as to be handy for overnight stops. She stopped her rocking and put an abrupt question to Kezzy.

'Are you'm sparkin', girl?'

Kezzy paused. 'No . . . not exactly.'

The woman's brows rose. She looked interested. She was looking for a suitable wife for her eldest son – a sturdy, ruddy-faced boy of sixteen who had already been giving Kezzy sly looks which she had carefully ignored.

Ma Dinion was looking even more interested. To her way of thinking, 'not exactly' was as good as no. 'How old are 'ee, might I ask?'

'Seventeen . . . eighteen come autumn.'

Kezzy rose to leave them, not too keen on the direction their conversation was taking. Shrewdly, she could see where it was leading. 'I must boil some water for my grandfather,' she said by way of an excuse to take her leave of them. 'He has lung-rot and can't sleep without inhaling garlic steam.'

Ma Dinion's sharp eyes moved to the deserted mine buildings. 'Knocked, is it?'

'Yes.'

'Lost thy pa and brothers, didn't 'ee?'

Kezzy thought it churlish not to reply. 'One brother and three cousins along with pa,' she said quietly.

Ma Dinion jerked her head towards the cottage. 'Thy grandpappy won't last long. Reckon you'm need good husband.' She twisted her wiry body right around so that she could better survey Eaglestone in the fading evening light. 'Never went horse, did yon bal?'

'No.' Kezzy was going to leave it at that but then she decided it would be wise to discourage the Dinions from entering the mine, perhaps just out of curiosity. Matthew sometimes took a turn up and down the tunnels to stretch his legs and she didn't want any of the tinners blundering into him. She chose her words carefully. 'We knocked the bal because it's dangerous. Regular slippy. And there's terrible fire-damp. Sometimes I can smell it clear across yard.'

Ma Dinion nodded her head sagely. 'Lost a brother to fire-damp blast over to Skale Downs.' She raised her voice, calling across to the menfolk. 'Heared that, did 'ee? Yon bal is slippy an' terrible wi' fire-damp so don't elly o' ye go in by mine.'

They nodded.

Kezzy was satisfied. She moved to go.

'What 'bout Garge? Do 'ee want he or nay?' demanded Ma Dinion loudly, stopping her.

Garge turned pink and grinned hopefully at Kezzy, liking the look of her slender body and full young breasts.

'I'm already spoken for,' Kezzy said in a level voice. 'He's away. At sea. We'll wed when he returns . . . whenever that might be.'

'Oh, you'm gone for a sailor,' Ma Dinion didn't hide her disappointment. 'Well, can't say as how I blame 'ee. Tinnin' be bad these days. Fish be better . . . Or copper . . . if'n 'ee can get it.'

She yawned and began rocking herself, lids drooping.

Kezzy wished them good-night and promised to bring them some eggs in the morning to cook for breakfast, the number of which would depend on how many chickens obliged.

At mention of chickens, Ma Dinion opened her eyes. 'What you'm should do, girly,' she told Kezzy, 'is tap on door o' henhouse at midnight. If hens cackle it do mean thy sailor'll never wed 'ee . . . nay, nor no other boy. But if'n cock crows! That do mean ye'll be wed by end o' year!'

Kezzy hid an amused smile and politely thanked her for the advice. She would, she assured Ma and Rose gravely, make the test one night very soon and discover her fate: spinster or bride. None on the moor knew better than she, daughter of Ruke the witch, that there were many strange powers in the world for whom the past, present and future moved as a single time. But superstitions and silly rituals such as this one suggested by Ma Dinion were no more than old women's widdles and not worthy of credence.

Next morning, the barn yielded fourteen good big brown eggs. Kezzy kept four for herself and Elyas and gave ten to the Dinions.

'Did ye do what Ma said an' tap on hens' door?' Rose asked her, grinning.

'No.'

'Bain't never wrong so don't ye forget to do it.'

'I won't.'

They moved on as soon as they'd eaten.

Matthew was strong enough now to climb up and down the ladder rather than be lowered and raised in the kibble. He emerged as soon as the Dinions had gone, glad to breathe fresh air and to stroll in the yard. He still hadn't the strength to help Kezzy with the heavy chores, though he would've gladly tried to if she'd let him. She didn't, saying firmly, 'I don't want you opening that wound again and maybe getting poison in it.' And although his helplessness brought him a bitter resentment, he stifled it and carried out those mundane tasks he could manage with his good arm, helping her to feed the chickens, or perhaps carrying a pail of water from the brook – anything that would keep him with her.

Watching them from the cottage, Elyas, who had now entered his seventy-first year, felt a great sense of relief. Here was a fine young man, indeed, to look after his beloved Kezzy. And there was no mistaking the secret looks they gave each other: deep and searching, with no shadows in their eyes. 'Reckon he'll be sueing for her hand afore month be out,' Elyas told himself contentedly.

Matthew never tired of looking at Kezzy, in particular, her eyes. He felt that if, at some other time, he met her and she was veiled from head to foot like the women of Arabia with just her eyes showing, he would know her. Her brows were curving wings of jet black above fine, clear, rather oriental-looking eyes. Her mouth, too, was quite lovely: a natural, healthy pink, the lips softly tilting at the corners as if she perpetually wore a faintly teasing smile. There was, of course, no sign on her of the paint and powder which was becoming increasingly popular with American women. In her simple cotton dress, with her long, dark hair flying in the breeze, she personified glorious, untouched Nature herself.

Kezzy was aware of his ardent scrutiny. And from beneath her long black lashes she subjected him to an examination which was every bit as close. He was, she thought, a good-looking fellow for all his wanness. His flaxen head was well set and he had an indefinable air about him that would have told her, had she not known, that he was a naval officer rather than Ma Dinion's 'sailor boy'. Plenty of good wholesome food was already putting flesh on his lean frame, returning it to its former muscular fitness. Kezzy was tall, but he was a good bit taller. She liked that. She also liked his deep voice with its strange rather musical accent.

They talked about many things, during the day as they moved about the yard (always with an ear cocked for Wart's warning bark in case Matthew had to hurry below ground to his secret chamber) or long into the night when Elyas was sound asleep. It was those quiet, idle hours Kezzy liked best, sitting with Matthew on his pallet in the lantern glow with his hand holding hers. Sometimes it passed through her mind that Dame Hannah Rogers would have plenty to say about propriety. And then she remembered the schoolmistress once telling her of her own secret sorrow: how she'd loved and lost a dashing army captain, and something told her that the dame would not be too disapproving of them.

Gradually, Kezzy learned almost all there was to know about Matthew and he about her, except that she avoided mentioning her involvement with Captain de Raddon and the flaskers – not because she didn't trust him with such a confidence but because she feared he might think her hoydenish. She wanted him to see her as a young woman of refined taste, not as some harum-scarum skiddamalank running with free-traders. And most of all she wanted him to think her beautiful. To that end, she took to scrubbing herself in the brook morning and evening, to wearing her good dimity dresses every day instead of the rough, patched garments she usually wore about the place. And she took to dabbing behind her ears a little of the expensive French scent which she kept hoarded in readiness to sell to the gentry in Exeter when next she delivered their cognac – though she knew not when that might be since, according to the Dinions, the moors still swarmed with dragoons searching for fugitives.

It was a mild though cloudy Saturday afternoon almost two weeks since Kezzy had found Matthew by Crazywell Pool. They were planting potatoes in the vegetable patch so laboriously evulsed from the stony terrain by Graeme and Isaac Hammett. Kezzy was considering aloud whether she should attend church the following day as she hadn't done so since Easter, almost three weeks past.

Although Matthew was loath to lose her sweet company for a whole morning, he encouraged her to go, saying, 'Perhaps you will hear some news. I ache to know how many of us managed to escape.'

She stopped what she was doing, a seed potato in her hand. She had almost forgotten Grote's visit while he, Matthew, had lain unconscious, and the advertisement from the *Western Daily Mercury*.

She said: 'Ninety-three prisoners escaped.'

He was stooping, digging the trench for the potatoes. Abruptly, he straightened up to gaze at her in surprise. 'Ninety-three! Are you sure? I mean . . . how do you know?'

She didn't want to mention Grote. She thought quickly. 'The tinners who stopped here last week. They said. I'm sorry, Matthew, I forgot to tell you.'

There was a pause while he digested this. Then, without any warning, forgetting that his shoulder and arm were still somewhat weak, he grabbed Kezzy around the waist and swung her high in the air with a jubilant whoop which set old Wart off hopping on his old legs and barking excitedly.

Kezzy shrieked with joyful amusement as he whirled her around until they were both quite giddy. He lowered her back to the ground, laughing down into her flushed face, reluctant to take his arms from around her warm, slender body.

'*Ninety-three*,' he said again, the delight manifest in his voice. This was better then any of them had hoped! They'd thought perhaps a score or so might manage to get away in the mêlée – but ninety-three! His smile faded and he looked solemn all of a sudden. 'Can we be sure? Perhaps the tinners were repeating rumour . . .'

Kezzy hastened to put him out of his misery. She shook her head. 'They had an advertisement, torn from the *Mercury*, offering five pounds reward for each fugitive caught and handed over to the prison authorities.'

He grinned. 'Well, imagine that! Five pounds for Moab and Lordy and John Dagge . . .' He stopped, the amusement draining from his face, sorrow shadowing his eyes. 'But not for Knuckles,' he murmured, a break in his voice.

'Knuckles?' queried Kezzy gently.

It was a moment before he answered. 'A young middy . . . only fourteen. He'd been a prisoner for over two years. They . . . shot him in the back.'

Matthew stooped again and began to dig, not wanting Kezzy to see the tears glittering in his eyes. Knuckles had been just ahead of him as the great seething mass of prisoners surged towards the gates and freedom. He, Matthew, had a tight grip on Prison Captain Gilpin, holding him hostage with the stolen pistol pressed to his quivering jowls. The guards had put up their weapons, afraid for Gilpin's life if they obeyed orders and fired upon the mutineers. Gilpin face saw only disgrace and ruin if he lived. His voice had rung out.

'Fire, you fools! Fire! Don't let the bastards get away!'

Two guards, younger, more hot-headed than the rest, had opened fire from the main tower. Men fell. Matthew didn't know for sure how many. As Knuckles went down, blood pouring from his back, he released Gilpin – who had been immediately swept away, cursing, by the throng. Kneeling in the dust, Matthew had cradled Knuckles's body. John Dagge had stopped long enough to shout urgently, 'Get out, Matt. He's dead, can't you see?'

So he left Knuckles laying beneath the stone arch. His poor young sightless eyes staring up at the words engraved in the granite: PARCERE SUBJECTIS. *Spare the vanquished!*

Well, their gaolers had never done that! mused Matthew with bitter resentment as he lifted another spade of soil, while he had been insistent that there would be no violence, no murder, that the uprising would be peaceable and no prison officers would be hurt. He had told Gilpin that was their intention when he broke into his quarters and took him hostage as he sat eating his supper of a fat capon and a loaf of fine white bread. Yet, Gilpin had given the order to fire – innocent, unarmed men had been cut down.

'By Jesu! I should have put a bullet through his gullet while I'd the chance and dang the consequences!'

The words burst forth from him involuntarily. Kezzy looked up from her potatoes to say gently, 'Don't torture yourself, Matthew. Better that you led a mutiny than be left to rot in that horrible place.'

He stopped digging and looked at her in surprise. 'Did I tell you I led the mutiny?'

Kezzy straightened up and smiled at him. He may as well know, she decided. 'The advertisement . . . it offered fifty pounds reward for the ring-leader.'

He met her eyes levelly. 'Fifty pounds, you say?'

'Yes.'

His face was impassive. 'And did this advertisement give the ring-leader's name?'

She couldn't help the corners of her mouth twitching. 'A most detailed description, Lieutenant Youngmay.'

He nodded. Then gave her a wry little smile. 'You could buy a great deal with fifty pounds. Pretty gowns and the like.'

That brought Kezzy's chin up. 'By the Lord Harry! Do you think I'd betray a man for a trumpery gown?' She was hurt that he could entertain the notion for even a moment and in jest.

'No,' he was quick to say. 'not you, Kezzy. But I was betrayed once . . . along with my shipmates . . . and all for a few pipes of tobacco.'

'Were you trying to escape?'

He dipped his flaxen head. 'We were digging a tunnel. Had been for more than a year . . . we were well beneath the inner walls. There was a Judas among us . . .'

His voice faded, his face hardened with the memory.

After a while, Kezzy asked him gently, 'Was that why you were flogged?'

His brooding eyes shifted to meet hers, eyebrows raising slightly in surprise because she seemed to know so much that he hadn't told her. Of course. She would have seen the scars on his back when she was nursing him.

'We were all flogged . . . those of us who'd worked on the tunnel.'

The mass of scar tissue on his back indicated that his own punishment, as ring-leader, had probably been more brutal than his fellow conspirators. She said, 'Did they flog the boy Knuckles?'

'Yes. He was so thin the lash opened his flesh to the bone.'

Kezzy shuddered. 'Poor boy.'

Matthew's hand suddenly sought hers, gripping it tightly. 'Was I wrong? Was I, Kezzy? To encourage them to escape?'

'No, of course you weren't. You gave them hope.'

'But if it wasn't for me . . . plotting and planning . . . they wouldn't have been flogged. Men wouldn't have died when the guards fired on us . . .'

'And how many would have died of starvation? Of disease?' she interrupted him. 'No. You did right and not a man among them . . . not even Knuckles and the others that were killed . . . would say different.'

Her words comforted him. He bent again to his digging.

The afternoon was almost done. The sky was darkening with approaching dusk. Matthew carried a pail of water from the brook and emptied it into the pig's drinking trough. He stopped for a while, leaning over into the sty to scratch the sow's broad pink bristly back. She grunted appreciatively. 'How are you, Thistle, old girl?' he asked her amiably. 'Given us a nice litter of piggies, haven't you?'

The sty was tucked away behind the barn so that the strong aroma wouldn't drift across to the cottage unless there was a good stiff nor-'easter to carry it. Matthew was hardly aware that Wart had given a sharp, warning bark in the yard. Suddenly Kezzy appeared.

'Quick. There's someone coming up the valley.'

He dropped his pail and made a dash for the mine, ducking low and following the shadows. Reaching the entrance, he scrambled down the first ladder and raced for his secret chamber. Kezzy tucked up her skirts and followed as quickly as she could to roll the two big stones across the entrance to the hidden tunnel. Returning to the surface, she emerged somewhat out of breath just as the horseman entered the yard. She'd fully expected the visitor to be Grote. It was Riding Officer Dorrity on a fine dapple grey.

'Peter!'

He looked around. Frowning slightly in surprise because she'd obviously just climbed out of the mine. 'Good-day to you, Kezzy.' His eyes went past her to the mine and she didn't miss the light of speculation in them.

'I was in by the bal,' she admitted casually.

'So I gathered.'

'Putting some wild daffodils on the grave.'

He stared down into her face. 'I'm sorry then that I didn't come earlier. I would have accompanied you . . . and paid my respects.'

She didn't take her eyes, wide and innocent, from his as she said: 'You may still do so if you wish it.'

She was clearly inviting him to enter the mine, proving to him that she had nothing to fear. He was quite sure that he would find freshly picked daffodils in the tunnel where the explosion had occurred: Kezzy placed flowers there every day during the spring and summer months. He didn't take her up on her offer. He swung down out of the saddle.

He said: 'I came because I was concerned for your safety.'

Her black brows shot up. 'But why? Oh, the dragoons! Well, yes, they have been here more than once and a rougher group of fellows . . .'

'Dragoons wouldn't hurt you,' he cut in tersely.

Her brows rose higher. So little did he know about that! 'Then who is it I must be wary of?'

'The escaped prisoners the dragoons are searching for.'

'Are they *very* dangerous, Peter?'

Her expression was the picture of innocence, yet he sensed that she was mocking him. He scowled. 'Might be. Men who've risked their lives to escape won't be easily taken again.'

His pale eyes took another speculative look over her shoulder at the mine entrance. Could he have glimpsed Matthew's fleeing figure? Kezzy wondered. He carried a spy-glass in a leather case suspended from his saddle so it was quite possible.

'You are welcome to search the mine, Peter.'

With grim levity he asked: 'And would I have better luck finding Yankees than contraband?'

She studied him for a moment. Then asked: 'Do you think I'm hiding a Yankee?'

'It wouldn't be the first time ye've harboured runaways, Kezzy.'

She bowed her head in acknowledgement, conjuring an image of him and his friend Jordan as boys, huddling in the hayloft as she smuggled food out to them. 'That was a long time ago, Peter. You were just boys . . . running away from a cruel master . . .'

She stopped, biting her lip. She had learned that it was best not to mention Captain de Raddon in front of Peter. His terrible experiences as an apprentice at Wheal Emma, and at the hands of the Lord Warden's perverted friends, had left him with an almost insane-hatred of the mine owner.

He spotted her reluctance to continue and knew the reason for it. Slowly and deliberately, he said: 'I haven't forgotten my vow, Kezzy. Nor will I . . . I'll kill him, one day. Rip out his filthy heart or pour a ladle of his own smelted metal down his vile throat!'

'Peter, Peter,' she sighed.

' "Vengeance is mine: I will repay, saith the Lord".'

Kezzy responded instantly with: ' "Be not overcome with evil, but overcome evil with good".'

He made an impatient gesture. 'Now you sound like Jordan.'

'Why do I?'

'Well, he's always talking of forgiveness and loving our enemies and carrying the word of the divine Jehovah.'

'He's joined the Methodists?' There was a faint note of disapproval in her tone. 'This new-fang religion' Elyas always called it, swearing that 'old way o' God-botherin' was good 'nough for any man to be baptised, wed and buried by.'

'He's a preacher for them. Considering he had no education they do say he's a great orator.'

Was there a hint of admiration in his voice for his boyhood friend?

'Haven't you been to hear him?' asked Kezzy.

The admiration was replaced by scorn. 'Fox preachin' to geese!' He nodded towards the brook. 'May I water my horse?'

'Yes.'

She wished he would go, but didn't want to appear concerned by his presence. She strolled with him across to the brook.

'The eagle has returned,' she said conversationally.

Immediately, he swung and gazed up at Eagle Tor.

'Hammetts always reckon 'tis good omen to have eagle back on her nest, don't they?'

'Yes. Things will be better for us now,' she told him confidently.

'I hope so.' He paused, watching her with his pale sensitive eyes. She had taken off her shoes and was wading in the water: her feet were long and narrow and very white, not broad and sunbrowned with wide, nobbly toes like the moorwomen who went barefoot. Her head was down so that her hair fell over her face, hiding most of it. 'Kezzy . . .'

He said her name softly so that she looked up in surprise. His serious face was even more grave than usual and his air of arrogant superiority had evaporated. He'd taken off his shako and was twisting it between his hands like a nervous boy about to bare his heart's secrets to his chosen sweetheart.

'Kezzy, I must tell you something . . .'

She guessed what was coming. She looked into his pleading, lashless eyes and wished that he wouldn't be so silly. She was used to boys declaring their interest in her and was quite able to deal with the situation. A polite, 'I'm promised to another,' was generally enough to quell their ardour. Not, she felt, Peter Dorrity.

'Peter . . .' she sought to stop him continuing, so that she wouldn't be forced to hurt his feelings.

He wouldn't be stopped. 'I love ye Kezzy. I want to marry ye.'

'God Almighty.'

'May I speak to Cap'n Hammett?'

'No, you may not.' Her retort was sharp and involuntary and she instantly regretted it when the colour rose in his cheeks, as if she had slapped his face, and his eyes shadowed with misery and disappointment. 'Peter . . . I'm not ready to marry anyone yet. I shan't be eighteen until All-Hallows.'

'Mary Beckwitt's same age as ye and she's been married this past two-year and with two babies to show for it and 'nother on way.'

'I'm not Mary Beckwitt,' said Kezzy briefly, this time purposefully curt in the face of his determination. She'd said what she had so as to avoid hurting his feelings. Had Matthew asked for her hand her reaction would have been one of exhilaration.

'I'll happily wait.'

She shook her head. 'No, Peter. That wouldn't be fair . . . not when I can't say for certain. You see, after Gramps has . . .' she paused, her eyes drifting to the cottage, unable to bring herself to say it. 'It may be I may never marry. Dame Rogers needs help with the school . . .'

He laughed suddenly, his taut face relaxing and his eyes glinting ruefully. 'Kezzy Hammett, spinster of this parish! Nay, I can't see that happening.'

Her mouth twitched. She folded her hands demurely in front of her ribcage and, in a voice which was a perfect imitation of Dame Roger's high, prim, agitated tones, said: 'Now, now, Master Peter, hope deferred maketh the heart sick.'

There was a long moment's silence. Then they were both laughing uproariously so like the good dame was her impersonation and so apt the saying. Elyas, watching from the cottage, scowled at the companionable picture they presented. He didn't like Dorrity. Not only was he a Preventative but, to Elyas's way of thinking, the worst sort of Preventative – a zealous one, the sort who'd arrest a man and think himself a fine fellow for doing it.

'He'd better not come askin' for Kezzy, the jumped up young hobbledehoy!' grumbled Elyas. 'Now, that Yankee boy . . . he's a fitty husband for she!' He chuckled to himself. 'An' her won't be turnin' he down when he do ask for she, I'll wager! Her's as full o' love for he as dog is o' fleas!'

By the brook, Kezzy's laughter died away as a question formed in her brain, a question to which Matthew would want to know the answer. She tried to sound detached. 'Have any of the Americans been recaptured, Peter?'

He was still grinning but in an instant his expression became grave. 'Fourteen, at the last count. And one found dead out on the moor with a slug in his guts. Of the fourteen, six did give themselves up before they starved to death. The rest were rounded up by the dragoons.'

'So there's still quite a lot of them missing?'

He was watching her closely. 'Folk are hiding them, no doubt 'bout that, tho' God alone knows where . . . or why. Every available riding officer and trooper has been out searching this past two-week. Every dratted barn, stable, cupboard and cave has been searched. I found one of 'em . . .'

'Oh?'

Again, his rueful little grin. 'Hiding in a pile of dung. *And* I had to take him in riding downwind of him.'

She didn't smile in response. 'The war is over, Peter. Why can't you leave them be?'

His mouth tightened. 'Of course we can't leave them be!' he said brusquely. 'They're escaped prisoners. They rioted . . .'tis a near miracle innocent people weren't amongst the dead and injured. As it is, a detachment of dragoons . . . six men and horses . . . were lost in a mire over near Crazywell.'

Kezzy was pulling at some young shoots of water-mint. She looked up at him, a frisson of alarm running through her at the mention of the dead dragoons. ' 'Twere always boggy over at Crazywell,' she said carefully.

Peter frowned. 'Strange thing is . . .' He hesitated, almost too embarrassed to finish what he was going to say.

'What?' prompted Kezzy.

' 'Tis only tittle-tattle, of course, but folk are saying as how the pixies must've tried to save them by pulling them out of the swamp with their belts. 'Twere all that was left of the dragoons . . . four belts laying on a clump o' reeds.'

Kezzy nodded. 'Well, they do right strange things, pixies. Why, they might even have led the dragoons into the mire in first place and only *pretended* to try and pull them out.'

He darted her a quizzical look, suspecting her of mocking him again. Her face was bland. She began plucking at the mint again.

She said: 'What will happen to them? The fourteen you've recaptured, I mean?'

'They've already been tried and sentenced to seventeen years' transportation.'

Her gasp of horror was audible. 'But that's unfair! Inhuman! They should have been released months ago and sent home like the French. They only took what was rightfully theirs . . . their freedom!'

His eyes narrowed, holding hers. 'Ye know a good deal about it, Kezzy.'

She snorted, tossing her head like a wild colt. 'Do you not think that the whole of the parish . . . the whole of Devon . . . isn't talking about this outrage? And do you know what they're saying, Peter? Do you?'

He didn't like it when her eyes flashed at him. 'What are they saying?'

'That to open fire on innocent, starving, brutalised men is nothing short of murder.' He stared at her, his long face still. 'By the Lord Harry, Peter! I would have thought that you of all people would have shown some compassion for the poor souls!'

Coldly, he said: 'If I did, my compassion would surely be as misplaced as thy own, Kezzy. We are speaking of men who stole a pistol and held it to the prison captain's head.'

'Then 'tis a damned pity that they didn't put a slug through his thick skull before he could give the order to fire on innocent men,' raged Kezzy, her heart wrung by the memory of Matthew's thin, pain-wracked body and his sorrow at the loss of his young friend, Knuckles.

Her fury turned Peter's face crimson. He set his shako squarely upon his head. 'I'll wish ye good day, Keziah,' he said stiffly, preparing to remount. 'I have my duty to attend to and time presses.'

'Then attend to it!' she snapped. 'Hunt down the Americans and drag them in chains before the authorities so they can be tried for mutiny and sent to rot in a convict hulk! But don't you ever show your face here again, Peter Dorrity. Do you hear? *Not ever!*'

She would have flounced away from him but he caught her arm. 'Kezzy . . . wait! Please . . .!' He couldn't let her go like that, couldn't bear the anger and disgust that burned so fiercely in her eyes at the thought of him hounding the prisoners. 'They won't be sent to Botany Bay. I'm sure of it.'

'Will they be pardoned, do you think?'

The hope in her voice was poorly concealed but he didn't appear to notice. ' 'Tis the ring-leader they want,' he told her. 'Naval lieutenant called Youngmay. Seems he's been stirring them up for months to mutiny. Fifty pounds reward was offered for him but that didn't flush him out so posters are to be put up in every town and village hereabouts inviting him to give himself up. In return, all the other fugitives will receive the King's Pardon.'

Kezzy chewed her lower lip while that sank in. Then said, 'And if he doesn't?'

'Then 'tis the boat for the lot of 'em.'

'How can they be sure he'll see the poster?'

'He'll see it,' answered Peter with certainty. 'All the escaped Yankees will, wherever they're lurking. News like that travels quick as a bee. Youngmay will waste no time giving himself up, ye can be sure of it. According to the prison captain, he isn't the sort to save himself at his comrades' expense.'

'No, he isn't,' she said absently, then realised what she'd said and quickly changed it. 'I mean, men like him would think of others first for sure.'

There was a silence. Peter stroked the grey's neck, loath to leave just yet but knowing that he mustn't linger much longer as he'd to call at Lamb's Down and one or two other farms over that way. There were reports of a weird misshapen figure being spotted in the area. It would probably turn out to be a waste of time: of late there had been a number of similar 'reports', most of which the authorities suspected were artful inventions to send the militia chasing in circles – which was precisely the result.

'I must go, Kezzy.' He swung up into the saddle.

She was absorbed with her own thoughts. His abrupt movement broke into them and she lifted her eyes to her face. 'What will happen to this man Youngmay if he gives himself up, Peter?'

'I don't know.'

'Will they flog him?'

'Oh yes, they'll do that. They must. He's committed mutiny. Then they'll either hang him . . . or, if he's lucky, send him to the penal colonies for life.'

'If he's lucky!' She didn't hide the bitter contempt in her voice. She turned again to go. Again he halted her, saying quickly, pleadingly: 'Kezzy . . . please . . .'

She paused, looked back at him.

'Say something nice before I go, Kezzy.'

She looked vindictive. Then her eyes softened. 'Good-bye,' she said, 'dear fool.'

Chapter Thirty-Two

'What did yon jackanapes want?' Elyas demanded to know the moment Kezzy came into the cottage after Peter had ridden away.

'He was asking if we'd seen any Yankees.'

Elyas chuckled. 'Do knowed from his'n own experience that ye've a soft heart, m'dear. I be proper s'prised he didn't want to take geek in hayloft in case ye've a couple of Yankees hid where'd ye did hide he an' Jordan.'

'I offered to let him search the mine,' Kezzy said with a smile.

Elyas gave another wheezing chuckle. 'He mebbe be Preventy man but he bain't half-witted. He knowed he wouldn't find so much as single hair off un Yankee's head!'

Kezzy was busy kneading their remaining flour into dough to bake for bread. She smiled across at her grandfather by way of response but said nothing. She saw no point in telling him that Peter had said he'd wanted to marry her since she'd no intention of accepting and it would only start Elyas off ranting and calling Peter an impudent young donkey and the like for daring to imagine a Hammett would wed a Preventative.

Neither did Kezzy intend saying anything about the bargain offered by the prison commissioners. Not to Elyas or to Matthew. Not yet. Not until she had thought it out calmly and quietly and decided what was best done. She knew she must tell Matthew sooner or later; he would never forgive her if she allowed his friends to be transported halfway around the world on a convict hulk while he remained in hiding, blissfully unaware of what was happening. Though Kezzy hadn't known him, really known him much more than a two-week, she'd discovered enough about Matthew to know that the prison captain's assessment of his character was right: he would give himself up the moment he knew about the posters. She would lose him. Probably for ever! Her hands, kneading the dough, began to tremble and something cold, far colder even than the eaglestone in her pocket, gripped her heart. *No! She wouldn't let it happen! She wouldn't let them take him!*

'What's for mossle, chield?'

Elyas's voice brought Kezzy back to earth with a start. She set the ball of dough near the fire to rise. 'There's some rabbit stew.'

He heaved himself up and swung across to the table on his crutches. Kezzy set a wooden bowl in front of him and brought the pot of stew from the hot slab. He watched hungrily as she ladled steaming vegetables and small pieces of tender dark flesh into his bowl.

'Elly bread, chield? Can't 'bide stew wi'out bread to dip in un.'

'A little.'

Until the new dough was baked she'd only half of a small loaf left over from the previous day. She gave it to him.

'Drat they bluggy millers,' he groused, 'sittin' on heap o' flour 'til price do rise even more.' He broke the hunk of bread in two and handed her back half, saying, 'Here, put good smear o' butter on that an' gi' it to thy Yankee boy wi' his mossle.'

She hesitated, knowing how Elyas loved his bread. 'Matthew doesn't care much for bread, I do believe.'

'Take it,' he insisted. 'He do need fattenin'. Skinny as a cat's elbow, he be.'

She took the bread and did as he said, covering it liberally with creamy yellow butter. She ladled soup into a tin mug with a lid and made her way across the yard to the mine entrance. She was becoming adept at climbing down the ladder carrying mugs or bowls of food and reached the first level without spilling a drop.

Matthew was glad to see her. He had been worrying in case he'd been spotted by whoever was approaching as he tore across to the mine and climbed into the shaft.

'It was a riding officer but he's gone now,' said Kezzy.

Matthew looked surprised. 'He didn't search the mine?'

'No. Peter . . .' she paused as his eyebrows went higher at this familiar usage of the Preventative's first name. 'Peter is sort of a friend. From when he was an apprentice over to Wheal Emma for de Raddon.'

'De Raddon?'

'Captain de Raddon.'

Of course! He wouldn't know about de Raddon and his mines, or that he was the Lord Warden of the Stannaries. So while Matthew ate, Kezzy told him something about de Raddon and the long-standing feud between the mine-owner and her grandfather. Yet, despite her shocking tales of witches hanged and brothers pressed and lost, there was, Matthew noticed, no obvious rancour in her sweet voice. Save for a certain hardness of tone it might have been gossip if every-day happenings and he marvelled at her quiet dignity.

'Do you not share your grandfather's hatred of this man de Raddon?' He felt drawn to ask her curiously. Matthew couldn't contemplate feeling anything but abject enmity towards Shem Frost. So much so that he sometimes dreamed he had Shem's bony throat between his hands and he was pressing the breath from his traitorous body.

'Yes,' answered Kezzy slowly, after a moment's thought, 'I hate de Raddon. But. . . . what is an old feud when there's more important business afoot?'

And so she told him about de Raddon's venturing, how she'd begun by simply hiding contraband for a few shillings. Then how she became 'tub-carrier', roaming the county dressed as a boy. He smiled at that, remembering his first vision of her in old jersey and breeches, her lustrous hair covered by a woollen cap. Even so, he'd known immediately that Kezzy was no boy.

'So you see,' said Kezzy, 'feud is a bitter thing to follow and won't fill bellies.'

He glanced at her with open admiration. This gentle, tender-hearted girl had risked her life and liberty to look after her crippled grandfather when most others would have allowed themselves to be beaten by such adversity as the Hammetts had faced. When he said as much, Kezzy blushed crimson and wouldn't allow that her blind, passionate loyalty to Elyas was anything unusual, though secretly she thought it quite delightful to be admired by Matthew.

They talked for a while longer in a desultory way. Then Kezzy brought their conversation around to something that had been puzzling her ever since she'd learned of the extreme measures to which the prison authorities were prepared to go to recapture Matthew, even to letting the rest go free.

'Matthew, was there some sort of personal vendetta 'twixt you and the prison captain?'

He glanced at her, surprised by her question.

'Old Blessed Guts . . . that's what we called Gilpin . . . hated me with a vengeance from the very beginning.' Matthew gave a humourless little laugh. 'He gave me a month in solitary for requesting permission to write a letter . . . I might add that it was to the Admiralty to complain about the conditions within his prison.'

That was enough to confirm Kezzy's suspicions. Gilpin undoubtedly saw Matthew as the worst sort of troublemaker; his hatred for this fine, fearless young American had probably become something of an obsession. He wouldn't care what became of the other prisoners just as long as Matthew was recaptured and made to suffer for initiating the mutiny in his prison.

Matthew had finished eating and was sitting quietly watching Kezzy as she sat deep in thought. In the lantern light, she had the whitest skin and the blackest hair. He moved towards her, taking her face in his hands, turning it gently towards his own. For a long time he just looked deep into her eyes. Then he lowered his head and kissed her gently on the mouth.

'Matthew . . .' she murmured his name against his lips.

'Shhh, don't speak, my love.'

His arms went around her and she trembled a little as he pulled her gently down with him to lie on the pallet. She didn't resist. She wanted, though half apprehensively, to discover what it would be like for this man to possess her finally. She was unprepared for the pleasure which seized her passive body as his hands moved over her, cupping her budding breasts and following the sensuous line of her hips, and she could have no more denied him than she could control the desire he was awakening within her. He tugged at her gown, almost tearing it and her cotton chemise and petticoat from her in his eagerness. Then he pulled off his own clothes. They held each other, lips against lips, flesh against flesh. She ran her fingers lightly over the ridged scars on his back and whispered his name in a voice filled with passion and promise.

'Matthew, Matthew . . .'

He drew back from her so that he could gaze at her fresh, healthy, naked body with eyes that glittered in the lamplight like twin sapphires. Kezzy lay quite still, aware of his fascinated gaze but feeling no sense of self-consciousness. Presently, she put out a hand and gently touched the pale golden hair on his lean, muscular torso. Despite the privations of prison life, his body was as strong and resilient as whipcord and steel. She moved her hand down over his flat belly: she knew what she was doing although never before had she touched another man in such an unashamedly sensual manner, or with such love and tenderness. He moaned slightly and lowered his head to kiss her breasts and her belly, his mouth travelling across her soft, warm flesh to the hollow of her collarbone, her throat. Their mouths moulded together and they kissed long and deeply, tongues exploring, eyes closed. He moved against her, thrusting, and her hips strained upwards from the pallet, her thighs whispering open to receive him.

He lay on her, probing, then an instant later penetrated her with one long, fiery movement which made her cry out and brought tears sliding from the corners of her eyes. Fearing that he'd been too savage, Matthew tensed and would have withdrawn but she gripped him more tightly as spirals of pleasure snaked through her lower body. Her face shone. He responded to her urgency, swiftly entering her again, her glorious softness surrounding him as they began to move rapidly against each other. The chamber was filled with the soft murmurings of their eager coupling. Kezzy gripped him tighter as her orgasm began to spread like a furze fire through her lower body.

'Oh, Matthew,' she panted, 'Oh, ohhh!'

His own carnal passion – so long dormant – soared as he began to strive feverishly for release. There was a moment of exquisite pain deep within his loins after which the sap of life burst forth from him into Kezzy's arching body with an involuntary, impulsive cry which echoed over and over in their stone cavern.

For Kezzy, the aftermath of this wondrous shared ecstasy was savage. As she lay there, very still in his arms, her cheek against the wiry pelt on his chest, she knew that come what may she wouldn't see him give himself up. The strength of determination rose within her. They were together and would remain so. Eaglestone would ring with the laughter of their children and grandchildren.

Matthew was peaceful, imbued with content. He felt Kezzy shiver though the chamber was warm from the heat of the lantern and their bodies were damp with sweat from their delightful exertions. He shifted his position so that he could see her face, pale, with smoothly flowing lines which gave it a sculpturally sensual beauty unlike the rather hard, flat faces of the farmers' daughters back home. Their eyes met. Matthew thought he caught a hint of some dark, troubled emotion lurking in the shadows of her depthless eyes. A strange sort of misery. Almost . . . guilt. Then it was gone. Her black, shining eyes were calm again.

'I love you, Kezzy,' he whispered without conscious thought because it was true. 'More than words can say.'

* * *

That evening, Elyas was terribly sick with lung-fever, the worst attack Kezzy had ever known him to suffer. She propped him up on his pallet to help his breathing and dribbled laudanum between his pinched, blue lips. His hands were cold to the touch so she went and got the woollen blanket from her own bed and added it to his, tucking the double thickness up to his chin. He smiled at her drowsily, muttered her name and something she couldn't make out. Every so often, he was seized by another fit of choking which flecked his lips with blood as he fought pain for breath. More laudanum. Eventually, the harsh rattling in his lungs quietened and his chest began to rise and fall more evenly as he fell into a deep sleep. She sat with him, the lamp shaded by an old flour-bag, for another hour, watching his yellow, waxen face. But he didn't waken and after a while she went out and stood in the yard, enjoying the cool air after the closeness of the cottage with its ever-smouldering peat fire.

A bat flipped silently over her head, delicate, out-stretched wings silhouetted against the clear, starry sky as it disappeared into the barn through a hole in the thatched roof. She must, Kezzy told herself, mend the hole before next winter. She'd never had to make repairs to the thatch before: her father or brothers had always done that but she had watched them often enough so felt sure that she could do a fair job. Unless Matthew . . .

Kezzy paused mid-thought. Even if Matthew was adept at thatching roofs, would he still be at Eaglestone come winter? As determined as she was to keep him there, she couldn't be certain. For once her *cohani* powers lay dormant and she could see no vision of the future. No image of them together as man and wife.

Another bat swooped across the sky and into the hayloft drawing her gaze to the barn. The chickens and the big old cockerel were shut in for the night since there was still a chance of frosts. What was it that Ma Dinion had said? Tap on the henhouse at night and if the hens cackle 'tis omen she'll never marry. On the other hand, if the cock crows she'll be wed by the end of the year.

'I'd have to be queer in the thatch to go along with such nonsense,' Kezzy declared aloud and emphatically.

She turned to go back inside. Yet something made her pause, her eyes straying again to the barn. Faith was sometimes greater by far than logic. And it would be rather fun just to see which *did* respond – biddies or rooster. She looked in through the cottage door to check that Elyas was still sleeping soundly, then crossed the yard to the barn door. After a moment's hesitation, she lifted her hand and rapped sharply on the weathered wood. Almost immediately came the disgruntled crowing of the old cock perched high up near the roof, well in advance of his wives' soft clucking and fluttering of feathers. The gratifying 'Cock-a-doodle-doo' barely registered with Kezzy. She was frowning in an occupied fashion at the barn door for it had swung open a few inches as she tapped on it. Surely she'd latched it! Unless of course Matthew . . . Yes, of course! Matthew probably went in the barn to fetch something while she was tending her grandfather and forgot to latch it again afterwards. Yet, he was always so careful about such things.

Another thought struck Kezzy as she stood pondering the reason for the unlatched door. *Where was Wart?* She looked about her but could see no sign of the old fox-hound.

'Wart,' she called softly. 'Here, Wart.'

She thought she heard a faint, answering whimper from within the barn. She paused the door fully open so that the pale, silvery light of moon and stars dimly illuminated the interior. She took a tentative step inside.

'Wart . . . where are you, boy?'

Again the faintest of whimpers, from behind the dark stack of peat vags. She made no move towards that shadowy corner but stood as if rooted just inside the door, her sixth sense warning her of the presence of some unknown element. She strained her ears, thought she heard a faint rustling.

'Who's there?' she demanded in a sudden, sharp tone. 'I know you're there, so you may as well show yourself.'

Kezzy wasn't prepared for what happened next. She half expected a runaway apprentice or a tinker to emerge from hiding behind the vags. Instead, the huge, copper-skinned, bald-headed figure of Lordy Sleeve, the half-Mohawk, loomed from the shadows.

'God in heaven!'

'I'm sorry if I frighted you, ma'am,' muttered Lordy apologetically. 'I feared I would.'

They stood staring at each other for a long moment in the half-light. Kezzy was, for once, so taken aback she was speechless. With the realisation that here was yet another escaped American, her heart began to cease its wild palpitations and return to normal.

'Come out here where I can see you better,' she demanded when she'd recovered her voice. But her tone was still sharp and her eyes snapped a warning that she'd stand no nonsense from him.

Lordy obeyed.

He presented an unusually formidable picture standing there in the moonlight, arms folded across his massive chest, rigidly proud despite his ragged prison garb. There was a snuffling and a slithering, and Wart appeared from behind the vags to crouch at the big man's feet, grey muzzle resting on his front paws, eyes rolling upwards towards the flat, brown face in adoration. Lordy looked somewhat embarrassed.

'Dawgs is like that when they're 'round me, ma'am,' he said ruefully. 'Won't bark, no, nor bite like they're s'posed to.'

Kezzy found herself smiling despite herself. This Wart dog in particular was a mean-natured hound who for years had shown hostility to all save the Hammetts. Even now, Wart growled at Matthew whenever he saw him.

'What do they call you?' Kezzy asked.

'Lord-Is-My-Shepherd Sleeve, ma'am.'

'Oh.' Kezzy bit her lip as her smile threatened to widen. Lordy saw and flashed her a wide, white-toothed smile in return, relieved that she wasn't yelling for her pa and brothers to come with their pitchforks or perhaps even an old fowling-piece.

'Proper name is Red Sleeve, ma'am,' he explained, 'but the good Quaker folks did reckon it were kinda heathenish to go through life with handle like that.'

'I see.'

'Folks mostly call me Lordy.'

That brought forth a quick exclamation from Kezzy. Lordy! Matthew had spoken of this giant of a man with affection. How surprised and pleased they would be to find themselves reunited! But she didn't reveal Matthew's whereabouts for the moment: first things first! 'Are you and your friend hungry, Lordy?'

Lordy's big, shining dome of a head wagged eagerly. 'We ain't had much in our bellies since I caught a rabbit yest'day . . .' He stopped as the significance of her words sank in. *You and your friend* . . . His expression turned to one of mortification because he'd given the game away.

Kezzy's acute hearing had picked up further faint rustling sounds from the direction of the vags. 'You may as well show yourself.'

He did so, hopping over the stack as agilely as a monkey to stand, grinning, beside Lordy. And if Kezzy had been startled by the hugeness of the part-Indian, her eyes widened with sheer disbelief at the sight of the misshapen, stumpy little man with long, pendulous arms and sharp pebble eyes set in a wrinkled, weathered face. He bowed in an almost courtly manner to her.

'Moab Austin, bosun's mate, the *Maryland*, ma'am, at your service.'

She dipped her own head in gracious acknowledgement, eyes twinkling at the incongruous pair. 'I think,' she said, 'there is someone you'll be rather pleased to see . . .'

In the event, Kezzy's use of the word 'pleased' proved to be something of an understatement. Their reunion with an equally astonished Matthew was a confusion of utter relief and delight. They hugged each other like brothers, slapping backs and whooping with excitement like a tribe of Lordy's half-relations. Lordy actually executed a strange, hopping dance around the secret chamber so thrilled was he, and Moab's brown monkey's face was streaked with tears of sheer joy.

'Jesus God! I've prayed for this!' said Matthew with deep feeling, his own sea-blue eyes shiny with emotion.

Kezzy slipped away, glad for them, leaving them to their raucous happiness. She returned shortly, however, with a crock of hot vegetables and boiled bacon upon which Lordy and Moab fell hungrily. She sat with them for a while, her back against the wall, hugging her knees, listening while they talked – Lordy and Moab sometimes together in their eagerness to tell Matthew of their adventures since they were separated amid the throng pushing through the prison gates.

Moab's malevolence and vindictiveness when he spoke of Captain Gilpin was overwhelmingly evident. His face became livid and his mouth distorted. ' 'Tis danged shame you didn't put a slug in Ol' Rotten Guts before he'd the chance to give order to fire, Matt. It would have been no more than he deserved. Good men were shot down in cold blood by the guards.'

Matthew's face was a picture of impotent fury at the memory. He said: 'I know that. Knuckles was among them . . . shot in the back.'

Lordy and Moab exchanged sorrowful glances. They were silent for a while, remembering the cheerful, plucky young middy with the ready fists.

'He was just a lad,' muttered Moab.

Matthew's voice was bitter. 'I really believed that if we foreswore violence then Gilpin would play the officer and gentleman and do the same.'

Moab sneered. 'That bilgy rat a gent! Bah! When the devil is blind!'

'Speakin' of rats an' Shem Frost in particky . . .' Lordy started to say then paused, looking uncertainly towards Matthew, knowing how opposed to unnecessary violence he was.

But Matthew had pricked up his ears. 'Yes, Lordy? What about Shem?' he prompted.

Lordy looked away from the narrowed blue gaze.

Moab gave a watery chuckle and spoke for him. 'Truth of it is, Matt, ol' Shem sorta met with an accident.'

Matthew's pale brows rose. 'An accident?'

'Aye,' said Moab, shaking his head with mock regret, 'there he was, takin' his ease behind the cellhouse enjoyin' a pipe o' Navy Plug . . .'

'And we all know how he earned that,' said Matthew grimly.

'Well, Lordy and me just happened by an' . . . that's when the accident happened. We sort of barged into him . . .'

'Accidental like,' put in Lordy.

'. . . an' would you believe it, Matt, he went down like the sack o' dung he is an' that ol' pipe o' his went clear down his throat. Jammed tight in his windpipe 'til his face turned sky blue and his eyes bulged outa his skull . . .' Moab stopped. He'd forgotten Kezzy's presence. He gave her an apologetic look. 'Sorry to shock you, ma'am, but Shem had it comin', as God is my judge.'

'I know all about Shem Frost, Moab,' she told him calmly.

'Miss Hammett believes that revenge corrodes the soul,' said Matthew, giving Kezzy a warm, faintly teasing glance which didn't go unnoticed by Moab and Lordy.

'Which isn't to say I don't understand it,' Kezzy responded primly, with an echo of Dame Rogers. But the gaze she turned to Matthew fondly belied her severe tone.

'Well, I say good riddance to the Judas,' growled Lordy, and none of them disagreed with that sentiment.

The talk turned to Matthew's own story. Moab and Lordy hadn't known he was one of those who'd been shot and now nothing would do but he must tell them how Kezzy had found him and brought him unconscious to Eaglestone. 'Though I doubt I know half of what happened myself, so modest is she,' Matthew told them with so fond a glance this time towards Kezzy, her cheeks turned pink. Moab and Lordy exchanged another knowing glance. The lieutenant was smitten, that was quite clear.

With a swift change of mood, Matthew suddenly asked: 'What of John Dagge? Do you know?'

They knew. Their dismayed faces told him that.

'Is he dead?'

Moab shook his head. 'Least, not yet mebbe.'

He knew that the *Maryland* purser and Matthew had been close friends, both at sea and in the prison. Both were colliers born and bred who had run away to sea as lads to escape the pits and to win their commissions the hard way.

Reluctantly, Moab told him what had occurred.

The three of them – Moab, Lordy and Dagge – had escaped together and had lived off the land for the first few days. Then the storm had blown up and they had sought shelter at a farm. The farmer had been good to them: hidden them in his barn and fed them despite the poor harvest. But it didn't seem right that all three should remain and be a burden to him, so they'd drawn straws and, after the storm had abated, Lordy and Moab went on their way. They were less than a mile away when they spotted a troop of dragoons riding towards the farm. They had returned and watched from the top of the rise.

'Took 'em a while, but they found Master Dagge and took him away. An' the farmer and his wife, God keep them, kind folk that they were,' said Moab miserably.

'What'll happen to 'em, Lieutenant?' asked Lordy anxiously.

Matthew's face was dark. 'Hang Dagge . . . if they haven't already. Imprison the farmers . . . or fine them.'

Kezzy almost contradicted him but managed to stop herself blurting out that all recaptured prisoners and those that succoured them were to be transported. It was agony withholding from Matthew the knowledge that he could so easily deliver them from their fate, but nothing like the agony she suffered at the thought of losing him. He was smiling across at her but guilt seared and stung her brain and she couldn't meet his eyes. She rose quickly: she had found out what she wanted to know. Her secret would remain safe: Moab and Lordy weren't aware that the authorities were prepared to bargain with Matthew.

'I must go. Gramps has brain-fever. I must watch him in case he wakes and needs laudanum.'

Moab and Lordy scrambled to their feet, unrestrained in their gratitude, not just for the food and for hiding them, but for the risk she was taking. She brushed their thanks aside with a little smile which softened her firm lips and assured them that they were all welcome to stay as long as they wished.

Matthew followed her out through the low, narrow tunnel and stood with her in the main alley. He took he hand and pressed it to his lips.

'Thank you, Kezzy. I don't know how I'm ever to repay you but I will . . . I swear it! I will!'

She stopped him with a finger against his lips. Her eyes were strangely bright. His words were like poisoned darts piercing her conscience. She was, she told herself and her heart turned as cold as granite, as guilty of betraying him and his friends – and the farmers who had succoured them – as Shem Frost!

Tell him! Tell him! Tell him!

She closed her mind to the stabbing voice of her conscience.

Matthew was watching her face, the face he knew so well, both awake and dreaming. Her eyes were wide, unmasked. He saw in them that something was deeply troubling her. 'What is it, Kezzy?' he asked her softly. 'Are you afraid that they will find us hiding here and seize you and your grandfather?'

'No. I'm not afraid,' she said quickly. *Except of losing you!* she nearly said, but bit her lip. 'No, they'll not find you. Won't look too hard, either. Mine has a terrible name for fire-damp.'

'Then what troubles you, my darling? Something does.'

She shook her head, forced a smile. 'Go back to your friends.' She stood on tiptoe and kissed him quickly. He would have held her, kissed her long and deeply but she dodged away from him with a merry laugh that didn't ring quite true. Then she was gone, climbing the slanting ladder as sure-footedly as a hill goat. He stood watching until she climbed out through the circle of moonlight and drew her lantern up after her.

It was suddenly very dark in the mine. As dark as the cramped, fetid dumb-box at the prison. Matthew shivered as if with a nervous chill as he tortured himself with the memory of his month in silent solitary confinement. If Gilpin got his hands on him this time, he would suffer a far worse punishment than that. Matthew told himself, worse even than a mere hundred strokes with the lash. Such was the prison captain's personal animosity towards him, he, Gilpin, would most assuredly 'have his blessed guts', given the opportunity.

Elyas's brain-fever had passed by morning.

'You'm makin' terrible lot o' porridge,' he remarked, watching as Kezzy dropped oatmeal into a large pot and poured on almost half a pail of water.

She gave it a stir. 'We've got two more visitors.'

'Eh?'

She raised her voice. 'Two more prisoners to feed.'

He thought about that, then asked: 'Can them sweat?'

She shrugged. 'They look to be in fair health. Better than Matthew. But then they weren't wounded.'

'Three good strong boys, eh?' muttered Elyas musingly. There was a glint in his old misted eyes. A glint of hope. Three good men could work Eaglestone. 'You'm throw handful o' sugar in pot. An' give they boys plenty o' cream wi' un, hear? Feed they up.'

She smiled across at him, reading his mind. Yes, it would be wonderful to hear the whim creaking again: to see the kibbles filled with ore rising to the surface. Good, honest tinning. That was the Hammetts' heritage. Not smuggled brandy and leghorn hats! Not dressing as a boy to escape the

Preventy men! Not de Raddon silver to fill their bellies and the laudanum flask!

'You'm dreamin', Kezzy.'

She shook herself. The porridge was boiling up.

'Yes, Gramps, I was dreaming.'

After she'd fed them all and swallowed a quick bowl of the hot oatmeal herself, Kezzy put on her best dress. Dame Rogers had helped her cut out and sew the crimson silk taffeta (a smuggled bolt from France which Kezzy, for once, had kept for herself instead of passing it on to the gentry at a handsome profit). Dame Rogers hadn't altogether approved of the finished garment. Her eyesight was increasingly poor but she could see enough to know that Kezzy's new dress was highly provocative, being a fair imitation of the sort of gown which graced the salons of the upper classes. The ladies of the Prince Regent's flamboyant court dictated fashion. No longer did they tightly corset themselves and strap their breasts. They had cast aside their hoops, elaborate wigs and heavy rich brocades and velvets in favour of fine muslins, taffetas and silks, simply styled and revealing as much of their bodies as decorum and the climate permitted.

When Elyas saw what Kezzy was wearing, he approved no more than had the dame. But whereby Hannah Rogers's protest had been limited to a murmured, 'Oh, Keziah my dear, do you think you *should*?' his was far more forceful and to the point.

'You'm bain't a-goin' anywheres in yon gerrup, chield. So 'ee might as well go an' put on thy Sunday frock. All done up like a townie gadder, whatever next?'

Kezzy checked her image in the piece of cracked glass hung on the wall. 'This *is* my Sunday gown, Gramps,' she told him calmly.

'You'm bain't reckonin' on a-goin' to *church* dressed like that, be you'm?'

'Yes.'

She took up a straw bonnet edged with crimson silk and a handsome red-plume and put it on, tying the ribbons in a flamboyant bow beneath her chin. Elyas's eyes bulged.

'Bain't proper, I tell 'ee!' he began to rant. 'What's matter withee all o' a sudden? Have 'ee got devil in 'ee or summat?'

She turned to face him with a rustle. She brought her cool, level gaze to bear upon his fulminating face. 'I'm tired, Gramps,' she said fiercely, 'of burying gold in the pig-sty and wearing rags . . .'

'You'm don't wear rags!' he protested.

She made a deprecatory gesture. 'Cast-offs, then. And floursacking petticoats and touzers and my mother's old straw bonnet!'

'You'm always look awlright to me,' he muttered.

'Well, I don't look all right to *me*. Not any more, Gramps.' She lifted the shimmering taffeta folds of her skirt. 'This has been paid for by my sweat, Gramps. I'm entitled to it. And I'm entitled to wear it to church like all the other ladies in their fine clothes.'

'Bah! Givin' thyself airs! They's entitled cos they be gentry. You'm tinner's daughter, chield, an' don't 'ee go forgettin'.'

Kezzy's chin came up. She stared hard at him for a moment. His own pale, reproachful gaze didn't waver. Then, tersely, she said: 'I've been educated and I know how to behave, and if that doesn't make me a lady I don't know what does. Besides, when I marry Matthew I shall be a lady official belikes. An *officer's* lady, no less.'

'Has un Yankee asked for 'ee yet?'

She hesitated. 'Not exactly. But he loves me . . . he said so. And I love him.'

Elyas snorted. 'Love bain't same as proper churchin'. Anyroads, he bain't free to marry 'ee. He's an escaped prisoner. An' if'n 'ee lay wi' he afore ye're churched then you'm nowt but sailor's shiner.' He saw her flinch at that and stabbed a finger at her. 'An' in that gerrup ye look like un. A reg'lar jill-flirt from down'long port.'

Her eyes flashed darkly at him. 'This gown is as good as any worn by any lady in this parish . . . if not better.'

'Then them must all look like reg'lar jill-flirts, that's what I says.'

'Nevertheless, Gramps, I've as much right to take my place in church with the best of them and that is what I'm going to do.'

Elyas scowled but kept a curb on his tongue as she picked up a small embroidered reticule and walked out with her head high and her scarlet ostrich plume nodding defiantly. He picked up his crutches and went and stood in the doorway, watching as Kezzy climbed up on the wagon and clicked to Rats.

'If'n ye were a *proper* lady ye'd have a fancy rig,' he called after her, 'not that ol' rattler an' a half-dead gossy to pull un.'

She didn't turn around. He watched until she was a tiny red dot at the foot of the valley. Abruptly, he chuckled, speaking softly to himself.

'Mebbe you be un lady, mebbe you'm bain't, chield. But one thing be certain . . . you'm a right good Hammett . . . considerin'.'

Still chuckling, he went inside and shut the door.

Chapter Thirty-Three

The village church was full with a handful of folk – farmboys and tinners – standing at the back. The moment that Kezzy entered, heads began to crane and the murmuring voices all but ceased. Mrs Creedy, seated at the organ, twisted in her seat to see who had caused such a hush to fall over the congregation and lost her place in the hymn Holy! Holy! Holy! Lord God Almighty! and had to begin again.

They were all there, thought Kezzy sourly as her gaze swept over their interested faces. All save de Raddon. Since his wife had died at the foot of the cliffs, he no longer attended the smaller parish churches. But the rest of the local gentry were there in the front pews; then the small mine-owners and farmers; then the tradesmen, among them the Wisdomes and the Beckwitts – young Tom Beckwitt gaping in utter astonishment at the glorious vision Kezzy presented. Yes, they were all there and staring at her as though she was an interloper instead of old Elyas Hammett's granddaughter whom they all knew.

Dame Rogers peered and peered through her quizzing-glass to see who had silenced them. She managed to make out a blurred crimson-clad figure and tut-tutted to herself: hadn't she known that gown would set tongues wagging? Her affection for Kezzy, and her loyalty, set her off waving to attract the girl's attention to let her know that there was room in her pew. Spotting the familiar, grey-haired, grey-gowned figure, Kezzy smiled and moved gracefully down the aisle to squeeze in next to her. As she did so, the congregation began buzzing again, only this time the topic of conversation was Keziah Hammett.

'Talk 'bout cattypilly into butterfly!' hissed Wisdome the miller admiringly to Smithy Beckwitt.

'Ay, one minute her be scriggy as un skellington, next thing, her be proper juicy med'n.'

The smithy's daughter, Jane, darted jealous looks at Kezzy's elegant ensemble 'How can likes of she 'ford taffety an' feathers?' she asked her mother sneeringly. 'Not from sellin' hens' eggs an' the like I'll be bound.'

'Hush, Janey,' reproved her mother with a nervous glance towards Kezzy, 'if'n her do hear her likely'd put evil eye on 'ee. Her do have witch's power like her ma.'

The Reverend Creedy appeared from the vestry and the service began with the singing of the hymn Lead Kindly Light. His sermon was, for once, mercifully short and he took for his text Luke 6:27: 'I say unto thee . . . Love thine enemies, do good to them which hate thee', which made a mockery of what followed: for the Reverend Creedy proceeded to address the congregation at length regarding the perils of harbouring fugitives. All Americans, he told them, were best given up to the authorities to be tried and transported. He went on to say that if any of them knew the whereabouts of the chief mutineer, Lieutenant Matthew Youngmay, they were welcome to approach him after the service whereupon he would be pleased to act as mediator thereby ensuring that whoever was misguidedly hiding him would suffer no reprisals.

'Thereby ensurin' fifty pound reward do go in Parson's purse,' growled Jim Beckwitt loud enough for them all to hear, whereupon Creedy turned a bright, angry red and scowled from the pulpit at the smithy. Beckwitt himself had two young American sailors hidden in a secret cellar beneath the kiddleywink at the back of his blacksmiths. The Yankees quite often joined the drinkers in the Brandy Keg, carrying pots to earn themselves a tot or two, and one of them was sparking Jim's daughter Jane.

It was apparent that others, like Beckwitt, were also succouring fugitives which was why the authorities were having the devil's own job rounding them all up. And despite the parson's impassioned plea from the pulpit, no one stayed to whisper in his ear information which might lead to Youngmay's, or any other prisoner's, apprehension.

'Perhaps, Burridge,' twittered Mrs Creedy to her husband as they stood at the church door as the congregation filed out, 'you shouldn't have chosen that text. They do seem to have taken your sermon to heart.'

Creedy scowled at her. 'Then they're fools, the lot of them. Just asking to be transported and I'll not lift a finger to help them . . .'

He stopped short, bowing low as old Lord Blachford limped by with a curt nod in his direction. 'God bless you, Your Lordship,' he said unctiously.

Since the morning was sunny and mild, Kezzy and Dame Rogers strolled a while in the little churchyard, stopping to pull a few straggly weeds from Beth Hammett's and her babies' graves and to place on them posies of primroses which Kezzy had gathered on the way. Kneeling there, thinking about Elyas's wife who'd died long before she was born, Kezzy couldn't help thinking, with a great sadness, that it wouldn't be long before her beloved grandfather lay alongside his wife. She shook the sad thought from her, got to her feet and shook out the folds of her gown with a rustle. Dame Rogers had said little, as if she was waiting for Kezzy to finish with her gestures of remembrance. Kezzy fully expected a tirade, or as near a tirade as her strait-laced companion could muster, to the effect that she had made something of a spectacle of herself by wearing her new gown to church. It had, thought Kezzy with a sense of satisfaction, caused quite a stir – even the gentry had raised their quizzing-glasses for a better look – the ladies enviously, the men goatishly. Yet, when Damn Rogers did launch into fervid condemnation, Kezzy wasn't the object of it but the Reverend Burridge Creedy.

'Does that man think that we would hand over these poor, unfortunate souls to the authorities on *his* say so?' the dame demanded hotly of Kezzy.

'I don't hold with it . . . not at all. Hounding them when the war is over because they weren't prepared to die of disease and starvation!'

The dame continued in much the same compassionate vein for a full five minutes, every so often raising her glass to note Kezzy's reaction. So manifestly concerned was she about the fate of the fugitives, Kezzy began to wonder if the schoolmistress had a Yankee hidden in the school cellar – the last place the dragoons would think to search. Of one thing Kezzy was sure: the dame suspected there were Americans hidden at Eaglestone. It wasn't so much what she said, as her quick, shrewd, searching glances. She trusted the dame as she would have her own mother, yet Kezzy felt it prudent not to mention Matthew. The fugitives' champion Dame Rogers might be, but the girl sensed that she wouldn't approve of the dashing young Yankee being at Eaglestone when Elyas was in no fit state to act as chaperone.

'And these posters!' the dame was saying. 'Mind, they're torn down almost as soon as the riding officers nail them up.'

Kezzy smiled faintly: she had torn down two herself on the way to church.

'Fifty pounds, they're offering for this poor man, Youngmay, as if he was some sort of cut-throat,' said the dame. 'Of course, if he *did* give himself up as the posters suggest, he'd save all those poor souls from being sent to the colonies next week . . .'

Kezzy's mind had been wandering but she pricked up her ears. 'Next week? It didn't say that on the posters.'

'Didn't it? Well, someone must have told me. Now, who could it have been? Ah, I remember! It was Mr Mutter . . . and he should know because it was his brother, Sam, and Sam's wife who were arrested for hiding a Yankee in their barn.'

Kezzy felt a chill of guilt. The Yankee was without doubt Matthew's friend, John Dagge. The Mutters – she'd attended the dame school with Sam's pretty young wife Nancy – were good, kind God-fearing folk. Just the sort who would help any poor wretch who came to their door. *Next week!* The chill turned to ice at the thought of them being herded on to a filthy convict ship, not to return for years and years.

'Mr Mutter went to Blackaven to ask the Lord Warden to help Sam and Nancy,' said Dame Roger.

'Oh,' said Kezzy, 'and what had Captain de Raddon to say to that?'

'He didn't see Captain de Raddon. He sent a message through his man Grote saying that he couldn't involve himself in the matter as the Mutters weren't tinners. Still, I suppose it was worth the attempt.'

'Yes, I suppose it was,' said Kezzy softly, remembering the time, long past, when she and the dame had approached de Raddon for help for her own brothers. Also to no avail.

Kezzy was deep in thought and started when the dame suddenly gripped her arm in bony fingers. She leaned conspiratorially close to Kezzy. 'I must tell you what Mr Mutter told me, Keziah. It really is most exciting.'

'Oh.'

'About Captain de Raddon. He has a very important visitor staying at Blackaven. A most illustrious personage!'

Kezzy was curious despite herself. 'Who?'

'The Prince of Wales!'

Kezzy's eyes went round. 'Prinny! At Blackaven!'

The dame's grey bonnet bobbed. 'Mr Mutter saw him perfectly clearly. Walking in the grounds with Captain de Raddon and a party of ladies and gentlemen. Mr Mutter said that at first he wasn't sure that it was His Royal Highness . . . never having seen him save on a coin. But he asked the Captain's head groom and he said that it was, indeed, the Prince Regent and . . . Keziah! Keziah! Where are you going, child . . .?'

But no answer came from the long-legged girl bounding between the gravestones in a most unseemly manner with her red skirt and bonnet strings flying behind her.

'I wish to see Captain de Raddon,' declared Kezzy imperiously.

The footman who had answered her knock bowed obsequiously, presuming the elegant caller was to join his master's houseparty, but as he straightened up he caught sight of her rickety wagon and shaggy moorland colt standing in the courtyard and some of his subordination desolved.

'Captain de Raddon is presently engaged . . . madam. If you have a calling card . . .'

'Tell him,' Kezzy interrupted impatiently, 'that Miss Keziah Hammett has urgent business with him. He will want to see me.'

The footman reluctantly showed her into the ante-room and left her. A few moments later, Grote came striding in. He stopped short, unable to hide his surprise at the stylish vision she presented. He positively gaped at Kezzy, so used was he to seeing her in patched dimity or her brothers' old clothes.

'What do 'ee want wi' the Cap'n, Mistress Keziah?' he asked when the power of speech had returned to him.

She shook her head. 'Not the Cap'n. Master Grote. I want to see His Royal Highness.'

Grote's small, hard eyes almost popped out. 'Ye can't do that . . .'

'I must. Where is he?'

There was something mesmeric about Kezzy's eyes.

'He . . . His Royal Highness is taking tea in the Italian Garden but 'ee can't go botherin' him there . . . Mistress Keziah!'

She was away and running, ignoring his angry shout. Grote immediately gave chase but his lumbering gait was no match for her agility and within seconds she had rounded the west wing of the villa and disappeared among the ornamental trees and shrubs.

'Drat her!' muttered Grote with feeling.

Kezzy hadn't the least idea in which part of the great cliff-top estate the Italian Garden was sited; she wasn't even certain what an Italian Garden was or how it differed from other gardens. It did occur to her, however, that since de Raddon and his royal guest were partaking of tea there, it must be situated fairly near the house. Moreover, since the back of the villa overlooked the sea, it must be inland. Keeping out of sight among the bushes, she skirted the big, dark, brooding house, widening her circle, ears straining for voices. After ten minutes or so, she was rewarded by the sight of two liveried footmen, one carrying a silver salver of sugared-cakes, the second bearing a vast silver teapot. She followed them.

The Italian Garden consisted of strange, fronded plants and exotic trees amongst which stood stone statues – mostly nude men and women, Kezzy saw with something akin to shocked surprise at such flagrancy. Here and there, in leafy arbours, were stone benches and it was the occupants of these who drew her attention as she peered out from the shadows of a clump of bushes.

She could see Captain de Raddon, resplendent in a wine-coloured coat, double-breasted with six buttons and knee-length tails as decreed fashionable by the Regent. His collar was high and faced with black velvet. His waistcoat was of white pique and his cravat was elaborately tied. Kezzy blinked, hardly able to believe her eyes: he looked, save for the livid scars on his face, almost personable. He had even discarded his old black horse-hair wig and wore instead one made of real hair, styled in the latest Regency fashion. He was deep in conversation with a handsome, white-skinned lady in a gown of almost immodestly gossamer-thin muslin. Her golden hair was piled high in classical emulation of the nude statues in the garden, and threaded with fine pearls. Pearls also adorned her plump neck and arms and were even set in her ears.

Kezzy's gaze moved on, searching.

There he was!

There was no mistaking Prinny's exquisite figure reclining on a stone bench carved in the shape of a gondola. His tight pantaloons were of the finest white virgin wool; his coat was of pale-blue silk-brocade with a high collar and large revers faced with dark-blue velvet. Above his snowy cravat – tied most intricately in his own special style – his indolent features, wide mouth, thick lips and fleshy jaw, were set in an expression of acute boredom. He seemed more interested in torturing some insect that had had the audacity to crawl near the Royal person than the lively, high-pitched conversation of the sumptuously gowned lady seated beside him.

Kezzy's attention was drawn to a sudden movement at the edge of the garden, directly across from her and near to Captain de Raddon. Grote emerged from the foliage, clearly intent on informing his master that an intruder was at large. She didn't wait for him to approach the Lord Warden, but, taking a deep, steadying breath, stepped from cover and walked swiftly across the grass to the Prince. Grote spotted her at the same time she saw him and, instead of approaching de Raddon, veered hurriedly towards her, striding over the ground, his dour face flaming scarlet with anger and embarrassment because she'd slipped past him.

'Away withee, girl, ye've no right to be here,' he growled.

Kezzy ignored him. Reaching the Prince, she sank into a low, graceful curtsey.

'Your Royal Highness,' she blurted 'I most humbly seek an audience.'

The Prince looked up in surprise, squinting his poor-sighted eyes to focus upon the figure in red. Realising that she was a stranger to him, he raised his glass for a better look as Grote arrived and grabbed her arm. He began hauling her to her feet so as to march her away. She twisted out of his grip but he made another lunge for her, caught the sleeve of her dress so that it parted at the shoulder seam with a popping of stitches.

'Oh, my new gown!'

Her anguished cry drew the attention of the twenty or so ladies and gentlemen. They ceased their own desultory conversations and stared interestedly at the scene being played before the Prince of Wales. Recognising Kezzy, de Raddon rose to his feet but remained disconcertedly where he was, uncertain whether he should or should not approach his illustrious visitor unsummoned.

Prinny liked what he saw through his glass. When Grote made another grab for Kezzy, he brushed him aside with a flick of his hand. 'Leave her,' he commanded.

Grote immediately fell back, eyes shifting towards the scowling de Raddon for guidance. The Lord Warden tilted his head sideways, indicating that Grote was to leave. He made the same gesture towards the footmen so that they, too, withdrew.

'And who have we here?' drawled Prinny. He was still quizzing Kezzy. Admiring the sheen of her black hair, how naturally the thick strands coiled about her slender, milk-white neck.

'My name is Keziah Hammett, sir.'

'And where are you from, Mistress Hammett?'

'From Eaglestone, sir. 'Tis my grandfather's mine upalong Dartmoor.'

'Kezzy!'

With a lusty shout, the familiar figure of Sir Ryden Bliss, almost as exquisite as Prinny in grey velvet and silk, bounded across to her. His plump, stupid features shone with pleasure at seeing her. 'I didn't recognise you for a moment, Kezzy. I've never seen you in skirts!' he neighed. '*Why* aren't you wearing breeches? I don't like you in skirts. And why haven't you brought me any cognac of late? And I need two dozen new silk kerchiefs. And some more of that pomade . . . the very sweet one. Like violets . . .'

Reproachfully, as though unaware that he was interrupting the Prince Regent, he babbled indiscreetly while the rest of the tea-party exchanged amused looks. Only de Raddon failed to be entertained; he shot Kezzy a warning look from beneath his overhanging black brows.

It was, however, the Prince who cut into the excited flow by exclaiming: 'Stab me! Do you *know* Mistress Hammett, Bliss?'

The child-like gaze shifted to regard the Prince. 'Oh, yes, Prinny! Kezzy is a *very* good friend of mine,' he giggled, then stopped abruptly, darting a look towards her. He looked anxious, flustered and woebegone all at the same time and those watching with growing interest saw that he was decidedly in awe of this slender young woman.

Prinny's jaded interest was well and truly caught.

'Very well, Mistress Hammett. You shall have your audience.'

'Oh, *thank* you, sir!' she breathed.

He rose stiffly from his stone bench because of the corset he wore to accentuate his waist as current fashion demanded. 'Come, my dear. We shall stroll a measure . . . while you tell us what is so pressing that our tea must be so rudely interrupted.'

Much to the amazement of all present, waiving any escort, Prinny set off into the shrubbery with the interloper. As a rule, it was the devil's own job to obtain an audience with him, particularly when he was at leisure. It was his greatest delight to make those who had business to transact with him wait for hours in some ante-room while he lounged, talking trivialities with his boon companions. What was even more surprising, Prinny forgot his tea completely so that the silver kettle had to be boiled again when, more than an hour later, he returned with Kezzy in the best of spirits. Moreover, his hand was linked through the crook of Kezzy's elbow in such a companionable fashion, that his long-standing favourite, Lady Hester Conyngham, the lady wearing the gossamer muslin gown, glared venomously after the pair of them.

Captain de Raddon gave Kezzy a questioning glance. She shook her head at him slightly, indicating that he'd nothing to fear on her account and that her business with the Prince Regent had nothing to do with free-trading. There was about her, de Raddon noted, a certain radiance; she was smiling happily and her eyes shone triumphantly. Clearly, her flattery had prevailed upon Prinny and he had granted whatever it was she wanted. In the event, it was the incorrigible Ryden Bliss who dared question His Royal Highness.

'Now, Prinny, do tell us. What favour have you granted Kezzy to put such stars in her eyes? Are you to give her a place at Court? Is that it?'

Prinny chuckled, shaking his head. 'Nay, nay, my good Bliss. Though Mistress Hammett would be a breath of fresh moorland air among my straight-backed ministers!' He had a sort of capricious good-nature that had nothing to do with righteousness or principles, and even less to do with any desire to be popular, but which could purge in a moment a long score of contemptible, cowardly, selfish behaviour at small cost to himself. Still chuckling, he said: 'We have most graciously agreed to pardon Mistress Hammett's intended. Some Yankee buck with a price on his head for leading a prison riot.'

'And all the other Americans, Your Royal Highness.'

'Did we say that?' he teased her in his lazy, drawling manner fluttering an eyelid at those nearest to him. They acknowledged him with indulgent smiles, amused by what had turned out to be a plea for leniency on behalf of a maid for her Yankee lover.

'Yes, sir,' she said firmly, 'you did. And all those who've hidden the escapers are to be free of reprisals.'

He shook his head in mock bewilderment. 'So many promises! You must have put a spell on us, Mistress Hammett. Stab me! You're one of these pixies in human form we hear so much about!'

They all roared with laughter at this witticism; Sir Ryden Bliss's maniac cackling louder than all of them. Child-like, he capered about Kezzy, shrieking: 'Kezzy the pixie! Kezzy the pixie!'

'Sooth, Prinny,' remarked Lady Conyngham with a contemptuous little laugh and a glance at Kezzy which was as cold and hard as emeralds, ' 'twould appear pixies are better at spells than stitching gowns! I do not think I have ever *seen* such a rag . . . save on a London trull!'

Kezzy eyes flashed at the insult. Before she could stop herself, she was uttering a sharp response. 'Madam, I know nothing of pixie spells or London trulls. But I do know that even our bal maidens wear drawers for the sake of decency.'

There was a sudden silence, all eyes turning towards Lady Conyngham who had risen in anger. The late afternoon sun streamed through the diaphanous folds of muslin revealing that she was, indeed, without underpinnings of any sort. Two bright spots of red rose in her white face.

The Prince guffawed, slapping his ample thigh in delight.

'Begad, Hester! The chit sets you lower than a bal wench. What do you say to that?'

If Lady Conyngham had anything to say, she didn't say it. After a second's pause, she threw back her head and joined in the uproarious laughter. Kezzy smiled faintly, her eyes lowered contritely. Her heart thudded with relief. The sudden silence which had met her cutting retort told her that to incur the Prince's favourite's displeasure was highly dangerous. She might have ruined everything for Matthew and the other Americans. Perhaps even made their situation worse, as now it was no secret that she knew the whereabouts of the chief mutineer.

But Prinny was as good as his word. There and then he summoned his secretary, Knighton, and had him draw up the document for him to sign, commanding his astounded and none-too-pleased host to see that it was carried forthwith to the prison authorities at Princeton.

'There!' declared Prinny, pressing his Royal Seal in the hot wax and with a flourish signing the document spread out upon his stone gondola. 'Now, Mistress Hammett, perhaps we may partake of our tay! Sooth, we are quite faint from lack of vittles!'

Kezzy stared at him with deep gratitude. It had taken her some time to persuade him that the Yankees weren't the dangerous, rebellious dogs they were coloured but just ordinary men driven by desperation to seek the freedom which was overlong due to them. She'd soon realised that he liked to be flattered and had lavished upon him emotional utterances such as 'Great and merciful Prince so beloved of his subjects.'

She felt a wild surge of happiness. The moment for which she'd longed and prayed for so long had come. Matthew was free! She fell to her knees beside the gratified Prince Regent and seized his plump, beringed hand, pressing her lips to it, tears of joy glittering on her long, sweeping lashes.

'God bless Your Royal Highness,' she whispered.

He patted her cheek. 'Be gone with you and tell your sweetheart the good news.'

As Kezzy rose to obey his command, she glimpsed de Raddon's dark, dangerous face through the mist of her tears. The unexpectedness of his expression, drawn and taut and as grotesque as a gargoyle beneath his fashionable wig, startled her. Their eyes locked for a long moment. What was it she read there? She wasn't sure. Anger, yes. But something else less definable. Then he looked away, pointedly turning his back on her to address himself to Lady Conyngham. Kezzy's sharp ears picked up his coarse, low-voiced comment.

' 'Twould seem the tinner's chit yearns for some Yankee fuckster. Well, she'd best beware. 'Tis said they suffer terribly with the French pox and their children are born deformed.'

Lady Conyngham nodded. 'So I've heard. Some of the mites don't even have heads! They run about like headless chickens!'

Kezzy's face flamed almost as scarlet as her gown with indignation. She pictured Matthew's pockless face; to suggest he had the French pox was pishary-pashary twaddle. She wasn't prepared to hear any more. With as much dignity as she could muster, she swept from the Italian Garden and made her way to where she'd left Rats and the wagon.

More than once on the way home she conjured the image of de Raddon's face with the peculiar expression it had worn when he'd learned that she was not only hiding a Yankee but intended to marry him. In a flash of understanding she realised what was behind de Raddon's hard look and spiteful remarks concerning the pox.

'Jesus God!' she blurted aloud. 'He's jealous!'

She shivered, as though the ominous notion brought with it a chill wind. Yet, there was about her a strange stillness and the moorland seemed bathed in a haze of lilac mist through which her *cohani* powers allowed a momentary glimpse of the future. She saw herself gowned in white with a wreath of myrtle set upon her flowing locks as she was carried to church upon a flower-decked wagon pulled by singing tinners. The picture changed and she was standing at the altar with her groom. There was a terrible silence. The spluttering candles flooded the church with light. She could, if she wished it, look upon the face of her bridegroom. 'Do not look!' urged a voice within her as the image began to fade. 'Let the vision go!' But she couldn't restrain herself from looking into the man's face, whence out of her mouth came a great and intense moan of dispair because it wasn't Matthew's face gazing lovingly back at her but John de Raddon's.

No! God in heaven, no!

Then a soft, stirring breeze wafted the lilac mist, and there came the sound of flapping wings against the stained-glass windows, accompanied by the brittle scratching of claws against the iron window frames, as if some great bird was trying to gain entrance. Kezzy's heart began to throb violently as a shrill sound filled the air.

'Kee . . . kee . . . keeiahhh.'

Strangely soothing, it drove away the dark presentiment. With a start, Kezzy was brought back to reality. It was almost dusk and she was almost home. Had she dozed while Rats plodded on, up the familiar track to

Eaglestone? Pray God it was a dream and not a vision!

'Kee . . . iahhh!'

Kezzy heard the piercing cry again and scanned the steely skies for the eagle. She didn't see any sign of the swooping dark shape but she sensed the great bird was there, spreading her invincible magic and watching over her.

Chapter Thirty-Four

'Must get 'nother Wart to guard yard,' ruminated Elyas between mouthfuls of apple-figgen and thick, yellow cream. 'Ol' Wart be past doin' proper job. Sleeps too much. Best drop he in leat wi' brick tied on he.'

Kezzy shot him a reproachful look. 'There's nothing wrong with Wart save his back legs are a bit cloppy, so just you leave him be.'

'An' we'm a-needin' new Rats. Best shoot he . . . they gossies don't take to bein' turned back on moor after livin' easy betimes.'

Kezzy had to smile at that. Rats's lot had been far from easy: the tough little colt had hardly stopped pulling and carrying since they got him some years before as a replacement for the previous Rats. She said: 'No one's taking a gun to Rats while I'm fit to stop it. He doesn't have much to do anyroads, just pull me to church on Sundays, when I go. He can live out his days here and welcome.'

'Bah! Waste o' oats an' hay. You'm too soft for ye own good, Kezzy chield.'

Kezzy's smile was impish. 'Your hindlegs are cloppy, Gramps, but I wouldn't drop you in leat with a brick.'

'Eh? What's that you'm a-sayin' bout me?'

'You heard, Gramps.'

'Bah!'

It was mid-day, three months after the fugitives had received their Royal Pardon. Kezzy was busy filling a dozen mossle bags with bread and cheese and great slices of figgen to take with canteens of water to the men working in the mine. For, as overseer, Matthew had formed a workforce from among his fellow countrymen – including Moab, Lordy and John Dagge – and had, to the Hammetts' delight, restarted Wheal Eaglestone. How good it was to hear again the creak of the horse-whim and the roar of the furnace! To smell the burning peat and see the thick, black smoke pouring from the chimney stack!

Below ground, a dozen or so men were driving a new tunnel west off Middle Alley near to the scene of the pitblast, but at a respectful distance from the Hammetts' grave. They were hulking copper. And plenty of it. The wall of bright green copper crystals which Elyas swore he'd glimpsed just before fire-damp brought the roof in on him was no figment of his imagination. There were two sturdy horses driving the whim as the kibbles came to the surface full of great lumps of copper ore to be spalled by another half dozen men with hammers until it was the size of rough gravel whence it was ready for market. John Dagge was in charge of selling, on account of the fact that he'd experience of trading as purser aboard the *Maryland*. Unlike tin, there was no fixed price for copper and, as the demand far exceeded supply, he always obtained with little difficulty the best price per thousandweight.

Having his beloved Eaglestone working again gave Elyas new life. There was nothing he liked more than to sit after supper with Kezzy, watching as, by the light of a candle, she made her entries in the stockwork ledger, adding her columns of neat, slanting figures and balancing the totals. And, as he watched her, Elyas silently marvelled at her ability, feeling a great sense of pride because the granddaughter of Elyas the tinner could add a row of figures quicker than even John Dagge who was, after all, a ship's purser.

Word soon spread. The Hammetts had struck copper. They were rich. That wasn't strictly true: the workforce of tributers took the lion's share. None the less, there was plenty of money left for the Hammetts as mine-owners, sufficient to pay for Elyas's medicines and to ensure that Kezzy had no call to risk venturing across the moor dressed as a boy to deliver moonshine for the flaskers. Once the Prince of Wales had pardoned the American fugitives, the troops of dragoons withdrew from the moors. Grote came to Eaglestone once it was safe, sent by de Raddon to ascertain whether the mine was, indeed, working and producing prodigious amounts of copper ore as rumour had it. He brought with him half a dozen hard-faced batmen but hurriedly withdrew when they were met by a score of American tinners armed with peekers. The message he was to take back to his master was quite clear: Keziah Hammett would deliver no more moonshine.

To begin with, backalong the beginning of May, Wheal Eaglestone had boasted nearly forty tributers and spallers. The numbers had gradually depleted as, three and four at a time, the men were summoned to Plymouth and given passage home aboard American merchantmen.

If Kezzy was honest with herself, she knew that one day very soon a warrant brought up the moor by an Admiralty clerk would bear the name Matthew Youngmay. It was something about which neither of them ever spoke, though sometimes Kezzy steeled herself to ask him the question that haunted her every waking moment and most of her dreams. *When that terrible time came, would he stay or go?* But the words would stick in her throat, so afraid was she of what he might answer. For never, not even as they lay together in the dark of her little stone-walled room at the back of the cottage, when Elyas had fallen into a deep soporific-induced sleep, did Matthew ever speak, as lovers were wont, of the future. Yes, he would whisper words of eternal love against her mouth as he held her to him. Sometimes, after they had made love, he would talk drowsily of his childhood in an overcrowded shanty near the Pennsylvanian coal-fields, about how he'd run away to sea and worked his way up from powder-monkey aboard a leaky Customs Service frigate to first lieutenant aboard the US *Maryland*. He told her of the *Maryland*'s short, bloody battle with *HMS Pelican* that had left her master dead and the rest of the survivors prisoners-of-war. He told her, in a calm, emotionless voice, of his incarceration, of the brutality and the privations. He told her how the vision of her lovely, compassionate face, briefly glimpsed beside Crazywell Pool, had not merely comforted him, but had saved his sanity and inspired him to think of escape. And over and over again, he would tell her in a voice hoarse with emotion that he owed his very life to her and that every beat of his heart, every breath, every nerve and sinew, belonged to her body and soul.

But he never told her he would stay.

Kezzy took the mossle bags and canteens to the mine entrance. On seeing her, the man driving the whim-horses reined them in so the creaking of the pulley wouldn't drown out the cow-bells when she tugged on them in the shaft. It wasn't long before a dusty face appeared in answer to the peal, eyes blinking in the strong sunlight, the candle set in clay atop his tin hat guttering in the warm breeze. Seeing Kezzy, the grimy face split into a huge, white grin.

'Hallo, Lordy,' she said smiling back at him, ' 'tis mossle.'

His grin widened and he licked his lips in anticipation.

'Might there be a slice o' your figgen for us today, Missy Hammett?' he asked hopefully. Lordy was particularly partial to figgen.

'There might.'

Eagerly, he slung the bags and the dozen small barrels of water on his back as if they weighed nothing and began his descent. Then he paused, came up the two rungs again, calling her back.

'Missy Hammett! The lieutenant says if you ain't too busy he'd be mighty pleased if you'll take a walk with him.'

Kezzy's heart beat a little faster as it always did at the thought of spending even a few precious minutes with Matthew strolling in the sunshine.

'Tell *Captain* Youngmay I'm not too busy.'

'Aye, aye, Missy. Danged if I can git used to callin' the lieutenant Cap'n when he ain't . . . least not proper *sea* cap'n . . .'

Still mumbling to himself, Lordy disappeared downwards.

The whim-driver had unhitched the horses to rest them and given them buckets of oats and two more of water. Kezzy gave him the rest of the mossle bags for the men working on the surface and he loped off towards the spalling ground with them. Seconds later, the clink-clink of iron on rock ceased as they dropped their hammers and fell upon the good, filling food.

Kezzy walked across to the brook and sat in the shade of a rock. The boggy ground along the bank was dotted with vivid yellow asphodel and beautiful, flush-pink bog-rosemary. Close by her, a patch of strongly aromatic boy myrtle was alive with bees. Myrtle!

A coronet of myrtle!

Involuntarily, she recalled the vision of herself as a bride adorned with myrtle which she'd had on her way home from Blackaven three months before and experienced the same terrible sense of foreboding as then. She closed her eyes momentarily, willing the image away. As though she would even think of marrying the stony-hearted, cruel-faced de Raddon! If she couldn't marry her darling Matthew, then she'd as lief plight her troth to Peter Dorrity . . . or even Tom Beckwitt. Anyone, including Old Nick himself, would be preferable to taking poor dead Emma's place in the Lord Warden's bed!

She heard a football and her gloom was instantly dispelled by the sight of Matthew approaching. His eyes shone, a vivid sea-blue, from the pale dust caking his face and dimming the gold of his hair. She gave him an impish grin.

'Good day, Captain Youngmay. I'm surprised you have the time to dally with bal maidens.'

He smiled at that, but the smile, Kezzy noticed, didn't reach his eyes and she felt a stab of unease. He dropped to one knee and planted a swift kiss on her mouth before rising again and going to the brook. Stripping off his shirt, he threw himself face down in the cold shallows, scooping the water over his head and upper body to remove some of the grime. Droplets of water glittered in the sun on his back, running in rivulets along the ridged scars. He shook the dust from his shirt and put it back on, leaving it open so the sunlight burnished his chest hairs to pure gold. He sat down next to Kezzy, an arm loosely draped about her shoulders.

'Did you see the eagles?'

She was immediately drawing away from him and scanning the sky excitedly. 'No! Where?'

He pointed. Kezzy squinted, following his finger to the rolling hills below Eagle Tor. Because the sun was at its highest and the shadows were at their shortest, the grassy slopes were a sunlit backdrop against which the antics of the eagle and her mate could be seen as they swooped and dropped in search of small prey.

'How strange, I've never seen the male before,' remarked Kezzy, shading her eyes the better to see the two birds.

'Perhaps he's the shy and retiring sort.'

'Well, shy won't feed hungry eaglets and I'll wager they've a brace of them sitting in yon nest. 'Tis mice they're hunting.'

'Shall we climb up and look?'

Kezzy looked horrified. 'We'll do no such thing.'

'Why not? Mebbe take a bag and get ourselves a good hunting bird to train.'

Kezzy gasped. 'You wouldn't!'

Then she saw that his blue eyes were laughing at her from his otherwise solemn face. He was teasing her: he knew how passionately protective she was about the eagles. She pulled a face at him and settled back against his chest again.

After a while she said: 'Is that what you do in America? Steal eaglets and train them as birds of prey?'

'Golden eagles. They aren't as big but they're just as vicious.' He looked down into her disapproving face. 'They aren't badly treated, Kezzy. And they get to hunt.'

Kezzy shifted irritably. 'But they're not *free*, Matthew.'

'No. They're not free,' he admitted softly. He knew what she was saying: *wasn't freedom everything?*

His arm tightened about her, with his other hand he cupped her chin, turning her face upwards to his. He kissed her gently on the mouth and felt her lips drowsily, sensually, open. One of her long, white slender arms coiled around his neck and she pressed eagerly against his lean and muscular body as he drew her with him until they were lying full-length upon a rich green bed of sweet-scented myrtle.

The very nearness of him flooded Kezzy with wild emotion. She craved his lustful kisses, his tender, urgent hands upon her body, to feel his heart savagely beating against hers. Life would be nothing without him.

'Don't leave me, my darling. Don't ever leave me,' she whispered.

Her words broke the spell. Abruptly, he released her and sat up, arms resting on his knees, gazing at the ground beneath his feet. Kezzy supported herself on her elbow, starting at him bemusedly. What had brought about the sudden change in him? She put out a hand tentatively, touching his arm caressingly.

'Matthew . . .' He sat in frigid silence. She withdrew her hand. 'What's wrong, Matthew?'

She knew the answer, even before he said in a voice filled with unutterable sadness, 'I must go home, Kezzy.'

Something cold, colder even than the tumbling brook, clutched at her heart. 'No! Don't say it!' She flung herself into his arms and clung to him. She began to sob, her whole body shaking convulsively.

'Please, Kezzy . . .' His voice faltered; he had the taste of ashes in his mouth.

'I won't let you go,' she wept desperately.

He took her face in both of his hands and gazed deep into her brimming eyes. 'Listen to me, Kezzy. Listen, my darling . . .'

But she wouldn't listen. She could only spill forth a great flood of words and feelings and pleas: saying anything that might make him stay, and all the while Matthew said nothing, staring down at her with an expression of sorrow and despair on his tense, grey face, for his mind was made up, cruelly hard though the decision was.

Suddenly Kezzy thought of her grandfather, saw him as clearly as though he was there, hoary-headed, pale-eyed, yet full of pride and dignity and thoroughly disgusted with her for weeping and wailing like some love-crossed flibbertigibbet. She caught her breath, swallowed hard, fighting to regain her equanimity.

She did not know that her face had altered, that the image of Elyas, solid and supporting and fond, had brought to her face an almost child-like softness which wrenched at Matthew's heart. He stared at the slanting dark eyes, still misty with tears, the bitter-sweet curve of her lovely mouth and for a moment found his staunch determination to put duty before love wavering. One word from her, one more plea, and he would cave in; he would stay with her at Eaglestone whatever the consequences. He found himself almost willing her to utter that deciding plea but she just stared back at him saying nothing and the moment passed.

Presently, in a voice that was strangely calm, she said: 'How long have you known?'

'Four days. The clerk came with the warrants early Monday.'

She nodded. She had gone to Wisdome's mill straight after breakfast to buy flour. There was still a shortage of grain but flour could be had for those who could pay for it. And with so much good copper ore coming out of Eaglestone, it was a luxury the Hammetts and their tributers could afford.

She steeled herself to ask the painful question. 'When must you leave?'

'Kezzy . . .'

'When?'

'Tomorrow.'

'Jesus God.'

'I should have told you. I . . . tried to . . .' he said brokenly.

She shook her head dumbly. Did it really matter? Would knowing on Monday have lessened the pain? In retrospect, she should have guessed. For he hadn't made love to her these past three nights. True, he had come to her bed – slipping by a snoring Elyas – lain entwined with her, kissed her, though not with such passion as he usually did, only to fall into a deep, restless sleep. She knew that he worked harder than any man at Eaglestone. Besides a long daily coore in by the bal, he took his turn at spalling the ore in the evening, wielding one of the big hammers until the sweat poured off him. And if such long, hard toil for the ultimate benefit of herself and her grandfather drained Matthew of his strength, what right had she to make still more physical demands upon him? Kezzy had asked herself as she'd lain wakefully beside his sleeping form the past three nights with her flesh aching to be claimed by his flesh.

'What of the other men?' she heard herself asking dully. 'How many go with you?'

'Moab and John and a half dozen more. But not Lordy . . . not yet,' he told her, voice rueful, as if he felt guilty because they, too, were deserting her.

'So they knew, also?'

'Yes. I . . . asked them not to say. Not until I'd told you myself.'

Silent and brooding, they sat gazing across the brook at the rolling vista of heather-clad hills, so close their bodies were almost touching, yet it seemed as if a great, thick wall of ice had grown between them.

After a while, Matthew said: 'I'll make sure a good man takes over as overseer.'

Kezzy couldn't keep the bitterness from her voice. 'And how long will it be before he, too, is given his passage home?' For a long moment the atmosphere was tense, then Kezzy put out an impulsive hand to cover Matthew's. 'I know I've no right to expect any of you to stay . . . of course you all want to go home . . .'

The blue eyes flashed. 'God in heaven, do you think that? That I *want* to leave you. Oh, Kezzy, Kezzy . . .' he gathered her to him, holding her rigid body tightly, his fingers tangled in her long hair. 'I *must* go back. I'm an American naval officer. If I stay, I'll be listed as a deserter. For ever branded a coward. Disgraced! Desertion is worse than mutiny, Kezzy. We'd have to live in the shadows . . . afraid of every knock at the door. Afraid of every stranger we happened across in case he was a bounty-hunter . . .'

She began to weep, clutching at him with clawed hands in her desperation. 'I don't care! As long as we're together, I don't care!'

'If they caught me I'd be dragged away in chains. Court-martialled. Hanged from the yardarm. No, Kezzy. No. What happiness would there be for us, living with a great black cloud hanging over our heads and blighting our lives together?'

She knew that he spoke the truth: what happiness, indeed? She also knew that just as the Hammetts were born tinners, Matthew, despite his mining origins, was born to the sea – perhaps through some long distant heredity that had taken generations to reveal itself again in his blood. To men like him, the salty tang of sea-air and the crash of waves against a wooden hulk carried with them as much pride and satisfaction as the creak of the whim and the thump of the stamps did to a tinner or copper-miner. Kezzy's sobs abated and her clutching hands relaxed.

'I'll come back,' he whispered against her hair.

She shook her head. 'No. Once you return to America you'll not come back.'

He wanted desperately to argue with her: to swear to God that he would return to her just as soon as he had been given his discharge in the proper manner. But the words wouldn't come. She was right: America was a world away with a great ocean in between. Moreover, getting his discharge probably wouldn't prove too easy. The United States Navy would bring pressure to bear upon him when they discovered he wanted to resign his commission for the sake of a dark-eyed tinner's daughter in Britain. No, they'd not discharge him willingly.

Kezzy let go of Matthew, drawing a little away from him. She shook her head in unhappy bewilderment. 'I can't believe . . . *tomorrow*!' she murmured.

She lifted her tear-stained face to his and Matthew's insides churned at the intense misery in her bright, sensitive eyes. He hadn't wanted to hurt her, would have given anything for it to be otherwise: anything save his honour. He owed her so much and loved her so deeply.

Impetuously, he said: 'Come with me, my darling. To America.'

The long eyes went round and it was as if a mist had lifted from them. Her ashen cheeks flooded with pink. 'Go with you,' she gasped, hardly able to believe what he was saying.

He took her hands in both of his, gripping them hard, his words coming rapidly. 'We can be married in Plymouth tomorrow. We'll find a parson who's more interested in a gold sovereign than calling banns. The master of my ship can't refuse you passage . . . not if you're my wife.

Why, if he's willing, then he can marry us . . . sea-captains can, you know . . .'

Her eyes were preternaturally bright. 'Can I go with you, Matthew? Can I really?'

He hugged her. 'Oh yes, yes, my darling! God in heaven! I must have been mad to even *think* of leaving you behind.'

'But where shall we live when we get to America?'

He laughed merrily. 'Oh, we shall not be paupers. A first lieutenant's money will keep a wife, never fear.'

'I shall wear my red taffeta gown to be married in,' declared Kezzy excitedly. *Anything but white silk and myrtle!* the thought occurred to her.

'And no man shall ever have a more beautiful bride! Oh, Kezzy, I love you so!'

He drew her to him again and kissed her passionately. As he did so, he felt her body suddenly tense and her lips turned to marble as her joy evaporated. She tore her mouth from his and pushed him away almost fiercely, something she'd never done before.

'What is it, Kezzy?'

'I can't go with you, Matthew.'

'Why not? You love me, don't you?'

'Yes, I love you . . .' Two tears escaped from her eyes. 'but I must stay here.'

'Why must you? What is there here for you?' he asked her wildly.

Elyas answered for her, his voice drifting across from the cottage door where he stood propped on his crutches.

'Kezzy! Where are ye, chield? 'Tis past mossle an' they hammers bain't workin' . . .'

'Your grandfather,' said Matthew, understanding dawning.

'How could I leave him?'

Her eyes begged him to understand that her loyalty to Elyas and Eaglestone flamed every bit as brightly as did his own loyalty to America and the US Navy.

'Keziah! Where you'm got to, chield?' came Elyas's plaintive, quavering voice again. He coughed, a harsh, rattling sound which carried clear across the valley. 'I'm a-needin' lung-syrup, Kezzy, an' I can't reach un down from shelf.'

'I'm coming, Gramps!' she called.

In a moment she was gone.

Elyas's fit of coughing grew worse during the next hour. By now, Kezzy had learned to recognise the symptoms of an impending attack of brain-fever: the high colour, the staring eyes, the aggressive, almost violent manner towards her. Having administered lung-syrup, which only served to loosen the thick mucus in his chest to help his breathing, she hastened to give him a large dose of laudanum. He was ranting and raving so much, and tearing his blanket to shreds, that she went out into the yard, searching for one of the men to help her since Elyas acquired the strength of three men while in the throes of brain-fever. She saw Lordy crossing to the spalling ground for his coore.

'Lordy. Help me please with Cap'n Hammett.'

The big copper-skinned man came immediately. Lifting Elyas in his huge arms as if he were a baby and tipping his head back so that Kezzy could trickle the laudanum down his throat. Then he laid him on his pallet and held him pinned down until it had taken effect and Elyas became drowsy.

'There you are, missy. He'll be right as iron in wink of an eye, poor ol' varmint.'

'Thank you, Lordy.'

'You just holla if you need me 'gin.' He ambled towards the door.

'Lordy.'

He turned. 'Yes, missy?'

'I'm sorry you haven't been given your passage home with Cap'n Youngmay and Moab and John Dagge.'

Lordy shrugged his massive shoulders unconcernedly.

'Don't matter, missy. I ain't frettin' none over it.'

He went out.

Kezzy stayed close to the cottage for the rest of that day watching over Elyas while he slept. Quietly she went about her tasks, cooking two big pots, one of vegetables, one of rabbit and chicken, for the men's supper. Lordy and Moab came at sundown to collect the food along with a basket of bread. Moab kept his eyes lowered, not wanting to meet Kezzy's eyes. She had been good to them; taken them in when they were fugitives with empty bellies. Now, at the first chance any of them had of a ship, they were off home, leaving her to cope as best she could, and for that Moab couldn't help but feel a sense of shame.

' 'Tis all right, Moab,' Kezzy told the wizened little man gently. 'I understand why you must go.'

'Do you, missy?' he asked, surprised. He'd been expecting her to upbraid them for letting her down when the mine was doing so well.

She made a wry grimace. 'The moors can't compete with the sea.'

He looked at her gratefully. She *did* understand. 'We're mighty beholden to you, missy, don't go thinkin' we ain't. But we're *sailors* not miners.' A faraway look came into his eyes. 'Ain't nothin' like a good swabbed deck beneath yer feet . . . the smell o' brine in yer nostrils . . .'

Lordy gave him a dig with his elbow. 'Grub's gettin' cold.'

Moab came out of his reverie and picked up one of the pots, he gave Kezzy a weak, apologetic little smile and followed Lordy out.

Matthew generally came to the cottage at supper time to eat at table with the Hammetts, but there was no sign of him that evening. His wooden bowl, trencher and tin mug stood unused on the table. Kezzy had no appetite for eating. She considered whether she should attempt to rouse Elyas and feed him some of the liquor from the rabbit and chicken since he'd not eaten since early morning but decided to let him sleep. If the brain-fever hadn't abated then she'd only have to give him more laudanum.

She heard Wart give a welcoming whine and looked out of the window.

Darkness had fallen but the sky was as clear as dark blue satin and there was a fair moon. Kezzy saw a figure move across the yard towards the entrance to Eaglestone. The fair head, silvery in the moonlight, the tall, slender silhouette, made his identity unmistakable. She slipped out after him, found him sitting on the low stone wall gazing out into drowning darkness. Her arrival disturbed a nightjar roosting in the heather and it rose up, uttering its long-drawn, purring cry. Matthew didn't look up at her; or draw her down beside him on the wall as once he would have. She stood waiting, not wishing to intrude. After a while, to break the brooding silence, she said, 'You didn't come in for supper, Matthew.'

'I . . . wasn't sure if I'd be welcome. I ate with the men.'

'Oh, Matthew . . .' There was a break in her voice and she put out a hand towards him. He seized it and pressed it to his cheek.

'Dear heart alive! I need you, Kezzy. I can't live without you! Make me stay! Make me stay and I'll . . .'

'No, Matthew,' she said in a faint, dull voice, interrupting his emotional plea. 'If I were to beg you . . . say the words that would make you stay, though God alone knows what they might be . . . I would be asking you to forfeit not just honour and reputation, but everything you have achieved. I would be asking you to go back to where you started . . . below ground, where the sun never reaches and the dust rots your lungs. No, Matthew, I'll not make you stay.'

After a pause he drew a deep breath, then tenderly pressed his lips to the palm of the hand he still held captured.

Kezzy said: 'Come, my love . . . come to bed. Love me one last time.'

So he did. With a passionate tenderness which fused their hearts and their minds as well as their bodies, and cemented their love so that it would survive whatever the future might bring.

Chapter Thirty-Five

When Kezzy awoke next morning she was alone. Her heart gave a wild lurch and she scrambled into her clothes, afraid that she'd find Matthew had slipped away before dawn without saying good-bye.

As she hurried through to the front door, Elyas was stirring, yawning and stretching his thin arms stiffly. 'Elly tea, chield?' he asked but she didn't stop to answer. She flew out into the yard, eyes desperately scanning the scene for Matthew. She felt weak with relief when she saw him over by the brook. His hair was wet and his broad, bare torso glittered with drops of water in the bright rising sun. He had washed both his shirts, his good white cotton one, once Huward Hammett's Sunday shirt, and his rough calico workshirt, and draped them over the bushes to dry. Kezzy felt a pang on seeing this: she would gladly have washed them for him if only he had asked her. Clearly, he felt he could ask no more of her now that he was going.

She went back inside and helped Elyas rise from his pallet and move across to sit at the table. Working almost mechanically, her mind busy with so many other thoughts, Kezzy filled a mug with hot water from the cauldron on the slab and added a handful of tea leaves, stirring until the water turned amber. Then she added a big spoon of sugar and a generous measure of cream. She placed the tea before Elyas who gulped it greedily between gasping breaths. It always helped his chest if he drank hot tea as soon as possible after awakening. Otherwise he would be seized by a terrible fit of coughing, often lasting nigh on an hour and which left him too weak to take food.

While he drank his tea, Kezzy put two big pots of oatmeal on to boil. When he set down his empty mug with a clang, she broke the news to him, saying in a loud, clear, emotionless voice, 'Gramps, Matthew is leaving Eaglestone this morning. He has his passage home.'

Elyas's watery eyes narrowed beneath his shaggy brows. 'Did I hear ye proper, chield? Thy Yankee be *leavin'*?'

'Yes.'

The eyes narrowed still more. 'Bain't takin' ye along wi' he?'

'No.'

Elyas looked relieved. 'Then good riddance. If'n he don't want to stay he don't want to stay, an' that suits us!'

Although he'd reacted with his usual stoicism, Kezzy knew that the old man was deeply disappointed. And deeply hurt. For himself, but mainly for her because she'd so openly declared her love for Matthew only now to be seemingly spurned. Moreover, she guessed that Elyas hadn't always been as sound asleep as he'd made out when Matthew crept by him. Somewhat defensively, she said: 'He's coming back, Gramps. As soon as he's properly free of the navy. Then we'll be wed.'

Elyas's response to that was to spit in the fire. 'He'll not come back from Yankee land, chield. So best 'ee look 'bout for 'nother shiner an' get ring on thy finger.'

Kezzy stirred the oatmeal unhappily, hating this talk of her marrying some man other than Matthew. To change the subject, she said: 'Moab and John Dagge and half a dozen more are also going.'

Elyas glowered. 'Ungrateful load o' hogs! We'll have to knock bal 'gin, rate they be a-leavin'.'

'We didn't have a setting day when they started,' Kezzy felt drawn to remind him of the fact that the men hadn't signed contracts which bound them to Eaglestone for any length of time. 'Anyroads, we can take on local men to replace them . . . all of them if necessary.'

'We'll do no such thing!' retorted Elyas furiously. 'They Yankees was awlright an' not too greedy but I'm a-tellin' 'ee, Kezzy, they local tributers will rob us blind o' copper. Ay, an candles an' tools an' Lord knows what else. On account I can't watch they in by bal, an' thee's but a maid.'

Kezzy spun to face him, chin up, hands on her hips. 'Are you saying I wouldn't make as good an overseer as Matthew?' she demanded, eyes flashing.

He held up a conciliatory hand. 'Don't start showin' hackle, chield. 'Course you'm right good overseer . . . you'm a Hammett ent you'm?'

'Well, then,' she said, tossing her head, somewhat mollified. She returned to stirring the oatmeal.

'I won't have it, Keziah,' Elyas told her determined back view. 'I don't hold wi' women an' maids workin' below grass. Never have. 'Tis too dangerous for they. I'll see bal knocked afore ye goes in by mine as overseer.'

She didn't turn around, saying loudly over her shoulder: 'Then I'd have to go back to flasking for Cap'n de Raddon.'

Elyas spat in the fire again. 'That scurf! Hidin' behind maid wearin' britches! Nay, nay, Kezzy, bain't proper, riskin' gettin' boated to do de Raddon's dirty work. I've been a-thinkin' this past three-month while that ol' mine has bin worked honest belikes. Ye'll not go deliverin' moonshine 'gin save over Elyas Hammett's dead body.'

'Oh Gramps . . . how would we ever manage?' Her voice caught and she left off her stirring and went to him, dropping to her knees beside him, her head resting on his bony arm. He stroked her thick, dark hair.

'Like I said, you'm best forget you Yankee an' get thyself wed. There be plenty boys leap at chance o' marryin' Cap'n Hammett's granddaughter. 'Specially wi' dowry like Eaglestone.'

'But I love Matthew, Gramps,' she whispered, tears pricking her eyes.

He didn't hear, patting her head comfortingly as he would Wart's and said: 'Now what 'bout they oats? Me guts is terrible empty.'

Eaglestone was coming alive. The men were appearing from the barn, blinking in the light, yawning and stretching and hungry for their breakfast. Usually, there was a buzz of cheerful voices and the occasional shout of laughter as they splashed each other with ladles of cold drinking-water from the buckets hung in the yard. But this particular morning there was an air of melancholy hanging over Eaglestone. The men were clearly dejected because Matthew was leaving, and with him cheerful, shrewd little Moab and wise-headed John Dagge. Even Lordy couldn't raise a smile when Kezzy called him to help carry out the pots of oatmeal. He, and all the others who were left behind, would soon be given their own passages home, but meanwhile there would be an aching void in their lives. Matthew had been their leader; guiding them, encouraging them, leading them to freedom and by so doing saving the lives of many of them who might otherwise have died of disease or starvation. They owed him a debt that none of them would ever forget.

Matthew didn't line up with the men for a bowl of hot oatmeal. He'd no appetite. Nor could he bring himself to face the ashen-faced Kezzy as she ladled out their breakfast. At least, not beneath the curious, sympathetic stares of the men. He went, instead, into the cottage to say goodbye to Elyas.

Elyas looked up from his bowl, saw who it was and frowned. 'So you'm off home then, boy?'

Matthew stood straight-backed, jaw jutting as though on the quarter-deck. 'I would like to return when I've resigned my commission, Captain Hammett. To marry Kezzy.'

The wiry grey brows arched. 'Dare says ye would, boy. Thing is, *will* ye return? Speakin' personal belikes, I don't reckon we'll see ye 'gin. Not once you'm back home 'mong other Yankees. How far is this place America, anyroads?'

Matthew's voice was hollow. 'A long way.'

'Eh?'

He raised his voice. 'A month away . . . with a fair wind.'

That settled it so far as Elyas was concerned. 'Ye'll not return, boy,' he said with deep certainty and went back to his bowl.

Matthew knew there was nothing he could say that would convince the old man differently. Only his actual return some time in the future would do that. If, indeed, he did return . . . Matthew brushed from him the very notion that he might not. Of course he would return! There would be nothing and no one to keep him in America once he was free of the navy.

'I'll never forget your kindness, Captain Hammett. Not yours, not Kezzy's . . .' His voice faltered as a lump came into his throat.

Elyas looked up, meeting the blue-eyed gaze. Suddenly he stuck out his hand for Matthew to shake. 'I won't say I ent dis'pointed you'm a-goin', but I'll wish ye God speed an' safe journey just the same.'

Matthew gripped the gnarled hand. 'God keep you, Cap'n Hammett.'

He went out into the yard.

Lordy had the whim horses hitched to the wagon in readiness to drive the departing Americans down the moor to Plymouth. Instead of starting work, the rest of the men had gathered to watch them leave.

Matthew looked for Kezzy without seeing her.

'Her be over by brook, Matt,' muttered Moab.

She was neatly folding the white cotton shirt he'd left to dry on the bush, having donned the calico one. Lost in thought, she didn't hear his approach and started when his shadow fell across the flat rock upon which she was folding the shirt.

'I was going to return the shirt to you,' he said.

'Take it. You'll be needing a fresh shirt when you get to America.' She took the bleached flour sack he was using as a gunny sack to carry his few possessions and put the shirt in it, pulling tight the drawstrings again. She handed it to him.

'Thank you. It's a good shirt. Finely stitched.'

'My mother made it for my pa.'

They were making conversation, putting off the dread moment when they must say 'good-bye' and part, probably for ever. They fell silent for a while, their eyes saying more than their lips ever could.

A great shudder ran through Matthew making it difficult for him speak without a tremor in his voice. 'The others are waiting . . . I must go.'

'I could come with you . . . to Plymouth,' Kezzy blurted.

'No!' His voice was abrupt. Then it softened as he said, 'That would be just postponing the torture.'

'When do you sail? Do you know? So I might think of you then.'

'In three days.'

'To think,' said Kezzy bitterly, 'for two weeks we shall be separated by just a strip of water. Not some great ocean.'

Lordy's apologetic voice boomed across to them. 'Beggin' yer pardon, Lieutenant . . . er, Cap'n . . . er, anyways, we best be gettin' long if I'm to be there an' back before sundown.'

Dear heavens, it was time! A sharp, searing pain gripped Kezzy's heart. Dry-mouthed, she stared at Matthew, all the things she'd meant to say to him at this moment forgotten.

His own eyes were suddenly luminous with tears. If only, he thought wretchedly, if only he didn't love her. His arm went around her, sweeping her to him and, as if to still her lips from saying words which might hurt them both still more, his mouth descended on hers with a quick, bruising force. He released her quickly, snatched up his sack and strode away from her.

Sick with dismay, her hands clenching into bloodless fists, Kezzy watched as he climbed up beside Lordy on the box and the wagon rolled across the yard towards the gap in the surrounding wall.

The men sitting, legs dangling, along each side and the back of the tail-board called out to Kezzy in low, sad voices.

'Good-bye, missy.'

'God bless you, missy.'

She unclenched one of her hands and forced herself to wave her kerchief as the team quickened and the wagon moved off down the valley at a brisk pace. She climbed a rock, not caring that she skinned her hands and knees, so that she could follow the wagon all the way down the valley and out across the wild, wind-blown land beyond. The mournful groups who had gathered in the yard to watch the departure began to break up as the men went about their work. But Kezzy remained like a sentinel on her rock, the breeze stirring her hair, the sun growing warm upon her skin. She watched, through eyes scalded with grief, until the wagon was a dot in the distance and she could no longer make out Matthew's erect figure and gleaming golden head.

Goodbye, my love! My only love . . . she cried silently after him.

But not once did he turn around.

Four days later, aboard the American merchantman *Caroline*, Matthew took from his sack the white cotton shirt so lovingly folded by Kezzy. It was his first evening at sea and he thought he had better wear it since he had been invited by the skipper to dine with the senior crew members. As he shook out the folds, something fell to the floor with a dull thud and began rolling gently to and fro with the plunging of the ship. Matthew retrieved the object and stood for a long time staring at it as it lay in the palm of his hand. It was smooth and oval-shaped, and a rather unusual shade of grey. It was Kezzy's most valued possession. Her eaglestone!

During the first week following Matthew's departure, the Admiralty clerk came twice to Eaglestone bearing warrants summoning yet more of the Eaglestone workforce to Plymouth to board merchantmen for their passage home. By the end of the second week copper-production had almost ceased. Only Lordy and three others remained and Kezzy had to drive the whim horses if any rate of production was to continue.

That itinerant band of tributers, the Dinion family, stopped a night at Eagle Brook and offered their services for a sixty-forty split of the copper ore – the lion's share to go to them. Kezzy wasn't against the idea – better a small slice of pie than none at all! – but Elyas flew into one of his rages, spitting copiously into the fire and ranting at Kezzy for even suggesting it.

'Why, you'm might as well just gi' they Dinions deeds o' bal. Do you'm really 'magine them would play us fair? Gi' us our forty 'cent share honest an' proper? Bah! You'm soft-headed, chield! I tell 'ee, they trav'lin' tributers be worse an' slyer un tinkers for a-takin' what bain't belongin' to they. Skin thy turds for tallow given half a chance!'

Elyas's mind was clearly made up, and with so much to do now they were so short-handed, Kezzy had neither the time nor energy to argue with him. So the Dinions moved on. But not before Ma Dinion surveyed Kezzy from head to toe and casually remarked: 'So you'm bin got by one o' they Yankees, have 'ee?'

Incredulity and blind panic rendered Kezzy speechless. She fought to gather her wits, trying to calculate the number of days since her last monthly flux. With a surge of relief, it occurred to her that it would be quite impossible for Ma Dinion to recognise any signs of pregnancy. For if she was carrying Matthew's child, she would have had to have conceived during their last night of love. Just sixteen days ago. No. Ma Dinion was simply scandal-mongering. She had to be!

Kezzy found her voice and hotly began to deny the suggestion. 'Oh no, you're quite wrong . . .'

'Well, you'm best to knowed that,' shrugged Ma Dinion, but her leathery features showed her scepticism. Her eyes darted, suddenly sly, towards the mine. 'Folk reckoned Hammett mine had gone horse but I never thought it. Mebbe slippy an' that, but plenty o' tin an' copper to be dug out o' there. Pity you'm bain't a-hirin' tributers.'

'My grandfather . . .' Kezzy began to explain.

'Oh ay,' dismissed Ma Dinion, 'Ol' Elyas do like to keep un bal in family.' Her sly eyes moved down over Kezzy's slender form again. ' 'Course, if'n you'm find 'ee has bin got . . . well, then, our boy Garge bain't too particular. He'll do 'ee favour an' take 'ee on. Ay, thy babbie an' thy mine . . .'

'That won't be necessary,' said Kezzy sharply.

'I bain't never wrong,' said Ma Dinion. 'When our Rosie were last got, I done presumed 'twere so within two-week o' ruttin'.'

Kezzy had trouble restraining her temper. 'For once, Mrs Dinion, you are presuming too much,' she declared icily and turned and strode away.

Ma Dinion called after her: 'Ye won't find many boys like our Garge willin' to take 'ee on wi' bellyful o' some Yankee's by-blow.'

Rosie Dinion joined her mother, her baby in her strong brown arms. She stared after Kezzy.

'Her don't look as though her's a-brewin', Ma.'

'Her don't believe it, but her is,' said Ma Dinion definitely.

Kezzy had been withdrawn ever since Matthew had left, and often her eyes were red and swollen from crying in secret. She would, however, make an attempt to put on a cheerful face while going about her work as mine-captain or when it came to overseeing Lordy as he served the men their meals from the big pots hung in the yard. This evening, however, she was extremely preoccupied, not even responding with a weak smile to Lordy's banter with the other three men as she usually did. And when they were all served, she went and sat on the wall, alone and desolate, staring down the valley into the creeping dark.

'Reckon her pinin' for her lieutenant,' muttered Lordy to the others, and they nodded sympathetically, feeling for her. They, too, missed Matthew's presence. Kezzy might incur their compassion but Matthew incurred their loyalty to the point of hero-worship. Most of those who'd gone made no secret of the fact that if Matthew had stayed, then they would have done likewise and settled on the moors as copper-miners, probably eventually marrying local girls. A few Americans had refused passage home, preferring to remain and marry English sweethearts. The young sailor who had been given refuge in Jim Beckwitt's secret cellar beneath his kiddleywink had asked for pretty plump Jane Beckwitt, had been accepted and the banns read. When Kezzy heard, through Dame Rogers, she had suffered a pang of envy because Jane was to marry her American sweetheart while she had lost hers. But she dismissed her jealousy as being unworthy and sent Jane her best wishes along with a pincushion that she made herself from scraps of red taffeta left over from her best dress and which she then sat up all one night to embroider with the United States flag on one side and the British flag on the other.

But Kezzy wasn't thinking only of Matthew as she sat brooding in the twilight. Paramount in her mind was Ma Dinion's thunderbolt. Despite instinctively rounding on the woman, Kezzy's own strange sixth-sense told her that what the shrewd old bal maiden had said was true and that she *was* carrying Matthew's child. Although how Ma Dinion could tell was a complete mystery since as yet there were no physical changes; her waist was as slender as ever and her stomach as flat.

What should she do?

As calmly as she could, Kezzy thought about that. She could tell her grandfather. He wouldn't be pleased. He would be sure to rant and rave about another mouth to feed and give himself an attack of brain-fever. So not Elyas; at least, not yet. Dame Hannah Rogers, then? Kezzy pictured her kind old friend dressed in mousey-grey, neat and prim. Oh dear! The dame would no doubt, be deeply shocked that Kezzy had joined the ranks of ruined women. But it was likely that she would know where to obtain certain special potions. The sort that would flush out her innards and bring on the flux. In truth, do as the bal maidens sometimes did when they found themselves in a similar desperate plight. *Get rid of the baby!* Kezzy shuddered at this drastic idea. No, whatever happened, she wouldn't do that.

Involuntarily, her hand went to her belly. ' 'Twould be murder,' she muttered aloud.

As would be throwing herself in the nearest deep water; the sad and tragic step taken each year by at least one ruined maiden from thereabouts. Besides, Kezzy swiftly reminded herself, how would her grandfather manage without her?

So, marriage.

The prospect, save to her beloved Matthew, filled Kezzy with dread. One after another, the dull-witted faces of the Dinion boy, Garge, Tom Beckwitt, and half a dozen more like them flashed before her eyes. Marry one of them and she'd be marrying a life of drudgery. She'd be a bal-maiden, no more, no less; a swede-grubbing, peat-digging, ore-washing chattal whose chief assets were a strong pair of arms, a fertile womb and a copper-mine. Yet, marriage was her only solution if she wasn't to live the life of a shamed outcast up there on the moor. Another face, tense with pale, serious, sensitive eyes, insinuated itself into her mind's eye like a picture in a frame. *Peter Dorrity.*

She did not love Peter – felt only a certain fondness for him, brief companion of her youth that he was, along with a great deal of pity for all that he had endured as a de Raddon apprentice. The poverty and cruelty and degradation, the bitter memory of which still held his spirit in chains. Perhaps marriage to her would help draw the curtains from the windows of his tortured soul. *If* he was still of a mind to marry her once he knew that she was with child by Matthew Youngmay. For Kezzy was determined that there would be no pretence regarding her condition. No entrapment. Peter was entitled to know the truth. Yet, if she married Peter, what of Eaglestone? Peter may have been a boy-tinner but mining wasn't in his blood like it was in hers. Perhaps he would prefer to remain a riding officer all his days and they would have to live in a little cottage down by the coast over to Salcombe. No more mining. No more moors. No more Eaglestone . . .

Kezzy dropped her head in her hands. A sob shook her body. 'Oh, Matthew, why did you have to go?' she whispered ardently.

Her unhappy reverie was interrupted by Lordy's voice calling urgently to her as he came lumbering across the yard.

'Cap'n Missy! Cap'n Missy! Come quick! Your grandpappy has taken a tumble and banged his skull. I reckon he's hurt pretty bad.'

Kezzy was up and bounding across the yard even before he was half through what he was saying.

The smashed cloam tobacco jar and its scattered contents, as well as a clay pipe with the stem snapped off, bore witness to the fact that Elyas had been filling his pipe propped on his crutches by the mantel-shelf when he lost his balance and fell, striking his head on the iron slab. That was how Lordy, returning the empty cooking pots, had found him. Before running to fetch Kezzy, he had picked up the unconscious old man and gently laid him on his pallet.

Elyas was grey-faced, eyes closed, blood streaming from a wound above his left eye. For a terrible moment when she first entered the cottage, Kezzy thought he was dead. But even as grief and blind panic gripped her, his chest rose and he let out a loud, wheezing groan.

'Cold water, quickly,' she commanded Lordy who had hurried in after her.

He snatched up a bowl and splashed water into it from the stoup in the corner while Kezzy found a piece of soft cotton to bathe Elyas's face. Once she'd washed away the blood, she found that, mercifully, the gash wasn't too deep. She pinched the edges together and held them with a wet cotton pad until the bleeding stopped. Elyas's eyelids flickered and opened. Like a wounded animal he gazed pleadingly up at Kezzy. She stroked his waxen cheek. His blue lips moved but he couldn't summon the strength to utter anything intelligible.

'Don't worry, Gramps. I'm here. I'll look after you.'

That night, Kezzy sat watching over him as he slept restlessly despite the laudanum. By morning, a good thick scab had formed on his head wound but he still seemed confused and could only mumble incoherently. Kezzy stayed with him all day, holding his cold, dry, fleshless hand. The faithful Lordy hardly moved from the doorstep, sitting there like some great, copper-skinned sentinel in case she needed him, which from time to time she did – mainly to lift Elyas while she pulled out the soiled cotton drawsheet from under him and replaced it with a clean one, for he seemed to have lost all control over his bodily functions. She tried feeding him with spoonfuls of warm milk but he coughed and spluttered and seemed in danger of choking. The little he did swallow was sicked up minutes later.

The second night, Kezzy brought her own pallet through and placed it near him so she could listen to his shallow breathing. She hadn't slept for thirty-six hours, yet she lay awake far into the night, watching the dying embers and the flickering candle, listening for any sound of change. This went on for three days and nights. Then Elyas seemed to rally. His colour improved and the dazed look lifted from his eyes. He still gasped for breath but managed a little warm milk and honey.

Later that afternoon, the Admiralty clerk put in yet another appearance with the final four warrants. The last members of Eaglestone's depleted workforce were to make their way immediately to Plymouth to embark for home aboard a merchantmen making ready to sail on the morning tide.

Lordy went to see Kezzy, to talk to her privately. He stood, shuffling his feet and twisting in his big hands the warrant he couldn't read, trying to find the words to say what he wanted to say.

'Thing is, Cap'n Missy . . . thing is . . .' he faltered.

'You want to go home, Lordy?' she helped him softly.

'Oh, no, ma'am . . . I mean Cap'n . . . this is best home I've ever had. The Quakers were mighty good folk to me . . . don't get me wrong. But, waal, I don't go too much for all that Amen-bawlin'. I reckon it's because I'm half-heathen savage an' changin' my name don't change that. The others, they've got wives waitin' for 'em. I ain't got nobody waitin'. So if it's all same to you, I'd like it mighty fine if you'd let me stay.'

It was the longest speech she'd ever heard him utter.

'Oh, Lordy . . .' she stopped, a lump in her throat, grateful tears swimming in her eyes. She put out a hand to him and he wrapped it in his huge brown fist in a strangely gentle way, as though it was a small frightened bird. She blinked the tears away and smiled up at him. 'I very much want you to stay, my dear, dear friend.'

He beamed, released her hand and with a look of sheer delight on his face tore his warrant to pieces and threw them on the fire.

'There! Now I gotta stay.'

Presently, the three who were leaving came to say their reluctant, sad-eyed farewells but only managed to stand tongue-tied until Kezzy smiled understandingly and said, 'Your families will be glad to have you home safe.'

One of them burst out: 'I've a child I've not seen yet, Cap'n Missy! I was pressed when my wife was five months carrying. Dragged off and her screaming fit to do herself damage, please God she didn't.'

A shadow passed over Kezzy's features as his words brought flooding back the terrible childhood memory of her beloved brothers, Graeme and Isaac, being dragged away by the press, never to be seen again.

'Yes,' said Kezzy, 'pray God she was delivered of a fine, healthy child.'

Somewhat awkwardly, one of the other men said: 'If we happen across Lieutenant Youngmay, can we give him a message from you, Cap'n Missy?'

Tell him I love him! Tell him I carry his child!

Kezzy ignored the shrieking inner voice.

'Tell him . . . if you *should* see him . . . tell him that I am perfectly well and hope that he is the same.'

They promised they would do so. She watched them go from the cottage door, waving until they were out of sight. Lordy was to take them in the wagon as far as Cornwood where, for a shilling or so, they would be able to find a wagoner to take them to the port. Lordy was reluctant to leave Kezzy and Elyas for even this comparatively short time but Kezzy was insistent; they had worked well for her digging copper and she'd not see them sail for home with blistered feet.

'Kezzy.'

She turned from the door in surprise as Elyas spoke her name in a voice which was surprisingly clear and firm. He was up on his elbows and smiling at her in the same way he always did when, before he was crippled, he returned from the coinage or perhaps from visiting his cousins up the moor at Cherry Brook. Yes, he was frail, but the light in his eyes told Kezzy that his spirit was never stronger.

She went to him and knelt down by the side of his pallet, her hands covering his. 'Gramps, you're better!' she exclaimed, relieved.

He shook his head, lips tilting wistfully. 'Nay, chield, the Master is callin' this ol' sinner.'

'No! Don't even say it!'

He lifted a palsied hand with a great deal of effort and touched her pale cheek. 'Now, now, chield, 'tis what's inside is the real life. 'Twon't just be snuffed out like penny dip when this ol' carcass is planted below grass.'

Kezzy was too moved to speak. Death was laying his hand upon her grandfather yet he wasn't in the least fearful. Indeed, he was strangely exulted.

'Help me sit up a bit, chield,' he croaked.

She hastened to do so, propping him up on a straw bolster.

She swallowed hard and found her voice. 'Do you want some lung-syrup, Gramps?'

'Nay, nay.' He patted his rattling chest. ' 'Tis just a touch o' the tilly-killy.'

She smiled faintly. He always said that, until the coughing started in earnest and she had to fetch his medicine. But for once the wheezing didn't worsen and he managed to get his words out without too many long, painful pauses while he gasped for breath.

'Kezzy love, I'm goin' to give in . . .'

'No, you mustn't, Gramps!'

Her eyes were wild, terror-filled at the thought of him not being there. Again, he lifted a weary hand and touched her cheek.

'Don't 'ee fret, chield. I bain't afeared to meet my Maker. There'll be bigger sinners than Elyas the tinner waitin' in line to face He.'

She must do something! thought Kezzy. She summoned her resources and said: 'As soon as Lordy gets back, let me send him for a doctor, Gramps. Dame Rogers will know of one who could get here before nightfall . . .'

Elyas shook his head. 'Nay, chield. I'm past blood-lettin' an' such quackery.'

'The minister, then. Let me send for Parson Creedy.'

'Faugh! That ol' God-botherer! Likely'd charge for sayin' prayer to see me over t'other side.' He paused a moment or two, but Kezzy knew he didn't want her to speak just then. 'I want to speak to 'ee, Kezzy m'dear. Since the good Lord has seen fitty to give me the breath.'

So it had come at last. Kezzy braced herself to meet it.

Elyas pointed to his seat in the corner by the fire. 'Lift seat o' settle an' bring me what's there.'

She knew what was hidden inside the box-like seat. A polished teak casket. None but Elyas had ever touched it, let alone opened it, and the younger Hammetts had always called it his 'Ark'.

'Now, you'm to take good care o' this box an' what's in it, chield.'

'I will, Gramps,' she solemnly promised.

'Ay, I know you will.'

He lifted the lid and stared inside for a while, a faraway look in his eyes. Then he put in a hand and brought out a thin gold band. 'I put this weddin'ring on my darlin' Beth's finger the day she became my wife. I want it buried wi' me. Will you see to it, Kezzy?'

'I promise it will be done, Gramps.'

He nodded, satisfied, carefully replaced the ring. Next he brought out a folded document, yellowing and ragged at the edges. 'This, chield, is most important of all an' 'tis all I have to leave 'ee. 'Tis deeds to Eaglestone.'

She took the document and carefully unfolded it, seeing that it was covered with Dame Roger's neat handwriting. She quickly read what it said, noting that the farmer from Lamb's Down bore witness to Elyas Hammett's squatter's rights and that ownership had been ratified by the Stannary in Plympton.

'Eaglestone do belong to 'ee now, chield, pack an' vardel,' said Elyas quietly, watching her face.

'Oh, Gramps . . .' her voice caught and her eyes swam with tears.

'No tears, not now or after I've gone. Do 'ee hear? I've had good life an' long family, God rest they all, so if you'm elly tears t'shed save they for them as were took young.'

He took back the document, folded it and put it back in his box. 'There bain't much else. This . . .' He lifted out a bangle, so blackened with age it was impossible to tell just by looking at it what metal it was made of. 'Mebbe I should have given this to 'ee afore now. 'Twere they ma's. Thy pa made un for she to mark thy birth.'

Kezzy took it, turning it in her hands. It was an unremarkable bangle, yet fashioned as smooth as silk beneath the discolouration.

' 'Tis muntz brass,' Elyas told her. 'Plenty o' copper in un so 'tis stronger'n ordinary brass an' can be rolled an' worked hot. Polish un up an' 'twill be as near gold lookin' as proper stuff.'

Her mother's! All this time and she'd no idea Elyas had it tucked away in his 'Ark'.

'I'll treasure it, Gramps,' Kezzy said gravely.

She'd spoken softly but he was watching her face and read her lips. Reverently, she kissed the bangle and handed it back to him to return to the box.

'There's just one other thing in this ol' box,' said Elyas, but he didn't immediately produce it. Instead he closed the lid and lay with one, crooked, pale hand resting on it. For a few moments he studied Kezzy. Then said: 'Ye've heard, I knowed it, what folks do say 'bout thy ma.'

'Being a witch?' she said candidly.

'Ay.'

'*Was* she, Gramps? Was she truly a witch?'

He didn't answer immediately. Again the faraway look came into his lachrymose eyes. Kezzy held her peace, waiting, sensing that at last she was about to hear the truth, uncoloured and unexaggerated and as painful as it might prove to be. Her grandfather drew a deep, rasping breath.

He said: 'Ay, chield. I reckon her were at that. Though it do hurt to admit it after all this time.'

The sun shone brightly and warmly outside, yet Kezzy shivered as though the chillest wind was blowing in through the creaking rafters and old wooden window-frames.

'But I'll say this,' continued Elyas, 'whatever powers Ruke did possess . . . an' they were right strong powers, stronger than just elly ol' gypsy *cohani* . . . her always used they for the good never for the ill. There's folks here'bouts wouldn't be 'live today if'n 'tweren't for thy ma an' her concoctions. Whenever her set foot out on moor her would come back wi' her apron full o' sprigs o' this an' that to make her potions. Yet, if'n barn did burn or a baby were born wi'out un limb . . . well, then folk would 'gin mutterin' 'bout havin' witch in they midst an' castin' they eyes at Ruke. Just to lick they fool selves clean.'

Again Elyas rested for a while, his head sunk broodingly on his chest, one hand resting on the closed box in his lap. Presently, wanting to hear more, Kezzy touched his hand so that he looked up at her. 'Gramps, I've never asked this because I always thought that one day, when you saw fit, you'd tell me . . . where is my mother buried?'

He stared at her for a long time, but he wasn't seeing her, Kezzy knew that. He was looking back. Suddenly he stirred himself and opened his box again. He took out a long plait of raven hair. Kezzy's eyes widened in astonishment: it could so easily have been her own, she involuntarily put a hand to the back of her head, momentarily forgetting that she no longer confined her abundant tresses, and hadn't done so since Matthew had begged her to let them hang free about her shoulders.

Elyas didn't proffer the plait to Kezzy to examine as he had the other things in the box but sat stroking its dark, still-glossy length in a sadly wistful manner. Presently, he said: 'Huward cut off thy ma's hair afore we buried her up'long Eagle Tor. Some folk do say that if'n 'ee cuts witch's hair afore burial her won't rise up 'gin in human form.'

'Did you . . . mark her grave?'

'Oh ay. Huward cut her name in stone slab a-coverin' she. 'Tis there, 'mong the heather, watched over by yon eagle . . .' His voice trailed. Then he seemed to shake himself and gently replaced the plait in the box. He closed the lid, then, lifting it in both hands as a priest might hold a precious relic, offered it to Kezzy. 'Here. Kezzy chield, take it. Take it an' let me go to my rest. Eaglestone be yourn now.'

With reluctant, trembling hands, Kezzy took the box. She dared not speak at that moment, knowing that whatever words she might try to utter would turn into deep-drawn, convulsive sobs.

Since her head was lowered, Elyas sensed rather than saw her struggle to retain her self-control. He put a hand beneath her chin, lifting her tense face. He patted her cheek. 'Now put un box back in settle an' run an' fetch me drink o' cold water from leat. All this'n talkin' has parched me.'

She rose immediately to do as he asked.

He watched as she snatched up a jug and ran out, leaving the door open behind her. From where he lay, Elyas could follow her fleet-footed progress across the yard towards the silver thread of icy water tumbling over rocks and down the valley until it gathered enough force to turn the big wooden water-wheel he and Huward and Graeme and Isaac had erected to pump the water from the mine.

Elyas's eye was carried far and wide over the rolling hills, decked more gorgeously in purple and gold than any king or queen, to Eagle Tor, regal and sombre and lightly shawled by the haze of summer. It was as if he had climbed that steep hill and stood atop the eagle's crag. How sweet the air! He could almost feel its coolness against his face. It seemed to rarify his bent, broken useless body, and lift his soul with the wings of an eagle. High, high, to the realms where no earthly eye could see . . .

Her equilibrium recovered, Kezzy returned, carefully carrying the jug so as not to spill and calling out eagerly as she entered.

'Here you are, Gramps! As cold as cold can be!'

But Captain Elyas Hammett was beyond recall.

Chapter Thirty-Six

Despite Dame Rogers's protests, Kezzy remained at Eaglestone with Elyas's body, and with just Lordy for company, for the three days until her grandfather was taken from there in his teak coffin to be laid to rest alongside his beloved Beth and their five babies. There was nothing to fear from the frail, waxen figure beneath the sheet in the corner of the cottage: her beloved Gramps wouldn't have hurt her when he was alive, let alone now he was dead.

Practically the whole of the tinning community came to Cornwood for the funeral. The church was filled to capacity and people overflowed into the churchyard and the village, blocking the main street and the little square. Kezzy, in a black dress and bonnet borrowed from Dame Rogers, occupied the front pew as chief mourner, with the dame beside her, similarly dressed, and with Captain de Raddon in his position of Lord Warden of the Stannaries seated across the aisle from them – an unexpected condescension since he generally sent one of the stannary stewards to represent him at tinners' funerals.

Despite her grief and the solemnity of the occasion, Kezzy found herself more than once casting a curious sideways look towards de Raddon. Gone were the rich, fashionable clothes and the fine, real-hair wig he had worn that day in the Italian Garden at Blackaven when in the august presence of the Prince Regent. Instead he wore his old, coiling, black horse-hair wig and the plain black coat he favoured while going about stannary business, adorned only by his gold chain of office with the big stannary seal.

During the congregation's hearty rendering of 'Captains of the Saintly Band', Kezzy became conscious of de Raddon's soulless, cynical gaze upon her. She waited until the last notes or the hymn had died away then turned her head and calmly and deliberately stared back at him. He didn't look away as would have been seemly under the circumstances but continued to regard her with a thin, sour smile on his lips and a speculative glitter in his severe eyes which fetched her heart into her throat. Did he guess her shameful secret? Kezzy wondered with a stab of alarm, then quickly dismissed the notion. What could de Raddon know of such things? A man without children? The absence of the flux suggested that she was, indeed, carrying Matthew's child. Nevertheless, she was barely a month pregnant even now. And she had confided in no one, not even her beloved Gramps. So unless Ma Dinion's scandal-mongering had reached the Lord Warden's ears – and Kezzy very much doubted he was interested in bal maidens' gossip – her secret was, for the moment, safe. Lifting her chin in haughty fashion at de Raddon, Kezzy turned away and fixed her eyes on Elyas's coffin, concentrating on the Reverend Creedy's droning eulogy. But all the time she was aware of de Raddon sitting not five feet away, and the same words kept echoing in her brain: what could de Raddon know of such things? A man without children . . .?

After it was over, de Raddon was the first to leave the graveyard, setting his gold-edged tricorne upon his head even before he was through the lych gate and striding off with his coat-skirts swinging to where Grote stood waiting with their horses.

Dame Rogers peered short-sightedly after him and tut-tutted. '*Well,*' she murmured to Kezzy, 'you'd have thought he'd have approached you and offered his condolences.'

'And forget the bad blood between him and Gramps? Captain de Raddon may be many things, but apparently not a hypocrite. I'm amazed he came at all, even if it is his duty.'

Kezzy, still with the dame beside her, went and stood by the lych gate to receive the condolences of the departing mourners. Jim Beckwitt and his family were among the last to file past her. Pretty blonde Jane was on the arm of her new, young American husband and it was abundantly clear that she was in the advanced stages of pregnancy. Kezzy, as she stood listening to the smithy's faltering words of sympathy, experienced a pang of envy because the newly-weds were so happy together. Jane had clearly given herself to her lover some time before their nuptials, yet no one would point the finger of shame in her direction. None would disdainfully mutter the words 'witch whore' or 'witch's bastard' as Jane passed by with her distended belly. None would seize her and shave her head so that all who saw her would know immediately of her 'sin'.

Kezzy began to shiver violently.

'Are you cold, Keziah?' asked Dame Rogers in surprise, for the afternoon was sunny and warm.

Kezzy turned her dark, shadow-ringed eyes towards the dame. Her face was ghostly white. 'No. I'm not cold.'

Dame Rogers touched her hand. 'Come and stay with me, Keziah. Even if it's just for a few days. Until you decide what you wish to do. Perhaps . . . perhaps you will choose to stay with me. Heaven knows, I need another, good, strong pair of eyes and a quick brain to help teach the children.'

'Thank you,' said Kezzy gently, 'but I do not think I would make a good schoolmistress despite the fine education you gave me. I have not the patience, I fear.'

'But how shall you live? You cannot run a mine! And who will look after you now that Captain Hammett is gone?'

It crossed Kezzy's mind to point out that over the past few years it was she who had done the looking after and had been the bread-winner. Out of loyalty to her grandfather she held her peace, and said instead: 'I have Lordy Sleeve.'

Dame Rogers looked quite shocked. She darted an anxious look at the Eaglestone wagon atop which sat the mountainous figure of the half-

Mohawk, his great bald head shining like copper in the sunlight.

'But Keziah, dear child, he is a perfect *heathen*!'

'Oh no, Lordy has been converted,' Kezzy hastened to reassure her to which Dame Rogers gave a disbelieving sniff.

'It really is too bad of Captain Hammett, I don't know what he was thinking of. He must have *known* he wasn't long for this world. He should have found you a husband long before now instead of waiting for that young American to make up his mind to propose. Tch, tch! Abandoning you like that after all you risked for him. *And* got him and his comrades a Royal Pardon . . .'

'Matthew didn't abandon me. He had to go home. He would have been listed as a deserter,' said Kezzy sharply; never before had she used such a tone to her dear friend but criticism of her darling Matthew stung her beyond endurance. Tears misted her eyes. 'He loves me, Dame Rogers! He wants me to wait for him . . .'

Dame Rogers patted her arm. 'Now, now, Keziah, you're overwrought. And hardly surprising. So harrowing, bereavement. But we must be sensible and think what is best for you. Your Matthew . . . my *poor* child, he won't come back. So best sell Eaglestone to de Raddon. We'll find a lawyer to ensure you receive a fair price . . .'

'Never!'

'Then perhaps one of the other big mine-owners . . . Captain Cudlipp or Captain Tavy . . .'

'I'll *never* sell Eaglestone.'

Dame Rogers sighed inwardly. When the devil was in a Hammett there was no conquering their stubbornness! 'Then,' she said firmly, 'you must marry.'

'Yes. I must marry,' acceded Kezzy slowly, thoughtfully.

Dame Rogers felt a surge of relief: she had been tolerably prepared for revolt at the very idea. 'Now, let us consider . . .' She closed her eyes the better to do so.

Kezzy fell silent for a while as she mentally mustered all the young local men who could be considered worthy of Kezzy and her copper mine. Kezzy, too, fell deep into brooding thought. For some reason, she couldn't get de Raddon out of her mind. Against her will, her mind's eye persisted in conjuring his face and the strangely jealous expression it had worn when he had discovered, that day in his Italian Garden with Prinny, that she was in love with a Yankee prisoner. Why should de Raddon care? What was she to him, other than his one-time tub-carrier and the granddaughter of his greatest enemy? Of course, he had, on occasions in the past, gazed at her with a totally different expression. One which Kezzy, as she had grown older and more comely, had recognised as unveiled lust.

Kezzy mentally shook herself. It was foolish to waste time musing about de Raddon. What mattered it if he viewed her jealously or lustfully? He was just a man! Albeit the most powerful in the parish. Moreover, he was the Hammetts' enemy, and therefore not worth another thought. Yet . . . what had been her answer when Matthew had asked her how it was that she didn't share her grandfather's utter hatred of de Raddon? 'What is an old feud when there's more important business afoot?' Well, Kezzy soberly reminded herself, there was still important business afoot. Finding a husband who could help her rear her child and work her mine! To those ends, the worst of feuds was best buried with the dead. Captain John de Raddon! It hadn't previously entered Kezzy's head to view him as a prospective husband. Until now.

Dame Rogers was saying something.

'I'm sorry,' said Kezzy returning to consciousness with a start. 'What did you say?'

'I said young Tom Beckwitt is a good-hearted lad . . . and a fine smithy like his father. A useful attribute when there's miners' tools to be kept honed. Then there's the Wisdome lad . . . rather young, I think. But what about that nice young riding officer . . . Dorrity? Now, *he* used to be apprenticed at Wheal Emma and would make a *very* fine captain for Eaglestone. And according to your grandfather, he always was sweet on you. So what about Mr Dorrity? Shall I approach him on your behalf?'

When there was no answer, she opened her eyes and looked about her. She was quite alone. She was just in time to see Kezzy, driven at a smart pace by Lordy, disappearing down the village street towards the coast road. She stood gaping after the wagon for a moment.

'Oh dear, Elyas,' she sighed, exasperated, aware of the small knot of people hovering by the lych gate, the Reverend and Mrs Creedy among them, waiting to be led back to her cottage for the funeral tea. 'Oh dear, Elyas, she might have waited to eat your ham before racketing off only the good Lord knows where . . .'

Blackaven House stood some sixty fathoms or more above the cove. The seaward side being a great sheer face of grey slate with a tumble of jagged, sea-lashed rocks at the base. The landward side faced ornamental gardens stretching to meadows and farms, with a wide, well-rutted approach to the front of the house along the cliff line.

The day was well advanced when Kezzy approached the sprawling villa with its ornate flying buttresses and squat-domed towers silhouetted against the darkening sky. The interior, she knew, was equally as foreboding, with its looming stone pillars and shadowy niches. There were rumours of ghosts, not least being the shade of poor, tragic Emma de Raddon who had thrown herself from her bedroom window on to the rocks far below and was now said to walk the long corridors wailing for the child she never bore her husband.

Climbing the stone steps to the big oak doors, ghosts were a long way from Kezzy's mind. She was far too preoccupied deciding on just what she was going to say to de Raddon – presuming that he was prepared to receive her at this late hour. But to her surprise, having given her name to the footman who answered her knock, she was kept waiting only a few moments before being led across the big, candlelit hall to the dining room. Once before, as a small child, she had been in that room. Hurriedly, she dismissed the memory, afraid that recollections might renew rancour and indignation, thus making it impossible to carry out the rather reckless plan she had in mind.

As the footman opened the door for her, she almost collided with a figure hurrying from the dining room. A tangle-haired wench with a shapely, buxom body barely concealed by her loosened bodice. She was gone in a flash, but not before she'd glared sullenly at Kezzy for spoiling her chance of a good dinner and earning herself a shilling or two for entertaining the Lord Warden in a bawdy fashion afterwards.

De Raddon still wore his wig but he had removed his coat and loosened his cravat. He lounged in a big oak chair at the head of the long, polished table laden with dishes – veal and lamb and a platter of game birds, with cauliflower and leeks. On the sideboard stood an array of bottles and a jug of ale; also a big apple cake, a truckle of cheddar, a great stilton, a bowl of blackberries and another of thick, yellow cream. A half-eaten chicken on the brass plate in the place set to de Raddon's left bore witness to the fact that the young woman had been despatched in all haste when Kezzy's arrival was announced.

'My apologies for interrupting your dinner, Captain de Raddon,' she addressed him civilly, advancing into the room.

He didn't rise or invite her to be seated.

'What brings you here so urgently on my heels, Miss Hammett, that could not be discussed before all of Cornwood? Or need I ask?'

Kezzy waited until the footman cleared away the half-eaten food left by de Raddon's late guest and had withdrawn in response to a click of his master's fingers. Candidly, she said: 'I haven't come to beg for flasking work if that's what you're hoping.'

That gave de Raddon pause. It was exactly what he *had* been hoping. None save she, disguised in her boy's clothes had delivered his moonshine so quickly, so safely, and without cheating him of at least a tub from every run.

'Then why have you come?'

'I have a proposition to put to you.'

He looked interested, picked up his glass and sipped the red wine, surveying her over the rim through narrowed eyes. Any proposition coming from Keziah Hammett must surely involve Wheal Eaglestone. He felt a stab of anticipation: for years he had coveted the Hammett mine. First as a tin mine producing the finest quality ore for miles around; lately, as a copper-rich mine.

'A proposition, you say?' he remarked casually. To appear too eager would undoubtedly put the price up quite unnecessarily. He fluttered a hand towards the vacant chair beside him. 'Then perhaps you should be seated and tell me what you have in mind, Miss Hammett.'

She didn't hide the disdain in her eyes as she glanced towards the chair he had indicated. Her chin came up. Did he expect her to sit at his table in his whore's place? When she did move, it was to the other end of the table where another chair stood, as ornately carved as his own, presumably, once used by the late Mrs de Raddon. Kezzy paused for just a moment with her hand on its high back, then drew it out and seated herself. De Raddon frowned but made no comment. Instead, he rose and, without bothering to summon a lackey, went and fetched a crystal glass from the sideboard and placed it before her, filling it with claret before returning to lounge once more in his own chair.

Kezzy took a sip of wine, glad of its fortification now that the moment had come to deliver the piece that she'd so carefully rehearsed on the way.

'You are without an heir, Captain de Raddon, are you not?'

He stared at her, hard and ill-humouredly, then barely perceptibly inclined his head. It was something of which he liked not to be reminded.

'Captain de Raddon,' said Kezzy in as calm a voice as she could manage, 'I am prepared to marry you and to give you a fine healthy son.'

There followed a long silence.

De Raddon's eyes bulged and the ridges of scar-tissue on his cheek, glimpsed beneath the loops of black horse-hair, stood out like crimson cords. Amazement for the moment quenched any other emotion but presently the rush of blood it brought to his face began to fade and when he eventually responded to her extraordinary proposal, it was in his usual crisp, authoritative, condescending manner.

'Are you saying, Miss Hammett, that you will *guarantee* to beget me a son and heir?'

Her answer came prompt, confident and clear. 'Yes, I am saying that.'

Just as her intuition had told her that she was with child before ever there was the slightest physical indication of it, so it told her that the child was a boy.

'Such confidence! I *almost* believe you, Miss Hammett.'

She met his eyes straight on, forced herself not to flinch at the strange hunger she saw there. 'You *must* believe me, Captain de Raddon,' she pursued quietly, 'else your name will die with you.'

There was something mesmeric about her steady gaze. By Jesu! he wanted to believe her! He rose, determined to break the spell, determined not to be influenced by whatever unearthly powers she might have inherited from her *didekei* mother. He went across to the sideboard and took his time refilling his glass from the decanter of claret. He felt her eyes boring into him. Only witchcraft could allow her to guarantee the future contents of her womb, he told himself. But did that matter? Wasn't it better to father a son by a witch than no son at all? And then there was her dowry. Eaglestone! It would be his at last since a woman's possessions automatically became her husband's on their marriage.

Kezzy's voice interrupted his considerations.

'There is one other thing I wish to say, Captain de Raddon. Regarding Eaglestone.'

He turned to regard her. 'Yes?'

'I am prepared to share equally with you . . . as my husband . . . all profits from the mine, but I will remain her sole owner. I would require you to waive all claim to it in writing before the marriage ceremony.'

His eyes glittered. 'And if I refuse?'

She rose, as if to leave. 'Then your nursery shall remain empty.'

'Confound your impudence, you eternal bitch!'

Her chin came up. 'I care nothing for your insults, Captain de Raddon. Our marriage would, of course, be one merely of mutual convenience. I need a husband . . . a protector . . . one who can help me work my mine. In return you shall receive a share of the profits and an heir for Blackaven. That, I consider a most fair proposition. Perhaps when you have had the chance to consider it . . .'

He moved towards her, crossing the room in a matter of strides, and seized her by the wrist. Pulling her towards him so that her face was a matter of inches from his own. She could smell the wine upon his breath and the heavy scent of the pomatum he used upon his wig. 'Very well, my lovely *sorcière infernale*,' he said, a note of raillery deepening his voice. 'I'll marry you and to hell with your damned mine!'

He crushed her to him savagely, deliberately hurting her because he knew that inwardly she was recoiling at his touch. He could feel her heart thudding as he kissed her hard. There was no answering passion from her mouth. He drew back his head to stare into her eyes and saw only disgust and revulsion mirrored there. 'Remember, Keziah Hammett,' he growled, 'remember that you came here of your own free will and must therefore accept all that you invite.' He kissed her again, almost contemptuously, and released her, only immediately to seize her wrist again as the bright gleam of metal caught his eye. He pulled back her sleeve to reveal the plain yellow bangle Elyas had bequeathed to her, now polished to an almost garish brightness which was why, for propriety's sake, she'd concealed it beneath her mourning clothes.

'Brass!' declared de Raddon disdainfully. 'A paltry, parting gift from your Yankee fuckster, I dare say.'

Kezzy felt a stir of anger at his jeering vulgarity, but she forced herself to remain calm as his eyes moved speculatively to her stomach, probing the black folds of her mourning dress. Reading his mind, she ran a hand over her flat belly so that he could see that there was no sign that she was with child. The success of her plan rested upon his believing totally that she was still a virgin.

She said: 'Matthew Youngmay and I have never lain together. Do you think that my grandfather would have permitted it . . . before I was properly churched?'

He lifted his gaze and stared hard into her eyes. She met his stare without flinching. It was true, he told himself, her grandfather was a martinet who'd not have allowed the Yankee to sully the girl. Sick and crippled as he was, he'd have watched the girl like an abbess her nuns! The suspicion left his face and Kezzy felt a surge of triumph.

He said not a word, but still keeping hold of her wrist, pulled her with him from the room and up a long flight of stairs. He pushed open the door of a room and propelled her inside. A tremor ran through her and her heart was fetched into her throat at the sight of the vast, canopied bed which dominated the room. De Raddon saw her stricken look and laughed hoarsely. 'Fear not,' he said, 'I shall not expect you to sacrifice your innocence until *after* the nuptials. Then, of course . . .' he paused significantly, his lips parting in an unpleasant smile which puckered his maimed cheek.

Kezzy bowed her head in acquiescence, lowering her long lashes modestly over her eyes as befitting a shy virgin. She was grateful that the evil moment hadn't, as she feared, arrived, though she knew that soon she must submit to his bodily demands: the sooner the better if he was to be completely fooled into thinking Matthew's child was his.

De Raddon went over to a silk-hung mahogany dressing-table. Taking a key from his pocket, he unlocked a drawer and took out a jewellery box engraved with the initials E.d.R. Opening it, he took out a pair of fine gold bangles and slipped them on to Kezzy's narrow wrist. They shone richly beside her bright brass one.

'A pre-nuptial gift,' he declared briefly. He closed the lid upon the valuable treasures Kezzy glimpsed inside against rich red velvet. He relocked the jewellery box in the dressing-table draw. 'Give me a son within the year and you shall have all that the box contains. I give you my word on it.'

Kezzy made no comment. She cared nothing for poor dead Emma's jewels. She cared only for the de Raddon name and the respectability it would bring to herself, to her son and the invincible strength it would bring to Wheal Eaglestone; for that alone Elyas would forgive her for taking his enemy as her husband.

'You shall stay here until tomorrow,' said de Raddon. 'I'll have supper sent up to you . . . unless you would care to join me at table.'

She was looking bemused. 'Why until tomorrow?'

He smiled his twisted, disdainful smile. 'Tomorrow we shall be married. If 'tis the banns that concern you, then worry not. The minister at Plympton St Mary will happily waive them . . . for a tub of old cognac.'

It was what Kezzy wanted: marriage without undue delay. Yet, she found herself looking desperately about her, as though a prisoner in the dead Mrs de Raddon's bedroom. 'But I've arrangements to make,' she faltered. 'I must tell Dame Rogers so she can be there . . .'

'I'll send word to her.'

'. . . and she must fetch me a gown. I can't be married in black.'

De Raddon crossed to one of the clothes chests and opened it. He seemed to know exactly where to find what he was looking for and in a moment extracted a white silk and lace wedding gown. He tossed it on the bed. 'There is your gown,' he told her. He bowed almost mockingly and went out.

Kezzy went and picked up the beautiful garment. It smelled faintly of sandalwood and had clearly been carefully stored so it was like new. Only she knew that it wasn't new: it had been worn by a previous eager young bride many years before. Touching the shimmering white silk and the fine French lace, Kezzy couldn't help feeling puzzled. It was quite impossible that she had ever seen Emma de Raddon in her wedding gown, yet it seemed so familiar. Going to a long cheval mirror, she held the dress before her and in a flash of recollection which turned her insides to quicksand, Kezzy realised why the wedding gown seemed familiar. *It was precisely the same gown she had seen herself wearing in her vision.* Flinging the gown from her in distaste, she threw herself upon the bed, her cheek pressed to the silk coverlet. She was worn out and near to tears. Suddenly, behind her closed lids she saw her grandfather's smiling face. He was just as she always pictured him: merry and eager and only slightly stooped with age. That vivid image of Elyas before he was ravaged by lung-disease and the pit blast had become a cherished mental recollection of Kezzy's. She sat up, took off her bonnet and tossed it aside. Then she went and tidied her hair in the mirror, pinching her ashen cheeks to bring some colour into them.

Taking a deep breath, she left the room and descended the stairs to the dining room.

Next morning, an astonished Grote was despatched with a message informing the minister at Plympton St Mary's that his services would be required later that day. Lordy was despatched, with a great deal of reluctance on his part, to Cornwood with a note Kezzy had written to Dame Rogers informing her of the 'good news'. Lordy, who had spent the night in the Blackaven stables, didn't think the 'news' was good at all.

'Suppose Lieutenant comes back lookin' for you an' finds you married to ol' scar-face?' he asked Kezzy unhappily.

He had no notion of how his words hurt her! She was trying so hard not to think of Matthew. 'The lieutenant isn't coming back, Lordy. I think we both know that. Now, begone with you or I'll begin to wish I had sent you back to America with the others,' she told him.

Mournfully, he set off in the wagon. Out of loyalty to the lieutenant, he wished there was some way of stopping the marriage taking place but couldn't think of anything save, perhaps, breaking de Raddon's neck. And then Cap'n Kezzy would be mighty cross with him for doing such a thing.

News of the impending marriage spread like a furze fire throughout the morning. Dame Rogers wasn't sure whether she approved or not of the match. Certainly, the suddenness of events suggested a lack of propriety, particularly when the bride was still in mourning for a close relative. Still, she did as Kezzy begged and put on her best dress and bonnet and set off in the wagon with Lordy to attend the wedding ceremony. Short notice though it was, they met on the road a number of other people who had heard the news and were setting off to ensure a seat in the church. The Beckwitt's wagon carried not only the entire family but also Mr and Mrs Wisdome from the mill.

'Must give Elyas's granddaughter proper support on her big day, Dame Rogers,' sang out Mrs Wisdome as the Eaglestone wagon sailed by. ' 'Especially her marryin' into gentry.'

'Proper support! Faugh! Proper nosiness, I call it,' observed the dame tartly as soon as they were out of earshot.

A mile or so further on, Dame Roger's path crossed that of Peter

Dorrity. He was watering his horse at a trough by the wayside and she bade Lordy rein in so she might alight to speak to the Preventative, whom she knew to be a friend and, she suspected, suitor of Kezzy's. He was, she also suspected, a great deal fonder of Kezzy than the girl perhaps realised, so it would be a kindness to have the news of her sudden betrothal and swift marriage to de Raddon broken to him gently by one who knew them both, rather than to have him hear it as idle gossip.

Peter touched his cap to the dame on seeing her, but she didn't waste time with niceties. 'Mr Dorrity, I have something to tell you,' she immediately began in a grave voice.

He listened, blank-faced. Then his features seemed to crumple as what she was telling him sank in. 'No . . . no,' he whispered, shaking his head. He looked for a brief instant like a madman, pale eyes bulging, lips trembling. His whole body tensed, as if he was about to spring at the bearer of such cruel tidings, and the dame took an involuntary step backwards out of harm's way. 'When are they to be wed?' he demanded wildly.

'Mr Dorrity . . .' she tried to appeal to him to be calm but he cut across her, savagely demanding that she answer him.

'When? Tell me!'

'Later . . . today, I think,' she revealed nervously, then wished that she had lied and told him next week, or a month hence.

'Where?'

'I'm not sure . . .'

Lordy, not liking the sharpness of Peter's tone, climbed down and lumbered up to stand protectively by the little schoolmistress. Peter's lip curled and he said: 'Fear ye not, fellow. The dame will come to no harm from me. 'Tis de Raddon blood I'm of a mind to spill. He shan't force Kezzy to be his bride . . . save over my corpse!'

He almost threw himself into the saddle, jerking the reins so that his horse reared and screamed as pain tore at its mouth.

'Wait, Mr Dorrity!' the dame begged agitatedly. ' 'Tis what Kezzy wants . . .!'

But his scornful expression told her that he didn't believe her. He hesitated for one last second, then he was gone, galloping towards Plympton.

They watched him go with anxious eyes. The dame hadn't expected that he would take on so. Undoubtedly, he'd harboured latent powers of jealousy regarding Kezzy but who would have imagined that news of the girl's marriage would, in effect, *derange* him. Peter Dorrity had always given the impression he was well in control of his emotions.

'Oh dear,' sighed the dame, 'Oh, dear . . . perhaps I shouldn't have said anything. Oh, dear . . .'

'He'd have found out soon enough, Miz Rogers,' said Lordy comfortingly. 'You weren't to know Preventy man ain't got all his oars in the water.'

Kezzy was glad to see her old friend's face amid those of so many strangers and embraced the dame somewhat tearfully. She was in the midst of preparations and a dressmaker had been summoned to ensure the wedding dress fitted perfectly.

The young Emma had been as slim as Kezzy so there was little that needed altering. The gown was very fine, though a trifle old-fashioned with its low tight bodice and vast skirts, ruched and flounced with a profusion of snowy ribbons and falls of delicate lace. At the time, it had well befitted the daughter of Plympton's leading banker, Thomas Clotworthy, and the bride of the then Lord Warden's son and heir to the mighty Blackaven estates. Dame Rogers had been in church that day years before and now recognised the gown immediately.

She sat perched on the edge of a velvet-covered boudoir chair in what had been Emma's bedroom, eyeing Kezzy's slender form through her eye-glass while the dressmaker made small pin-tucks here and there ready for stitching. She said nothing until the woman had finished and had taken the dress away. Then she could no longer hold her tongue.

'Oh, Keziah, my child, *think* what you are doing!'

Kezzy put on a silk morning *saque*, again once belonging to Emma de Raddon, and turned to face the dame. She was pale and deathly tired, having tossed and turned all night in the big canopied bed, haunted by the shade of the unhappy woman who had once lain there, but there was a determined glint in her eyes.

'I *have* thought,' she said, 'and I know what I must do. This marriage . . . 'tis for the best. I'll do no better.'

The dame couldn't argue with that, though something told her that Kezzy would have been happier by far with daft young Tom Beckwitt or the Wisdome boy. Either of them would have treated her with more kindness than Captain de Raddon. Dame Rogers hid an involuntary shudder; his decadence was no secret and she dreaded to think what depravities his new young wife would be forced to endure.

Kezzy was watching her friend's expressive face and read her mind. She went and knelt beside the dame's chair. How she longed to reveal the real reason she was prepared to marry the hideously disfigured whore-monger who had been her grandfather's greatest enemy; moreover, marry him knowing full well that he had led the mob who had hanged her mother. But she dared not. For her own and her unborn child's sake she must confide in no one. One indiscreet word – perhaps some time in the future when extreme age had befuddled the dame's brain – would be all that it needed to arouse de Raddon's suspicions concerning the child she carried and which would be his son and heir.

'Please understand,' Kezzy adjured, 'that if I cannot marry Matthew then I care not who I marry. And since I need money to invest in Eaglestone . . .'

Her voice faded, but it was clear what she was saying: money and power were powerful aphrodisiacs. She would stomach a gross husband for the sake of Eaglestone.

'Eaglestone, always Eaglestone!' snorted the dame impatiently. She was about to upbraid Kezzy for what she considered was misplaced loyalty to a delapidated pile of stones and a smoke-blackened stack, but stopped herself, remembering that the mine was also the grave of Huward and Jamie, and the three Hammett cousins, Jake, Cleve and poor, simple Ebert. Her tone softened and she touched Kezzy's wan face lightly. 'I did so want to see you happy, child . . . married to a good, kind man. Surely, after such adversity, you deserve more than this . . . a dead woman's fripperies and married to a lecher thrice your age!'

Abruptly, Kezzy rose and turned away, the sea-green robe fluttering about her. In a hollow voice, she said: 'Let be, Dame Rogers. This marriage is of my own choosing. I am well content.'

Dame Rogers frowned. 'That was what I told Mr Dorrity,' she started to say then stopped wondering if she should concern Kezzy with his outburst.

'Peter? You've seen Peter?'

'On the way here.'

'Did you . . . tell him? That I'm to be wed today to Cap'n . . . to John?'

'Yes. I thought it would be better coming from me . . . only . . .' The dame paused again. She didn't have to tell Kezzy that Peter had taken the news badly.

'What did he say, Dame Rogers?'

'He . . . Oh, Kezzy, he wouldn't do anything stupid, would he?'

'He threatened to kill John, didn't he?' asked Kezzy softly.

'He was distraught. I'm sure he didn't mean what he was saying.'

Kezzy shook her head, her face grave. 'He has threatened to kill John more than once. His anger goes so deep . . . and with good reason. But murder . . . no, somehow I don't think he would commit murder, poor Peter.'

Poor, mad Peter, thought the dame, praying that Kezzy was right.

At noon, the dressmaker returned with the altered garment. She was accompanied by a pair of giggling maidservants who, in the absence of a proper lady's maid, were to dress the bride. One carried a freshly picked posy of white rose-buds; the second, a wreath of white myrtle, the sight of which made Kezzy quail.

'Must I wear it?' she whispered,

They looked surprised.

' 'Tis proper, mistress,' ventured the dressmaker. 'Plenty of myrtle, plenty o' cradles.'

The maid servants nudged each other and began giggling again. They were silenced by a stern look from Dame Rogers.

Resignedly, Kezzy allowed them to set the myrtle upon her brow and stood for a long moment before the long mirror gazing at her reflection. Gone was the Kezzy of old – wild, free, moorland Kezzy. Replaced by an elegant young lady with a paper-white face and eyes which glittered like two pieces of polished coal. An iciness gripped her emotions, as if never again would she know love or warmth.

Matthew, oh Matthew! She cried his name silently, wistfully. If only it was he who awaited her at the altar!

' 'Tis time, Keziah,' murmured Dame Rogers as the French lacquered clock on the mantel chimed once.

Kezzy straightened her shoulders and took the posy the maid handed her with a curtsey. 'I'm ready,' she said.

In later years, when Kezzy looked back upon that day in the summer of 1815, she could recall it all so vividly.

She remembered being carried from Blackaven House all the way to Plympton St Mary's upon a flower-decked wagon pulled by singing tinners from Wheal Emma and Wheal Blackaven. All along the way people came swarming to see her pass by as news of the approaching bridal procession spread from village to village. Their cheerful rustic faces were a blur but she could recall that they threw her hazelnuts to ensure fertility and called bawdy remarks.

'God bless thy marriage bed, m'dear!'

'May 'ee have a long family startin' from t'night!'

Almost before she knew it, she was being led down the aisle by the curate, precentor and choirboys to stand beside the richly dressed, stiff-backed figure of her bridegroom. She remembered seeing his face, the scar prominent and fiery as if it was but recently that the skin had been scorched by fire-damp instead of years past and feeling the horror of fascination. He looked at her in a cold-eyed fashion, almost boredly, as if he wanted the formalities over and done with, and Kezzy remembered suddenly thinking: this isn't real, it's a dream, a vision which soon would fade. She would awaken and be lying in her little room at Eaglestone with Matthew sleeping beside her and Elyas snoring in the adjoining room.

But it wasn't a dream and the minister's voice as he joined them in matrimony echoed in her mind down the years to come, as did John de Raddon's gruff, almost brusque responses and her own voice, firm, clear, almost defiant. She remembered returning along the aisle on her husband's arm amid the rows of smiling, deferential faces, and seeing Dame Rogers's troubled expression, her thin, pale lips moving in silent prayer for Mrs Keziah de Raddon's happiness. Then the congratulations, the bowing and kissing of hands, the rakish grins of de Raddon's gentlemen friends and the steely, jealous smiles of their ladies who secretly didn't approve of this fresh and lovely newcomer to their exalted circle. How old she made them seem! She had no need of *poudre* and *rouge* or to torture her hair in end-papers.

It was the journey back to Blackaven House for the sumptuous wedding feast, that the entire household and a number of de Raddon bal maidens had stayed up all night to prepare, which was later to become a nightmarish mingle-mangle as Kezzy's brain sought to blot it out. Only vaguely did she recall being helped into the Blackaven landau with its coiled snake emblem on the doors and rich blue-velvet interior. Her husband climbed in beside her and at the head of a long procession of coaches, chaises and gentlemen farmers riding fine horses, they set off.

The newly-weds travelled mostly in silence, absorbed in their own thoughts. Now and then de Raddon made some desultory remark, deliberately courteous, and Kezzy would respond in the same way. Sometimes he would slant a look at his lovely young bride, eyes sombre and weighing rather than admiring or affectionate.

He thought: such naivety! To imagine that her American would stay with her in that Godforsaken place once he had his freedom. Yet, she had achieved considerable status in the community by marrying John de Raddon, Lord of Blackaven, so perhaps she wasn't so foolish after all. Initially, it had occurred to him that Kezzy was pregnant and seeking a way out of her dilemma, but she had convinced him that it was not so. And he wanted to believe her. The nursery at Blackaven had been empty so long. So he was happy to accept that she had married him partly for position and partly to assuage her wounded pride at being left by her naval officer, not for a moment did he suspect her real motive.

They were almost home, wending their way along a track through a thickly wooded part of the Blackaven estate, heading towards the clifftop track which would carry them to the house, when the crack of a pistol and a shouted 'Halt in the King's name' caused the Blackaven coachie to rein in his startled, plunging team, also bringing those following to an abrupt halt.

'What in God's name . . .!' de Raddon vented an ejaculation of annoyed impatience.

Ahead of them, the late afternoon sun dappling through the boughs glinted on silver buttons, pistol and carbine. A lone figure barred their way.

'Damned riding officer!' snarled de Raddon, craning his neck to see. 'Does the fool think we carry a run of moonshine on our wedding day?' He signalled to Grote, leading the band of men acting as outriders. 'Ride forward and inform him who he has had the audacity to delay.'

Grote moved to do so, but the riding officer's voice rang out and his pistol moved so that it was pointing directly at Grote's head. 'Stay where ye are, fellow. My business is with thy master.'

'Why, 'tis Peter!' burst out Kezzy in astonishment and her husband scowled at such familiarity on her part.

Behind them, men were cursing and women twittering in alarm because, having heard the shot, their immediate reaction was that they were being held up by a highwayman. One or two women actually swooned, but in the main they set to tearing the rings from their fingers and the jewels from their ears to hide in their bodices until word was passed back along the line of carriages that they were in no danger. The 'highwayman' was merely a riding officer. And a very young one at that.

Peter Dorrity's voice rang out again, and this time Kezzy felt a stab of alarm at the wild, shrill note of menace it contained.

'Stand up, John de Raddon, Lord of Blackaven.'

For a moment Kezzy thought her husband wasn't going to move, then, slowly, he rose to stand tall and erect in the open landau, hands clasped behind him, his heavy Lord Warden's chain across his chest.

'Well, fellow? What do you want with me? I trust for your own sake that you do not take your sovereign's name in vain.'

'The King has invested in me the authority to bring to justice and see punished those who violate the laws of this land. And, by Jesu! ye've worked a deal of cruelty and wickedness in thy time, de Raddon.'

De Raddon gave a savage laugh. 'What nonsense is this? A tub or two of cognac . . . is that what troubles you, fellow?'

Peter sneered. 'Flasking? That's just part of it. A gentleman's crime, almost, and a fine front for the rest of your evil doings. Ay, there's not much I haven't fathomed, de Raddon. Wrecking! Slavery!'

His tremulous voice rose to a maniacal pitch, silencing those behind who began straining their ears to hear the accusations he was levelling at the Lord Warden.

'How many seamen have perished 'pon rocks in Blackaven Cove, de Raddon? How many young apprentices have ye sold into a life of debauchery? How many innocents' lives have ye ruined?'

The colour ebbed and flowed in de Raddon's face.

'Hold your tongue, you impudent cur!'

But Peter wouldn't be stopped. 'How many, de Raddon?' he persisted in his high-pitched, nervous voice. 'Scores? Hundreds? Or so many that ye can't even remember?'

Kezzy sat frozen in horrified fascination. When she had spoken to Dame Rogers about her concern for the de Raddon apprentices, the dame had intimated that certain practices were the privilege of certain of the gentry. Never had she imagined that de Raddon's nefarious interests were so widespread. To think that she had voluntarily given herself in marriage to a man so steeped in iniquity! Jesus, God, grief must have robbed her of her senses!

Kezzy became aware that Peter had kneed his horse into a position whereby he still held them all at pistol point but could see her more clearly. She met his gaze straight on. There was hell in his hollow, burning eyes, usually so pale and solemn. The sort of hell she'd seen in mad Sir Ryden Bliss's eyes on occasions.

He bowed slightly to her, mockingly. 'So . . . Mrs John de Raddon, Mistress of Blackaven,' he sneered. 'What would Elyas Hammett think of ye now, Kezzy? Married to his enemy . . .'

Kezzy flinched, as though he'd struck her. 'Don't, Peter,' she pleaded softly, wishing that she could explain so that he understood her plight and not look upon her as a traitor to her grandfather.

De Raddon stood motionless and silent, watching Peter with narrowed, inimical eyes, as if he'd just realised that he was facing a madman. A dangerous lunatic consumed with bitter resentment and burning hatred.

A complete hush had fallen, broken only by the chink of bridles and the sweet piping of a wood lark in the branches above. The wedding guests leaned from windows, some, those in open carriages, stood up for a better view of the scene ahead. They hadn't expected such grand entertainment.

Peter's voice was angry, accusing, as he said: 'I warned ye, Kezzy. Told ye many times that one day I'd kill de Raddon. Well, that still holds good whether ye've wed him or nay.'

De Raddon tensed. 'Don't be a fool, boy. Put up your pistol. Kill me and you'll hang for certain . . . if my men don't tear you limb from limb first.'

Peter ignored him. He remained staring at Kezzy with tortured eyes. 'Ye cannot love him. Ye cannot want to share his loathsome bed or beget his evil spawn.' A sob burst from him. 'I won't let him ruin your life like he ruined mine! I won't . . .!'

'No, Peter . . .!'

There was a loud crack and de Raddon was hurled sideways as the ball shattered his throat. He fell across Kezzy, twitching and convulsing and spurting blood over the pure white of her wedding gown.

At the same time that he fired, Peter startled his horse with a kick that made it leap into full speed so that the volley of slugs fired by de Raddon's men passed his shoulder, the heat so fierce they could have missed him by mere inches. He swung and galloped through the trees, de Raddon's men and some of the wedding guests in pursuit.

Kezzy stared down at her dead husband as if mesmerised. His flesh was already turning the colour of wax and his jaw hung slackly. But his eyes were the worst part: they seemed fixed upon her face and held a look of angry astonishment.

Behind her, women were shrieking and swooning. Some of the male guests circled the landau, their shocked faces peering in at the bloody scene of carnage. Dame Rogers hurried up, pushing through them to climb in next to Kezzy.

'Oh, my dear,' she said, aghast. 'Oh, my dear . . .'

Kezzy looked up at the sound of her voice. But she could only shake her head. She could not speak.

Lordy took off his coat and used it to cover de Raddon, then lifted the corpse so Kezzy could be helped down. Minutes later, Grote arrived back, the other riders streaming behind him. He dismounted and went and stood before Kezzy. She stared at him for a moment. Then her eyes shifted to the faces of the other men, and she saw the same thing in their eyes. Peter Dorrity was no more.

Poor, mad, tortured, degraded Peter . . .

Into Kezzy's mind flashed a picture of him and his friend, Jordan, as boys hiding in the hayloft at Eaglestone. Two apprentices running away from a cruel master. She hadn't known *how* cruel. How could she? She was but a child herself then and without any real knowledge of the world beyond the valley. How safe her world had seemed. Standing there in her blood-stained finery, almost forgotten by the milling crowd eager to view the lifeless figure in the landau. Kezzy was suddenly encompassed by an overwhelming desire to be back at the cottage in the comforting shadow of the chimney stack, beneath the hunched jagged rocks of Eagle Tor.

Was the eagle still there? she wondered. Or had it, too, left the moor now that Eaglestone stood deserted? Even old Wart had given up the ghost and died in his sleep two nights after Elyas. And Lordy had brought Rats down and turned him out in Dame Rogers's orchard to end his days in peace.

Grote was saying something. Kezzy came out of her thoughts.

'What's that you say?'

Grote repeated himself. 'Yon murderin' varmint didn't 'scape us, Miz de Raddon,' he told her with great satisfaction. 'Preventy man paid for what he done, good an' proper. His hoss lost un footin' 'long cliff an' them both went a-crashin' on rocks in Blackaven Cove. Smashed to pulp . . . won't be much left after sea's finished wi' un.'

Peter's mount, Kezzy knew, was as sure-footed as any wild gossie and chosen by him because of that since his duties had so often taken his across the treacherous, stony moorland. She doubted that the poor beast had lost its footing in such fine, clear conditions. More likely, Peter had purposefully set his horse's head at the edge of the cliff having finally wreaked the revenge which had simmered within him for so long. For sure, Kezzy told herself, he'd never have let his baying pursuers take him alive.

Aloud, she said: 'So he *did* escape you, after all.'

It was some days before the reality of her situation sank in: that she was a widow almost as soon as she was a bride and not yet eighteen years of age. Kezzy was kept too busy to brood. First, there were the interminable fittings for widow's weeds. Hurriedly, the dressmaker who had so recently fitted her wedding gown upon her was summoned and a number of black gowns, also once Emma's, and worn when her mother had died, were carried in on a waft of sandalwood. Some of these were to be made over for Kezzy's immediate use, while others, from plain black velvet graduating to grey, lilac and black-trimmed white satins and taffatas, would appear at intervals since Kezzy would be expected to wear mourning for at least two years.

Since the Prince of Wales was to be represented at the obsequies by the Prime Minister, Lord Liverpool, who was conveniently spending a month with the Pitt family close by in Lyme Regis, Dame Rogers – who knew about such things from her days as governess to the de Raddons – informed Kezzy that her entire household must wear *grand deuil* rather than just black armbands. All of which meant further delays before the funeral, with much ceremony and knelling of bells and beating of muffled drums as befitted a Lord Warden of the Stannaries, could take place. Although Kezzy had not loved him, and could not therefore mourn him as a real wife should, she found the last honours extremely harrowing, especially following so closely her grandfather's burial – so simple and moving by comparison.

Kezzy found the interment in the de Raddon family vault in the bowels of the church particularly disturbing. Her husband's coffin was set upon its stone couch between that of his father, the previous Lord Warden, and that of his young sister, Georgina, who had succumbed so tragically to smallpox aged only fifteen. Through her heavy black veil, Kezzy read the brass plate on the rather plain-looking coffin lying at his feet:

EMMA DE RADDON
1773–1814

Poor, barren Emma! To die, like Peter, on the rocks at the foot of Blackaven Cove! The unusual lack of funereal adornments was an indication of de Raddon's lack of esteem for his first wife. Kezzy shivered suddenly. The minister, the same one who had conducted the marriage ceremony two weeks before, noticed and concluded her trepidity was due to emotion. He sought to console her by edging close to her and, indicating the empty plinth across the top of the newly interred coffin, murmuring, 'Do not grieve, Mrs de Raddon, by the grace of God you shall one day be united in death with your husband.'

His words had the effect of turning Kezzy's shivers to violent trembling.

And so it was over. Without any issue to succeed him, or close relatives to lay claim to any part of the vast de Raddon fortune and estates, Keziah de Raddon, granddaughter of Elyas the tinner, became sole mistress of Blackaven and Eaglestone and, hence, the most important mine-owner in all of Devonshire.

Before the month was out, Kezzy was wondering how much longer she could stand her bleak new home with its army of muttering, sullen-faced servants. She knew what they whispered behind her back. Lordy told her. She was a witch. She had put a spell on their master. The riding officer had been her lover. Together they had plotted to murder de Raddon and to gain control of his fortune. Having done so, the witch had cast another spell, sending him crashing to his death. Yes, she knew what they said! And the rumours passed from household to household, from maid to mistress, from manservant to master, until the drawing rooms were seething with gossip. And when Kezzy entered the church and walked down the aisle to the front de Raddon pew a hush would fall over the congregation. People would cross themselves as she walked by and men would look down at the floor for fear of meeting those dark eyes and being bewitched like Captain John de Raddon.

And there were those that feared Kezzy not because they believed in her witchery, but because of the power her new wealth and vast mining interests gave to her. Moreover, during that first month she had improved the conditions of the tinners by increasing their wages out of hand when to pay more than the stannary maxima was a punishable offence, and had barred women and children from working below ground. The other mine-owners had no choice but to follow suit, or be left with just old men to dig their tin and copper while the fit, young men all went to the de Raddon mines on 'setting day'. There was even talk that the Prince Regent would make her the first female Lord Warden of the Stannaries in her late husband's shoes – a rumour that made Kezzy more enemies than anything else that was said about her.

All this, and more, she prised from Lordy. Sometimes she lay awake at night tossing and turning and plagued by night-hags. What would her enemies say when they realised she was pregnant? As soon they surely must, for she was already beginning to suffer the throes of morning sickness which preceded the growing of her belly. Would her enemies not insist that here was proof that Peter was indeed her lover? Proof that she was a witch? Perhaps they would march upon Blackaven House and seize her and take her to Gibbet Hill and there hang her like her mother. Kezzy would awake bathed in sweat, sobbing and trembling from such nightmares but would be comforted by the images she conjured of Elyas. She would, he seemed to be telling her, always be safe at Eaglestone, which was why one morning, when the kitchen skivvies were hardly stirring, Kezzy rose and dressed in the dark and crept out to the stables. As if by magic, Lordy appeared at her side as she lifted down a harness. She put a finger to her lips, then pointed to the Blackaven wagon. In a matter of minutes they were rolling through the big, wrought-iron gates and along the cliff road.

'Where is it you've a mind to go, Miz de Raddon?'

'Eaglestone,' she told him simply. Then, after a pause, added, 'and 'tis not Miz de Raddon, Lordy. 'Tis Miz *Cap'n* de Raddon.'

The morning was perfect. The turquoise summer sky cloudless above the distant tors. Butterflies thronged the heather and young rabbits darted here and there, white scuts bobbing. From a good distance away, they could see the smoke pouring from the Wheal Eaglestone stack. Kezzy had sent Jordan there as acting overseer to get the mine restarted. He had thrown himself into the task with fervour and had in no time at all hired a first-class workforce and replaced the antiquated machinery with new, steam-driven pumps. The Eaglestone copper harvest promised to be the best for miles around.

Kezzy had Lordy rein in at the foot of the valley and climbed down.

'Go on up to the brook and water the horse . . . I'll be along shortly,' she told him.

When Lordy had gone, Kezzy sat down on a rock and unpinned her hair, shaking it free so that the warm breeze could catch at it. She closed her eyes, enjoying the afternoon sun on her face. How Dame Rogers would tut at her for going out without a shady straw. She could almost hear the wavery voice: 'Oh, my dear, you'll roughen your skin and be as brown as a bal maiden if you don't cover up.' And then she heard her grandfather's voice, taking her side, 'Leave she be, Hannah. Her's so pale her could do wi' a bit o' colour in her cheeks.'

Kezzy started as the new Eaglestone engine rent the air with a piercing steam-whistle that told the tinners it was time to break for croust. Was it that time already? She must have dozed off. She knew she should make her way up the valley to begin her inspection of the workings but she was loath to move yet awhile. She felt a flickering sensation in her belly. Had she imagined it? No. There it was again. Life! Protectively, she placed a hand over her still-flat stomach and smiled a gentle, contented smile. Her son wouldn't have to scratch in the earth to fill his belly. Or walk miles to and from a dame school to be educated. He would have a tutor! He would have *everything* that she and the other Hammetts never had!

Everything, but a father's love, reminded a nagging inner voice.

Presently, she caught movement a good distance down the moor.

Shading her eyes, she made out a horse and cart. The driver clearly felt his old flatboard was too rickety to risk a broken wheel upon the stony, rutted moorland, so he was setting his three passengers down just where the well-used Cornwood track began to peter out.

Tinkers, thought Kezzie. No, more likely travelling tinners in search of work. Well, if they could sweat, no doubt Jordan would take them on. She watched the trio begin their climb, bundles on their backs. One of the men, dressed in waistcoat and breeches and with a tricorne set low over his face against the bright sun, was the more agile of the three. He was also much taller that his companions and his long, muscular legs soon carried him far ahead of them. Moreover, they didn't seem to be climbing with the same urgency, content to dawdle and let him get well ahead of them.

Squinting against the sun, Kezzy thought there was something oddly familiar about his loose-limbed gait. Her heart began to hammer and she rose for a better view on legs that trembled so violently they could hardly support her. Her eyes went to the two men behind. Their figures were also familiar: the one sturdy and straightbacked, the other bow-legged and almost dwarf-like in stature. John Dagge and Moab Austin! Her eyes swung back to the tall figure climbing doggedly upwards. Dear God, Kezzy prayed, don't let it be a cruel trick of light! Let it really be him!

The man stopped to catch his breath. He took off his hat to wipe his perspiring brow with his cuff. His hair shone bright golden in the sun. With an exaltant cry of 'Matthew!' Kezzy took a stumbling step towards him, her arms outstretched.

He looked up at the sound of his name echoed from high above him and from the way he tensed Kezzy knew that he had spotted her standing there among the heather. Then she was running, leaping and bounding over the rough ground, black skirts flying, hair dancing in rich profusion about her shoulders.

'Kezzy!' he shouted. 'Kezzy!'

He threw down his bundle and began running to meet her.

Yet, instead of throwing herself into his arms, Kezzy stopped a few feet from him and stood there, suddenly shy. Matthew also halted. His face she saw, was gaunt, older than she remembered. Could a man age in so short a time? Clearly so. Matthew's blue eyes were examining her face, also noticing the changes. She had lost a little weight, the roundness of childhood, so that her features were sharper. Now there was a fragile maturity about her which hadn't been there before. Her skin was the colour of magnolia and her wondrous almond eyes seemed almost too big and dark for her face. He saw in them all the misery and strain of the past weeks and felt a great surge of guilt because he was the cause of most of it – according to Dame Rogers with whom he had spent half an hour on his way up the moor. And if she had berated him, hadn't she also assured him that, once Kezzy was over her initial shock, she would welcome him warmly?

Kezzy said: 'I never believed . . . never thought I'd ever see you again. I prayed, oh God how I prayed, but I didn't think . . .'

Her voice trailed as a lump rose in her throat.

He delved in his pocket and brought out her eaglestone, holding it towards her in the palm of his hand. 'This brought me back to you, Kezzy. I thought when I left, that what I felt for you would soon fade. Oh my darling, how wrong I was! If anything, my love for you grew. Then I found your precious eaglestone and I knew what a fool I was. All the way to America I could think of nothing else but getting back to you as soon as I could. Because I knew there could be no future without you.'

Kezzy felt a rush of joy. Hesitantly she reached out a hand and closed her fingers over the stone in his palm. His fingers closed over hers and for a long while they stood like that. Holding hands. Neither speaking. But Kezzy saw that there was anguish as well as tenderness in Matthew's face, and his brooding blue gaze kept moving beyond her to the smoking stack. She knew what was in his mind. When he had left, she was just a tinner's granddaughter with little more than a middling-sized mine for her dowry. But in those few weeks since they had been apart she'd become the wealthiest woman in the parish. She opened her hand and showed him the eaglestone.

'Do you see this? Well, since it brought you back to me I count it the most valuable thing I own. I would swap all that I have for it.'

She took a step nearer to him. Her full red mouth was upturned towards him as if in readiness to meet his own. In an instant she was in his arms and responding to his kiss with swift, equal passion oblivious to the grinning Dagge and Moab seated on a rock a discreet distance away. After a while, she drew away from him and held him at arms' length, her head cocked on one side and an impish gleam in her slanted eyes like the Kezzy of old.

'And what of your mistress?' she asked sternly.

Matthew looked perplexed.

'The sea.'

He gave a heavy sigh and responded in the same teasing manner. 'My staunch attachment to her has begun to waver . . . due to certain other attractions.'

'And what of your master . . . the navy?'

He sighed again. 'I fear that I am once again a fugitive from the authorities. A deserter.'

'Then we must hide you. And not let them take you from us. Not ever.'

His brows rose. 'We? Us?'

Kezzy didn't answer. Just stood smiling at him, her eyes strangely bright. Deep in his spirit, Matthew sensed what lay behind her lightly spoken words and enigmatic expression. A new, joyous feeling flooded him. It seemed to start in the region of his heart and spread right through his body, suffusing him with warmth and love. Yet, he asked the question almost timidly: 'Is it so? Are you . . .?'

Kezzy nodded, still smiling. 'Yes, Oh yes,' she whispered. 'I'm carrying our child . . . our son.'

He drew her to him again and bent his head to rest his cheek against her hair. 'Oh, my love,' he whispered as she clung to him, weeping tears of sheer happines, 'oh, my love.'

The steam-whistle sounded again, signalling the end of croust-time. The ear-jarring noise echoed through the valley and carried all the way to the top of Eagle Tor where the eagle sat on her nest. This new sound made her uneasy and she ruffled her feathers. Her restlessness disturbed the two egrets huddled beneath her. They had been quiet for a time but now they began to move, pushing their open beaks upwards and demanding to be fed with thin cries of 'Kee. Kee. Kee.'

Their mother stood, bowed her head and stretched her massive wings ready for flight.